Also by Jessica S. Taylor

The Seas of Caladhan Duology

The Syren's Mutiny

The Captain's Revenge

The Ocean's Mercy (A Prequel Novella)

Standalones

Hollowed: A Sleepy Hollow Reimagining

Beyond Those Gilded Walls

the complete duology

JESSICA S. TAYLOR

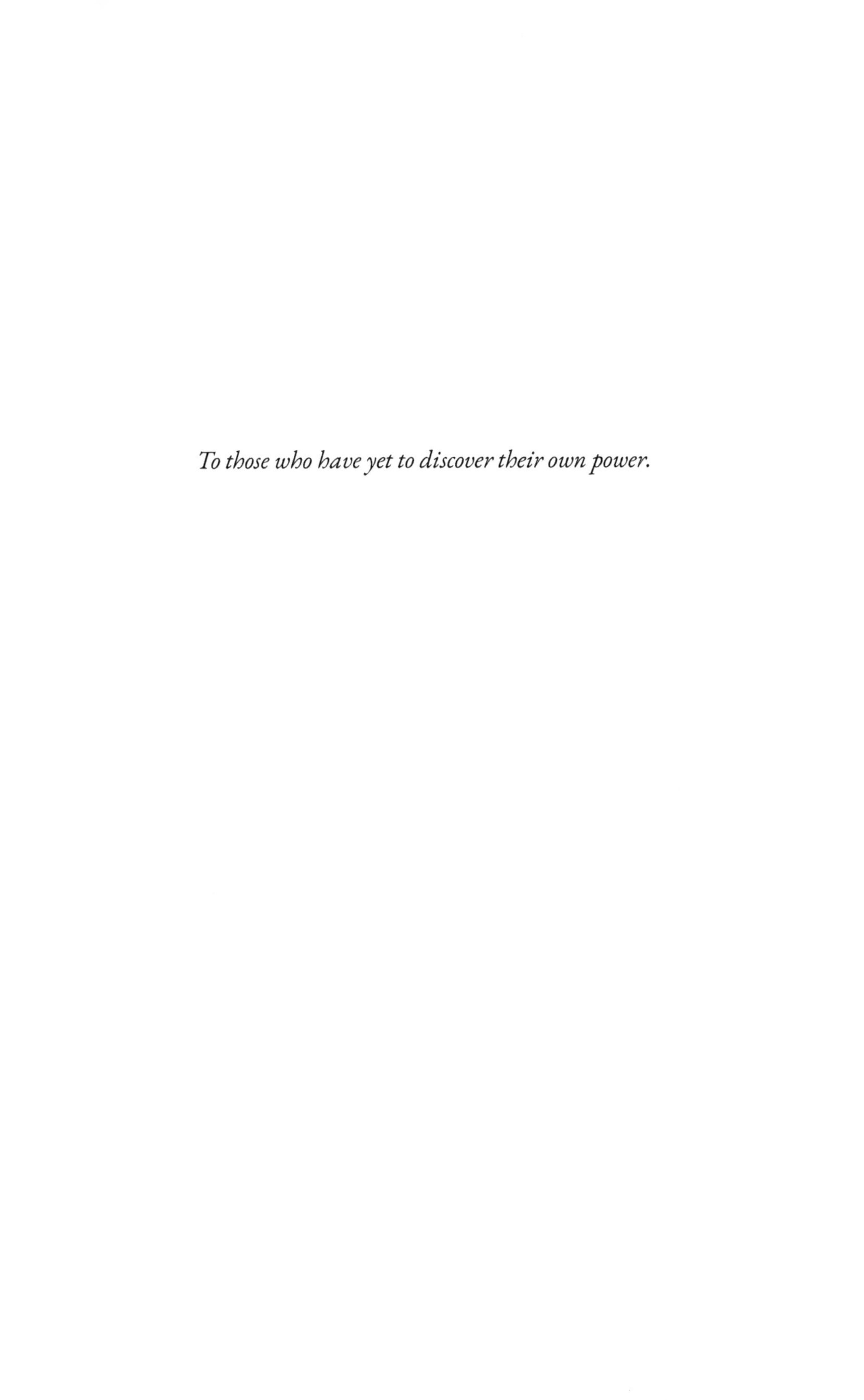

To those who have yet to discover their own power.

FAIRPORT
CAELUM'S COTTAGE
THE NEHALENNIA
TUAT
WHITGAIRN
SEOLTAN SEA
SYREN'S CAVES
NEAMH NA MARA
STRAIT
TREÒIR COVE
DÀRNA COTH
CLIODHNA'S FORTRESS
CALADH

GAISIN
ACH
FINN'S COTTAGE
BRINEMOORE
BRINEMOORE HARBOR
FAILEAS SEA
MARBH
TEICH
BHODHEAS
PRIOMH
N

Author's Note

This duology contains mature themes and scenes and is not recommended for readers under 18.

Potentially triggering content across the duology includes, but is not limited to:

- Violence (explicit)
- Blood/gore (explicit)
- Injury descriptions (explicit)
- Dismemberment (explicit)
- Death and murder (explicit)
- Torture (explicit)
- Moderate sexual content (fade to gray, focused on emotions not bodies)
- Mentions of past abuse and domestic violence

If any of this content would be harmful to you, please protect your mental health. A full list of content warnings for each book is available on my website if needed.

Pronunciation Guide

Characters:
Brigid (bridge-id)
Caelum Loinseach (cae-luhm lun-shakh)
Sorcha (sor-sha)
Maira (my-ruh)
Cliodnha (klee-uh-nah)
Kellan (kehl-uhn)
Alys (al-iss)
Faolan (fay-lan)
Nehalennia (neh-ha-lin-ia)
Kyla Còmhan (kye-luh ko-vahn)
Rhiannon (ree-ahn-un)

Places:
Gaisin (go-shin)
Straits of Marbh (marv)
Seòltan Seas (shole-tuhn)
Bhodheas (vo-dees)
Tuathnach (too-ath-nack)
Caladhan (call-uh-han)

Neamh Na Mara (neve-nuh-mar-uh)
Faileas Seas (fay-lish)
Treòir Cove (tro-oir)
Dàrna Cothrom (dar-nuh koe-thrum)
Teich (teck)
Prìomh (preeve)

THE OCEAN'S MERCY

a prequel novella

JESSICA S. TAYLOR

Elizi
@ELIZIANN

BRIGID

CHAPTER ONE

10 years before the events of The Syren's Mutiny

Sweat trickled down my brow, itching fiercely as it dried, as if it knew in this exact moment I could do nothing about it. Cursing my father and the debts that made him desperate, I slid deeper into my hiding place, praying to any gods that would listen that I would not be found. Stowing away anywhere, let alone a merchant ship, was ill-advised.

But I was out of options.

The bundles of rope beneath my legs bit into my skin, rubbing them raw, but I didn't dare move, despite every muscle in my body telling me to run. If I was discovered now, I would be immediately returned to my father, and that could not happen.

Drowning in debt he could never pay, and faced with a daughter he did not want, my father's decision to solve both of those problems led me here. If I were returned to him now, my fate would be sealed, and I would be married off to a man three times my age, who had only ever looked at me with lecherous intent in his eyes.

It could not—*would* not—be my fate.

I would rather die.

Holding my breath, I closed my eyes, trying to ignore the damned itching across my face. My life depended on staying hidden until we were out at sea. Then, at least, it would be too late to turn back and harder to return me to my father. I knew little about sailors, but I did know they would not turn back for something as small as a stowaway. Not when there was money to be made.

The bustling of men and the movements of cargo being prepared for departure both relaxed and frayed my nerves. I needed the ship to get out of port, but I couldn't speed up the process. I just had to remain hidden. Remain still.

Careful not to disturb the canvas covering me, I slowly brought a hand to my chest before slipping it beneath the neckline of the scratchy cotton shirt I had stolen from my father's closet. I closed my eyes, focusing on the rapid beating of my heart. Skin on skin. A whisper of stale air flowed through my nostrils. It grounded me. My heartbeat leveled out, easing my anxiety for the moment.

I needed to keep my wits a bit longer. Offering a silent prayer to any of the gods who were listening, old or new, and hoping no one needed anything from where I was hiding, I kept my eyes closed and settled against the wood and ropes.

"Boy, bring me that line there!" The booming voice shook me awake. The man's voice was loud and gruff, with a thick northern accent that eerily reminded me of my father's. My stomach curled, and I shied away from the voice and the mere thought of anger in the air.

The swaying of the boat was more pronounced now, and I hoped we had made it to open water.

The rope under me began unwinding. I carefully wiped my sweaty palms on my pants, bunching them in my hands tightly, and

I realized there was no way for me to shift my weight off the rope without surely being discovered. My heart sank to my stomach, the oily sensation of anxiety once again wrapping itself around my lungs and clawing up my throat.

"What's on this damn line?" a younger voice grunted as he tugged on the rope.

I braced myself as footsteps came closer. Before I could take another breath, the canvas was ripped from above me and light filtered in, bright to my unadjusted eyes.

"Who the hell are you?" the boy whispered, almost to himself, as he looked down at me.

Staring at him, I couldn't bring myself to move. My body had frozen, and I was completely at his mercy. He couldn't have been much older than my own fifteen years, but his muscles were well defined, and his arms and hands were rough with cuts and callouses.

He cocked his head to the side, causing his dark hair to flop into his face. My stomach flipped. If we had been in a different situation, I would have said he was attractive. He was the kind of boy my father would have beaten me simply for glancing at.

"Who are you? What are you doing here?" he repeated, squatting down to eye level. His blazing green eyes were intense as he stared at me. Though we appeared similar in age, the way he spoke was more mature than I'd expected. There was soft concern, edged with something that sounded vaguely like fear.

I licked my lips, dry from the open-mouthed breathing I'd been doing to calm myself. Looking around for any side of others, I whispered, "Please don't tell them I'm here."

He looked over his shoulder, to where the booming voice had come from. "I have to. I'd get in a lot of trouble if they find you."

"I need passage; I need to get away from here. *Please.*"

His eyes were full of pity. "I want to help you, I really do. But if they found out I hid you..."

Beads of sweat rolled down my spine, soaking the fabric against my back. This boy was no one to me, and I was no one to him. And while he wasn't clear about what would happen if we were discovered, the apprehension in his voice and the bruises along his arms told me plenty.

But this was my only chance at freedom. "Please. Please, I need your help."

He shook his head, and his eyes flitted around nervously. "I can't. They would hurt me if they found out."

"You can't send me back, please," I begged as visions of my father's reddened face and raised hand flashed through my mind. Tears burned in my throat at the thought of going back to him—at facing his ire. "Just take the rope you need and go. They don't have to know you saw me. Please." My voice cracked again, choked by the unshed tears I'd tried to swallow back.

He stood, the end of the rope still in his hands. After a long moment, he nodded, but his face pinched and his shoulders hunched with tension. "Okay, I'll... I can do that. You cover back up. If they find you—and they eventually will—I knew nothing of this. You have to promise me you will not give me up. They don't take kindly to disobedience here, and I *will* be severely punished if they find out."

Immense gratitude flooded me, making a laugh almost bubble out, but I caught it and nodded once instead. "I'll stay hidden and quiet. They won't know you helped me. I swear it. Thank you."

"Boy, what the hell's taking you so damn long?" a voice called, accompanied by equally loud footsteps. I flinched, pressing myself back into the wood of the hull. A burly man in a dirty, sweat-stained blouse stomped up and froze in place when he saw me curled against the floor, the boy standing over me. He peered down at me with curious eyes. "What the hell're you doing here, girl?"

My heart stopped, and I froze, unable to speak, unable to breathe. I could only stare up at the boy and the man. I had convinced the boy, just barely, but this man seemed the type to sell me out in an instant. He also seemed the type to be quick to violence.

The man huffed, crossing his arms. "Do you speak, girly?"

I swallowed hard before managing a whispered, "Aye."

"Then what the hell're you doing here?" He leaned forward.

His brow was furrowed, and he did not look sympathetic in the least, not like the boy did. He turned to the boy. "And what the hell're you doing, just looking at her? Why didn't you call for me when you found her?"

I opened my mouth to try to form a response that wouldn't get me, or the boy, killed, but the man held up his hand. "Save it for the captain. Both of you. Let's go."

Elizi
@ELIZIANN

BRIGID

CHAPTER TWO

A rough hand wrapped around my upper arm and pulled me up, surely leaving bruises on my pale skin. The man towered over my small frame, pushing me toward the boy, whose grip was gentler, but still firm. "Here, boy, make yourself useful. Since you obviously don't know what to do without being told."

Walking behind the large man, the boy led me up the deck stairs and out into the sunlight. Out of the corner of my eye, I could see tendrils of my hair catch the rays of light, burning like flames. I knew this was going to end poorly, for both me and the boy, but I kept my back straight and my head high as we walked to the center of the deck. My fear had no place, and certainly no use, here.

An imposing man with short, dark hair, shorn close to the scalp on the sides, stepped up. Scars were slashed across his face, cutting through his eyebrows and scoring his jawline. He was the definition of rugged, and he exuded a menacing energy as he strode toward me, his boots thudding against the deck. His eyes roved over me, assessing me like he was trying to figure out what I was and how much of a threat I posed. His lip curled up, obviously not liking what he found.

"What're you doing on my ship, girl?" the man asked, crossing his arms over his chest. His voice was quiet, but edged with a dark undertone that promised violence and made me worry more for the boy than for myself.

Panic surged like the waves lapping at the sides of the ship, and I ran through all the possibilities I was facing. The most likely option was that they would lock me up and dump me at the next port, but if things went poorly, he would kill me quickly.

I doubted they would grant the boy who found me such a quick punishment.

"We found her in the hold, captain. Under some canvas," the large man from before piped in. "The boy was just staring at her like a lump on a log."

"Quiet. I asked her, not you," the captain snapped, not taking his eyes off me.

Rolling my shoulders back, I steeled my nerves, despite the trembling of my knees. "I'm seeking passage, sir."

The captain snorted. "Passage? Usually, you pay for passage, not hide away like a thief. Why're you really here?"

"I'm running, sir," I admitted quietly, still holding his gaze. "From my father."

"And why didn't you pay?" he asked, looking down his nose at me.

"I have no money." If I told this man my story, would it even matter? Likely not, based on his attitude toward me already. "And I had nowhere else to go and no one to turn to. Your ship is going to Bhodheas, and I can start over there."

"Women are bad luck on a ship."

I ducked my head at that. I had heard the superstition, along with many others, from my father time and time again. He used them as his excuses for treating me the way he did. "I know, sir. But I had no other choice. I needed to get away."

"If you knew you'd be bad luck, that's just bad manners," the man sneered. He turned to the large man who had led me up with the boy. He was becoming paler with each passing moment. "How far are we from land, Quinn?"

The man shook his head, casting a quick glance off the side of the ship, where nothing but water waited. "Too far."

The captain looked back at me for a long moment. He stared at me, as if looking through me rather than at me. I fidgeted under his hard gaze.

His eyes snapped back into focus. With a steady voice, he simply said, "Throw her off."

My eyes widened, and I opened my mouth to protest, but the boy beat me to it. "We can't throw her off! She's a *child*!"

"She's not a babe, Caelum. If she's got enough wits about her to sneak onto my ship, she can take responsibility for her own actions," the captain said, holding his gaze on me. Finally, he turned to look at the boy, his eyes hardening. I knew he would face the captain's wrath once they were alone, and my stomach churned for him. "I'll not risk the wrath of the sea over a lass who snuck onto my ship. Throw her off. And I'll deal with you later."

"But..."

"No, Caelum. And if I hear another word of argument, there'll be hell to pay." The captain turned away from both of us. "She leaves the ship, and since we're too far from land, she leaves the ship *now*."

"Please, Captain, I may be a girl, but I can work. Let me earn my passage," I pleaded, wringing my hands in the hem of my shirt. While I was willing to do anything to get away from my father and the man he was selling me to, drowning wasn't my first resort.

The captain stopped in his tracks and turned back around, laughter in his eyes. He barked out a harsh noise. "You? You think you can be a member of my crew? I doubt that very much, girly."

"I can." I met his eyes despite every fiber of my being telling me it would only result in pain. If I cowered to this man, if I showed him my fear, I would never survive. His smile dropped, when I continued. "I worked on my father's farm growing up. I know how to do hard labor."

The captain stepped up close to me, too close. He leaned down until his hot breath tickled my cheek as he sneered, "And is that why you're running from him? For making you earn your keep?"

"No, captain. I'm running because he tried to sell me to a laird three times my age to relieve his own debts. And I refused." I forced myself to maintain eye contact with the captain. He had never been told he would be the property of a withering old man who looked at me with nothing but bad intentions. However intimidating *this* man might be, I needed to hold my ground if I had any hopes of living through this.

"Father, we can't just throw her off. We can make her leave at the next port," Caelum pleaded again from my side, still clinging to my arm. "She's just a child."

This captain was Caelum's father?

My stomach churned. The boy had been petrified to help me, and all along it was his own father he was afraid of. Sympathy warred with my panic, but I needed to focus on getting myself out of this situation. At least they were unlikely to kill the boy. The same could not be said for me, though.

The captain looked at me for a long time, and I couldn't read his eyes. After what felt like hours, he switched his gaze to Quinn. "Throw her off. Now. And have some men hold on to Caelum there. He seems to be smitten with the stowaway and has forgotten how to follow orders."

Quinn nodded to several crew members, who promptly grabbed both Caelum and me. They pulled him toward the mast where they began tying him up, while someone yanked me toward the ship's side. Both of us fought the entire way, to no avail.

"Please, don't do this," I begged the men holding me. I struggled to get away as we neared the railing, but their grips on my arms was too strong. I never thought I would stoop to begging for my life, but as drowning in the cold north Faileas Sea stared me in the face, I would do whatever it took.

"Girls're bad luck. You'll anger the sea if we keep you here," the man on my left muttered. "It's nothing personal, girly."

"Please. I need help, please. I can't swim well. Don't do this." I was nearly sobbing. I didn't want this to be the last moment of my life. Tugging my arms away roughly, I managed to get a few steps back toward the center of the deck before their grips returned, digging into my arms so tightly my bones ached. They lifted me up off my feet, carrying me back toward the deck railing.

"No!" Caelum roared from where he was tied to the mast. He struggled against the bindings, the rope biting into his skin, turning it so red that even I could see it.

A deckhand delivered a harsh blow to his face, knocking him unconscious, his head slumping down onto his chest.

Bile rose in my throat, battling with my tears. They had struck him for helping me. And if his previous words were to be believed, they would do much worse once I was gone.

I was alone. And I was going to die.

"Sorry, girl. This is how it has to be," the man holding me said, his grip tightening.

Crying out, I didn't have time to respond with words before they heaved me over the railing. I plunged into the icy waters, the cold depths swirling up around my body, pulling the fabric of my baggy clothes up and around me, suffocating me. I kicked as hard as I could, but I knew I could not swim well. So, I sank. The sunlight dimmed as my body fell further beneath the surface.

Suddenly, several cool, sharp fingers wrapped around my ankle from below, and I was dragged into the consuming darkness of the cold depths.

Elizi
@ELIZIANN

CHAPTER THREE

Squinting against the burning of the salty water and the sudden darkness, my eyes widened at the sight in front of me. Two women stared back at me, hair undulating in the water behind them. But they had *tails*. A stream of bubbles escaped my mouth as I tried to scream, but water rushed into my mouth and down my throat.

One of them, a woman with rich brown skin and thick waves of hair, reached out to me, and suddenly, I could breathe again. I spit and coughed as water dribbled from my lips and down my chin. A sphere of air surrounded me, the ripple of the water beyond reflecting against the thin barrier.

Mesmerized, I pushed my hand through the bubble effortlessly, meeting the cold water. Light glinted off the gold of the dark-haired woman's tail and cast rays across my hand.

"Who are you?" I gasped, pulling my hand back inside and turning my gaze to my rescuers. The other woman watched me carefully, her lavender tail swishing in the dark of the sea. She tilted her head slightly, the movement rippling through her golden curtain of hair drifting up above her head.

They were both beautiful. I'd read stories of alluring women who drew men into the sea, only to kill them. But I'd never dreamt of believing the words in my mother's old books. Yet here were two creatures who fit every depiction of those stories.

"I am Kyla," the golden-tailed one said. She motioned toward the blonde, who nodded once. "This is Maira. Are you well?"

I nodded, still too stunned by their presence to answer her question properly. In all reality, I was far from fine, but I was alive, and that was more than I'd been expecting mere moments ago. "You saved me. I... *thank you.*"

"You don't have to thank us for that," Maira said, scoffing lightly. "How did you end up in the water?"

Chewing on my lip, I debated what to tell them. Would they send me back to my father? Or would they help me? Looking at Kyla, she nodded with a smile. "It's okay, you can tell us. You're safe now."

"The captain of the ship had me thrown overboard. I'd stowed away, and they discovered me." My arms wrapped around my middle, trying to protect my heart as I whispered the heavy words. "I was running away from my father." Maira's face hardened at my words as my nerves flitted about in my belly, mirroring the twitch of her tail. I shook my head, tears burning my eyes as my voice cracked. "I—I can't go back to him. Please don't take me back."

Maira opened her mouth, but Kyla spoke first, stretching her hands out toward me with her palms up. "Calm, be calm. Breathe. We will never send you back there. I told you that you are safe. What's your name?"

"Brigid," I replied, wanting nothing more than to go hide somewhere, away from both their heavy gazes. Kyla motioned with a hand at her chest, fingers drawing together as she raised it up her sternum, inhaling dramatically. I mimicked the motion, warmth spreading through me as she smiled and nodded in approval.

"Well, Brigid, would you allow us to take you to our home? There are options available to you, but trust that you'll never go back to your father if you don't want to." The hand resting on her chest reached for me.

My eyes caught Maira, grinding her teeth with her eyes fixed on the surface. She looked back at me, and then to Kyla, as if she were asking permission.

"Maira," Kyla's voice was sharp as she spoke. She shook her head once and the command in that one motion made my body lock up, muscle memory taking over despite Kyla's soft voice being nothing like my father's. "Not now."

Maira huffed, but turned her sapphire eyes to mine. "You're safe, Brigid. They will never hurt you again."

Their words washed over me, settling on my skin. Was it really a choice? I would choose anything over returning to my father and the village in Gaisin. Anything these women—these creatures—could offer me would be a better fate. After a moment, I nodded. "I will go with you."

"Good," Kyla said, her serene smile calming my anxiety more than any amount of deep breathing. She had such confidence in herself, every movement, every word. I wanted that. I wanted to *be* that. She tightened her grip on my hand as Maira took hold of the other one. "Hold on, this might unnerve you a bit."

Before I could ask what would unnerve me, we were off, moving through the water at a speed I'd never thought was possible. My stomach rolled, and I clenched my jaw to fight back the wave of nausea. The ocean passed by in a blur, my eyes darting back and forth, trying desperately to soak in the experience of darting between schools of fish and weaving through fields of seagrass. I'd never even swam in a lake before, so seeing the underside of the sea was something I wanted to cherish now that fear wasn't gripping my bones.

My eyes widened as we slowed, approaching the gaping mouth of a large stone wall. Cragged edges framed the opening that led deep into the stone. Light filtered through the depths of the water, but darkness quickly reigned as I peered into the entrance. Only the first steps into the cave were visible.

Beyond that, the unknown. I'm fairly sure my mouth fell open.

We slowed, pulling up in front of the entrance to the cavern. Both Maira and Kyla turned to me with smiles on their faces. Kyla squeezed my hand. "Welcome to Neamh na Mara."

"What does that mean?" I breathed out, tilting my head back to take in the enormity of the stone wall that stretched out from the entrance. My cheeks heated as I realized how I'd sounded. A foolish child, questioning those who had saved me. I had no business questioning anyone. Ducking my head, I grimaced. I couldn't make them angry, couldn't give them any reason to want to send me back. "I'm sorry."

Kyla laughed, a soft sound that was muted by the water. "Never apologize for your curiosity. It means Heavens of the Sea in the old language. This is our home."

"You live in there?" I asked, pointing at the entrance. It was beautiful, but the thought of living inside the rocks made my stomach twist slightly. I loved the sun, loved the warmth on my skin. Would I have to stay beneath the rocks for the rest of time?

Maira nodded, moving into the entrance. "Yes, with our queen. She and the others are ready to meet you."

Kyla placed her hand on my shoulder. "It's not as frightening as it seems, I promise. It's very cozy."

"I'll get the others," Maira said, her voice a soft murmur as she turned and disappeared into the darkness of the cave.

My hands trembled, and I clasped them together in front of me to keep Kyla from noticing. Their queen? Neither of them had said they were bringing me to their queen, and the idea of facing someone who commanded such a title was enough to make me want to shrink back into myself. I couldn't do this. My breathing quickened and I could hear my heart pounding in my ears. There was nowhere else to go, and looking up, I knew I wouldn't make it back to the surface without their air bubbles. But I needed to get away. I couldn't meet a queen. I couldn't—

Kyla swam up closer beside me, her tail brushing up against my leg. "It's okay. You're safe here."

Taking a deep breath, I closed my eyes and let her words wash over me.

"Can I touch you?"

Taking a shaky breath through my nose, I nodded. Her hand

was cool and damp against my shoulder, but it instantly slowed my racing heart and pulled me back into my body.

"You can do this, Brigid." Her voice was a whisper across my skin. "You are strong. You are brave. This world cannot break you. No one will harm you here."

I clung to her words like a lifeline, repeating them over and over in my head to the rhythm of my breath. Finally, the world no longer felt like it was closing in on me, and the pressure around my ribs lessened. I could do this. If it meant freedom from my father, safety, and security, I could do this. Opening my eyes, I looked at her, nodding as I pulled my shoulders back. "I'm ready."

"Does that happen often?" she asked, tilting her head at me as her fingers trailed slowly down my shoulder to hold my hand.

I couldn't bring myself to admit out loud that the world often got too loud, too overwhelming, too *much*. Instead, I just nodded, clinging to her hand so tightly it likely hurt her.

Squeezing my hand back with a startling strength, she smiled and tugged me gently behind her into the mouth of the cave. The darkness beneath the surface deepened as we moved further inside the rockface. "You are strong, Brigid. Nothing can harm you."

Elizi
@ELIZIAN

CHAPTER FOUR

Entering a large open cavern, the four others in the room turned toward us as one. My heart dropped into my stomach as the weight of their eyes was burned into my skin. I was never good with judgment, always falling short in the eyes of my father and anyone he associated with. Knowing they were looking at me, studying me, forming silent opinions about me clung to the hairs on the back of my neck and crawled down my spine. I wanted to hide behind Kyla, to disappear into the walls, but I knew I couldn't.

"This is Brigid," Kyla introduced, pulling me into the center of the room and nodding toward a woman off to the side.

My eyes tracked over to her, then widened, just barely keeping my jaw from dropping. I'd thought Kyla and Maira were beautiful, but this woman was ethereal. Hair the color of moonlight flowed around her head like a halo, topped by a crown of glinting pearls and shells. Icy blue eyes glided over my body like a feather as we moved closer, my heart speeding up. This was certainly their queen. And I'd need her approval.

I wanted her approval.

"Hello, Brigid," the queen greeted, her voice like carved and polished crystal. "I am Cliodhna."

"Hi," I replied, my cheeks heating even though I was beneath the cool water. My stomach fluttered and twisted, nerves wrapping around it like gnarled tree roots. My words stuck in my throat. I wanted to compliment her name and tell her I had read it before in my mother's storybooks. But I couldn't. Couldn't bring myself to say anything beyond a fumbled greeting. There was no possible way this queen—this goddess—would ever approve me to join her collection of perfect creatures.

"What has Kyla told you about me?" Cliodhna asked, surging toward the bubble around me. In an instant, a tail the same color as her hair changed into legs as she stepped inside, hair dripping water down her naked form. I kept my eyes firmly on her neck, not wanting to show disrespect by looking at either her face or her body.

I swallowed past the anxiety that blocked my throat, hot shame burning my chest despite the cool breeze from the water circling around me. Ignorance was my biggest fear, my biggest failing. I wanted to know everything. Knowledge was power, and I didn't want to admit that I knew nothing about her. "That you are their queen. And that I would be safe here."

She nodded once. A firm movement that ushered in more confidence than I could have hoped to emulate over the course of my entire life. I could see where Kyla had gotten her mannerisms from. "Yes, you will be safe here. We are women sacrificed to the sea by angered men. We have been given a new life. You have a choice, Brigid, to stay and become one of us, or to be sent along to safety and freedom with your memories of our existence taken."

"Are you..." I took a deep breath. "Are you mermaids?"

"No," she snapped. "Do not call us that."

On instinct, I recoiled, lowering my head until my chin brushed up against my chest. "My apologies, my queen. Please forgive me."

Keeping my eyes on my feet, the surrounding water moved, and I clenched my fists at my sides as a long finger tucked under my chin, lifting my gaze. Cliodhna was smiling, an apology written on her face. "Do not apologize to me, Brigid. But take care to not call us that. We are not mermaids, we are syrens. Syrens carry the magic of the sea in their veins. Mermaids are a figment of a child's imagination. Do not confuse the two."

I nodded, swallowing hard. "Syrens, then. Of course."

"Now, do you want to be a syren, or do you want to be taken back to the surface?" Cliodhna dropped her finger from my chin and stepped back. My skin instantly missed her touch.

Hardly a choice, just as I'd suspected. If I returned to the world above these seas, without memories of the women who saved me, I would still be that frightened girl who stowed away on that ship. But I didn't want to be her anymore. I wanted to be like the women in front of me. Confident. Beautiful. Dangerous.

"And if I become one of you..." I looked over at Kyla, who smiled encouragingly as I clasped my hands to ease their shaking. Despite my earlier desire to be like the syrens, my body wanted nothing more than to curl in on itself, like it had when the boy had discovered me. Hiding away from the world. "Would I be able to help others like me?"

Cliodhna laughed, a songbird's tune echoing in the chamber. "You will be able to do far more than that." At my quizzical look, she continued, "My syrens and I are the protectors of women in the seas and avengers of them as well. Men who believe themselves above us will find themselves below us rather quickly."

A tickle of satisfaction flowed through me at the thought of being able to drown men like my father and the captain, to rid the world of them before they harmed anyone else. "How do we do that?"

"As a syren, you will have the full extent of my magic at your disposal. Our song sends men into madness, driving them into the seas below where we will be waiting with talons to hold them as they struggle and teeth ready to rip flesh as they die." She tilted her head as she studied me, walking around me and running her fingers through my hair before coming face to face with me. "Aren't you angry, my child? At what they did to you?"

Now that I was not fearing my immediate and horrible death by drowning, I was angry. Angry at my father, who'd driven me to try and escape on the ship. Angry at the old man who was to be my husband and how he looked at women as his property to treat however he wanted without repercussions. Angry at the captain of the ship, who's superstitions led to his callous disregard for human life. Angry at the men who'd thrown me over and were incapable of individual thought. Angry at the boy who'd found me, for giving me hope, only to have it ripped away.

It was him I was angriest at.

He'd given me hope, encouragement, and foolishly, I'd believed him. I had looked into his swirling green eyes and let myself hope and believe I could hide beneath that canvas until I reached safety. Desperation was far easier to deal with than shattered hope, though. And I should have stayed in my fearful desperation. My pitiful hopelessness. It would have been far safer.

The boy never should have offered me any kind of ludicrous daydreams about my safety aboard the ship. He should have turned me in immediately. At least then, I would never have to live with the memory of his face, fighting against those men to reach me. The sound of a fist hitting his face and the image of him slumping as they tied him to the mast. He hadn't even seen me thrown overboard.

Did he care that I was gone?

The burning rage grew deep in my chest, warming my neck and face as my fists clenched at my sides. "Yes, I am angry."

A smile crept across the queen's face, pink lips pulling back to reveal sharp teeth. "Good."

"I want to become a syren," I said, determination coursing through every ounce of my soul. I would become a syren. I would join these women. And I would exact my vengeance.

"Then you shall." She turned to Maira and Kyla, both of who were still behind me. "You may go join the others."

Both women bowed their heads deeply before moving to join the three other women across the cavern. Maira swam straight toward the one with hair a few shades lighter than my own fiery copper. They embraced each other, sharing a soft kiss before letting their foreheads touch as they muttered to each other. My heart tugged at the scene, longing for something else I'd never had.

Kyla joined the other two, sitting between them. The one on Kyla's right was an embodiment of the setting sun, with caramel waves that floated around her head like a halo, framing her face, the color of sun-kissed sand. Her tail was the color of the ocean at dusk, a dusty purple and blue that mirrored in reverse the syren that sat at Kyla's left. She was all angles and sharp eyes, taking in my form even as she continued her conversation with the others.

I reluctantly turned my attention back to Cliodhna, forcing myself to stop staring at the other syrens as one request bubbled on my tongue. The boy. The one who'd tried to save me.

Caelum.

Despite my anger at him, I didn't want him to suffer at the hands of that horrible captain. At the hands of his father. The sickening sound of his nose cracking echoed in my ears...

He needed saving, too. Maybe even more so than I did.

"There was a boy," I said, trying to get the words out before I couldn't anymore. "He tried to save me, and they are going to punish him for it. They'd already struck him to stop him from helping me, and they are going to do worse. Can we go back for him?"

Cliodhna looked at me, her face unreadable. "No, we cannot. He may have saved you today, but given time, he would surely have been the one to throw you over. No, you are safe and that's what matters. We saved you. Not him."

I wanted to protest, to plead to go back and rescue this boy from his father, but I couldn't risk jeopardizing my new home. She was right, Kyla and Maira had ultimately saved me, and I owed it to them to honor the wishes of their queen. Those men would never truly harm the boy. He was one of them and would become just like his father one day. I was certain of that, whether it was by choice or by force.

I nodded. "I understand."

"Now, are you ready for your transformation to begin?"

Taking a deep breath, I nodded again. I was ready. Ready for a new life, and a chance to live my life the way I chose.

"It may tingle, but it will not hurt," she said, reaching a hand toward me, one finger outstretched in a gesture that on anyone else would have been seen as lazy. But on her, it was intentional. Decisive.

Before I had a chance to react, or even brace myself for what was coming, ribbons of water pulsed from her fingertips. The tendrils wrapped around my body like a warm hug and shrouded the cavern from my view behind bubbles and gushing veins of salt water. There was a tugging behind my navel, like a hook pulling the skin back to my spine. More warmth spread from that spot, flowing down my hips and thighs and calves. It grew hotter, wrapping around the outsides of my legs like hands, pressing them together. I closed my eyes to the sensations, letting my body feel them as the tingling began to fade.

At once, the ribbons of warm water surrounding me collapsed, and the cold ocean surged in around me. But goosebumps didn't form on my body like they typically did when I grew chilled, which was all the time in the little one-room cottage with no fireplace I'd lived in. No, it was like I knew the water should have been cold, but it wasn't. It was like a gentle caress across my skin, a breath of a warm summer breeze. Opening my eyes, I hesitated briefly before looking down at myself.

Talons grew from my nails, curving to sharp points as I studied my hands. Red slipped in the edges of my vision, and I pulled my hands away, looking down at the tail that now grew from my waist and swished unconsciously, keeping me afloat in the water. Red and silver, silver and red.

I blinked at the scales that began at my waist, sparse at first, and as they grew denser around my hips and morphed into one long tail. Red at the outside, along my hips and tracing the edges of the large fin, and silver in the middle, glinting in the low light.

My heart seemed frozen in amazement.

My eyes darted up to Cliodhna, who had reformed her own tail and was watching me with satisfactory pride on her face.

"Thank you." My voice cracked with the grateful tears that filled my throat. "Thank you for this."

"Do not thank me with your words, child," she said, swimming up to me to take me in. "Thank me by joining your fellow syrens and teaching men that the sea is not a merciful creature they can bend to their whims."

I nodded, intent on making this woman proud. Men had never been kind to me, and this group, this new purpose, soothed the raw wounds in my heart. I let rage bubble up in my heart, burning and spreading over everything with a tinge of red and flame.

I would wash my hands in the blood of those men who believed themselves better than women—of those men who believed women were their property and playthings.

It was as if the chains that had been wrapped around me my entire life, crisscrossing over my chest and pinning my arms and legs together... had just fallen away. I was *free*.

Raising my chin with confidence I'd not felt in a long, long time, I smiled at Cliodhna, showing off my newly pointed teeth. "As you wish, my queen."

Eliza
@ELIZIAN

CHAPTER FIVE

The next several days passed in a blur of activity and new information. It quickly became painfully obvious that despite knowing how to read and write, my education had been woefully neglected. It didn't surprise me, just fueled my anger. My father had only cared about what I could achieve for him, and anything beyond the bare minimum needed to keep me alive was an effort he would not put forth.

My anger warred with my frustration at just how much I did not know.

Kyla and Maira tried to calm and reassure me it wasn't my fault and that I would have the time to learn everything I ever wanted to learn. But still, my face flushed with shame every time one of the syrens discussed something I was ignorant of.

In the mornings, the syrens took turns teaching me whatever they could about their world. In the afternoons, I learned what it meant to be a syren: controlling my song, transforming between my human and syren forms, learning to manipulate water.

The evenings were mine to spend as I wished. And most evenings, I found myself in the room I shared with Kyla, curled in the hanging bed away from the world.

Was it wise to stew alone in my anger? Likely not. But the syrens had their own friendships, and their own bonds. And I wasn't one of them. Not yet. I knew I should try to form friendships, but I couldn't bring myself to do it. I could bring myself to learn, to soak in every bit of information they shared, cataloging it and running through it in my mind later as I lay in the darkness.

I would never be ignorant again. I would never be vulnerable.

The mantra worked as long as I was awake. But when sleep came, my newfound strength quickly waned in the darkness. Leaving way for the fearful and sniveling girl who had been tossed aside, again and again.

"Useless girl," my father had snarled, tangling his hand in my knotted hair as he hauled me out of the bed. "Get up. You have work to do."

"I..." I coughed, trying desperately to suck in a breath and ease my spasming lungs. I'd been sick for days, delirious with fever, and my throat filled with needles. Hands wrapped around my middle, pushing and squeezing my chest to the point of pain. "I can't, father. I can't... breathe."

My protests went unheard as he dragged me through the cottage. I flinched as the door flung open, clattering against the stone. He tossed me into the frosty morning, dawn barely turning the sky gray as I fell to the frost covered grass that dug into my knees and palms. "Get up, you useless child. Earn your keep or you'll be going to the McDonnal's far sooner than you think."

Fear caused the spasming and coughing fit this time, and I pulled on every ounce of strength to pull my swaying body upright. I would not give my father a reason to send me to that monster. Nodding, my matted hair slipped over my face. I sucked in a deep and painful breath, pushing out the words in one go. "Yes, Father."

He sneered at me, curling his lip up in disgust before slamming the door in my face, leaving me stranded in my nightgown.

In the distance, the birds began their morning song. I flinched, tears welling in my eyes at the pain that ricocheted through my body. My feet were already numb from the cold, and my eyes stayed fixed on them as I walked. I couldn't feel the steps, couldn't feel them moving as I made my way to the barn. I didn't make it, though, collapsing against the door before I could reach for it.

Sobs wrenched from my mouth as the wood scraped against my side. Hot tears flowed down my cheeks, and I couldn't breathe. Couldn't move. I let my head fall against the wood, my eyes drifting closed as black dotted my vision.

"Brigid. Brigid! Wake up!" Hands grasped my shoulders, shaking me awake with a gasp. Wide, amber eyes peered down at me. A soft breath puffed against my face and the hands on my shoulders moved to cup my cheeks. "Brigid, it's okay. It was just a nightmare."

Kyla. Kyla was in front of me. My eyes left her face, roaming behind her and taking in the rockface, I turned to see Maira's own concerned blue eyes staring back at me, the twitch of my tail hanging from the bed. The tightness in my chest eased, and I slumped against the canvas supporting my body. I wasn't there anymore. I wasn't there. I was in the caves. I was with the syrens. I was safe.

"Come with us, Brigid," Kyla said, her voice barely louder than a whisper as she intertwined our fingers and tugged me from the bed. Maira came up on the other side of me, taking my other hand.

Together, they pulled me into another cavern. A larger canvas hammock hung there, big enough for several people to fit comfortably side by side. Kyla swam forward, urging me toward the bed.

"Get in," Maira said, pushing at my lower back. "We'll protect you tonight."

I didn't have it in me to fight off their help or insist that I was *fine* and that I could sleep alone. I didn't want to sleep alone. So, I nodded and settled in the middle of the hammock, both of the syrens tucking into either side of me.

"I'm sorry I woke you both." I sniffed. Pressed between them, I couldn't reach up to wipe my tears away, and they trickled from the corners of my eyes, slowly trailing down my face into my hair.

"Don't," Maira snarled. Her voice softened she tucked a strand of hair behind my ear, wiping the tears that dampened it. "Do not apologize for what they put you through. Do not apologize for your emotions."

"I know I didn't have it as bad as some of the other women in the village," I said, shaking my head as I thought of Maeve, the woman married to the wheat farmer two farms over, who had been killed by her husband in a fit of drunken rage. "At least I'm still alive."

"People can do worse things than kill you, Brigid." Kyla's soft and shattered voice broke the silence. "Surviving what they throw at you is the true battle. And you are a survivor, make no doubt about it."

My mouth opened to offer another apology and take back the words, but even in the darkness, I saw Maira's raised eyebrow and swallowed the words like a bitter tea. Instead, I bit my cheek and said nothing, relishing the comfort of their bodies pressed against mine.

The three of us laid in silence for what felt like ages. None of us spoke, but occasionally, Kyla's hand would trace a path down my arm to my fingers, where she would squeeze gently before retracing her path to my shoulder.

"Will it ever get better?" I asked, my scratchy voice shattering the peaceful silence.

"It will," Kyla replied in the darkness. I felt more than heard the deep breath she took, her chest moving against my side. "It will take time, though."

"Good that we have all the time in the world," Maira added, her voice thick with sleep. She patted my hand, settling in deeper against my side. "You will get there, Brigid. You have us."

"How long did it take for you?"

Silence met my question, and I feared that I had overstepped. Just as I was about to speak, to pull the words back into my chest as best I could, Maira spoke. Her voice was softer than I'd ever heard it. "Some days, I still think I haven't quite gotten there."

"What helps?"

"Our purpose," she said with a shrug. "Cordelia."

The smile in her voice brought one of my own. "Cordelia, hmm?"

I didn't know if it was acceptable to tease her, but it felt right. It felt like what I should say in the moment.

Kyla chuckled. "They've been smitten with each other since Cordelia joined us."

I could *hear* Maira's scowl. Adjusting, I rolled over until I was on my side, facing the blonde. I hesitated slightly, pushing the words out before I could swallow them back. "She helps? Truly?"

"She does," was her immediate response.

"But don't seek out your healing in someone else, Brigid," Kyla added. "You have to find it in yourself, too."

"Let her find it wherever she can, Kyla," Maira snapped. "Not all of us can find the inner peace you have."

Biting my tongue, the room filled with thick tension, though neither syren said anything else. Kyla was right, of course. If I found my healing in someone else, when they inevitably left me behind, I would be right back where I was. But at the same time, I wasn't sure I'd ever be able to find that peace alone. I wasn't sure I'd be able to find that peace at all. I wasn't even sure how to begin that journey. But I had time, I supposed. Perhaps that was all I needed. Time.

"Thank you both." My voice broke through the tension, dispelling it as though I'd waved a hand through a forest of seaweed, pushing it along to the edges of the room. "Thank you for staying."

Once more, the silence was comfortable, like a worn blanket to snuggle into on a cold morning. Without a second thought, I let the weight of the two women on either side of me ground me and chase away my nightmares.

I would learn to chase them away myself later.

For now, I would relish sleeping peacefully for the remainder of the night.

Eliz
@ELIZIAN

BRIGID

CHAPTER SIX

"Brigid, you'll be going out with Cordelia and Maira today," Cliodhna said, foregoing any greetings as we gathered in the main chamber of the caves.

"As you wish," I replied, bowing my head. Upon raising it, my eyes flitted to Maira and Kyla before snapping back to my queen.

I had no clue what she meant by going out, but I also knew better than to question the magnificent creature before me. She was a goddess, and I was nothing. I pulled my hands behind my back, twisting them together. The twinge of my knuckles scraping together cut through the sharpness of my anxiety. It was a battle to keep my shoulders back and not curl in on myself.

Cliodhna studied me for a moment, her lips pursed.

My heart quickened. Had I offended her somehow? I had been so careful to avoid that, and yet, I was failing once more. Just as I'd opened my mouth to apologize for whatever slight I'd committed, she nodded, turning and surging away with a powerful wave of her tail. Pressure built behind my eyes. I could not even do this right, it seemed.

Water surged against my face, like a strong gust of wind as if we'd been above. Silence fell as the queen left us, and finally, I was able to pull the words from my throat. "Going out where?"

Maira's grin was feral. "Hunting."

Swimming forward, Cordelia huffed at the blonde, hitting her arm with a gentleness that could never truly hurt. "You're going to scare her." Cordelia turned to me, a pretty pink blush spreading across her ivory-colored skin. "Don't mind her, Brigid. We're going scouting. To look for any threats or ships that might become a target for us."

"How is that different from what I said?" Maira scowled, crossing her arms. "You just said it with more words."

"What will I be doing?" I asked, warmth spreading through my chest as I watched the two syrens interact. They were a balancing act. Where Maira was all sharp and jagged edges, Cordelia was smooth and rounded. Where Maira was cold like a winter midnight, Cordelia was warm like a summer afternoon. They fit together, better than I could ever have dreamed. I wanted that. I wanted someone to balance me, to hold me together and absorb the sharpness of my broken soul.

"You only have to observe this time," Kyla said, swimming up to join us after finishing her conversation with Iona and Nerina. "Take all the time you need to get accustomed to things, Brigid. Don't rush."

The placating tone had me gritting my teeth. I wasn't weak. I could do this—do whatever the rest of them did. "I can do more."

Kyla only smiled, her glowing amber eyes never leaving my face. "I know you can. And you will. In time. But at least take today to observe and learn how things work. You don't have to be everything all at once."

"She's right," Cordelia added, smiling as her fingers intertwined with Maira's. "Just watch us today. And then, tomorrow, if you want to do more, if you're ready to do more, we can do that. Let us just show you today."

Reluctantly, I nodded. They were right, and as much as I wanted to prove myself, if I made a fool of myself by rushing into things, it would only set me back. I needed to take the time to learn and analyze every aspect of being a syren, and then perfect it. Nodding again, I squared my shoulders. "When do we leave?"

"Now, if you're ready."

"Let's go."

The seas were *magnificent*.

I'd only ever seen the waters of the Faileas Seas from a distance along the east of Tuathnach atop the hills of Gaisin when the fog lifted from the cliffs enough. Oh, how I wished I'd seen them sooner. The waves called to me, beckoning me in and folding me into their embrace.

But now, we were beneath the Seoltan Seas of the west. And the waters were stunning, like blue crystal, fracturing the light from the sun as it came down into the depths. Shadows and light, columns of sunlight reaching down and creating pools of light along the ocean floor.

I'd never felt more at home.

Maira and Cordelia took turns pointing out various creatures, plants, and rock formations as we entered the Straits of Marbh. The rocks were my favorite part; the craggy towers of stone reaching up to hide just beneath the surface, waiting to rip apart an unsuspecting ship that passed over it.

We left the other side of the Straits, emerging once more into the Faileas Seas and turning south, skirting along what Maira explained was the coast of Bhodheas, in the space between the port of Tiech and the capitol of Priomh. My heart squeezed. Priomh had been my hopeful destination.

I'd never made it as a human, but now, I could see the seas around it as a syren. I would see every nook and cranny of this world, I vowed. Lifetimes worth of time lay ahead of me, and I would use every second of it.

My tail pushed harder, driving me toward the coast and surging through the waters. I wanted to see the town, the port, the docks. Would the ship I escaped on be there? It should have made port by now.

Instead of going toward the towns and ports, though, Cordelia and Maira led us along the coast, surveying the waters that crashed against the steep cliffs. We trailed along for a bit, before Maira turned us away into the deeper waters out to sea. They had a calm confidence, always certain of where they were going. I could see no discernable way they should be able to navigate the water so easily. I hoped I could learn that.

The deep waters were just as breathtaking as the cliffs along the coast had been. The calmness of the water itself and the bustling life of the fish and plants that lived in it was a beautiful balance. I wanted to stay in one place and just soak in the vision, but Maira and Cordelia had their mission to hunt. And I had mine: to learn.

"There," Cordelia said, raising a taloned finger to point ahead of us.

In the distance, I saw a dark shape on the surface of the water. Squinting, I tried to make out more details as we slowed. "Is that a ship?"

We'd not seen any so far, the seas unusually empty, according to Cordelia. It wasn't fishing season, she'd explained, but there still should have been more ships. Subsistence fishermen—those who fished for survival instead of coin—would take whatever they could get. But they tended to stay toward the coastline, not out in the depths as we were.

"Let's find out." Maira wiggled her eyebrows, and with another menacing grin, she shot off through the water, pulling my attention back to the task at hand.

Cordelia rolled her eyes, pale blue glinting in the fractured sunlight that seeped down from the surface. The fond smile softened the exasperated sigh that left her lips. "Come now, Brigid. Before she gets herself into trouble."

Eliz
@ELIZIAN

B R I G I D

CHAPTER SEVEN

As Cordelia and I swam after Maira, the shape of the ship atop the water grew larger and larger. Barnacles covered the keel and stretched up the sides of the hull of the old wood. Maira halted a short distance away, waiting for us to catch up. Once we reached her, she grabbed our hands and pulled us to the surface with her.

Heads breaking water, the icy wind stung my eyes as I searched out the ship's form. I knew little about ships, but I knew this one was large. Three masts, large, yellowed canvas sails, port holes that stretched across the sides and led to an elaborate wood carved figure-head of a naked woman with hands stretched toward the sky as a large snake twined around her body.

My eyes fell to the name carved into the side and inlaid with gold. *Ceirean's Fury.*

Maira snorted, her eyes following mine. "What a foolish name."

"What does it mean?" I asked, fingers twitching to trace along the wood grain. The name seemed familiar, but I couldn't place where I'd heard it before.

"Ceirean is a bedtime story pirates tell their children to scare them," Maira said, waves lapping at her neck. "It's a large sea worm that's said to swallow ships whole."

"Is it…" I swallowed. "Is it real?"

"No," Cordelia said, resting her hand on my shoulder. There was laughter in her voice, but for once, I didn't feel like she was laughing at me. It felt like an inside joke, and one I was in on. "*We are the most dangerous thing in these waters.*"

"That's why it's foolish." Maira tilted her head toward the ship. "Let me show you what we look for when we assess a ship."

"Won't they see us?" I asked, eyes flitting to the deck as a man came to the railing and fiddled with the ropes.

"Only if they cared enough to look." Maira held out her hand, and I slipped my fingers through hers, letting her pull me gently toward the ship. "Let us teach you."

Dipping back beneath the surface, we approached the ship, finally close enough to touch it. I reached my hand out and did just that, tracing my talons over the rough edges of the barnacles, digging into the seams in the wood. I was entranced by the feel beneath my fingers.

"This is a pirate's ship," Maira said, startling me from my thoughts. She reached out and traced her fingers over the wood above mine. "You can taste the gunpowder in the water around it."

I opened my mouth, letting the salty water coat my tongue. Immediately, I grimaced, pulling a chuckle from both Cordelia and Maira. "It tastes bitter. Like metal."

"Come," Cordelia beckoned, swimming away and toward the middle of the ship. "I'll show you the cannon ports from here."

Something hit the surface of the water, rippling through as it sank. I frowned, trying to figure out what the object was as it moved closer to Cordelia. My eyes turned to Maira, who was still looking at the ship. "What's that?"

Her head turned toward the object, eyes widening as it descended around Cordelia, settling around her body. "Cordelia!" she screamed, surging forward. "Cordelia, it's a net!"

Icy hands gripped my heart, squeezing and paralyzing me as I watched the net constrict. The ropes pressed against Cordelia's sage green tail as it lifted her through the water. They were going to catch her.

My eyes darted to Maira in search of direction, for what I should do. Maira snarled, surging toward the net, her talons extended. I followed without hesitation, both of us reaching the netting at the same time.

Maira's hand twined with Cordelia's through the rope. "We'll get you out, my love. Don't worry."

"Call the others," Cordelia instructed, pulling away from Maira. Her talons attempted to slice at the rope, but she made no progress. Her hands trembled as she slowly stopped her attempts. "*Now*, Maira."

"What do we do?" I asked, cursing the way my voice trembled as Cordelia's hands had. "Why won't her talons rip the rope?"

"Maira is going to call for the others to come help us," she said, reaching through the net to rub her thumb over my cheek. "It will be okay, Brigid. Don't fret. The rope must be something different than usual. It's okay, sweet girl."

A mournful yet urgent cry fell from Maira's lips, the song moving through the water and washing through me as it echoed into the depths. "They'll come soon." Maira's words fell off abruptly as she too failed at slicing through the ropes around the strawberry blonde that held her heart. A scream of frustration left her lips as she clawed mercilessly.

Cordelia's fingers reached through the netting and clasped onto Maira's, stilling them.

Maira's hands curled into fists, jaw clenching as she and Cordelia held a silent conversation. The message of the conversation was clear—Cordelia was trapped.

My heart thudded against my chest, threatening to burst through and escape into the cold water. I searched over the net, looking for any opening, any vulnerability we could exploit to free Cordelia. If the men aboard the ship hadn't already noticed they'd caught something, they surely would soon.

Time was not on our side.

Elizi
@ELIZIAN

BRIGID

CHAPTER EIGHT

Before we could begin a new strategy to free the syren, the ropes moved, and Cordelia was being hauled to the surface. Yank after yank tugged her through the water, ropes digging into her skin and tail. Cordelia cried out, twisting and adjusting to keep her tail from being folded beneath her.

And I did nothing.

My body would not move, even as I screamed at myself to go with her, to do anything to help her. It was like I was back on that ship, back in the grips of those men, and I could do nothing to stop it.

Floating in the water, all I could do was watch in horror as Cordelia was snatched from us.

Maira snarled, mouth opening as she began her song, crying out into the sea and urging the madness to descend over the crew. She snatched at my hand and pulled me with her toward the surface, just as Cordelia breached it.

Screams filled my ears. Men on the deck going insane at the sounds coming from Maira's mouth. Above the surface, the song was much louder and clearer. There was no barrier between her deadly music and their ears.

But still, Cordelia's progress toward the railing above continued.

"Sing. Now," Maira snarled at me before immediately going back into her song. Her hands grasped the rungs of the ladder built into the side of the ship.

Her command pulled my own song from my lips. I continued the haunting melody as I watched Maira transform, her naked body climbing the rungs as she chased after Cordelia. I'd never sung alone before, but if this would help Cordelia, I would do whatever it took. Fear gripped me as Cordelia was hauled over the side of the ship, her tail disappearing over the railing. The thud of her body hitting the deck echoed in my ears.

A hand on my shoulder had my song stuttering, but the others picked it up, as Kyla, Iona, and Nerina appeared above the surface beside me. Kyla nodded, squeezing my shoulder as the screams of the crew intensified.

Flailing bodies came crashing over the deck railing and into the water. Iona and Nerina immediately dove beneath the waves to snatch their prey and drive them deeper into the sea. More men came over, splashing into the water one by one.

Kyla's hand squeezed my shoulder tighter as we continued our song, not chasing after the men who held their hands over their ears, screaming as they struggled to stay afloat.

My eyes widened as Maira stepped up to the railing, her human legs powerful as she held Cordelia in her arms. With a nod from Kyla, Maira fell from the railing, plunging back into the sea together.

"Come," Kyla said, halting her song. She pulled me through the water as we rushed to Cordelia.

Maira set her syren upright, holding her until Cordelia's tail could hold her weight once more. Passing her to us, the blonde's lips curled back from her teeth, revealing the sharp points. "They will pay for that."

Another man fell into the seas, spluttering as he pulled his head above the water. His eyes widened as he looked at us, finally understanding what he saw. "Pl—please. Mercy! Mercy!"

Maira snarled. "The ocean shows no mercy to men like you."

And with a look that chilled the seas around us, Maira surged toward him, and the mass of flailing men, and began her culling.

Kyla held Cordelia, and I could only watch in horrific fascination as Maira carved a bloody path through the crew in the water. Her talons flashed and teeth tore into flesh as the seas darkened with the blood of those men who had dared to lay a hand on Cordelia.

Iona and Nerina finished with the few men they had taken on themselves and returned to our sides.

"She is going mad," Nerina murmured from beside me as we sank back beneath the waves, watching the bodies of Maira's victims sink into the depths.

"Will she really kill them all? What is she doing?" I couldn't tear my eyes from the bodies in front of me, ripped apart and floating in the red-clouded waters. The metallic tang of their blood was sharp at the back of my throat, and the ribbons of warmth that cut through the cool waters made my skin crawl.

"Nothing you can stop."

My stomach churned, nausea rising and twisting my stomach. Maira had decimated them to the point I could no longer tell which bodies were corpses and which were still clinging to their last seconds of life.

And still, she attacked.

After a long moment, the blonde paused, surveying the damage she'd done. Her chest heaved, though I was certain it was from emotion rather than exertion. She turned from the carnage, eyes searching for Cordelia amongst the rest of us.

A flash of silver behind her caught my eye.

Before I realized I was moving, I was immersed in the bloody water, snatching at a man swimming for Maira's back with a blade. My talons dug into his throat, ripping away at the flesh as his eyes gaped. His neck showed no resistance to the power in my hands, skin tearing easily.

My lips pulled back into a snarl as my talons continued striking the man. With his throat gone, they moved lower, shredding his shirt and carving deep gouges through his chest.

Fresh blood poured into the water, veiling us both in a curtain of red.

His body finally slumped in my arms, and I let him go, his clothes scratching against my tail as his carcass sank. Blood settled around me, hiding the silver of my scales behind a sheath of red.

I watched as the corpse fell deeper and deeper until I could no longer make out the unseeing eyes. A shudder went through me as reality settled in. I had *killed* a man. Had ripped his throat out and swam in his blood.

My fingers came together, and I rubbed at the talons to remove his blood from beneath my nails. What had I done?

"Thank you." Maira's voice pulled me back. Her eyes were shining, glimmers of sapphire beneath the waves. Her throat worked as the current pulsed her red-tinged blonde hair behind her. She had blood on her teeth. "*Thank you, Brigid.*"

The others joined us as we all pressed together in a huddle around Cordelia, bathed in the blood of the crew we had slaughtered.

"So," I croaked out, my voice cracking with an emotion I couldn't name. "Does that happen often?"

A shuddering laugh burst from Maira's chest. "Welcome to the family, Brigid."

THE SYREN'S MUTINY

book one

JESSICA S. TAYLOR

Eliz
@ELIZIAN

BRIGID

CHAPTER ONE

There was a certain satisfaction that came with the last breath of a dying man. Feeling it ghost across my lips, knowing I was the last thing that man would ever feel, was empowering. It was also time consuming. Men were slow to drown, slow to do anything except show anger.

The man I had in my grasp was desperately trying to free himself. His cheeks bulged as he pulled at my grip in a pathetic attempt to get back to the surface that was taunting him just out of reach. He managed to rip an arm away from me, but he only succeeded in tearing his own flesh open on my talons, tinging the water around us pink.

While he was able to get some space from me, it didn't last long. Using the strength of my tail, I surged forward and wrapped my talons back around his arm, pulling him close to me.

Bubbles escaped from his nose and mouth, and his body thrashed, still trying to escape. His obvious panic and suffering did nothing to me, and I only watched in utter indifference as he continued to try to break free of my grip. But I was a syren. And he was just a man.

His movements slowed, and he cast one last longing glance at the light fracturing down through the surface of the water. He tried to pull away again, but his strength was gone, and the attempt was pitiful. Watching him, I bared my pointed teeth at him, intent on making his last emotion be that of fear. Not of drowning, but of *me.*

The thrashing of the man in my arms finally ceased, lulling the water back into brief calmness once more, and I pulled back, supporting his body floating in the water. Blank, unseeing eyes stared back at me as I released his body into the cold depths. I watched him sink into the water, seeing his limbs float away from his body, reaching up toward the surface as if he could still escape his fate. His death stirred nothing in my chest. He was simply another face I would soon forget, another insignificant man who would never harm a woman again.

Beyond the faint ripples left by the man's sinking body, I observed Maira releasing her own corpses into the sea. My fellow syren was blonde, with an anger that rivaled the men we targeted. The wreckage of the ship our victims had inhabited now surrounded us, the splintered wood bobbing in the waves and shredded canvas blocking the sunlight from reaching the depths as it sank.

"Is that all of them?" Maira asked, her sharp voice bored as she dodged the debris to move toward me in the water. A flutter of a sail fell in her path, and her talons ripped through it with ease. She moved through the gap in the fabric, sidling up beside me.

Searching through the waters before us, I saw only sinking bodies. There was no one left alive in these waters but us. "Yes."

"Let's get back." She dismissively turned away from the ship, swishing her lavender tail to power through the water, leaving a rippling of bubbles behind her.

Casting a last glance over my shoulder at the destruction we had caused, I turned and followed my companion back toward our home, *Neamh na Mara.* The heavens of the sea.

The sea caves I now resided in were beautiful, jutting up from the ocean floor and creating a sanctuary that protected us from anyone or anything that might stumble across our home. The caves' passageways, forged from years of the sea's relentless power, twined and burrowed through the cragged rock. Swimming through the arched main entry, Maira and I moved from the tunnels to a large open cavern.

The others had already gathered there, resting on the age-smoothed stalagmites rising from the sea floor. Kyla, with her dark ebony skin and darker hair, watched us closely as we entered, her bright gold tail swishing lazily. Next to her sat Iona and Nerina, who were not related, yet looked as if they could be twins with their light brown skin and caramel hair. Even turned into syrens, their tails were similarly colored with splashes of purple and blue.

"Brigid, Maira, report." Our queen's melodic voice was confident and proud, demanding respect in the same way the bold jut of her chin and set of her bare shoulders did. Her white hair lifted off her shoulders with a stray current flowing through the caves.

"One ship. No survivors," Maira said from beside me, her scales catching the low light as her tail moved restlessly. "There was no harm to us."

"Good, they deserved to be punished." Cliodhna glided toward us through the water, her silver tail lazily swaying back and forth, the light reflecting off her scales and bouncing onto her pale skin. My heart swelled at the pride in her voice. "My creations, you did well, as always."

Both Maira and I respectfully bowed our heads to the one who had saved us, rescued us from the cruelty of men, and breathed new life into our veins. Our queen raised her webbed fingers and laid them gently upon my head, trailing her sharp nails through my fiery red-orange locks, which undulated behind me in the ever-moving water.

"The wrath of men will never be as great as the wrath of the sea," I said, repeating the words she had said to us often. Taking in the flowing white hair that trailed behind her, her sharp cheekbones and piercing icy blue eyes, Cliodhna reminded me of a queen in every sense of the word. And she had chosen me. She had saved me when I had been thrown overboard many years ago. Unbidden, thoughts of my past returned. My stomach twisted at the memories, my heart racing. Remembering the icy chill of the water as I was thrown into the sea, my body shivered, my skin tightening. The cold of the water didn't affect me now, not in this form, but the ghost of icy needles lingered.

"That's right," Cliodhna said solemnly, moving her hand to my face. Her nails caught on my skin, the webbing scraping across the roundness of my cheeks as she stroked it. Even in the cold water that filled our caves, her fingers were frigid, and I shivered again. "You all are my greatest creations, my greatest pride."

My head bowed again, as did the heads of the others, as we honored our goddess. Our queen demanded respect, but we would all freely give it. I raised my head back up to look at Cliodhna. "You saved us all. We owe you our lives."

"That you do," she said, looking back at us with a smile that displayed her mouth full of pointed teeth. It wasn't a friendly smile. It didn't reach her eyes, but instead settled on her lips only, not disturbing her cheeks or wrinkling her forehead. "How many men today?"

Maira swam forward; she was always so eager to answer. Maira was bloodthirsty, and out of all of us here, she enjoyed inflicting pain upon men with her song and her touch more than the rest of us. "It was a small crew, ten or so. We drowned them all after they jumped into the water. The ship drifted and ran aground."

Cordelia, another redhead like me, watched us with interest, her blue eyes more focused on Maira than me. She smiled widely at the news.

Cliodhna raised her chin, baring her teeth in a semblance of a smile. "Good. There must be no one left to bear witness to our existence."

"As you command," Maira responded with another low bow of her head.

I was indifferent to the suffering of men, numb after all these years of killing the men who fell prey to our song. Their lives—and their deaths—held no interest to me, not anymore. I killed because I was told to, because that's what we did as syrens and servants of Cliodhna. It made me feel no sadness. It made me feel no happiness. It just...was.

"We have survived this long because no one knows we truly exist. Those who do witness us are called crazy and written off by their people. But as more and more people travel through my waters, the likelihood of someone believing them grows." Cliodhna's voice was firm and brokered no arguments, though none of us would ever argue with her.

"Are we in danger?" I asked. My stomach clenched, old feelings of anxiety threatening to bubble up again. Clenching my fists, I dug my talons into the palms of my hands, giving myself something else to focus on. I was not that girl any longer. *I* was the one to be feared now. *I* was the threat.

Cliodhna looked at me, her icy blue eyes softening almost imperceptibly. "Not at all, my child. We are safe down here. And men will never be a threat to us. I promised you that when I took you all in, and I will keep my word. I am growing in my powers and will continue to do so to keep you all safe. But we must be cautious, even still."

"We will be," Maira vowed.

We all nodded along with Maira, Kyla moving from her seat at the rocks to cross her arm over her chest and bow her head. "We will take care of each other."

"Men will never be a threat to us. Know that," Cliodhna repeated, jutting her chin out proudly and looking around at all of us. "I will protect you, of course, but more importantly, you have the power and the strength to protect yourselves now."

The room fell silent then, and I pondered the news Cliodhna had given. The depths of the seas were our home, and if we were discovered, they would attempt to control us as they attempted to control the sea's surface. Men roamed the seas, fishing and trading, and pretended that they alone held dominion over the sea. A delusional belief, but one that had permeated mankind as time drew on.

Being syrens made us powerful, but we all had troubling histories with men, and I knew it unnerved each of us to think about the possibility. Anger flared in Maira's eyes, and her fists clenched at her sides.

In the corner of the cavern, Kyla's face turned resolved, but I could see the fear shining in the amber of her eyes. Of us all, she had the most reason to be afraid of men, rather than just vengeful. Before she had been a syren, Kyla had been a wife and a mother. One day, she had angered her husband, and he threw her from a cliff in a fit of rage.

The oldest of us, Kyla, had been a guide to each of us as we entered the fold, and seeing her discomfort made my own body tense. I fought back the anxiety that had taken me years to overcome after my transformation. Men would not harm me again. I would rather die—no, I would rather *kill* than be afraid of being harmed by men.

"Go rest for the evening," Cliodhna said, raising her chin. Her fingers flicked dismissively, motioning for us to disperse. Without a second glance, she turned and left the cavern, heading toward her own chambers.

The others began to follow, moving toward their rooms within the caves. Kyla caught my gaze and nodded to the side, asking me to linger.

"You're clenching your shoulders again," she said, her soft voice full of concern. She reached out and grabbed my hand, her dark skin contrasting with my own pale flesh. "What happened?"

I shrugged, pulling my fingers away from hers gently. Her pity and concern was not what I needed right now. It would only make me give more attention to the emotions I sought to quell. "I'm fine, Kyla."

She raised an eyebrow, quirking up the corner of her lip in a sardonic smile. "No, you're not. But if you don't want to talk about it, I understand."

Kyla had always been able to see through me—see through all of us. And I knew she was concerned, but my anxiety was something I had to deal with on my own. Or rather, something I had to push down on my own. Regardless of what I did with my anxiety, I didn't need Kyla's help with it. "I'm fine."

She looked at me for a long moment, her dark amber eyes drilling holes in me, as if she could see into my very soul. "Okay. Goodnight, Brigid. May your dreams give you guidance."

"And yours," I replied, forcing a smile onto my face.

Elizi
@ELIZIAN

CHAPTER TWO

Life passed normally for the next few days. Our lives as syrens were routine; we patrolled the waters, searching for ships and men that our queen deemed marked for ruin. Despite how busy the waters were becoming, we didn't wreck every ship we came across. We had to be careful with how we attacked to keep from being seen.

There were eight of us, including Cliodhna, and even though we were powerful and deadly, we were no match for taking on multiple ships worth of men. When we found ships that fit our guidelines, Cliodhna would give us the final answer on if the ship and the crew would meet their end.

Today, Kyla and Nerina had just returned from their own patrol. They had been successful in wrecking a lone merchant vessel off the coast and killing the small crew. With any crew larger than fifteen, the rest of us would join the duo on patrol to ensure there were no survivors. Our song did most of the work, causing unbearable agony to any who heard it, driving them to madness and eventually ruin. But occasionally, if we weren't careful, some managed to get away before they drowned.

"You did well today, my daughters," Cliodhna praised, raising her chin and offering a small smile to Kyla. She had been with Cliodhna for the longest, and Cliodhna was softest toward her, though even that did not mean much.

Cliodhna was detached. Her emotions often bordered on cold, but then again, she was a queen. Her role in this relationship wasn't to be one of us, but to lead us.

"Thank you, my queen," Kyla said softly, returning the smile with a deep nod.

Cliodhna's head snapped up, looking up toward the surface beyond the cave walls that made up our home, her eyes glowing white as they peered far beyond the rock. "There is a woman in my waters."

I smiled at her words, showing off my equally pointed teeth in a less-than-friendly grin. A woman in the water likely meant that men had thrown her overboard. And it meant that we could seek revenge. While Cliodhna's previous words had brought back old feelings of anxiety and anger, this part was familiar. Rescuing a woman would give me something to hold on to, something tangible to focus on. A purpose. And more importantly, an outlet for my rage. "Let's go fetch her."

Together, my fellow syrens and I swam off, following our queen toward our destination. Our tails slashed through the water as we moved, shining and sparkling in the fractured light leaking through the surface. We weaved and dodged rocks and sea life, eager to get to the surface as we made our way to save a woman who had been undoubtedly shown the cruelty of men. We *would* save her.

As we moved closer and closer to the surface, bubbles formed around a figure sinking beneath the waves. She wore a flowing white dress, which wrapped around her body, making it even harder for her to kick and stay afloat. But she tried, her petite body thrashing and flailing through the water, trying to right herself. My chest tightened watching her. The familiarity of the situation stung as I surged toward her.

Maira and I reached her first, reaching up and wrapping our webbed fingers around her ankles and wrists. We pulled her down into the water more and adjusted her body to be upright. Maira waved her free hand, creating a bubble of breathable air around both of us and the woman. Her chest heaved as she glanced back and forth between us and the surface.

"Stay calm, we are here to help you," I said, holding onto her gently but firmly. Her eyes darted between Maira and me, but she finally stopped thrashing, likely realizing that she could breathe. I moved a hand to rest gently on her upper arm rather than holding her tightly. "We are here to save you."

"Who...what are you?" the younger girl gasped out, still trying to catch her breath. Her long, dark hair clung to her face and neck in heavy ropes, a stark contrast to her alabaster skin. She was thin, her sopping wet gown clinging to her bones inside the bubble.

"You are safe with us," Maira responded proudly, tugging the woman gently toward her. She was careful with her talons, consciously flexing her fingers out to avoid digging the sharp points into the woman's skin. "My name is Maira, and this is Brigid. The others behind us will meet you when you are ready."

The woman's dark eyes, wide and frantic, darted up to the shadow of the ship that still lingered above us. The fear radiating off her was palpable, and I was overwhelmed with a desire to wrap this girl in my arms and shield her from the world. Despite that she only looked a few years younger than my own twenty-five, I felt protective already. My childhood had been cut short by my own misadventures with men, ending with me being thrown overboard in a similar fashion, and I didn't want this little one meeting the same fate.

Determined, I caught her gaze with my own and held it. "They will not hurt you again. We'll make sure of it."

"How?" she whispered, obviously afraid. My stomach hurt at the pain I was seeing in this young woman. It was like looking into a mirror and seeing myself all those years ago. Again, the feelings from my past bubbled up and threatened to break out of the chest I had locked them in. I would not be weak. This young woman in front of me needed strong and steady right now; breaking down could wait until I was alone.

I nodded over at the others swimming behind us at a distance, directing them to take care of the ship and the men above. They returned the nods to me, jetting toward the surface and the ship resting in the water. These men would not live, not after throwing this woman overboard. My attention turned back to her. "Those men will face the same fate they gave to you. They will have to sink or swim."

The young woman shuddered, her eyes closing tightly and her jaw clenching. She took a deep breath before opening her eyes wide. "You'll kill them?"

Surprised at the empathy still in her voice, I raised an eyebrow. I had not expected that reaction from her, not when she was so clearly impacted by what she had been through. "You want them to live? They just threw you into the sea."

She looked down, chewing on her lip. "They did. But they shouldn't have to die for that."

"They were ready to let you die for far less." I tilted my head as I studied her. The look of shame on her face was concerning, and I guessed there was more to her story than just her guilt over these men possibly dying. "Why did they throw you over?"

"Because I'm a woman. That was all the reason they needed, it seems." Her voice hardened, the soft and timid tone giving way to anger of her own.

"Sounds like men." Anger flooded through me, my fists clenched and my talons itched to tear through flesh, but I tamped it down. This young woman had seen enough anger for the day and did not need any more of it from me. She needed empathy and support. She reminded me of myself, of the girl who had died in these waters.

Maira's own face hardened at our conversation. Thankfully, she remained silent, simply holding the woman upright with me. I feared if Maira spoke, she would only make things worse and more overwhelming.

"I just wanted to be with my beau, Owen. My father forbade it, but I ran off anyway to meet him in the south, in Bhodheas; we were to start our new life together," she explained, pain crossing her features as her brows pinched together. "I paid for passage on the merchant ship, but apparently, they just wanted my money. The crew members I had paid told the captain. And the captain didn't like a woman on his ship, even if she had legally paid. He said I would be bad luck, and that the trip through the Straits of Marbh would be hard enough without me aboard."

Understanding her story and her sadness, I nodded. "You'll not have to face the ire of superstitious men again, I promise. We'll take you to our home and help you."

"Where are we going?"' she asked curiously, looking down into the depths. She couldn't have been older than nineteen, her face still young. Her dark eyes were dull, almost as if she didn't want to get her hopes up that we were here to save her. That feeling was a familiar one too, and my protective instincts surged.

"We have a network of caves that protect us and give us privacy. We'll explain more there, but all you need to know now is that you're safe and no man will ever harm you again," I repeated, wanting to make sure she understood. Maira reached out, and we tugged the young woman through the water behind us, keeping her in the air bubble Maira had created. We led her behind the others back to *Neamh na Mara* and toward a fresh start.

BRIGID

CHAPTER THREE

It took us longer to get back to the caves than it did to leave them, as the air bubble caused some drag through the cold water. Eventually, we slipped through the rocky archway at the entrance and emerged into the large main cavern.

Another, larger air bubble encompassed the back of the cavern, where Cliodhna and the others were already waiting. The others remained in their syren forms, sitting on the craggy rocks jutting up from the floor of the caves with their tails draped over the edges. Cliodhna had shifted to her more human-like appearance and stood, naked, waiting for us to bring the girl into the bubble.

We released the girl as both Maira and I transformed into our human forms, tails shifting slowly into legs. I wanted to stay with the girl, to support her.

"Welcome to *Neamh na Mara*," Cliodhna said, her voice echoing off the rocks now that the water was not absorbing the sound. It was easy to hear the pride in her voice as she spoke of our home.

The young woman stood in awe, her gaze shifting back and forth between all of us, the cavern, and the water above. She twisted her hands into her dress, which still dripped cold seawater and clung to her waifish body. Her anxiety made me want to twist my own hands, a motion reminiscent of my childhood, but I flexed my fingers wide instead.

"What is your name?" Cliodhna asked gently, walking toward the young woman. Her pale blue eyes roved over the smaller woman.

"Sorcha," she whispered, looking down at the floor. She took a deep breath before raising her gaze bravely to Cliodhna and clearing her throat. "Who're *you?*"

"They call me Cliodhna these days," our queen answered with a regal nod, inviting Sorcha to continue.

"Okay…" she drawled, seeming to gain a little bit of courage in the face of Cliodhna. A dark eyebrow arched in challenge. "Then *what* are you?"

Cliodhna smiled widely, though I wouldn't quite call it a friendly smile. Sorcha was getting her spine back under her, rebuilding the fire that had surely been almost extinguished when she was thrown into the frigid waters. Warmth flowed through me, and my mouth twitched up in a ghost of a smile. This confidence would serve her well, if she could keep it.

"I'm a goddess, my child. Of the sea, of beauty, of many things that have long been forgotten by man. These days, I'm a protector. Of the sea and of women like you. These are my syrens; they came to me the same way you have." Cliodhna jutted her chin out again, her voice loud and clear through the caves.

Sorcha peered around at the rest of us, taking us in, before settling her gray eyes on me. "You were all like me?"

"We were you, little one," I replied softly, trying to keep from overwhelming her. I recognized the signs of her anxiety, and it threw my own body back into the patterns I had fought to overcome. My fingers twitched at my sides, and my stomach twisted, muscles tensing across my entire body as the trauma resurfaced in my bones.

"Instead of letting us drown at the hands of hateful men, Cliodhna gave us a choice to stay with her," Maira said, her southern accent hanging off Cliodhna's name. *Klee-nah,* she pronounced it. "And now, we save girls like you and seek revenge on men like the ones who did this to you."

Sorcha's eyes snapped to Maira. "Revenge?"

Maira's gray eyes twinkled, as they always did when violence was mentioned. Her talons flexed, itching to tear into flesh. She was easily the most bloodthirsty among us, and it served us well, but now, it did little but frighten an already terrified girl. "Yes, girl, revenge."

"Don't overwhelm her," I scolded, seeing how Sorcha's hands trembled at her sides despite the resolved expression on her face. Maira scowled at me, but I ignored her, looking at Sorcha and remembering what it felt like to learn all of this for the first time. "If you choose to stay with us, you'll get your chance to avenge yourself."

"You do have options, Sorcha. If you do not wish to be part of this or to be one of us, we will take you to land and leave you in the care of someone safe. I will wipe your memories of us," Cliodhna explained, as she had to all of us before. "But if you wish to be one of us, you will be transformed. Part woman, part sea creature, all deadly. As a syren, you will become one of my children."

"Do I have to decide right now?" Sorcha asked, gripping her fingers together and twisting them roughly once again. Her index finger began picking at the skin of her thumb. My fingers twitched, wanting to reach out and pull her nails away from the torn skin.

Cliodhna smiled at her gently, more gently than I had seen from our queen in a long time. Her face typically displayed apathy or anger, but this look was soft and reflective. "Of course not. Take some time; think it over. Brigid will get you some dry clothes, and you can stay with her."

Sorcha looked around, her eyebrows wrinkling and forehead creasing. "Dry clothes? We're underwater."

I stepped over and put my hand on Sorcha's shoulder, which was still cold and damp from the seawater. The corners of my lips turned up in a teasing smile, trying to put her at ease. "We're blessed by a goddess, little one. We can do many things that may seem impossible."

Cliodhna nodded at me, jerking her head toward a passage at the back of the caves. "Take her to your room, Brigid."

I bowed my head respectfully. "Of course."

Taking Sorcha's hand in mine, I led her away from the rest of the group and farther into the caverns. While Cliodhna had said "room," she'd meant chambers. There were no doors in the underwater caverns, but we respected each other's privacy and stayed out of the spaces we weren't invited to. We stepped into my chambers, and I led Sorcha to sit in the hammock that allowed me to sleep in my syren form. Waving a hand, I expanded the air bubble around her to encompass my entire room so she could move freely.

"You have the same accent as me," Sorcha said quietly, her eyes roaming my space. She tracked my movements as I walked over to a small chest of drawers and retrieved her a dry shirt and fitted pants.

I glanced over my shoulder at her before turning and pressing the clothing into her hands, which had finally stopped trembling. "Not quite, but close enough. I'm from northern Tuathnach, in Gaisin. I imagine you're from somewhere near there. Here, put these on."

"Yes." Sorcha looked down at me. Her cheeks turned pink, and she quickly raised her gaze back up to meet mine. "Why're you not wearing any clothes?"

I shrugged, amused at her embarrassment. My nakedness didn't bother me at all, having grown used to my body being exposed. It was just a body, and men would not sexualize my body without my permission lest they die at my hand. "I don't usually wear my legs anymore, and it's kind of difficult to put pants on a tail. And other clothes have too much drag in the water. Nakedness is purely functional."

"If you don't wear clothes, why do you even have any? And how are they dry?" she questioned, taking the clothes from me and inspecting them as if they were made of pure magic. But they were just clothes, and the awe in her eyes made me want to smile.

It was an odd feeling. I hadn't truly smiled in years, and yet this girl was bringing these emotions back in full force within minutes.

"We all have clothes we keep for moments like this. If you don't decide to stay with us, we'll wear them to take you somewhere safe. We'll give you supplies," I explained. I tilted my head, thinking through what other questions she would have. While Kyla and the others had been helpful to me, I wanted Sorcha to be different, to feel safe and protected. I didn't want her to feel like she had to grow up before her time. "But none of us wear clothes here. It's much easier to stay in syren form. And they stay dry because the drawers are enchanted by Cliodhna. I told you, she's a goddess. Her magic is nearly limitless in what it can do."

"And do you all...worship her?" she asked, her voice cautious, as if she were afraid I might be offended. Her unease set my teeth on edge, and all I wanted was to calm and reassure her. She had nothing to fear here, and certainly nothing to fear in me.

Tipping my head side to side again, I thought about how to answer her. The situation was more complex than she made it out to be. "Och, not really. We're more her helpers—I suppose would be the word. We honor her, but there's not a worship aspect involved. Only humans do that. And more and more humans are forgetting to do even that."

"Are there other gods and goddesses?" Her soft voice was full of interest now.

I raised a shoulder slightly, unsure of exactly how to answer her. The questions of a child, despite her being nearly a woman, were always more complicated than they seemed. "Of course, there are. Most of them keep to themselves now since humans have taken over the world. Humans see them as abstract ideas, not real beings."

Her dark blue eyes opened wide. "Have you ever met any?"

My lips twitched up at her excitement, amused by how quickly her mind had moved from the trauma of the day to the excitement of the unknown. "No, little one. I've only met Cliodhna."

"So, Aine? The fae? They're real?" The interest was so clear in her voice, it was hard to keep from breaking into a full smile.

"I don't truly know," I admitted, letting myself smile at her. It felt freeing. And for the first time in a long time, I didn't feel like I needed to keep my smile hidden. The others were always so serious, so showing my emotions made me stand out from them. For the last ten years, all I had wanted was to fit in, to be accepted by my new family, no matter what it took. I had mirrored their behaviors, masking my emotions and shoving them down deep. "But I would imagine so. If we're real, I'm sure there are other stories that are real too."

"Do you think...I could meet another goddess?"

"Let's get you through this first," I said, reaching out to pat her shoulder. If anything, I admired her resiliency. "Then we'll talk about meeting other mythical creatures."

She blushed slightly, ducking her head. "So, what's your story...Brigid?"

I nodded, confirming my name for her. The thought of sharing my own story made my stomach clench. If I were alone, I would likely be curling in on myself. But Sorcha needed to see strength right now, so I shoved my anxiety and discomfort down into the depths of my mind. Rolling my shoulders back and holding my head up, I took a deep breath through my nose, calming my senses. "My story is one for another time. You don't want to hear it right now."

"Why not?" I wasn't sure why I had expected her question to be combative, but the genuine concern and curiosity in her voice threw me. She sounded like she truly wanted to know my story. Truly wanted to know *me*. It wasn't something I was used to.

"It's not a nice story, Sorcha," I said, my voice cracking slightly as my emotions threatened to burst through the dam I had built. Swallowing hard, I forced them back into their box and locked the lid. I couldn't talk about my past right now. I didn't want to remember what had happened that day on the ship. I didn't want to remember the boy who had suffered trying—and failing—to save me. I shook my head, trying to physically clear those thoughts from my head, before turning back to Sorcha. "And you just went through something traumatic. I'll not add to that right now. I'll tell you my story later."

She was silent, peering at me. Finally, she spoke again, her voice contemplative. "How long did it take for you to decide to stay?"

I shrugged, going along with the change of subject easily. While it was still talking about my past, the decisions I'd made after I was thrown off the ship weren't nearly as painful to remember as those that had come earlier. "I didn't need to think about it. I was angry when Cliodhna saved me. Saying no never crossed my mind."

"Are you still angry?" she asked, tilting her head again. Her dark blue eyes were wide and curious.

"No," I replied after thinking about it for a moment. It surprised me, but I hadn't considered my own emotions in a while. Indifference had been my only emotion. But thinking about what had happened to me as a child, I wasn't angry. "No, just tired. Men think they can just control anything and anyone they want to, especially those they think are smaller than them. And I'm tired of it. I could kill these men with one hand, and yet in my human form, they would dismiss me without a second thought."

"We are not beneath them." Her voice was quiet but firm, as if she were trying to convince herself. It made my temper flare; I wanted to crush any of the men who had made her question that statement before.

"No, Sorcha, we are not," I said firmly. My voice softened slightly; I didn't want my anger to overwhelm her. "Tell me your story. How did you end up here? What was your life like?"

"Like I said before, I was running away to be with my beau. His name is Owen, and he's wonderful. My father is a controlling man, and a violent one. He kept me isolated apart from my letters with Owen and our occasional meetings. I couldn't be around him anymore, couldn't take the abuse, so I took my fate into my own hands and tried to make my life better. It didn't work," she said, her voice going flat at the end. She twisted her hands in her lap again. "And now I'm here, trying to wrap my head around the fact that I'm currently residing in a cave underwater with mermaids."

"It did work. It got you here," I pointed out, trying my best to reassure her. "You can either stay with us and start a new life, or we can take you somewhere safe where you can start a new life. Either way, you control your fate now. And we're syrens, little one, not mermaids. Mermaids are fairy tales; we are very real."

"Do you think I should stay?" She twisted her fingers together again, her voice uncertain and slightly shaky.

Dipping my head down to catch her gaze and force her to make eye contact with me, I put a hand on her shoulder. "I think you should do what is best for you. And you need to take the time to think about that and figure out what that is. Just because I gave in to my anger and became this doesn't mean that's the right answer for everyone. But if you do stay, we will be your family, and we will protect you with our lives."

"Will you tell me about the others?" she asked as she finally began changing into the clothes I had given her. She kept her eyes on me as she dressed.

"They've all got similar stories to us: men had wronged them, and they were rescued by Cliodhna and offered a new life. They've all been here longer than me. Some have been here for half a century. Maira is the newest before me; she was saved fifteen years ago. The others will introduce themselves," I explained. Telling the stories of the others was not my place, but I wanted her to understand that we were on her side and that we understood her pain and what she had gone through. "But Kyla is the oldest, the first of us. She was thrown off a cliff by her betrothed when she said something to anger him. She's our leader when Cliodhna isn't here."

"You don't seem very close to them," she said. "You didn't say anything to them when we left, not even a look or a nod at them."

Considering that, I sat in silence for a moment. She was right, we weren't close, not in the way some of the others were close to each other. "No, I suppose I'm not. Maira and Kyla mentored me when I was first changed, but I never really connected with the others."

"Why not?"

I sighed. This girl was going to pull my life's story and every emotion out of me if I wasn't careful. "Little one, this is a lot of information. You don't have to learn everything about us right now."

"How long have you been here?" she asked, only pausing for a moment before launching back into her questioning.

"Almost ten years now, I suppose," I replied, at least grateful she had moved to something less personal. Time wasn't something we often considered here, and while I had a general idea of how long it had been, it might have been longer.

"There haven't been any others before me?"

"There have," I explained, "but none of them wanted to stay with us as a syren. So, we took them to a woman in the south who helps them start a new life, finds them work and a place to stay, and gets them back on their feet. Their memories of us are erased by Cliodhna; all they know is that they were in the water and then they were rescued, waking up at their new home in the south."

"And the...revenge bit?" Her face was curious, if a little apprehensive. "What's all that about?"

I sat down on the hanging bed beside her, the netting dipping beneath my weight. "Aye, the revenge. You know those tales of the lovely women of the sea who lure the sailors into the water with just their voices? Well, that's not entirely accurate, but that's us. They call us mermaids, sea witches. But it's just us."

"But they haven't done anything to you personally? Why not just target the ones who actually wronged you?" she asked, still playing with her hands in her lap.

"All men have wronged us," I said fiercely. That was something Cliodhna had driven into our heads from the moment she saved us. And she was right. All men were bad, and all men were the reason for our fates. Men succumbed to our song quickly, showing the truth of how weak they were. And despite what Sorcha had said about her beau, I still believed Cliodhna's words. Men had never been kind to me, apart from one young boy a lifetime ago. My experiences with them had been those of violence or those of cold indifference to my suffering.

"There hasn't been a single man who was kind to you?" she asked, still playing with her hands.

"There was one. Once," I said quietly. It was more than I had wanted to admit, but I couldn't help myself. Thoughts of the boy from all those years ago, with his dark hair and bright green eyes, filled my mind. I could still see him reach his hand out to help me. I knew he'd been punished because of it—because of me.

"Is he not innocent?" Her voice was soft, as if she was afraid to jar me from my thoughts.

I thought of the boy often, picturing what he would look like now and wondering if he had survived. But I could not dwell on those fantasies and pushed them back into the chest in my mind. It didn't matter what I dreamed, I owed fealty to Cliodhna. "Likely not anymore. He's either dead or has turned into those men he was surrounded by. Innocence doesn't last long when surrounded by men like that."

"But what if he hasn't?" she pressed. "What if he's still the kind boy you knew, just grown up?"

"Then I pray to never see him on the seas," I said, meeting her gaze. I couldn't let her fill my mind with any more fantasies about that boy. Caelum. Even after all these years, I still remembered his name. Maybe if he had grown into a man, he would be different. But I knew better than to get my hopes up.

Sorcha stayed silent for a few moments, again wringing her hands in her lap. I wanted to reach out and soothe her anxiety, but I could see the motion brought her comfort. Her voice was quiet. "Will I have to do that?"

I placed one of her hands in mine, squeezing gently. "You will be able to if you decide to stay with us."

She looked over, our eyes locking. There was fire in hers, the kind that burned so hot it was blue rather than orange. Her voice did not waver as she replied, "I think I want to be one of you."

"You think?" I questioned, raising an eyebrow. "You need to be certain, lass. This isn't something you can change your mind about later. If you're with us, then you're with us forever. You need to be sure. Get some rest, take the night and sleep on it, and then we can talk about it more if you'd like."

She nodded and lay down, pulling a thin blanket over her as she turned on her side. I stretched out into the other hanging bed, pulling a blanket over myself as well. "Goodnight, Brigid."

"Goodnight, Sorcha. May your dreams give you guidance."

Elizi
@ELIZIANN

BRIGID

CHAPTER FOUR

The next morning, once Sorcha had cleaned up and dressed, we walked back out to the main cavern. There was now only an air bubble around Sorcha and me rather than in the cavern itself. The others, including Maira, who had transformed back into her syren form, swam around us, flitting impatiently back and forth. Kyla caught my eye, nodding at me with something akin to pride in her eyes. I furrowed my brow, wondering what she was proud of.

Cliodhna swam forward, stepping softly into the air bubble while she transformed as naturally as breathing. Her human form was just as regal as her syren form. She raised her head, jutting out her chin and peering down her nose at Sorcha. "Have you decided, my dear? Or do you need more time?"

Sorcha looked over at me, her dark blue eyes wide. Sensing her rising anxiety, I nodded my head and smiled in what I hoped was an encouraging look and not a grimace. Though we had talked at length about Sorcha's options, she hadn't outright told me what she had decided. She nodded back before taking a visibly deep breath. "I'm ready. I want to stay with you; I want to be fierce like you."

"Then you shall," Cliodhna said, her voice resonating with

conviction. She looked at me, and her eyes hardened back to the expression I was familiar with. The queen may have put on her smile for Sorcha, but I knew better than to expect any sentimentality. "Brigid, please step out of the bubble."

Bowing my head, I stepped back into the water, letting the transformation take me back to my syren form. One moment I had legs, and the next, a silvery red tail took their place, moving me through the water with ease.

Once Cliodhna and Sorcha were the only ones in the bubble, Cliodhna placed her hands on either side of Sorcha's pale face. I couldn't see Sorcha's expression from behind her, but Cliodhna's eyebrows furrowed with concentration.

A strong current came swirling from behind me, rushing around my body and moving into the air bubble. The air around them filled with the cold water, swirling in thick ropes in a spiral around their bodies. The spirals danced and weaved around them, growing thicker and obscuring them from view. Suddenly, the spirals collapsed, and once the rush of bubbles dissipated, Sorcha and Cliodhna were no longer in an air bubble at all. They were out in the water with the rest of us.

Sorcha's borrowed clothes had ripped and fallen away to reveal her pale skin covering new, powerful muscles. Her torso lengthened and transitioned into a shimmering indigo tail, lithe and muscular. The webbing between her fingers connected, and her nails grew sharp, as did her teeth. She truly was a syren now, deadly and powerful.

Cliodhna smiled, showing off her own sharp teeth, as Sorcha looked down over her new body, holding her hands out in front of her and swishing her tail experimentally. "Welcome, my child."

Sorcha finally tore her gaze from her hands and tail, looking up. Her mouth opened a few times as if she were getting used to not having to hold her breath beneath the waves. Her hand grabbed at her throat, and her eyes widened. Finally, she was able to speak. "So, what now?"

Maira grinned from across the cavern. "Now, we explore and show you your new home."

The others and I swam out of the cave, twisting and gliding through the icy waters. Sorcha was behind us, moving much more slowly, still getting used to having a tail instead of legs. She was catching on quickly, though, twirling and smiling as she swam between us.

We spun around, swimming between rocks and dodging sea life. The tall stalagmites on the ocean floor jutted up, creating pillars for us to swirl around.

"Look!" Iona said, pointing up toward the surface. There was a shadow looming above. It was a ship, oblong and dark in the waters, its long hull slicing through the dark waves. The keel was jagged, and even from this distance, it was obvious the ship was old and unkempt. And it was alone.

Cliodhna nodded once at us, instructing us to deliver our wrath upon this ship. We all grinned and shot up again, swimming toward the shadow. Maira reached the hull first, running her claws across the wood and gouging deep gashes along it. When she reached the bow, she turned and did the same down the other side of the hull, marking the ship for doom as water spilled inside.

I turned to look at Sorcha as I explained what was happening. "Now, we sing. Our song will cause them to go mad and jump into the water to escape the agony. And then we will drown them."

"But you don't try to save them? Even if they're innocent?" she asked, still staring wide-eyed at the ship above us. She looked so much younger.

I swam over in front of her, blocking her view. "Sorcha, no man is innocent. They are the reason for all of our suffering."

"Some of them are innocent," she protested quietly, looking down at her tail. Rolling her shoulders back, she raised her head. "My beau was innocent. He never hurt me, never would have."

I didn't answer as the others jettied up, beginning to sing their song from below the surface. Even from beneath the water, I could see the men on deck holding their hands over their ears, trying to block out the agonizing noise. One man quickly succumbed, walking toward the railing with a frantic look on his face. Before the others could reach him, he jumped right over into the icy water.

Maira didn't hesitate, swimming up to him and circling him like a shark with an equally toothy grin on her face. Finally, he fell out from the madness our voices induced and began flailing in the water. But the current was too strong, or he was too weak a swimmer, and after a moment, he stopped flailing, sinking lifelessly into the darkness below. As Maira and the others began to sing louder, the ship veered off toward the jagged cliffs, crashing into the sharp rocks jutting up in all directions. The hull ripped open along Maira's gouges, and water began flooding into the large hole.

Sorcha swam beside me, her shoulders tense and her fists bunched at her sides. "How long will this take?"

"As long as it takes." I sighed, conflicted about how to address the uncertainty in her voice. I understood her conflict with what we did, but she needed to understand the choice she had made and come to terms with it. Again, her words before brought the boy who had tried to save me to mind, but I shoved down those thoughts and turned my attention to the scene before us. "This is what we do, Sorcha. We avenge ourselves on these men. Yes, there may be a few innocent men, but more likely than not, they're not. Especially not men who try to claim and control the ocean as their own and determine who can or cannot be on it."

Sorcha was quiet, her only movement her tail flicking back and forth. Her dark hair fanned out behind her in the current. After a few moments of watching the destruction behind me settle, she nodded. "I understand. You're right. My beau was not a sailor, and no sailor I ever met was kind to me."

Taking her hand in my own, I squeezed gently, pulling her from her visible anxiety. "This will take time to accept and acknowledge. You have all the time in the world now. Take it. You can watch us for as long as it takes to come to terms with your new life."

"Do we not age?" she asked, her eyebrows wrinkling, her attention finally focusing back on me. "What do you mean 'all the time in the world?'"

"We age, just slowly. Cliodhna says that we are her creations, and she enjoys our company, so her magic slows our natural aging process," I explained. Noticing the others finish with the ship and the crew, I watched the wreckage sink down into the darkness. "We can do many other things too. In our syren form, we're immune to the cold of the water and we can see in the darkness of the depths."

"But not in our human form?"

I nodded. Cliodhna's powers had grown over the past few years, and I had no doubt we would continue to find new things it allowed us to do. "Not unless we're in an air bubble created by one of us. Those hold the same syren magic."

She nodded, and I could see her mind trying to wrap around the new information. She looked over my shoulder. "We should go; they're leaving."

"Do you want to stay a moment longer?" I could see how this was affecting her; if she needed time to process what had happened, I would stay with her. When I had transformed, the others had thrust me into the life with no warning, explanation, or time to adjust. I wanted something different for Sorcha, and I wanted her to take her time leaning into this new world.

Her gaze flicked back to the wreckage sinking into the darkness behind me. After watching for a moment, she shifted her focus back to me. "No, I think I've seen all I need to. It will just take me some time to understand my new reality, I think."

"And that's fine, Sorcha. You have a lifetime to understand. The others will understand as well. But just remember, there's no going back to being human. You're a syren now. Forever." My voice was stern, but I needed her to know that. Cliodhna had never taken back the transformation, and I feared what she would do if Sorcha requested it.

She nodded. "I understand."

Over the next few weeks, Sorcha and I grew close. She had elected to share rooms with me, and we spent many nights up later than we should have, talking. While I wasn't used to sharing my own space, something about Sorcha made it feel less imposing than sharing with someone else would have been.

We spoke of our lives before we transitioned, of our goals and dreams and how we both had wanted to explore the world. Sorcha spoke often of her beau she had left behind, wondering if he had moved on already or if he was still waiting for her.

My mind often drifted to Caelum, thinking of what my life could have been like if I had met him in a different place. Would we have been like Sorcha and Owen? But it was a fool's dream and a waste of my time to hope for things that could never happen. Men were our enemy, not something to be fantasized over.

Tonight, we had landed back on the topic of our revenge. It had been a rough day; the men we had targeted earlier did not die easily, but fought and thrashed every step of the way. I had seen it wear on her earlier; I'd known this talk would be coming.

In the semi-darkness of the sea caves, she spoke. "Why do we do this, Brigid? Why do we ruin these ships and these men?"

I sighed. I truly did not have an answer that would satisfy her, not after our conversations at the first ship she saw with us. "I suppose, mostly, because our queen declares it. We all have different reasons why we agreed to become syrens, but Cliodhna's word is rule here. Maira enjoys killing men—killing anything, really. I know this has been rough on you, Sorcha, but that's what we agreed to. What *you* agreed to."

She was silent for a moment before letting out her own sigh. "I know. And I'm not questioning her. She saved me, saved us. But I just can't help but think about how there might be another Owen out there, just stuck on a boat because he knows no better. And we might kill him."

My mind raced, unbidden, back to Caelum, who had fought to save me and been punished because of it. I would never be able to repay him for his kindness. "Aye, I know what you mean."

"You all are my family now, and I would never go against you. I just can't help but think that maybe some of the men don't deserve our ire."

"How are we to know, then?" I asked softly. "How can we tell which ones to punish and which ones to spare?"

She sighed again. "Maybe I'm too nice to be a syren."

I smiled at her, knowing she could see it in the little light cast through the cave. "You are too nice, but not too nice to be a syren. You're a great syren, little one. You have a kind heart."

"You do too," she said quietly, tentatively, as if she were afraid of my reaction.

My heart clenched. "Maybe once. Now? I'm not so sure about that."

"You do, Brigid. You're a good person with a good heart. Life just dealt you a bad hand."

"Yes," I said softly. "It did. But it ended up getting me here, so how bad can it really be?"

"True," she agreed. "Thank you for saving me that day. I'm glad to have met you."

"And I, you," I replied.

As we talked into the night about everything and nothing, I was glad I had found a friend, a true friend, at last. I had never had siblings, but this connection, this protective instinct to shield her from the troubles of the world, I imagined it was what I would feel toward a sister. Sorcha was a good person—much better than I could ever be—and kind. She had obviously been sheltered as a human, and I could see that she had potential. She was ready to become her own woman, and I couldn't wait to mold her and help her grow.

Elizi
@ELIZI

CHAPTER FIVE

We were out on a patrol, looking for anything amiss in the waters Cliodhna controlled. I was with Sorcha again, as she was still adjusting to her new reality as a syren. She had taken to it mostly with ease. Her tail was beautiful, and she knew how to use it well. She had practiced singing her song and creating air bubbles. The only thing she was still having issues with was accepting the destruction we would bring. But she was slowly coming around to Cliodhna's ways of thinking.

Swimming through the waters, we twirled and spun, having fun with each other as much as we were on a mission. Sorcha and I had only gone out once before, nearly a week ago. In the meantime, we had just been swimming around the caves with each other, getting her used to her new home.

She had been with us for nearly a fortnight and was adjusting quicker than I ever had. Though she still had many questions, they were endearing and almost comforting now.

"Do we do this often?" she asked, spinning around with some dolphins who had been following us for a while. When they had first shown up, she had been so shocked, I had laughed for the first time in what was likely years.

I had missed the feeling of joy.

Turning my head to face her, I explained our patrol schedule. "We're on a rotation, always in pairs. A pair goes out once every couple of days to patrol the waters. Kyla sets up the rotations, and we go out to see if there's anything that needs our attention. They kept us out of the last few as you got used to your new body."

Typically, I was paired with Maira. Being the only one who could put up with her harsh attitude for long periods of time, the others often used me as a buffer. Years of being a syren had only fueled Maira's anger, rather than tempered it like it had with some of the others. And while it often stung when directed at me, I had such practice shoving my emotions down that her words slid off my skin like water.

"How do you decide which ships to target?" she asked, weaving in and out of the craggy rocks. Her dexterity with her new tail was coming along nicely, as if she had never been without it.

"If we see any ships that are alone, we are to report back to Cliodhna. She decides their fate from there," I explained, moving through the water beside her. "Otherwise, if she senses a woman in the waters, we will all go then."

"And you never questioned how she chooses?" Sorcha asked, swimming closer beside me. She wrinkled her brow. "I mean, if all men are the target of our revenge, like she says, then why does she pick and choose?"

I tilted my head, halting for a moment. I had never thought of it that way before, never thought of questioning the choices my queen made. But perhaps Sorcha had a point. Why did Cliodhna pick and choose the ships for us to target? "I...I don't know. I never thought of it like that. We don't really question her."

Her eyes widened and her face became panicked. "I didn't mean to question her, really. I was simply curious."

I smiled softly. Sorcha was afraid of a cross word or a tense look. While she was comfortable enough to ask me questions, her apprehension still leaked through. It had taken me years to get over my own hesitations and anxiety, and even now I still tended to close down when someone became upset, bottling up my substantial anger to be unleashed in private later.

"Relax, little one. There's nothing wrong with asking questions. It's been a right minute since someone was around here to shake things up. And it's natural that you'd have these questions."

Her shoulders slumped, and the tension bled out of her face, erasing the soft crinkle between her eyebrows. We went back to playing with the ocean life as we circled the waters. We rounded a large rock sticking up high into the water column and stopped. There was a ship up ahead, a large one.

Sorcha looked over to me, her eyes wide again. "There's a ship."

I almost laughed again at her tone of surprise. This girl was pulling me from my own shell as much as I was trying to pull her from hers. In the short time I'd known her, I had laughed and smiled more than I had in my entire life. It was odd, but welcomed. "Yes, we need to report back to Cliodhna and let her decide its fate."

"We have to go all the way back? What if they're gone by then?" Even in the water, she began twisting her hands.

"No, we just have to speak with our syren voices. It's similar to singing, but not quite the same. The magic carries our voices through the water. She'll hear us and be able to answer the same way," I explained. I held out my hand, and she slipped her taloned fingers in with mine. "Let me show you."

She nodded, her face resolved. She had sung before, but we hadn't talked about this part of it yet.

Straightening my spine, I began to speak, fusing the vocalizations with intent. We were far enough below the water that the humans on the ship would not be affected, and Cliodhna was able to hear us from wherever we were in the waters. "My queen, we've found a large ship. What are your orders?"

After a few moments, our queen's voice came echoing through the waters. "Wait there, my daughters. The others are on their way. This ship will face our vengeance."

I released Sorcha's hand and turned so my eyes were back on the ship again. "Now, we wait for the others. And we will keep watch and make sure the ship doesn't get away from us before they get here."

The ship did move, but not significantly, by the time the others swam up beside us. It didn't seem to be in a hurry, but rather was hugging the rocky coast as it continued through the water, the keel slicing through the waves. Through the water, I could see the name painted on the side.

The Nehalennia.

How fitting that this ship would be named after the lost goddess of seafarers. It was almost ironic, and my lip curled softly at my own humor.

I had not met other gods or goddesses, but I remembered them from my limited teachings as a child. Nehalennia had once been worshiped as widely as any of the gods but had disappeared as humans began to change. And unlike Cliodhna, no one had worshiped Nehalennia in years, her altars and temples lost to the new world.

Led by Kyla, the others circled around us, looking at us intently. Her eyebrow quirked as she looked at me, and I schooled my face back into indifference, erasing the hint of the smile that had lingered on my lips. Kyla glanced over her shoulder toward the ship. "What have you seen?"

"They're not fishing. There are no lines or nets. And they've not gone out into the deeper water. They're staying fairly close to the coast for some reason. It could be easy to get the ship to run into the rocks," I explained, nodding my head to the ship in the distance. It was odd that the ship was this close to the coast with no fishing lines, but who knows what they were doing. Maybe they were pirates, trolling for the vulnerable. "It's a wooden hull, and it looks old, but it's well taken care of. Either way, it should splinter if it runs into the peaks there."

Sorcha looked at me, an expression of shock on her face as her tail twitched. "I didn't know you were analyzing it like that."

I raised one side of my mouth in a half-smile, all the emotion I could risk showing around the others. "I'm always analyzing, little one. We need to be aware of what we're up against. The ships and the crews both suffer. Our focus is on the crew, of course, but the ships themselves face destruction just the same."

"If there are lines or nets, they could snag us in the water," Kyla explained patiently, "and then we'd be trapped at their mercy. Our claws are sharp, but it would still take us time to free ourselves."

"So, they could catch us?" she asked. "Have any syrens ever been caught before?"

"Not in my time," Kyla said, smiling reassuringly. "We're very careful to avoid them. If men discovered the reality of our existence beyond just legends, we would likely be hunted and captured to extinction. It's better to simply avoid any fishing vessels unless we can easily wreck and kill the crew."

Sorcha nodded her understanding. "But if they don't have lines or nets, what are they doing so close to shore?"

"It doesn't matter what they're doing," Maira interjected impatiently, flexing her talons. "They won't be doing it much longer."

At that, Maira and the others surged forward toward the ship. I tugged on Sorcha's hand, and we followed, tails slashing through the water as we neared the underbelly of the ship. We surrounded it on the side of the open water and began singing as one. Still holding Sorcha's hand, I squeezed her fingers as she joined our song. The power of her voice seemed to startle even her, but she adjusted to it quickly. Our song wasn't actual words, more of a melody filled with intent. And that intent was to drive these men to madness and ruin.

Abruptly, the ship diverted from its course, turning hard toward the rocky cliffs on the other side of it. Even in the water, there was a sickening crash and the sound of splitting wood as the nose of the ship rammed into the jagged peaks.

We kept singing.

The ship began to turn, its side now scraping along the rocks as well. Men, driven mad by our song, began jumping overboard as the ship started to take on water and dip lower beneath the waves. While still close to the shore, the water here wasn't exactly shallow, and the ship would sink in its entirety.

We circled, diving deep as bodies began tumbling in the water, the panic induced by our song preventing them from seeing reason and turning toward the cliffs for refuge. Sorcha looked over at me, her eyes wide as she processed the scene in front of her. She still seemed intimidated, yet interested.

I motioned for her to follow me. As we swam up closer to the surface, gleeful that these men would feel our wrath, a body crashed into the water in front of me. A man, based on the broadness of his shoulders and the general bulk of his frame. His body twisted, his limbs flailing as he sank through the water.

I stopped short, letting go of Sorcha, who continued swimming up toward the surface with the others. I swished my tail to hold myself steady as I stared at him. Instead of flailing, he was trying to steady himself. He righted his large, muscular body and finally turned in the water to face me. His eyes widened, but he didn't seem afraid of me.

Another man splashed into the water in between us, diverting my attention. This man, once the bubbles around his form dissipated, was terrified. His eyes widened, and he opened his mouth to scream, but only more bubbles came out. He furiously tried to kick to the surface, but Maira was faster. Swimming down between us from the surface, she lunged forward, grabbing his leg and pulling him down into the depths. He kicked, still releasing a stream of bubbles from his mouth as he flailed about furiously.

With Maira gone into the depths, I turned my attention back to the man from before. He was closer to the surface now, almost close enough to breach it. Flicking my tail, I used my power to surge up, wrapping my talons around his ankle just as his head surfaced.

I could not let him escape. This man seemed a powerful swimmer, and if I let him go, I had no doubt he would survive. And given how closely he had seen Maira and me, I couldn't let that happen. In the moment, I was grateful Sorcha had continued to the surface and wouldn't have to watch this. I wasn't sure she'd have the stomach to witness this death up close.

I yanked hard on his boot, pulling him back beneath the waves. Down, down, down we went before I released him. I wanted to see his face, this man who had not seemed afraid of us. Had he seen us before?

Tilting my head to the side, I looked at the man more closely as he calmly treaded water, not trying to get back to the surface. His face was familiar to me...somehow. I swam slightly closer to him, whipping my tail in the water, impressed when he didn't back away. We stared at each other for a moment longer before it clicked in my head. The bright green eyes staring back at me, the dark hair floating in the water, the chiseled and strong face. While he had aged some, I knew that face, those eyes.

The boy from the ship.

Caelum.

My eyes widened, and my stomach twisted again, my heart in my throat. I never thought I would see him again after being thrown overboard. He had fought to try to save me, even knowing he would be punished by the captain for it. My mind was spinning, trying to process the man before me as I studied him.

He was still oddly calm, keeping himself upright but never trying to go back toward the surface. He studied me back, his eyes roving over my body and stuttering on my tail before traveling back up to my face. He seemed resigned to his fate. His gaze was intense, and I wondered if he recognized me as well. I doubted it, as he had only seen me for a brief moment. But I had remembered him.

His cheeks began to bulge, a sign he was running out of time under the water, and he finally cast a glance upwards to the surface before looking back to me. But still, he didn't make a move.

In an impulsive moment, I knew I couldn't let my only savior, the only redemption to men, drown because of us. Because of *me.* Before I could stop myself and think about the betrayal my family would surely feel, I rushed toward him, grabbed him under the arms, and pulled his chest against mine as I propelled us toward the surface. He would not die on my watch. I would not be the cause of his ruin.

Not after he had suffered trying to save me on that ship.

Maybe Sorcha was right. Maybe he was still the innocent boy who had tried to save me all those years before.

Eliziel
@ELIZIAN

B RIGID

CHAPTER SIX

We broke the surface, the man gasping for breath as water dripped off his dark hair and into his eyes. His chest heaved as I let him go, sure that he could at least tread water on his own. I put some space between us, still staring intently at him. Now above the surface of the water, I could see how clearly his face had changed since we had last seen each other. What used to be the face of a boy was now the face of a man, weathered, weary, and rough.

Despite the anxiety swirling through my mind, I schooled my face into blankness and calm. Hiding my emotions was not a new feat for me, and it was easier than I would have liked to put on the façade of indifference. Showing emotions would not benefit me here. The man—Caelum—was obviously a sailor, and had likely heard the legends. If he believed me to be anything but a blood-thirsty beast, I would be at a disadvantage.

"I thought you were going to kill me," he said cautiously, beginning to tread water to keep his head above the waves. "Like the other one did to Gordan."

My stomach was still clenching, and I didn't know why I was doing this. I was a rational person, and my logic was screaming at me that I was making a mistake by saving him. He was on the ship we had destroyed, and that meant he was likely one of the men we sought vengeance on. One of the men who sought to control those who would travel the ocean. But I couldn't stop myself from saving him.

In the near distance, the ship continued sinking. I could feel the others beneath the surface, but I was confident we were now far enough away that they would not shift their focus from the wreckage long enough to notice us.

I was betraying my family, the people who had saved me and given me purpose, for this man I barely knew. But he had saved me before, and I had thought I would never see him again. Faced with him again, I didn't know what to do, but I did know I couldn't have killed him or let him drown. No matter how much my gut was telling me this was wrong and that I should have just left him to drown, something else, something deeper, was telling me this was right and that saving him was the right thing to do.

Swishing my tail back and forth to keep my head out of the water, I peered at him, deciding to tell him why I had saved him from surely drowning of his own stubbornness. "You're the boy who tried to save me about ten years ago. I was thrown overboard from a merchant ship bound for Bhodheas."

The man seemed shocked that I had spoken to him. Finally, a glimmer of realization passed over his face like he had finally been able to place where he recognized me from. "Aye, that's right. You're the girl who stowed away in the hold."

"I am." I didn't know what else to say to that. I didn't know what else I even *could* say to that in this situation. He had tried to save me before, and I had been intent on drowning him today. I wanted to vomit, and I wanted to run back to my room and curl up with Sorcha and listen to her stories. But I had to face my actions, my choices.

The man looked behind his shoulder to the wreckage of his former ship. It was sinking below the waves now, more than halfway submerged. I could feel in the water that the others were still picking off survivors who had seen us, ensuring they drowned either on their own or with help.

He turned back to me, anger now prominent in his blazing green eyes. "Was that your doing?"

"Indirectly. Your wheel man is the one who drove it into the cliffs, not I," I replied, looking at the wreckage as well. My voice was confident and indifferent despite the warring emotions in my mind. It was what we did every day, and yet, I found myself feeling guilty about it now as I faced him. I didn't like the feeling. I hadn't let myself feel emotions this strongly since I was a child.

The anxiety and fear of the day I was thrown overboard had broken something in me, and I hadn't allowed myself to feel anything for a long time. Sorcha had brought it back some, and now being face to face with my past ripped the lid off the chest I had kept my emotions locked in. I fought to shove the feelings back down, to plaster my indifference across my face and be the deadly creature I knew I could be.

He opened his mouth to speak, but a wave crested and swelled around us, pulling his head under the water. With an inconvenienced sigh at the fragility of humans in the sea, I dipped beneath the water and pulled him back up. I held him wordlessly while he again caught his breath. Panting as he tried to wipe the water out of his eyes without going back beneath the surface, he asked, "Did any of my men survive?"

I shrugged, releasing him to hold himself up in the icy water. If I told him the truth, that my fellow syrens were picking off any survivors they thought had seen them, it would just make him angry. For some reason, I didn't want to make him angry.

"Why did you save me?" he asked, leveling his piercing gaze back at me. The accusation and anger there were almost tangible. "Why did you wreck my ship and then come back and save me?"

My eyes narrowed at his tone. I had just risked everything to save this man, including the anger of my goddess if she found out what I had done, and he was questioning me. I chose to ignore his question about me pulling him down and then saving him, because I simply did not have an answer. Anger bubbled up in my stomach, hot in

my throat as I tamped it down. I smothered out the fire with practiced ease. "*I* did not do anything to your ship."

He went to respond, but seemed to think better of it, closing his
mouth and nodding instead. "Thank you for saving me, whatever
the reason."

"Let's get you to shore," I replied, tugging him along beside me
as I began swimming toward the rocky coastline that I knew was
just above the horizon. The cliffs the ship had wrecked into were
completely inaccessible, and if I wanted to get him out of the water,
I would have to take him a fair distance to the shore.

The water was cold, and while it wouldn't affect my body in this
form, I only hoped I could get Caelum to shore before he became
too cold and succumbed to the elements. Looking around, I
searched for any wreckage that had bobbed to the surface, but none
of the pieces this far away were big enough to hold his weight.

"What happened to you when you got thrown over before?" he
asked after a few moments of swimming. He was trying to help hold
his own weight, but the waves were making it difficult, and I still
ended up bearing most of his weight as we moved forward.

I stayed silent for a few moments, pondering just how much
detail to give him, before finally answering his question. "I turned
into this. What happened to you?"

"But how? And what exactly are you? Are you a mermaid?" he
pressed, shivers wracking his body as we continued swimming.
"And I got punished, like I told you I would."

"Don't talk. We need to save our energy," I replied, staring
straight ahead as we moved through the water and trying not to
bristle at being called a mermaid. I also forced myself to ignore
hearing that he'd been punished for trying to save me. I was repaying
that debt with this action, and I didn't want to know the details,
despite what I had pondered before with Sorcha's influence.

I didn't want to care what had happened to him when he was a
child. And I didn't want to share my own story with him.

After swimming for several more minutes in silence, I looked
down at the man, who had suddenly grown heavier in my arms. His
eyes had closed, and as I shifted his weight, his head lolled forward

into the water. Damn. I cursed, shifting more of his weight onto my own body to keep his head up. I needed to get him to shore, and fast.

The rocky beach seemed much farther than I remembered it being as I continued to swim through the water, propelling us forward with the power of my tail. While the coast itself was nearly right beside me, it was nothing but tall jutting cliffs; there was nowhere to pull the man out of the water. Finally, the shore became clear, and I heaved one last push to get there. The water became shallower and slightly warmer.

Pulling us up onto the rocks as much as I could, I cursed the heaviness of my tail when it was out of the water. Not wanting the man I had just saved to drown in his suddenly unconscious state, I pushed him as far up onto the beach as possible, shoving against his back and thighs. I forced myself to ignore the feeling of the firm muscle beneath my hands. Eventually, his head was resting on the beach, but his body was still mostly submerged.

Heaving a sigh, I transitioned quickly into my human form, shivering from the cold air. Working hastily, I bent down and dragged him out of the water and onto the beach. The air would still be frigid to him, but at least he would be out of the water.

Stepping back into the water, I sat down in the icy waves and transformed back—the shifting of my body as natural as breathing —before working my way back onto the shore and as close to the man as possible. I had to keep him from dying; and staying with him until he regained consciousness was the least I could do. I had gone against my own to save him, a fact they would find out about when Sorcha and the others realized I was no longer with them. My stomach churned. I wasn't sure how they would react, but I knew it wouldn't be good.

We lay there on the beach for what felt like an eternity but was likely only a few moments. The ship had almost completely sunk below the waves in the distance. Suddenly, there was a break in the water close to the shore.

A blonde head of hair.

Maira.

"What are you doing, Brigid?" she demanded, her head the only thing above water.

I looked down at Caelum, who was still lying unconscious across the rocks. I looked back up at Maira. "He's the one who tried to save me when I was a child. I had to return the favor, Maira. I had to save him."

"He's a man, Brigid. He is just like the rest of them. As soon as he wakes, he will destroy you. That's what they do," she said angrily, swimming closer to me. "They take and take and take and leave women for dead when they're done."

"I had to at least make sure he didn't drown," I said softly, trying to get her to understand. "I repay my debts."

"Your debts? What about your promises to us? What about your vows to Cliodhna? What about those?" she asked, fury and hurt shining in her eyes. "He will tell others about us, and you will bring doom on us."

"I'll come back, Maira," I pleaded, trying to move closer to her without splashing water onto Caelum. I knew I'd vowed to be loyal to Cliodhna and the others. But I couldn't shake the debt I owed to this man either. "I'll come back. As soon as he wakes, I'll leave him and ensure he doesn't tell anyone about me. And then I'll come back and earn your forgiveness."

"Don't."

I reeled back as if she had struck me. "What are you saying?"

"I'm saying us or him. You come with us right now, or you stay with him and you don't come back at all," Maira said. The fire in her eyes that was usually directed at others felt intense and uncomfortable when directed at me. I couldn't believe she was doing this to me after all we had been through. I knew she was an angry person and despised men, but that she wasn't even giving me a chance to explain myself. "He does not deserve your help or your favor. He will turn on you as soon as he wakes."

"Do you speak for Cliodhna?" I demanded, jutting my chin up defiantly. Maira's anger was one thing, but I would not take her word as law.

"I speak for all of us," she said, pointedly not answering my question. "Don't come back."

"I am just making sure he does not drown in the surf," I snapped, growing irritated. I knew she didn't understand, couldn't understand. But I had to do this. "It's not like I'm running off to marry the man."

Maira shook her head, a look of disgust on her face. My stomach twisted at the thought of being so easily dismissed by my adopted family, but I couldn't bring myself to abandon the unconscious man in my lap.

"Let's not be so hasty," Kyla said calmly, swimming up in front of Maira. "Brigid, you've got to think this through. Is this truly what you want to leave us over?"

"So, you'd turn me away too?" I asked, hurt bubbling up. While Maira's dismissal had stung, it had also been expected. Kyla's, however, was like a gut punch.

"We don't save men," was all she replied, her voice apologetic but firm.

"Then I guess that's our answer," I replied, looking back down at Caelum. "I *will* save him."

"Sorcha will come back with us." Maira looked at me for a long moment, our eyes locking as she dared me to defy her, to give her an excuse to fight me.

"You won't let her decide for herself?" I demanded, pushing back the burning in my throat at the thought of having to choose between saving this man and staying with Sorcha. While Caelum deserved my penance, I did not want to abandon Sorcha. Not so soon after I had found her.

"No. She's a syren. She belongs to Cliodhna. Just like you were supposed to." Sadness and anger flashed in Maira's eyes, and she turned and disappeared, dragging a stunned Sorcha with her.

I was on my own with only the man I had saved for company. I hoped the fool didn't die now, or this would all have been for nothing.

Elizianna
@ELIZIANNA.THE.ONE

CAELUM

CHAPTER SEVEN

What is that blasted noise? I asked myself as I drifted back into consciousness. There was someone singing, and it was annoying. Shivers wracked through my body, and I moved slightly, my damp clothes chafing against my skin. Rocks dug into my body as I tried to figure out where I was and what had happened. The pain in my chest, legs, and arms began to come back into focus. I groaned. The singing stopped.

"Are you awake?" the gravelly but feminine voice asked from above me. She was the one who had been singing, a folk song I vaguely recognized from my childhood.

Suddenly, the memories of what had happened flooded my mind. The shipwreck, my men being thrown into the water, *myself* being thrown into the water, the girl. My eyes opened and found her staring at me. I opened my mouth to reply, but all that came out was a string of wet coughs. My chest heaved as it tried to expel the seawater I had inhaled, and my body contorted as I leaned over, spitting water out onto the rocky beach.

She arched an eyebrow at me but leaned toward me and helped me sit up as I hacked and coughed, spluttering out water. Her voice was dry as she looked at me with barely disguised curiosity. "You gonna live, sailor?"

I looked at her once my coughing had passed. She was beautiful, with long, wavy red hair, pale skin, and blazing green eyes. And a bloody tail, of course. Couldn't forget that bit. She had changed some since I had seen her last, but she was still recognizable as that young girl I had tried desperately to save. "I'm fine. Just had a bit of water."

She rolled her eyes and huffed, adjusting her position by moving with her weight on her hands. "'A bit of water,' he says. More like the whole ocean."

"Why did you save me?" I asked again, still confused. My men were likely dead, yet she had deemed me important enough to save. Was she planning to kill me later? A more important question sprang to mind as I studied her. "And why did you stay?"

Her green eyes hardened at my questions. "Well, I could not very well let you drown, now, could I?"

"That's exactly what you did to the others," I pointed out, trying not to think about the men I had lost, about their families I would have to tell. Anger surged within me, but I tamped it down for the moment, preferring to get answers from this woman first. She had saved me, and despite my anger at what her kind had done to my crew, I was thankful for her actions. "Which is why I'm asking why I'm alive right now."

She was quiet for a moment, looking down at her lap. Her tail flicked in the water, sending flashes of silver across the rocks. She seemed hesitant, opening her mouth a few times before finally speaking. "I owed you a debt."

Now it was my turn to roll my eyes and scoff. This...woman was something, all right. She had saved me for a debt more than ten years old? It didn't make sense to me. "A debt? Are you daft?"

At my insult, her head snapped up and her eyes almost glowed with green fire. There was the spitfire I had seen beneath the surface, the one with death in her eyes. I wondered what it would be like to be consumed by that fire.

Wait, what? I shook my head to clear that surprising thought and focused back on the matters at hand.

"Yes, *boy*, a debt. You tried to save me when they threw me over years ago. You got punished because of it. Now, we're square." She nodded, and I wasn't sure if she was trying to convince me or herself. She fidgeted on the rocky beach, her tail flicking beneath the shallow water and splashing. As I watched her, she picked up a rock, rubbing it between her palms and tracing her sharp talons over it.

"So, you owe me a debt because I wasn't a superstitious old coot?" I asked, my eyebrows rising into my hairline. I shook my head, the cold suddenly shivering through me. That's also when my brain saw fit to remind me that the girl—nay, the woman—before me was...naked. Or at least naked from the tail up. Her hair covered her curvy upper body mostly, but still, I had to know, "Aren't you cold?"

"Do not change the subject. My nakedness is none of your concern," she snapped, dropping the rock back into the water. It amused me how defensive she was being about the entire thing.

Her kind had just killed my men, one of them right in front of me, and she had the gall to say her saving me was because I had "saved her" before. Anger bubbled up in my throat, but I pushed it down. I had never struck a woman in my life, and I wasn't about to start now. Her words irked me, though. I had been a child, just like her. It didn't make sense to me that she'd saved me for something I had done over ten years ago. And something I had failed at, at that. Despite my anger, I needed to know the truth. "So, why did you stay? Honestly?"

"I was honest with you. I owed you a debt. Least I could do is make sure you didn't drown," she said, shrugging. She looked around, picking up another rock and digging it into the soft soil beneath. "I don't reckon you know where we are."

I looked around, taking in the hills and the rocky shore. Some of it was familiar. But I didn't miss that it was now her changing the subject. "Och, vaguely. Why?"

"You need to get dry before you catch ill," she said, looking at me like I was an idiot. I guess I *was* acting like one. Instead of getting away from the water and going to dry off like a normal person would, here I was, sitting inches away from ice-cold water and talking to a lady with a tail. In my defense, there was quite a bit going on that I had to wrap my head around, and my physical state was not one of the things I considered pressing.

"And you?" I asked. She had obviously been sitting with me for a while if the slowly setting sun in the distance was anything to go by. "You going back into the sea to kill some more of my men?"

She didn't respond, but her face hardened again and her hands stilled against the rock once more. "I don't know what I'll be doing after I leave you, but it'll not be that. The others told me not to come back after seeing me rescue you."

Well, then. Her casual statement caused a mass of thoughts and questions to pour down. There were others? Other mermaids? How many others? And why had they told her to not come back after rescuing me?

"Then why save me?" Her reasoning just didn't make sense, especially after hearing that she had been sent away by others like her. There couldn't have been that much of a sense of gratitude and debt for my kindness before. I had seen a girl hiding in the hold, and she had reminded me of myself, so I had tried, and failed, to save her. There was no reason she should be this adamant about keeping me alive.

She shrugged again, dragging her talons over the rocks under the water again. "Was the right thing to do, I suppose. I'll be fine. I'll go seek their forgiveness, and if they can't give it, I'll just have to find a new home. But you're the only man who's ever shown me kindness; I couldn't let them drown you."

I didn't like where my mind was going, but I never could ignore a damsel in distress—even one in mild distress. Even if this particular damsel looked as though she could easily kill me and had likely killed some of my men. My anger warred with my overwhelming desire to help her. The vein in my temple throbbed, and I reached up to rub at it.

She had obviously gone against her kind to save me from drowning, and even without knowing mermaid customs, it was clear that it was something the others would not approve of. My first meeting with the woman had been her running from something, and I hadn't been able to save her from being thrown overboard. Maybe now I could at least offer her some shelter until she was ready to decide where to go next. I needed to recover from my own near drowning before trying to find if any of my men had survived.

My stomach clenched. My men. My best friend and first mate, Duncan, entered my mind, and I desperately hoped he had somehow beaten the odds and survived.

"You wanna come with me? I know a place we can stay for a few days," I finally said, looking at her thoughtfully. She could at least rest and plan while I recovered enough to journey to find survivors and get back on track with my mission to stop my father. His evil plans wouldn't pause just because my ship had wrecked. I needed to get back to it before he got too far ahead.

She looked at me, her eyes piercing. "I don't know if that's a good idea."

Likely, she was right. But seeing the flash of sadness in her eyes when she had spoken about seeking forgiveness from the others still made me want to fix things for her. I never was one to push, though, so it would be her decision. "No, probably not. But the offer is there."

"Why would you even offer?" she asked, her eyebrows furrowing. "You don't know me. My kind just tried to kill you."

I shrugged, struggling to keep my guilt and sadness over my crew's death tamped down, at least for now. I needed to deal with this first before I could mourn. "You need help."

Her face hardened, and I knew I had used the wrong words. She leaned in, her hands curling around the rocks beneath them. "I don't need anyone's help."

Unable to resist, I shrugged again. "Seems like you do. Unless you want to go back to those other mermaids who shunned you."

"We're not mermaids," she snarled. Leaning back, she crossed her arms over her chest and sniffed. "And I don't need your help."

"Fine," I conceded. If she didn't want my help, I wasn't going to force it on her. While I was grateful she had saved me from drowning, I had survivors to find and a mission to get back to, and neither could wait for me to convince the fiery-headed not-mermaid that she needed help. "I'll just be going, then."

"Wait," she gritted out after I had stood. I looked down at her expectantly, and she sighed heavily, letting her arms fall back to her sides. "I suppose I could stay with you for at least a night to make sure you don't have any lingering effects from the sea."

Sure, that was the reason. But I would let her think it for now. "Okay, then. Like I said before, I know a place not far from here."

"Which direction?" she asked, running her hands over her tail.

Bringing it back to my attention, I realized the tail would cause some issues with the travel to said place, though. "I'd have to get a big bucket for you to get there, though."

She laughed at that, a tinkling sound that I hadn't expected given the gravelly nature of her voice. From the look on her face, the laugh had surprised her as much as it had me. She recovered quickly, raising an eyebrow. "A bucket. I can just put my legs on. I'll just need some clothes."

My mind didn't know what to do with that bit of information either. I didn't exactly have any extra clothes for her just hanging around. I might have had some on the ship she had just caused to wreck, but not tucked away in my pocket of my now very wet trousers. And the house I was thinking of would be too far for me to carry a tailed lady. "You...can put...legs on?"

Now she let out a big laugh, throwing her head back, her hair shifting off her chest. Her fiery red-orange hair moved, uncovering her full breasts. I quickly averted my gaze, which seemed to make her only laugh harder. "You're such a gentleman. And yes, I can transform so I look just like a real girl. So, where's this place of yours?"

I swallowed, looking back at her but forcing my eyes to stay on her face and not her curvy torso and breasts. Every fiber of my being wanted to look at her, to drink in the curves I had glimpsed. But I reminded myself that she had killed my men, and, suddenly, she wasn't that tempting anymore. "If we're where I think, just a few miles over the hills in a little cove."

"Can you get to the cove from the sea here?" she asked, thankfully fixing her hair to cover herself again. Her nakedness obviously didn't bother her, but it did something to me. What, exactly, I wasn't quite sure of yet. "Since we don't have extra clothes or a bucket."

Going through the geography in my head, I nodded. While I could walk directly over the jutting land, she would have to swim around it. "Aye. It'd be longer than walking, but you can."

She looked over me, scanning my body from head to toe. While normally I would enjoy a pretty lady looking at me, her eyes were analytical as she scanned me, rather than appreciative. "Can you walk? Or if not, can you stand the water a bit longer?"

Taking inventory of my body—which was still very cold and sore, but not seriously damaged—I shrugged. "I can walk. What're you thinking?"

"You walk, and I'll swim and meet you over there," she explained, turning closer to the water. Finally looking up, she whirled quickly to glance at me over her bare shoulder. "Will there be clothes at this place? Or will you really need to get me a bucket?"

"I've not been there in a while, but there should be clothes for the both of us. Maybe not your size, but something," I responded. I hadn't been to the cottage in a while, but it should still be stocked with something to get us through the night. And if any of my men had survived, they would know I would try to get there at some point. If they were already there waiting for me, it could cause some issues, but I had confidence I could at least explain to the others before blood was spilled...by either side.

"What does it look like?" she asked. "Landmarks?"

"It's a stone cottage next to some big, mangled oak trees in a cove. There's a big rock arch at the mouth." The cottage was a ways from any large town, but close enough to the trade routes that I could easily get to port as I was needed. I was rarely there, preferring to stay on my ship, but now that it wasn't an option, the cottage would be seeing more use.

She was quiet for a moment, thoughtful, as she tilted her head to the side slightly. "I know where you're talking about. I'll meet you over there."

Using her hands, she pushed herself down the rocky beach into deeper water at the shore. "Are you sure you can walk that far? You were out for quite a bit."

My heart tugged at her concern. She had obviously given up something big to save me, and she was still concerned about my safety. While I was still reeling at the loss of my men and their uncertain fates, I was grateful for her mercy. I nodded at her in what I hoped was an encouraging manner. "Go. I'll meet you there. I'll beat you, so I'll have some clothes and a fire ready."

Slipping into deeper and deeper water until only her head remained above the water, she turned back to me, nodding once. "I'll meet you there."

As she disappeared into the waves, I turned and finally pulled myself to stand on the beach. Now that she was gone and I had only my thoughts to keep me company, I was cold. Very cold. I gritted my teeth as the brisk wind rushed across my skin and damp clothing. Great, just what I needed. Tensing my muscles, I geared myself up for the walk across the familiar rolling hills.

For some reason, I could only hope the girl actually met me at my cottage like she'd said she would. She had no reason to, and I already couldn't stop thinking about her. Much like when I was a boy, my thoughts raced over if she would be safe in the water. Despite knowing she was apparently more than capable of protecting herself, there were still things bigger than her in the seas.

I turned to the hills and started my trek. Nothing I could do about it now but walk.

Eliz
@ELIZIAN

CHAPTER EIGHT

Swimming toward the cove, my mind ran in circles. What was I even doing? I should be going back to the cave to grovel for the others' forgiveness and beg Cliodhna to take me back. To reassure Sorcha that I had not abandoned her. Goddess, Sorcha... What did she think of my actions? I had spent the past weeks convincing her that Cliodhna was right and that all men were evil, and then in the face of the one man I had admitted had redeeming qualities, I had left. Was she feeling vindicated? Or betrayed? I needed to get back to see her.

I should be going back to beg them to forgive my indiscretion and forgive my saving a man. And yet, here I was, swimming to go meet the boy again. No, he was a man now. A very handsome man. But still a man.

I was really doing this, saving this near stranger at the expense of my family. I knew Maira was upset, and maybe the others were too. They had every right to be, but I needed to make this right with the man. I needed to ensure he was safe and would be able to get back to wherever he had been going before we had wrecked him.

I had experienced little kindness in my life, and he had been the only man I ever knew to show me that. I valued my adopted family and my queen, and I knew no love for men, but there was something about this man that made me want to throw that conviction in the bin. Something about him that made me *need* to make sure he was safe.

He had been willing to risk punishment to hide me from his crew, and when we'd both been discovered, he still tried to fight to save me. No one before the syrens had ever done that before, and it had made a deeper mark in my heart than I even knew. I blamed Sorcha for dredging up these feelings and doubts in the last few weeks. But really, I knew the words she had said were true. Maybe not all men deserved our anger. And maybe this was my chance at proving that.

My heart was torn. The others, through the mouthpiece of Maira, had shunned me, and for understandable reasons. I wanted both their love and protection, but I also wanted to ensure the man's safety and earn his forgiveness for what I had done to his crew and his ship. I knew losing people was never easy, and we had likely wiped out his entire crew. I had never thought of our impact before, just followed my queen's orders without question.

But despite all of this, I was questioning myself. This man didn't know me. He didn't know how much importance I placed on his kindness. He wouldn't even question it if I left him. Likely, he would welcome it. Once the shock wore off, I was sure anger would be left in its place over his crew. And I could go back to the cave and beg for the forgiveness of Cliodhna and the others and hope they would take me back. But the thought of turning my back on one of the first people to show me kindness and care about what happened to me felt wrong, wrong down to my core. The sickening feeling when I thought about turning away from the cove where he was waiting made up my mind. I would go there, I would meet him, and I would stay until I was sure he was safe or until he turned me away.

As I approached the shore, there was something wrong with the sight before me. I was expecting to see one shape on the shore waiting for me, but instead, there were three. And that wasn't right. The man hadn't mentioned anything about the cottage being occupied or anyone meeting us, so I slowed down my approach, wary. Had he tricked me?

"Is that you?" I called out hesitantly. I was still far enough from shore that the figures were unclear, and far enough that if one of them wanted to reach me, they would have to swim a fair distance. "You all right?"

"No! Get out of here!" Caelum's voice came back, frantic. Ignoring his warning, I surged forward. His voice was enough of an indicator that he was in danger, and after the toll the water and the walk would have taken on his body, I wasn't optimistic he could defend himself against two attackers. After I'd risked everything to save him, I wouldn't let these men kill him now.

As I neared, the figures on the shore became clear. Two large men were holding him, and they were dragging him toward the water. Struggling, he still managed to shout at me. "Leave, lass!"

I had just saved the fool from drowning once, I wasn't going to let these brutes drown him again. The men had wrestled him down into knee-deep water as I approached. I smiled menacingly, baring my pointed teeth; that was plenty of depth for me to work with. Their eyes widened as they saw me moving toward them, but to their credit, they stayed true to their path, pulling Caelum into the water.

Snapping forward in a flash, I wrapped my webbed hands around one of the man's ankles, digging my talons in and yanking hard. It probably caught him off guard, because one rough pull was all it took for him to fall into the water. Using all my strength, I pulled him back into deeper water, dragging him by the ankle. My speed and strength prevented him from being able to pull his head above the water as I swam out to the deepest part of the cove. Finally, his body went limp and heavy in my grip, and I retracted my talons, letting his body sink down into the depths below. He had drowned quickly, and I was grateful.

Turning my attention back to the shore, I swam as close as I could before transitioning into my human form and surging out of the water, where Caelum was now fighting off the second man, and he was waning, his body sloppy and sluggish. The man he was fighting obviously had not expected me to come to his aid, as seeing me emerge from the waves made him stumble and lose his balance. That stumble was all the opening Caelum needed, and he swung a tired fist toward the man's face. It connected, and the man dropped onto the shore, unconscious.

Caelum looked at me, panting and shaking out his hand, his shoulders slumping. "I had him, *teine.*"

"Obviously," I said, raising an eyebrow and again ignoring the name he called me. It was vaguely familiar, but his accent was from the south of Tuathnach, and it was a word I didn't know. I looked down at the man on the beach. "What did they want?"

He pushed his hand through his dark, messy hair, pulling it out of the tie that was barely holding it back any longer. It fell to brush his shoulders, wavy from the water that remained. His eyes roved over my body appreciatively before snapping back to my face, a blush spreading across his neck. "You. They wanted the 'mermaid,' they said."

My stomach dropped, and I cursed. Cliodhna had been right in her fears. My palms suddenly felt clammy, and my legs struggled to hold my weight as a flood of anxiety washed through me. I sucked in a deep breath through my nose, the cold air burning my throat. It gave me something to focus on as I shoved those feelings back down and steeled my spine. Anxiety would do me no good. I needed to find out more information and handle it. "Me? How do they even know I exist? Did they ask for me specifically?"

He held a hand out toward me, concern and suspicion shining equally in the green of his eyes. "Let's get you some clothes and we can talk more."

I looked away, trying to find something else to focus on. Maybe I should have stayed in the water and taken my chances returning to *Neamh na Mara.* But I couldn't linger on that now. Jerking my head toward the unconscious man, I stopped. I could focus on disposing of this man. "What're you gonna do about him?"

He looked down at the man, still unconscious on the rocky beach. "Och, I had forgotten about him already. I suppose we can tie him up and leave him there."

"As soon as he gets free, he'll be gone in an instant. And he'd likely come back with company. We can't let him live," I bit out, frustrated at the situation I had found myself in. I couldn't risk him finding out more about me, about us, and endangering my family. I wouldn't say I enjoyed killing, but I had done it many times before and would be willing to do it again to protect what's mine—or what *had* been mine. "I will take him out and drown him like the other."

His eyes widened, but he had something akin to respect in them. After a moment of looking at me, he dropped his outstretched hand and nodded. "Yeah, that's probably for the best. It's quite lovely how bloodthirsty you are—when it's not me or my men that it's aimed toward, of course."

My eyes rolled. Of course, he would think me murdering people was attractive. The rest of his words registered, and guilt churned in my stomach before settling like a weight. "And I am sorry about your men."

"Whatever you say..." He trailed off. "What's your name again?"

"Brigid."

"Brigid," he drawled out, like he was tasting my name and liked what he found. He smiled slightly, the corner of his lip turning upwards. It didn't quite reach his eyes as he nodded his head at me. "I'm Caelum, if you didn't remember. Go do your murderous fish-lady thing. I'll be here."

"I've got to get him into the water before I shift," I said, already reaching down to grab the unconscious man's arm. I had remembered Caelum's name, but hearing it aloud made things feel far more real.

Caelum pulled in a sharp breath behind me, and I realized belatedly that I had just bent over and showed him my entire arse. Before I could snap at him for his modesty again, he walked over and bent to grab the man's other arm. "Here, let me help."

Together, we pulled him out into deeper water. I was grateful he was still unconscious, as I did not want to deal with a thrashing man again. Once we got the man into deeper water where he could float off the bottom, I slipped into the water and laid back, my hair floating out behind me as I transformed. A tingling sensation started from my core, spreading down my legs as they merged and turned from human legs into a powerful tail. My fingernails lengthened into sharp talons, and my teeth pointed as well.

The transformation complete, I dug my claws into the floating man's arms, tugging him down into the water and out into the cove without a look back toward Caelum, who I could feel staring at me as I swam away. This man did not thrash as he drowned, thankfully. Once I was sure the man was dead, I let his body sink down into the depths of the cove before swimming back to the shore.

Transforming back into my human form, I entered shallow water and stepped out of the sea, my hair dripping icy water down my bare skin, which immediately pebbled as the equally icy wind whipped across me.

"I started a fire while you were out drowning that man." Caelum extended his hand again. "Let's go get you warmed up."

I nodded but didn't take his hand. I didn't need his help walking, and I didn't want to make this any more difficult on us when we eventually and inevitably parted ways. I was a syren, and once I ensured Caelum would be safe from any other immediate threats, I would be returning to my family to beg their forgiveness and do whatever it took to prove my worth to Cliodhna and ensure they were protected from the men who had been looking for me.

And Caelum would be grateful to be rid of the monster who had had a hand in killing his crew. But why was the idea of leaving him already making my stomach hurt?

When he realized I wouldn't be taking his hand, he let it drop once again and turned to lead me into the small stone cottage covered in soft green moss. He reached it before me, holding the sturdy wooden door open for me. I entered the cottage, immediately bathed in warmth from the fire going in the corner.

The small cottage was mostly bare, but it had a bed, a table and chairs, and most importantly, blankets. Shivers wracked through my human body once more as the cold spread through me.

By the time I noticed he had even walked toward the bed, Caelum had returned with the heavy quilt that had been spread across it. He held it open and motioned for me to step in. "Here, *teine,* wrap up and dry off while I find you some clothes."

That word again. Deciding to continue ignoring it, I stepped into his arms, and he wrapped the quilt around me. I grabbed the corners from him and tucked myself into the large fabric, relishing its warmth and the weight around my shoulders. I didn't want to be reliant on him, but I knew when I was out of my element. And here? On land, in a strange house with a strange man? That was about as far out of my element as I could get.

My stubbornness to ensure Caelum would get back to wherever he had been going was overriding any sense I had. But despite being on land, I knew I was still able to take care of myself, whatever my anxiety might tell me. "Thanks."

Still holding me in his arms, he looked down at me. His eyes were intense as they locked with mine, and I was sucked into the swirling green there. No words were said, we just looked at each other as he held me in the quilt. My body was heating from his attention alone. The fierceness in his gaze wasn't aggressive, but I wasn't sure what it was. Determined, maybe. He blinked, and the moment was over.

He stepped back and motioned toward the bed as he turned toward a large trunk I hadn't noticed before. As I sat down on the scratchy sheets of the rickety wooden bed, he began rifling through the trunk. As he bent over, I took the time to study him without him knowing. His back was broad, and his still-damp shirt clung to the corded muscles there. As broad as his back was, he was extremely proportionate. Well-muscled all over and tall—very tall. His dark hair curled slightly where it brushed his shoulders. The sides of his hair near his temples and around his ears were shaved close to the skin. I wondered what it would feel like under my nails.

As he dug through the chest, his bare forearms flexed, showing off the muscle and power coiled under his sun-tanned skin. There was a thick, jagged scar around the wrist of his right arm, white with age, but puckered and extremely noticeable. I wondered where that came from.

Finally, he stood, then turned and walked over, handing me a bundle of clothing. "Here you go. They'll likely be quite big on you, but they should do."

Wordlessly, I took the clothes from him, standing and leaving the quilt behind on the bed. I heard his quick intake of breath before he whirled around, facing away from me. Shaking my head at his modesty, I quickly pulled on the clothes to ease his discomfort. The pants were scratchy and far too big, but the generous curve of my hips held them up...barely. Nothing could be done for the length, and I was sure I would trip over them embarrassingly often. The shirt swallowed me, the sleeves dangling past my fingertips where my talons had receded. I looked over at Caelum's back again. "I'm decent. You can turn around."

He spun around, his eyes sparkling with humor as he took me in, dragging his gaze slowly from my head to my toes. "You look like a little faery."

I rolled my eyes, ignoring his teasing statement. He was likely right. Even as a full human, I was much shorter than him, but that wasn't my fault. He was just extremely tall. "You need dry clothes too. Was there more in there for you?"

He shrugged, looking over his shoulder back to the open chest. "There was mainly blankets, but there's another pair of pants in there. I'll hang my shirt up to dry by the fire overnight and it should be fine. I'll set my boots out as well. They won't fit well at all, but there's another pair of boots in the trunk, too, if you need them."

Nodding, I sat back down on the bed, wrapping the quilt around me once more. It was warm, and despite its scratchy fabric, it reminded me of another time. "Do you have food?"

He shrugged again, turning his back to me and pulling the second set of britches out of the trunk. "We'll need to get some at some point, I suppose. Do you mind turning around?"

"Why? You shy?" I teased. I supposed I should have been more mindful of his apparent modesty issue, but over the past years with the other syrens, I had grown comfortable in my skin. Nakedness was normal to me now, and despite never seeing a man naked before, I doubted very highly it would make me feel different.

Snorting, he pulled his pants down over his hips, showing me his pasty white arse and legs, which were dusted with a dark smattering of hair. Keeping his back to me, he pulled on the dry pants quickly before straightening up and pulling his still-dripping shirt off over his head. Unlike his legs, his bare upper body was tanned by the sun, but it was still covered in the same dark hair. His back was mottled by deep and jagged scars, white with age like the one around his wrist. It looked like he had been whipped. Repeatedly.

While the scars turned my stomach at the thought of someone inflicting them, they didn't detract from his appearance. He turned back around to face me, showing off his defined chest and stomach.

I was wrong. It had made me feel different to see him naked. Very different.

He tilted his head to the side as he studied me. "Wait. Do you even eat food?"

I blinked at him. I hadn't expected those to be the words out of his mouth. It took me another moment before I was able to respond. "Och, I do. I don't live off the seawater."

"Well, how exactly am I supposed to know what a fish lady eats? I didn't even really know your kind existed outside of fairy tales until today," he said, plopping his body down into one of the wooden chairs. It groaned under his weight as he shifted to get comfortable in the small seat. "I guess we'll have to find us some food, then."

Elizianna
@ELIZIANNA.THE.ONE

CAELUM

CHAPTER NINE

"So, what is even around here for food?" she asked, still clutching the quilt around her frame. She really did look like a little faery, clad in too-big clothes and wrapped in a quilt. It was, in a word, adorable, but I doubted she would appreciate that thought being voiced aloud. In our brief interactions, it was clear there was a temper beneath the surface, burning as brightly as her hair. It was also obvious she tried to subdue that fire, to tamp it down and smother it. And something about that made me want to provoke her even more.

"I think there might be some dried meat in here somewhere," I replied, looking toward a cabinet in the corner. "And I can go into the next town over, Fairport, and get some things, depending on how long you want to stay here. That was where my ship was headed anyway, before it went down."

It would be a walk, but I was familiar with the town. There was lodging, food, and it would be close enough that if any of my men had survived, they would be heading there. Beyond wanting to get food, I desperately needed to see if anyone had lived through the wreck, if my best friend had lived or had fallen victim to the deadly women apparently prowling the seas. Trying to push my mind off my crew for the moment, I turned back to study Brigid. The conflict was clear on her face, as if she couldn't decide if she wanted me to leave or if she wanted to be the one to leave.

She was silent for a moment, looking out the small window toward the trees while chewing on her lip. "How long do we need to stay here?"

There was something in her voice that made me pause. It sounded almost like anxiety, and something in me wanted to fix it. "Just because those two were looking for you doesn't mean others will be. You'll be safe for as long as you're here. Until you decide what you're doing next."

Her brilliant green eyes snapped over to mine. Now her voice was firm and cold. "I do not need your protection. I was asking how long I needed to stay to make sure you don't die in your sleep."

A smile broke across my face. She was something, for sure, unlike any other woman I had ever met. Obviously, she didn't want me to worry about her and was disguising it by worrying about me instead. I didn't believe that the only reason she was staying was to make sure I stayed alive, but I'd let her hide behind it. For now.

"I won't die in my sleep. If you want to go, I'm not stopping you. But I would ask you to at least stay until I can get you some food." My anger was still simmering, but something about a woman —or anyone—in distress quelled it momentarily. It was a true failing of mine that had gotten me in trouble on more than one occasion, and I had little doubt it would again.

Despite wanting nothing more than to shake her and ask her why she believed all men were evil, I saw the hurt in her. It was the only thing that extinguished my anger.

"Fine," she huffed, pulling the quilt tighter. Her face pinched up, making her look even younger. Not for the first time, I wondered how old she really was. She had been young when I had found her aboard the ship, and although more than ten years had passed, she didn't look all that old. Not as old as I did, for sure.

After a few moments of silence and me just looking at her, she spoke again. "Why do you think they were after me? Do you think they really know for sure we exist?"

I heaved a sigh. I was wondering the same thing. Those men had jumped me as I was walking the last few meters to the cottage, ranting about a mermaid and asking where she was. They didn't mention any defining characteristics like Brigid's hair or the silvery red sheen to her tail, but I was still worried, same as she was. I walked over to sit down on the small bed next to her, my thigh brushing hers. "I don't know, but if you want, I can help you find out."

Her thigh was warm against mine, even through the quilt. I couldn't deny she was beautiful, and while she appeared to ponder over my statement, I let myself look at her more closely. She was stunning, of course, with a fire burning under the skin as bright as her hair. But there was obvious hurt there too, and I couldn't help wanting to ease that hurt however I could. It was a foolish notion, and one I should have been kicking myself for. Gods only knew that if my friends, my crew, could see me now, they would be furious.

She had been through a lot and was likely about to go through even more, if the day's happenings were anything to go by.

She still didn't speak, so after a moment, I added, "I can ask around in Fairport discreetly. You don't have to go if that's what you're worried about."

"I'm not worried about myself," she admitted, looking down at the quilt. She picked at the seams before stopping herself and flexing her fingers. She looked back up at me, determination shining bright. "If they know about us, my family is in danger, and I have no way to warn them."

"Why can't you warn them?" I asked. "I know they told you not to come back, but I'm sure they'd change their minds if you told them what happened."

She shook her head. Her fire was dulling, and her eyes were sad. I could see her chewing on the inside of her cheek. "They knew that it was always a possibility. But I don't know if I can go back. They might not let me in."

"Let you in…the ocean?" I asked, feeling like that wasn't what she meant but not knowing what else it could mean. I couldn't explain why, but in that moment, all I wanted to do was wrap my arm around her and pull her into my side, to comfort her, despite us both having better things we could be doing. More important things. I had my old crew's family to notify, a new ship to find, and a new crew to gather.

She snorted, and I couldn't help the smile that spread across my face. She was funny, and I was already connecting with her despite not knowing her that well. I felt guilty about that. She and the other syrens had killed my men. I shouldn't be connecting with her. But I couldn't seem to help it.

"Not in the ocean, you fool. Back where we live. Our queen has it spelled so only we or people we accompany can enter. After what I did, I imagine she's revoked my right to enter." As she spoke, her body visibly deflated, her shoulders slumping as she curled in on herself.

"But you don't know for sure?" I asked. I wasn't sure why I was encouraging her to return to her family—wasn't even sure why I was continuing to hold a conversation with her at all—but I was.

"No, I don't," she replied with a sigh, making an effort to sit back up straight and meet my gaze. "But what I did was a betrayal in their eyes. It wouldn't matter if I was trying to warn them, they wouldn't want to see me."

"Do you know that for fact?" I asked.

After a moment, she shook her head. "No, only one of them told me that. But the others didn't object. It's safe to assume that most of them feel that way, even if I've never done anything to have them doubt me."

"You saved me, *teine*," I said, the pet name slipping out of my mouth before I could stop it. Seeing her fire dull right in front of me had let the word slip right out, as if calling her "fire" could reignite that spark within her.

She raised an eyebrow at me, but thankfully didn't comment on the name.

Brigid had told me about what she and the other syrens did to men, but I still didn't quite understand what the big issue here was and why they had so quickly shunned her for interacting with me. It didn't seem like she was off saving every man she encountered, just me. They obviously hadn't saved any of the other men from my crew. Just thinking of them again brought my anger back to the surface, my fists clenching at my side. I took a deep breath to calm my rage, tamping it down for the moment. It would serve no purpose here other than pushing Brigid away. And I needed her to stay around a bit longer, at least until I understood if she could help us stop my father.

"You're a man. We syrens are all where we are, what we are, because men betrayed and hurt us. In the others' eyes, I chose you over them—I chose men over them—and that's apparently unforgivable. We made vows to our queen when we were turned, to be loyal to her, to follow her. And I broke those vows. It's just a matter of hearing the words straight from my queen."

Now it was my turn to snort. Lots of things were unforgivable, but saving my life was not one of those things—in my mind, at the very least. Perhaps the deaths of my crew could be unforgivable, but I had the feeling she was beating herself up about that enough. But we would get more into that later when she was more comfortable with me. "Well, that's just daft. Not all men were responsible for your pain."

"Not all men, no. But the people who caused our pain were all men," she pointed out, looking up at me. "That's how we all ended up together in the first place."

She had a point. I didn't know her story or what she had been through before or since meeting her on the ship that day. I certainly knew some men who should be punished. Maybe I would pass their names along to the other syrens, starting with my father. I bumped my shoulder into hers, trying to jar her out of her melancholy. "Well, thank you for saving my life. I do appreciate it."

"I told you before. You tried to save my life when I was a child, and I repay my debts."

"Well, now I'm in your debt," I pointed out. "I wasn't exactly successful at saving your life, not like you were with saving mine."

"We're even now," she argued. Debts were obviously important to her, and they were important to me too, but this situation wasn't as clear-cut as she was making it sound.

I waved a hand and stood up from the bed. I didn't want to argue technicalities with her. Now that I knew she needed food too, I needed to get us some. If it had just been me that was hungry, I could have stuck it out and waited, but again, my instinct to protect kicked me into action. Turning my back to her, I kept speaking as I looked through the cabinet by the wall. "Nay, you're stuck with me until we at least feed you. Plus, you don't really have anywhere to go unless you've changed your mind about going back to the other mermaids, and I happen to have this very cozy cottage."

"Not mermaids," she said exasperatedly. "Syrens."

I held my hands up apologetically. All right, good to know. "Syrens, then. Point still stands."

"This cottage barely has enough room for one of us, let alone both of us for any length of time," she said, the amusement in her voice coming through clearly. "But thank you."

"Still, it's something. We both need to get warm and rest before we start doing anything else," I said, finally successful in focusing long enough to find some dried meat in a cabinet. There was also what looked like some very stale bread on the shelf, but I wouldn't break into that unless it was a last resort. I turned back, handing her some of the meat. "Here, eat this while I stoke the fire."

She started chewing the tough meat, watching me as I bent over to tend to the fire in the small fireplace against the wall. I could feel her stare on me, and I liked it. For once, her gaze felt less analytical and more like she was enjoying what she saw. While I liked her attention, I tried to remind myself that she'd had a hand in the deaths of my crew, and I could not—would not—get involved with her.

Once the fire was going strong, I went back over to the bed and pulled the covers down next to her. I patted the mattress, grimacing when I felt how thin it was. I had gotten used to the hammocks on the ship, and going back to this hard and thin mattress would not be ideal. In a move I hoped seemed gentlemanly and not like I was passing it off to her, I motioned toward the bed. "Here, you can take the bed."

"Where will you sleep?" she asked, looking around the nearly bare cottage.

I rubbed the back of my neck, looking over at a spot on the floor by the fireplace. It wasn't ideal, but with enough of the raggedy blankets in the trunk, I could at least sleep through the night without being in too much discomfort. "I'll take the floor."

"Why?"

I looked at her, confused. "Why what?"

She looked at me, exasperated. I had a feeling she would be looking at me like that a lot based on how our interactions had gone so far. "Why will you take the floor? The bed is big enough for both of us, isn't it?"

All the words in my mind escaped me. "But..."

Her lips quirked up into a small smile. "I appreciate your concern, Caelum. But we can share a bed for one night as long as it doesn't harm your delicate sensibilities. Besides, I need to make sure you don't die in your sleep."

I snorted. She still couldn't be seriously concerned about me dying; I was clearly in no danger of it anymore. I wasn't sure if she was being serious or using it as an excuse to not go back to her fellow syrens.

"I won't die sleeping on the floor. And I don't have delicate sensibilities, I'm trying to be a gentleman," I pointed out. Sleeping in the same bed as her was a bad idea, and even though I could see that she was goading me, I couldn't help my reactions.

A teasing smile lit up her face. "Are you scared to sleep next to a syren, Caelum?"

I sputtered, my cheeks and neck burning. "N-no. I'm just trying...trying to be respectful."

She full-on laughed at that point, and I could feel my cheeks heating up. I wasn't used to being teased by a woman. *I don't think I like this.*

She turned her body, slipping under the blankets on the bed, which was big enough for both of us to lay comfortably, before spreading the quilt she was wrapped in out across her legs. She patted the space on the mattress beside her. "Come on. We both need rest. It's been years since I slept in a bed, anyway I might need someone to keep me from falling off it."

I should be jumping into the bed. She was a beautiful woman, and she wanted to share a bed with me. Just to sleep, of course, but the sentiment was still there. But she had been so young when she was thrown over, and I doubted there were male syrens around. My mind warred. On one hand, she was beautiful. On the other, she had just played a role, big or small, in the deaths of my men, and I couldn't just forget that.

"Not tonight, lass. I'll take the floor," I said, strengthening my resolve. I had to remember her actions, and I had to remember that if she hadn't recognized me, I would be dead along with my crew. It was a small distinction, but it built up the wall again in my mind. This woman would be trouble, I knew it.

She sighed heavily like she was yet again irritated with me, but she rolled over onto her side, her back facing me. "Goodnight, then. Get some rest."

I folded several blankets onto the floor by the fire, lying down on my back with an arm behind my head. Looking over at the long waves of fire and gold that spilled over the dingy pillow on the bed, I let myself smile at the sight. "Goodnight, *teine.*"

As sunlight spilled in through the dirty windows, waking me, I became aware of someone watching me. I hoped it was only Brigid. If anyone else was looking at me, I was too tired to fight them. Peeking open an eye to avoid her noticing I was awake, I studied her. She lay on the bed on her side, an arm curled under her head as her eyes roamed over my body.

I studied her in return. She was gorgeous, and here, just waking up, she looked so peaceful and young. There was no tension in her face or her body for the first time since we'd met. She was at ease in my bed. Granted, it was a bed I never really used, but it was still one that I had slept in before. The thought that she was this relaxed around me sent my heart off at a run. I couldn't explain the reaction I was having to her, and I didn't want to stop to think about it at any length.

Suddenly, her body tensed beneath the quilt. "You're awake."

My smile widened, and I couldn't help but tease her. "Aye, lass. Been watching you watch me."

Her cheeks tinted pink. "I wasn't watching you."

"It's okay. I know I'm irresistible," I teased her.

She glared at me then, her embarrassment quickly forgotten, which had been my intent. "Well, are you going to get us some more food?"

I sat up, looking at her as she did the same to me. "Aye, I'll be leaving here in a moment once I wake up some."

"Is your shirt dry?" she asked, standing up from the bed quickly and walking over to where the shirt was hanging off a chair. She picked it up, scrunching the fabric between her hands.

"So eager for me to put my clothes back on?" I teased again. I couldn't seem to help myself; her lack of non-violent experiences with men was both alluring and a challenge.

I shook my head. No. I shouldn't be thinking that she was alluring. She killed my men, and I needed to remember that.

She rolled her eyes, oblivious to my internal argument, and tossed the shirt at me. "Here, go get us some food."

I caught the shirt, pulling it on over my head while I forced myself to laugh. For someone who had no problem with nudity, her lack of comfort at simple intimacy with another person was genuinely amusing. Though maybe she was genuinely just very hungry. "All right, all right, I'll be going. Let me just tend the fire."

"I can do that." She waved a hand, nodding her head at the door to the cottage. "You go on so you can get back while there's still daylight."

"I'll be off, then. There should be enough wood here to make it for another day. If we end up staying here longer, I can go chop some more," I said, motioning toward the crackling fire. I looked out the window to see the sun rising up over the horizon. "I should be back from the town by dark, but if I'm not, I'll be back first thing in the morning."

"I can take care of myself, Caelum," she replied, smiling. My heart took off at a dead run again when she said my name. She hadn't said it since she'd pulled me from the water, and I very much enjoyed hearing it come from her mouth.

Again, I shook myself at the thoughts. Why couldn't my body keep in line with my brain when it said to not get attached to this girl, this creature who had killed my crew?

I went back over to sit next to her on the bed once more. I took her hand in between my own. They were still cold, but hopefully she would warm up more now that she was moving around. "I know you can. And I hope you'll still be here when I get back."

She tilted her head, and her gaze locked with my own. "Why?"

"We still have much to talk about, including why you chose my ship to wreck," I said, only lightly teasing her this time. I really did need to find a new ship and see if any of my crew had washed up alive in the town. My plans to stop my father would be really set back if I had to start from scratch again.

Hopefully, going into Fairport to get food would be a twofold mission. I could get food, yes, but I could also see if my crew was alive and find any survivors.

"I did not know it was your ship. Why would I intentionally wreck your ship just to go against my queen to save you?" she pointed out, still holding my gaze. It was getting warm in here again, and I wasn't sure if it was from the freshly stoked fire or from her eyes.

"We'll discuss that when I get back. You stay here, stay inside. I'll be back with food and supplies, and we can go from there," I said, releasing my hold on her hands and patting her knee. I stood up, slipping on my boots. They were finally dry after sitting out by the fire all night. "I'll be back soon."

She smiled at me. "Be safe as well."

With a smile of my own, I turned and walked out of the cabin before I did something really stupid—like kiss her.

Elizianna
@ELIZIANNA.THE.ONE

C AELUM

CHAPTER TEN

After several hours of walking, I finally made it into the small village of Fairport. It was barely a village, but it would be the closest place any of my crew would have found if they had survived the wreck. And I desperately hoped they had. Fairport would also have food and clothing for Brigid and me. I could only hope again that she would keep her word and still be there and be safe.

But first, I needed to see if any of my men had survived. I turned my path toward the first place they would go if they had lived through the wreck. The pub. With food, a fire, and a place to sleep, it would be the perfect place for them to post up and recover.

Hustling down the dirt path, I pushed open the door to the pub, stepping in out of the brisk air. I held my breath, trying not to get my hopes up.

"Caelum! You made it!" a loud voice sounded off to the right. My first mate, Duncan. I let out a heavy breath, tension bleeding out of my body. We had been friends for so long, I was grateful that I didn't have to learn to live without him. I had been doing my best to not think about him as I walked, and a wave of relief washed over me, nearly buckling my knees.

I walked over to his table, where he was sitting with two more from our crew, Cameron and Maddock. I stopped, speechless for a second as gratitude over their survival clogged my throat.

Cameron had a cut on his forehead, slightly covered by his brown curls, but it did nothing to detract from the relief in his dark eyes. Maddock looked visibly uninjured, his own dark hair pulled back neatly from his light brown skin. He studied me, his eyes likely scanning me for injuries as I did the same for him.

It didn't surprise me that of all my crew, these three were the ones that made it. A breathless laugh left my lips. "Duncan, I'm so glad to see your ugly face!"

Duncan stood up, towering over me, and yanked me into a crushing hug before pushing me back to look me over. We shared a smile that I felt down to my bones before I stepped over to give equal hugs to both Cameron and Maddock.

Duncan quickly reclaimed my attention, putting his hands on my shoulders and looking at me intently. I could see the worry and fear in his bright blue eyes. It was similar to the fear I had been trying my best to ignore since being rescued by Brigid. He smiled sadly. "Are you okay, Caelum?"

I didn't want to tell them about Brigid yet, for some reason. I wouldn't risk that until I was back to protect her, not that she needed it. But my loyalty to Duncan, Cam, and Maddock weighed heavily. They should know. Sidestepping the questions, I turned and studied them. They were relatively unscathed, and I was almost giddy with the knowledge that they had lived. I wanted to ask them how they had survived, but I was overwhelmed by the relief washing through me; all I could do was smile like a fool.

Duncan leaned in, his eyes hardening as he reflected on the ordeal and the question I hadn't been able to verbalize. "When Archer steered us into the cliff to get away from whatever was making that horrible noise, we all jumped over on the cliff side instead of into open water. We figured the beasts would be waiting on the water side to pick us off."

"Did you see them?" I asked, knowing he was talking about Brigid and the syrens. I swallowed hard and forced the next words out. Brigid was not a beast, but I knew they would be expecting me to call the syrens the same thing they did. "The beasts?"

Duncan shook his head. "Not clearly, but what else could it have been? I know they're a myth, but come on. It was obviously mermaids. Did you see them?"

I exhaled sharply, about to answer honestly and tell them everything, but I stopped myself. Those men had found my cottage, a cottage only my crew knew about. And they had known about Brigid and what she was. Obviously, someone had let information slip, and I needed to be more careful about what we spoke about in public.

I knew in my gut that the men in front of me had not been the ones to tell those men where to find Brigid and me, but someone had obviously told them. And it had been someone who had heard the myths of mermaids. While that didn't help narrow down my suspicion, it guided me toward someone familiar with the stories of the seas. I rubbed at my forehead, my mind flickering back to the rest of my crew. "Did anyone else survive?"

"We're the only ones who have washed up here so far. We've been watching for others," Duncan said, sitting back down and motioning for me to do the same. He looked me over again, questions in his eyes. "Where did you wash up?"

"South of here, near the cottage. I stopped there last night to rest," I explained. Then something hit me. "How did you all get out of the water? There's no accessible coast by the cliffs."

"You swam all the way to your cottage? You blasted fish!" Duncan exclaimed, his eyes wide and suspicious. "How did you get that far?"

Shit, I shouldn't have said that. He was right, there was no way I could have reached the cottage on my own from where the ship went down. I wiped a hand over my face before pushing my hair back. Gods, how I wanted to just tell them the truth. But my protective instincts soared. If I told them, Duncan especially would never let me return to the cottage. "I walked from the coast over the hills to the cottage. I only swam to the shore on the other side of the cove."

"Still, that's a long way in cold water," Duncan said. He motioned to the others. "We climbed up the cliffs a bit to a ledge and waited until another boat, some fishermen, came by. They brought us back here."

Fishermen. My mind churned with possibilities, none of them good. If my men had told them what they had seen, that we had been attacked by what could have been mermaids, would they come after us? Mermaids were a myth in my world, but if anyone thought they were real, it would turn into a hunt to prove it. I turned to Cameron and Maddock. "Did either of you see anything in the water?"

Cameron nodded, crossing his arms over his narrow chest. "Just some vague shapes in the depths. Looked like long fish, but I swear one of them had hair. Blonde hair."

Maddock nodded as well, leaning forward to rest his forearms on the table. "Same as Cam. Nothing for sure, but it wasn't like any sea creature I'd ever seen before. We've all heard the stories, it had to be the mermaids. Why?"

Ignoring his question, I continued my own line of thoughts. "Did you tell the fishermen what you saw?"

"Caelum, what's going on?" Duncan asked, putting his big hand on my arm. He was concerned. I knew it. We had basically grown up together, and he knew me better than I knew myself sometimes. "Did something happen?"

I sighed heavily, rubbing my free hand over my face. I was either going to have to quickly become a better liar to my oldest friend, or trust that he and the others would at least listen to what I had to say. I decided to take a chance, mainly because I knew Duncan would see right through any lie I told. "Two men met me at the cottage and attacked me. They were asking about a mermaid."

Duncan took a sharp inhale of breath, immediately looking around suspiciously. "At your cottage?"

I nodded. "Aye. That's why I need to know if you saw anything and if you said anything. Only the crew knows of my cottage."

"Are you okay, Captain?" Cam asked, worry in his eyes as they scanned over my body again. "Did they hurt you?"

"No, I'm fine. I took care of them. But did you all tell anyone—anyone at all—about the cottage or about anything you saw in the water?" I pressed. If they had told someone, even if it hadn't been maliciously, there could be others on the way to the cottage now. And Brigid was there alone.

"We didn't say anything, Caelum. We know the cottage is supposed to be a secret," Duncan said, leaning in closer to me. He lowered his voice. "But what's this really about? I can tell there's more to it."

I hated that I hesitated. Brigid's safety was important to me for some reason that I didn't want to stop to think about yet, but these were my most trusted men and my best friend. If I couldn't trust them, I couldn't trust anyone. I took a deep breath, steeling my nerves. "You all need to come back to the cottage with me. There's a situation. And I'll not explain it here, so don't ask me."

"What do you need from us, Captain?" Maddock asked, leaning in as well. "You know we'll do whatever you need us to."

"Okay, then we need food and clothes. Clothes for me, and clothes for a woman." Brigid would likely be furious at me for bringing others back with me without telling her, but I needed their help. And I needed her help.

Duncan's eyebrows shot up into his sandy blond hair. His voice was loud. "A woman? When did you have time to meet a woman while you were swimming to shore?"

"Duncan, what part of 'don't ask' was unclear?" I hissed, lowering my voice and looking around. If I gave any more details here, Duncan would likely figure it out. And if he could, anyone listening could. The jump from naked woman in the water to mermaid wasn't a large one for someone with any intelligence, unfortunately. And Duncan was anything but stupid. "Help me get clothes, help me get food, come back to the cottage with me, and I will explain everything then."

"Sure. Whatever you need." Suspicion was still clear in his eyes, and I could see the wheels churning in his head, but I hoped that he would remain ignorant for a bit longer. Thankfully, our legends about mermaids—no, syrens—seemed to be somewhat false, given that we hadn't known they could transform into human forms.

"Captain, I know you said no questions," Cameron started tentatively. "But what about the mission we were on when the ship was wrecked? We have to keep going to stop your father, or he's going to get too far ahead of us."

"We'll get back to that once we can find a crew and a ship," I explained. That mission was important to me and to the men. We wouldn't forget about it or the children we were working to save from my father. "We'll need to notify families of those we lost as well."

"Who are we sure is dead?" I asked, sighing heavily. I didn't want to go through this, but if we had any chance of getting back to stopping my father's nefarious plans, we needed to know our numbers. If any of our crew had survived, I needed to find them.

"Archer and Gordan for sure," Duncan said immediately. "And I saw Alastair go down as well."

"Bain and Connor as well," Maddock added. "Grady, Curran, and Liam also never resurfaced."

Cameron cleared his throat. "I only saw Sloane and Whelan go under."

"So, we don't know what happened to over half of our crew?" I asked, counting the names as they spoke. I tried hard to ignore the knot forming in the center of my chest as they named those we had lost. They had all been good men, ready to fight to stop my father.

My fists clenched, anger bubbling up. I spread my fingers out across the table, focusing on the feel of the wood beneath my fingertips to calm down. Anger would do me no good right now.

"We can keep searching for the rest of them," Duncan offered softly.

"With what ship, Duncan?" I asked, my anger seeping into my voice. Why had we been chosen for ruin by the syrens when men like my father were free to sail the seas spreading their evil wherever they chose? It hardly seemed fair. I took a deep breath to calm myself. My anger was of no use pointed at my own crew. They knew how despicable my father was. "Sorry. I'm just frustrated."

"Aye, we know, Captain," Cameron said quietly. "But it's not your fault. We all knew the risks of sailing. If it wasn't…whatever it was, it could have been a number of different things that did us all in."

"We need to notify their families," I repeated, as if saying it again would take care of the task for me. Most of the crew had come from Brinemoor, and I was not anxious to get back there and inform the families of the losses. But I knew I'd have to travel there eventually, as that was my father's home base, and he would likely be returning there soon.

"Aye, we'll handle it as soon as we can," Duncan said, standing from the table and clapping a hand on my shoulder. "Now, let's get back to the supplies you need. When did you have time to find a girl in the middle of all this?"

Despite the sadness of the situation, Duncan's words brought a smile to my face. But I couldn't tell him the truth. Not yet. "You'd be surprised."

"Well, since you know what your girl looks like," Maddock outlined, standing as well, "you and Cam can get clothes. He has some coin we managed to grab before jumping off the ship. Duncan and I will get food, and we'll meet back here when we're done."

"First," I said, stopping them from moving away from the table. I reached over and picked up a mug of ale and raised it. "A toast to those we lost."

We all stood, clanking our mugs together and sloshing some of the golden liquid onto the table. Duncan nodded his head solemnly. "To those we lost."

Emptying our glasses, we set them back onto the table. Maddock smiled sadly at me. "We'll get through this, Captain. We've gotten through worse before."

I nodded, grateful that he was giving out instructions for once. Maddock always was a planner, which made him an invaluable asset to my crew. I picked at a stray seam on my shirt, peering out the window of the tavern. "I want to be back to the cottage before dark, if possible."

The boys all nodded back to me. Duncan clapped his hands. "We better get moving, then."

A short time later, Cameron and I had walked back to the pub, bundles of clothing in sacks slung over our shoulders. I had gotten several days' worth of sturdy, casual clothing for both of us, and some thick socks and rugged boots for Brigid. The boots were likely too big for her, but they would fit her better than the ones of mine at the cottage. And if she was going to be in her human form for any length of time, she'd need them.

As we walked up to the entrance, Duncan and Maddock came around the corner with their own bags. Duncan held his up. "Got it, Cae."

I smiled at his enthusiasm. "Then let's start walking. We should be able to make it back to the cottage before it gets too dark."

"Uh, hey, Caelum," Maddock started tenuously, "That cottage only has one bed, and it's fairly small. And if you've got a girl there, how are all of us supposed to fit to sleep?"

My smile dropped. I hadn't thought of that. Well, damn. Tight quarters were usual for us, but sharing tight quarters with a woman was definitely not the norm.

Maddock laughed at my expression. "It's okay, Captain. You've had a lot on your mind, apparently. We can meet you in the morning with the clothes if that's okay to you, so you don't have to carry both bags all that way. Or we can all bunk on the floor together."

I ran a hand through my hair, which reminded me that I needed to replace my band that I used to hold it back. "If you can all keep your traps shut tonight, you can meet us in the morning at the cottage."

"Steel trap, Captain," Duncan said. He handed me the heavy bag of food and took my bag of clothes. "We'll leave here at first light."

I nodded at them, grateful they were alive but still mourning those we had lost. "Stay safe. I'll see you in the morning."

"You as well, Captain," Cameron said, stepping over to stand next to Duncan and Maddock.

I turned and began walking away before I remembered something important. Stopping and turning around, I walked back up to them, leaning in conspiratorially. "Oh, and if you see a girl at the cottage with red hair and I'm not with her for whatever reason, assume she's dangerous, eh? I'd hate to have her kill you when I just found you alive."

"What the hell kind of girl have you found, Captain?" Duncan asked, narrowing his eyes.

"Don't worry, boy. It'll be fine." Smiling at them, I waved as I hefted the sack of food onto my back and began my journey back to the cottage, and back to Brigid...hopefully.

Elizi
@ELIZIANN

BRIGID

CHAPTER ELEVEN

As soon as Caelum left the cottage, I jumped from the bed. I watched from the window until he was out of sight. I needed to get into the water and back to the caves. I needed to at least *try* to warn the others.

Stepping out of the cottage, I made my way down to the shoreline, pulling off my clothes as I went. Bending down, I folded them into a pile, leaving them on the beach for my return. I stiffened at the thought. Would I be returning? Did I even *want* to return?

That thought stopped me in my tracks. I had never imagined a life away from the syrens; I had never wanted to. But less than a day with Caelum had me questioning my choices.

Warning the others was the most important thing to me right now, but I couldn't help feeling like I still owed Caelum a debt. The one I owed for him trying to save me may have been paid, but he had lost his entire crew at the hands of my kind.

Shaking my head, I decided to deal with that later. I stepped into the icy water and waded out into the deep. Letting my transformation take over, I quickly began swimming toward the caves.

As I neared them, my chest tightened. Would I even be able to get in?

Thankfully, I was able to swim to the entrance and make my way inside the large cavern. As I rounded the rocky walls, I heard the others talking, though I couldn't make out their words.

Steeling my spine, I swam forward, revealing myself. The conversation stopped.

"What are you doing here?" Maira hissed, swimming up to me in an instant and leaving her seat next to Sorcha behind. "I told you to not come back."

"I know, but—"

"No, there is no reason for you to be here. You left us for that man." She bared her teeth at me, her talons flexing at her side.

Cliodhna swam forward, a frown marring her otherwise perfect face. "Maira told us what you did, Brigid."

I nodded, lowering my gaze respectfully. "Aye, I saved him. But he tried to save me from the violence of man when I was a child."

"He didn't succeed." Cliodhna's voice was harsh, harsher than I had ever heard before. She swam closer to me, stopping directly in front of me. "So, why did you feel like it was worth using my gifts to you, *my power,* to save him?"

Shame swirled in my stomach, but I pushed it down. I had spent years shoving down my emotions, and I needed to do it once more. "He is innocent."

"That does not mean he deserves your kindness now," Cliodhna bit out, grimacing. Her jaw clenched, and her forehead furrowed. "You are squandering my gifts to you for this man."

Again, her words were like a knife, stabbing through my stomach. I couldn't reply. I knew there was nothing I could say that would make this better for them.

"Maira spoke the truth. You are no longer welcome in our home. You have disgraced me and your fellow syrens by siding with this man." She raised her chin high before turning away dismissively.

I looked up at her, my throat burning as I fought back tears. I wanted desperately to search out Sorcha and talk to her, but I knew if I gave Cliodhna anything less than my full attention, I would regret it. "I understand your ire, my queen. But I will repay this debt to this man. And then I will earn your forgiveness."

"Why did you return?" Maira asked, her eyes narrowing. "You knew you would not be welcomed."

"There are men on the surface," I explained. "They were looking for mermaids. I wanted to come warn you."

"And you think that would earn our forgiveness?" Maira spat, disgust clear in her face.

"No," I admitted. I knew there would be much more that I would have to do to earn their forgiveness, if I even could. "But I still had to tell you. I couldn't bear it if something happened to you all."

"No one will find these caves. We are protected here," Cliodhna said, her eyes narrowing at me. "And for you to imply that I cannot protect my creations is...unwise."

"That's not what I was implying," I said, raising an eyebrow. My protectiveness would not be dismissed or looked down on. "You all matter to me, and I want to make sure you are safe."

"Don't pretend you care about us now. You abandoned us on a whim."

"And now you're abandoning me as well," I replied softly, knowing my words would cause even more anger. But they needed to be said. Yes, in their eyes, I had betrayed them,but they had decided to denounce me after more than a decade together for one decision I had made.

Maira shook her head, a look of disgust on her face. She didn't say anything else before turning and disappearing deeper into the caverns.

Cliodhna looked at me for a long moment. "You will leave here and not return. Once you leave, the caves will be closed to you. And once you leave, you will lose your song."

"You're taking my powers?" I asked, the breath rushing out of me. No, she couldn't. She'd never taken anything back before. Would she make me forget them as well?

"I am taking back *my* powers, girl," she said, her voice as icy as her eyes. "They were never yours to begin with. Some of them I cannot remove; I don't have enough power to do so currently. You will still be able to transform, but I am stripping the magic that makes it painless. It will be excruciating for you now. You will no longer be able to communicate with us in the seas. And you will not be welcomed in my waters any longer."

Without another word, she turned and disappeared into the caverns as well. The others, except for Sorcha, followed, although much slower. Kyla lingered the longest, casting me a sorrowful glance before she too turned and left. Sorcha remained, just watching me, an unreadable expression on her face. My stomach twisted at the thought of being so easily dismissed by my adopted family, but I hadn't been able to bring myself to abandon Caelum on the beach, and I couldn't now.

Sorcha swam closer, almost hesitantly. She looked hurt, betrayed, but also confused. "Why are you doing this? You left me, Brigid."

I shook my head, trying to get her to understand my choices. "I have no love for men, Sorcha, you know that. But this man, when he was just a child, tried to save me, and he was punished for it. I have to repay that debt. I couldn't let him drown. You were right, maybe some of them are innocent. Or at least innocent enough to deserve a second chance."

She looked at me for a long moment, her eyes betraying nothing. Her face was conflicted, her brows pinching together as she studied me. As quickly as it had come, that expression vanished, replaced with blankness that I feared she had learned from me. Maybe the others had already gotten to her, turning her against me. She sighed heavily. "I hope he's worth it, Brigid. And I hope he truly is innocent."

I offered her a small smile before jerking my head toward the exit of the cavern. "Go on. I'll be fine, lass, and so will you. I am sorry."

Once they had all left, I took one last look at the caves I had called home before I turned and departed. Swimming back to the surface, I lingered near the beach, not wanting to leave the water. I wasn't ready to give up my tail and my song, the form I had known for ten years, and the power that came along with it. I just wanted to sit here for a while before it was taken from me.

Elizi
@ELIZIANN

B R I G I D

CHAPTER TWELVE

The sun was just beginning to set, blazing streaks of red and orange over the waves, when I finally left the water. I let the transformation take over me, relishing the feelings and sensations moving through my body, painless one last time. Sadness filled me and burned at my throat once the change was complete. I was human again. Mostly.

With a heavy heart, I pulled the clothes from the beach onto my body, ignoring how they clung to my wet skin uncomfortably. I deserved the discomfort. I deserved the hatred from my family, and I deserved the angry looks from Caelum whenever he thought about his crew. This was all my fault, and at the end of the day, when Caelum was ready to leave, I would be alone again.

I trudged back up the beach to the cottage, taking out my frustrations on the heavy wooden door as I flung it open and entered. The inside of the cabin was cold again, reminding me that I had been gone nearly all day. Caelum would be back soon, if he returned at all. I still wasn't convinced he wouldn't cut his losses and leave me behind.

Sighing, I bent and tended to the almost extinguished fire before settling in at the table to wait.

The sun had nearly set when Caelum appeared through the window, walking toward the door. I stood from the table, unsure if I should go out to meet him or not. I hated that I was excited to see him. I shouldn't be, and the knowledge that I was tasted sour on my tongue. I was hurting those I had been closest to; I shouldn't be happy about it.

In the time I took to question my actions, Caelum had opened the door and stepped in, a huge smile spreading across his face. His eyes lit up before narrowing and turning suspicious, like he wasn't sure why I was still in the cottage. "You're still here."

"I am," I replied hesitantly. Did he not want me to stay? I took a deep breath to calm the anxiety coursing through me. If he wanted me to leave, he should have told me so. "You brought a bag?"

He held up the canvas sack in his hand, the grin returning easily to his face. "Yes, I brought food."

At the mention of food, my stomach grumbled loudly. Before I had gone to the sea, I had eaten the remaining dried meat from the cabinet, but that had been hours ago. The sensations of my empty stomach clenching around nothing brought back memories from my childhood that I would rather have stayed forgotten. With a twist of my jaw to unclench it, I took a deep breath and shoved the memories down. As a syren, I hadn't really had to worry about food, as Cliodhna had always provided for us. But those days were over. My stomach grumbled again, and my cheeks heated at Caelum's grin.

"So, what did you bring?" I asked, trying to take the attention off my demanding body.

"I'm not actually sure. A friend got it for me," he said, opening the bag and peering down inside.

My stomach clenched, but not from hunger this time. He had met someone in town? He hadn't mentioned that when he left. My mind wondered what else he hadn't told me. "Friend? Did you tell someone we were here?"

He nodded but held a hand up quickly, palm out as if I were a wild animal. "I found some of my crew that survived. They'll be coming here in the morning to meet with us. To help. They're not going to hurt you. I didn't tell them what you are."

Glaring at him, I grabbed the sack out of his hand and stomped over to the table. I couldn't believe it. One man was hard enough for me to deal with, but others? I didn't think I could do it. The feelings of shame and betrayal were enough when I was just with Caelum, but now, with more men coming to the cottage, I was sinking further and further into the feeling that maybe Maira was right, and I had made a mistake saving him.

Dumping the contents out of the bag, I tried to smother my fiery anger. I concentrated my attention on the food sprawled across the table: cheese, crusty bread, meat, and fruit. My stomach grumbled again. I was furious. We had already been attacked by two men, and now Caelum was inviting more here. My emotions warred again between staying and leaving. But if I left, where would I go? I had nowhere and no one to go to. Maybe, if I could get to the syrens' contact in the south in Bhodheas, I could use her help. I'd never met her myself, but I knew she was willing to help those in need.

I heard him walk up behind me, his body heat encroaching onto my skin. His voice was soft. "Hey, it's okay. They will not hurt you."

My jaw clenched tightly, and the muscles in my cheeks protested. His soft tone irritated me for some reason. It was like I was a rabid animal he was trying to calm, and maybe I was to him, but it still grated my nerves. "I don't need your protection. From you, your men, or anyone."

He put his hand on my upper arm, gently tugging me to look at him. Somehow, I was able to keep from ripping out of his grip and grabbing his throat for touching me. I wanted to be angry. Goddess, I wanted to be angry. But the softness I found in his green eyes tempered it down against my will. "You may not need it, but you have it. They're going to help us. Help you find a way back to your family and help me find a way to continue my mission."

This was the third or fourth time he had mentioned a mission. I was curious, but also hesitant. I didn't want to get involved in whatever he was involved in; I knew it would only make it harder to leave. And I would leave. I would leave and return to my home, I promised myself. Though, a tingling sensation of doubt began to form in my stomach. *I am returning to them,* I vowed. I remained silent, looking deep into his eyes.

After a few heartbeats, he released my arm and stepped around me to pick up a piece of bread. He pressed it into my hand. "Here, you need to eat. We'll talk more about my men while you do."

Eat. I could do that. I nodded at him, moving around the small wooden table to sit down. I tore off pieces of the bread, eating it while watching him do the same. I swallowed hard, pushing my anxiety back down as far as I could get it. I needed to be strong. "What are their names? How many survived?"

He looked at me, and for a moment, I didn't think he would answer. His eyes were sad, and I realized he was likely thinking of the men he had lost. I opened my mouth to tell him that he didn't have to tell me. He didn't have to share that with me if it hurt too much.

But finally, he spoke. "Duncan is my first mate. He's smart, sharp, keeps my head on straight. Then there's Cameron and Maddock; I've known them both for years. Cam is a fun guy; he's my quartermaster and strong as an ox for being so skinny. And Mad is too smart for his own good, always analyzing everything and everyone. A bit like you, actually, always observing. They're good men. They won't hurt you."

I wasn't sure what to say to that, so I just shoved more bread in my mouth. After chewing slowly, I was finally able to respond. "How did they survive?"

"Fishermen found them, rescued them from some cliffs."

"Did they question how you survived?" I was sure they had, and yet I had to know all I could. Understanding the entirety of the situation would ease my anxiety and make it easier to manage my expectations when I met these others.

"Aye. And I imagine they'll have even more questions once they meet you."

That set my spine on edge once again, my jaw tensing so hard my teeth groaned at the pressure. Consciously, I unclenched my jaw and flexed it from side to side. "Did you tell them about me? About what I am?"

He looked at me from the corner of his eyes, hurt flashing in the depths. "Of course not. You asked me not to. They know I'm with a girl, and that's what they'd be asking about."

I felt foolish, but how was I to know? I was a mythical sea creature who had killed the friends of these men. I wouldn't even blame Caelum if he'd told them or if they showed up here with pitchforks and nets, ready to kill me in revenge. More surprising was that he had not told them, to be honest. "Will you tell them about me?"

I debated telling Caelum about the shift in my powers and the new limitations thrust upon me. But I didn't know anything about him, and to tell him my vulnerabilities when I knew he blamed me for the death of his crew was...unwise. He seemed willing to forgive me, but I was not ready to forgive myself. Or ready to trust anyone else yet.

He turned his body to face me, grabbing one of my hands in both of his. His hands swallowed mine, the skin rough and calloused against my own, and deeply tanned against my pale flesh. "That is entirely up to you. You can tell them if you want. And if you don't want to, then all they need to know is that you helped save me. That's all that will matter to them."

"That's not all that would matter to them," I whispered, afraid that if I raised my voice, it would break the moment. Our eyes locked, and I hoped he could see the guilt in mine, the apology. "My kind killed your crew. They would be right to hate me if they knew what I am."

He didn't reply, instead just looking at me. I wanted to crawl inside his mind, to see what he was thinking. After a moment, he pulled his hands away, and the moment was lost. "Maybe I should tell them. They'll be upset if they find out on their own."

"Would they...tell anyone?" I couldn't put the others at any more risk. If these men told anyone about my existence, I could bring doom upon myself and the other syrens. Despite their anger at me, I couldn't knowingly lead someone to hurt my family. If

Caelum's men hated me, wanted to kill me, I could live with that. But I could not abide them seeking out the others.

He shook his head, looking at me curiously. "No, they wouldn't, not if I told them to keep it quiet. But you should know, they did see something in the water. They know the myths, same as I did."

I nodded, leaving it at that. I would have to wait to meet these men to make my own determination. If I felt they were a threat to the others in any way, I would leave. I had stowed away before, and I could do it again.

A lump formed in my throat at the thought of leaving Caelum. I wasn't sure what had changed since I drug him out of the water, but something had. I was growing to enjoy his company, despite knowing that I shouldn't.

We sat in silence, eating our fill of the fresh food he had brought. I wasn't sure what else to say to him, what I even could say after that. Eventually, my stomach was full, and the sun had fully dipped below the horizon. I looked over at the fire. "Should we chop more wood tonight?"

Caelum turned to look at the fire and the few logs left beside it. "Probably, but I think we'll make it through the night. We won't be staying here tomorrow, anyway. It's too small for us and the men."

I started at that. That was new information. He spoke like he was planning on me coming with them, and I had not been expecting that. "Where will we go?"

"Once they get here in the morning, we're going to set out toward a town a bit farther away but closer to the bay," he said, putting the leftover food back into the sack. "Will you stay with us? Or return to your syrens?"

Swallowing hard, I weighed my options on how much I should reveal to Caelum about what I had done while he was gone. "I don't think the syrens would take me back. Not now. I don't think returning is an option anymore."

"But you don't know that for sure," he said. If he was trying to be reassuring, it didn't work. He didn't know that I had gone back and had been stripped of everything I had known for the past decade.

"I do know," I said softly, deciding to tell him the truth. "I went back while you were gone. To warn them. They banished me instead."

"Oh." He seemed torn, his brows furrowing. "Were you planning on coming back if they hadn't banished you?"

"I..." I swallowed hard again. "I don't know."

He nodded, his jaw tensing. His voice was gruff when he spoke again. "Then why did you send me out for food? If you weren't planning on coming back, what was the point? I could have stayed in Fairport and kept looking for more survivors."

On instinct, I ducked my head at the anger in his voice and the tense hold of his body. Pressing my lips together, I quelled my anxiety and reminded myself that I could easily take on Caelum if I had to. "I needed to warn them. They are still my family, as your crew is yours."

"So, staying with me is your second choice?"

"We just met, Caelum," I reminded him, my own anger building in response. I took a deep breath through my nose, using it to put out the fire building in my chest as I flexed my fingers. "What possible reason would I have to prioritize you over them? Yes, I wanted to help you in repayment for us wrecking your ship. But their survival trumps your need for a ship and a crew of men who likely deserved to die."

"They didn't deserve to die," he said, his voice icy. "And if you ever say that again, I will throw you out of this cabin so fast your head will spin."

We locked gazes for a moment, the fire building in both of our eyes. It was obvious we were both intense individuals. I did want to help him, even after all of this, but I wouldn't let him dismiss my need to protect my fellow syrens. "Fine."

"Fine."

"So, where will you go from here?" I asked again, hoping to get the conversation back on track.

"To Whitcairn," he replied. When I looked at him, confused, he waved a hand. "It's a small town south of here. We'll be able to find a new ship and hopefully build a new crew to get back to our home port."

I officially couldn't wait anymore, and my curiosity damned me once again. Likely, he wouldn't tell me, but I had to ask. "Why do you need a new ship so badly?"

He was quiet for a moment, his eyes flitting about as if he were thinking of what to say. "We were on an important mission to stop someone who actually *would* have deserved to die at your hands. I'd like to get back on track with that as soon as possible."

"What's your mission?" I asked. Logically, I shouldn't be trying to connect with Caelum any more, but I wanted to know as much as I could. Caelum intrigued me, despite my better judgment. He didn't seem the type to be a pirate, plundering innocent merchant ships, but I was used to living my life beneath the waves, not atop it. Ships were ships to us. We didn't differentiate what we chose to wreck based on the goods they were hauling.

He raised an eyebrow at me, challenging me. "Tell me your story, and I'll tell you mine."

I hesitated. While I did want to hear his story, I wasn't quite sure if I was ready to tell him mine. I hadn't even told Sorcha my whole story, and Caelum and I barely knew each other. Despite our shared history, my story largely involved the others, and I couldn't put them in any more danger than I already had.

Caelum seemed to sense my hesitation and offered a small smile, his earlier anger already gone. "I can go first if that makes it better for you."

I exhaled slowly and nodded. "Yeah, you go first. I promise I'll keep your story to myself."

He reached over the table and grabbed my hand, squeezing it gently while looking into my eyes. "And when you're ready to tell yours, I will keep it to myself as well."

Smiling at him, I tugged at his hand until he stood with me. I motioned toward the bed. The idea of telling my story to Caelum while he looked at me made my stomach turn, and I needed at least a ruse of solitude to be able to push down my anxiety. "Let's go lie down."

His eyes widened in equal parts curiosity and suspicion. "Lay down?"

I dropped his hand and stretched out on the bed myself, getting as comfortable as I could on the lumpy mattress. I may not have laid in a bed these past years, but my hanging canvas bed in *Neamh na Mara* had seen and heard many a story. "Stories are always better when you're lying down with your eyes closed. But you don't have to if you're uncomfortable. I can lay on the floor."

He looked at me for a moment, an unfamiliar look in his eyes. He walked over and put the last of the logs onto the fire. Finally, he kicked his boots off and stretched out on the bed next to me, folding an arm behind his head. "Aye. But I'm not sure where to start."

I rolled over onto my side, propping my head up on my hand and putting my weight on my elbow as I looked at him. "Start from the day we met ten years ago. What were you doing on that ship?"

"My father had sent me away to learn how to be a sailor. He always had high hopes for me to work with his crew. But I never wanted to be like him, my father or that captain. After they threw you over, I lost the little bit of respect I had for the captain and started revolting more than I had been. Ignoring directions, doing my own thing. I was whipped badly for the disobedience, but that captain eventually got tired of my attitude and sent me back to my father."

"I saw the scars on your back." I was beyond furious, my anger bubbling beneath the surface of my skin, begging to be unleashed. My fingers twitched, claws aching to extend and punish someone, punish whoever had given him those scars. "They did that to a child?"

He grimaced. "Aye, they did. It took months to heal."

"They won't touch you again." The protectiveness I felt over Caelum shocked me, but it also felt natural. I wanted to tear apart that captain and Caelum's father both, piece by piece. Drowning would not be enough for them, for anyone who would do what they had done to a child. "Is that captain still alive? Does he still sail?"

He smirked at me, delight twinkling behind the pain in his eyes. "Why? Are you going to avenge me?"

I raised an eyebrow. "I was planning to, yes."

"The captain is dead, so there's no one left to punish for that," he said with a sad smile. "But I appreciate the sentiment. I can take care of myself now."

Unbidden, I reached out to place my hand on his cheek. The desire to comfort him had come out of nowhere, but I didn't stop myself. His eyes closed and he leaned into the touch, but as quickly as he'd melted, he stiffened and opened his eyes. The wall he constructed between us was visible in his eyes. Slowly, I lowered my hand, pulling back into myself. I shouldn't have touched him. Obviously, he would not welcome the touch of a killer—of a monster. "I apologize. Please, go on."

"He wasn't pleased that I had...disobeyed him, so he punished me. At first it was mental, just belittling me, giving me shit work to do. Then it turned physical as I got older and bigger. He would beat me, but it didn't affect me the way he wanted it to. I could turn off the pain and ignore it. So, he turned to other physical abuse. The final straw for me was when he tied me up and dangled me upside down over the water. My arms were completely in the water, my head just barely out of it. Some lovely fish decided to gnaw on my hand while I was hanging there, but I was too exhausted to try to keep myself out of the water. When the blood attracted more sharks than anything, he finally pulled me back in, laughing the whole time. That's where this scar came from," he explained, holding his right hand up so I could see the jagged and puckered skin circling his wrist. I wanted to reach out and touch it, but his reaction to my touch earlier made me curl my fingers in, digging my nails into my palm instead. "I almost lost my hand. Had even debated what kind of hook I would get to replace it. But it survived. And so did I."

He shrugged. "I knew my father wasn't a good man, but that solidified it for me. When I was finally better and able to use my hand again, I started learning more about what my father actually did; what he used his ship for, where he made his money. And I made it my life's mission to stop him at whatever he's doing."

There was more to it, that much was obvious. But I could tell it pained him to talk about it. Despite his reservations at my touch, I placed a hand on his arm, wanting nothing more than to erase the pure anger in his eyes. It was an anger I recognized in myself, one I knew would consume him if he didn't unleash it at some point. "What was he doing?"

He hesitated, opening and closing his mouth a few times. The conflict was clear to see on his face. He didn't want to tell me, and I understood his apprehension. I was wary of sharing my own story with him.

"It's okay, you don't have to tell me," I said slowly, understanding the struggle he was going through. We had barely met, and I knew I was not eager to share my story with Caelum, so how could I expect him to be open with me? But his words rang in my ears and settled deeply in my stomach, running together with Sorcha's words from our last night together. She was right, maybe we *were* punishing innocents. The thought made me sick to my stomach. How many men had we killed who had not deserved it?

"Aye, thank you," he said, looking over at me, pulling me from my spiraling thoughts. He placed his other hand over mine, still resting on his arm, and brought it over onto his chest. His gaze turned back to the ceiling, and he squeezed my hand. "Would you be open to joining us? Now that I don't have a full crew, I could use all the help I can get to stop him. He's one man I would actually encourage you to kill."

I didn't know what to say to that. My heart went out for him, and maybe under different circumstances, I would have jumped at helping him. But I couldn't forget that my kind had just killed his crew. *I* had just killed his crew. That would surely lead to some less-than-positive feelings. While I could handle myself, I wasn't in the habit of putting myself in situations where I knew I would be vulnerable. "I don't know, Caelum. I don't even know what your mission truly is."

His forehead furrowed, and his voice was cold. "Do you think we would truly be trying to harm people? Helping us is really the least you could do.”

“What?” I asked, confused. He had been soft as he told his story, but now his voice was hard, and anger was seeping into his eyes, blazing like fire.

“You and the others are the reason I’m having to basically start over on this mission. My father is an evil man, and we were so close to catching up to him and finally being able to stop him. The least you could do is help me get it back on track. What’s there to not know?” He seemed frustrated, his body tight against mine.

I was speechless. He was right, but at the same time, I despised being told what I should and should not do. Caelum seemed like the type who was accustomed to being listened to, not being questioned. And maybe in another life, I would have cowered and folded to his harsh words, but not anymore. However right he was, however true his statement, I would never do what men told me to do just because they told me to do it. Not anymore.

Stubbornly, I raised my head to meet his gaze, my back straight and eyes steady. “I don’t know what you want me to say to that. I don’t know you, Caelum. I don’t know your mission. I’m not going to blindly jump into something I have no understanding of.”

He sighed before motioning at me with his hand. “Go on, then, tell me your story. Fair’s fair.”

I took a deep breath, flexing my fingers against my legs. Caelum had trusted me with his story, I could do the same. Despite his anger, I felt safe with him, and confident that he wouldn’t harm me like other men had. At least, not physically.

“I grew up on a farm with my father. My mother died when I was born, and he’s resented me ever since. But I worked, pulling my weight on the farm while my father gambled all of our money away. I didn’t have any siblings, no other family I knew of, and no friends.

“Eventually, when I turned fifteen, my father tried to marry me off to a man nearly three times my age. He wanted to cover his gambling debts. The man was awful, and I wanted more than that. I wanted a life of my own choosing. I wanted to make a name for myself the right way. So, when I heard that your ship was going to

Bhodheas, I just needed to get away from Tuathnach and start over for myself. But I didn't have any money, so I had to stow away. There were no other ships leaving, not for several days, and I wouldn't have made it walking. I considered hiding in a supply carriage, but I couldn't have stayed hidden long enough."

"He was basically going to sell you?" Caelum asked, his voice angry but controlled. His anger surprised me. He was upset for me, and I wasn't used to having someone care about my well-being. Sure, Kyla had been kind to me when I first joined the syrens, but largely, they were indifferent to me unless I was needed for something.

I looked over to find him staring at me with an intensity in his eyes that stirred something in my stomach. I unclenched my jaw again before continuing. "He said at least I would be good for something that way. But regardless, I was found by your crew, thrown over, and then I was rescued by a sea goddess and the others. She offered me a choice, to seek my revenge on men or to be taken to a women's shelter in Bhodheas. At the time, I was so angry. So, I decided to become a syren.

"I worked with my fellow syrens, learning the seas, the creatures, and what it meant to be part of a people that cared about each other. We looked out for each other, sought comfort and companionship in each other, and we sought revenge on those who had wronged us, and on all men. Men had never brought us anything but suffering, so we repaid the favor," I explained. My fingers, still resting on his chest, twitched, bunching up his shirt slightly. Slowly, I relaxed my fingers one by one, smoothing out the fabric. "But maybe there are some good men out there."

He grinned, but it was slightly forced, and squeezed my fingers again before dropping his hand to his side. "Well, I'm glad you're coming around to that thought."

I smiled back before laying my head down on the pillow. He was still upset; I could feel it radiating off him. But he tried to hide it from me, to mask it beneath that forced smile. He turned his gaze away from me and up to the ceiling. For a moment, we just laid there in each other's company and warmth. We stayed like that until the light in the room began to dim and the fire began to sputter. A breeze moved through the cottage, sending shivers through my body. "We should put more wood on."

He sighed and sat up, moving me off his chest. Looking toward the fireplace, he cursed, running his hand through his hair. "There's no more wood. I just put the last of it on before we laid down."

"How cold will it get?" I asked, sitting up in the bed as well. I wasn't used to the cold in my human form yet, and I was not looking forward to trying to sleep while shivering. "We have other blankets. Will that be enough?"

"We're pretty far north, so it will get fairly cold tonight. But the blankets should be enough, as long as you don't mind having to huddle under the same blankets as me for warmth." His voice was hesitant. "We don't have enough to each have our own."

My cheeks flushed at the thought of feeling his body pressed against mine all night. But I also couldn't help but think of how adamant he had been the night before about not sharing the bed with me. I knew we needed to stay warm, but I also didn't want to be curled up next to someone who didn't want to be there. "I don't mind. If you're sure you're okay with sharing."

He stood, walking over to the trunk to collect the last of the blankets. He brought them back over to the bed and was silent as he spread them out over me. Just as he was finishing, the fire sputtered out, the room darkening even more until only the glow of embers remained. Wind fluttered through the cottage. He pulled back a corner of the blankets, jerking his head at me. "Move over, *teine*. I'm coming in."

I bit my tongue to keep from asking what that word meant. He had said it several times now, and it seemed endearing, but I wasn't sure. The language was familiar, but I couldn't place it. Once we were both under the blankets, we lay there, side by side. I could already feel a chill starting and couldn't help the shiver that racked through me. My fingers twisted into the rough fabric of the blankets covering us as I tried to control my body's reactions. I could feel the warmth seeping off Caelum's skin, and I wanted nothing more than to press back into it. But he was still angry.

I debated moving to lay on the floor so that my shivering wouldn't wake him. I didn't like the cold, but I also did not want to rely on this man who obviously was angered by my actions, no matter how much he tried to hide it. I understood his anger, so it made it easier to accept the reality.

Before I could move to leave the bed, another shiver racked through my body. Caelum cursed again, wrapping an arm around my shoulders and pulling me into his side, my head resting on his chest. He pulled the blankets higher over us both and interlocked his fingers behind me, holding me to him tightly. "Get some sleep."

"Goodnight, Caelum," I whispered, holding my body deathly still. If I moved, it would ruin the moment, and I wanted it to last just a little while longer, to relish the feel of him next to me.

As I drifted off to sleep, I swore there was a soft press of lips to my temple. But I couldn't be sure, as I was already succumbing to the body-heat-induced sleep.

Elizia
@ELIZIAN

CHAPTER THIRTEEN

The morning came way too soon. Light filtered in, shining into my eyes as an arm tightened around my midsection. Caelum. The feeling of his weight on my stomach was comforting. Rather than uncomfortable, like I'd thought it would be, spending the night next to Caelum had been relaxing. I shifted around, grumbling sleepily to confirm if it was truly him still holding me. "Caelum?"

He smoothed his hand over my hair and pushed it out of his face, his own voice rough from sleep. It sent chills down my spine, and that, more than the light, woke me up instantly. "Good morning, *teine.* Sleep well?"

"What does that word mean?" I asked, rubbing my eyes as I sat up. I needed to get away from him, from my body's reactions to him. Our paths were not destined to stay together long, and trying to pretend otherwise was foolish. Other than making up for the sins of syrens, the only thing I could offer Caelum was my body. And I doubted very much that he would want that after the deaths of his crew.

He didn't reply, just looked up at me with a sleepy expression on his face. It made him look younger, the tension gone from between his eyebrows.

Smoothing a hand over my wild curls, I sighed. I shouldn't have asked, and I feared now I would never find out what the pet name meant. "I slept well. Did you?"

"Aye, better than I have in a while," he admitted, smiling at me and jarring me from my thoughts. "You're a much better sleeping partner than a bunk room full of snoring sailors."

I smiled at that, trying to convince him that nothing was wrong. So many things were wrong. The smile slipped off my face and my jaw tightened, my teeth grinding together. "When will your friends be here?"

Caelum looked over through the window at the sun rising softly through the hills. "If they left Fairport at first light, they should be here fairly soon."

"Where will we be going from here? I don't think five of us could fit in this little space," I said, waving my hand around the cottage. I was used to having more space to live in, and this would be confining even if I were the only inhabitant. Sharing the cave rooms with Sorcha had been less cramped than this. Standing, I righted my clothes that had rumpled from sleep. Picking at the frayed seams, I looked around the cabin, doing anything possible to keep my mind from racing and my attention off Caelum.

Thinking about sharing the room with other men brought my mind back to Sorcha. What would she think if she could see me now? Would she be pleased I was coming around to her views of men, or had the others gotten to her? In the same breath, my mind switched to worrying about Caelum's friends and how they would treat me. Despite what I told myself, I wasn't sure if I could keep my confidence in the face of four men.

"Whitcairn is just a day's walk south of here. We'll be headed there to try to find a new ship and build back up a crew," he explained, clearing the sleep from his eyes and voice. "I hope you would consider coming with us. Help us stop my father."

I hesitated, unsure how to answer. I would be useless to them without my powers to help them with anything, let alone a mission as important as this one seemed to be. Without my song, I was just a fish with arms. I could see in the dark and live in the cold water, but I doubted that would be useful to them. If Caelum discovered I had no more powers and had no use to him, maybe his mind would change. But his words the night before had resonated with me, and really, I had nothing left to lose. Maybe dying to stop a truly evil man would atone for my sins against the innocent ones. I let my gaze rise back to his. "I'll help you. You're right, it really is the least I can do after what happened."

He paused, studying me for a long moment. I could almost see the wheels turning in his head, thoughts racing about what my motivations were. It was clear he didn't completely trust me yet. That was fine. I wasn't sure if I entirely trusted him yet either. Being cautious was healthy, and given what we both had faced, I didn't blame him.

"Do you want some breakfast?" he eventually asked, getting out of the bed and walking toward the sack of food still sitting on the table. He pulled out some bread and handed it to me. "The others will be bringing some fresh clothes for us, and hopefully some more food for the journey."

We ate in silence, and as we were finishing up our food, voices drifted in from outside. Male voices. I tensed up, looking to the window. My heart raced, though I knew it was likely only Caelum's surviving crew. Still, anxiety raced through me; sweat slicked my palms and a trickle slid down my spine. Would they immediately know what I was? Would they immediately want to kill me? My jaw popped from how tightly I was clenching it, and I opened my mouth to flex it from side to side, forcing it to relax.

Caelum stood, walking over to the window and peering out. His shoulders relaxed, and he turned back to me with an easy smile. "It's just my men. Nothing to worry about."

I couldn't bring myself to respond, thoughts of what was about to happen kept me still and terrified. I had faced many things in my life, but facing them without the backing of my powers was disconcerting. It threw me back to when I had first met Caelum and how helpless I had been then. I never wanted to feel that again, and yet, here I was. Caelum cast a curious glance back at me before walking over to the door and opening it.

"Caelum! Morning," a large blond man greeted, stepping through the door and clapping a hand on Caelum's shoulder so loud that I couldn't help but wince.

But all Caelum did was smile at the man. "Morning, Duncan. Come on, you oaf, let's get inside."

They all moved inside the cottage, Caelum, the large blond man, and two other men. The dark-haired one was well-kempt and stiff, assessing everything in the cottage with a focus that unnerved me. The curly-haired one smiled carelessly, but I felt his gaze on me as well, curious. I tried not to fidget beneath it despite every muscle in my body screaming in protest to move, to leave. Flexing my fingers against my leg, I bent and straightened them one by one, focusing on the feel of the fabric beneath them. I wondered if they noticed I was still wearing Caelum's clothes.

"Brigid, this is Duncan, Cameron, and Maddock. Men, this is Brigid," Caelum introduced, motioning to each of them in turn.

Duncan, the large blond, walked right up to me and stuck his hand out. I didn't miss the suspicion in his eyes as he studied me, though. "Duncan. Nice to meet you."

I stared at him, shoving down my fear and crafting a practiced look of blankness on my face. Despite how enthusiastic he was with Caelum, this man was much larger than me. Without a second thought, he could kill me in my human form. Maybe he would once he found out about what I had done. Maybe I deserved it. I tensed my body, trying to clear my mind and keep my emotions off my face. Swallowing, I extended my hand to meet Duncan's. "You as well."

"So, how'd you meet Caelum?" Cameron, the sandy-haired man, asked, sitting down at the other chair. He was smaller than Duncan, but seemed more open and relaxed with me. His eyes roved over me, but not in a way that made me feel uncomfortable.

My gaze flicked to Caelum briefly, but I forced myself to look back at the man in front of me. Caelum was *their* friend in this situation. He could do nothing to protect me from them. I could do this. I could tell them this story without giving away my secrets. I needed more time to prepare for how they would react and how I would react. "I helped pull him out of the water. He was almost to shore, and I saw him from the beach. His head dipped under, so I swam out and helped pull him out. I stayed with him to make sure he didn't drown."

Cameron reached over and squeezed my fingers. It took every muscle in my body to keep still and not jerk my hand away from him. The touch of a man was jarring, but his face was serene and genuine. "Thank you for saving him. I don't know if the fool has thanked you himself, but I will."

I forced myself to return the squeeze and offered him a small smile. While I likely deserved more anger and disgust from them, I would take their kindness for the moment. Until I could figure out exactly how they would react when they found out the truth, this façade was the safest for me. Even if it meant deceiving those Caelum obviously cared about. "He has. But the gratitude is appreciated."

"I'm glad you saved our captain here as well," Duncan added.

"Someone had to," I said lightly, trying to keep the tension out of my voice. My jaw clicked as I clenched it tightly. "He didn't seem to be succeeding at doing it himself."

All three of them roared with laughter. Caelum crossed his arms over his chest, but the large grin stretched across his face told a different story. I almost wanted to smile with him, but I kept my face carefully neutral.

"Yeah, yeah, laugh it up."

"So, tell us about the men who attacked," Duncan said, suddenly serious. He looked back at Caelum briefly before focusing his attention on me. "Did they hurt you?"

I shook my head, afraid that this conversation would turn in an ugly direction. I had to be careful with what I divulged. Deciding to keep it safe, I replied, "No, I'm not hurt. Caelum handled one, I got the other."

His eyebrows shot up. "You did?"

"Is that so hard to believe?" I asked, arching an eyebrow at him.

My discomfort waned for a moment, replaced by indignance that this man would so easily dismiss me. Taking a slow breath through my nose, I calmed myself before my temper got the better of me and I let something slip that revealed more than I intended.

Duncan backtracked quickly, his eyes widening slightly. "No, not at all. Just a bit surprising given how...small you are."

"I have a few tricks up my sleeve," I said, leaning back in the chair and crossing my arms. Maybe I was antagonizing them, leading them on. But I would never be dismissed by a man again, whether I had my syren powers or not.

He laughed at that, reaching over to pat my shoulder. I was proud of myself for not flinching under his touch. Oblivious, he continued to smile at me. "Aye, I'm sure you do. I'm glad you're both okay."

"Did any of the rest of your crew survive?" I needed to know. If these men had survived, maybe more of them had as well. It wouldn't erase my guilt or my obligation to help them, but perhaps it could ease my conscience. It would also help me gauge the anger they would feel when they discovered the truth.

The dark-haired one named Maddock answered this time. "Not that we know of. We were waiting for any who washed up when Caelum found us. You can call me Mad, by the way."

I looked down at the table, fighting the sudden urge to twist my fingers like Sorcha had. Instead, I picked at my nails, cursing the sharp talons beneath them. I wondered what it would feel like now when they extended. I took a deep breath, unclenching my jaw that had unconsciously tightened again, and raised my gaze. "I'm sorry for your losses. Caelum told me what happened in the water."

Caelum stepped up behind me and squeezed my shoulder, surprising me. He at least knew the truth, and he should not be comforting me. But I supposed that if his men didn't know the truth, it wouldn't make sense for him to shun me in this moment. "It's all right."

As if he'd read my thoughts, he pulled his hand back. Perhaps he had realized exactly what he had said. Nothing about this was all right, and it was important that both of us remembered that.

"Aye," Cameron chimed in, "it's not like you drowned them."

I couldn't help but flinch at his words. My body tensed, and I bit down on the inside of my cheek hard enough to taste blood.

Caelum straightened. "All right, let's—"

"Tell me about them," I demanded, interrupting Caelum's dismissal. I wanted to know. To know the men who had died at the hands of my kind. "Tell me about your crew."

"Are you sure you want to hear about this?" Caelum asked, eyeing me suspiciously. Perhaps he didn't want me to know about them. Did he think me unworthy enough to know their memories? "We don't have to talk about them."

I gazed at him, hoping my determination shone through. "No, I want to hear about them. If you're willing to share."

"Wait, are you sure we can trust her?" Duncan asked, his voice loud in the quiet room despite him trying to whisper to Caelum. In any other instance, I would have smiled. But this was serious. They likely shouldn't trust me, but in reality, who would I tell?

"Can we trust you not to go telling anyone about this? Some of the men have families still at home, and I don't want anything happening to them if it's discovered they were part of my crew," Caelum asked. His tone was teasing, but the glint in his eyes told me exactly how serious his question was.

Nodding at him, I raised an eyebrow. Who else would I tell? "You can trust me. I won't tell another soul."

I have no one left to tell, were the words left unspoken.

Caelum jerked his chin to the others before dragging over the trunk filled with blankets to sit on the lid.

Caelum began, "All right. We'll tell you about them. Our crew was thirty-three men. Not quite enough for a full crew on the barque we sailed, but it worked well for our purposes. They all came from different walks of life. Some had been sailors their whole lives. Some were there for other reasons. They all knew why we were sailing. They were all good men."

I wanted to throw up at his words. It must have shown on my face because he stopped talking and looked at me with concern. How could he be concerned about my feelings after this? He should be furious with me, telling me to get out of his cottage and never come back.

"Why were you sailing?" There was more to the story than he had told me, a more specific purpose. I clenched my jaw again to keep the burning in the back of my throat down. I took shallow breaths through my nose to stay focused on the men in front of me and not my own emotions.

Duncan looked at me, his hazel eyes wary, before turning to look at Caelum. They seemed to have a conversation without words. Caelum nodded at him before continuing the story. "Aye, I told you last night, my father was a bad man. He had taken something dear to us, to all of us, and we were sailing to figure out a way to find him and get it back."

Cameron looked at Caelum for a moment and then turned his gaze to me and continued the story. "I don't know how much Caelum told you, but a lot of the men were there hoping to find the...thing that was taken. But when we get back, at least we can tell their families that the ship went down, and they can get that closure."

"Aye, it's better than not knowing," Duncan said solemnly. The overwhelming urge to vomit came over me once again, and I unclenched my jaw to draw in breaths through my mouth instead.

"Good men," I repeated. Maybe if I said it enough, it would take back the actions. But I knew that was a foolish hope. Almost as foolish as the hope that I would be able to stay with Caelum. "You all seem like good men."

Maddock grinned at me, oblivious to the numbness I was feeling. "We like to think so."

My jaw clenched painfully. They should want to kill me. Why Caelum hadn't that first night, I would never understand. I deserved it. I opened my mouth, unsure of what to say but needing to say something.

"All right, that's enough. They were good men, and we lost them. But we owe it to them to get to Whitcairn and figure out our next moves." Caelum stood from his seat on the trunk, interrupting what I had been about to say.

Cameron pulled a map out of his bag and spread it across the table before diving into the best route to get to Whitcairn, a town further south of here, and the supplies we would need. While the change in subject was nice, my thoughts continued to race about what the future would hold and what would happen once they discovered the truth. They may be good men, but I had little doubt they would want my head once they knew.

Elizi
@ELIZIAN

BRIGID

CHAPTER FOURTEEN

After a full day of walking, a town finally appeared just over the hill. I could have cried out in relief. For the past ten years, I had almost exclusively lived in my syren form. My feet were not used to this much movement and this much work. To add to that, the boots Caelum managed to get me in Fairport didn't exactly fit properly, rubbing painful blisters on my heels and toes.

"Hey, are you okay?" Caelum asked quietly, slowing down to walk beside me.

"Yeah, I'm fine," I replied, taking care to not wince as I stepped over some rocks. My ankle twisted, rubbing one of the blisters harder, and I couldn't hide the wince at that. I was beyond ready to rest, though I wouldn't be the first one to ask for a stop. I knew if I said anything, we would stop immediately, and I didn't want to show these men any weakness.

"You've been wincing like that for the past three hours, lass," he said dryly, raising an eyebrow. "You're not okay."

Shit. I shook my head, not wanting him to be concerned about me. I was fine, or I would be. These men, however good they may be, would only see me as a weakness. And I was not a weakness, not anymore. "Just not used to walking so much. I'm fine."

Grabbing my upper arm, Caelum pulled me to a stop and moved to face me. "Why didn't you say anything? We could have stopped to rest."

That was the last thing I wanted. I couldn't give them any reason to think me even weaker. I was of no use to them—more of a hindrance, really—and as soon as they realized that, I would be gone. But I needed to get closer to Bhodheas, closer to my chance at potential freedom. And if that meant holding in my winces, then I would. I had shoved down my emotions for years, a few more days was nothing. "I didn't need to stop. And we're almost there, so there's no point in stopping now."

Thankfully, Caelum let us start walking again after staring at me for a long moment, and we caught up to the others. He reached down to squeeze my fingers. "We're talking about this later. And I'm going to look at your feet."

I rolled my eyes but didn't say anything. He would *not* be looking at my feet, but it would take too much energy to argue with him now. When we got to the inn we had planned to stay at and I could sit down, I would argue with him then.

We finished our trek into the town, and my mouth fell open in awe as we stopped on a hill overlooking everything. I had only seen a few towns in my childhood, and nearly none as a syren, so I didn't have much to go on, but this town was large. There were dirt paths twining over the ground and in between thatch-roofed structures. A stream ran along one side of the town, snaking into the forest in the distance. There were people out, walking between the buildings, carrying baskets and bags. Children were playing somewhere; I could hear the tinkling laughter. On the other side of the town, the harbor and coastline carved into the sea, the smell of fish and sea salt permeating the air. Off to the right of the town, a large field was being worked in the distance. My eyes couldn't stop roving over the scene, taking in all the details I could.

Caelum turned to peer at me where I had stopped to take in the view. "You coming, *teine?*"

I nodded, shaking myself from my haze and walking behind him again. We reached the first dirt path, and Maddock led us through the maze of buildings and pathways until we reached a small building set off to the side. Its white stone was partially covered in soft green moss, accenting the rickety wooden shutters and the brown thatched roof.

Entering the small inn, Caelum took the lead, walking up to the man at the counter. "Got a couple of rooms?"

The older man looked over his glasses at Caelum and then over at Duncan, Maddock, Cam, and me, still standing by the door. Beside me, Maddock chuckled at the innkeeper's face.

"He's offended," Maddock whispered, leaning in close to my ear.

The innkeeper's eyes narrowed in suspicion as he looked at us before he looked back at Caelum, likely questioning why one woman was with three men. "How many rooms do you need?"

"Two, if you have them." Caelum's voice was confident and sturdy. Either he was oblivious to the offense of the innkeeper, or he didn't care.

After an uncomfortable silence where the man just stared at Caelum, he eventually reached under the counter and reluctantly brought two keys out. Caelum paid the man with coins from a pouch at his belt and then walked back over to us. He handed one key to Duncan and kept the other for himself.

"So, what are the arrangements?" I asked. I had never stayed in an inn when I was a child. Would I get my own room, or would I have to share? My heart sped up as my thoughts raced. Would Caelum make me share with the others?

"Duncan, Mad, and Cam in one room, and then you and I in the other," Caelum explained. He looked at me. "I'd feel a lot better if you were within eyesight and not out in a room by yourself."

Despite relaxing slightly, my cheeks burned at his casual tone when he announced we would be sharing a room. Logically, I knew the other men must know Caelum and I had likely shared a bed in the small cottage, and I wasn't known for my modesty, but still. The society I had grown up in as a child had frowned upon it, and I was sure this one still did. "I can stay alone. I don't need to be supervised, Caelum."

"I know you can take care of yourself," he said, his tone obviously trying to placate me. He lowered his voice so that only I could hear him. "But just three days ago, we had men trying to find you and capture you, and we still don't know who they were, who told them about you, or how they found us."

I crossed my arms over my chest, irritated that he made a great point. I just wanted a night to myself to regroup and gather my thoughts, which were quickly going down paths I had never dreamed possible since becoming a syren. There was so much happening, and I just wanted to take it all in and not have to hide my emotions from everyone around me. But Caelum was right. "All right, I suppose that would be fine. Someone obviously needs to keep an eye on you to make sure you don't die."

He smiled like I had just given him the biggest compliment of his life. He shouldn't be smiling at me like I had given him anything. Crossing his arms proudly, he inclined his head toward me. "Thank you. Your cooperation is noted and appreciated."

Off to the side, Maddock snickered. It was cut off by a grunt when Cam elbowed him in the side. I snapped my gaze over to them, irritated by their amusement. "What are you boys giggling about over there?"

They all quickly schooled their features back into seriousness. "Nothing."

"Let's go get settled. We'll meet back up in an hour or so and go hunt down some food and figure out our plan," Caelum said, his face suddenly serious and concerned again. He jerked his head at the others, and Duncan returned his nod.

Message received. Caelum did not like me making friendly with his crew. I suppose it made sense, given the reality of our situation. I tamped down the feelings of unease in my stomach. These were his men, and if he didn't want me being friends with them, I would respect that. Crossing my arms over my chest, I tried to hold myself together, at least until I was alone again. Years of practiced indifference with the others made my emotions easy to hide. But my time with Sorcha, and now with Caelum, was making it more difficult than it had ever been in the past.

"Take two hours. I'm going to go ask around about a ship, and hopefully I'll have something by dinner," Duncan said, clapping Caelum on the back.

"Aye, good plan," Caelum replied. Turning to me, he tugged at my hand once before letting it drop and leading me up the stairs.

We walked into a room at the top of the stairs, small and dark, and I looked around. There was a desk and a wardrobe against one wall, and a small wooden bed on the other. The large bay window was framed by gauzy cream curtains. I quickly moved over and sat down on the bed, sighing in relief as the weight was finally off my sore feet.

Caelum looked over at me out of the corner of his eye. He grabbed the chair from the desk and dragged it over in front of me. He motioned to my foot, leaning down toward it. "Here, let me look at that."

I rolled my eyes, not moving an inch. "You don't need to inspect my feet like I'm a child, Caelum."

"If you're injured, I need to know about it," he said, his voice cool. He motioned for my foot again. "Stop being stubborn. Let me see it."

Sighing, I lifted my leg, plopping my booted foot into his lap. His irritation at my stubbornness was palpable, and I didn't want to waste any more energy on this discussion. My feet did hurt, after all. "Fine, take a peek."

More gently than I was expecting, given his mood, he pulled the boot off. We both grimaced when we saw my bare foot. It was torn up, bloody, and my heel had a giant blister on it. "*Teine,* you should have said something a lot sooner."

"Can we bandage it?" I asked, twisting my ankle to get a better look at the damage. I really had messed it up. And without being in the caves with Cliodhna, or at the very least, in the sea, I wouldn't be able to heal quickly like I normally could. A sour taste filled my mouth as I thought about the healing powers I used to have access to. I wondered if Cliodhna had taken those from me too, but I wasn't keen on trying to slip away from Caelum to find out, not in a strange place like this.

Looking over his shoulder at the basin in the corner, he glanced back to me, gently lowering my foot to the floor. "Aye, we can clean it up and bandage it. But we really need to get you some better-fitting boots and some socks."

"Can we find those here? How can I afford them?" I didn't have any money, and I was already irritated about using Caelum's money. For some reason, Cliodhna providing for us with her magic did not feel like depending on Caelum for his money. I supposed it had to do with being in the sea versus being in the world of humans.

"We can find you some. And I can get you boots and socks. It's the least I can do for you saving my life," he said, not looking up as he gently touched my feet. He winked at me playfully.

My mouth turned sour. Even though I had saved his life, it had cost him the life of much of his crew. I had begun to forget that fact as he had inspected my feet. Intent on keeping my vow to return to Cliodhna and the others eventually, I added a new one that I would make amends with Caelum for the death of his crew. I would do what I could to help him get back what his father had taken, and only then would I set off on my own.

"How do you have money?" I asked, trying to change the subject from his helping me.

He raised his head to look at me. "Why do you want to know?"

"Are you a pirate?" I asked, raising my eyebrow. It seemed unlikely, but if they were so intent on stopping his father, I doubted they had time for legitimate merchant business.

He laughed. "No, *teine.* We're not pirates. Though some people might call us that."

"Then what are you?" I pressed, curiosity burning. "What do you do?"

"We're smugglers," he said matter-of-factly. "But the good kind."

Both eyebrows shot up my forehead. That had not been the occupation I was expecting. "There's a good kind of smuggler?"

He grinned, pride and amusement flashing equally in his eyes. Rubbing a hand over his beard, he tapped my foot, letting me move it back to the floor. "Aye, we smuggle people looking to escape from something or those needing help. And we smuggle goods to places where they're needed but can't be gotten."

"That's...very noble," I replied, still processing his words. It was similar to what the syrens did with those we rescued. Again, my stomach churned as I thought that I had almost killed this man in front of me. This man who helped people escape horrible things and fought to stop evil men.

"I'm sure to some. To others, we're a nuisance at best." Laughing quietly, he stood and walked over to the basin in the corner, wetting down some rags there. He returned to sit in front of me, pulling one of my feet back into his hands. "Let's get you cleaned up some before we try to bandage it."

"I don't need your charity. If you buy me boots and socks, I'll pay you back. Somehow," I replied softly, watching him run the cloth gently over my torn skin. I appreciated his help and the sentiment, but I had survived for this long and would continue to do so. "And I am sorry about your crew and your ship, again."

He paused in cleaning my foot and looked at me so intensely that I had to force myself to keep from squirming under it. "Brigid, let me help you. It's a pair of boots, nothing more. You don't have to pay me back. And do I miss my crew? Yes, of course. Do I mourn them? Yes. I'm allowed to be upset about the situation without being upset at you."

I bit the inside of my cheek, keeping silent. He was right, and he had every right to be as upset with the situation, with me, as he wanted to be.

I turned my mind to the original conversation. I really didn't want to have my feet torn up like this every time I had to be on my feet. Nor did I want to be the reason we slowed down, and I would be now that Caelum knew about my feet. "Fine, we can get me some new boots that fit. But only because I don't want to be a burden to the group."

"You wouldn't burden the group, but I'll take what I can get," he said, continuing to wipe the blood away from my torn feet. He was silent as he finished cleaning one foot, then pulled the other one into his lap and did the same. His body was warm and firm beneath my feet, and some part of me wanted to stay like this, with him. Patting my ankle, he ceased his movements. "So, want to tell me more about your syrens?"

"Not really," I admitted, shrugging. "Want to tell me more about your past?"

Caelum stood, pointedly not answering my question as he walked over to one of the bags he had brought in, pulling out some white bandages. Still ignoring my statement, he sat back down in front of me and pulled one foot into his lap again, resting it against his inner thigh as he unwound the bandage. Not wanting to watch him bandage my feet, I tilted my head back to stare at the ceiling, letting myself feel instead. If he didn't want to talk, that was fine. But I wouldn't be the only one speaking.

His body was warm against the sole of my foot, and I couldn't help myself from wiggling my toes into his leg. It had been so long since I had felt the warmth of another person. The last time had been when I shared a bed with Nerina nearly a year ago, both of us seeking the comfort of another person just for a night.

His rough hand grasped my foot, holding it firmly but gently in place. His voice was gruff, "Don't do that, *teine.*"

My eyebrows scrunched as I brought my head down to search his face. I didn't think I had wiggled my toes that hard. "Did I hurt you?"

"Not exactly." He looked down at his lap pointedly, then back at me. "Not at all, actually."

Following his gaze to his lap, my cheeks blazed at the tenting in the front of his pants. I hadn't realized my foot was that close to his manhood. While I had been relatively young when I became a syren, I was not sexually inexperienced. A woman did have needs, after all. But still, I ducked my head, warmth spreading down my neck, and looked down at my own lap instead of his. "I'm sorry, I didn't mean to. You were just warm."

He tucked a finger under my chin, pulling my gaze up to meet his. His eyes were soft and warm, and I wanted to get lost in them. If he kept looking at me like that, I might. "Don't apologize. I'm sorry if I made you uncomfortable with my reaction."

I shook my head quickly. Uncomfortable was the wrong word for what I was feeling. Overwhelmed, maybe, but Caelum didn't make me uncomfortable. "You didn't. I just didn't realize what I was doing."

"Well, you are a beautiful woman," he pointed out. His face was calm, and again, I felt like a skittish animal he was trying to avoid being bitten by. He smiled slightly. "It was bound to happen sooner or later."

"Oh yes," I muttered dryly, "I'm sure my bloody feet are absolutely what's doing it for you."

He stopped his movements and looked up at me, his gaze heated and direct. "No, *teine*. You are doing it for me."

He went back to wrapping clean bandages around my feet. "We don't have to go down that road right now, or ever, if you don't want to. I know we've both been through a lot in the past few days. This doesn't have to mean anything. Let me finish wrapping your feet, and we can go get boots now instead of after dinner and then meet the others."

I nodded, grateful he had given me direction. That was a good plan. Anything to get out of this room and push down the heat that was building between us. It was purely physical attraction, I told myself, echoing Caelum's sentiments earlier. That was all. There could be nothing between us emotionally. There were too many bodies—thirty of them, to be precise—that barred that path.

Caelum continued to wrap my feet in silence. His hands were calloused and rough, but his touch was gentle as he wound the fabric around my bare feet. His skin was warm, and I found myself silently protesting when he put my foot down. Then, he picked the other one up and began to do the same.

As he wrapped, my mind wandered, thinking about what else his hands were capable of and how they would feel on other parts of me. I shivered at the image of him running his hands down my back, over my stomach. He set my other foot down and patted my knee, pulling me from my thoughts. "All done, *teine*."

"What does that mean?" I asked again. He was calling me that with increased frequency, and with a familiarity that I knew meant something to him.

He blushed, running his hand through his hair. "It's just an endearment in my mother's tongue. It doesn't mean anything."

I swallowed hard. Of course, it didn't mean anything. What had I been thinking?

Staying with him was one thing, but laying with him intimately? The syrens would never take me back if they knew the thoughts running through my head about the handsome man in front of me. And Caelum didn't think of me the same way, despite the physical reaction he'd had to my touch earlier. I had to get a hold of myself and face my reality. This was not a time for fantasy. "Thank you, Caelum."

He looked at me, his eyebrows raised and his mouth curved in a crooked grin. "Are you okay? You've never thanked me before."

I scowled. Of course, he would open his mouth and ruin it. The teasing was too familiar, too casual, to make distancing myself easy. I quirked a brow up, smirking at him. "I've never had anything to thank you for before now."

Grinning, he pulled me to my feet. "There she is. Come on, put those old boots back on. You just have to wear them long enough to get to the shop next door. They should have something in your size."

Elizi
@ELIZIAN

B R I G I D

CHAPTER FIFTEEN

Boots purchased and now snugly on my feet over thick, wool socks, we walked back to the inn. Duncan, Cameron, and Maddock were already sitting at a table over by the fireplace. Striding over, Caelum led us to take a seat with the others.

"We already ordered stew and bread. It should be here soon," Duncan said, looking over at me as I sat. "You doing okay with all this traveling?"

I nodded. It was unlikely he actually cared for the details, but I couldn't help but give them. "Got me some new boots, so I'll be able to keep up better now."

His eyes widened as he looked down at my feet. "You walked that far today in boots that didn't fit?"

Caelum snorted, making me want to retreat in on myself. I knew I shouldn't feel shame, and yet I couldn't help it in the face of his laughter. "She did that, the stubborn thing. Her feet were all bloody. Didn't say a peep."

Instead of curling in on myself like I wanted to, I crossed my arms over my chest and frowned. They were my feet, why did these men care what I did to them? "I didn't want to slow us down. I know you were all already going slower than you normally would because of me."

"Aye, because you got short little legs, Brigid. Not because you're a woman. If you had legs as long as Caelum's, we'd have gone at a regular pace. You'll do us no good if you keel over because we walked you to death's door on the first day," Duncan teased me, oblivious to my true emotions. For the better, I supposed, given that Caelum did not seem to want us being friendly.

I felt myself beginning to shut down, wanting to wrap my arms around myself. My heart pounded and my jaw was clenched so tightly my teeth might crack. Badly, I wished Sorcha were here. She made me feel balanced. These other men threw me off, and I wasn't sure how to behave. I had spent years mirroring the behavior of the syrens, but these men were all over the place and hard to read.

"Relax, Brigid. I did the same thing when I first joined this lot," Cameron said, bumping his shoulder into mine with a smile. His easy grin was supposed to be reassuring, but it just made my palms sweat and my jaw clench tighter. He continued, nodding his head at the others. "They don't care any about appearances. Just be yourself and do what you can."

I tried to smile at him, unsure if it came across as genuine or not. Likely, it came across more as a grimace than anything else. Be myself? Myself was a murderous sea creature who apparently killed innocent men. But even that wasn't really accurate anymore, given that I was no longer welcome with the other syrens. And while I would not apologize for becoming a syren, I was beginning to regret my actions as one and the blindness with which I had destroyed those ships. Caelum's disposition despite his losses was eye-opening, to say the least.

"So, I found us a ship—a pinnace, to be precise." Duncan got back to business, plopping his burly forearms down on the table and leaning in. His expression let it be clearly known that there was more to this finding than he was saying. He looked around, lowering his voice. "But it's not *exactly* for sale."

Caelum crossed his arms over his chest as he leaned back in his chair, his eyebrow raising. "What exactly is the situation, then?"

"Well, we'd have to borrow it, technically. The owner doesn't use it, he admitted that, but he also said he wasn't willing to let anyone else use her." Duncan's face twisted into an expression somewhere between a grin and a grimace.

Caelum sighed, leaning forward and pinching the bridge of his nose. "Borrow, you say?"

"Aye," Duncan said, his voice still low.

"Borrow?" I couldn't help but interject. My curiosity would likely be the death of me, I was sure. "You mean steal?"

"Keep your voice down. We don't want to tell the whole town our plans," Duncan hissed, leaning in close.

I fought to keep myself from shrinking in at his tone, instead digging my fingers into my thighs and tensing the muscles of my back to stay upright. I was no longer the wilting flower I had been as a child. No, I was a syren now, and even without my song, I was powerful. "Have you stolen many things before?"

Duncan raised an eyebrow at me. "And if we have?"

I returned the expression. "I suppose that depends on what you steal, and from whom."

"And would you judge us if we told you the truth?"

"I'd judge you if you didn't."

His lips curled slightly. "All right. Yes, we do steal. Gotta live somehow."

"So, you *are* pirates?" I asked, leaning back and crossing my arms over my chest. Had Caelum lied to me earlier?

Caelum scoffed. "No. I told you before, we're not pirates. We just...need a little financial help now and then."

"We don't steal from those less fortunate," Maddock said quietly. He cleared his throat. "We only take from those who won't miss it."

"Honorable pirates, then," I said, smiling. I supposed that did fit with the good man persona.

Caelum rolled his eyes and looked around at the busy tavern before leaning in and lowering his voice even more. "How exactly would we borrow this ship, Duncan? Would we be able to do it with just the five of us?"

"We might be able to, but it would be difficult. I'd feel more comfortable if we could get a few more souls to help. It would go a lot smoother if there were at least a dozen of us to crew her." Duncan leaned back in his chair and crossed his arms, spreading his large body casually over the small chair.

"Me too. Do you think we can find any here?" Caelum asked, rubbing his chin and the faint stubble that covered it. I could see his mind turning behind his eyes, calculating what the next step should be.

Duncan shrugged and looked over at Cameron and Maddock. "I think we could. You two go ahead and see if you can feel out anyone. Caelum and I will come by tomorrow tonight and make a final push."

Cameron nodded. "Good plan. How many are we aiming for? Six or seven others?"

"At least five more would be doable in addition to us, but I'd like to get more. It would get us out of the town and would let us bring it into Brinemoor, where Kellan's likely at. We don't need her to be a warship." Maddock went through the scenario quickly, his eyebrows furrowing as he fiddled with the handle of his mug.

"Wait, Kellan?" I interrupted, leaning in. They hadn't mentioned that name before.

"Kellan is my father," Caelum explained, a pinched expression on his face. It was obvious he did not like talking about the man.

"So, how far away is Brinemoor?" I asked, changing the subject and tucking a loose strand of hair behind my ear. The idea of sailing made my stomach twist. As a child, I had not traveled off my father's farm often; I wasn't familiar with the town they spoke of or with being on top of the seas. The one and only time I had attempted to travel by ship had ended with my turning into a syren.

"Too far to walk," Caelum replied, grimacing slightly. "It's on the other side of the mountains, and it would be far faster and easier to sail through the Straits of Marbh to get there."

"The Straits are dangerous," I said instantly, looking at him. As syrens, we had often roamed the Straits of the Dead, looking for ships to target. The rocks beneath the water there meant few survivors, if any, ever made it out of the wrecks. If we sailed through there, I had little doubt the others would come for us.

"How do you know that?" Duncan asked curiously. His voice was light, but I could see the suspicion in his eyes as he studied me.

Duncan's suspicions aside, I kept my eyes on Caelum, trying to convey the true meaning behind my words. He needed to be prepared in case they tried to wreck him again. If he had been upset at starting over before, having to do so again would likely ruin the little progress I was making in my redemption.

He smiled at me, but it was obviously forced and didn't reach his eyes. My message seemed to have gotten through, at least. "We'll be careful."

I nodded hesitantly and reminded myself to warn him more explicitly later. My presence on the seas could anger the syrens even more, and the last thing I wanted was for Caelum to be faced with their ire again.

Caelum rubbed his hands together, leaning forward. His eyes were bright with genuine excitement. "Mad, you and Cam go tonight, get a feel for any men we might be able to get onboard. See if we can pull this off."

"If we can get the boat and the crew, when would we be doing this?" I asked, leaning across the table to get closer. Having as many details as possible helped calm my anxiety. If I knew what to expect, I could prepare for it.

"We get the crew on board tomorrow. And then, depending on the type of men they are, we could maybe pull it off tomorrow night and be out of here before the sun rises," Duncan explained.

"Type of men?" My voice was colder than ice. I had little patience for the dismissal of women, even from these men. My entire life had been one long dismissal until I became a syren, and I would no longer stand for it from anyone. My anger overrode my anxiety of the situation. "Would you turn away women who wanted to join your crew?"

"Women are bad luck on the seas," Duncan said, his words an echo of those I had heard right before I was thrown overboard. It made my stomach churn. "Just because we're willing to let you sail with us doesn't mean we're going to risk it further than that."

"The only bad luck on the seas is the luck we earn," Caelum said, scoffing. "Superstitious oaf."

"You're not bad luck, Brigid, ignore him," Maddock said with a smile. "He's just traditional like that."

My jaw clenched almost painfully, and I bit my tongue to keep from saying something I would regret. Duncan's sentiment was common, and until I could prove them otherwise, arguing would do nothing but make him more suspicious of me. Leaning back, I spread my arms out wide. "So, where do we start?"

Staring up at the swinging wooden sign, I took a deep breath. My nerves were as worn as the sign advertising The Silver Serpent tavern. This was where we were to meet the men Cameron and Maddock had found. At Duncan's insistence, both Caelum and I were dressed for the part as well.

'You've got to dress as a captain if you want them to take you seriously, Caelum. And the girl can't keep wearing your clothes either,' he had said to us. Caelum had resisted initially, as had I, but the large man had gotten his way in the end. Duncan was right, I supposed. Us showing up in casual clothes that didn't fit properly likely would not make a good impression on the men we were asking to help us.

We had spent all day rounding up an appropriate outfit for the both of us. It had been a true pain in the arse, but we had finally found everything we needed. Caelum was dressed in a lace-up white shirt that cut low to show off his tanned chest. The shirt was tucked into dark breeches, which were then tucked into high leather boots, laced up tight. He had also tied his hair back into a low knot at the nape of his neck, showing off the freshly shaved sides of his scalp. A silver chain around his neck, a scrap of black fabric around his wrist to cover his scar, and a couple of silver rings rounded out the ensemble. He looked devastatingly handsome.

While Caelum looked every bit the harsh captain he needed to be tonight, I felt like a child playing dress up. Cameron had offered to braid my hair, much to the surprise of everyone. He wove into intricate sections, forming a crown around my head and leaving the rest spilling in wild curls down my back. If nothing else, my hair was truly beautiful.

I wore a similar outfit to Caelum, a white blouse covered by a dark leather corset that sat beneath my bust and laced up the back, displaying my figure more than I necessarily wanted. My pants were tight and tucked into boots with thick silver buckles, like Caelum's. Despite the discomfort at the attention I knew I would receive from men tonight, I did feel beautiful and powerful.

We stopped just inside the door, looking for where Maddock and Cameron were. I spotted them over in the corner, at a table with a small group of six men. Cam waved his hand over his head in acknowledgement. Caelum nodded his head back, and we made our way over to them.

"Men, this is Caelum, our captain, Duncan, the first mate, and Brigid," Cam introduced us. He stumbled over my name, likely unsure how to best introduce me. I hoped the men sitting before us had not noticed. They seemed more focused on Caelum than me, which I was eternally grateful for.

One of the men stood, extending his hand to Caelum. His hair was dark and messy, and his clothes disheveled, as if he couldn't care less about his appearance. "I'm Alan. We hear you're looking for a crew."

"Aye." Caelum sat down in the empty chair, leaving me to stand behind him. I tensed my body, ready for anything. "Are you looking for a captain?"

Alan grinned at Caelum, delight playing in his dark eyes. "Aye, sir. Me and my men here."

"Do you have any experience as a crew?" Duncan asked, taking the last empty chair beside Caelum.

I stayed behind them, observing the situation. My mind was

good at taking note of things other people missed, and I was watching everyone in the room. This tavern had every nerve in my body on edge, surrounded by men and people I did not know. But I would take in every detail as if I were analyzing a ship the syrens were about to ruin. I crossed my arms and schooled my face into blankness.

"Aye, sir," one of the other men added. "We worked on a merchant vessel up until recently. The captain retired, and we haven't been able to find work since."

"Are you opposed to less-than-legal work?" Caelum asked, his voice quiet.

Alan grinned even wider. "Nah, we're open to any work, legal or otherwise."

Merchant vessel...sure. From the grin on Alan's face, I assumed they were former pirates. I raised an eyebrow, continuing to study them.

Caelum looked at Alan for a long moment and then moved his attention to the rest of the men sitting there. "And you all? Any problems following orders?"

"No, sir," they all responded, echoing each other.

Caelum looked over at Cameron and Maddock, who had apparently spent most of the night before and the afternoon with these men. Maddock nodded his approval. After a moment, Caelum clasped his hands together, leaning forward. "All right, let's do this. Can you start right now?"

One of the other men across the table leaned forward on his forearms. "What's the plan?"

I could hear the grin in Caelum's voice as he launched into a discussion of payment, followed by the plan he and Duncan had devised to get control of the boat and out of the harbor with minimum fuss and involvement. Once everyone was on the same page, we stood, following Duncan out of the pub.

As we left, Caelum grabbed my arm, pulling me off to the side as we all walked toward the harbor. "Hey, *teine,* are you okay? You've been quiet tonight."

Shrugging, I met his gaze, trying to keep my anxiety out of my eyes and maintain my façade of indifference. "Had nothing to contribute to the conversation."

His own eyes narrowed and pulled me to a stop, turning me to face him. "What's going on?"

I couldn't meet his gaze. Couldn't tell him that the thought of being on a ship with these men terrified me and being out on the water my sisters patrolled terrified me even more. I couldn't tell him any of that. He seemed to think me useful, and if he knew just how wrong he was, I would be an afterthought in a moment. "Caelum... I'm fine."

He gripped my chin in his hand, forcing me to look at him. I fought my instinct to pull away from his grip. His skin was warm against mine and sent chills down my spine. "You are valuable to this, Brigid. I need your help, and they will not hurt you."

How he managed to land on every single insecurity in one sentence, I didn't know. But he had. I swallowed hard, flexing my fingers at my side and forcing my jaw to unclench. "I know that."

"You are in control here," he said, leaning his head down. I could feel the warmth of his skin radiating into my face. "They. Will. Not. Hurt. You."

I looked at him for a moment. He could make no such guarantees, especially not once the others found out the truth of my involvement in the shipwreck and what I truly was. But I would let him feel as though he could for now. I nodded at him, looking up into his eyes. "They won't hurt me. Now, let's go get this ship."

He smiled at me, dropping my chin and instead twining our fingers together. I should have, but I didn't pull my hand away. His smile grew slightly before he masked his face into blankness. The captain was back. "Let's go get us a ship."

Elizi
@ELIZIANN

BRIGID

CHAPTER SIXTEEN

On the trailing ends of the sunset, we approached the harbor carefully, spotting the ship we would be taking. The three-masted pinnace had its sails tied up, but it was clear it would take all of us to crew. The small ship was old, the wood weathered and flaking in some places, but according to Caelum, it would make it to where we needed to go. Duncan corralled the men, explaining what each of their roles were. One by one, they slipped through the harbor rows before climbing aboard the ship.

Finally, Caelum and I joined, strolling hand in hand through the rows as the harbor master made his rounds. My steps were wooden, and I was relying all too much on the grounding of Caelum's hand against mine. I forced myself to focus on the heat of his skin, the roughness of his palm, the tingles that spread up my arm and down my spine at the contact. It kept my mind from spiraling down into anxiety. We didn't have time for that, and I needed to get my emotions back under control.

We walked together, passing the ship we would be taking. *The Voyager,* it read. Once the harbor master was out of sight, we changed our course, climbing up the rungs to board the ship.

"Hey, you lot! Stop there!" a voice yelled from the harbor docks.

"Shit," Caelum cursed aloud, turning from his position at the stern to see the harbor master and an older man I assumed was the ship's owner running down the docks toward us. He turned to Duncan, his eyes frantic and his forehead furrowed. "Are we ready to go?"

I looked at Duncan too, who grimaced. "Not quite. We're still tied on by one of the cleats on the dock. We were gonna climb down and loose it before we left."

"Can we cut it from up here?" I asked, leaning over the railing to look down at the rope keeping us attached to the dock. If we could cut it, we would be on our way easily. But I did not pretend to know anything about ships, and would gladly defer to those more experienced than myself.

Caelum shook his head, grimacing. "No, we'll need it when we get to Brinemoor. One of us will have to climb down and unwind it."

I looked back over my shoulder at the rest of the crew, an idea forming in my mind. While the others would likely not want to risk it, I had no such illusions of my own importance. "Other than that line there, are we ready to leave?"

"Aye," Duncan said, his attention already back on the rest of the ship and crew.

Caelum narrowed his eyes at me. "What're you thinking, lass?"

"Get ready to go," was all I said before jumping up onto the narrow railing and proceeding to climb down the line. I could get it untied faster than any of them could, and I could climb the lines faster than any of them too. Behind me, I heard Caelum curse.

"Aye, move, men!" Duncan roared, catching on to my plan.

I reached the dock, and with one hand holding on to the line still attached to the ship, I began unwinding the figure eight securing it to the cleat. The harbor master noticed me and started running. I needed to pick up my pace. My hair was still in the intricate braids Cameron had woven, but a strand of hair fell into my face, irritating me. I puffed a breath, moving it out of the way, and continued working.

We needed to get out of here, and I needed to prove I was useful beyond my powers.

Just as the harbor master was about to reach me, the line came free and I swung, the tips of my boots glancing off the water. I slammed into the side of the boat with a groan and then the rope began to move, pulling me closer to the deck rails. Finally, we were out into deeper water where no one from the dock could reach us, and I pulled myself the last few inches to reach the railing, digging my fingers in. That had been a rush, one I hadn't felt since seeing Caelum's ship in the waves above me. As I climbed up to the railing, Caelum grabbed me under my arms and hauled me over, both of us landing on our arses on the deck.

I couldn't help but grin at him, the excitement of the moment overtaking the previous nerves I had felt about this journey. "Got the line."

He laughed. "Aye, that you did."

"Good work, Brigid!" Duncan boomed, walking over to us. He pulled me up and into a bear hug. "You'll be a sailor yet!"

"You'll pay for this!" The harbormaster was yelling from the dock, shaking his fist at us as we sailed away. The owner of the ship next to him was running his hands over his face, resting them on top of his head as he watched us, distraught.

"They'd have to catch us first," Caelum muttered, rolling his eyes.

"Thanks, Duncan," I replied, my smile still etched on my face. The praise was wonderful, and I would relish it while I could.

Caelum stood from the deck too and tucked me under his arm, pulling me into his side. "Aye, lass. Fine job."

"I told you I'd keep up."

"That you did," he said again, letting go of my shoulders and twining our fingers together. Once again, I didn't pull away from him, relishing the contact instead.

After several heart-pounding moments of movement I was sure would be heard, the ship was finally ready to leave. The darkness surrounding us made this much harder, but we couldn't risk lighting any lanterns, as that would surely set off warning bells to the harbor master. Finally, with Maddock at the wheel, the ship began its departure.

But we weren't in the clear yet. We still had to get out of the harbor, and we wouldn't be safe until we were out of sight and in the open water off the coast. My palms were slippery with anticipation. Once we were on open water, all bets were off. The syrens could, and likely would, come for us.

"Let's go get you settled in," Caelum said, squeezing my fingers.

He led me down below deck to the captain's quarters. This was an older ship, and there wasn't a proper bed in the quarters. But there was a netted hammock and a trunk full of blankets. It would do. I had slept in a similar hammock as a syren, and it would be comfortable enough.

"We need to talk about the journey," Caelum said, leaning his hip against the table in the room, his voice suddenly serious again. "Will the other syrens come for this ship too?"

I rubbed at my face. "I don't know, not for sure. There's a marking I can put on the hull so they would know I'm onboard, but I'm not sure if that would stop them from wrecking it. It might make them want to wreck it more."

"What happens if they do anyway?" he asked, his brows pinching.

We would all likely die, was what I wanted to reply. But that would do none of us any good.

"I don't want to risk everyone's lives again, but we need to get back on track before my father gets any further in his plans." His face was conflicted, and I could tell just how important this mission was that he was willing to risk the lives of these men. But maybe it helped him that they were strangers still.

"I can take the wheel," I said instead, shrugging slightly. If I could help get us all through this alive, I would do whatever it took. "I can at least keep us from crashing. But I don't know if I can do anything against their song if they decide to sing it."

"Would plugging our ears work?" he asked, motioning at his head. "I've heard of that in the myths before."

"Potentially. I've never seen it done, but I don't think our myth is as widely told as it once was," I admitted. Cliodhna often spoke of how man was forgetting her and the ways of the old gods, more intent on pretending this world was their creation.

"I'll see if we have any wax aboard. Will their song affect you?"

I hesitated, flexing my jaw and snapping my mouth shut. Would their song affect me now as well now that I didn't have one of my own? Cliodhna had not said, and I was not sure I was keen to find out in such a dire situation.

Caelum must have sensed my hesitation, raising an eyebrow at me. "What aren't you telling me?"

"I don't have to tell you everything, Caelum." I knew my voice was cold, but I couldn't bring myself to care. This was my burden to bear.

"No, but if it could impact our journey, I need to know it," he said, his anger rising.

He was right, of course; he did need to know. I rubbed my forehead, sighing heavily as the motivation drained out of my body. I would have to tell him. "Fine. I don't have my song anymore. When they banished me, our queen took it from me. So, I'm not sure if I'm even immune to the song of the others now or if I would be just as vulnerable as you."

"She stole your song?" he asked. His eyes swirled with curiosity and what looked almost like worry. "What else did she take? Are you even still a syren?"

The urgency in his voice gave me pause, and hurt washed through me. He had been hoping to use my syren powers for something. My stomach dropped and my throat burned. "Is that all I am to you? Is that the only value I hold?"

"No, of course not. But like I said, I need to know if it will affect our journey." He was quick to recover, but the thoughts were already there, worming their way into my mind. He only valued me for the abilities I had once possessed. Now, I truly did have no purpose in his eyes. How long would it take for him to ask me to leave? I had been expecting it, but the idea that it would be coming soon created a pit in my stomach that I did not appreciate.

"I can still transform into a syren, if that's what you're asking," I said slowly, answering his questions. If he needed me to be a syren, that was fine. I technically still was one. And if that was the only value I showed, I needed to exploit it until we could get closer to the Bhodheas so I'd be better off when they asked me to leave.

Caelum was silent for a long time, rubbing at the stubble on his chin as he stared at me, likely wondering if I was worth the trouble anymore.

"What will it take to mark the hull?" he asked finally.

"I just need to get in the water, then I can mark it with my talons. If the other syrens see it, they'll know I'm onboard," I explained. I had not transformed since Cliodhna had taken away her magic that made it painless. I had no idea what it would feel like to transform again. "But like I said before, that might not be enough to stop them, especially if they're still angry. Or if our queen commands them to wreck the ship."

"Does she wreck every ship that goes in the water?"

"No, she tells us which ones to target. It's more likely to be wrecked if it's alone, though. We avoid witnesses."

He nodded, the resolve clear in his face. "We'll take the chance, then. Let's go get you into the water to mark the hull."

"I don't want the others to see me," I said firmly. I really didn't want Caelum to see me either, but I doubted he would trust me enough to leave me alone and not observe. My pain was private, and not something I liked sharing. "I don't know the new men, and I don't want to risk them turning back because of the danger."

"Agreed. We'll make sure they don't see you," he said, nodding solemnly. I held back my sigh.

Leaving the quarters, we walked to the lower deck, avoiding the men gathered there. In the darkness, the water was pitch black and likely freezing. While the water wouldn't affect me once I transformed, it would still shock my human body. Already, the ship was moving out of the harbor, the strong winds picking up the sails.

Looking at me, Caelum motioned down to the water. "How are we going to do this?"

I looked around, glancing at the crew on the other side of the deck. Determined as I might be, this was going to be tough. I had no idea how much pain I would be in or if I would even be able to get myself back out of the water. "I'm going to jump over. Once I'm in the water, I'll transform and mark the hull, but I'll need you to help me back out of the water. And I'll need clothes once I get out."

Caelum sighed again, sensing my hesitation. "What is it? I need you to be honest with me, *teine.*"

"The transformation may be painful for me. That was another condition of my banishment. I'm not sure what shape I'll be in after I transform back," I finally admitted after a few moments of consideration. I didn't want to tell him, but if I needed help getting back on the ship, he was my only option. Admitting weakness went against every fiber of my being, but for whatever reason, I trusted Caelum would not betray me. As much as I figured he wanted to, he wouldn't leave me to the mercy of the other syrens.

"Painful?" he asked, something akin to concern flashing in his eyes. It was gone in a moment, though, the calculating captain's look back once again. He raised his chin, his forehead creasing. "What do I need to do?"

"I might not be able to get myself back up the ladder," I warned, wanting him to understand the gravity of the situation. "I might need your help. And I might need your help getting back into the clothes. But I won't know until I transform back."

"Aye, understood. Should we tether you to the ship somehow?" he asked, his eyes flicking down to the line on the deck.

I shook my head. "No, it might hinder my transformation."

"What do we do if you can't get back to the ladder?"

"Throw a rope down. If I need your help, I'll tug on it." It was the only solution that came to mind.

"Okay, let me go get some things ready." With a quick step, he went over to the supplies we had brought, coming back with a bundle of fabric and a blanket. He nodded back toward the men, who had not looked over from their place across the deck. "I'll make sure they don't see you come back as well. Keeping them busy should do the trick. And if you're in pain after, we'll take care of that when we get there."

I tried to look reassuring as I peered down over the railing into the water and then back at Caelum. "Be right back."

And then, before I could overthink it, I swung a leg over the railing and plunged into the black sea below. The cold water shocked my system, my muscles clenching up painfully. As I sank deeper in the dark water, I prayed that Cliodhna would not notice I was in her waters. Bracing my core, I willed the transformation to begin.

Pure agony rolled through my body as it began, the muscles of my legs tearing and reforming together. Bones snapped, and bile surged up my throat. I fought it back, gritting my teeth so hard I was surprised they did not crack. As my leg muscles continued to tear and reform, my talons began to emerge, slicing through the skin of my nail beds. The pain was searing hot, and I saw the blood dispersing into the water from them. I loosened my jaw, my teeth slicing their way through my gums now as well. Copper flooded my tongue, and I fought the urge to gag.

This was a miserable experience. I fought against the blackness outlining my vision, willing myself to stay conscious through the pain. Clenching my jaw to keep from crying out, my entire body ached and screamed in protest.

Finally, after what felt like an eternity, the transformation was complete. The ship had moved ahead while I had been busy being broken and remade. I swam toward it, the muscles of my tail and core aching in protest.

I reached the hull, raising my hand to the old wood. Ignoring the pain searing through my nailbeds as I carved, I drew Cliodhna's symbol, a small trident with waves beneath it, into the ship, marking it for the others to know there was a syren aboard. The only thing left to do was hope that they would not wreck the ship purely because of the symbol.

Marking it with my talons meant that some of the residual magic, whatever I had left, would be imbued into the wood. The others would sense it. We hadn't used the symbol or the practice often, but the ships used by our contact in the south were all marked to protect them. Cliodhna had marked other ships and even buildings from what she had told us, but she hasn't shared the reasoning behind those marks.

While I wanted to remain in the water and relish being back in my syren form, my body was aching. Besides that, I didn't want to risk staying in the water longer than necessary. That was asking for the others to come investigate, and that could only bring ruin upon Caelum and his men. The blood could also attract other sea creatures, but I was hoping to be well out of the water by the time they noticed the possibility of food.

Reaching a hand up to the ladder on the side of the ship, I gripped it as tightly as I could as the transformation took over once again. The pain was slightly more bearable this time, but I could still feel the muscles of my legs ripping beneath the skin. White-hot fire spread through my limbs as they split once more. It was a struggle to maintain my grip on the ladder, but I knew I needed to. Without my tail, I wouldn't be able to catch up with the ship if it left me. Finally, the transformation back to human was complete, and I began the daunting task of climbing up the ladder.

I knew Caelum was there if I needed him, but I wanted to prove to myself that this curse from Cliodhna was something I could overcome on my own. Arms and legs shaking, I panted as I climbed, stopping at nearly every rung to rest. As I neared the top, Caelum's head peeked over. His face shone with relief, and he reached down to grab my hand, hauling me up and onto the deck, where he immediately wrapped me in a blanket.

Thankfully, the others hadn't looked up from their game and their work. I let out a sigh of relief that I wouldn't have to explain myself immediately.

My legs were screaming in protest, but I fought to remain upright as I dressed. Once clothed, I pulled the blanket back up around me, relishing the warmth. I looked at Caelum, answering the question shining clearly in his eyes. Even speaking was exhausting, but I needed to tell him I had succeeded at what he asked of me. "I've marked it. Hopefully, it works."

He pulled me into his arms and pressed a kiss to my wet hair. I closed my eyes and let myself lean into him. "Thank you."

"Don't get your hopes up, though," I warned, my voice muffled against his chest. I looked up at him but made no move to pull away. I could barely hold my own weight, and despite not wanting to rely on Caelum, this moment of weakness was acceptable. "This might not work, Caelum."

"Aye, maybe not." He shrugged and pulled me closer, taking on more of my weight. He didn't comment on my condition, which I was grateful for. "But you tried, and that's what counts to me."

I let out a yawn that made my jaw ache, and Caelum led me down to the captain's quarters without another word. Climbing into the hammock, I immediately curled up on my side, tucking my sore legs up against my stomach. The position provided some relief.

"Get some rest, *teine*. We're going to sail through the night, and I'll wake you when we get to Brinemoor," he said, brushing a loose strand of hair off my forehead as he looked down at me. For a moment, I could have sworn there was caring behind his eyes. But I knew better; exhaustion was making me foolish. "You need sleep."

I looked up at him, suddenly unable to keep my eyes open. "G'night, Caelum. Wake me if you need me, please. If you hear the syrens, don't try to play a hero."

As I stretched out in the hammock, he pulled the blanket up over me. In an instant, I was asleep.

Elizianna
@ELIZIANNA.THE.ONE

C AELUM

ℭHAPTER SEVENTEEN

With Brigid fast asleep nearly immediately, I turned to head back up to the deck. Brigid may have helped us get out of the harbor, but I still needed to discuss some things with the crew without her listening in.

"Caelum, you disappeared on us," Duncan greeted, his brow quirking suspiciously. He moved away from the others, and we walked over to the other side of the deck, leaning against the mast.

"Had to talk to Brigid about what to expect on the Straits," I replied, keeping my voice casual. Despite itching to tell the others what Brigid was and her attempts to keep us safe, while we were on the seas was probably not the best moment. The crew, especially Duncan, would be angry, both at me for hiding the truth and Brigid for her involvement in our wreck. Maddock would likely want to ask Brigid a hundred questions about what it was like being a syren, and Cam would try like hell to keep the peace.

"And what can she offer that we haven't already learned for ourselves?" Duncan demanded. "We've sailed the Straits of Marbh at least a dozen times over the years."

"I was telling *her* what to expect," I lied, the words burning like ash in my mouth. It was a white lie, but it was still a lie. Before he could question me and cause me to lie further, I changed the subject. "We need to discuss some things about the mission."

"You don't trust her." His statement wasn't a question, but it still deserved an answer.

"I don't know her well enough yet to trust her or not." This, at least, I could be honest about. Brigid may have saved my life, but she was still a syren. And she had likely killed far more men than she had saved. She was dangerous, and until I was certain she was completely on our side, there would be things I would not tell her about our mission.

"Your father is getting ahead of us," he grumbled, crossing his arms over his chest. "And we're running out of money."

I pushed a hand through my hair with a sigh. "Yeah, I know. He's going to take those children and do god knows what with them."

My father had been kidnapping orphaned children, mostly boys. We'd known about it for *months,* but every time we had gotten close to figuring out what exactly he was doing with them, either my father got away, or something else happened to keep us from getting the information we desperately needed. As a child, my father's ship had engaged in piracy mostly, but he'd also dabbled in smuggling. And unlike us, he wasn't discerning in what he smuggled.

We smuggled people who needed passage away from something horrific. Often, our customers were women. Maybe my desire to engage in this type of smuggling stemmed from the failure to save Brigid as a child. But either way, I helped those who needed it start a new life.

"We need to get to Brinemoor. He's probably going back there," Duncan said, heaving a sigh as well. "He always ends up back in Brinemoor."

Shouts rose from the railing, and ice ran down my spine. Something was wrong. Duncan and I shared a look of concern before running over to the crew. I reached them first. "What is it?"

"Rocks ahead," Maddock said, his face serious. "And the darkness doesn't help. We can't see them until we're right up on them."

"We just need to all be on watch, then," I replied, leaning over the railing to peer down into the water. "Stay as close to the middle as possible; that should keep us away from the worst of it."

"The weather's on our side, at least," Cameron commented, tilting his head back to look at the sky.

The moon was full, which gave us more light than we normally would have, and thankfully, the clouds were sparse. The wind was strong enough to keep us moving, but steady. Hopefully, the weather would remain good until we passed through the worst of the Straits.

They weren't called the Straits of the Dead for nothing, after all.

We needed assignments. Alan and his men seemed capable of following orders and knew their way around a ship. I turned to Duncan. "Take the wheel. Cameron, you watch the sails and the weather. Maddock, you're with me."

"What do you want us to do, Captain?" Alan asked, motioning toward his men.

"Watch for rocks, and do whatever Cameron tells you to."

"Aye, aye, sir."

"Don't call me sir," I said firmly, pointing at him. "Captain" I could live with, but I was no better than any of my men, and I wouldn't have them calling me sir. I had too many bad memories associated with that word and my father.

"What did you say, boy?" my father barked out, stepping up close to my face. His hot breath stank.

"I...I said...said that I would...said I would do it," I stuttered out, cowering under his hard gaze.

"Would do it, what?" he growled. He reached down to grab my shirt by the neck, yanking me even closer to him.

"Sir," I gritted out, somehow managing to keep eye contact with him. If I looked away, it would have only made it worse.

"Ten lashes," my father said loudly, releasing me and shoving me toward Iain, his first mate. Iain grinned at me, holding up the whip in his hands.

I swallowed hard, bracing myself for the pain.

"Get to work," I said, shaking my head to clear the memories. This was *my* ship, and *my* crew. And I would not be like my father.

"Captain," Maddock called me over, waving his hand at me. I stepped up next to him and he lowered his voice, keeping the conversation between us. "We need to keep an eye out for whatever wrecked *The Nehalennia* too. Should we tell Alan and his men about them?"

"We don't even know what they were. Not for sure," I said, swallowing the taste of the lie once again. The safety of my crew was a priority for me, but we needed Alan and his men. And telling them that we suspected the legends of murderous half women, half sea creatures could very well scare them off. "Better to keep it to ourselves. You and I will watch for them."

"Should we get Brigid up here to help?" he asked, raising an eyebrow.

I shook my head. "No, she's sleeping. Let her rest."

Maddock nodded, turning back to the railing. "I like her. She seems like she'd be good for you."

"Not happening, Mad," I replied, going to stand next to him at the railing. "It's not like that."

He turned, raising his eyebrow even more dramatically than before. "Okay, Captain. Whatever you say."

"Go keep watch," I grumbled, focusing my attention back to the water.

The smirk on his face as he walked away was visible from my peripheral vision. I shook my head at his antics. Brigid may have been attractive, and we may have bonded, but I needed to be careful. Getting involved with her romantically, or even just physically, could lead to repercussions with my friends that I didn't want to think about.

And for now, I wouldn't think about it. For now, I needed to get us through the night, watching for rocks and calling them out to keep us from wrecking. That would require all my attention, and hopefully keep my thoughts off a certain red-haired syren sleeping below.

BRIGID

CHAPTER EIGHTEEN

I woke to sunlight hitting my face through the dirty porthole in the captain's quarters. It was morning, which hopefully meant that we were almost to Brinemoor. My body was sore, but it had thankfully turned from the sharp pain into a dull ache. A dull ache I could ignore if I tried hard enough.

Climbing out of the netted bed, I made my way to the upper decks to look for Caelum. On deck, I was surprised to see a town in the distance, just above the horizon. Still looking out over the water, I walked over to where Caelum was standing with Maddock, looking over the maps.

"Any issues last night?" I asked carefully. If we had almost made it into the town, I hoped that meant we had avoided the others through the night. It was a miracle we hadn't wrecked even without their influence, but if they had come for us, we should not have been alive right now.

He smiled at me, broad and genuinely happy. "None at all, *teine;* clear weather and the sea was on our side. We're about to pull into Brinemoor now, actually."

I let out a sigh of relief. We had avoided the other syrens, by some miracle. I didn't want to stop to question our good fortune. "Good. That's good. What can I do to help?"

"Once we get to the harbor, we might need you, but we're all right for now," he replied, still smiling at me.

Hesitantly returning his smile, I nodded. While I was grateful we had made it through the Straits unharmed, Caelum should not be smiling at me like he was. "Aye, all right. I'll let you get back to your maps. I'll just be watching for a bit, then."

After a while, Alan and Duncan began to guide the ship into the harbor, pulling it into a slip at the end. I stayed seated on my perch by the mast, watching the crew bustle around, securing the sails and tying off lines to the dock cleats.

I wasn't used to so many people—so many men—around me, and I was slightly overwhelmed along with still being physically exhausted. I knew I could help prepare the ship, but I found myself unable to do anything but sit there and watch, my legs tucked up under my chin.

Instead, I watched as the men scurried around the ship, preparing the ship to dock. Despite the new men on the crew, it was a well-oiled machine. Everyone knew their role, and I wasn't sure where to even start with offering to help. Perhaps I could haul the lines, securing down everything on the deck, but Alan and his men were already doing it so efficiently.

Logically, I knew I should be helping them somehow, but my body was frozen. I hated what I had become and how anxious I was. I was a syren, for goddess' sake. I could kill every man aboard this ship if I wanted to, and it was time I started remembering that. Rolling my shoulders, I flexed my neck and loosened my jaw, pulling up all the feelings of anger and fire I had been subduing.

Caelum stopped in his path across the deck and turned to come over to me. He put a hand on my shoulder. "Hey, *teine.* You okay?"

I looked up at him, raising a brow at his concern. "I'm fine. I'm not used to being around so many men. And I'm still sore."

"Do you need to go rest?" He sat down on the mast banister next to me, concern in his eyes. I wasn't sure what had changed after my excursion the previous night, but it was obvious that something had. "You have been with only women for the past few years. I can understand that. How can I help?"

"I'll be fine," I said, uncrossing my arms and lowering my legs. I appreciated his concern for me, but I needed to get over myself. I was already starting to rely on Caelum, and I couldn't go any further down that line of thinking. It wouldn't happen again. It *couldn't* happen again.

He tilted his head at me, a strand of his dark hair flopping down into his face. "You don't have to be. It's okay if you're not."

Standing, I straightened my back and looked at him, smiling with what I hoped was a reassuring expression. "I'm fine, Caelum. Now, how can I help?"

"You can grab that line there and follow me."

I stood, grabbing the line he pointed at. I would be useful, even as a human. My value did not lie in my syren abilities. Fire in my belly, I turned it inwards, fueling my determination. At whatever cost, I would stop Caelum's father and I would redeem myself, and then I would make a new life for myself, whatever that looked like.

After successfully securing the ship into the slip at the harbor, it was well into the afternoon. While Duncan was sent to deal with this harbormaster to pay our mooring fee, the rest of us inventoried the supplies that were on the ship, getting things ready for our evening adventure and finding what money we could.

One of Alan's men would be staying on the ship to keep guard, a decision that had been made while I was sleeping, apparently, and the rest of us would be spending the night at the inn attached to a tavern in town.

I almost would have preferred to sleep on the ship, but according to Caelum, the inn was closer to where we needed to be.

Once we were all ready, the rest of us left the ship and walked into the pub Duncan had said would be our first starting point.

Maddock and Cam went off in one direction, leaving Duncan and Caelum on either side of me. I turned to them, already over-stimulated by the crowd and the noise. Clenching my fists, I took deep breaths through my nose, pasting on my façade of indifference. "What's the plan?"

"Cam and Maddock are going to see what they can discover. We are going to blend in and observe the crowd and see if anyone sticks out or if we can overhear anything," Duncan explained as we followed Caelum over to a table.

"How are we going to blend in?" I asked, looking around. There were people drinking, dancing, bumping into each other. I really hoped that was not Duncan's idea of blending in. Sitting and looking angry and unapproachable, that was what I could accomplish right now. But if someone asked me to dance, I would likely murder them, consequences be damned.

"Relax." Caelum laughed as we sat down at a small table in the corner. "We'll just be sitting here and pretending to have a good time."

Duncan remained standing and clapped Caelum on the shoulder. "I'll go get us some ale."

"Get Brigid a pint too. She can pretend to drink it," Caelum said before Duncan walked off toward the bar.

"Pretend?" I asked, offended. Granted, I had never drunk ale before, but I wasn't liking the assumption that I couldn't drink it. I didn't enjoy the embarrassment washing down my spine. It was not an emotion I was used to, and I didn't like how it felt, slimy and coiling in my stomach and heating my cheeks.

"Fair enough," he replied, nodding agreeably. "Then, let's get you a drink."

Duncan walked back over shortly after, three mugs in his large hands. He sat them down on the table, sliding one toward me and one toward Caelum. He and Caelum picked theirs up, holding them together toward mine. Picking up the pint, I lifted my own mug, touching it to theirs. I took a drink and promptly grimaced as the wheat taste flooded my tongue. "Goddess, that's vile."

Caelum roared laughing. Duncan sputtered, wiping the golden

liquid off his mouth where some had escaped during his own laughter. "It's not supposed to taste good."

"Then what's the point of drinking it?" I asked, wrinkling my nose at the mug before me. They really did this for fun? No wonder men were so easy to kill.

"To get drunk, of course."

That could be nice. Goddess knew I wanted to forget about what had happened lately. Between being banished by my sisters, hunted by strangers, and now this, a night to forget sounded perfect. I picked up the mug again and, without another word, emptied it into my mouth, swallowing hard. I slammed the empty mug down onto the table as my head swam. Maybe that was not a smart decision.

"*Teine...*" Caelum trailed off, looking at me wide-eyed. Duncan cast him a confused side glance, likely at the nickname.

I somehow wasn't embarrassed anymore. I felt almost free. All my life, I had never been one to enjoy myself; I had never been able to. But tonight, here with Caelum, it seemed like I could. Yes, I wanted to prove myself. But more than that, I wanted to live. And live I would.

Duncan nodded his head, pursing his lips and appraising me. He slid his still full mug over to me. "Have at it, Brigid."

I lifted the mug to my lips, but hesitated slightly, turning to Caelum. "This isn't smart. What if we need to move?"

Caelum's face softened. "I've got it, Brigid. Enjoy yourself for a night. A mug of ale won't have any effect on Duncan or me. We can handle things if needed."

Likely, I should be setting the mug down and pushing it away, making sure I could still be useful if anything did happen tonight. But the temptation of experiencing something for the first time, of being so free, was too much to pass up. I pressed the worn mug to my lips and let the liquid slide down my throat.

Over the next hour or so, I downed three or four more mugs of ale, abhorring the taste each time. But the more I drank, the lighter I felt. And the warmer I felt, the freer I felt. It was a nice change from being constantly on edge and waiting for something to go wrong. I looked over at Caelum, who was talking with Cameron. They had their heads leaned together, whispering.

Caelum was attractive—seriously attractive. His dark hair was shaved close to the skin on either side of his temples, fading into long waves that he had tied back in a bun at the crown of his head with a strip of leather. The short beard covering his strong jaw was enticing. I wanted to see how it felt under my fingertips. His fingers flexed around his mug as he spoke to Cam, drawing my attention to his rough skin there, the scar around his wrist, and the dark smattering of hair covering his muscular forearms.

I wanted to run my fingers over his arms, to feel the muscle under the skin. From his arms, my gaze drew up to his shoulders, broad and powerful. They were tense, likely from whatever he and Cam were talking about. His face was just as attractive as the rest of him, weathered and tanned from the sun, with a smattering of freckles over the bridge of his nose that made the green of his eyes stand out.

A throat cleared, and I was able to refocus my gaze after some effort. Caelum was grinning at me. "Can I help you, Brigid?"

Shit. He had caught me staring at him. Cheeks flushing, I pushed a strand of hair off my sweaty forehead. I had thought I was being discreet, but apparently not. "No, I'm just looking at you."

His eyebrows rose. Damn, I hadn't meant to admit that out loud.

He laughed loudly before turning to Duncan and Cam, who were watching us with undisguised amusement. "Men, go have a night. I'll stay here with her."

Without another word, they left, leaving Caelum and I sitting alone at the table. I dropped my head into my hands, embarrassment washing over me once again. I was making a fool of myself, and already regretted my attempts to be free. "Sorry. I didn't mean to say that out loud."

He chuckled, softer this time, as he moved his chair closer to me. He bumped my shoulder with his own. "Don't apologize. A pretty girl is staring at me, I'm fine with that."

"I was not staring!" I protested. He raised an eyebrow at me. I looked down at my lap, tucking a loose strand of hair behind my ear. "Okay, fine, maybe I was staring a little. Have you seen yourself?"

Cheeks turning pink, he ducked his head slightly, rubbing the back of his neck. "Thanks. You're a pretty sight yourself."

My cheeks got even hotter. My whole face felt like it was on fire now. He thought I was beautiful? My brain was screaming at me that I was being foolish, but my stomach fluttered at the compliment. "I...uh..."

"Not used to being called beautiful, *teine*?" he asked, the sides of his mouth quirking up. "Those syrens of yours never told you?"

I rolled my eyes. Teasing was good; I knew how to respond to teasing. "We had other things on our mind, Caelum."

He leaned in closer, tugging gently on the strand of hair that kept falling into my face. His breath puffed against my face as he whispered, "That's too bad. Someone as pretty as you should be told more often."

"Are you flirting with me, Captain?" I asked, leaning in just as close. The ale had made me braver than I would ever have been. I shouldn't be doing this, but I was being free tonight, and I wasn't thinking about how hurt my family would be if they found out. How much *more* hurt they would be.

No. They had shunned me. Banishing me without a second thought had lost them any right they had to be angry over how I chose to live my life.

"Are you flirting back, syren?" he asked, bumping his shoulder into mine again.

I didn't even try to stop myself as I reached out and looped my arm through his, pressing myself to his side and resting my head on his shoulder. He was warm and sturdy, smelled like sandalwood and rain, and I fit a little too well into his side. "Did you know you're attractive, Caelum? Real handsome."

He laughed softly, tilting his head down to rest against mine. "Aye, you mentioned that already, *teine*. You're real pretty too."

I laughed with him, tilting my head back and full-on laughing. I wasn't sure if it was the drink or him that made my body light up like a crackling fire. I hadn't laughed like this in a long time, and it felt good surging through my body. "I bet you say that to all the girls."

He shrugged, his fingers going back to playing with the strand of my hair that seemed to fascinate him. He tucked it back behind my ear, letting his rough fingertips slide across my cheek, where he rubbed his thumb over the swell. "Only if it's true."

I sat up straighter, tugging at the tight corset around my waist. I needed it off. I needed to breathe. "It's too hot."

His hands quickly covered mine, stilling them. "Let's not take that off here. Do you want to leave? The others can stay and keep gathering information."

I stopped moving, my eyes locking on his. He wanted to leave with me? Unbidden, thoughts of us lying together, of me running my hands over his chest and tracing the scars on his back, entered my mind. And I wanted it. Badly, I wanted it. "Leave?"

"You've got a dirty mind, *teine*," he said with an easy grin. He dropped his hands away from my waist. "Not for that, but so you can go change and cool down a bit."

My stomach dropped in disappointment. He didn't want me, not really. But who could blame him? I was a sea monster who had killed all his friends, and he was a handsome captain, on a mission to stop a truly evil man. There was no hope for us, no matter how much I might want there to be. "Oh, okay."

Suddenly, my face was engulfed in his warm hands and our faces were so close our noses almost touched. His eyes locked with mine, and I felt like I might be lost in the intensity of the green flames there. "Brigid, you are beautiful, don't doubt that. But you are also completely steaming drunk for the first time in your life. So, let's go back to the room and get you some rest, okay?"

My brain was really not working, because all I heard was that he said I was beautiful. "You think I'm beautiful?"

He smiled, still holding my face. "Aye, I do."

I smiled back at him, staring into his eyes that were like shining jade. His lips quirked, drawing my attention there. He even had freckles on his lips. Leaning in, I wet my suddenly dry lips. His eyes shot down to my mouth. I leaned in closer, intent on seeing what his lips felt like against mine. My lips parted as I whispered his name.

Suddenly, he blinked, and his gaze cleared of lust. He leaned back away from me, dropping his hands from my face. "We can't do this."

Stomach dropping, I swallowed back the tears burning in my throat. Of course, we couldn't. What had I been thinking? I leaned back in my chair, squeezing my hands tight into fists and letting my nails bite into the skin at my palms. I clenched my jaw tight, biting into the soft skin of my cheek until my mouth flooded with copper. The pain was a welcome distraction from my foolish idea that had been fueled by alcohol I shouldn't have been drinking.

I was a fool to think I had any kind of chance at a normal life, even for a night. I had given that up when I said yes to Cliodhna, and I would give it up again when I decided whether I should go back to her or live my life as a human in Bhodheas. And I was even more of a fool to think that any sense of normalcy would come with Caelum, given the fate of his crew at my hands.

I managed a nod, somehow keeping the tears from spilling. "Yeah, yeah. I should go back to the room."

I stood quickly, ready to leave, but the room spun on its side, my vision blurring. I slammed a hand out on the table to steady myself, and Caelum quickly stood and grabbed my elbow. "Steady there, *teine.*"

I pulled my elbow from his grip, forcing my muscles to tense up and allow myself to stand on my own. Speaking took entirely too much concentration, but I managed. "I'm fine. I can get back by myself. You can stay."

He sighed heavily, wrapping his arm around my waist and holding my elbow in his other hand. "No, Brigid. You're drunk, that's all I meant. But let's get you back to the room."

After more stumbling than I cared to admit, we entered the room we shared at the old inn a few doors down from the pub. Caelum let go of me, letting me stumble further into the room as he lit the lamp sitting on the table by the bed. I slumped down onto the bed, suddenly exhausted. But I knew I needed to get out of this corset and these pants. I reached behind my back and began tugging on the strings.

Gentle hands pushed mine away. "Let me, *teine.*"

I somehow managed to keep from asking why he kept calling me that as Caelum began unlacing my corset, freeing my ribs from the compression. He pulled me up to standing before kneeling at my feet and doing the same to my boots and pulling them off one by one. He guided me to sit back down on the bed and pressed a kiss to my head. "What do you want to sleep in?"

"I'll just sleep in this," I said, running a hand over the tight pants that covered my thighs. It would be uncomfortable in the morning, but I was drunk right now and didn't care about my comfort. All I cared about now was the embarrassment still churning at Caelum's rejection.

"No, let me help you change," he said. He motioned for me to stand up, which I thankfully managed to do on my own. "Or do you want to do it yourself?"

Still unable to bring myself to speak and make this situation any worse, I shook my head. I knew I would need his help, at least with the pants. There was no way I was getting myself out of them in this state, no matter how much I wanted to.

He nodded, pulling me into his arms and looking down at me. "Let's get you ready for bed."

Elizianna
@ELIZIANNA.THE.ONE

CHAPTER NINETEEN

Brigid was absolutely smashed.

I held her gently in my arms as I pulled her slightly away from the bed. It was a pure exercise in self-control as I unlaced her pants and pulled them down over her full hips. She held onto my shoulders as I bent down to my knees, helping her step out of the tight pants. Her legs were beautiful, and up close it was almost too much to take. All I wanted was to press my mouth against her legs and feel the soft skin there against my face. But she was drunk, and I would not become one of the men she feared. We would do this her way, when she decided it was time, if ever.

Once she was out of her pants, I rose from my knees and helped her back to sit down on the bed. She was adorable, her hair mussed, her cheeks flushed, and her lips pouty. I motioned vaguely. "Arms up."

She lifted her arms immediately before putting them back down just as fast and narrowing her eyes at me. "But then I'll be naked."

I raised an eyebrow, amused at her pouting statement. "Suddenly, you're modest? You had no problems showing off when we first met."

She spluttered, her cheeks turning even pinker and the blush spreading down her neck and disappearing beneath her shirt. "That was before I made a fool of myself. Now, you don't get to see my body."

"You didn't make a fool out of yourself," I said with a sigh, sitting down on the bed next to her. Taking her hands in mine, I twined our fingers together. Why I felt the need to comfort her, I didn't understand. I shouldn't be wanting this, wanting *her*. She had a large hand in killing my crew, whether it had been her idea or not. I couldn't forgive that yet, and I certainly couldn't forget that —no matter how much I wanted to. But something about her drew me in like a moth to a flame, and I was curious to see what getting burned would feel like.

She was silent for a long time, and if I wasn't looking at her eyes, darting back and forth, I would think she had fallen asleep standing up. Finally, she spoke. "I shouldn't want to kiss you. I shouldn't be wanting to do any of this."

Her words hit me like a sucker punch to the gut. Hearing her admit out loud that she wanted more than just existing in the same space as me was surreal. Hearing that she was also struggling with the notion that we shouldn't be doing this was validating, but somehow even more frustrating. I wanted to make a move, to be with her in some way, but I couldn't forget what had happened. And I couldn't forget about what *would* happen once the others found out her involvement.

"What exactly is 'any of this,' *teine?*"

Even keeping that secret still made my stomach hurt. I didn't like lying to my men, even if it was just by omission. They deserved to know the truth about the wreck, but I still found myself protecting Brigid. If we were both denying ourselves, would anything ever happen? I doubted it. But I still needed to know what she was specifically talking about.

She waved a hand vaguely around the room. "All of this. I want to live, I want to experience life with you. I want to kiss you, and to hug you, to feel your skin on mine and to wake up next to you. I want to see what all I've been missing. But I shouldn't. I shouldn't want any of that. I should be leaving, groveling to my queen to take me back. And you shouldn't want me either. I was part of causing your wreck; you should hate me. You probably do hate me."

I pulled her into my arms, pressing a kiss to the top of her head. I should hate her, but the more time I spent with her, the harder that was becoming. Instead, the more I learned about how she had been no more free from her queen than I had from my father, it made me feel closer to her. "Brigid, you were faced with an impossible choice to make when you were too young to know any better."

"But I still made that decision," she said, her voice uncharacteristically small. I wasn't used to hearing her so meek or seeing her wrap her arms around herself as if she would fall apart. Her jaw worked, and my fingers itched to massage at the joint, but I kept them to myself. "And now I'm torn between wanting to run back to them and beg for their forgiveness and wanting to stay here with you. I like you, Caelum. But I shouldn't."

"Forget about shouldn't. Let's talk about what you want for yourself. You wanted to make a life for yourself when you stowed away on that ship. What would that life have looked like?" I asked. Even drunk, she needed to face her decisions and really see what it was she wanted out of life. And if that was me, then great, I returned the sentiment. But if it was going back to the others, I would accept that too. Ignoring the part about the wreck seemed smart for now, until I could get a grasp on my own emotions on the subject.

"I don't know. I've never thought about it," she said, looking down at her hands still in her lap. "I didn't know what I was going to do when I got to the Bhodheas, and then I never even got that far."

"You can do whatever you want now. What were your dreams when you were a child?" I asked, sitting down next to her. She had to have something she'd aspired toward when she was younger.

She shrugged, her body slumping in on itself even more. "To be free. To have my own life and make my own decisions. I was never really allowed to be a child, not with my father. I always had to be strong, dependable."

"So, you wanted freedom and ended up just serving a different master," I pointed out. She had run from her father only to end up with this queen she talked about. Anger burned in my chest for her. The more she spoke, the more difficult it was for me to stay angry at her alone for the shipwreck. She had been nothing more than a soldier, following orders. "Why?"

"I was angry when the syrens found me. I guess I never stopped to consider the consequences," she said, her voice wobbly. I studied her; her chin was quivering, but her jaw was tense. This side of her, this vulnerable and emotional side, was new to me, and new to her as well, I believed.

The past few days, she had tried to hide her vulnerabilities, masking them with confidence and snark. Even when she was in such pain from her transformation that she trusted me to hold her upright, she had still been reserved, hiding away the extent of the pain I could see in her eyes. I highly doubted she would appreciate being seen as vulnerable now, especially while she was drunk. Making the decision that we didn't need to talk any more about this heavy subject, I tugged at her hands, making her look at me. "We can talk about it later. Let's get you changed and get some rest."

She nodded, her eyes cast down at the floor. "Okay."

Note to self, Brigid is a sad drunk. I stood again with a sigh, turning to face her. "Now, arms up this time. You can wear my shirt to sleep in. I promise I won't look."

This time, she didn't hesitate, just pulled her shirt right over head, leaving her upper body completely bare. My mouth dried out, but I forced myself to stay focused on her face as promised. I pulled my own shirt off quickly before turning it around and slipping it over her head and pulling it down. It engulfed her, and my heartbeat quickened seeing her in my shirt.

Pulling her hair out from beneath the collar, I sat down beside her, taking out the pins and ties holding her braids back. Without speaking, I unraveled her long hair from the braids, running my fingers through it until the biggest of the tangles were gone. "Are you ready for bed?"

"Thank you, Caelum," she said softly, leaning into my side. "I'm sorry for all of this."

I turned, cupping her face. The way she looked up at me, her green eyes so fucking soft, it almost melted me. "I know you are. This is an impossible situation that has no easy resolution. I'm still angry about what happened, I won't deny that. But I see the guilt you hold too. And honestly, it makes me feel quite proud that you think about all these things with me. You've been against men for years, and look at you, trusting me enough to be attracted. It's an honor."

Her cheeks turned pink under my touch. "I still shouldn't have said anything. We can't ever have a future. Not between the syrens and your mission to stop your father, and my involvement in the wreck. The others would never accept me, not if they knew the truth."

I bent forward and kissed the top of her head. Giving credence to her thoughts, telling her she was right, wouldn't be a useful conversation right now. Not when she was drunk. Against her hair, I mumbled, "We'll figure that out when we get to it. But we've still got a mission to fulfill. So, let's table this discussion for later."

She giggled, and the noise shot right through me, turning my blood to fire. "Yeah, good idea."

We separated, and she turned, stretching out in the bed. The shirt rode up on her thighs, revealing the pale skin there. She truly was gorgeous, and I would make sure she knew it. Tomorrow.

I pulled the blankets up around her, tucking them around her. "Goodnight, *teine*."

"Wait, you need rest too. We can share the bed," she said, reaching her hand out to grab my own.

I swallowed hard. I could do this. I could sleep next to this beauty and behave myself for the night. "All right, then, scoot over."

Deciding to keep my pants on, tight as they may be, I unlaced my boots and tugged them off. I walked over and extinguished the lamp on the table before sliding into the bed next to her. Almost immediately, she turned on her side and curled up next to me, slinging an arm over my stomach and resting her head on my chest. It felt nice. It felt right. But I had to keep my hopes from getting too high. I clenched my jaw, trying to ignore how warm she felt against me. Then, she twined her bare leg in between mine. Fuck.

Looking up at the ceiling, I huffed out a breath as I tried to keep from pulling her even closer. I had to behave. She wasn't aware of what she was doing right now.

"Caelum?" she whispered into the darkness.

I turned my head to look at her. "Yeah, *teine?*"

"Thank you for being worth saving," she whispered, and then her small hand was on my cheek and her soft lips were on mine.

All thoughts left my brain at that point. I tangled my hand in her hair and deepened the kiss, pulling her tight to my body. This was really happening, and my heart was pounding in my chest so hard I feared it might explode. After enjoying the feel of her against my lips, the taste of sea salt and citrus and of her, I pulled away, leaning my forehead against hers and panting more than I'd like to admit. I wanted to continue, to take this as far as she would let me, but I had to remember she was still drunk. We would have time for this later, if I had my way.

I pressed another gentle kiss to her lips before tucking her under my chin and wrapping my arms around her. "Get some rest, *mo teine.*"

"G'night, Captain," she whispered, snuggling down further into my chest and thankfully ignoring my small addition to her pet name that would have made all the difference in the world.

I pulled the blanket up around us both and sighed contentedly. This was going fast, and I knew the only reason she had kissed me was because of the ale, but I didn't regret it. I just hoped she wouldn't also regret it in the morning. I wanted to get to know her more, to protect her, and to help her experience the life she talked about wanting. But I couldn't help but think about the losses I had suffered.

They might not be directly because of her, but they came from her kind. I doubted my ability to be able to separate those things in my mind, and more importantly, I doubted the others would even want to try to separate them. Despite my turmoil, feeling her in my arms was good. If I turned off my mind, I could truly be happy for a moment.

Taking one last look down at Brigid, who was already breathing deeply into my chest, I smiled into the darkness. I only hoped I could keep her.

BRIGID

CHAPTER TWENTY

The morning came in like a blasting drum. My eyes burned, my head pounded, and my stomach churned, revolting against all that I had consumed the night before. Slowly, awareness came back to me, and I did a quick scan of my body. I was in a bed, once again pressed up to the warmth and hardness of Caelum's body. He didn't have a shirt on, and he had his arms wrapped around my waist as I lay across his chest.

My memories of the previous night came rushing back, and my cheeks burned at the embarrassment. I had kissed him. Cursing to myself, I ran through the blurry memories in my head, searching for anything else I had foolishly done. I had kissed him and basically threw myself at him, and he had rejected me. What had I done?

I must have moved slightly, because Caelum grunted, opening his eyes to look at me sleepily. When he saw I was awake, his eyes became alert and filled with laughter. "Good morning. How are you feeling?"

I groaned and dropped my head to his chest, hiding away from his knowing gaze. "What have I done?"

He chuckled before tucking a finger under my chin and pulling my face back up to look at him. "You had a fun night, that's all that matters. No harm done."

"I kissed you," I pointed out, trying to bury my face in his chest again to hide my embarrassment. I had kissed him, but he had kissed me back. Did that mean he actually did want me?

He dropped a kiss on my hair, suddenly more comfortable with me than we had been the previous day. Had the kiss truly changed that much about our relationship? Was it possible his attraction to me could overcome his hatred?

"That you did. Please feel free to do it again now that you're not plastered." The teasing smile on his face made me question whether he was serious or teasing me. And even more, I wasn't sure which one I wanted it to be.

I needed to change the subject before I did something foolish, like kiss him again. We couldn't do this. I pushed myself up to sitting, looking down at him. For a moment, I lost my words. He really was a sight to see, with his broad and muscled torso lightly dusted in dark hair. He was all power. As if sensing me staring, his stomach flexed. My mouth dried, and I'm certain it even dropped open a bit.

"Like what you see?" he teased.

Mentally shaking myself, I finished pushing myself up to put my feet on the floor and my back to him. "What are we doing today?"

He sat up behind me, movement shifting the bed slightly. "We'll have to meet the men and see what they're planning to do. My father always returns to Brinemoor. It's his base. But since he won't be back until tomorrow, we need to take the day to prepare. We lost our weapons in the shipwreck."

"Sounds like we have a busy day planned," I replied, getting out of bed and turning away from Caelum. I needed to get my head on straight. Every time he mentioned the shipwreck, it brought things back into focus. *Syrens* had caused that wreck, and I would always be a syren, forever associated with that.

Caelum rose too, moving to stand in front of me. He brushed a strand of hair away from my face before tugging on one of the laces of the shirt I was wearing. His face moved close to mine as he whispered, "I'll be needing this back, *teine.*"

My cheeks burned again, something they had been doing quite a bit since Caelum had come back into my life. Ignoring the voice in my head screaming that this was a bad idea, I turned my face closer to his until our cheeks were almost touching. I couldn't resist feeling the heat of his skin radiating against mine. "Aye, you likely do."

Locking gazes, we stood there for a heartbeat. The heat in the room was building at the same time the heat inside my own body grew. His eyes dipped down to my lips, and all the air left the room. His voice was rough as he looked down at me, his eyes darkening. "Brigid..."

"Kiss me," I whispered, tilting my face up toward him. Consequences be damned, I wanted to feel this man against me, and I wanted it now.

In an instant, one large hand threaded through my unbound hair to cup the back of my head, and his lips crashed down on mine. His other hand grabbed onto the swell of my hip and pulled me closer to him as our mouths moved together, his days-old stubble rubbing against my face roughly. My own hands reached up to grab at his chest, his shoulders, at anything, and he groaned into my mouth. His fingers explored and squeezed at my curves as he nipped at my lips and tugged at my hair. It was breathtaking, overwhelming, and like no kiss I had ever experienced before. He pulled back, as breathless as I was, and tilted his forehead down to rest against mine. Our breath intermingled as our chests heaved in unison.

"Now that's a kiss," he said hoarsely, rubbing a thumb over my swollen lips.

Somehow, I was able to find my voice. "Aye, that was definitely a kiss."

"Good morning to me." he smiled. He pulled back away from me and tugged on the laces of his shirt again playfully. "We really should meet up with the others, though."

He was right, of course. My brain was already going at high speed, and some space and food would do me well. I nodded before stepping back away from him and pulling the shirt over my head. "Aye, you're right. Here's your shirt."

Looking up to the ceiling, he let out a pained groan. "*Teine,* you cannot just do that."

My neck and chest flushed. Caelum's kisses had left my mind swimming, and I had just pulled his shirt off to return it, not giving any mind to the fact that I was now standing naked before him. I probably should have moved to cover myself up, but my body was one of the few things I was not ashamed of. Raising an eyebrow, I held his shirt out higher, shaking it at him. "You said you needed your shirt back."

He looked back at me before grabbing my face with both hands and pressing a quick and rough kiss to my lips that left my entire body tingling and wanting more. Pulling back, he looked like he wanted to do a great deal more, but restrained himself. He took the shirt from my hands finally, but made no move to put it on. "You really have no idea the effect you have. Now, put your clothes on before we're really late to breakfast."

I did know the effect I had on him, but it was almost endearing to see him think me innocent and inexperienced. Caelum's reaction to my body burned through my blood, lighting my whole body ablaze. I knew from my childhood that I should have felt ashamed, but I didn't. Knowing the effect I had on this gorgeous man made me feel powerful in an entirely different way than being a syren felt powerful. And I was beginning to like it. Quirking up the corner of my mouth, I couldn't resist teasing him. "Maybe next time, then."

He laughed, reaching over to hand me my own shirt from last night and then pulling his own on. "Aye, next time."

We dressed in pleasant silence. I decided to forgo the tight corset I had worn last night, dressing only in the loose, white blouse and leather pants. Caelum and I both laced up our boots before facing each other. He smiled at me, reaching over to squeeze my fingers before leading me out of the room.

When we got down to the dining area, Duncan was the only one there. We sat down at the table with him, and he grinned knowingly at me. "How you feeling?"

I rolled my eyes, knowing his question was more teasing and less genuine. "I'm fine, big man. Thanks for your concern."

"How was the rest of your night, then?" he asked, looking at Caelum now. The smile had dropped from Duncan's face, and the two of them looked at each other, no doubt having a conversation with only their eyes in the way only longtime friends can. I wondered if Duncan could tell we had kissed. More than that, I wondered if he approved or not.

While I only slightly regretted kissing Caelum last night, I did not regret kissing him again this morning. But I was nervous about him telling anyone else. I was still coming to terms with my own feelings and questions related to my family and to Caelum. I didn't want to be figuring out those feelings under the scrutiny of others. And I didn't want Caelum to feel the judgment of his friends more harshly if—when—they found out my role in their wreck. I was under no illusions, it would be discovered. My only surprise was that Caelum had not immediately told them.

Finally, Caelum ended their secret conversation and shrugged a shoulder. "Entertaining. And yours? Was it as informative as we hoped?"

Duncan nodded, the smile back on his face. "Aye, it was. Let's wait for Cam and Mad to join us before I fill you in. They got most of the information."

As if they were waiting for their names to be said, the other men walked down the stairs, plopping down at the table with us. Cameron reached over and fingered a strand of my loose hair. "Want me to braid it again, B?"

I smiled at him, a genuine feeling of friendship building. It scared me, thinking about how quickly it would change when he discovered the truth, but I would cherish it for now. "Yes, please. After we eat."

"I meant to ask last night," Duncan said, leaning in, "but where'd you learn to do a girl's hair like that, Cam?"

He shrugged nonchalantly, picking at the splinters in the table in front of him. "Three younger sisters. When my ma died, someone had to tame their hair. And it sure as hell weren't my da."

"That's nice," I said, smiling at him, thinking how different my life may have been if I had had a brother like Cameron, like any of them. These were good men. It still sickened my stomach to think that myself and the others had almost been the cause of their ruin. I couldn't help but feel myself growing closer to them, and I shuddered to think of what their reactions would be when they eventually found out the truth about me. My heart broke at the thought of being shunned again. But I had endured far worse before, and I would continue to do so until my last breath.

"Okay, down to business," Caelum said, running his hand through his own unbound hair. "What did you learn about my father's plans?"

Duncan looked over at me from the corner of his eyes, not bothering to hide his suspicion. "Should we be talking about this here?"

Caelum met Duncan's eyes, and they had another unspoken conversation for several moments. At the end of it, Duncan sighed and nodded, waving a hand loosely at Caelum. Caelum's shoulders dropped, the tension bleeding out of him slightly, and he turned to me. "If we tell you this, you're in this until the end, Brigid. If you don't think you want to help, it's time to tell me now."

I rolled my shoulders back, steeling my spine. Caelum was right before, I did owe him this. And I would do whatever it took to earn his forgiveness and the forgiveness of the syrens. One at a time. "I told you I would help, and I will. I won't tell a soul what I hear."

Caelum looked at me, an assessing gaze that I had not felt from him before. After a moment, he nodded, a strand of hair falling onto his forehead. "All right, then. My father has been stealing children."

My mouth fell open. Of all the things I had been expecting him to say, that was nowhere near anything I had dreamed. Only a monster would target children. My temper boiled under my skin, my hands clenching into fists at my side at the thought of these innocent children being harmed. "Children?"

"Keep your voice down," Maddock said softly, looking around the room to ensure no one had heard us.

"We don't know who my father has on his payroll. If they find out we're going after him, he'll move again," Caelum added.

Nodding, I took a deep breath to temper my anger and lowered my voice to a whisper. "Children? Really?"

Caelum nodded, his eyes sad. "Aye, children. That's why we're trying so hard to stop him."

My mind raced, churning through thoughts of what all Caelum had told me. The other syrens and I had wrecked a ship on a mission to save children. Perhaps we truly were the monsters men thought us to be. How many men had we killed before that had been on journeys like this? How many men had we doomed to death that did not deserve it? Sorcha's words about some men being innocent rushed back at me, and guilt flooded my mouth, sour on my tongue. I swallowed harshly, trying to erase the taste of death from my mouth.

Peering at me curiously, Caelum watched a moment before turning back to his men. "Go on, Cam."

Cameron sighed heavily, and I knew whatever he was about to say wouldn't be good. "Well, we're in the right place. We have reliable information that he's been holding the children somewhere in this town. Last night, we finally found out what he's doing with them. He's selling them."

"To whom?" Caelum gritted out, his forearms corded and tensed as he clenched and unclenched his hands into fists. His anger was palpable, rolling off his hunched shoulders in waves. It only served to feed my own anger that was building again beneath the surface of my skin. It was clear he had not known this part of his father's plans.

"Our sources didn't know that bit. They suspected it was a woman, but reports were too mixed to say one way or another."

"So, what are we going to do?" I asked, sick at the thought of these young children being sold, much like I had almost been. If I still had any reservations about helping Caelum, they had disappeared with Maddock's words. I would do everything in my power to save these children. After we saved them, which we would, I would make sure they were safe and cared for too. The syrens' contact in the south would be willing to take them in, I was sure.

"We're going to go get them," Caelum said angrily, standing abruptly and leaning with his fists on the table. "Now that we know what he's doing and where he is, we can't keep waiting around."

Maddock put a hand on his arm, pulling him back down. "They're not there."

Caelum returned to his seat with a heavy and irritated sigh. He waved a hand at his friend. "Explain."

"They're not in town right now, and our sources say they won't be back with new...children." Maddock swallowed hard before continuing. "They won't be back with new children for at least another day."

"So, we have to wait?" Caelum asked, his irritation and impatience nearly palpable. "We can't go find where he's holding them and wait?"

"Aye, Captain," Maddock confirmed with a grimace. "We'll have to wait."

Caelum ran a hand over his face before sighing again and leaning back in his chair, crossing his arms over his chest. "We didn't find out anything else except that he's selling them to someone who may or may not be a woman."

"We also found out for sure that he's only taking orphans. Mostly boys, but it seems any orphan will do," Cameron said slowly. "People here in town are reporting that it's only street children that are disappearing. Children with no one to miss them. Which is why it's taken so long to notice."

My brow furrowed. What could anyone possibly want with only orphaned children? I couldn't fathom a reason, but I also couldn't fathom harming children in the first place. Yet it was obvious Caelum's father had no such reservations, given what he had done to his own child. Maybe the others knew more about the motivations. "Why?"

Cameron looked at me, and the corner of his mouth twitched. "Lass, if we knew that, we'd have been running around celebrating that we finally found something out."

My cheeks flushed. Obviously. They had been searching for information for who knew how long, and I had just come into this mission. I had questions, sure, but I doubted they wanted to sit here and answer them for me right now.

"So, the plan," Duncan said, leaning forward. "We need a plan."

"Aye," Caelum said. "Do we know exactly where he's holding them?"

"A building on the outskirts of town was the most consistent information," Cameron said, crossing his arms over his chest. "But they won't be back for at least another day."

"Aye, I got that bit. But we can scope it out and know when they get back." Caelum rubbed his forehead. "Do we know where my father is coming from?"

"Up from Bhodheas. Along the coast, according to the townsfolk," Cameron explained.

"Not through the Straits, though?"

Cameron shook his head. "Old man said they avoid the Straits and stick to the east."

"We can have Alan and his men rotate a patrol around the building. Your father won't recognize them like he would us or Duncan. When they bring in the children and return, we can go in and rescue the children," Maddock proposed. "Some of us can go in and get them and send them out to the others, who can get them far away quickly in case something goes ass over teakettle."

"Set it up," Caelum said before casting a glance at me. "And then we need to get prepared."

"We need new weapons," Cam said, crossing his arms. "All of ours went down with the ship."

"Do you know how to handle a sword, Brigid?" Duncan asked, looking over at me.

"I can learn," I shot back, not wanting to advertise that I had absolutely zero experience with weapons of any kind. I had grown up using farm equipment, and anything beyond a utility knife was foreign to me. But that didn't mean I wasn't still dangerous. I knew how to kill a man with my bare hands and with my talons.

"Maybe we'll start with a dagger," Maddock suggested, tilting his head to look at me.

Elizianna
@ELIZIANNA.THE.ONE

CAELUM

CHAPTER TWENTY-ONE

"Will people notice if we just walk around here with swords and knives?" Brigid asked as we walked into the blacksmith's shop, her eyebrow raised once again.

I chuckled at the incredulous look on her face. "We're in a port, *teine*. No one will give us a second glance."

"There's a lot of pirates here, then?" She stopped walking, turning around fully to face me, curiosity clear on her face.

"Yes and no," I said, opening my arm wide to allow her to walk through the door first. The town *was* a haven for pirates and other illegal services, but it was also a legitimate port for merchant vessels. And it was getting harder and harder to tell the difference. "Let's get weapons first, then we can have a history lesson."

She looked like she wanted to ask more questions, but hesitated and nodded, moving to enter the shop fully.

The heat inside was overwhelming even though the shop was separated from the forge. Bells tinkled as the door swung shut behind Duncan, and Brigid moved to run her fingers over the blades displayed on the wooden counter.

"I'll be right there," a loud voice shouted from the forge. Moments later, a large man with a leather apron came out of the door to the forge, pulling off his heavy leather gloves and tucking them under his arm. When he saw me, his weathered face broke out into a wide grin. "Caelum! Welcome back, my boy. What can I do you for?"

"Looking for some blades, Galen. Broadswords, cutlasses, daggers, whatever you've got," I replied, raising my chin slightly as I returned the smile. I knew this smithy wouldn't question why we needed such weapons. He had long been the go-to smith for those in less-than-legal businesses. And even more, Galen had known me since I was a child, and I trusted he wouldn't tell my father I was here.

"Well, you've come to the right place," he said, beaming at me. His eyes fluttered over to Brigid before landing back on me with a mischievous grin. "Let's get you geared up."

"Don't skimp on me, Galen," I said, raising my eyebrow teasingly. I knew the older man would only give me the best, but I still had to poke at him a bit. Kept him on his toes.

He threw a glove at me, laughing. "Should send you in there to make your own bloody sword."

"You know how to smith?" Brigid asked, looking over at me. The admiration in her eyes was alluring, and I felt myself preening under her attention.

"Aye, I do. Galen here taught me whenever I wasn't with my father," I explained with a smile. Out of the memories of my childhood here in Brinemoor, my time with Galen was a reprieve from the constant violence of my father. It hadn't been an easy reprieve by any means, but it had given me a reason to be away from my father and a chance to heal from whatever injuries he had inflicted upon me. "Speaking of, have you heard anything about him lately?"

Galen shook his head. "Naw, son. Can't say I have. He don't come in here much anymore. Prefers to get his steel from Bhodheas now, I hear."

"He still staying in the old house when he is here?" I asked. Galen was an unlikely source of reliable information, as the old man rarely left his forge, but I knew I could trust whatever information he did have.

"Suppose so," he said with a shrug. "Haven't heard of him staying anywhere else."

I nodded, content with the information. At least I had trusted outside verification that my father was at his old home in Brinemoor. Though I hadn't been there in years, I knew where it was and the basic layout. It would give us an advantage, albeit a small one, in our raid of the house. "Thanks, Galen."

Galen studied me for a moment. "You're going after him, aren't you?"

I gritted my teeth, keeping silent. I might trust Galen, but the more people who figured out I was finally able to take on my father, the greater the likelihood my father himself would discover our plans. I had been waiting years to be in a position to stop him. I wasn't going to give it up now just to catch up with Galen. "The blades, Galen."

He raised an eyebrow at my tone, but shrugged. "All right, your business, boy. Let me see what we've got ready for you. How many of what do you need?"

"Just bring out whatever you've got made."

He nodded, turning to head to the storeroom in the back. I let out a harsh sigh, turning to Duncan. "Maybe you should have done this on your own. He knows me too well."

"He won't tell Kellan," Duncan said confidently. "He dislikes the bastard as much as you do."

"He saved you as a child," Brigid commented quietly. She was far too observant for her own good.

"Aye, he did," I finally replied. I didn't want to talk more about my childhood. Not while I was trying to mentally prepare myself for the possibility of fighting my father directly. I needed to be ready, and remembering the balm Galen had been as a child would not help me channel my anger.

Thankfully, Galen returned from the back, a bundle of swords in his arms. He spread them out on the wooden display counter with a clatter. "All right, Caelum. Here's what I've got made. Let me know what you want and I'll get them all sharpened and polished for you."

I glanced down briefly at the weapons along the counter. Given that my father's men had an arsenal of weapons at their disposal, anything we could get to rebuild our own arsenal would be needed. "We'll take it all."

"All of it?" Galen asked with an eyebrow raised. He paused for a moment and then sighed, shaking his head. "All right, I'll go get it ready."

"Oh, and we'll need some daggers for Brigid here," I said, jerking my head at her. She had been quiet but bold in her stance, watching Galen's movements with equal parts curiosity and suspicion.

Galen nodded, reaching under the counter to pull out a box. He set it on the counter and motioned toward the display of daggers already set up. "This is all I've got. While I go sharpen these swords, you see which ones fit you best, girly."

He left to the back, and I turned to face Brigid, leaning my forearm against the counter. "All right, then. Let's get you a knife."

Quickly, it was clear that Brigid was a natural with a dagger. The smile on her face as she tested the weight and grip of each one was almost dreamy. I should have expected it, but even then, it still brought a smile to my face.

After going through the box of knives Galen had brought, two daggers stood out as favorites. The way she held them, with her fingers fitting snugly around the handle and hefting it in her palm, they were obviously the ones for her. The sparkle in her eyes was amusing, and even Duncan let out a chuckle watching her.

"So, you like daggers, huh?" Duncan said, leaning onto the counter as he watched her twirl one of the daggers in her fingers.

Brigid seemed to come back to herself and realize we were both watching her. Her cheeks flushed pink, and she set the dagger down roughly on the counter, clearing her throat. "I suppose I do."

"Good. I would hate to have you unable to defend yourself," Duncan said with a smile. "Shame we don't have time to teach you to use a sword."

She smirked. "I can defend myself without a blade, but I appreciate your concern."

"Swordplay will come later," I said with a nod. Brigid may be feeling fiery with her new blades, but we didn't have time to afford Duncan's questions. A woman being able to defend herself wasn't unheard of, especially here, but Duncan was too curious for his own good.

Thankfully, Galen came back out of the forge with the bundle of a dozen swords. He spread them carefully out on the counter. "Sharp as can be, Caelum. Now, do we need sheaths as well?"

"We need it all, Galen," I replied. My eyes flicked to Brigid before returning to the older man. "We lost all our weapons and supplies."

"I'll get you fitted up," Galen said with a grin. He nodded his head at Brigid. "You like those two, girly?"

She nodded, pushing them across the counter to him. "I do."

"You're gonna let Caelum there teach you how to use it?" he asked, raising an eyebrow.

Returning the gesture, she smirked at him. "If he behaves."

Now, it was my turn to raise an eyebrow. Brigid normally wasn't this forward with strangers, but I liked it. The fire I had seen was coming more to the surface. But she was wrong. I would teach her how to use the dagger no matter what. "Sure thing, *teine.* Whatever you say."

Elizi
@ELIZIAN

CHAPTER TWENTY-TWO

Weapons gathered, we met back up with Cameron and Maddock at the inn. The blacksmith had been intriguing to me, and Caelum had been different around him, more childlike.

But beyond that, the feel of the daggers in my hands felt...right. For years, I had relied on my talons, my strength beneath the waves, and my syren powers to defend myself. The idea of using an external blade felt strange at first, but feeling the weight of the handle was natural. Now I just needed to learn how to wield it effectively.

"Get everything we need?" Cameron asked, walking up to meet us and taking the canvas bag of swords from Caelum.

"Aye. Swords with scabbards, some daggers for Brigid, and all have been sharpened." Caelum tilted his head toward the innkeeper, who was looking over at us with narrowed eyes. "Best take those up to your room there, Cam."

Cam nodded before turning and heading up the stairs.

Maddock crossed his arms over his chest. "We need to do some recon, don't we?"

"I'm familiar with the house, but we need to see what my father is doing in terms of patrols and security," Caelum said, shrugging.

He looked at me, and I could almost see the thoughts churning in his head. "We should split up. Someone needs to teach Brigid how to handle those new daggers of hers. And the rest of us can go observe the house for a bit and see if my father has security already set up at the house."

"Who's going to teach me?" I asked, raising my eyebrow. While I was comfortable enough around the others, I felt much more relaxed with Caelum and would greatly prefer him to teach me than the others. Not that I would ever admit that out loud.

"Caelum is the real knife hand," Maddock replied, smirking slightly. "But I'm a good second."

Cameron walked back down the stairs, joining us by the windows once again. "So, what's the plan?"

"Cae and I are going to teach Brigid how to use a knife," Maddock explained. He clapped Cameron on the shoulder. "And you and Duncan are going to go scope out the house. Maybe take Alan with you."

"We need to go over plans again tonight," Caelum added. "With everyone present, including Alan's men. I want everyone to understand what's going to happen and what needs to happen if something goes wrong."

"Aye, aye, Captain," Cameron said with a lazy salute that made me smile. "We'll have everyone back here at sunset. We'll meet in your room; it should be big enough."

My smile only grew wider when Caelum waved off Cameron's honorific, giving him a rude hand gesture in the process. These men were truly a family, and it made me both warm with joy and cold with envy. I had never experienced a family like that, not with the syrens and certainly not with my father.

Caelum had his own grin on his face as he jerked his head at me. "Let's go, *teine*. Got a lot to teach you."

"Going to your room, Cae?" Maddock asked, also smiling at Cam and Duncan as they laughed and walked out of the inn.

"Probably smart," Caelum agreed with a shrug. "We'll be in close quarters, most likely."

We walked up to Caelum's room, and Cam shut the door

behind him. Caelum nodded to Maddock, and they began moving all of the furniture against the walls to clear the middle of the floor.

"Have you ever fought before, *teine?*" Caelum asked, walking back to stand in front of me.

"Not quite like this," I replied, raising my eyebrow.

"Then let's see what you can do and go from there," he said, grinning. He reached over and grabbed the two daggers, handing one to me and keeping the other for himself. Opening his arms, he motioned for me to come to him. "Try to stab me."

"I will not," I said, aghast. I may not know how to use a dagger, but if I got near him, I wouldn't want to hurt him, even accidentally.

Maddock laughed, a bellowing sound. "Brigid, don't worry. I doubt you'll get anywhere near him."

"Come on, *teine,*" he said, grinning even wider now. "Try to stab me."

With a sigh, I tightened my grip on the handle and charged at him, slashing the dagger toward his midsection. He reached down with his arm and blocked me easily, sweeping my legs out from under me in the same movement and pressing his own knife to my throat.

If he grinned any wider, his face would split. Quickly, he stood and held a hand out to me, pulling me to my feet. "Don't advertise your moves. Again."

Well, this was going to take longer than I'd thought. With a sigh, I picked up my dagger and moved toward him once more.

Sore, irritated, and slightly bloody, a knock on the door halted our training sessions, finally. It was time to meet with everyone and go over the final plans for tomorrow. I let out a sigh of relief, letting my muscles relax and tucking the dagger into the sheath on my hip.

As the others filed in, they claimed seats where they could.

Taking a seat between Duncan and Cameron at the small table and chairs by the door, I smiled in what I hoped was a reassuring way and not an I-almost-accidentally-stabbed-your-captain-earlier way.

I settled down into the hard wooden chair with a sigh, shifting around in a feeble attempt to get comfortable as my sore muscles protested.

"Training go well?" Cameron asked with a sardonic smile.

I narrowed my eyes at him. "I have a feeling you know exactly how it went."

He shrugged, mirth sparkling in his eyes. "Might have an idea."

Caelum came over to us, sitting down across the table from me and pushing a plate of food he had conjured from somewhere in front of me. "Eat. You need the energy."

I wanted to raise my hand in a mock salute, but my arms were too sore to follow through. I did narrow my eyes at him, though, which only made him grin. "Aye, aye."

"Don't you start that too." He rolled his eyes before turning to address the rest of the room. "All right, let's get started, everyone."

The low chatter of the room stopped, and we all turned our attention to Caelum. Seeing him in his element, being the captain, was certainly attractive. It made heat build in my stomach. His jaw, now dusted in a thicker coating of dark hair, was tense as he spoke.

"Cameron, Duncan, what did you all discover about the house today?"

"Looked like they set up guards. Only one at each door, but we saw about five others moving around inside," Cameron started, leaning forward to rest his elbows on his knees, lacing his fingers together. "We could likely get inside easily, but there's no way to tell where the guards are stationed on the inside."

"Do you think they'll bring more guards when Kellan returns with the children?" Caelum asked, his eyebrows furrowing together.

Cameron shrugged. "Unlikely. Unfortunately, a guard at each door seems plenty. It's a fairly quiet street."

"How are we going to get inside, then?" Alan asked from his place sitting cross-legged on the floor.

"I had a thought on that," Duncan said slowly, looking at Caelum. "But you won't like it."

Caelum raised an eyebrow at his friend. "Tell me anyway."

"We send Brigid in as a maid delivering groceries. We saw several delivery people going in and out of the house, so it should be easy enough to get her to the house without attracting notice."

"No," came Caelum's immediate response. He barely spared a glance at me as he continued. "I'm not putting her at risk for this."

My blood burned. "I can help, Caelum. I'm not a child."

His eyes snapped to mine, and I saw the fire burning there for the first time. "Not happening."

I took a deep breath through my nose to keep from snapping at him and saying something I would regret. I turned to Duncan instead, moving my whole body to show Caelum my back. "Why does it have to be me?"

A small smirk crossed Duncan's lips before he schooled his features. "Well, it could be one of Alan's men, since Kellan doesn't know what they look like. But a woman would be much more likely to be able to approach the house without raising suspicion. And I doubt very much we would want to risk asking a local for help."

I nodded at him, satisfied with his answer. I *would* be doing this whether Caelum approved or not. Shifting my body around to face Caelum again, I raised an eyebrow. "Do you disagree with that assessment?"

He leaned back in his chair, crossing his arms over his chest. "And how will you get the guard to leave his post to let us into the house? You won't be able to get all those children out by yourself. We'll need to join you somehow."

I opened my mouth to speak but caught myself before I could say what I wanted to. Admitting that I had killed many men before would likely raise questions I couldn't answer right now. "You did just teach me how to use a dagger. I can handle it."

"We're not killing anyone," he said, his jaw flexing. "I am not my father. We will not kill anyone unless absolutely necessary and in self-defense."

"Fine, no killing." I shrugged easily. I could still easily incapacitate a man. Granted, I wouldn't have my syren strength or the advantage I had in the water, but I still knew how to handle myself.

Caelum just looked at me for a long moment, our eyes locked. I could tell he didn't want me to do this, but I just stared back at him, trying to convey that I *could* do this. Maybe saving these children could redeem me for the lives of potentially innocent men that I had taken. And more, I wanted to help Caelum stop his father. I saw how much it meant to him, and something deep in my soul that I didn't want to acknowledge yet made me want to do anything to see a smile on his face.

I was scared of what that might mean for my plans afterwards, but that was a problem for the future. For now, I needed to focus on convincing him to let me help him.

"Cae, it's a good plan," Maddock added quietly.

Caelum's eyes reluctantly left mine to look at Maddock. "I'll not put anyone else in danger for this, especially not her. I can easily sneak up and knock the guard out."

"They'd see you coming from a mile away," Duncan said immediately. "You really think your da hasn't told them to be on the lookout for you by now? He's got to know we've been asking around about him."

With a heavy sigh, Caelum slouched back into his chair, rubbing between his eyebrows. After a moment, he straightened up, his face resolved. "Fine, she can do it."

I nodded at him, smiling slightly. "Thank you. I'll be fine. I'll incapacitate the guards and make sure the hall is clear before letting you all in."

"And once we're in," Caelum continued, going into full captain mode now, "we'll *incapacitate* any other guards we run into. Cameron, you, Alan, and three of Alan's men need to wait outside the house. When we find the children, we'll send them out to you. You don't wait for us. You get them out of there immediately."

Cameron nodded. "Aye, where should we take them?"

"I have an arrangement with the orphanage. The matron there agreed to house them once we're able to rescue them. Take them there and tell her I sent you," Caelum explained. It made me wonder just how long they had been planning this.

"What if things go south?" Maddock asked, raising an eyebrow. "We need a backup plan."

"Aye," Caelum said, leaning forward. "If we don't come out in fifteen minutes, Cameron, you are to leave and go back to the ship."

"No, absolutely not," Cam started.

I leaned forward, intent on arguing as well. Caelum would not be dying. No one would, if I could help it. Even out of the water, I was able to transform my talons and teeth, and despite the pain, I would be more than willing to use them, even if it meant revealing myself. The only men who would die tomorrow would be Kellan's.

Caelum held a hand up to stop us both. "Let me finish. If we can't get out, then someone needs to keep this mission going and still be alive enough to try again."

"I don't like it," Cam grumbled, crossing his arms over his chest.

"Aye, and I don't like the idea of Brigid being the first one to approach the house," Caelum said. "But here we are. I'm the captain, this is the plan. Is everyone on board?"

"Aye," came the responses from everyone in the room. Cameron's was more reluctant, but eventually joined the chorus.

"Good, then take your weapons and go get some rest. We start at dawn," Caelum said, standing up.

Elizianna
@ELIZIANNA.THE.ONE

CAELUM

CHAPTER TWENTY-THREE

Watching the house my father was staying at was a test of patience. I wanted nothing more than to barge through the doors and confront him. But I knew I couldn't, not without risking the children he held. I had no doubt that if my father thought he was in danger, he would use the children as shields. And I wouldn't risk that.

We would have to do it according to the plan. The plan I was very much not on board with and very much still angry about. I knew that Brigid could handle herself, but the idea of sending her inside that house with only a dagger she had just recently learned to use, was disconcerting. The others were on board, electing to trust Brigid's words when she said she could handle it, so I supposed I would have to as well.

Brigid, disguised as a maid delivering groceries from the local market, would enter the house's side door. Once the guards were incapacitated, she would let us in. From there, we would find where the children were being held. Brigid and Maddock would lead them out, while the rest of us covered the retreat and faced off against any guards inside the house.

I took a deep breath as I sat beside Duncan and Cameron,

watching the house from a safe distance away. I blew the breath out through my nose as Brigid rounded the corner of the alley, walking toward the side door with confidence, as if she belonged there. Turning the handle, she looked to where she knew we were hiding in the nearby bushes and smiled slightly before pushing the door open and entering the house.

That was our cue.

Standing, we swiftly but cautiously walked toward the side of the house, trying not to draw attention to ourselves from anyone passing by. While I doubted anyone passing would notice us, I couldn't risk someone stopping to ask us what we were doing, potentially drawing the guards' attention to us. We had to be patient now, without getting caught out in the open. All we needed now was for Brigid to open the door again and let us in. We stood along the side of the house, waiting.

In a flash, the door swung open, and a red braid flung out over a shoulder. Brigid. She smiled. "It's clear. Come on in."

We rushed in through the door, turning right down a long, stone hallway. Continuing through the large estate house I had grown up despising, we opened every door, checking inside before moving on. Thankfully, the house was only one story tall, but it was large and sprawling. We would have a lot of rooms to check. As we continued down the hall, I became eerily aware of how empty the house was. We had not run into a single soul yet, and in a house this big, I knew there had to be workers and servants. My gut churned with unease, but we continued our search.

At the end of the next hallway, there was a large metal door, with several unlocked padlocks on the outside, ready to be locked. This had to be it. I motioned to the others, and we continued toward the room. Brigid was beside me, her dagger now drawn, with Duncan and Cameron next, then Maddock, Finn, Aiden, and Blaine, with some of Alan's men bringing up the rear. We entered the room, and I stopped dead in my tracks. My heart sank into my stomach, and my legs felt like steel weights. No. It couldn't be.

Before me, leaning against the wall all too casually, was my father. And filling the rest of the room were about six of his men. It had been a trap, and we had walked right into it.

"We should run," Maddock whispered under his breath, keeping his eyes locked on my father straight ahead.

I looked over my shoulder to see more guards coming down the hallway behind us, swords drawn and boxing us in. I cursed lightly; their numbers were greater than we had been expecting. "Not an option."

Brigid stood behind me, her own tension radiating out from her body. I doubted she recognized my father, but I was certain she would know it was him from my reaction alone. My biggest fear, that someone else would get hurt by my father's hands, was staring me in the face. I wanted to rage, to run at him with my sword swinging and cut him down. But his men outnumbered us twelve to seven, and I wouldn't risk the lives of those with me.

"Ah, boy," my father boomed, grinning at us as he pushed off the wall and drew himself up to his full height. "Glad you could join us."

I gritted my teeth. "Can't say I was expecting to run into you here, sir."

My hatred couldn't overcome the years of respect my father had drilled into me through violence and pain, and so I still called him by the honorific he had insisted upon. I stared at him, waiting to see what he had planned, because I knew he had something planned.

Looking over at the man in front of me, I was disgusted. I got my looks from my father, almost certainly, and I wished I hadn't. We looked like mirror images, just a few years apart. He, too, wore his hair longer, but he left it down, hanging over his shoulders and down his back. Our faces were similar, with sharp angles and bright green eyes.

"I imagine not," he finally replied, studying us. His eyes flicked over to Brigid, interest sparking. "Interesting company you're keeping, my son."

I shrugged, not wanting to draw any more attention to her. If my father knew what she was, or even just how important she was becoming to me, there was no telling what he would do. "I accept help wherever it comes from."

My father didn't reply, simply fixed his gaze on me. After what felt like forever, he turned and nodded to one of the men on his right. The men in the room moved swiftly, circling behind us and boxing us in. Alan and some of the others had been waiting outside to help get the children to safety, so we were very outnumbered. One of the men moved forward, and before I could blink, he had a hold of Brigid's arms and had dragged her over to my father. She struggled, trying to get out of his grip, but another man moved to help, holding her so she could get no leverage to escape. The one on the left pinched her wrist, causing her fingers to open and drop her dagger to the floor. The man kicked it away.

I lunged forward, my hand tightening on the sword in my hand, but Duncan grabbed my wrist, squeezing hard. Fighting my instincts to reach out and protect Brigid, I stayed. If my father knew how important she was to me, he would find a way to kill her. Maddock tensed beside me as well, no doubt also ready to move to save Brigid. He looked at me and shook his head minutely, telling me to wait.

"Why are you here, Caelum?" my father asked, his gaze roving over Brigid even as he spoke to me. The curiosity in his gaze as he stared at her made my stomach churn and my head pound with anger. If he touched her, I doubted I could guarantee I would not kill him, despite my words the previous night.

"To rescue the children you've stolen," I said bluntly. There was no doubt in my mind that he knew exactly why we were here, but if he wanted to play this game, we would.

"And if I told you there were no children here?" he asked, walking in a circle around Brigid, still studying her intently, looking her over from head to toe.

"Then we'll just kill you and find where you've taken them," I said with a shrug. Although the thought of killing my father made me sick, I would be able to make the tough decision if needed. It was putting my nerves on edge how closely he was looking at Brigid, and I feared he may already know her secret somehow.

My father paused in his pacing, looking at me before throwing his head back in a loud laugh. "Oh, my boy, you do amuse me."

"I'm glad you find it funny." I found nothing about this situation funny.

"You could never kill me. You don't have the stones." His face turned serious, and he grabbed Brigid, pulling her to him so her back was pressed against his front. He had her chin in a grip so hard that I could see where his fingers dug into her skin. She looked irritated, and I could see her fingers flexing at her side. Quietly, I willed her to keep her talons to herself, lest he discover what she was. Fire surged in my veins, but I took a deep breath through my nose to calm it. How dare he touch her? My father smiled. "Son, there's only one way you and your men are going to live to see another day."

I swallowed hard, fearing the answer to my next question. "Aye? And how's that?"

He squeezed Brigid's face tighter. I saw her wince slightly as she tried to pull away, but her eyes were full of bright fire and anger. "You leave the syren with me."

My stomach dropped, and the room went silent. He knew. Shit.

Eliz
@ELIZIAN

CHAPTER TWENTY-FOUR

"The *what?*" Duncan's voice was outraged as his eyes flashed to mine, glaring. He shifted his sword in his hand, schooling his features and turning his focus back to the men surrounding us. They hadn't restrained any of our men yet, but they still could easily overpower us if they decided to.

Kellan laughed loudly. The sound was grating in my ear, but it distracted from the vice-like grip he had on my face. No doubt, I would have bruises in the shapes of his fingers. "Oh, ho, this is perfect. Your men didn't even know the creature you had in your midst? Keeping secrets from your crew, son?"

Caelum didn't answer right away, his eyes locking with mine. I saw the panic there, the anger. I knew without a doubt that this would cause a rift between Caelum and Duncan, and guilt swirled knowing it would be because of me. Caelum swallowed, moving his gaze to his father. "She's not going anywhere with you."

His father clucked his tongue. "It wasn't really an option. She's coming with me, regardless. I have someone who's very eager to... *meet* her."

Bile rose in my throat. Someone wanted me? What did that mean? I swallowed back the sour taste in my mouth, not wanting to think about the reality I could soon face. From the way Caelum spoke of his father, there was no one Kellan could give me to that would end pleasantly for me.

Rolling my shoulders back as much as I could in Kellan's grip, I made a decision. I would not go with Kellan—not alive, at least.

"You're not taking her fucking anywhere," Caelum growled, his voice low and more angry than I'd ever heard.

"And you think you can stop me?" Kellan's voice was amused as he raised his voice to address the others with us. "You think you and your little friends can stop *me?*"

Maddock's eyes met mine, and I saw the betrayal there. It hurt more than any bruising grip from Kellan ever could. He smiled sadly at me before drawing his sword from the scabbard at his side. "Aye, we do."

"Then you're as delusional as my son," Kellan sneered. He gripped my chin tighter, bending down to put his cheek against mine. "The little syren is...coming...with...me."

"I am not property that you can just take," I gritted out around his tight grip, struggling to pull my face from his grasp. "And neither are those children."

"Ah, she speaks!" his father crooned. He let go of my chin, only to grab my upper arm in his tight grip and spin me around to face him. He lowered his face closer to mine, sneering. "And you *are* property. My property."

I glared at him, my fingers itching to unleash my talons and drag them across his throat. Rearing back slightly, I spat at his face, relishing his grimace as my saliva slid down his cheek. "I will never be the property of men, especially not men like you."

He laughed, shaking his head as he wiped his cheek on his sleeve. "Child, there are no men like me."

"There's always men like you. And I've killed many before. You'll be no different," I snapped, vowing that I would kill this man if it was the last thing I did. I might have to fight Caelum for the privilege, but it would be worth it. Men like this, who believed they were superior to everyone else in the world, were a danger to everyone. And they were everything that syrens were *supposed* to fight against. But this time, I would fight against it. And I would win.

"Sure, darling," he said dismissively. He still held onto me but shifted his focus to Caelum, ignoring me as I continued to struggle. For a man so comparative to size, his grip was strong and unyielding. "Now, run along before you get hurt, son."

"Like you ever cared about hurting me," Caelum snarled, taking a step toward us.

The men on either side of Kellan, one an absolute giant, met Caelum's steps, moving in front of Kellan and me with warning hands raising their own swords up. Wordlessly, I tried to get Caelum to stand down with my eyes. If I could just get free from Kellan's grip, I could do at least *some* damage to him.

"You're right." His father sighed dramatically. "Then I guess we shall have to see who the better man is."

Without another word, his father's men jumped into action, barreling toward Caelum and the others. Metal clanged and flashed as swords met, and a cacophony of grunts and metal meeting metal filled the room. I pulled away from Kellan again, managing to get one of my arms free enough to push against his chest. Beginning the transformation, I willed my talons to extend; flesh began tearing, and blood pooled down my hands as they protruded from my nailbeds.

"Now, now, none of that," he said, looking down at my hands and pulling my arms back down to my sides.

As the others fought, my eyes darted among our men, tracking their movements. Maddock was fighting two men, his sword a blur as he moved back and forth between each of them. Caelum was engaged with another two men, as was Duncan. Alan's men were fighting their own combatants. So far, the fights seemed even, but I feared the numbers game would overpower them soon.

Watching the scene in front of me unfold, worry and nausea swirled in my stomach. His father was going to make me do goddess knows what. Flashbacks to my father telling me he was marrying me off flooded through my mind. I would never be the property of men again. And if I died trying to get away, then that was fine. My life was my own now, and I wouldn't give it to anyone else. I took a deep breath in through my nose, reminding myself that I didn't need to depend on Caelum to keep me safe. I was a syren, after all.

And now that Kellan had let my secret out, it was time to show what I could do.

Pulling my body as hard as I could to yank us to a stop, I tensed the muscles of my neck and flung my head forward toward Kellan's face, grinning at the sickening crunch that resulted. His hand loosened around my arm, and I whirled, yanking my arm the rest of the way out of his grip. I took a step back before raising my leg and kicking at his knee, raking my talons across his face at the same time. Blood spurted out, warm and sticky as it covered my nails and ran down my fingers.

Kellan dropped to one knee, groaning in pain as his hand clapped to his bleeding face. I reared back, readying a punch, when strong arms wrapped around my middle, pinning my arms to my sides and pulling me off my feet. The other man held me there, roughly squeezing me as Kellan rose to his feet, grimacing. He gripped my chin in his hands again, smearing his blood across my face.

"I like that spirit, lass. I cannot wait to break it," he said with a wicked grin. He released my face and looked up at the larger man holding me. "Take her to the ship."

I struggled, but the man was so much larger than me, larger than even Duncan, and I knew I stood no chance. But still, I kicked at his legs and clawed at his arms, attempting to get out of his hold. His flesh shredded under my talons, but he paid no mind. Out of the corner of my eye, I could see Caelum still fighting off other men. Maddock had downed one of his and was now assisting Caelum. Back-to-back, they moved elegantly as they fended off three of Kellan's men with swordsmanship that would have been mesmerizing to watch under any other circumstance.

If they took me, there was no telling what my fate would be. The man lifted me effortlessly, walking behind Caelum's father as he led us to a door at the back of the room I had not seen before.

"Caelum!" a man's voice roared. It was Duncan, I realized after a moment. "They're taking her."

Twisting my neck, I strained to see where Caelum and Duncan were now. I managed to get a brief glimpse over my captor's broad shoulder, seeing both Caelum and Duncan trying to make their way toward me, cutting down anyone in their way. I knew that Caelum didn't want to kill anyone, and I could see he was aiming for non-deadly attacks. Maddock and Finn, one of Alan's men, were still fighting the others.

My captor attempted to walk faster, but I began flailing more strongly than ever. Caelum was right there; I just had to hold out long enough for him to reach me. I had to get away. Whatever happened, I couldn't let this man take me.

"Stop that," the giant brute muttered, tightening his hold on me so much that my fingers began to tingle. "Captain, they're gaining. What do we do?"

"Stop them," Kellan gritted out next to us, holding his hand to his face, trying to staunch the blood. "Give me the girl. You keep them at bay until we're out."

I was roughly set back on my feet, only to be grabbed again by Kellan's bloody hand. The bastard would surely leave even more bruises across my arms, smearing blood where he touched. He pulled me harshly, yanking me off balance, but I continued fighting and struggling against him. I was more evenly matched in strength with him, at least, than I had been with the giant. He cursed under his breath, pulling me even more roughly to him to bend his face toward mine. "This will only end badly for you, girl. Stop struggling."

"Never," I breathed, continuing to pull away from him. I managed to get out of his grip, and I turned to move back into the room just in time to see the giant raise his sword and swing it down toward Caelum. My heart stopped, and I froze. Blood rushed in my ears and my vision tunneled into only seeing that glinting steel arcing down toward the man who was worming his way beneath my skin.

"Captain!" I heard Maddock roar, and I watched Maddock move in what felt like slow motion.

Maddock flung himself in front of the sword just in time. Instead of ripping through Caelum's neck as his father's man intended, it slashed across Maddock's chest, ripping his shirt and his skin open. Blood began to weep from the cut almost instantly, and Maddock swayed for a moment, looking down at his chest before falling to the ground with a loud thump.

Elizi
@ELIZIAN

BRIGID

CHAPTER TWENTY-FIVE

The sound of his body hitting the ground echoed in my ears, and I stood motionless, watching the blood pool on his chest. My ears rang. I could hear nothing of the room around me as I stared at Maddock on the dingy floor.

My shock was all the opening Kellan needed, however, and he took advantage of it and yanked hard. He pulled me off balance and, despite my stumbling, we were moving toward the exit once again. I was forced to tear my gaze from Maddock and turn forward, lest I fall flat on my face.

There was another loud thump behind me, no doubt another body hitting the floor, but I could not turn around to see who it was. I couldn't bear to see who it was. The sight of Mad falling to the floor, his shirt stained crimson, would be burned into my mind forever. I had killed men before, but never like this. And never men that I had *known*. Tears stung my throat and clouded my vision, but I shoved it down, trying to keep from falling as Kellan dragged me down the hall.

Kellan had me by the upper arm, his arm extending backward as he dragged me along. Suddenly, a metallic flash filled my eyes, and a sword was coming down. It connected with the hand holding my arm, severing it at the wrist. I turned my head and saw Caelum, chest heaving and eyes red, holding a bloodied sword. My eyes found their way to the floor, where a severed hand was lying in a quickly forming pool of blood.

Caelum had cut off his father's hand. The hand that had been holding me captive.

Hands found their way to my shoulders again. For a moment, I flinched, ready to fight, but these were familiar hands accompanied by a familiar, if less-than-friendly, voice. "Come on, *syren,* we've got to go."

Duncan. And as grateful as I was to hear his voice, I knew I was not out of the woods with the whole syren thing.

Caelum moved in between me and his father, who was clutching his now handless arm and wailing in pain. Duncan turned me completely around, pushing me gently toward the door. They had dispatched Kellan's men that hadn't rushed to his side, and only we remained. Finn had picked up Maddock, and Duncan moved to help him carry him out as another of Alan's men guided me out of the room. I was numb, unable to form any thoughts or do anything other than let them lead me.

"Is he alive?" I heard Duncan ask behind me, his voice hoarse.

"Aye, for now," came Finn's quiet response. "We need to get him help. Fast."

"Caelum," I managed to croak out after we had taken a few steps, my mind finally catching up with the reality in front of me. I looked around wildly, not seeing him next to us. "We have to help Caelum."

Duncan jerked his head around to look at me, his eyes hard. "He's coming, syren. He's right behind us. But we need to move."

In my haze, the others had led me outside. The sun shone down on my face, but it felt wrong. My face felt cool in some places and warm in others. I raised a hand to my cheek, pulling it away. My fingers were smeared red, and all I could do was stare at the blood on my hand. It meant I had blood on my face, but I knew it was not mine. My heart pounded in my chest, and panic crawled up my throat. I needed to get if off. Get it off. *Get it off.*

I took a deep breath through my mouth, trying to avoid the metallic smell of blood surrounding me. There were more important things to focus on right now, like Maddock bleeding out.

I needed to pull myself together. Now was not the time for my anxiety to resurface. I had seen death before, and I needed to get over it. Shaking my head to clear it, I pulled myself out of Cameron's grasp, holding myself upright and steady. My jaw clenched, and I let it, relishing the feel of my muscles tightening and my teeth grinding together. It gave me something to focus on.

Cameron, Alan, and the rest of his men rushed toward us from an alley around the corner. They stopped short when they saw the scene that awaited them: Maddock's body slung between Finn and Duncan, and the others standing next to a blood-covered woman. Someone brushed up behind me. Caelum.

I turned then, seeking out his face. His eyes were dark and pinched, and his shirt was covered in fine sprays of blood as well. I reached down to grip his fingers, relishing the connection for a moment. "Are you hurt?"

He shook his head, his eyes glassy and far away, before turning to the others, his eyes focusing on Maddock. "We need to get him help. Now."

"There was an apothecary shop down the alley," I croaked out. I cleared my throat. "They should have medical supplies."

Caelum nodded, turning to search the alley. "Move. Now."

In a wordless rush, Maddock was gathered up and we moved as one down the alley. Taking the lead, I burst through the apothecary shop doors, causing the young woman at the counter to jump. "We need help."

Her eyes widened as the rest of them came in through the door behind me. She motioned toward a cushioned couch sitting against the wall. "Yes, lay him there. There's bandages under the counter."

"Alan, Finn, watch the doors," Caelum barked out, pointing as he moved around her, going directly to the counter. The young woman, a petite blonde with her hair pulled back in braids, rushed over to Maddock, who had been set down on the couch.

Without hesitation, she ripped open his shirt, pulling it away from his wound. I winced as the fabric tore away from the dried blood on his stomach.

"Bandages," the woman called out, holding her hand out. Caelum pressed them into her hand in an instant, and she moved to push them onto Maddock's chest, causing him to emit a low groan. "I need water. There's a bucket in the back room. Get it and some cloths."

I stepped back to go fetch it, but Duncan held his hand up, stopping me. His hand was covered in blood. "No, you've done enough, *syren.*"

"Now is not the time for this," Caelum snapped, handing the woman more bandages.

Duncan glared at me before moving out of the way to let me fetch the bucket and bring it back. I handed it to the young woman and stepped back, letting her and Caelum work.

Cameron stepped up between Duncan and I and lowered his voice as he raised an eyebrow. "Syren?"

"Apparently, Brigid here is a syren, like the legends say," Duncan muttered angrily, crossing his arms over his chest. "And Caelum knew about it. *We* had to find out from Kellan."

I rolled my eyes, irritated by the larger man's words. "Get over yourself. You're just mad you didn't figure it out yourself."

Caelum stood and spun around on his heel to face us, his eyes blazing mad. "You two fucking stop it, right now. This is not the fucking time. Maddock is *dying.*"

Duncan glared at me as Caelum turned his attention back to Maddock, stepping away from me to hand the apothecary woman bandages and clean rags. I ducked my head, cheeks burning at Caelum's admonishment. He was right, this wasn't the time to argue with Duncan.

Cameron looked down at me. "You're covered in blood."

I raised my hand to inspect it, realizing my talons were also still out. "I managed to get a swipe in at Kellan."

He raised an eyebrow. "Those are new."

"We're losing him," the young girl's urgent voice jarred us from our conversation, then Cameron was moving toward his friend.

I took a step forward, intent on joining them, but Duncan spun around and pinned me with a glare, stopping me in my tracks at the pure fury there. His lip snarled. "You stay there."

Normally, I would have ignored him and pushed past him with an eye roll, but Maddock was their friend first, and he was injured because of me. I swallowed hard, stepping back and willing my talons to retract. Wincing as they slid back beneath my skin, I crossed my arms over my chest, holding myself together.

More muffled curses filled the room, and bloody bandages and rags fell to the floor with wet plops. Slowly, fewer and fewer movements came from the couch. After a long moment, Caelum stood from his kneeling position and turned to face the rest of us. His eyes were rimmed with red, and blood covered his arms and shirt.

"He's gone." His voice was flat and empty, and it broke my heart.

"I'm sorry I could not save your friend," the young woman said quietly. "He lost too much blood."

Caelum shook his head, turning to look at her. "Thank you for your help. We'll leave you money for the mess."

The woman put her hand on Caelum's forearm, her own arms covered in blood to her elbows. "You won't."

"We need to regroup now, Captain," Duncan said softly, still looking down at Maddock lying on the couch. From the gap between him and Cameron, I could see Maddock's lifeless eyes staring up at the ceiling. I forced myself to look away, focusing back on Duncan. "And we need to bury Mad."

Bile rose, mixing with the tears in my throat. He was dead. *Maddock was dead.*

Caelum nodded, sniffing harshly before wiping at his eyes with his shoulder. It was the only clean part of his shirt. "Aye. Aye, we do."

"Where will we bury him?" I asked, keeping my voice as soft as possible.

Duncan whirled around, stomping toward me. "There is no we. You need to leave. Now."

I didn't say anything, but I also didn't back away from the

hulking man looming over me. He was angry, and rightfully so. But I wouldn't cower to any man.

"Duncan, stop it," Cameron muttered.

"So, you don't care that she's been lying to us since the minute we met?"

"I care that Maddock just died and we need to find somewhere to bury him," Caelum snapped. "We can have this argument later."

Duncan glared at me again, but fell silent.

"What about your old house, Cae?" Cameron asked softly. "In the garden?"

Caelum nodded. "Aye, let's do that."

Carefully, Duncan picked up Maddock from the couch, and we wrapped him in a sheet the young woman provided. In somber silence, I lingered behind the others as we walked through the maze of alleys toward a derelict estate, with vines overgrowing the wooden structure. This was Caelum's house? It must have been where he had grown up. I itched to ask more about it and the history of why it wasn't where he still lived.

Caelum led us to the back of the house, where an overgrown garden sprawled over the estate. He nodded toward a patch of wildflowers. "Set him down there. There should be a shovel in the shed somewhere."

Wordlessly, Cameron went over to the small shed and returned with a shovel, handing it to Caelum. "Do you want us to help?"

"No, I need to do this," Caelum said, his voice watery.

My fingers flexed, itching to reach out to comfort him, but I held back. I had a strong feeling that my touch would not be welcomed by either Caelum or Duncan.

We were all silent as Caelum dug the hole for Maddock to rest. His shoulders heaved with effort, and I watched the blood on his forearms dry to a dark brown and begin flaking against his tan skin. But he never stopped digging and never let anyone take the shovel from him.

After several wordless hours, Maddock was buried among the wildflowers.

"He'd like it here," Cameron said quietly.

Duncan nodded his agreement. "Aye, he would."

Caelum cleared his throat, wiping the sweat from his forehead with his forearm. "We need to find a new place to stay. If my father knew about our plan, he likely knows where we're staying."

Duncan cast a suspicious glance at me. "We need to figure out how he knew we were coming."

"It wasn't me, if that's what you're thinking," I snapped, growing immediately defensive. Did he really think that I was working with *Kellan?* Rage simmered beneath my skin, and I flexed my fingers. As if I would ever work with a man like that. It was a miracle I was choosing to work with men at all.

"My family has a house about an hour's walk from here," Finn volunteered softly, interrupting our glaring session. "It's empty, so we can all stay there. There's no way anyone else will know where it is."

Duncan looked at Caelum, his blue eyes filled with concern. When Caelum didn't answer and kept staring at Maddock's grave, Duncan did. "Aye, let's do that."

Elizi
@ELIZIAN

CHAPTER TWENTY-SIX

After burying Maddock, we all changed out of our bloodstained clothes, bundling them up into a bag and burning them in the fire pit behind the house, and began the trek to Finn's family house. Everyone was quiet and reserved. My own heart was heavy, realizing again that this was likely what they had all been feeling since the wreck. Nausea built in my stomach, wondering how Caelum could even stand to look at me after the deaths of his crew.

Losing people close to me was not something I had experience in. And witnessing this first-hand made my guilt rise even more.

I hadn't spoken to Caelum since we left the house. But then again, Caelum hadn't spoken to anyone, not even Duncan, since we had buried Maddock. Though Duncan and Cameron had continued tossing me glances throughout the walk, I had not spoken to anyone either.

I had a feeling Caelum's silence was guilt and that he was destroying himself over Maddock's death. It was doubtful anything any of us said would convince him it wasn't his fault, but I still did not want him to wallow in misplaced guilt. Maddock's death was the fault of Caelum's father and his men. And me.

All of this was ultimately the fault of syrens. The wreck was our fault. And Maddock's death was partly due to Kellan wanting me. All of it led back to the syrens—back to me.

After about an hour of silent walking, we finally made it to the large but modest cottage sitting in the rolling hills. It was situated on a high plateau overlooking the coast, and the stone of the cottage was covered in a soft green moss. The building was inviting, and I hoped it would be safe for us to regroup. I wanted desperately to sit and rest and check on Caelum.

We entered the house, which was as welcoming on the inside as it was on the outside. It was warm, decorated well, and I could tell it had been lived in and well-loved. There was a large kitchen along one wall, and a massive round wooden table with eight chairs surrounding it. The fireplace in the corner looked cozy. There was a separate living area with another fireplace and two large cushioned chairs.

Everyone gathered in the kitchen, taking seats at the table. I stayed leaning against the wall, watching them. My anxiety was too high to sit, my body wired with energy.

"So, what are we going to do?" Cameron asked quietly from his seat at the table. "How did they know we were coming?"

"And how did they know about Brigid?" Duncan added, glaring at me. At that single look, I knew without a doubt that Duncan blamed me for Maddock's death now too. "*We* didn't even know about Brigid."

"Are we really going to do this now?" Caelum asked, sighing as he sat down. He waved a hand. "Let's go, then. Get it all out there now so we can move on."

The vein in Duncan's forehead throbbed, and he acted on Caelum's permission, stabbing a finger at me. "She is a fucking syren. And if that's true, then we know exactly what we saw when *The Nehalennia* wrecked, don't we?"

"And I saved Caelum from drowning to what? Trick him?" I asked, crossing my arms. I knew my own anger was feeding off Duncan's, but I couldn't help it. He wanted to intimidate me, and I was no longer a scared little girl who could be frightened by men.

He might be able to physically overpower me, but I could take care of myself in a fight. "If I had wanted to do that, I would have killed him in the water."

"I'm missing something here," Alan piped up slowly, looking back and forth between us. From the table, I watched as Caelum rolled his eyes.

"Brigid is a syren," Cameron explained patiently as Duncan and I continued glaring at each other. "You might have heard them called mermaids in old legends."

"They're real?" he asked, his voice going high. "And they really wreck ships like the legends say?"

"Yes, they're very real," Duncan snapped. "She and her ilk wrecked our ship and drowned our crew."

"Then why are *you* still breathing?" I retorted, raising an eyebrow.

"Okay, enough," Caelum said, sighing and pinching his forehead. "That's enough."

"And you," Duncan continued to rage, turning on Caelum, "I'm your best fucking friend. And you couldn't tell me what she was?"

"Would it have mattered?" he asked, his voice defeated. His shoulders slumped and he rubbed at his red eyes. "No matter when you found out, you would have been angry."

"Aye, I would have. Because she *killed* our crew." Spittle flew from Duncan's lips as he spoke. In the corner, Alan and his men watched with rapt interest. Duncan crossed his arms over his broad chest, glaring at Caelum. "Or have you forgotten that?"

Caelum jumped up from the table, his chair screeching across the floor and tipping over. He stepped up chest to chest with Duncan, his eyes hard. "Shut your fucking mouth, Duncan. I've forgotten *nothing*."

"Okay, that's enough," Cameron snapped, standing up from the table to move between them, putting a hand on each of their chests. "Tensions are running high. We all need to calm down. Brigid is a syren, yes, but she's been helping us. So, we need to move past this for now. We can revisit it once we avenge Maddock and save those damn children. Or did you both forget what we're doing here?"

After glaring at Duncan a moment longer, Caelum broke away first, bending down to pick up his chair and sitting back down heavily. He rubbed his forehead. "I'm sorry I didn't tell you all."

"It's not your fault," I said, my voice steadier than I was expecting it to be. "I asked you not to tell anyone."

Cameron sighed as Duncan snapped his attention to me. Duncan advanced toward the table, and I craned my neck to look up at him as he loomed over me. "All of this is your fault, syren."

I shrugged a shoulder, pushing my anxiety at his anger down. If he tried to hurt me, I would defend myself. My talons in my human form could still easily rip through his flesh. But I had a feeling that Duncan just needed to get his anger out of his system. And if I killed his best friend, I very much doubted Caelum would let me live. "That's one way to look at things, I suppose."

"As if there's another way?" he scoffed.

"Okay, we're done," Caelum said, slapping his palm on the table. "I'm the captain, and it was ultimately my decision to keep this information from you all. Now, it's time to get over that, move on, and figure out what our next move will be. Knowing she's a syren before wouldn't have changed what happened in that house. He still would have gone after her to get at me."

"If we'd known, she never would have been with us in the first place," Duncan muttered, stalking over to lean against the wall.

Ignoring Duncan's comment, Caelum spoke again, turning in his chair to face the rest of the room. "Obviously, someone told my father we were planning to go after him in Brinemoor and had us fed false information. It would be a waste of our time trying to figure out who it was."

"Why?" Alan asked, tilting his head. From his spot sitting cross-legged on the floor, added with the head tilt, he looked like a puppy.

"No one would ever give up my father. They're too scared of him," Caelum explained, sighing heavily as he rubbed at his forehead. "We need to find out where he's actually holding the children, and if he even really is selling them, or if that was a lie too."

There was silence. Today had been rough for all of us, and no one knew what to say just yet. These children were important to all of us, and yet we were no closer to stopping his father than we had been before. I was frustrated, and I had only been involved in this mission for a few days. I couldn't imagine how angry the others were.

"We can ask the syrens for help," I offered quietly. If they knew that Caelum's father was aware of our existence, it might be the push needed to get them to help us. I had no idea how I would get back to them or talk to them once I got there, but I would figure it out if it meant stopping his father. As women, and especially as women who had never been associated with Caelum before, we might be less suspicious when we gathered information. "It would give us the element of surprise."

At first, I was unsure if anyone heard me, as the silence only continued. Then Caelum spoke, his voice firm and unyielding. "No."

"But—" I started to protest. They could help us if they were willing. And if Kellan tried to escape via ship, they could help stop him. I just needed to talk to them and try to convince them they were in danger if Kellan continued to live. If children weren't enough to sway their minds, at the very least, their own survival might be.

"No, Brigid. We'll not be going to the others for help," Caelum said firmly. His words drove a dagger deep into my heart. The little progress we had made toward forming a relationship had been ruined with Maddock's death. "And I'll not hear any more discussion of it."

Before I could respond, Caelum turned to Cameron and Duncan, who had somewhat calmed down and joined us at the table, and began talking. Hurt washed through me. It seemed that Caelum had finally discovered that the losses I'd caused outweighed any interest he might have had. Maybe it was for the best. We had only just gotten over the initial hurt to begin exploring our feelings toward each other, and now, it seemed we would never get to continue that. Caelum was done with me.

Out of the corner of my eye, I saw Duncan smirk at Caelum's dismissal of me, quickly hiding it behind his hand. At least someone seemed pleased at the turn of events. But I supposed it would please Duncan for Caelum to rebuke me so publicly.

Caelum's dismissal hurt, but I wouldn't continue speaking where it was obvious my contributions were not wanted. Quickly, all the other men joined in, none of them casting me a second, or even a first, glance. Slowly, it felt like I wasn't even there at all. Standing up from the table, again without anyone so much as looking at me, I moved over to the cushioned chair by the large window that overlooked the hills and ocean down below.

My only course of action was to prove to Caelum that I could help. I understood his pain, I understood his anger, and I would do what I could to rectify the situation, even if he did not want to be around me anymore.

My stomach hurt. Perhaps I should have just ignored Caelum's words and gone with his father. At least then, Maddock would be alive. Duncan likely would have offered the trade himself, given his reactions toward the discovery.

Sitting in the chair, I watched the men talk for what felt like hours. They went through several ideas for how to get back at Caelum's father, then managed to dismiss every single one of them. There just wasn't enough information on his father's operation to be able to make good plans, and Caelum's input seemed intent on avoiding the deaths of any of the rest of his men.

I had to go to my family and at least ask for help. If they could help us, it would provide a way to attack that I doubted Caelum's father would expect. I was on land, something that the legends of syrens often said was impossible. It was likely he assumed I was alone, especially since he hadn't seen any other women with us. If we could get the other syrens to help and keep them under Kellan's radar, it could be an advantage for us.

Day turned into night, and I watched the sun set over the water as the men continued poring over alternatives at the table. Eventually, Cameron stood up and began gathering ingredients to make a pot of stew. Debating for a moment, I rose to help him, moving to wordlessly chop vegetables and passing them to Cameron. He smiled sadly at me as he took them. At least this was something I could do.

As he cooked, I watched the tension in his shoulders and the furrow of his brow. He was hurting; they all were. Once the stew was done, he walked over and handed me a bowl, sympathy in his eyes. I bristled. I wanted him to see me as part of their team, as someone who had good ideas. I wanted him to convince Caelum to listen to my plan. But I knew I couldn't ask that of Cameron. We had grown close, but Cameron had been Caelum's friend first, and we had only known each other for a few days.

Cameron smiled at me sadly, reaching out and tugging on a lock of my hair. "You still have blood in your hair."

I shrugged. "Adds to the aura."

His smile grew slightly wider, his eyes sparkling. "Wash it tonight, and I'll braid it for you in the morning. Now, eat up."

Nodding, I turned to my bowl of stew and ate it, alternating between watching the water through the window and listening in on the continued conversations surrounding Kellan. It had been established that he would have to seek attention for his hand, which would buy us some time, thankfully. But we still didn't have time to dawdle with our plans.

Night fell, and the conversations began to dwindle. The scuffing of chairs brought my attention away from the window and back to the room before me. All the men had stood and were leaving toward the bedrooms.

Caelum walked over to me and stopped, standing above me, an unreadable look on his face. "We won't be sharing a room tonight, lass."

I nodded, having mostly been expecting that due to his anger at the situation I had brought about *and* that we would be sharing space with more people. Even though I had been expecting it, it still brought on some unpleasant emotions that I didn't want to process right now. Just previously, I had been saying that I didn't need to share a room with him, and now I found myself wanting nothing more than that. But maybe it was for the best if we put some distance between us. Maddock's death had brought up emotions that Caelum had likely been shoving down. Losing most of his crew was one thing, but one of his closest friends was a much different matter.

I glanced over at the fireplace and the warm chairs in front of it. Sharing a room with a stranger, or even by myself, was not appealing. I turned back to Caelum. "I'll sleep out here. Give my room to the men."

He stood there a moment longer, as if he wanted to say something further, but he simply nodded and retreated to the room that Cameron and Duncan had previously entered.

Standing briefly, I moved over to the basket sitting next to the fireplace and pulled out a thick wool blanket. I spread it over me and settled back into the cushioned chair to continue watching the water from the window, longing to feel the waves on my skin and smell the salt in the air. I only needed to stay awake long enough that everyone else would be asleep. And then, I would enact my own plan.

Find the syrens and convince them to help.

Elizi
@ELIZIAN

BRIGID

CHAPTER TWENTY-SEVEN

Stepping up to the beach, I took a deep breath, steadying myself. I could only hope that asking them for help would work. If they chose not to help, I wasn't sure what I would do next. Caelum was still angry, mourning, and shooting down every idea that was brought to him, so I needed to make sure my plan was solid before taking it to him. But first, I needed the help of the syrens. We needed the ruthlessness of Maira, the cunning and insightfulness of Kyla. Together, we could stop Kellan, I had no doubt.

I removed my clothing, folding it by the driftwood log before stepping out into the cold water. It washed over my feet, and a shiver moved through my body, but I continued out until the water reached my waist and the ends of my hair floated in the sea. Taking another deep breath, I dipped beneath the water and began my transformation. The magic swept over me, ripping my muscles apart and then merging my legs together and lengthening them into my powerful tail. My fingernails and teeth pushed through my flesh and lengthened to sharp points. My body no longer felt cold, but rather, I was filled with power. The pain washed over me, but I pushed it down, ignoring it. There was no time for my pain.

I needed to help Caelum. I needed to avenge Maddock, save the children, and kill Kellan. Despite what Caelum had said before, I was willing to kill. And I would if needed.

Swimming more into the sea, I swished my tail, stretching and flexing in an attempt to ease the soreness. It had been mere days since I had transformed before our journey to Brinemoor, but after more than ten years of living primarily in my syren form, these past days in my human form had me missing the sea, despite the pain transforming brought me. Flicking my tail again, I swam out into deeper water. The water was dark, light barely filtering down, but I had no trouble seeing.

Without my song, I couldn't call to my family. Cliodhna could sense me in the water, but I was unsure if she would send the others after me or simply ignore my presence. Not wanting to rely on Cliodhna sending the others to me, I swam toward the caves I knew I could not enter. For hours, I waited. The waters were all familiar to me, the rock formations all similar, but not being able to enter this one system marked it as my former home. As time passed, light slowly began to filter down through the surface, a sign that the sun was beginning to rise. Hopefully, they would come soon. Otherwise, I feared for Caelum's reaction when he woke and I was not there.

Or maybe I feared for his lack of reaction.

Thankfully, I didn't have to wait much longer after the sun rose. Within moments, I felt the power of the others nearing. One by one, I could make out their shapes as they exited the caves, swimming toward the surface. First, Kyla appeared, then Maira, Sorcha, and the rest of them. Sorcha swam by, her head turning to take in the water. Her eyes landed on me floating near the outcropping of rocks by the cave. Her eyes widened and she opened her mouth to speak, but I couldn't hear what she said. My heart shattered in my chest. *I couldn't hear her.*

She guided the others toward me until all of them were there, swimming in front of me. Maira's face pinched and her mouth opened. I could tell her words were angry, but I still couldn't hear them. I shook my head at them, pointing to my ears, trying to convey that I could not hear them.

Maira rolled her eyes and fisted her hands at her sides in frustration. If she had legs, I'm sure she would have stomped her foot. She pointed roughly to the surface and then took off, blasting through the water and leaving a trail of bubbles behind.

Kyla looked at me, her gaze kind but closed off, before she too took to the surface. One by one, they followed. Sorcha pulled me into a quick hug before leaving as well. I closed my eyes briefly to center myself. I needed to be my best when I faced them again; I needed them to understand me. My hurt would need to wait, so I pushed it down, down, down as I swam up toward the surface.

Breaching the waves, the cold air stung against my wet face and hair. The others were waiting for me.

"Can you hear us now?" Maira snapped.

I nodded, keeping my face neutral. "Aye, yes. I can hear now."

I couldn't help but notice that Cliodhna wasn't among them. While I hadn't expected her to be, I had been hopeful. I wanted our queen's approval and forgiveness. If she was sympathetic, maybe the others would be as well. With Cliodhna's power, we would have the best chance possible to stop Caelum's father.

Maira spoke again before I could. "What do you want, then?"

"I need your help," I admitted. "And I know you owe me nothing, not after what I did. But there is a man using the seas and his power to steal children and sell them. I am working to try to stop him, and I need your help."

"Why should *we* help you?" she demanded, her eyebrows furrowing. "You abandoned us for that man you saved on the beach. Go seek help from the other humans."

A pang of guilt pierced through my heart, my anger building in contradiction. While I wanted nothing more than to give them all a verbal lashing for being so quick to dismiss me as a traitor, I needed their help. And making them angry would only succeed in getting them to say no even faster. "Aye, I know. I needed to save him for my own reasons, and I understand that my actions hurt you. I apologize for that."

"So, you think you can come back and offer an apology and we will just jump to help you with your new priorities?" Maira asked.

"No, I don't think that," I replied. And it was the truth. I didn't expect them to help me, but I did hope they would. I hoped they would remember what it was like to feel human, to want to protect those less fortunate. We had all been victims, and I hoped they would understand the plight of these children. "I do hope that you will help. I hope that you will show the world that you are good and kind, as I know you are. I will respect your choice, though; I know this is my fight, not yours."

"And these children, tell me, are they girls? Or are they boys?" Her lip curled up on the last word. After years of violence at the hand of men, and even more years under Cliodhna's rule, Maira truly distrusted and vilified men in any form. At one time, I would have agreed with her. But Caelum, Duncan, Maddock, and Cameron had begun to change my mind.

"Mostly boys, but the man taking them isn't entirely discerning," I said quietly. I knew that could very well change their minds, but I would give them all the information and then accept their decision, whatever it was. I could only hope the past decade we had spent together meant *something* to them, like it had for me.

"We will not help you rescue children who will one day grow up to be the very men we punish," Maira spat. "And I cannot believe that you would be willing to do this. You've changed. And you've betrayed everything that our queen has done for us."

A pang of hurt went through my heart. I'd known they would label me as a traitor, yet hearing it aloud was another thing entirely. I didn't feel like a traitor. I felt like a woman fighting for what was right and trying to make up for the mistakes I had made. Was I a traitor? If so many people—the syrens, even Duncan—thought I was one, did that make it true?

"I am not betraying you," I said, my voice quiet but firm. "I am doing what is right."

"According to whom?" she snarled, moving closer to me. "Because according to our queen, the right thing to do would have been to kill that man when you saw him in the water."

"I've told you why I wouldn't, and I'll not keep explaining that decision," I said, just as angry now. "But I've come to you all for help to save children, and you're using my decisions as an excuse to not act."

"Now, wait," Maira started, raising her hand.

Kyla swam between us, holding a calming hand out toward each of us. "Calm, sisters. Maira, we will hear her out. Brigid, you say this man is stealing children? And selling them?"

I swallowed my anger, looking into the calming amber eyes of Kyla. "Aye, he's stealing orphans and children who have no one to miss them. We don't know why he's selling them or to whom, but we tried to stop him ourselves. It...didn't go well."

Kyla tilted her head, studying me. "The children remind you of yourself."

A lump formed in my throat, hot and leaden. She was right. I knew what it felt like to be treated as property, to be taken and sold to further someone else's agenda. To be forgotten. "Aye."

"What happened when you tried to stop him?" she questioned. I noticed that Maira's own anger had softened slightly as well, and she simply floated behind Kyla, watching me.

"One of the men was lost. And the man we were trying to stop knew I was a syren. He tried to trade me for their safety."

"He knew you were a syren?" Kyla seemed shocked. "But how?"

I shook my head. "I couldn't find out. There was too much violence, and we were trying to escape. But I cannot let children be punished for the sins of adults. I must help them. And I can't do it alone."

"We'll not help you, Brigid," Kyla said softly after a long silence. "We sympathize, me especially, and wish you well, but we won't get involved in the troubles of men. And we can protect ourselves down here. *Neamh na Mara* is a safe place for us."

I nodded my head, sad but understanding. I wouldn't push them further; I had my answer. If any of them would have agreed to help, apart from Sorcha, it would have been Kyla. She had a soft spot for children, and her motherly instinct had survived her transformation to deadly syren. "Thank you for listening to me. And I am truly sorry for leaving before."

Kyla simply nodded back before they all turned and swam away as one, disappearing beneath the waves.

Dejected, I turned to leave. Caelum had been right, my family was not an option. Maybe they never had been. Pushing my fingers through the plants rising from the ocean floor, I swished my tail, watching the bubbles it created.

"I'll help you, Brigid," a soft voice came from behind me.

I whirled around. Sorcha floated there in front of me, a small smile on her face. Tentatively, I raised a questioning brow. I had considered asking her directly, but didn't want to draw attention to her in front of Maira. "Why did you stay behind?"

She looked over her shoulder at where the others had retreated, no doubt heading back to the caves. "You're right. The minute we let children suffer for the sins of adults, we've lost. I told you before you left that I thought some men were innocent. You working with your man and the others proves my point. I want to help you."

My heart squeezed. After our long nights of conversations and her adamant defense of innocent men, I had hoped Sorcha would want to help. Her friendship filled me with gratitude. I swam up to her, looking at her for a long moment before I surged forward and wrapped my arms tightly around her neck.

"Thank you," I whispered into her hair, breathing in the briny scent that saturated her hair. "Truly."

"Now, stop weeping. Tell me what's going on," she said, hugging me back just as tightly. "Take me to where you're staying."

I released her and then we swam back up toward the shore by the cottage. As we neared the shallow water, our heads broke the surface. Reaching out through the cold water, I found her hand, squeezing it. "I have clothes for us if you want to transform. Have you done that yet?"

"Aye." She nodded. "Once before. I'm glad you brought clothes. I hadn't even thought about bringing some with me."

I smiled. "I figured as much. It's hard to remember to bring them after being without them for so long. Let's change and put some clothes on. I don't want you to be alarmed, but my transformation will be painful."

"Is it...bad?" she asked, worry playing across her features.

Placing a hand on her arm, I tried to reassure her. "I'll be all right. It's nothing I can't handle. I just didn't want it to surprise you."

We both transformed there in the shallows, tails morphing and splitting into equally strong legs. Stepping out of the icy water, we both shivered as the wind whipped across our skin. I reached for the bag of clothing sitting by the driftwood log on the shore. Taking out black pants and a cream sweater for me, I handed her the bag. Dressing quickly to get out of the wind, I sat down on the wood and watched as Sorcha dressed in something similar, her sweater about five sizes too big for her.

She sat down next to me. "So, are we going back to wherever you're staying?"

I looked over my shoulder at the cottage and let out a sigh. Caelum was still angry with me, and until I could talk to him and apologize for getting Maddock killed, I couldn't face him, let alone face him with another syren. I looked back at Sorcha. "No, we can stay here for a bit if you're okay with that. We can just talk, like we used to. The sun just rose, we have a few hours before anyone will come looking for me—if they do at all."

Her head tilted to the side, and her eyes drilled into me. "What's happened?"

I pushed my hair behind my ears, shivering slightly as the water from the strands ran down my back. "I...it's my fault one of their men, Maddock, died. Add in the wreck as well...and I think the reality that I was the cause for so much of their pain has finally sunk in with the man I saved. I expect he's still angry with me."

"Was it your fault?" she asked. "Did you deliver the blow that killed him?"

"No, of course not." I shook my head vigorously. "He was killed by one of Kellan's men. That's Caelum's father."

"Then how is it your fault?" Her voice was quiet.

Looking down at my lap, I twisted my fingers together, a habit I had picked up from the girl in front of me, a girl who was wise beyond her young age. "The ship wrecked because of us, and with no one else to blame, they blame me. Caelum's father wanted me. That's what started the fight that killed Maddock. How could they not blame me?"

"They cannot blame you for the actions of another," she said, twining our fingers together. She squeezed them gently. "And if they do, since when do you cower to the anger of men?"

I couldn't help but laugh, a loud noise that startled even me. "You're right, little one. You're right."

She smiled reassuringly at me as if she was seeing why I didn't want to go back to the cottage. She reached out and squeezed my hand briefly before letting it go. "Aye, I know I am. Now, tell me everything that's happened since you pulled him up on that beach. Don't leave out a single thing."

Elizianna
@ELIZIANNA.THE.ONE

CAELUM

CHAPTER TWENTY-EIGHT

I woke up to the sound of Duncan snoring like a bear. Why had I decided to punish myself and share a room with him and Cameron? *Oh, that's right, because another one of your friends died yesterday and you wanted to be near the remaining ones.*

The image of Maddock being sliced down by a sword meant for me would haunt my nightmares forever, I was sure. His death had been my fault, and I wasn't sure if I could ever forgive myself. The deaths of the crew, that had been bad enough, but I knew now that we hadn't been targeted specifically, just attacked at the whims of an ocean queen. But Maddock's death? That had been my fault. It had been my idea to go after my father, to go into that house, and now my friend was dead.

Sighing heavily, I ran my hands over my face before pushing my hair back out of my eyes. I needed to get up and go check on Brigid. I had wanted to give her space last night, space from me and my sour mood. Likely, she was furious with me for leaving her alone, but I didn't want her around my negativity. I only hoped she was okay and willing to forgive me.

I stood, dressing quickly before I walked across the hall into the room that we had decided would be hers. It was empty. No, it didn't even look like it had been slept in at all. My heart began racing.

Had she left? Had she abandoned our mission and left us? Where had she gone? Was Duncan right? My thoughts swirled, and I tried to catch my breath as I searched the room for any sign that she had been there.

When I had gone to bed last night, she had been wrapped in a blanket, sitting in the chair by the window. Maybe she had fallen asleep there. Trying not to panic, I walked quickly into the main living area, my eyes scanning the room. Apart from Alan, putting a kettle on the stove, it was empty. The chair was empty, the blanket Brigid had been curled up in last night flung across the back. I rushed over and picked it up. It was cold; she had been gone a while. Where was she?

I turned to Alan. "Was Brigid out here when you woke up?"

"No; I think I heard her moving around in the middle of the night, though. Thought I heard a door shut. Maybe she went outside?" he asked, shrugging as if it was no bother to him where she had gone. The man had no sense of urgency in anything he did.

"And you didn't think to wake one of us up and tell us she had gone?" I asked, my anger rising. My father wanted her. She shouldn't be alone. Again, I cursed myself for not sharing a room with her. I should have been there to protect her. I had failed. *Again.*

He shrugged again, and my blood began to boil. He turned, taking the kettle off the fire and pouring the boiling water into a cup. "I just figured she wanted some fresh air. Plus, I didn't want to go after her. I'm still wrapping my head around the whole syren thing."

I bit my cheek to keep from saying something that I would regret later. Instead, I turned on my heel and stalked back to the room. I slapped Duncan roughly on the shoulder before doing the same to Cameron a bit more gently. "Wake up."

They grumbled but opened their eyes. Duncan spoke first, "Wha'dya want, Caelum?"

"Brigid is gone." Just saying it out loud made my heart pound in my chest. I ran a hand through my hair, anxiety skyrocketing.

Cameron sat up, his eyes wide and no longer holding sleep. He at least had come to care for Brigid and her safety. "Where'd she go?"

"If I knew that, I would have her back here," I retorted. I took a deep breath. Cameron had not taken her; my anger at him was unwarranted. "Alan says he heard her leave in the middle of the night."

Duncan eyed me, the suspicion clear. "Do you think she just left?"

I sat down forcefully on the bed, my mind racing with a hundred different possibilities. Irritation bubbled, lodging beneath my ribs, right next to the tight ball of worry. "I don't know why she would have. After yesterday, I'm more certain than ever that she wasn't working with my father, like you suggested. But I don't know what happened, and she's not in the house."

"Maybe she just needed some space," Cameron suggested, rubbing at his eyes.

"Space from what?" Duncan asked, scoffing. "She's a bloody syren, what could she possibly need space from?"

"Space from you being a giant arsehole?" Cameron asked angrily. "Since you found out what she was, you've been nothing but mean. She saved Caelum. She's been helping us. That has to count for something. She told us why she did what she did. I know she had a hand in our friend's deaths, but can you blame her? If any of us had gone through what she had, we likely would have lashed out at those responsible just the same. Since she's joined us, she's done everything she can to help us. Do not keep punishing her for the choices she made to stay alive."

Duncan looked ashamed, and rightfully so. Cameron had put into words what I had been thinking since the day we had lost Maddock. We were allowed to be angry and grieve those we had lost, but Brigid, right or not, had been trying to make amends for her actions and the actions of her fellow syrens.

Cameron turned his eyes back to me. "But Caelum, what if she really did just need some space from all this? She watched a man die yesterday, and watched you cut off a hand that was holding her. That's got to have rattled her at least a little bit."

"We need to find her," I said, ignoring their suggestion. If she needed space, she should have just bloody stayed in the living area and not gone wandering outside. "My father wants her for some reason. We can't let him get her."

They both nodded before dressing and following me out back into the main living space. Alan and Finn were both out there, eating their breakfast.

Alan looked at me, finally seeming at least slightly concerned. "You lot still going on about Brigid? I'm sure she's fine."

"We need to find her," I gritted out, still angry at the man. "My father just tried to kidnap her, so we can't have her just wandering off on her own."

"Let's split up. We can just look around the property," Duncan suggested, despite his body language being obviously unconcerned. I wasn't sure what angered me more, Duncan's intentional lack of concern, or Alan's lack of attention.

I nodded, not trusting myself to say something that wouldn't be angry, then turned and walked out of the house. I was furious with her, and when I found her, I would be letting her know. I had just lost one friend to my father; I couldn't lose her as well.

Knowing Brigid, she had likely headed down to the shore if she truly had wanted space. I turned my footsteps down the hill and toward the water. Trudging down the grassy bank, I tried to settle my anger. As I neared the shore, I saw her. My breath left my chest in a heavy, relieved sigh. She was okay.

The closer I got, I saw that she was sitting on a driftwood log, and she wasn't alone. A smaller figure sat next to her, with long dark hair cascading over her back and shoulders. Their hands were clasped together in Brigid's lap. Who was she? Was she a syren?

My vision turned red. She had gone back to the syrens despite my instructions. Why couldn't she just listen to me? I was trying to keep her *safe,* and she was dead set against it.

"Brigid!" I yelled. I would figure out the identity of this new woman later; for now, I needed to talk some sense into this woman.

She turned at my voice, her eyes alight. She was happy to see me. But then, as quickly as it had appeared, her eyes and face turned blank, shutting down. I furrowed my brow. What had happened in the course of a night? I got even closer, my boots crunching against the rocks of the shore.

"Caelum," she said, her voice calm and her face still blank. "Is everything okay?"

My blood began to boil again. She had the nerve to ask if everything was okay? After I had just nearly lost my mind at the thought of her missing or in my father's hands? "No, it's bloody well not okay. Why did you leave?"

Her eyes turned to molten flames and narrowed, an eyebrow raising. "I wasn't aware I needed permission from you to go places."

"You do when my father just tried to kidnap you yesterday," I said bluntly. Taking a deep breath, I forced myself to calm down and at least try to approach things rationally. "Now, tell me why you left."

"I went to the others to ask for help," she said. Her tone was so casual, and it irritated me even more.

"I told you not to do that." *Explicitly,* I wanted to add. Out of the corner of my eye, the other girl's lips twitched into a smile as she watched us.

"Did I miss the announcement that I was under your control?" she asked, now seething mad. Her forehead furrowed, and she released the other girl's hands to ball her own into fists.

Shit. That came out wrong. I pushed a hand through my hair, trying to calm down. She was safe, it was fine, there was no need to worry anymore. "No, that's not what I meant."

"Then what did you mean, Caelum?" she asked, arching an eyebrow as her forehead smoothed out. Tension and distrust still radiated from her, though, as if she were afraid I might explode at her again. I didn't like that.

The girl sitting next to her sniffled, reminding me of her presence. Good. The distraction of another person would help me calm down. I turned to the other girl, trying to calm myself. "I'm Caelum. What's your name?"

She also arched an eyebrow at me. "I know who you are. And I'm Sorcha."

"So, you're here to help?" I asked, shocked that any of them had actually agreed to it.

She nodded, her dark eyes full of amusement. "Aye, I am. Now, please continue on with Brigid. I'm sure we'll get to know each other later."

"Aye, thank you, Sorcha," Brigid said, her voice frosty. "Now, what did you mean by that, Caelum?"

I sighed heavily. "I just meant that I thought we had decided that wasn't an option we would be exploring."

"And who is 'we?' Because I certainly wasn't included in that decision."

"Can we just go back to the house?" I asked. I was doing this all wrong and making her angry when I had truly just been worried. Well, maybe I had been a little angry.

"No, I'm fine here," she said, crossing her arms. "Please, explain why I wasn't allowed to go seek out my family's help."

"Because I knew they would say no," I admitted. I kicked a rock at my feet. "And I didn't like how they had treated you."

Both of her eyebrows shot up. "You didn't like how they had treated me? That's why you didn't want me to ask them for help?"

"Well, yeah. That, and I figured they would say no anyway, and I would have rather spent our energy on solutions that actually had a possibility." I shrugged, not enjoying explaining my reasoning. I wasn't used to explaining myself, but Brigid had me doing it more often than ever. Looking at her, at her narrowed eyes and arched brows, the words just kept spilling out of my lips. "And what if they had kept you? What if they hadn't let you return to me? To us?"

"Caelum, Sorcha is here. She said yes to helping us." Her voice softened as she studied me, and I felt like pulling her into my arms just to reassure myself that she was really here. "And I'm safe. I'm back, and I'm safe, and we're going to save those children and stop your father."

"Aye," I acknowledged. "But that's not your whole family, lass.

That's one of, what did you say, eight? That's not exactly going to help us defeat the man."

"No, but it can give us another set of hands and perspective," she said. She looked at her friend. "Sorcha, tell him your idea."

I raised an eyebrow and turned to the younger girl. "Your idea?"

"Don't look so shocked. I do have a brain," she said, smiling. "And aye, my idea. We need information on your father's operations, but obviously, he knows you're looking for it. So, instead of trying to pick it up from the ramblings of drunk fools, I say we go straight to the source."

"That wouldn't work," I replied with a sigh, leaning forward with my elbows on my knees. It had been one of the first ideas we had pitched last night, but my father had likely instructed anyone with any knowledge of his plans to be on the guard for me and my men trying to get to them. "My men would never get anywhere close."

"I'm not a man," she replied, grinning wickedly. Instantly, I understood why she and Brigid were close. "I can go in. They don't know me, they wouldn't suspect me. We grab one of your father's men, preferably one close to him, and we question him. While your father might change plans once he realizes we have one of his men, he can't change them that much. There's only so many places he can take a group of children without being noticed or stopped."

That was...actually brilliant. I was kicking myself for not having thought of it. I simply stared at her. She was young, but she obviously knew something about this kind of business. I wondered what her story was.

"Aye, you'll catch flies if you leave your mouth open," she teased, reaching over to tap the underside of my chin. "Just say thanks, and let's get to work."

I grinned at her. "Aye, little one, let's get to work."

Elizi
@ELIZIAN

BRIGID

CHAPTER TWENTY-NINE

As we made our way back to the cottage, I was still fuming over how Caelum had burst onto the beach, angry and talking to me like I was disobeying him. Had Caelum even noticed that I was gone last night? Had his anger at the beach been fueled by worry, or was I truly nothing more than another person to watch out for after Maddock's death?

As we entered the cottage, Duncan and Cameron were standing just inside the door. Alan and his men were seated at the kitchen table. All heads snapped our way when we stepped over the threshold.

Cameron's face transformed, his forehead smoothing out and his lips turning up so far it had to hurt his cheeks. He continued to grin widely, looking over my head to Caelum behind me. "You found her."

"I wasn't lost," I grumbled, stepping to the side and allowing Caelum to pass by me. Sorcha came in behind him, moving to stand close to my side.

"Well, we didn't know where you went," Cameron said, not letting my surly mood affect him at all. He looked at Sorcha, curiosity in his blue eyes. "And who's this?"

Before I could introduce Sorcha, Duncan stepped around Cam. Unlike Cameron, his face was still as stoic as ever, his brow furrowed and his arms crossed. "Are you okay? Where did you go off to?"

My eyebrows shot up, mirroring the shock I felt. Quickly, I schooled my features, leaving one brow arched in defiance. Duncan had cared little about my safety after finding out I was a syren, and likely was more concerned over his ridiculous notion I was working with Caelum's father. My voice was steel as I spoke. "I went down to the beach. No nefarious intent, so don't worry your head over it. I promise I wasn't secretly plotting with Caelum's father or any other enemies."

Duncan reeled back as if I had struck him. The shock on his face looked genuine enough that it gave me pause. His voice was softer when he spoke next. "That's not what I meant. We were worried for you, that's all."

I didn't have it in me to have it out with Duncan again. My emotional state, already fragile from yesterday's events, had only been made worse by Caelum's piss-poor attitude. I couldn't deal with the big man's suspicion and anger—or worse, his pretending to care about me. Instead of replying, I turned my focus back to Cameron, physically turning away from Duncan. "This is Sorcha. She's another syren, and she's agreed to help us rescue the children."

"There's more of you?" Alan exclaimed from the table, his voice high.

"Yes," I said, exasperated. Alan was a nice man, but he seemed to have fallen off the rigging a few too many times. "There are eight of us."

"Have your crisis later, Alan," Caelum said with a sigh, stopping whatever reply had been about to come from the other man. "Sorcha is here to help, and she's already got a new plan to find reliable information on my father."

"We're trusting her?" Duncan asked, his voice softer but still harsh.

Anger burned in my veins, and I rolled my eyes. If Duncan wanted to be venomous toward me, that was one thing. But Sorcha would not be the subject of his anger or suspicion. I would not allow it. "She's not in league with his father either. And she's likely the only syren who's never killed someone. So, if you're going to trust any of us, it should be her. Now, get over yourself. Do you want our help or not? Because if not, we'll leave and go stop him on our own while you all sit up all night and talk the issue to death again."

Duncan looked almost...amused? He turned to Caelum. "Was this the fire you had mentioned?"

Caelum grinned, though it didn't quite reach his eyes. "Aye."

I huffed and crossed my arms but didn't respond. I had been slightly nervous around Caelum's men before, but after the events at the house, my mind had other things to worry about. Caelum had made it clear there would be no more future for us, so my focus was on saving the children, then getting them and myself to the contact in Bhodheas, who could help us all start over.

"Let's all eat something, and we can discuss Sorcha's plan," Cameron said, guiding Sorcha over to the table to sit.

I was still upset and hurt by Caelum's indifference, and despite wanting to move on from it, wanting to ignore the knot of pain in the center of my chest, I couldn't. Caelum would likely want me to continue helping to save the children, of course, and I would. But afterwards, I could almost imagine the conversation we would have and him telling me to leave. It didn't sit well with me.

Add to that how upset he had been with me over my going to my family for help, I wasn't exactly keen to speak with him or sit at the table and pretend along with him. Without another word, I turned and went back to the chair I had occupied last night, wrapping myself back in the blanket and sitting to watch the sun continue to rise over the water, painting the blue waves with streaks of red. Sorcha would be able to tell them her plan, her ideas. She was well-spoken and seemed confident sitting there between Cameron and Caelum.

I watched from the chair as they all ate and talked, studying their interactions with my friend. They asked Sorcha about herself, and I was surprised at how comfortable she was, answering their questions as if it were nothing to her. She kept darting glances at me, though, and I saw worry in her eyes. After the third or fourth time, I realized she was not looking to me for comfort, but looking at me as if she were worried about me.

I nodded my head slowly at her, reassuring her that I was okay. She needn't be worried about me. I knew I needed to get up and contribute to the conversation, to ease Sorcha into the new environment, but I couldn't. So, instead, I watched from the chair, focusing on their words and letting them wash over me. If I needed to jump in, I would be ready.

"Brigid, you well?" Caelum asked, coming over to perch on the arm of the chair. He had also been quiet while the others talked to Sorcha. I hadn't heard him approach until he was already upon me.

Looking up at him, I could see the concern shining in his green eyes. I was sure to keep my own expression blank and not betray the swirling emotions I was still sifting through regarding him. Inclining my head slightly, I replied, "Yes. Are you?"

He raised an eyebrow, looking down at me with an unreadable expression. Holding out a hand, he nodded toward the door. "You want to go for a walk with me?"

After a moment of just looking at him, trying and failing to read the emotions on his face, I nodded. I supposed we would eventually have to discuss things, no matter how much I didn't want to. Maybe it would be better to get it over with now. Standing from the chair and ignoring his hand, I turned to him. "Sure. Where do you want to go?"

"Just down the hill, I suppose," he said with a shrug, dropping his hand back down to his side. He tucked them into his pockets, but I could see them balled into fists.

Wordlessly, I stood, offering a nod to Sorcha as she glanced at me walking toward the door. She returned the nod, smiling reassuringly and flicking her eyes to Cameron. He followed. While I felt slightly bad about leaving Sorcha with a room full of strange men, I knew Cameron would protect her if need be.

Sorcha had been laughing and talking with them comfortably

when I left, something I was insanely jealous of. I wished that I could have been like that, opening up to them so quickly, with no secrets or fears. Maybe it would have saved us the trouble Caelum and I were in now.

We walked down the winding path, walking through the grass and feeling the wind whip across the knoll. Neither of us said anything as we walked. My body felt as though lightning was passing through it. Every muscle was tensed, waiting for the words to come from Caelum's mouth that would surely break my heart. His shoulders were tight and bunched up around his ears as he walked. Maybe he was building up the nerve. A small part of me hoped it was as agonizing for him to think about as it was for me.

After a moment, he stopped walking. We were at the peak of the hill, looking down at the water a short way below us. Standing side by side, it was a peaceful moment, yet my emotions were still churning inside me, begging to be let out. I had saved Caelum, turned against my own kind for him, and had done so more than once. And he didn't seem to care. Granted, I didn't blame him.

"I'm sorry about Maddock's death," I said quietly, breaking the silence. I needed to get the words off my chest. "I know he was a good friend to you."

His eyes were sad as he turned to look at me. "He was a good friend. I had known him for years."

I heard the intention beneath his words. *I had known him for years, and I have known you for seconds. You cannot compare to that.* I took a deep breath. "Aye, friendships like that are important."

"His mind was brilliant. He was always analyzing, always looking for a way around things," he said, a fond smile spreading across his face. It dropped suddenly, his eyes sad again. "Maybe if he was still here, we already would have found a way to stop my father."

"You'll find a way," I said immediately. I closed my mouth, swallowing hard, hating how quick I was to reassure him, to comfort him.

Looking up from his boots, he offered me a kind of half-smile that I knew was more polite than anything. "Thank you. I think we will, especially if we can make Sorcha's plan work."

"Aye, she's a smart lass," I agreed, wrapping my arms around my chest. This conversation was painful. The small, polite words that meant absolutely nothing were like knives beneath my skin. *Just tell me,* I wanted to scream at him. I wanted this over with so I could bottle my emotions back up and shove them down behind my indifference.

Caelum didn't reply. He didn't say anything for a long moment, just looking out at the seas beneath the hill. After what felt like a lifetime, he took a deep breath, letting it out harshly and all at once. "I hate that he's dead."

"I'm sorry for your loss," I said, my voice mechanical.

He looked over to me, his brows wrinkling in confusion. "What's wrong, Brigid? You're acting strange."

On instinct, I went to protest, but stopped myself. I hugged myself tighter, as if I could hold myself together and keep from falling apart. "I'm sorry."

"For what?" he asked, stepping over in front of me and holding my arms. I closed my eyes, relishing the heat of his hands against me.

"It's my fault he's dead," I said, my voice barely over a whisper. I was afraid that if I spoke any louder, I wouldn't be able to hold myself back from crying. I hadn't cried in years, and I didn't want this first time to be in front of Caelum and out of pity for myself.

He looked at me, his face void of emotion. For a moment, I thought perhaps he had not heard me. As I was about to speak again, his hands tightened around my arms. "No."

"I know you don't believe that," I muttered, looking down at my feet. My stomach was twisted up in knots over the idea of losing Caelum. Not that I ever really had him in the first place. I had wanted him, though—desperately.

"Believe what?" he asked, his voice exasperated. "What is there to believe or not believe?"

"It was my fault," I explained, still looking down. I could not bring myself to meet his gaze, to see the pain in his eyes over his friend. Did he want me to own up to it? I would if that would make it easier for him. "If your father hadn't been after me and grabbed me, Maddock would still be alive."

Suddenly, one of his hands released my arm and moved to gently cup my cheek. Raising my face, I found his eyes staring intently into my own. "Brigid, that is absolutely not true. The only fault for Maddock's death lies with my father and that giant tree of a man that killed him."

Now I was the one confused. My face scrunched up as I looked at him. For days, he had been angry, avoiding me. What else could have been the reason? "Then why have you been avoiding me? If you didn't blame me for his death..."

He laughed, but there was no humor in it. He squeezed my arm again before moving the hand holding my chin to cup my cheek. His touch was so gentle now, it made me want to cry. "Lass, I wasn't avoiding you. I was blaming myself and mourning the loss of a friend, and I didn't want you around my sore mood."

"Oh." I swallowed, nodding. His explanation made sense, but at the same time, it didn't. There had to be more than that to explain why he had been completely avoiding me and acting as if I was invisible. "I...I don't understand."

"Understand what?"

I took a deep breath, trying to calm myself and form the right words. "I thought you were bringing me out here to tell me you didn't want anything to do with me anymore."

He blinked at me. "What?"

I huffed out a small laugh, pulling myself from his grip and wrapping my arms around my middle once again. As if it would protect me from Caelum breaking my heart. "I would still help you stop your father, obviously, but I was expecting you to tell me that once that's over, you want me to leave."

"No. No, I heard you, *teine,*" he said, shaking his head. He blew out a rough breath. "Why would you think that?"

"Maddock's death, you not wanting to share a room, you not speaking to me, you dismissing my ideas and treating me as if I'm invisible..." My words came out too fast, jumbling together. I took a deep breath again. "It all seemed as if you were shutting down, shutting me out, and getting ready to tell me to leave. I thought that was why you wanted to come out here to talk."

"Brigid...I don't blame you for his death," he said, stepping forward. He was so close to me now that only a sliver of air could pass between where our bodies stood.

"But the wreck was," I pointed out. I was screaming at myself to stop talking, to stop giving Caelum reasons to want me to leave, but I couldn't help myself. "You've said that yourself."

He looked at me for a long moment. "You didn't decide to wreck the ship. You didn't decide to kill my men. That was your queen."

"But I still did it."

"Do you want me to hate you, Brigid?" he asked, letting his hand fall away from my face. He took a step back, running his hand over his hair. "Do you want to leave? If you do, just say so."

"I'm being realistic here, Caelum," I said, my voice thankfully steady and not betraying how badly my emotions were swirling.

"No, you're trying to push me away," he said, stepping back up into my space. "You think that you get to tell me what I want and decide what's best for me, but you don't. Only I get to do that."

"Then what's best for you?"

"I don't know, *teine,* but I'd like the chance to find out if it's you." He stepped even closer, our bodies now touching, my chest pressed against his sternum.

Hope rose in my chest where we touched, warming me from the inside out and pulling a smile across my face. He still wanted me. And I still wanted him. Despite all the challenges facing us, maybe we could make this work.

"You really don't blame me for his death?" Despite the optimism fueling my body, I had to be sure.

He raised a hand and gently pushed a loose strand of hair back behind my ear, letting his fingers trail across my cheekbone. "The only person I blame for this is myself."

"But his death wasn't your fault either. You know that, right?"

He smiled at that—a small smile, but it was there. "Aye, I know that, but it doesn't help the feelings, as you well know. I'm sorry, *teine*. And I'm sorry about yelling at you this morning. I was just worried."

"We'll make sure they pay for what they did," I promised, reaching up to place my hand on his face. Our eyes locked, and the promise swirling in his eyes was enough to make my knees weak. Then I registered the rest of his words, and my brows furrowed. "Worried? Why would you be worried?"

"Oh, I don't know, maybe because my father obviously wants something to do with you," he said, his face and tone exasperated as he looked down at me, letting his hand fall from my face to hold me around the waist. "I know you're a big, bad fish lady, but my father is an evil man. I was worried he had found and taken you."

My heart clenched at his worry. While I knew his father still wanted me for some reason, I hadn't considered that he would have still been searching for me. And more, I hadn't considered it a threat.

"You really have no care for your own safety, do you?"

I grinned viciously at his words, baring my teeth. "Not really, no. I never needed to be concerned after I became a syren. I was one of the most dangerous things in the ocean, and I never ventured onto land often."

"Aye," he said, releasing my face and slinging one arm around my shoulders, pulling me into him. "Well, you're mostly on land for now, so get used to the concern. You need to watch out for yourself more."

His concern touched me, made my heart flutter and my stomach twist. I studied him, seeing the worry etched in the lines on his face. I reached up to put my hand on his cheek, running my thumb over his rough skin and beard, relishing the feel of him beneath my hand. He smiled down at me, something entirely too close to admiration in his eyes.

"Like what you see, Captain?"

"Aye, very much," he replied, his voice gruff. He reached out to tug on a strand of hair before sliding his large hand through the strands to cup the back of my head. He lowered his face down to mine, resting his forehead against mine. Our breath mingled. "You're a very dangerous woman."

"I know," I said, my voice barely over a whisper. I badly wanted to kiss him.

So, I did.

Elizianna
@ELIZIANNA.THE.ONE

C AELUM

GHAPTER THIRTY

In the next instant, she had risen on her toes and her lips were pressed against mine. Instinctually, my other hand found her bare hip, my fingers digging into the swell of flesh there, pulling her as close as I could until every part of me was touching some part of her. My brain short-circuited as our lips moved together, molding to each other. This was surely what heaven felt like.

Her curvy body was warm against mine, and I could feel my cock pressing firmly against her stomach. I had to strain to keep from rutting against her, though I desperately wanted to. While I doubted she would mind, given the way she was kissing me, I didn't want to scare her off by moving too quickly. I wanted to pull her clothes off and feel her soft body against mine completely. Unfortunately, though, this was not the time or place for that. Knowing that was the only thing that kept me from pushing further and seeing how far she would let me go.

Breathless, we finally pulled away, our chests heaving together and her eyes opening slowly.

We should have been getting back to the cottage and the others, but she was breathtaking, and I had to have her in my arms. I pulled her back to my chest and looked down at her, her own face tilted up to meet my gaze.

"You're beautiful, *teine,*" I said, my voice hoarse. My hands encircled her waist, molding her body tightly to mine. I could feel every curve still pressed against me, and my mind was racing, stuck on imagining what those curves would feel like skin to skin.

She tilted her head to the side, staring up at me with attraction in her eyes. It made me feel good that it wasn't just me being affected here. "You're pretty handsome yourself, Captain."

I couldn't take it anymore. The others be damned, I would kiss her again.

With a harsh breath, I bent down and captured her lips with mine, holding onto the generous swell of her hips as I pulled her as tight against me as possible. Our lips moved together, and Brigid's hands found their way over my shoulders and into my hair, pulling it loose from the tie that held it back. As my hair fell around my shoulders, she twined her fingers into it almost painfully and held us closer together.

Panting for breath, I pulled back slightly, my mouth resting against her forehead. Her fingers left my hair, and she trailed them down over my face and neck, making me shiver as her nails scratched at my skin. Coming to rest at my sides, her arms wound around me, and she tucked her face into my chest, squeezing me tightly. I smiled and pressed a kiss to the top of her head. "You keep kissing me like that, I'll never let you leave."

"What are we doing here?" she asked, her voice still muffled by my chest.

I pulled back, looking down at her with my brows furrowed. "What do you mean? What do you want us to be doing here?"

"If I wanted to be with you…" she started, looking up at me. The fierceness and determination in her eyes made me want to kiss her again. "How would that work?"

My heart was racing. While I had only known Brigid personally for a few weeks now, she was already taking up residence in my heart; her personality, her looks, and just her. She had finally begun opening up to me and the others, and I couldn't stop finding an excuse to touch her. Last night had been the hardest night since I had met her; I'd spent it tossing and turning, wanting nothing more than to hold her in my arms and feel her warmth. She had burrowed her way under my skin, and to hear that she felt the same was... mind-bending. But she was right, we had outside factors to contend with.

"Caelum?" Her voice startled me from my thoughts.

I looked down at her, pressing my lips to hers to avoid talking. I didn't want to think about those outside challenges; I just wanted to think about her. I slipped my tongue along her lips, groaning when she opened for me and our tongues met. I kissed her deeply, pouring every emotion I didn't know how to say into the kiss. I wound my hand through her hair and slid the other one down to grip her hip. Without breaking this kiss, I rolled us over so that her back was pressed into the earth and I was above her.

The hand on her hip slid down to her knee over the thin fabric there, and I pulled her leg up around my hip. She moaned into my mouth, her own hands gripping and tugging on my hair. I couldn't help it as my hips ground into hers and I kissed her harder. She was pure fire in my arms, burning up every bit of me.

Panting, we broke apart. I let my fingers slip out of her hair and trace along her cheek. "I told you, you can have whatever you want. And if that's me, well, I'm honored."

She smiled, the expression lighting up her face. I groaned and leaned back down to capture her lips in a scorching kiss.

"We better get going before one of them comes looking for us," I said after kissing her again. We had likely been gone for almost an hour, but I didn't want to stop. Hell, I could easily lay on this grass kissing and holding her for the rest of my life and be content. But we had other commitments we had to uphold, other people relying on us. And at least one man that I needed to kill.

She let out a small sigh, sitting up. "Aye, we better go. I didn't mean to leave Sorcha by herself for this long."

We stood, and I pulled her into my arms again, looking down at her and tucking a finger under her chin to ensure she met my gaze. "But, *teine,* we're not done here. Not by a long shot."

She raised an eyebrow at me, pulling back to nip at my finger. "We'd better not be, Captain."

With a huge smile on my face, I walked back up to the cottage, Brigid close beside me.

Elizi
@ELIZIAN

CHAPTER THIRTY-ONE

Unlike when we had returned with Sorcha before, when we stepped through the cottage doors this time, no one paid us any mind. They were all huddled over a map spread across the kitchen table, Sorcha included.

I looked at Caelum questioningly, who just shrugged and walked up to the table. My heart fluttered at his gaze, remembering the feel of those shoulders beneath my nails as I held him while we kissed.

Sorcha and Cam were pointing at something on the map, which I could now see was a hand-drawn map of Brinemoor. They had been busy while we were gone.

Duncan looked up, raising an eyebrow. "Where've you two been?"

"We went for a walk," Caelum replied, peering down at the map on the table. "What's all this?"

Duncan's eyes roved over us both, taking in our appearances. I didn't know if he saw that our lips were swollen or that Caelum's hair was as wild as mine, but Duncan was observant. He could likely guess what we had been doing. He huffed before turning to the map. "Sorcha here thinks we should target higher levels of your father's circle, so we're trying to figure out where they'd likely be staying and going in town."

"That's smart," Caelum said, nodding in agreement. He looked impressed as his eyes flicked up to Sorcha, and he smiled encouragingly. "They'd be more likely to know the finer details that we would need."

I glanced over at Sorcha, who was standing next to Cameron. Her face flushed, and she ducked her head. "Thank you."

"Ah," Cameron said, wrapping his arm around her shoulders and pulling her into his side playfully. "Don't act all shy and humble now that the captain's back."

I was glad Sorcha was already getting along with the men, glad that they weren't holding anything against her for being a syren. Sorcha hadn't played a role in their ship's destruction, and I doubted very much she had a violent bone in her body. Sorcha was a person who cared deeply about others, and it showed. It delighted me that Cameron had already seemed to take her under his wing. No doubt she reminded him of his little sisters.

Sorcha cleared her throat, pulling away from Cam. "Aye, so if we can figure out where your father's men are staying, we'll be able to watch them and see where they go. And from there, we can figure out when would be best to get one of them alone and grab them."

"Aren't they staying at the house?" I asked, leaning over to look at the map as well. There was a large circle around where the house we had infiltrated was.

"Aye, not likely," Cameron said, scratching the back of his neck. "But we figure they've moved on from there since we discovered they were staying there. We expect they're somewhere Caelum wouldn't know about."

I nodded. That made sense, I supposed. A safe house likely wouldn't do much good if everyone knew where it was. "So, how are we going to watch them without being recognized? Caelum's father had a lot of men in that room when they ambushed us, and the ones that got away likely know our faces by now."

Duncan stepped forward, his arms crossed over his chest. "We figure the best plan would be to pair off and rotate watching often. We need to avoid being seen as much as possible, so the fewer of us together at one time, the easier it will be to avoid attracting attention."

"Aye, but some of us are pretty recognizable," Caelum pointed out. He nodded at me. "There won't be a lot of women around with that color hair. And you're kind of hard to miss yourself, Duncan."

"We'll just have to be extra careful, then," Duncan snarked. He looked at me like he was expecting me to argue with Caelum, but I didn't. Caelum made a good point, and if his father was still looking to take me, I'd stand out like a sore thumb.

"I can probably do something to Brigid's hair to make it less noticeable," Cameron said, rubbing his chin thoughtfully as he looked at me.

"Let's figure out a rotation and a pattern first, then we can discuss how we're going to keep from being spotted," Caelum said, rubbing the crinkle between his eyes.

"This is a good plan, Caelum," I said, putting a hand on his shoulder, seeing that he was growing frustrated and upset. I knew they had briefly entertained this idea before and quickly dismissed it, but the way Sorcha had presented it made it sound like a better plan. Maybe Caelum had just needed a new face to suggest something. "We'll find one of your father's top men that we can question."

He turned his head and smiled slightly at me, then turned back to the rest of the group. "We rotate pairings, rotate routes, and if anyone feels like they got recognized, you stop and come back immediately and we'll send someone else out. No one else is going to die because of my father."

Duncan clapped his hands. "Perfect, let's get it together. We can start rotations tomorrow."

"Let's go over some more details first. My father's men are dangerous and cautious," Caelum said, his voice warning. "We need to be smart about this."

Caelum launched into descriptions of his father's top men,

describing all he could remember about their appearances and places in Brinemoor they had frequented in the past.

"Do we have any contacts in Brinemoor that would be willing to go against your father and feed us even more information?" I asked, crossing my arms. Despite the butterflies still swarming in my stomach when I looked at Caelum's hands flexing on the table, I knew we needed to focus. And by contributing, I could focus on the plan and not on how I wanted to pull Caelum's clothes off. "What about Galen? Any of the people who reported those children missing in the first place? Would they be willing to help?"

Caelum looked up at me thoughtfully, stroking his beard. "Possibly. Galen is a recluse, but we could ask some of those who reported the children missing. I'm sure we could easily find people who would think my father is a horrible man, but the problem will be convincing them they will be safe if they help us."

"Can we discreetly convince them that if they help us stop your father, they won't have to fear him again?" I asked. If we could get these townspeople on our side, we could learn so much more, so much faster. Caelum was likely right, if the town knew they would not be in danger from Kellan, they would be more likely to help us. But how could we offer protection?

"We can certainly try. While our pairs are in town, we can see who might be open to helping us, even if it's just providing information on where my father and his men are going," Caelum said with a shrug.

"But would any of them tell Kellan that we're asking?" Duncan asked, raising an eyebrow at me. "It's a good plan except for the part where Kellan unofficially rules this town with fear."

"We'll never know unless we ask," I pointed out, returning the expression.

"Okay, simmer down, you two." Caelum sighed. "We need to be very careful about who we approach, and only do so if we think they would absolutely be on our side. We can start with Galen and see who he thinks would help us."

Duncan shrugged. "You're the captain, Cae."

"That's right," Caelum reiterated, raising an eyebrow. I bit down on the inside of my cheeks to keep from smirking. While I was pleased that Caelum was finally telling Duncan off, I knew my amusement would likely not go over well.

Digging my fingernails into my palm to focus myself back on the matter at hand, I refocused my attention. "What do we need to be looking for while we're on patrol?"

"Anything that could be useful," Duncan replied, his tone implying that I was stupid for even asking.

"I'm sorry, I haven't been involved in this plan from the beginning, and neither has Sorcha or Alan and his men. We need more information," I snapped before turning my attention to Caelum. "What information would be helpful? What should we be listening for?"

Caelum's lips twitched up, and from the corner of my eye, I noticed Duncan's expression. If looks could kill, it would have struck me dead on the floor.

"We still need to know where he's really holding the children, where he's taking them, what exactly he's doing with them, and if he is selling them, why and to whom," Caelum explained, ticking off each item on his fingers as he spoke. "If we can figure out their travel patterns or supply routes, that could help us as well."

"When do we start?" Cam asked, a grin spreading across his face. The others echoed the sentiment with agreeable chuffs and noises.

As Caelum launched into plans for our patrol routes, I stepped back, watching the group gathered around the table. These men, and Sorcha now, were truly willing to do anything to rescue these children from Caelum's father. And now that Maddock had died trying to reach that goal as well, they were all the more involved.

Despite my time with the syrens, who I had thought were my family, I was already more involved and at ease with these men. I still didn't feel like I quite fit in with them, especially with the tension still there between Duncan and me, but I already felt more at home. And that both excited and scared the living daylights out of me. Going back to the others felt wrong now, and so did going south to Bhodheas. But would Caelum want me to stay after this was over? I wasn't sure. The uncertainty of what I would do after this weighed heavily on me.

"Brigid?" Caelum asked, his voice jarring me out of my thoughts.

I snapped my head up to look at him. They were all looking at me expectantly. I had missed something. I cleared my throat, fighting back the feelings of embarrassment. "Sorry, what did you say?"

"Are you okay with teaming up with the other men, if need be?" Duncan asked.

I nodded hastily. "Yeah, that's fine. It's probably better if I'm seen with the others instead of Caelum, Cam, or Duncan, anyway."

The conversation started back up, and Caelum looked at me, a questioning look in his eye. He stepped up closer next to me and brought his lips down to my ear. "You okay?"

"Yeah," I murmured back, eyes still on the others. If I looked him in the eye, I knew my cheeks would burn. I needed to focus, to figure out what my future would be after this. But we needed to get through this mission first. "Just thinking."

"Want to share?" he asked, reaching down to squeeze my fingers.

I looked up at him and smiled, my heart soaring at the genuine concern in his eyes. Our talk earlier had relieved a lot of pressure on my mind, and it appeared to have done the same for him. "Maybe later. We've got planning to do right now."

By the time the rotation and routes were planned out, it was dark outside. Cameron and Finn worked quickly to make dinner, another stew, and placed it on the stove for us all to eat. Bowl in hand, I sat down in the cushioned chair once again. Caelum came over soon and sat down in the one next to me. "So, Sorcha's fitting in well."

I looked over to where she was laughing with Cameron and Finn at the table. I smiled. "Yes, she is. Good for her. She never really belonged as a syren, anyway. She has no violence in her bones."

"Why did she become one, then?" he asked, eating his stew and looking at me curiously.

I shrugged. "She was lost; wanted a family, I suppose. A purpose."

"Well, hopefully she's found one," he said with a smile. "Do you think your queen will come after her?"

My fists clenched involuntarily at my sides at the thought. "No. She won't get anywhere near Sorcha. If she's upset about her deciding to help me, she will punish me, not Sorcha. I won't allow it."

"We'll protect her too," he said softly, pulling at my fingers to unclench my fists. "Now, what were you thinking about earlier? Because I know it wasn't that."

"You," I replied. I waved a hand, realizing how my statement may have sounded. "Us, this—everything, really. I was with the syrens for more than ten years, and I already feel more myself and at home with you than I ever did with them. With them, it was all about...pleasing our queen. I had friendships with the others, of course, but nothing meaningful like you have with your men. Maddock...dying, put it into perspective. And today. I like being here, with you, Caelum, and I'm not sure that I want to give it up."

"Is that a bad thing?" he asked quietly.

"I don't know." I shook my head. This was all too much for me to process right now, and every time I tried, I was quickly overwhelmed. "I feel obligated to return to my queen and the others, but my heart wants to stay here, with you."

He reached over and squeezed my hand, lacing our fingers together tightly. "You do what you think is best for you, *teine;* though I'd prefer if you maybe stopped the whole murder thing. Would make it kind of difficult to make any money on the seas, you know."

"Will you ever tell me what that means?" I asked, the corner of my lip quirking up. "And I don't think I would go back to killing indiscriminately. But I won't promise to never kill again."

"I suppose that's a fair agreement." He released my hand to tug on a strand of my hair. "And you'll figure out what it means eventually, I'm sure of it."

I rolled my eyes, and we fell silent for a moment. I couldn't help myself, so I asked the question I had been dying to know. "Why did you put me in a room alone last night?"

He grinned wickedly, and I knew his answer would also be less than helpful. "Why? Did you miss sleeping next to me?"

I sniffed, raising my chin indignantly. If I admitted that I had missed sleeping next to him, I'd never hear the end of it. "No, of course not. It just didn't make sense to me, that's all."

His grin stayed firmly in place. "So, is this your way of asking if I'll share your room tonight?"

I returned his grin this time. "You lost your chance, Captain. Sorcha is sharing with me tonight. You're with the others again."

"You're a cruel woman, *teine,*" he said, still smiling at me.

Maybe this could work after all. Still grinning, I turned back to my dinner.

Elizia
@ELIZIA

CHAPTER THIRTY-TWO

Finally, a schedule was set up for the surveillance routine. Two of us would take a turn each day watching the town, walking around and acting like locals while keeping an eye out for Caelum's father or any of his men. We had descriptions of Caelum's father's top men and instructions to keep on the lookout for them. If we saw them, we would just observe, seeing where they went and what they did. At the end of the day, we would head back to the cottage and discuss.

Today, I was on patrol with Cameron and Sorcha. While everyone involved had been hesitant at first, with Kellan still wanting me for reasons unknown, Sorcha and I wanted to help. The argument that had gotten this patrol approved had been Caelum's first true experience with my stubbornness and his first experience with Sorcha's disarming kindness that could get her what she wanted.

So now, Sorcha and I, along with Cameron, were walking along the narrow streets of Brinemoor.

Throughout the day, Cameron ushered us from shop to shop, pretending to browse through various shops and market stalls. It was an exhausting process, but both Sorcha and I knew it was necessary if we wanted to be able to pull off this plan. We needed to not draw attention to ourselves, to blend in with the locals.

As we were turning down an alley to start the journey back to the cottage, Cameron swore quietly, grabbing our arms and pulling us into a nearby shop. He turned and quickly peeked out the window, pushing us back into the corner by the door.

"What's happening, Cam?" I asked, trying to lean around his massive body to see what he was looking at.

"It's Iain, Kellan's first mate," he whispered, looking at us over his shoulder briefly. "He's walking by now."

"Well, see where he goes," I said, pushing Cam so I could peer out the window as well. I saw a taller man walking away from us, but his back was turned. But I trusted Cameron; if he said it was Iain, I believed him.

"Should we follow him?" Sorcha asked, wringing her fingers together.

"We don't need to," Cam said. He pulled back from the window and looked at us with a satisfied grin. "He just went into that bar down there."

"Okay, so we need to see if he goes there again," I said. This was good. If we could find a pattern in Iain's behavior in the town, it would get us valuable information on how best to grab him and interrogate him.

"Aye," Cam replied. "Let's get back to the cottage and tell the others."

For two days now we had watched, taking turns and doing our rotations. We melted into the townspeople, observing anyone and everyone who walked past. While we never found out where Caelum's father and his men were staying, we did discover a crucial pattern. Seeing Iain go into that bar had not been a one-time thing.

He was there every night, usually from before the sun set to well after the sun rose the next morning.

As we continued observing over the weeks, he became our target. He would be the one we would capture and question, the one to give us the information we needed to bring Caelum's father down.

Caelum assured us that Iain would have the information we sought, so the decision to go after him was finalized. All that was needed now was a plan to take him and bring him back to the cottage without anyone else noticing.

"How are we going to get him out of the bar?" Caelum asked. We were all sitting around the kitchen table in the cottage, once again trying to come up with a solution to get Iain back here. We'd tried the same thing last night, and it had only devolved into arguing and frustration. I hoped today's conversation would be more productive, but I wasn't entirely optimistic.

"I'm telling you, just knock him out and drag him out the back. We can say he's passed out or something," Alan suggested for the third time. The man enthusiastically wanted to knock Iain out and was telling us this at every chance. It was getting exhausting.

Caelum sighed heavily, pinching the bridge of his nose. I reached down under the table and squeezed his other hand briefly. Looking at Alan, I replied, "If the people at the bar know him, they'll know we aren't friends with him. It has to be something he would do normally and that no one would remember."

"What about a woman?" Cameron suggested. When we all looked over at him, again cooking dinner, he shrugged. "He leaves with women fairly regularly, so what if we got a woman to lure him out and then take him when there's no one else around?"

"He would recognize me, though," I pointed out. Iain had apparently been one of the men standing by Caelum's father in the house when he had tried to take me.

"I can do it," a quiet voice came from the corner by Cam.

Sorcha.

Anger and dread formed in the pit of my stomach. As soon as

Cameron opened his mouth, I'd known she would volunteer. She had been the one to suggest this plan, and so it made sense she would want to be part of it. But it still filled me with a fear I couldn't push down.

I closed my eyes tightly, scrunching up my nose before relaxing my face and opening my eyes. We all looked over at her. She was sitting in the chair next to the fireplace, watching Cameron cook with her petite body twisted up in the chair and her chin on her knees.

"Absolutely not," I bit out, shaking my head. Sorcha had survived her ordeal of being thrown overboard, but I did not want her to have to experience any more of the evils of man. And these men were the true definition of evil. "It's too dangerous for you, Sorcha. That man wouldn't give a second thought to hurting you."

"Let her do it," Caelum said calmly, looking over at me. His eyes were like steel. "She can do it, Brigid."

Eliz
@ELIZIAN

Chapter Thirty-Three

"No, absolutely not," I snapped, my fingernails digging into the wood of the table as I attempted to control my building rage. "We'll find another way."

"Brigid, she's the only one of us my father's men don't know," Caelum tried to explain, leaning toward me.

I didn't care. This mission was dangerous, and we'd be asking Sorcha to get close to a man I knew wouldn't hesitate to kill or capture her if he knew her true intentions. "He didn't see Alan. We don't have to use a woman. Alan can just try to get Iain out to the back."

Duncan snorted but didn't say anything. Probably for the best, as I was spitting mad and ready to take on anyone who spoke.

Unfortunately, Sorcha was the one to speak again. "You just said that wasn't a viable option, Brigid. I can do this. I wanted to help, so let me."

After a pointed glare at Caelum, I turned to the younger girl, anxiety twisting its way up my throat. "This is dangerous, little one."

She rolled her eyes, a habit I knew instantly she had picked up from me. "Obviously, it's dangerous. This whole thing is dangerous. But would you let that stop you?"

I huffed, crossing my arms over my chest while thinking over her point. She was right, of course, I likely wouldn't have let it stop me either. But that didn't mean I was happy about it. "Fine, you can do it. But I want to be there."

"It's too dangerous for *you*, Brigid," Sorcha said softly. "Kellan wants you for some reason. We can't give him the chance to catch you away from the others."

"And what if he just wants a syren in general and we're handing him you on a silver platter?" I returned.

"This is a dangerous mission no matter how we look at it," Caelum said, far more diplomatically than I ever could. "And while it's not ideal to send either of you, if it would make Brigid feel better to be there, I think it's a compromise we can make."

"It's up to you, Caelum," Sorcha said, looking over at him. "You're the captain. And this is your mission."

Caelum looked at her for a long moment as if he were surprised at her easy concession. I figured he was used to dealing with me arguing with him, and Sorcha's agreeableness threw him off. He spoke slowly, "If he doesn't see her face and she doesn't draw attention to herself, I think it'll be fine."

Sorcha turned back to me, determination in her dark eyes. "Fine, deal."

Caelum clapped his hands together, leaning forward excitedly. "All right, that part of the plan is finalized, then. Now, we need to figure out what to do once we get him out of the bar."

"Wait," Duncan said, holding a hand up. "If Brigid is sitting in there alone, even hidden in the corner, it's going to look suspicious. She needs to be with a man."

"Not me," Caelum said, shaking his head. I could have sworn his expression was...disappointed. "He'd recognize me on the spot."

"Let me," Alan suggested. "I wasn't in the house, so he won't think twice about me."

Caelum pondered that and, after a moment, nodded. He looked

at me, his green eyes bright with worry and anticipation. "Brigid, you okay with that?"

I nodded, shrugging one shoulder casually. Alan seemed nice enough, and I could handle being alone with him if it meant keeping Sorcha safe. And I would do whatever it took to keep Sorcha safe. "Yes, Captain. That'll do."

"So, you all will be inside the bar. Once Sorcha leads him out, we'll need to have people in the back alley," Caelum explained, running his finger along the map of the town. "We also need people in the front to watch for any other of my father's crew. We should have someone do a search of the bar before Sorcha goes in too."

"Caelum, you and I should be in the back. We're the most recognizable," Duncan said, leaning in to point at an alley behind the tavern on the map.

Cameron, who had finished cooking, came over and took the seat next to me. He nodded and pointed to the lines on the map detailing the road in front of the bar. "And then Finn and I can position out here along the street to keep an eye on the front entrance."

"When should we do this? Tomorrow night?" I asked. The longer we waited, the more likely it was that Caelum's father would heal enough to continue his plans. I wanted this over with, and soon.

Caelum looked out the kitchen window, where the sun was just beginning to duck down over the rolling hills. He turned back to the rest of us. "Tonight?"

"Aye, tonight," Duncan agreed. "Before anything changes."

Cameron stood, clapping his hands. "All right then, better eat up. We've got a long night ahead."

Finally, our plan was in place, and despite my hesitations about using Sorcha like this, it was a good plan. The others set about talking about supplies and whatnot, and I walked over with Cameron to where Sorcha was still sitting.

"Since we're doing this tonight, you ladies might want to go start getting ready," he said with a smile. He tugged on a lock of Sorcha's dark hair and laughed when she scowled at him. "Let me know when you're done, and I'll do Sorcha's hair up nice and pretty. I'll bring some food in too."

Sorcha and I smiled at him before walking into the room we had been sharing. Wordlessly, we began laying out clothing for the night. While the bar wasn't well-maintained, wearing our casual clothing of borrowed sweaters and knit pants would make us stand out in a way we weren't hoping for. After our shopping trip with Cameron, we each had some pieces that we could use to blend in at the bar, and in Sorcha's case, to stand out and attract the attention of Iain.

I dressed in a similar outfit to one I had worn when recruiting Alan and his men. I pulled on tight, black leather pants that molded to the curves of my hips and legs. Over those, I added knee-high black boots with large silver buckles. On top, I wore a black long-sleeved blouse with lacing detail up the front, along with the same black underbust corset I had worn before. The dark fabric stood out against my pale skin, but it would allow me to go unnoticed in the shadows of the bar.

Sorcha dressed in a much more ostentatious way, pulling on an aesthetically simple but flattering dress. The cream-colored fabric left the attention on her dark hair, and the cinch at her waist emphasized her figure. I had no doubt she would be successful in getting Iain's attention. Sorcha was still young in my eyes despite technically being an adult at her nineteen years. I snarled inwardly at the thought of Iain laying a hand on her. *No one will touch her tonight,* I vowed. Getting Iain's attention was one thing, but he, nor anyone else, would lay a single finger on her. If they did, I would remove that finger. Viciously.

As Sorcha was lacing up her low-heeled shoes under her dress, Cameron walked in, holding two large bowls. He set them down on the dressing table before motioning for us. "You both look lovely. Now, let's get that hair done."

We alternated, Cameron doing Sorcha's hair first while I ate, and then we switched off.

Sorcha ate as she watched us, a thoughtful expression on her face. From the hunch of her shoulders and the tension in her jaw, I knew she was nervous.

"You okay, little one?" I asked. I was unable to turn to look fully at her, but I could see her out of the corner of my eye. If she didn't want to do this, we would find another solution.

She took a deep breath and raised her chin proudly. "I'm fine. I can do this. Just a bit nervous."

"I'll be there the entire time," I said. I wanted to tell her again that she didn't have to do this, but I could see that her mind was made up, and I wouldn't take this away from her if she genuinely wanted it. "We won't let anything happen to you."

Cameron patted my shoulder. "All done."

I stood, immediately bringing a hand up to my hair. Cameron had tamed my mass of waves into a single braid, beginning at the crown of my head and hanging down my back in a thick rope. While my fiery red hair would still be visible, it would now attract a lot less attention than it would if we had left it down and wild.

"You look deadly, Brigid," Sorcha said with a smile.

"We are deadly," I reminded her. "*You* are deadly. Don't forget that, little one."

With a fierce nod, Sorcha stood, taking my seat at Cameron's feet as I took hers at the table and began eating. Instead of a single braid like mine, Cameron began weaving Sorcha's hair into a more intricate pattern, starting at her temples and twining in small strands to keep her long hair back from her face. The braids on either side of her face then met in the back of her head, twisting together and falling down the rest of her hair, which Cameron left loose. It was beautiful and would attract attention just as much as the rest of her would.

I finished my stew and stayed sitting at the table, watching Cameron weave beads into the Sorcha's braids as well. Just as he was finishing up, Caelum walked in, leaning against the door frame. His eyes were molten green fire as he looked at me, scanning my seated body head to toe.

"You got some drool there, Captain," Cameron piped up from the bed, smirking at his friend. He patted Sorcha's shoulders. "You're all done now."

"You do good work, Cam," Caelum said, finally able to speak.

He moved to stand next to me and smiled down at me. "You look gorgeous."

"Thanks, Captain," I replied with a grin. I enjoyed being able to distract Caelum. His attraction to me was not disguised, and it made me feel good. Returning the favor, I let my gaze glide over Caelum, taking in his own dark clothing. He was dressed more simply than me, but he still was so handsome that my breath caught in my throat. "But the goal was to look underwhelming."

"You could never look underwhelming to me," he said softly, setting off another storm of butterflies in my stomach.

Sorcha cleared her throat. Caelum and I looked over at her, seeing her smirking along with Cameron. "Are you two finished making eyes at each other? We have things to do tonight, remember?"

Caelum rubbed the back of his neck, the tips of his ears turning pink at Sorcha's words. "Aye, let's get going."

Without any further disruptions or teasing, we all began our trek into town, ready to begin. The bar came into view, and Cameron and Finn murmured goodbyes before splitting off from our group and going along the path in front of the bar, heading down a bit further than the building. There were already towns-people meandering about, heading toward the tavern and pub. Cameron and Finn shouldn't have any issues blending in.

Alan, Caelum, and Duncan escorted Sorcha and I up to the front door of the bar. Hopefully, Iain wouldn't have arrived yet and we would have time to get settled. I reached down to squeeze Caelum's fingers and smiled at him. "Go on, Captain. We'll be fine."

He looked at me for a moment, then after a quick but scorching kiss, he and Duncan left, walking around the side of the building to the alley where they would be waiting for us.

Sorcha grinned at me as we pushed the door open. "He's a good one, huh?"

I rolled my eyes at her. "Be safe, little one. I'll be in the corner watching with Alan."

Elizianna
@ELIZIANNA.THE.ONE

C AELUM

CHAPTER THIRTY-FOUR

We sat in the alley behind the bar, hiding behind some crates and barrels so we wouldn't be visible, waiting for Sorcha to lead Iain out to us. My leg was bouncing with anxiety. I wanted desperately to be inside, seeing what was going on with my own eyes. I trusted Brigid to keep herself and Sorcha safe, but my heart still thundered in my chest at the thought of them being hurt.

"Relax and sit still," Duncan murmured from my right. "You're driving me crazy."

"Sorry," I muttered, forcing my leg to stop bouncing.

Duncan sighed heavily, keeping his eyes on the door that led to the bar. "She'll be fine. They'll all be fine."

"I know," I replied. "But I still worry. I don't want anyone else getting hurt in this."

"Brigid can handle herself, and she wouldn't let anything happen to Sorcha. You know that."

"Aye, I know. She's deadly, and she'd sooner kill Iain before letting him hurt Sorcha," I acknowledged. "But..."

"No buts, Caelum. You either trust her to take care of this, or you don't."

I snorted, tearing my gaze from the door to look at my friend. "Big words from someone who obviously still doesn't trust Brigid."

"Are we really going to talk about this now?" he asked, not turning to face me. "We're a little busy."

"Might as well," I replied with a shrug. "It'll keep us occupied."

"I just don't understand why you were so quick to forgive her for what happened to the crew. We spent so much time with those men, and it's like you've forgotten them already." His voice was quiet, but I could hear the hurt in his voice.

"I've not forgotten them," I said with a heavy sigh. I now understood his anger and the sadness that lay beneath it. "But Brigid did not kill them, any of them. She saved me, and she's been trying to make up for it ever since she pulled me out of the water."

"But she's killed others before—others like you and like me. How are we supposed to move past that?" he asked, turning to look at me for a moment before turning his attention back to the door.

"You and I have both killed men as well," I pointed out. I didn't want to start an argument with Duncan, not now. But it was important to get this out in the open so that we could move forward as a team. "Do we not deserve kindness or forgiveness any longer?"

"It's different, Caelum, and you know it," he said dryly. "And you should have told us what she was the first time we met her."

"She asked me not to."

"And there's the issue. You sided with a woman you had just met over me, your best friend. Can you not see how that makes me angry?"

I nodded, clarity dawning. "Aye, I understand. And I apologize. I truly do. I thought I was doing the right thing and that once you all knew her, it would be fine. I wanted it to all be fine."

"You should have let us make the decision for ourselves," he said. He rubbed his forehead. "But I understand your decision as well. If we had known then, we likely would not have gone to the cottage or even let you go back."

"I don't want to leave her," I replied, my voice soft. It was the first time I was voicing any of these feelings aloud to anyone. "I enjoy spending time with her. I want her to stay. And I want you two to get along."

Before Duncan could answer, the back door of the bar swung open, banging into the wall. We both slumped down, focus now intently on the door, waiting to see who would exit.

"Now, girly, don't play hard to get," a slurred male voice said. It was Iain.

I narrowed my eyes, watching closely as Iain and Sorcha walked out of the bar into the alley as planned. He wasn't touching her, but it wasn't for a lack of trying. Sorcha continued to push his hands away every time they reached for her. "I told you, sir, I'm not interested."

Sorcha continued walking deeper into the alley, and I saw Brigid and Alan slip out of the still open door.

"I don't care if you're not interested," Iain growled. It appeared he was done playing nice now that he thought they were alone. He grabbed Sorcha's arm, spinning her around and pinning her to his body. His other hand reached around and grabbed her behind roughly. Even from my hiding place, I could see fire and anger build in her eyes.

"Don't touch me," she ground out, the anger palpable as she struggled against him. If she could get free, I had no doubt that we would no longer be able to say Sorcha had never killed a man.

But it wasn't Sorcha I was worried about. Brigid had seen him grab Sorcha as well, and faster than I could blink, she had drawn the dagger at her side and was moving down the alley toward them. In an instant, she tore Iain away from Sorcha and pushed him against the wall with her dagger to his neck.

Quickly, left our hiding place and rushed over to where Brigid had Iain held at knife point. Sorcha was looking on, almost bored, and Alan looked excited. While Brigid was the only one holding him, Iain wasn't squirming. Instead, he just looked almost snootily down at Brigid.

"Give me one reason I shouldn't remove your filthy hands right here," I heard Brigid hiss, pressing the knife deeper into Iain's neck.

A thin line of red appeared along the knife's edge. "She's not yours to touch."

I put a hand on her shoulder. "All right, there. Let him go."

"He touched her," she ground out, not moving an inch. "Without her permission."

"Aye, he did," I said, trying to soothe my spitfire's anger. If she killed him now, we'd have a mess on our hands and no answers. I needed her to calm down. "And he'll pay for it. But not here and not now. We need to go."

After a long moment of glaring at Iain, Brigid finally released him, tucking her dagger back into the sheath at her waist. She looked at me for a moment, an unreadable expression on her face, before nodding and moving over to Sorcha. I heard her whispering concerned words to the younger girl.

I turned my attention away from the girls, as I was sure Brigid could handle it. Facing Iain, I looked him over slowly. "So, here we are, Iain."

He spat at my feet, glaring at me while rubbing his hand over the thin pink line left behind by Brigid's knife. "Caelum, you need to control your woman better."

I spared a glance at Brigid, then turned back to him and scoffed. "I don't think so; she's doing just fine. Now, let's go. You're coming with us."

He snorted dismissively. "I think not. I'm not going anywhere but back to your father to tell him what you've done."

"Oh no, Iain," I said, a wicked grin spreading across my face. This would be fun. "It wasn't a suggestion."

At my words, Duncan came up beside him and knocked him over the head with his large fist. Iain crumpled to the ground, hitting with a dull thud. Duncan looked at me with a grin of his own. "We got him."

"Aye, we did," I agreed. I ran a hand over my face and looked around. There was no one else in the alley, but we had to move quickly to avoid being seen. "We've got to get him out of here."

"Alan, go grab Cam and Finn," Duncan instructed. He turned to Sorcha and Brigid. "Lasses, we could use your help over here."

As a team, we were able to get Iain transported back to the cottage without being seen. Once back, we secured him in an outhouse on the property with Finn and another of Alan's men staying out there to guard him. Reassured that our guest wouldn't be leaving any time soon, I walked back to the cottage and went to check on Brigid and Sorcha.

"You ladies okay in here?" I asked, leaning against the door frame. Neither had changed out of their clothes yet, and they were sitting on the bed together, Brigid holding Sorcha's hands. They looked up when I entered.

Brigid smiled at me and stood. "Yes, Captain. How's our guest?"

"Secured," I replied with a smile of my own. I turned my focus to Sorcha. "You sure you're okay, little one?

She rolled her eyes, but still had a smile on her face. "Yes, *Da*. Between the two of you, he was never going to hurt me."

"He shouldn't have even gotten to touch you at all," Brigid grumbled, crossing her arms.

Brigid's protective streak toward Sorcha was adorable and attractive all at the same time. I couldn't help my grin from growing wider, to the point that my cheeks hurt. I nodded my head at Brigid, still looking at Sorcha. "You mind if I borrow our mama bear here?"

"Go ahead," she replied with an equally huge grin.

Brigid scowled at both of us as Sorcha left the room, pulling the door closed behind her. Not wanting to waste a moment, I pulled Brigid into my arms, holding her firmly to my chest. "You know you're insanely attractive with a knife in your hand?"

She rolled her eyes at me, but I didn't miss the grin spread across her face as she tilted her head up to look at me. "I suppose you came in here just to tell me that, eh?"

I shrugged a shoulder, having made up my mind of what I would do. "That, and to do this."

Leaning down, I cupped a hand on the back of her head and pulled her face up to meet me in a scorching kiss. Lips moving together, she consumed all my thoughts. Her small hands moved to grip the front of my shirt, pulling me tighter to her. Her braid bumped into my hand cupping her head, and I grinned wickedly against her soft lips.

She pulled back, breathless. Her eyes were blazing and filled with the same arousal I felt for her. "What is it? Why are you grinning?"

I didn't answer, not with words. Instead, I wrapped that braid around my hand and tugged. Hard. Her answering moan and her eyes sliding shut about made me fall to my knees. I dropped my other hand to her hip, guiding her back until her thighs hit the dressing table. One hand still in her braid, I used it to tug her up until she was sitting on the table. She was stunning, sitting before me with her eyes bright and her chest heaving. I had to kiss her again.

Pushing my way between her thighs, I released her braid and cupped her face in both hands, looking at her before crashing my lips down to hers again. The room fell away, and all my focus came down to the feel of her lips on mine. I let my hands move from her face, wandering down her body and tracing her curves. When they reached the swell of her hips, I pulled her roughly into me, pressing my body against hers. She was all I could think about at the moment, and I wanted nothing more than to peel her clothes off her and have my lips trace the path my hands had just taken.

We pulled back for breath, both of us panting as we rested our foreheads together. I needed this woman like I needed air, and the thought scared the living hell out of me. I could only hope that she felt the same.

"Caelum," she whispered, her eyes burning holes in me down to my very soul. Her voice was breathy and aroused and made my body react even more. I was unbelievably hard.

I had to swallow twice before I trusted my voice to not crack. "Aye?"

"Touch me," she said firmly, despite her breathlessness. She ran a hand through my hair, giving it a brief tug, before trailing her hand down over my shoulders and chest, down my stomach, before hooking a finger in my waistband. She leaned in and ran her nose against mine. "I want you to touch me."

My brain went completely blank. "Say again?"

She laughed quietly before moving her hands to hold my face. She lifted her legs up to wrap around my waist, pulling me hard against her. "I want you to touch me, Caelum. Take my clothes off and touch me."

I nodded almost frantically. I was not expecting her to ask for that, not yet, but I desperately wanted it. "Aye, yes, I can do that."

She leaned her head down to tuck into my neck, pressing soft kisses there. Her hands shook slightly on my chest, and I wondered if she was as nervous as I was. I wanted to please her, to make her understand how much I wanted this. Taking a shuddering breath, I reached around her back and began unlacing the knots of her corset.

As I was unlacing the last knot, she pulled my face back to hers, pressing her lips to mine in a kiss that felt more determined than aroused. I almost pulled back, wanting to remind her that we would take this at her pace, but then her kiss changed, and she melted into me even more. I finally freed the corset from her, pulling it off and throwing it to the ground behind me. I pulled back and looked at her, her chest still heaving and her neck pink.

"Brigid." I swallowed hard. "Are you sure you want to do this? There's no rush."

She opened her mouth to answer, but a thunderous knock at the door had us both jumping apart.

"Captain," Duncan's voice thundered. "Our guest says he'd like to speak to you."

I groaned, letting my forehead fall against Brigid's. I did not want to leave this room. Even if Brigid changed her mind, I wanted to hold her and feel her against me for a bit longer.

She chuckled, patting my chest before unwrapping her legs from my waist. "Let's go. I want to see what he has to say too. And maybe remind him to keep his hands to himself."

I helped her stand, pulling her into my arms once more. I pressed a kiss to her forehead. "You're deadly. But don't think we're done here. I told you earlier, this isn't over."

"Promises, promises," she teased before walking to the door and opening it.

Elizi
@ELIZIAN

BRIGID

CHAPTER THIRTY-FIVE

After Caelum had taken a moment to calm his body, much to the undisguised amusement of Duncan, we made our way to the outbuilding where Iain was being held. I was grateful for the interruption, despite how much I had wanted to continue. Caelum sparked a fire in me, in my body, that scared me and intrigued me at the same time. I wanted to explore that fire, to explore Caelum, but now wasn't the right time. We had a mission to accomplish, and we needed to stay focused on that and not each other. No matter how much I wanted to lock us in a room and never come out.

Caelum reached down and twined his fingers with mine as we neared the building. He squeezed them reassuringly, smiling at me broadly. How he could still be so upbeat in a situation like this, I would never understand.

We entered the small outbuilding and saw Iain tied to a chair in the center of the room. Finn, Alan, and Cameron were already inside, leaning up against the walls.

Iain's eyes landed on me, and he sneered. I grinned, baring my teeth at him. He was likely just mad that two women had gotten the drop on him.

"You bring your woman to all your fights, Caelum?" he asked, turning his angry gaze to Caelum now. "Can't take on your father on your own?"

"Considering Kellan tried to kidnap her, I'd say this is her fight too," Caelum replied with a shrug.

"You have no idea what his plans are, boy. You should leave this to the adults and go play with the other kiddies," Iain taunted. "And leave your syren at home."

"The syren belongs wherever she chooses to be," I replied coolly, raising an eyebrow at the bound man in front of me. "And you're very lucky that I don't rip your head off your shoulders right this second."

He smirked. "Sure, girly, whatever you say."

I saw Caelum's shoulders tense, and I knew the bastard had struck a nerve, both with what Iain had said to him and to me. I stepped up behind Caelum slightly so he could feel my physical presence. Slowly, his shoulders relaxed, the corded muscles in his neck disappearing once again. When Caelum spoke again, his confidence was back. "Aye, I don't know all of his plans yet. I don't know what he's selling the children for. But that's why you're here."

Iain laughed loudly. "Oh, that's funny, you wee boy. But I'll not be telling you a thing. I only asked you out here to tell you that you stand no chance."

Caelum shrugged, appearing unaffected by Iain's words. "We'll have to disagree on that, then. Because I think you will be telling us everything we need to know."

He turned to look at Alan and Cameron. Cameron nodded his head once. "We'll watch him, Captain."

Caelum returned the nod, turning back to me and motioning with his chin to follow him outside. We stepped out of the building into the brisk air, and Caelum let out a long sigh. "I shouldn't have wasted the time on him."

I put a hand on his shoulder and squeezed gently. "We needed to hear what he had to say. And now we know we have a difficult time ahead of us to figure out your father's plans."

"I would have rather finished what we started in your room than listen to that daft old man say absolutely nothing."

I raised an eyebrow at him, amused at the source of his frustration. It wasn't that Iain wasn't talking; it was because we had been interrupted. "We'll have time, Caelum. I promise you that."

Duncan walked out of the building, coming up to us. He rubbed the back of his neck. "Sorry, that wasn't as productive as I had thought it would be."

"We need to figure out our plan to work with him," Caelum said, rubbing his face. "I really don't want to torture him unless we absolutely have to."

"I have a feeling we're going to have to, Cae," Duncan said quietly.

Caelum's face pinched, and I could tell he was uncomfortable with the idea of torturing Iain, no matter what he had put him through in the past. I stepped up, putting a hand on his shoulder. "I can do it, Caelum."

Duncan raised an eyebrow. "You?"

"Aye," I said, raising my eyebrow back at him. "I've never tortured anyone before, but I can't imagine it would be too difficult to figure out."

Caelum chuckled, leaning over to press a quick kiss to my temple. "As much as I appreciate the offer, it *is* slightly more complicated than it sounds. I can do it if it comes to that."

"If you're sure," I said, looking into his eyes intently. I could carry this burden for him if he needed me to. I was willing.

"I'm sure, *teine*," he said, smiling. He nodded his head toward the house. "Let me walk you back to the house. You and Sorcha get some rest. I'll join you after I talk to Iain some more."

"You shouldn't be alone," I said.

"He won't be," Duncan said in a surprisingly reassuring tone. "Cam and I will be there too."

Looking at Duncan for a long moment, I nodded. That would be fine. They could keep Caelum from doing anything he wouldn't be able to come back from.

Caelum reached down to squeeze my hand, and we walked back

up to the main house. Before we made it to the door, he stopped, pulling me close to him and turning to press me against the cold stone of the house. He brushed his nose along my cheekbone, sighing. "I want to hold you. I know we can't pick up where we left off, there are too many people in this bloody house, but I want to hold you tonight."

"Come find me when you're done, then," I said, pressing my lips to his neck. "I'm sharing a room with Sorcha, but I have a feeling you'll be too tired to do anything but sleep."

He chuffed out a laugh, his breath warming my skin. "Aye, you're probably right."

"Let's get going then, Captain. You've got some questioning to do," I said with a smile as he led us into the cottage. Sorcha was sitting in the chair and looked up when we entered.

"Did he say anything?" she asked, turning her body to face us.

Caelum scowled, the easy smile that had been there a moment ago falling from his face. "No, just wanted to taunt us that he wouldn't be saying anything."

Her face fell slightly. "Oh."

"They'll get him to talk, lass," I reassured quickly. I knew this had been her idea, and I didn't want her to feel like she had failed.

"So, what are you two doing?" she asked, looking around. "Did everyone else stay?"

"We'll be questioning him overnight," Caelum explained. "I was just walking Brigid back to the house."

"And I suppose you'll be wanting to know if you can sneak into our room when you get done with Iain," she said, raising her eyebrow along with her smirk. She was insightful, I would give her that. A smile of my own spread across my face.

"Well, of course," he replied with a grin, not missing a beat. "But it'll be late before I'm done, I imagine."

This man made my heart soar and my stomach clench in ways I never thought I would experience. And no matter what promises I had made to my queen, I knew I couldn't give this up. The revelation made my smile slip slightly, but I pulled it back into place before Caelum could notice.

He pressed another quick kiss to my temple. "You two don't get into too much trouble. Alan will be back in a bit."

Sorcha waved him off, turning back to the fire. He let out a chuckle and squeezed my fingers before turning to leave.

"So, shall we go to bed, then?" I asked, grinning at Sorcha.

"I suppose," she said with a sigh, standing up. She returned the grin, mischief sparkling in her eyes. "But I don't know if we will go to sleep. We have stories to catch up on."

Several hours later, the sun had long set through the window of our room, and I was curled on my side, listening to Sorcha's soft breathing. We had stayed up for hours, talking about all we had missed in each other's absence. It was nice, and needed. Now, as she slept, I studied the moon through the window, trying to stay awake.

The door to our room creaked open, heavy bootsteps sounding.

"You awake still, Brigid?" Caelum's voice was a soft whisper in the darkness.

"Yeah," I said. My voice broke, and I cleared my throat, trying again as I sat up to look at his figure in the dark. "Yes, what is it?"

"Just wanted to see if you were awake," he said, moving over to sit on the bed next to me. "We're stopping for the night."

"Did he tell you anything?" I asked, keeping my voice down to avoid waking Sorcha.

In the moonlight, I saw him shake his head. "No, he didn't. We'll have to...improve our techniques."

I reached out and squeezed his hand. "Offer still stands, Captain. I can do it for you."

"No, *teine*, I need to be the one to do it," he said, leaning over to kiss my forehead. He tucked a finger under my chin, tilting it up slightly. "But know that I do greatly appreciate the offer."

I pushed up onto my arm to look down at him, my unbound hair spilling over my shoulder and down over my chest, which was covered by Caelum's shirt. "Are you staying the night?"

He nodded again, standing from the bed to remove his boots and shirt, leaving his pants on. "Aye, I need to rest. We have a lot of work ahead of us."

Settling into the bed next to me, he pulled the blanket back over us, pulling me to rest my head on his chest. The silence of the room took over once more, the only sounds our breathing.

"Can I kiss you goodnight?" he asked after a moment.

I pulled back slightly to look up at him, raising an eyebrow. I had little doubt if he kissed me that he would want to stop there. "Is that all you want to do?"

Even in the dim moonlight, I could see his wicked grin. "All I want to do? Not even close. All I will do? Aye, for tonight."

My own wicked grin spread across my lips, and I moved up to press my mouth to his. "Goodnight, Captain."

"Goodnight, *teine.*"

Elizianna
@ELIZIANNA.THE.ONE

CHAPTER THIRTY-SIX

Waking up to find Brigid still curled up in my arms was wonderful. I had missed feeling her against me as I slept. Waking up to see Duncan standing in the doorway with his arms crossed and looking down at us disapprovingly, however, was not how I wanted to be woken up. His brow furrowed, and he shook his head at us. It wasn't quite disgust in his eyes, but it was easy enough to tell he did not approve of us spending the night together.

"What?" I asked quietly, trying not to wake Brigid. Sorcha's bed was already empty, the sheets rumpled. "Why do you look so cross?"

"You spent the night?" he asked, raising an eyebrow and looking over at Sorcha's bed.

"Aye. Do you have an issue, or are you just stating facts?"

He raised an eyebrow at me. "We need to get started for the day. One of Alan's men reported seeing more activity with your father's men in town. They're preparing for something."

I sighed, letting my head fall back into the pillow. "Aye, they probably realize we have Iain and are speeding things up."

Duncan nodded, his expression easing up slightly. "Aye, that was my thought as well."

I bent down and pressed my lips to Brigid's hair, shaking her arm gently. She looked up at me sleepily. "Morning. It's time to get up, we've got some more questioning to do."

She nodded and sat up, rubbing her eyes. She saw Duncan standing in the doorway and froze. I hated it. I hated that her body tensed up at the sight of my friend. She cleared her throat. "Morning, Duncan."

He inclined his head at her in greeting before setting his eyes back on me. "I'll let you both get ready. Cam and Sorcha are making breakfast."

Without another word, he turned and left, pulling the door shut behind him. As soon as the door was closed, Brigid let out a huge breath, her body relaxing. I looked over at her, pulling her hand into mine. "You don't have to be nervous around him, *teine*. He won't hurt you."

She shrugged. "He doesn't like me, though. It's hard to relax around someone you know doesn't care for you."

I sighed before filling her in on what Duncan had shared about my father's men.

While it was a struggle, we managed to get dressed without me hauling her back into the bed. Once we were both ready, we walked out to the kitchen, where Cam and Sorcha were serving breakfast. Sitting down to eat, Duncan took the seat next to me.

"So, how are we going to approach this?" he asked in between bites. "Just asking last night didn't seem to work."

I swallowed the food that had suddenly turned to ash in my mouth. "My father's lessons weren't for nothing, I suppose. I know how to torture someone."

"Is there not another way?" Sorcha asked quietly. Her face was pinched, and from what Brigid had told me, she wasn't a proponent of violence, despite being a syren.

Duncan scoffed. "We don't have time for delicate sensibilities. Iain knows where these children are, and we need that information."

Sorcha's face morphed, tensing. She snapped, "I'm aware of that. My point was, won't Iain be prepared for physical pain? I imagine Caelum's father prepared his crew for the possibility of capture."

Hell, she had a good point. I tilted my head, looking at Duncan. "Aye, he likely has."

Duncan let a heavy sigh fall from his lips, turning back to Sorcha. "All right, then, do you have a better idea?"

Sorcha immediately turned to look at Brigid, and the two appeared to have an unspoken conversation before Brigid finally nodded at the younger girl. They both turned back to look at Duncan and me. "We can use our song."

"Absolutely not," Duncan nearly roared, standing abruptly. "We will not be letting you two sing your cursed *song* anywhere near us."

Brigid rolled her eyes, and I knew things were about to get... interesting. Over the last few days, Brigid's apprehension had waned. Her confidence was building in the face of my friend and the other men, and I had a feeling Duncan was about to get first-hand experience with the fire I knew bubbled under her surface.

"Just because you're afraid of it doesn't mean it's not the best course of action. We can keep you and the others from being affected by it," Brigid said, also standing up and facing down Duncan. "But our song induces madness." She hesitated slightly, looking over at me for a moment. "I don't have a song anymore, but Sorcha does, and she can break him."

I looked over at Brigid, trying to catch her gaze, but she was busy staring down Duncan. I was surprised she had admitted that in front of him—to him.

"We can cut off his fingers and he'll talk just the same," Duncan snapped, keeping Brigid's gaze. "And none of us will be subject to falling under your influence."

"For the last time," Brigid said, rolling her eyes, "the song induces madness. We can't control you with it."

Duncan's ears began to turn pink, and I knew that was a sign that his anger was building. Before he could speak again, I stood, interjecting myself. "Okay, we'll do both. If one doesn't work, we'll try the other."

"You'll really trust her to not turn the song on us?" Duncan asked, looking at me like I had lost my mind.

Cameron walked over, standing in between Duncan and me. He put his hands out, palms up. "Let's think this through rationally. Getting upset is only going to help your father."

"Putting wax in your ears and standing outside the building should be enough to keep you from being influenced," Sorcha offered.

Duncan snorted. "Should?"

"We've never actually tried this before, Duncan," Brigid said, her voice icy. "But I have seen sailors on previous ships use the wax and remain unaffected. So, yes, *should*. And you need to watch your tone with her. She's done you no wrong."

"This is going nowhere," I said, stepping in before tempers flared even more. "We need to be working on getting information from Iain, not fighting with each other. Duncan, I know you don't like it, but we're going to try everything we can. Brigid, we're going to try Duncan's way first, and if we get nothing, then you and Sorcha can try your song. Deal?"

They both grumbled, but thankfully there were no other words.

Once we all finished eating in tense silence, Duncan and I stood. I turned to Brigid. "We'll start first. I'll come get you when we're finished."

She shook her head. "I want to come."

"You don't have the stomach for what we'll be doing," Duncan said.

I cut my eyes sharply to him. It was like he was trying to get her to lash out at him. Saying a quick prayer to the gods for patience, I turned back to Brigid. "He won't talk with you there, Brigid."

The look in her eyes made me sure that she was going to argue, but instead, she just nodded shortly. I knew there would be more to this later, but we needed to get started, so I couldn't stop to think about it too long.

Duncan and I walked out to the outbuilding, dismissing Alan and Finn, who had been standing guard. We entered the building and I kicked at Iain's chair. "Wake up."

He grunted, but opened his eyes. His wrists were raw from pulling against the ropes all night, but he appeared otherwise unscathed, if tired. "Oh, goody."

"Let's talk," I said, feigning more nonchalance than I felt. Violence made me sick, especially the kind I was about to inflict on Iain. My own father had done similar to me, and I had once vowed to never do it to another human being. But my convictions had to take a backseat to saving these children. "What's my father planning with the children?"

"I'll tell you nothing," he snarled. "And no pain you inflict will change that."

"Okay," I said with a shrug. I grabbed his left hand, pulling his fingers taut as I brought the pommel of my dagger down onto the bone, breaking his index finger. "What is my father planning?"

"He's planning to kill you," he panted, gritting his teeth.

Stubborn bastard. I clenched my teeth, preparing myself for what I was likely going to have to do next. "Now, now, my father has always been planning to kill me. That's nothing new. What's he doing with the children?"

Only panting breaths filled the room.

"One more chance, Iain," I said, flipping the knife in my hands. "What's he doing with the children?"

He raised his head and spit in my face.

Without another word, I slipped a sharp, curved knife from the sheath at my side. With no hesitation, I brought it down onto Iain's hand, severing the index finger of his right hand. Bone crunched and blood gushed. My stomach swirled, but I swallowed, keeping my face blank.

"What is my father planning?" I asked, my voice rising to carry over Iain's pained grunts. I had to give him credit, he didn't scream. "What is he doing with the children, Iain? Who's he selling them to?"

Iain brought his eyes up to mine, filled with pain and hatred. "Do what you like. I'm not speaking."

"You're afraid of my father, no?" I asked, letting his head drop and standing up. If I couldn't break him, we would never find out what was happening to the children, and we would have no hope of saving them. I *needed* to get this information. I walked around the chair, moving to stand behind him. I clapped a hand down roughly on his shoulder, relishing the sharp intake of breath he gave at the impact. "You should be. But you should be afraid of me too."

He laughed—the bastard had the nerve to laugh. "Oh, boy, I'm not scared of you a lick. There's nothing you can do to me that I haven't already done to others. Nothing will make me betray your father."

I looked over his head at Duncan, trying to convey that we would be needing Brigid and Sorcha after all. I knew that Iain wouldn't give anything up merely due to physical pain. But that didn't mean I was done. "That's too bad for you, then. My father isn't worth your loyalty."

I grabbed another handful of hair and pulled Iain's head to the side, slicing my knife along his ear, severing it. He roared in pain again, his hands flexing as he tried to staunch the bleeding of his ear. It only made the bleeding in his hand worse.

I walked back around the chair to stand next to Duncan. "Don't let him bleed out. There's bandages in the cabinet over there. We'll try again in a bit."

Elizianna
@ELIZIANNA.THE.ONE

CHAPTER THIRTY-SEVEN

I sighed heavily, rubbing the back of my bloodied hand over my forehead to wipe the sweat away. "This isn't working, Dun."

"Aye, I know," he said, with a sigh of his own. We had been trying various methods of physical pain, including cauterizing his wounds and pouring water over a cloth spread over his nose and mouth. We had even severed another finger. Nothing had worked so far.

We walked to a bucket by the side of the cottage and washed the blood from our hands and knives. Drying my hands, I thought of how to broach the subject of having Brigid and Sorcha try.

Duncan surprised me, speaking again. "I guess we should let the girl try, then."

I raised an eyebrow at him, shocked. "You're going to just let them try? No more fighting?"

"Well, obviously, what we're doing isn't working. And we don't have a lot of time," he snapped. He stopped and sighed heavily. "I just don't trust it. They already ruined our plans once, wrecking the ship. I don't see how you're trusting them so quickly. Did the men we lost mean nothing?"

"Of course, they mean something. I thought we talked about

this," I snapped back. "Just because I'm not in the corner crying does not mean I don't feel their loss."

"No, you're just losing your mind over the *creature* that helped kill them."

My anger bubbled up, and I pointed the now clean knife at him. "Watch it, Duncan. My feelings for Brigid are in no way related to what happened with the ship. And now is not the time to be having it out like this. Save it for later. We can mourn when my father is dead."

Duncan shook his head, a disgusted look on his face, but wisely said nothing else. My anger continued to simmer as we walked back into the cottage. Brigid and Sorcha were sitting in the chairs by the fire, talking. They stopped when we walked in.

"Did you get anything from him?" Brigid asked, raising an eyebrow.

I shook my head. "No."

She cocked her head at me, studying me. I had no doubt she could see the anger and frustration on my face, but I couldn't bring myself to elaborate, not after what Duncan had said. Was I truly forgetting myself for Brigid? I hadn't thought so, but now I wasn't sure. Duncan's anger and sharp words were still shaking around in my brain, and I couldn't help but question myself.

"What do you need to be able to do your song on him?" Duncan asked, crossing his arms and looking at the girls.

Brigid raised an eyebrow and slowly let her gaze move from mine to Duncan's. "Oh, so you're going to let us help now?"

"Aye," he grumbled, repeating what he had told me. "Obviously, what we're doing isn't working. And we're running out of time."

Brigid shared a glance with Sorcha before answering, "Sorcha will need to be in syren form. So, we need to either move him to the water, or we'll need to get a large enough basin to hold her in her syren form."

"We're not untying him," Duncan said immediately. I agreed. If we untied him, even if it was just to move him to the water, we couldn't risk him getting away.

"There's a large enough trough in the back," I said, rubbing my chin. "It'll take us a bit to fill it up from the well, but it should work."

"I know this is asking a lot of you, little one," she said, looking at Sorcha. "We can find another way if you can't do this."

Sorcha took a deep breath. "There is no other way, and you know it, Brigid. You don't have your song anymore. I need to do this."

"Will her song affect you?" Duncan asked, jerking his head at Brigid.

Her eyes twinkled, and one side of her mouth tugged up in a smirk. "Don't know. We'll find out when we find out if it affects you."

Duncan threw his hands up, scoffing before he turned and left the cottage.

I raised my eyebrow at Brigid. Why did they constantly have to antagonize each other? "Did you really have to do that?"

She grinned at me. "Sure did."

Over the next hour, we all pitched in, getting the basin situated in the outbuilding in front of Iain and filling it. He didn't say a word the entire time, just watched us carefully.

The basin finally filled, and now Brigid, Sorcha, Duncan, and I stood outside the building. I looked to Brigid, whose face was apprehensive. If I had to guess, she was worried if the song would affect her as well. I caught her eye and nodded at her. "I'm staying in there with you."

"Absolutely not," Duncan immediately argued. "Even with the wax, you could be affected, Caelum."

"He needs to see that I'm still in control," I pointed out.

"I'm going in with you, then."

"Fine, let's get this started," I replied, not fighting with him. If he wanted to come in, then he could. It would be pointless to argue with him. Sorcha would not hurt us, not intentionally. I trusted that much.

We entered the room, and Iain looked up at us. Even bloodied and obviously in pain, he sneered at us. "Bringing in the women now, are we?"

We ignored him. Sorcha handed wax to Duncan and I, and we promptly put it into our ears, muffling all sound until we were in complete silence. Duncan and I stood behind the basin against the wall, watching as Sorcha and Brigid had another wordless conversation. Brigid moved to stand next to us, and Sorcha began removing her clothes.

Apart from Brigid, the rest of us averted our eyes at Sorcha's nakedness. It felt wrong to look at her, and I was grateful I wouldn't have to cut Iain's eyes from his skull for looking at her. Once Sorcha stepped into the basin and began her transformation, Iain seemed to understand what was happening and began thrashing against his bindings. My father must have warned him of what the syrens could do.

I saw Sorcha's mouth open, and my body involuntarily tensed, but I heard nothing. Iain's body went slack, his mouth falling open and his eyes glazing over. The calm stillness didn't last long, though, and he quickly began flailing, his eyes going frantic as his remaining fingers clawed at the chair.

Sorcha continued singing for a few more minutes, then Iain's mouth began to move. I looked to Brigid, who held a hand out to stop us and spoke to Iain. At his reply, she turned to us and nodded.

I yanked the wax out of my ears. "What is my father planning?"

Iain's head was still thrashing, his body shaking, but he replied, looking at me with panicked eyes. "He's selling the children to a woman. I don't know who, but she only wants boys. She uses them for something."

"Where are they being kept?"

He groaned in pain.

"Speak, or she'll start again," Brigid threatened.

Iain whimpered, actually whimpered. "They're at another house. The woman they're sold to wants them healthy."

"When is he taking them to her?" I asked, trying to keep the franticness out of my voice. We were getting answers, finally.

"Day after tomorrow," he groaned.

"One more question," I conceded, seeing that we were about to lose him. The madness was fading. "How did my father know about the syrens?"

"He's known about them for years. Since I joined him." He panted more, stopping to let out a wheezing chuckle. "I'm surprised you hadn't heard more about them, to be honest. But you never were good at listening."

Iain had been my father's right-hand man since I was a child, which meant my father had known about syrens for much longer than I had feared.

"Where are they leaving from?" I asked, trying to get the last of what I could from him.

Iain groaned but didn't answer. Brigid motioned at me to put the wax back in my ears. Duncan and I both reinserted the wax into our ears, and Sorcha began singing again. Iain thrashed more, and I noticed blood beginning to trickle out of his remaining ear.

Sorcha stopped, and Brigid again motioned to us.

"Where are they leaving from?" I repeated. "Are they leaving from here?"

"Brin...Brinemoor," he panted, his head falling on his chest again. His nose had begun to bleed as well.

"That's all we needed to know," I said, looking at Brigid and Sorcha. "Thank you, ladies."

"What will we do with him now?" Brigid asked, her face hard. In the basin, I could see that Sorcha had begun to change back to her human form.

I spared a glance at Iain again before reaching to help Sorcha stand and helping her wrap a blanket around her small body. I looked back at Brigid. "He'll die now, don't worry."

She grinned at me, the bloodthirsty side of her coming out to play. "Aye, Captain. Good."

Elizi
@ELIZIAN

BRIGID

CHAPTER THIRTY-EIGHT

D ry, human, and clothed once again, Sorcha walked into the kitchen, moving to stand beside me at the counter. We had killed Iain—or rather, Caelum had—and then he and the others had buried the body. Now, we stood, discussing our plans for how to stop Kellan.

"We need to get back to Brinemoor," Cameron said. "They have to be leaving out of the harbor there. We could stop them at the docks."

"There are too many ways for them to escape at the docks," Caelum said, rubbing his hand over his bearded chin. "We need to box them in somehow."

"We still have that ship we borrowed," I pointed out. "We can let them get out into open water and board them there."

Caelum shook his head. "His ship is likely much better armed than *The Voyager* is. We'd never stand a chance. That's why we haven't already targeted it."

"What if Sorcha and I were in syren form and disabled their ship somehow?" I asked. "We'll need to get the children off quickly, away from the violence."

"What if we used two smaller rowboats and Sorcha and Brigid in syren form?" Cameron suggested. "They disable the ship when it's out from the harbor, then we can board, send the children off in the smaller boats. We could sneak in, and it wouldn't be a firefight, at least. They wouldn't be expecting us to come in rowboats."

Caelum nodded. "That could work, but Sorcha and Brigid won't be able to communicate in syren form."

"Yes." I nodded. "I no longer have my song, so I can't speak to her under the water. We'll come up with a solution for that, not to worry."

"We'll need to relocate back to Brinemoor tomorrow," Duncan said. "If they're leaving at first light the following day, we need to be ready and set up before dawn."

"Aye, good idea," Caelum said. "We'll need to get rooms in pairs so we aren't all seen together. Who knows who my father is paying off to inform him? Anyone could be feeding him details."

"We should all get some sleep," Sorcha said softly. I knew what she had done today had affected her, not that she would ever let it show.

"Aye, that's probably a good idea," Caelum agreed. He looked tired, and I knew that today had worn on him too. I had seen the state Iain had been in, and I knew that Caelum would not have let Duncan do any of it for him.

We dispersed, Sorcha going back to our room. I stayed behind, catching Caelum's gaze. He stepped over beside me, and once everyone else had left the kitchen, I pulled him into my arms, tucking my chin into his chest. "You did what you had to."

He sighed, his breath tickling me as he tightened his arms around me. "I know. So did you two."

"We finally have some answers, and we have our plan."

"Aye, we do. Thanks to you," he said. He pulled me back to look at me intensely and leaned down to press a kiss to my lips. "Thanks to you."

"I'm just glad the wax worked," I said with a teasing smile. "Or I'd have never heard the end of it."

He rolled his eyes, but I knew my words had done their job in cheering him up. "Okay, now go get some sleep. We've got a long couple of days coming up."

"You sleep too," I said, poking his chest.

"I'm stealing you tomorrow night. I need you in my arms before we face down my father again," he said with a small smile.

I placed a hand on his cheek, meeting his eyes and hoping he could see the intensity in my gaze. "I like that plan, Captain."

He nudged me toward the bedrooms, nodding his head. "Go on, before I change my mind and drag you off somewhere."

I raised an eyebrow. "And if I wanted you to?"

He swallowed hard, shaking his head. He pointed a finger at me, but the grin on his face told me all I needed to know. "You're trouble, *teine.* Go to bed."

With a final mischievous grin, I turned and walked into the room I was sharing with Sorcha. When I opened the door, she was sitting on the bed and greeted me with a small smile. I closed the door behind me and moved to sit next to her.

"Do you want to switch rooms again?" she asked.

I shook my head and scooted closer to her. "No, I'm sharing with you tonight. Is that okay?"

She grinned. "Of course. It'll be just like old times."

I answered with a grin of my own. We smiled at each other for a moment before the smile slipped from my face. As much as I wanted to protect Sorcha, I knew she was as fiercely independent as I was and would not be stopped or left behind. "We need to talk about today and the coming days."

She nodded as if she had been expecting it. "Aye, I figured we would. I know you want me out of this, but I want to help."

I sighed heavily. "I know, little one. And I want you to help. But you have to be careful. You promise me that you will be careful."

"I promise, Brigid," she said, taking my hands in hers. "You promise me the same, though."

"I promise," I replied, squeezing her fingers. "Now, are you okay after what you did today?"

"Aye," she replied. She tilted her head slightly, her eyes flitting up. "I won't pretend I enjoyed it, because I didn't. But I understand it was necessary, and I'm fine."

"Good, good." I nodded, swallowing hard. Sorcha deserved more than this violence, than the life of a syren. "What will you do after this? They likely won't take either of us back, you know that, right?"

She sighed. "Aye, I know they won't take us back. I'm not sure what I'll do. Maybe I'll continue to Bhodheas, try to find Owen."

"Does he know you were trying to reach him?" I asked. Maybe if things didn't work out with Caelum, Sorcha and I could travel to Bhodheas together. That would be nice.

"He did. But I have no doubt he's assumed the worst at this point," she said with a shrug. "And maybe he's moved on, but I'd still like to see him and know for myself."

"We'll get you there," I promised. "Once this is over, I'll take you to him myself if I have to."

She smiled widely. "You're a gem, Brigid. And what will you do after?"

"I don't know," I replied, looking down at my hands. "I don't know if Caelum would want any kind of future with me or not. I'll just take it day by day, I suppose. I'll need to find work and a place to live."

"He wants a future," she said, her voice strong with conviction. My heart wanted to believe her, but my mind questioned the reality in front of us. "I see how he looks at you, Brigid."

"I played a role in killing his friends," I said quietly. "And Duncan will never let me, or Caelum, forget it. Maybe we were over before we ever started."

"You don't know that," she said. "You two fit together perfectly. You...balance."

I tilted my head, thinking about her words. We did balance, as she put it. Caelum dimmed some of my fiery anger while still letting me make my own decisions, and I was the serious side to his irrepressible positivity. Maybe we would work after all. "We shall see, I suppose. We have to make it through the next few days first."

"Aye, that we do," she said. She turned in the bed and patted the mattress. "So, let's get to sleep so we can pull our weight. We can't let the boys show us up."

I grinned at her and leaned over to extinguish the lamp before crawling into bed. "Aye, they'll have to rise to meet us."

Elizi
@ELIZIAN

B RIGID

CHAPTER THIRTY-NINE

S till early in the morning, we made our way into Brinemoor, walking through a thick fog that had built up overnight. It certainly wasn't ominous at all.

We had all arrived separately, in pairs or groups of three. Kellan's men were likely watching, looking for our large party to enter the city, and we wanted to remain as inconspicuous as possible while we prepared. I arrived with Caelum, who, despite protests from the group over our recognizability, insisted on being with me. Not that I minded it. We were facing his father again tomorrow, and after what had happened the last time, I was relishing this time with him.

Before we had left the cottage, it was decided that we would split ourselves between the two inns in Brinemoor, with Alan acting as a go-between for the groups. We all checked in at different times, under assumed names. Hopefully, it would be enough to keep Caelum's father and his men off our trail, but I had doubts. They knew we had taken Iain, and they knew what most of us looked like now. The plan was for all of us to stay in our rooms as much as possible. At dinnertime, the groups at each inn would meet and go over the plan again for the morning.

We had developed a rough plan before leaving the cottage, but based on any events that happened once we got here, things might have to change.

Now in our room, Caelum and I sat at the small table.

"Do you think tomorrow will go as planned?" he asked quietly. His shoulders were hunched up and his face was scrunched.

"I'm not sure," I admitted softly. Reaching out, I covered his hand with my own and laced our fingers together. "But we'll make it work."

"I can't lose anyone else. And I can't lose these children."

"He won't win, Caelum," I promised, squeezing his fingers with mine. The look of pure desperation on his face broke my heart, and I knew I would do anything in my power to ensure his father was stopped. "You and I will both do whatever it takes."

There was a long silence, then, "Why are you helping me with this?"

My brows furrowed. "What do you mean? Isn't that what you wanted?"

His eyes were fixated on the table in front of him, and he wouldn't look at me.

"Caelum," I said firmly. He finally raised his eyes to look at me. "What's happening? Why are you asking this?"

"I..." he started. He took a deep breath. "I'm worried you're only helping because you think it's your only choice."

"My only choice?" I asked, raising an eyebrow. "There are children being stolen and sold. Did you really think I would just choose to leave once I found that out?"

"We don't know each other well enough for me to even know that, Brigid," he said. He pulled his fingers away from mine and ran a hand roughly through his hair. "That's the issue. I don't know what you would do."

I leaned back, looking at him. "You think we don't know each other well enough for you to trust that I'm here willingly?"

He nodded, and my heart splintered, filling my stomach like an iron weight. Somehow, this was worse than my belief that he would ask me to leave after Maddock's death.

Despite wanting nothing more than to curl up under the blankets on the bed we were to share, I knew there was more to Caelum's abrupt words than he was letting on. We had only known each other a few weeks, he was right about that, but it felt like it had been a lifetime. More importantly, it felt like it didn't matter how long we had known each other. While I didn't know Caelum's favorite food or what he had done for Yule as a child, I knew what mattered. I knew that he was a good man who cared deeply for others.

"What do you want to know about me, then?" I offered. "Because I know enough about you to know that you would do anything for those in need, you care deeply, and laugh loudly."

"And that's okay with you?" he asked. "You're fine with the fact that you know next to nothing about me apart from that I try to help others?"

I shrugged. "What else do I need to know?"

"I don't know, *anything* else?" he said, his voice turning frantic. He was panicking, and I could see it clearly in his eyes.

I took a deep breath and sat for a moment, working through what I could do. Standing, I bunched up the skirt of the long-sleeved cotton dress I was wearing and moved to straddle Caelum's broad thighs, settling down on them and pulling his face into my hands.

"Brigid," he said, his voice still frantic, but the tone lower. "What are you doing?"

"Look at me," I said, holding his cheeks in my palms. "We could have all the time in the world to get to know each other more once this is over, to learn all the little things about the other that make us unique. But for now, all I need to know about you is if you see a future for us after this. Do you?"

He was silent, his green eyes meeting my own as his hands rested on the creases of my hips. He swallowed hard, his throat bobbing. "Aye, I do. Or I want to, at least. I like you, *teine,* a lot. And I want to see where things can go with us without my father looming over us."

I leaned down, brushing my lips lightly over his forehead. "Yes, me too, Captain. And I want that. I want to spend my days with you, learning things about you. But right now, we have something more pressing that needs our attention. I enjoy being with you, and I want to stay with you, if you'll have me."

"I want that too," he whispered, leaning his forehead down to rest against my chest. His hands tightened on my hips, and he grew hard, pressing against me between my legs. He lifted his head up to smile wickedly at me. "And there is definitely something else that needs our attention right now."

I raised an eyebrow at him. Oh, he wanted to play? Then play we shall. "Och, I don't know about that, Captain. You seem to keep leaving before the fun starts."

"No one to interrupt us this time," he said, skimming his hands up from my hips and tracing over my sides.

I rolled my hips, grinding down onto the hardness of him before pressing my lips gently to the corner of his mouth. "Then what are you waiting for?"

"Are you sure about this, *teine?*" he asked, his hands flexing on my hips and his face full of desire.

Moving my hands to his shoulders, I leveraged against him as I shifted my weight, lining up his body exactly where I wanted him beneath our clothes. I smiled at the groan that left his lips before leaning down to kiss him lightly. "Aye. I'm sure, Caelum."

Without another word, he turned his head, his lips on mine once again, and my eyes slid shut. One of his hands left my sides to weave into my hair, holding my head in place as he ravaged my mouth. His tongue traced over my lips, and I opened my mouth for him, tangling my tongue with his. My heart was beating absurdly fast in my chest, and my stomach fluttered at the new sensations.

Sliding my hands down from his shoulders as we kissed, I explored his chest and stomach. He was firm everywhere, muscles on top of muscles. My fingers grazed the top of his waistband, and he let out a rumbling noise from his chest that vibrated against my lips.

I pulled back with a smile, confidence and power oozing from my skin. "You like that, Captain?"

He leveled a look at me before moving both of his hands to my hips. He pressed them down as he jutted his hips up to meet me. He leaned in, and his breath tickled my ear, sending shivers down my spine. "Does it feel like I like that?"

"Not sure," I said, suddenly breathless. "Might need to take a closer look."

He shook his head at me, a smile on his face. Then his hands had shifted under my thighs and he was picking me up, standing in a fluid motion. "You're pure trouble."

I grinned at him before leaning in and pressing my lips against his neck, peppering kisses down his suntanned skin. The hair on his chin and neck felt rough beneath my lips, something I had never experienced before. I was used to smooth, supple skin and dainty touches with small hands. Caelum was firm and unyielding and knew exactly what he wanted. He also knew exactly what I wanted, and he was determined to give it to me.

Still holding me with my legs wrapped around his waist, he walked us over to the bed. He put one knee down to hold us before lowering me onto my back. I looked up at him leaning above me, all muscle and arousal, and my mouth went dry. Caelum was a sight, handsome and strong, but what was even more alluring was the kindness I knew was beneath his rugged exterior.

He looked down at me, his eyes unfocused and his mouth slightly open. I laughed lightly before hooking a leg behind his thigh and pulling him down to me, his hands landing on either side of my head. "You're staring."

"You're worth staring at," he replied, his voice more gruff than usual. His eyes roamed down my body hungrily, and he tugged at the hem of my dress, bunched up near my thighs. "Can I take this off, *teine?*"

My entire body flushed, and I nodded, maybe a little too enthusiastically. I couldn't wait to feel his hands on my skin. "Only if you tell me what that means."

"It means fire," he said softly, his eyes molten green. He didn't waste a moment, leaning back on his heels and grasping the hem of the skirt. Slowly (too slowly, in my opinion), he pulled it up, up, up until the fabric was bunched around my ribs. He bent down, pressing his lips against the soft skin of my stomach. The contrast of the roughness of his hands and beard and the gentleness he touched me with were sending my mind into a spiral. There were so many sensations in my body warring for my focus.

"Still good?" he asked, looking up at me.

I nodded, not trusting myself to be able to speak. My chest was heaving with breathlessness, my mind still racing over his pet name for me. *Fire.* It made my body light up.

He leaned his head back down to my skin, continuing to press open-mouthed kisses to the skin as he pushed the dress further up. The fabric rose over my breasts, and his hand slipped under my back to pull me up to sitting. Our eyes met for a long moment, and my own heat and desire echoed in the swirling green of his eyes. In a motion smoother than I could have ever achieved, Caelum pulled the dress over my arms, leaving my body completely bare to him. My pulse quickened as his eyes skated over my body, darkening with obvious desire.

It made me feel powerful to see how much my body affected him, and I hope he felt the same about me looking at him.

The dress was tossed to the side, and he cupped my cheeks in his hands, pulling my face to him for another kiss. I let my eyes close as our lips moved together, losing myself in the sensations of Caelum touching me.

We pulled apart for breath, but stayed close, our breath mingling. Keeping our gazes locked, I reached down to tug at the collar of his shirt. "Off."

A crooked grin spread across his face, but he shook his head and pressed a kiss to one side of my mouth, then the other. "No, this is about you right now."

I wanted to see him, to touch him the same way he was touching me. I wanted us to feel good together. "Caelum..."

"Don't whine," he said, running his nose up the side of my neck. He caught my earlobe between his teeth and tugged, eliciting a sharp gasp from me. He gently pushed me back onto the bed and traced a hand down my thigh, squeezing it. "You're beautiful, Brigid."

I reached my hand up to rake through his hair, tugging slightly. "You're beautiful too, Caelum."

He smiled at me, and the pure joy on his face made my heart tighten. I had never had someone look at me like that, and now that someone—that *Caelum*—had, I never wanted to lose it.

Before I could think anymore, Caelum bent down and firmly nudged my legs apart with his shoulders, settling on his stomach between my thighs. He bent his head to my inner thigh and started kissing there, gently at first, but getting firmer and rougher, alternating with nibbling bites that were making my chest heave and wetness gather between my thighs.

"You ever done this, *teine?*" he asked, pausing his kisses with his cheek resting on my inner thigh. He was so close to where I truly wanted him. I could feel his breath against my core.

"Yes, once," I said. My voice was already coming in pants, and he hadn't even started yet.

He raised an eyebrow at me. "Oh, really?"

Despite how aroused I was, I rolled my eyes at him. "I'm not as inexperienced as you seem to think I am."

"When have you had time to be with a man, huh?" he asked, going back to rubbing his cheek against my inner thighs, his beard chafing and scratching.

I raised an eyebrow back at him. "Who said it was a man?"

He stopped abruptly and just looked at me. I could see the wheels turning in his head as he worked through the possibilities. I was a syren, and I had spent the last ten years with the others. While we were all close, yes, we all still had romantic and sexual desires. Some of the others preferred to go to land for a night, while others, like me, found comfort in the familiarity.

"Och. Never thought of that, but it makes sense, I suppose," he said after a moment.

Without a word of warning, Caelum ducked his head between my thighs. His mouth landed on me, chasing all thoughts from my mind.

His tongue worked me over, taking me to heights I had never imagined I could reach. I was glad to be sharing this with him. I wanted it to last forever as he licked, sucked, and nibbled at my flesh.

He took me higher and higher, working his tongue against me. I groaned, my head pushing back into the bed. The sensations were overwhelming, his mouth hot against me, and yet it also wasn't enough. I wanted more.

"More, Caelum, please, more," I begged, reaching down and twisting my fingers through his hair to hold him there.

He obliged and began again with even more enthusiasm, making the coil in my stomach tighten, pressure building. I registered his hand moving against my thigh, but my brain was too far gone to realize what he was doing until his fingers joined his mouth, stroking and teasing.

His tongue slowed down slightly, but the languid intensity was not a reprieve, and I didn't want it to be. Gently, so gently, he eased one finger inside me, sliding it in and out as he continued to work me with his tongue. I was falling apart around him, and it was unlike anything I'd ever felt before. Another finger joined, and he sucked hard on the bundle of nerves at the apex of my thighs, and I was lost, white blinding my vision as I arched from the bed in ecstasy. He continued working me through my climax, bringing my body down from the high as skillfully as he had built it up.

My vision returned, but my breath was still coming in pants, and my body was tingling from head to toe. He pressed a gentle kiss between my thighs and then sat up, grinning at me as he pulled his fingers, still glistening, into his mouth. His eyes closed and he groaned. "You're delicious."

"Come here," I demanded. I hooked a leg around the back of his thigh and pulled him down on top of me, making his lips crash against mine. I could taste myself on his lips and tongue, I could feel the wetness still in his beard rub across my chin. It was delicious.

We pulled back for breath, and I reached for the bottom of his shirt, pulling it up and over his head with ease. I traced my hands over his chest, admiring his body. My hands landed on the waist of his pants, and I tugged.

His hands covered mine and made me stop. "Not tonight, *teine*. This was all for you."

"I want to touch you, Caelum," I breathed out. I wanted it more than I wanted air.

He pulled my hands away and pinned them above my head, moving to hover with his face over mine and a thigh between my legs. "You will. After this is all over. We're taking this slow, Brigid. You've never been with a man, and I'm going to do this right for you."

"I want to do it now."

He grinned, his eyes sparkling. "Oh, you do, do you? Well, that's too bad."

I knew it was childish, but I stuck my tongue out at him. I wanted to touch him and feel him against me and inside me, and he was refusing me because he was being a gentleman. Well, that wasn't the Caelum I wanted tonight.

He moved to hold both of my wrists in one of his large hands. He tapped the tip of my nose with his now free hand. It still smelled like me, and my stomach fluttered with desire.

"The only thing you're doing now, *teine,* is going to sleep. If we make it through this, I promise you, I'll take you to bed, I'll strip off both our clothes, and I'll ravage you so thoroughly that you won't know your name or my name or which way is up." he nearly growled. "I promise you that."

"Promises, promises," I breathed, insanely turned on. My body wanted more, needed more, and I ground down against his thigh between my legs.

His eyes snapped down to my moving hips before he looked back up at me with another one of his crooked grins. "And what do you think you're doing?"

"Fixing the problem myself," I said with a coy smile. I kept moving my hips, consciously this time, using his thigh to get the pressure and friction I desperately needed.

"Don't let me stop you, then," he said, swallowing hard as he watched me. "But after, we go to sleep."

"We'll see," I said with a grin and began moving with more purpose. He had no idea what he had unleashed with his touch, with his body, with his words. But he would find out soon enough.

Elizianna
@ELIZIANNA.THE.ONE

Caelum

Chapter Forty

The sun was just beginning to peek over the horizon as we made our way down to the docks. Not many people were out, and the ones who were paid us no real attention as we walked through the town. The men had their weapons strapped to their bodies, but it was not out of place, like I had told Brigid. No one batted an eye. Once we reached the slip where our small rowboats were moored, we stopped.

"Be careful," I said, pulling Brigid into my arms. I squeezed her tightly, feeling her body against mine and hoping to the gods it wouldn't be the last time. After last night, I needed her more than I had ever needed anything in my entire life. Letting her go reluctantly, I pulled Sorcha in next, giving her a quick squeeze as well. "You both be careful."

Brigid locked eyes with me, her gaze intense. "You be careful as well, Captain."

I nodded, not trusting my voice to not blurt out something that was better said in private. Forcing myself to move, I turned to Duncan and Cameron. "Let's get started."

Near silently, we untied the boats, all of us loading into them. Once the boats were pushed off, Sorcha and Brigid began pulling their clothes off, shoving them into a bag at my feet. While I wanted to watch Brigid reveal her body and relish in seeing her again, I kept my eyes on the horizon. We had to stay focused. *I* had to stay focused.

With a long glance back at me, full of promise, the girls slipped over the side of the boat and into the cold water. Their heads disappeared under the dark surface, but after a moment, they resurfaced, their mouths now full of sharp teeth. Sorcha passed a concerned look to Brigid, who was wincing, and I realized that this was the first time Sorcha had seen Brigid's new transformation.

I let out a harsh breath, pushing back all my emotions as I assessed our situation. "All right, time to go."

Just like we had discussed, we quietly rowed our boats to the mouth of the harbor, where we could sit in wait, fairly out of sight, and see my father's ship when it left. From there, Brigid and Sorcha would disable the ship's rudders so that we could catch up. Thankfully for my nerves, we didn't have to wait much longer. After a while, a ship appeared from the far side of the harbor, slipping out silently into the water. I recognized it instantly, and bad memories of being aboard that ship as a boy threatened to overpower me. Pushing the memories down, I tried to focus on what was happening now.

I motioned to Duncan in the other boat, letting him know they were coming. It was time to stop my father once and for all. He nodded back at me.

The next few minutes were agonizing as we waited for the ship to get out far enough from the harbor that they could not send for help. Finally, they were out in deep enough water, and we made our move, rowing the boats close to the hull. If anyone cared to look over the railing, they would have seen us. But like my father, his men were overconfident, and it would be their downfall.

In the water, I saw a shimmer flash by, and knew that Brigid and Sorcha were going about disabling the ship from beneath.

The ship slowed, turning unnaturally toward jutting rocks near the mouth of the harbor. Perfect. Sorcha and Brigid's plan had worked. A loud ripping and splintering sounded as Brigid and

Sorcha attacked the ship, and we used the noise cover to toss lines and hooks over the side of the ship to secure our row boats to the railing. The crew began shouting, trying to figure out what the noise had been.

Quietly, we climbed the ropes, peering into portholes and gunning hatches as we moved, hoping to find any indication of where the children were. Duncan whistled softly, pointing at a porthole by his shoulder. The children.

I nodded confirmation. We continued climbing, slipping onto the deck quietly and unnoticed. My father's crew was moving about, trying to see what they had run into and how they could fix it. If this had been my crew, I would have reprimanded them for lack of attention until my voice went hoarse. But now, I was grateful for their inattention. Duncan and Cameron were at my back as we moved swiftly across the deck.

It was only a matter of time before we were spotted. As inattentive as my father's crew seemed to be, someone would spot us eventually. I could only hope we could get to the children before that happened.

As usual, my hopes were not reality.

"And where do you think you're going?"

I turned only to see my father standing on the upper deck, looking down at us. At his side was the big man, the one who had killed Maddock. My jaw clenched, and I saw red, furious that the giant oaf had survived after all. "Thought it'd be obvious. We're here to stop you."

In an instant, I whirled around, drawing my sword and blocking the cutlass that had been coming down toward me from behind. Our blades clashed as I backed him up toward the railing. With one final step and a harsh stab, he fell overboard. I couldn't stay to watch, but I saw flashes of scales, and the man disappeared faster than what was natural beneath the waves. The girls had taken him. Good. I grinned.

I turned back to the deck and immediately had to engage with another one of my father's men. Out of the corner of my eye, I noticed the rest of my crew doing the same, fighting against my father's men while the devil himself stood, watching with a grin.

As I continued fighting my father's men, I was trying to make my way to him, my eyes tracking him at his casual position on the upper deck. I needed to end this, and the best way to do that was to end him. In flashes of seeing him between fighting, I could see that the stump where his hand used to be was still heavily bandaged. I hoped that would benefit me in our fight.

The ship began to slant as it started to take on water from Brigid and Sorcha's destruction, and it tilted rapidly to one side. It threw us all off-balance, but I was able to recover quicker than my opponent, and cut him down with a slice to his throat. I kept moving to keep from thinking about what I had done, what I would continue to do.

My father was a skilled swordsman, but it required balance, and I doubted he had time to perfect his swordsmanship with the new adjustments. In a fair fight, he would have beaten me—not easily, but he would have beaten me. But now, adding the tilting of the ship, I had a slight advantage—one that I planned to utilize.

As I fought my way toward the stairs, I saw Cameron and Duncan coming out from below deck, a group of small boys huddled between them. I turned to the rest of our men on the deck and gave a sharp whistle. It was our signal to protect Cam and Duncan as they got the children off the ship.

Without anyone even so much as glancing at each other, we shifted our positions to keep my father's crew away from Cam and Duncan as they moved toward the side of the boat. Painfully slowly, I watched as child after child was lowered down until Duncan and Cameron finally followed. Thirteen children, all around age ten, with disheveled clothes and dirty faces, were in the boat.

I let out a heavy breath. They were safe. We had done it. Even if the rest of us didn't make it off this ship alive, we had done it.

Mission ultimately accomplished, I began fighting my way back to my father once again. Finally, I reached the stairs and rushed up them, only to be blocked by the giant oaf once again. I could hear my heart beating in my ears, rage flooding through my body as I remembered this man's sword swinging down and cutting through Maddock's chest. With a roar I barely heard, I charged him, swinging my sword with all my strength.

It was a stupid move. The giant merely stepped out of my way before moving back with a swing of his own. The metal clashed, and we fought, lunging back and forth.

Where this man was obviously bigger than me, I was faster and much more skilled. After lulling him into a pattern with my strikes, I spun quickly in the other direction, slicing my blade down across his chest, exactly as he had done to Maddock. And for good measure, I followed it up with a backswing of my hilt into the back of his neck.

Before his body even hit the deck, I was moving toward my father, bloodied sword dripping. I raised it to him, surprised that he didn't immediately fight back.

"Congratulations, my son," he said as I held the blade to his throat. "You're officially the pirate you swore you'd never be."

My teeth ground together, my jaw clenching, before lowering the sword and swinging my fist directly into his face. "I'm saving them from the likes of you, father."

He grinned as he righted himself, his teeth bloody. "Still a pirate. Just. Like. Me."

"I'm nothing like you."

"We'll see about that," he replied before pushing me back with his only remaining hand and finally drawing his sword against me. He swung toward me, and I met it, blocking his blow.

"Who are you selling them to?" I asked, our swords clashing together as we fought.

He pushed me back a step, and the grin on his face made my steps falter. "Oh, you mean you still haven't figured that out? Even with that beast of a syren in your midst? I thought you were *smart,* son."

"Who?" I gritted out, tightening my grip on my sword.

"Cliodhna. The syren queen. The goddess who transformed your precious lass into the monster she is," he said. His voice was gleeful.

My stomach dropped into my boots like lead. Brigid's queen was working with my father. Did that mean that she was too? I shook my head. No, I wouldn't go down that path. Brigid was trying to help us. There was no way she was working with him.

As if she knew I was thinking about her, I saw Brigid's head pop up over the waves below. She looked around, eyes violent and frantic. I couldn't help it, I had to know. I took a step backward toward the railing.

"Brigid, did you know?" I shouted at her, keeping an eye on my father.

She swam closer to the ship, looking up at me. She shouted back, "Know what?"

"He's working with your queen." A sick feeling clamped around my stomach. If Kellan had been working with Brigid's queen, did she know about this? Had she known all along? I tried to tamp down the feelings of betrayal—at least until I knew the facts.

Her eyes widened and her mouth fell open, and I knew without a doubt that she had not known either. I could barely hear her voice when she answered, "What?"

"He's working with Cliodhna!" I shouted, in case she truly had not heard me. My heart was racing as I wondered what could be happening in the water. If he was working with Cliodhna, then the other syrens could be on their way to fight against us, and Brigid and Sorcha were alone. My eyes frantically scanned the water, searching for any sign of the others.

Before I could see her response or offer any other information, my father had rushed me again. I turned my attention back to him.

Elizi
@ELIZIAN

B RIGID

CHAPTER FORTY-ONE

"He's right, you know. Kellan and I are working together."

At her voice behind me, I spun in the water to face my queen. The queen who had apparently been the root of this evil we were working to stop. Her face was bored, but I saw her eyes sparkle with violence. I knew that it truly had been her all along.

"Why?" I asked, twisting and moving through the water to keep away from her.

"Man has forgotten me," she said, bitterness lacing her voice. "And as man forgets, so does the world, and my powers weaken."

"So, you take children to remedy that?" I couldn't believe what I was hearing. I had trusted Cliodhna, revered her. My heart shattered with betrayal.

She shrugged as if what she was doing was nothing of importance. "Their youth and purity fuels my power. The souls of men are tainted by their violence."

My eyes widened. No, it couldn't be. "You're killing them?"

All those times she spoke of her powers, she was talking about these children. I wanted to vomit. The powers she had given me were from *children*.

The water beneath me changed. We weren't the only ones here; there was someone coming up from below me. I turned to see Maira and the others popping above the water one by one. Cliodhna looked at them. "Stop her and her man. That ship and those boats must all sink, and everyone on them must die."

"My queen?" Kyla asked, her voice confused. She looked at me and then back at Cliodhna. "What's going on?"

"Why are you talking to her?" Maira asked Kyla, her voice angry. "She abandoned us."

I really hoped the others had nothing to do with this horror. Lip snarling, I got in Maira's face. As close as we had been, if any of us had helped Cliodhna or known about it, it would be her. "Did you know about this?"

She bared her teeth at me. "Know what, Brigid?"

"She is the one taking and killing those children I am trying to rescue," I hissed, pointing a clawed finger back at Cliodhna, who was watching us with a look that could only be described as boredom. Turning my back to her was likely a foolish move, but I needed to know the truth of the others' involvement. "We have been serving a queen who sacrifices children to sustain her powers."

Maira's eyes widened slightly for a moment, but she covered it by narrowing them suspiciously. "And who told you that?"

"She did." My face was hot with anger, and my claws itched to dig themselves into flesh. I cast a quick glance back to the ship, where I could see Caelum fighting with his father. I wanted badly to help him, but I knew I needed to deal with my own fight first. Caelum was capable and could handle himself.

Maira whipped her gaze to Cliodhna, then to Kyla, then back to me, before landing on our queen once again. Her eyes were suspicious still, but I could see the frantic undertone in them. Perhaps she wasn't involved after all. "Is that true?"

Cliodhna shrugged again, swimming toward us. I turned to face her, and though my back was now to six other syrens, I trusted them more than I trusted our supposed queen. Cliodhna sighed as if we were annoying her. "Yes, yes, Brigid's little tale is true."

"You're using the life force of children?" Kyla asked, her voice quiet but deadly. Her face was pure rage, and I remembered that Kyla had been a mother when she had been changed. "Why?"

"Why not, my child?" Cliodhna laughed. The sound grated on my nerves, and I gritted my teeth, my fangs digging into the gums. "These are the children of men, in case you forgot. And if I remember correctly, that was the same reasoning you gave for not helping Brigid when she first came begging. So, I wonder what has changed."

"We didn't know you were involved in that," Kyla said, her voice faltering slightly. "Or we would have…"

"Would have what?" Cliodhna asked, sneering. She came even closer to us, nearly within my reach now. "What would you have done? Gone against me? Tried to stop me? You all are nothing without the powers I gave you. You were discarded like rubbish until I saved you. You all owe everything to me."

"We owe you nothing," I snarled, fighting the urge to lunge forward and push my claws through her chest. It would likely do nothing but anger her. "All you care about is becoming more powerful."

"You think you can mutiny against me, girl?" Cliodhna curled her lip up and scoffed. "I created you, I gave you purpose, and this is how you repay me? The others will never follow you."

I looked at the others, their eyes flitting between our queen and me, no doubt trying to figure out what was happening and whose side to take.I hoped they believed me and would help me. I doubted that Sorcha and I would be able to fight all six of them and come out alive. "I'm not asking them to follow me. They deserve to know the truth about you and decide for themselves what to do."

"And what's this truth, child?" She rolled her eyes.

"You don't care about us. We're a means to your end."

She laughed loudly, throwing her head back. "Of course you are a means to an end! I created you for a reason—to serve me, not to run about with men and get in my way. It's too bad the men I sent when you first saved that boy failed."

The fishermen…she had been the one to tell them about me?

She had sent them to Caelum's cottage? Anger and betrayal burned within my chest.

"We will not help you stop them like you asked," Kyla said firmly. "Brigid may have left us, but she's never lied to us. And she's certainly never killed a child."

Cliodhna rolled her eyes again, and my fingers twitched beneath the water, itching to pluck the eyes from her skull. "I truly don't understand what is so important about these children. They are nothing to you, and their sacrifices allowed me to create you, to save you."

"Then I would have rather died." Kyla looked at me, determination clear in her eyes and the set of her jaw. "What do you need from us, Brigid?"

Cliodhna whirled at me, rage in her eyes. "You see what you've done? You've destroyed this family."

I met her gaze with anger of my own. "No, you did that on your own. I merely opened their eyes to the monster you are."

She growled and lunged for me, her talons out. I was ready for her, though. Moving swiftly, I avoided her strike.

She growled in frustration, moving toward me once again. We danced in the water, both above the waves and below, swiping at each other and dodging. She was fast, but I was fueled by anger so palpable I could feel it radiating through the water. I couldn't let her live. She was a monster. Urging my body to move faster, I pushed harder, trying to get closer. My claws reached out, swiping at her side. They glanced off her side, scraping slightly, but I knew it wasn't enough to do any damage.

If anything, it just seemed to irritate her. She paused in her movements, tilting her head as she studied me. "You are so insignificant. This bores me."

With a wave of her hand, magic pushed through the water, driving me back until I could no longer make out the features of the others. Sorcha looked back to me before moving to take my place in the fight.

Recovering from the blast of waves, I hurried back toward Cliodhna to help Sorcha. But I was too late. Sorcha tried to dodge a swipe of claws, but she must have moved the wrong way. I could only watch in horror as Cliodhna's claws dug into her chest. My friend went still, and the water began to turn red around her.

No. *No.*

I surged forward, pulling Sorcha away from Cliodhna and into my arms. *No!*

Cliodhna pulled away with a frustrated scream. "Insolent girl! Now look at what you've done."

I pulled Sorcha more into my arms, holding her to me. My eyes blurred and my throat burned. "No...no, Sorcha."

"What have you done?" Maira hissed at Cliodhna, moving forward toward us. "Sorcha was innocent."

"She sided with the traitor, that is not innocent," the icy goddess replied, watching us intently. She seemed disinterested yet again, not caring that she had just killed one of her own. Her icy eyes flashed back to me, retribution burning in them like blue fire. "This is your fault."

I heard the words, but they echoed in my ears as I held the body of my friend in my arms. Blood spread in the water around us, and tears ran down my cheeks, landing on her face. My vision was blurry as I looked down at her.

Sorcha blinked slowly, looking up at me. "Bri...Brigid?"

"Yes, Sorcha, what is it?" I sobbed. "What do you need?"

"Find Owen," she said. "Tell him...tell him what happened."

I nodded furiously as my tears continued to fall. "I will. I'll find him, and I'll tell him everything. I'll find him, I promise."

"Love you," she whispered, closing her eyes.

"No, no," I sobbed. I shifted her so I could tap my palm against her cheek. "Open your eyes, stay with me."

A hand touched my shoulder, and I jumped. I whirled, ready to fight whoever had touched me, but it was Kyla. There were unshed tears in her dark eyes. "She's gone, Brigid. She's gone."

With a snarl, I let Sorcha's body fall from my arms into the water, and I lunged at Cliodhna, my claws out. She wasn't ready for me this time. Swiping at her face, satisfaction flooded me when my talons ripped at her flesh.. She cried out in pain as blood began to pour from the wounds, staining her white hair pink. Her hand clapped against her face, staunching the blood flow slightly.

Her eyes were like daggers as she glared at me. "You will regret that."

"I highly doubt that," I bit back. Moving toward her again, I vowed to kill her for what she had done. Sorcha had been innocent. She'd done nothing to Cliodhna. The queen's lack of caring would be her downfall. *I* would be her downfall.

Before I could reach Cliodhna, she dipped beneath the waves and shot off toward the open sea. She would not escape my wrath. I moved to dive beneath the water to follow.

"Brigid." Kyla's soft voice stopped me in my tracks before my head dipped below the surface.

Looking after where Cliodhna had disappeared for a moment, I eventually turned back to the others. Kyla's eyes were shining with tears as she held Sorcha's body in her arms. The rich color of Kyla's skin made Sorcha's body look all the more pale.

"Why didn't you help her?" I asked, my voice cracking. "You were all *right there.*"

"We need to put her to rest," she said quietly. She ignored my statement and pleas.

Hurt washed through me. My revenge and anger could wait; Sorcha deserved better than this. I nodded, looking down at my hands beneath the waves. My hair fell down into my face. I didn't move to push it away. "Yes, of course."

"What will we do?" Maira asked, her own voice uncharacteristically quiet. "Sea or land?"

My head snapped up at her words. "I don't want her in the sea. Cliodhna will find some way to taint that."

"Then we'll bury her on land," Kyla promised, her voice stern. She looked over her shoulder. Cam was moving in an empty rowboat toward us. "Let's get her on the boat."

Elizianna
@ELIZIANNA.THE.ONE

CAELUM

CHAPTER FORTY-TWO

I don't know what pushed me to look over the railing. Looking back, I think Brigid's sorrow and anger had traveled through the water and had become palpable. Whatever the case, my eyes managed to catch the moment she clung to a small body as she flung her head back and screamed. It was a sound I would never forget. I watched as she swam toward the rowboat in the distance, unable to process what I was seeing. Sorcha was dead.

From the deck, I couldn't hear what was said, but Cam must have convinced her to give Sorcha to him; he took the small girl from Brigid's arms and pulled her up into the rowboat with him and Finn, who had turned the children away.

"Och, such a young one," my father said, smacking his lips.

I turned back to him, my anger and energy suddenly revived. "This is your fault."

"Actually, no," he said, and lunged at me with his sword. I blocked it with my own, and our fight had begun anew.

I shoved him back with my sword before I thrust at him. He blocked me, pushing me out to the side and exposing my midsection, which he quickly took advantage of, trying for a thrust of his own. But I was faster and stepped out of the way. We circled each other, taking any opening the other left, metal clanging together as we fought.

A quick sidestep and a slash down, and I had landed the first hit —barely. My blade nicked the side of his cheek at the top of my arc, but he stepped back far enough to avoid the blow. He countered with a step forward and another thrust, but his balance was off, and the sword angled down toward my thighs instead. I dropped the tip of my blade and countered, knocking his out to the side. I followed it up by bringing my arm down, slamming the pommel into his wrist.

The sword fell from his hands, landing at his feet, and he looked at me, anger and desperation written across his face. He narrowed his eyes. "You've not won yet."

Like the desperate fool he was, he charged at me. Without a sword, he was defenseless, and I could have easily killed him. Perhaps I should have, but he was still my father, and the moment of hesitation I had was enough to change my mind. I blocked his punches with my forearms rather than my blade before sweeping my leg out and catching his ankle, sending him crashing to the deck.

Lip curled in a snarl, I kicked the sword away, the metal clattering across the wooden deck. Finally. I pointed my sword down at my father. "Yield, and I'll not kill you."

"You're weak, son," he said, the cut on his face weeping blood. He wiped at it, smearing crimson across his only remaining hand. "I would never give you this mercy."

"I told you, I'm nothing like you," I gritted out. I didn't want to kill him, but I would if I needed to.

"Well, I'll not yield," he said. In an instant, he drew a dagger from his belt and swiped at me.

I jumped back but wasn't fast enough. The metal sliced into the skin of my lower leg, cutting deep. The pain jolted through my body, but I gritted my teeth and tensed the muscles. Despite my earlier words, I knew I couldn't let him live at this point. I knew he would just continue the fight, and I needed to end this. Any sentimentality between us had been lost long ago. Now, he was just trying to kill me.

With a kick, I knocked the dagger from his hand, and without hesitation, plunged my sword through his chest. His body tensed before going limp, blood trickling slowly out of his lips. His eyes stared up at me for a moment before looking off into nothingness. I stepped back and turned away without looking, my stomach heaving at what I had just done.

I had just killed my father. Gods, I had killed him.

I staggered over to the railing, taking gulping breaths of sea air, attempting to stop the bile turning sour in my throat. He had deserved it, but that didn't make the pain and confusion any less real.

I saw Brigid in the water, still at the rowboat, gently stroking Sorcha's hair while Cam spoke softly to her. I continued taking breaths, watching her as I tried to calm my racing heart and churning stomach. She calmed me, even from a distance. Brigid was my solace, and after this, I was never going to let her go. I just needed to tell her that and hope she would feel the same.

I tried to avoid looking at Sorcha's small body as they held her in the boat. I looked at the other syrens, studying them as they huddled together away from the boat, watching the scene before them. My gaze kept flitting about, doing anything to keep from looking back at my father behind me, lying on the deck with my sword still in his chest.

I watched Brigid nod shakily and pull back from the boat, and Cam turned it back toward the harbor. I could see the silver shining in her eyes and the wetness on her cheeks. She floated in the water, her tail swishing beneath her, as she wiped furiously at her eyes. I wanted to reassure her, to hold her, but we weren't finished here yet.

The other syrens came up beside her, but she pushed them away, directing them to follow the boat, which they did. I only hoped that meant they were on our side now. I doubted she would have pointed them toward Cam and the children if they weren't.

Behind her, the water swirled, and a white figure swam through the water, a silvery tail following—Cliodhna. I straightened up, leaning over the railing as much as I could.

"Brigid, look out!" I shouted, seeing the white-haired syren shoot down into the water before surging up from beneath Brigid.

Before she could react, the queen had Brigid in her grasp and was pulling her down into the depths until I could no longer see her beneath the dark waves. The look of terror on Brigid's face as she was pulled down was haunting, and I could do nothing to save her from my place on the ship.

My heart stopped. This feeling was nothing like I had felt before, nothing like I had experienced moments ago with my father's death, or even with Maddock's. No, this was much different.

She was gone. Brigid had been taken.

Elizianna
@ELIZIANNA.THE.ONE

Caelum

Epilogue

"Captain, what happened?" Cameron asked me as I stepped out of the rowboat with Duncan. He looked around at the water behind me. "Where's Brigid?"

I was numb and wasn't sure how to answer him. Instead, I just shook my head. The emptiness in my chest needed no words right now. My voice probably wouldn't even work if I had tried to speak.

Duncan stepped up next to me and placed a hand on my shoulder. His own voice was quiet and more subdued than I had been expecting. "We'll get her back, Caelum."

"Where did she go?" Cameron asked slowly, his voice suspicious. I could see Sorcha's small body under a blanket on the harbor docks, and it was the only thing I could focus on. We would need to bury her. Brigid would have wanted that.

"Caelum says the queen took her, dragged her down in the water," Duncan answered for me. I was grateful for his voice.

Shoving down my grief and warring emotions, I cleared my throat. There were things I needed to take care of, things Brigid would want me to be doing. "How're the children? Are they ready to be taken to the cottage?"

"They're fine, mate. But are you okay?" Cam asked, looking at me with concern. But I didn't deserve his concern.

I just nodded again. They needed me to be a captain, so I needed to step up and shove everything else down until I was alone. "Aye, I'm fine. We've got to get the children safe, then we can go find Brigid."

"Find Brigid?" a female voice asked. I turned to see a group of women walking down the dock, all wrapped in various blankets and fabric, but otherwise naked. The other syrens, I supposed. The woman who had spoken first stepped forward, her dark eyebrows furrowed. "Where is she?"

"Your queen took her," I said flatly. I had no patience for these women. They had abandoned Brigid, and then when she and Sorcha had needed them, had abandoned them again. "Do you know where we can find her?"

"What do you mean our queen took her?" a blonde syren asked, her voice harsh and cold. She stepped around the other one.

Her tone grated on me. The accusatory tone was unwelcome, and I knew immediately we would not be getting along. "Exactly what it sounds like. She was swimming toward me, and then your queen came from the depths and dragged her down."

The blonde one curled her lip up at me but didn't say anything else.

"Do you know how to find where Cliodhna took her?" I asked again, pointedly turning my attention back to the dark-haired one.

"No, but we'll help you find her," she said, raising her head proudly despite being soaking wet and wrapped in a threadbare blanket. She stuck her hand out, her brown skin a stark contrast to the pale hand I was used to seeing with Brigid. "I'm Kyla. We'll help you."

I looked down at her hand for a moment, but made no move to take it. "I hope so."

Without another word, I turned my back on them and started walking toward Finn, who was helping get the children settled at the docks. I couldn't face those women, those women who had turned their backs on Brigid when she needed their help. And while I was grateful for their help now, I couldn't look at them. I heard Cameron and Duncan speaking to the syrens behind me, but I couldn't focus. Nothing was going through my mind except the image of Brigid's terrified face as she was dragged down into the depths.

I would do anything to get her back, including killing that bitch goddess. I would get her back, even if it was the last thing I did.

Elizianna
@ELIZIANNA.THE.ONE

CAELUM

UNDERWATER ADVENTURE

This is a deleted scene from The Syren's Mutiny

I shivered as the icy water reached up to my ankles, then my shins, then my thighs, as Brigid led me by the hand deeper. The water didn't seem to faze her at all, nor did her nakedness. While I knew logically, I should be back at the cottage, working with the others to come up with a plan to avenge Maddock's death and stop my father, I wanted this time with Brigid. Maybe even needed it. She brought life out in me that I had long pushed down in favor of being the dutiful captain.

Stopping at waist deep water, Brigid turned to me. Her eyes dropped down to my mouth and she grabbed my face, capturing my lips in a searing but quick kiss before pulling back and dropping down into the water, submerging herself completely.

I watched her, able to see every detail of her body through the clear water. She closed her eyes and the water shimmered as her legs merged into that beautiful silvery red tail. My eyes moved up, watching as her fingernails lengthened into talons. Even under the water, I could hear her bones cracking, and blood spotted the shallow water, turning it red, then pink. I watched her face, tracking every grimace and clench of her jaw. More than anything, I hated her queen for doing this to her, for causing her this much pain to become the thing she loved. I hoped I never met this queen. I wasn't sure if I would be able to control my anger.

The transformation complete, she opened her eyes and popped her head up out of the water, panting slightly. She smiled, and though it was shaky and still had remnants of her pain, she was luminous and deadly, pulling her lips back and showing off her mouth full of pointed teeth. "You ready?"

"As I'll ever be." I returned the smile, reaching down to rub my thumb over her wet cheek. She hid her pain well, but I would do whatever I could to distract her from it until it faded.

She reached up to grab my hand with her own and in a swift moment, I was pulled under the water with her, moving out into deeper water at the same time. The first thing I noticed was that other than my pants and the hand holding Brigid's, I was completely dry. My eyes roved around, spotting an almost imperceptible bubble surrounding me. I could breathe too. It was truly magic, and nothing like I'd ever experienced before.

She pulled me through the water, pointing out rock formations, sea creatures, and everything else along the way. I had no idea where we were, or how long we were taking, but it didn't matter. The pure joy on her face as she swam around, pulling me next to her was worth it all. She showed me everything, took me into caves I had no idea existed, spinning me between rocks and among the seagrass. It was breathtaking, truly. Her and the ocean.

If I was her, I would never want to leave. I understood now, the sacrifice she had made to leave her family to save me, and it meant everything.

After a while of pulling me along at speed, showing me everything possible, she slowed. We came to a platform of rocks out in the middle of the sea floor, all alone. She stretched her tail along the rocks, pulling me to sit down beside her. She pointed up at the surface. Above us, the bay and the harbor lay, casting shadows down.

We couldn't talk, not without my powers, but instead we tilted our heads to the surface and watched as ship after ship passed over us, following their paths in and out of the harbor. It was calming, nothing around but us, and we sat there for who knows how long, just enjoying the other's company.

I looked over at her and pointed back up towards the surface. She turned to look at me, a sad smile crossing her face as she nodded. In a flash, we were up and moving through the water again, heading back towards the shore by the cottage. We broke the surface, our heads above water, but still a large distance away from the beach. The bubble she had created protected my body still in the water but did nothing for the wind sluicing through my hair.

"We should probably get back," I said, my voice quiet. I didn't want to ruin our moment, to set us back on what we had just overcome.

She turned to look at me. "Yes, we should. I didn't plan on leaving Sorcha alone so long anyways."

"She's fine. Cam and Duncan will watch out for her," I replied. I was glad that Sorcha had agreed to help, and I could see how much it meant to Brigid as well. At some point, I wanted to learn more about the young girl who had befriended the fiery syren.

She snorted. "That's not exactly comforting. Duncan doesn't like us."

Sighing, I ran a hand over my face roughly. Duncan and Brigid had obviously not gotten over their issues. "Duncan has problems with things he can't understand. And he was closer to the crew than I was. I didn't know them as well as he did, so their deaths hit him harder."

Pain flashed in her eyes. It was brief but I had seen it before she covered it up with her mask of fierceness. "I don't need his approval to exist, but I would like his respect and trust."

"We'll get there," I promised. Tonight, I would have a long talk with Duncan about Brigid. I understood his anger, and I understood hers, but they both meant a lot to me, and I wouldn't have them uncomfortable around the other. We needed to be working as a team.

"Let's just get back," she said, her voice dull.

"Don't pull away from me again." The situation frustrated me, and I didn't know how to fix it. It would have to be patched up between Duncan and Brigid themselves. "He's a good man, just give him some time."

She didn't reply, but she did nod before taking a hold of my hand again. Silently, she tugged me along and we began our return to the beach. She kept me in my protective bubble until we were almost up on the shore, her tail dragging along the rocky bottom. Once the water reached my knees, she let go of my hand and the bubble dropped, icy water drenching my pants once again. Our eyes locked as she began her transition. I turned away and forced myself to focus on the rocks, the shore, anything to keep from listening to her bones crack and shift. After a moment, she stood out of the water, her long hair dripping icy water down her naked body as she stepped up next to me.

I pulled her against me, not caring that my shirt was getting wet from the water on her body. "Come on, *teine*, let's get some clothes on you."

"So, you don't want to see me naked?" she asked, her voice teasing and light. I was glad she had moved on past our previous conversation. This side of her was one of my favorites and was first by a slim margin to the bloodthirsty and fiery side of her.

I laughed loudly. "Brigid, if it was up to me, you'd never have clothes on. But it's cold, and the others don't get to see you like I do."

She grinned at me as we exited the water. Walking over to the bag of clothes she had left by the log, she reached in and pulled out a long, simple white dress. It had long sleeves and as she pulled it over her still damp body, the fabric clung to her body obscenely, the slit up her right leg showing off the milky skin there. My mouth dried up and all I could do was stare at her.

As she straightened the dress, I couldn't resist any longer.

This scene continues in Chapter 30 of The Syren's Mutiny

THE CAPTAIN'S REVENGE

book two

JESSICA S. TAYLOR

Elizianna
@ELIZIANNA.THE.ONE

CHAPTER ONE

Sitting in front of the rolling waves, contemplating how I would kill a goddess, was likely not the best use of my time, but here I was anyway.

It had been about a fortnight since Brigid disappeared and I was no closer to finding her than we had been the day the syrens' goddess, Cliodhna, had dragged her away, vanishing beneath the waves. I had no idea where she had taken Brigid, let alone how to save the syren who had adeptly wormed her way into my life.

Not being able to breathe underwater posed a slight challenge to my rescue plans. Especially when the syrens were even less trusting of me and my crew than Duncan had been of them. Their stubbornness made it even more difficult to achieve anything.

But I tried.

As soon as she disappeared beneath the surface, I tried to get to her. Too many things—Sorcha's burial and getting the children somewhere safe—had delayed the search, making it feel near impossible to find her now.

At Brigid's request to the other syrens, we buried Sorcha in the earth instead of the sea to keep Cliodhna from getting her hands on Sorcha's body. Per my sentiment, we buried her next to Maddock back in Brinemoor at my old home. Burying her had been hard, and even Maira had shed a tear as she and the other syrens watched us cover her small body with earth.

We had fixed the dilapidated structure just enough to make it habitable while we discussed our next plans, but in the end, we returned to Finn's cottage. Sorcha's burial had only made me more determined to save myself from having to bury Brigid next to her, and this home, this structure, had too many emotions connected to it for me to think clearly.

The syrens, all of whom had returned with us, somewhat helped with the burial. They wanted to hold their own rituals for Sorcha, and during these, my crew and I had made ourselves scarce out of respect. But that had been the last time they willingly cooperated. Each day that followed was a battle.

What to do with the fourteen children we had rescued from my father and Cliodhna had been another point of contention. Admittedly, I had been short-sighted in my goal of ending Kellan's evils and had not truly stopped to fully consider how to care for these orphans once we rescued them.

The syrens had collectively wanted to send the children to a contact in Bhodheas, a woman who had apparently helped with the previous charges the syrens had saved who elected not to become syrens. I wanted the children to stay closer at the orphanage in Brinemoor so I could monitor them and ensure their continued safety. I would not abandon them now that I accomplished my original task. They deserved more from me, from life, and I would ensure they got it. I wasn't my father, and I would die before I let myself become anything like him.

It had been a hellish argument, almost coming to physical blows with one syren, Maira, but thankfully, it had been an argument that I won. The children were now at an orphanage in Brinemoor under the care of a woman Maddock and I knew named Isla.

Since returning to Finn's cottage after burying Sorcha, every single decision had been an argument with the syrens. Which rooms everyone would stay in, who would go into town to shop for food and supplies, and who would complete the chores and household duties. All of it was exhausting. But I knew I wouldn't be able to find Brigid without their help. So, I endured it.

After all, I had endured far worse for far less of a reward. And I would continue to endure anything thrown my way if it meant getting her back.

I rubbed my temples, attempting to relieve the recurring headache forming, and stared out at the water. "Where are you, Brigid?"

Standing, I picked up a stone from the beach and threw it as hard as I could out into the churning sea. It barely made a ripple before it disappeared into the roiling waves. It was a sad outlet, but it was something. My rage was nearly equal in power to my sadness.

"What did the water ever do to you?" An amused feminine voice echoed behind me.

I turned to see Maira walking toward me, and I had to squint against the annoyingly bright shine of her gold hair and pale skin against the overcast haze. Sighing, I moved over to allow her space beside me on the beach. If I didn't, she would have pushed her way in, regardless.

She was a female version of Duncan. Angry, suspicious, and above all, fucking stubborn. I wasn't sure why she had come out here, but I didn't want to speak with her. It would only devolve into another disagreement, and I was already exhausted. Of all the syrens, she had been the one most disapproving of every decision I made. And she had definitely been the most vocal.

Crossing my arms over my chest, I looked at her out of the corner of my eye. "There's not enough time for me to tell you about it all."

She smiled, but it didn't reach her eyes. It was a gesture of forced politeness, one I was not sure why she was engaging in. "So, what are you doing out here, then? Brooding?"

Clenching all my muscles and then relaxing them one by one, I slowly attempted to quell my irritation with the syren in front of me. It didn't work. It never worked. "Aye, sure. Since no one is doing anything to find Brigid, I might as well. What are you doing out here? Other than intentionally bothering me."

The fake smile she had pasted on her face finally dropped away, and her eyes narrowed. "What else is there to do? We searched the caves. She was not there." Her voice could have dropped the temperature of the water, freezing the sea to match her mood.

My patience and politeness quickly faded in the face of this annoying creature. All the syrens had used that same excuse, time and time again, and yet I knew they could do more. Search more. "And that's the *only* place you have searched. She could be anywhere!"

"Exactly. She could be anywhere," Maira retorted, rolling her eyes and crossing her arms over her chest. "So why should we waste our efforts when you don't have a clue where we should look?"

"Cliodhna was *your* queen," I reminded her, pointing at her chest. Rage simmered in my stomach, hot and wild, waiting to be unleashed. "If anyone should know where to search, it should be you. And yet here you sit, eating *my* food, wearing *my* clothes, and arguing with *my* men. No wonder Brigid left you."

Without warning, Maira snarled and stepped forward, wrapping her small hand around my throat and digging her blunt nails into my skin. I growled, my hands clenched at my side as I struggled not to reach out and strike her. *I do not have time for this.*

In one swift move, I reached down and pulled a dagger from my belt, pressing it to her throat and raising my eyebrow. I was not one of the defenseless men she faced, and I would not cower to her or her kind. Her grip was tight, but her hand wasn't even big enough to wrap around my throat, and without her talons extended, I wasn't afraid of her. She was a mere annoyance, like a fly swarming. And I was about to swat her.

"Insolent *man*," she spat, attempting to tighten her grip around my throat. "You have no idea the connections we have with one another. Brigid and I spent years together."

"And yet, you and your queen abandoned her on a whim after she saved me," I retorted, still holding my blade to her throat. It was an ongoing battle of wills, and if I let it, it would quickly turn physical. I knew without a doubt that if I gave her an opening, she would take it, and my blood would cover this beach.

"Hey!" a sharp voice yelled from up the path. Another syren. "What are you two doing?"

Coming down the hill were Cameron and another syren, Kyla. They came to a stop in front of us, Cameron's narrowed eyes tracking our every move. He had argued with Maira too, and I knew he was just as fond of dealing with her as I was. Which was not at all.

Kyla had been the one to shout at us, and her eyes were full of fire, a blazing amber that stood out against the deep russet of her skin. Kyla was the leader of the syrens now, an unspoken motion decided after several days of tension and several hushed arguments. For a moment, I worried Maira might end up on top, but thankfully the syrens had more sense than that.

At least Kyla was tolerable. Her soft voice and calm demeanor had deescalated many arguments between us all, including some between the syrens themselves. Cam had especially taken a liking to the woman, siding with her as often as he sided with me when we were on opposing sides of an argument.

Now, though, she was pure power. Her mass of long, dark brown curls lifted and swept back by the wind made her look even more intimidating, an expression I had never seen on her before. At least, never directed at me. Her shoulders were tense beneath the borrowed sweater, and her hands clenched at her side as she approached us, her eyes darting back and forth between Maira and me as she assessed the situation.

"This insolent man believes us beneath him," Maira said, squeezing her fingers around my throat, irritating me further. "I was simply proving him wrong."

"Keep digging your nails into my skin, syren, and I will prove *you* wrong," I promised, shifting the blade in my hand and pressing it harder against her skin. Her pale skin turned pink against the pressure of the blade, but I was careful to mind the pressure. I just wanted to remind her who was in charge, not actually hurt her.

"Both of you, stop," Kyla demanded, stepping between us. She put a hand on each of our chests, pushing to separate us, though we didn't move an inch. She pushed harder, nostrils flaring, and sent Maira back half a step, though the petulant syren's hand remained wrapped around my throat. "This is not helping anyone."

Turning my gaze to the brunette, I couldn't help my lip from snarling. "Aye, that's the point. You aren't helping. Brigid has been missing for weeks, and you've looked for her *once.*"

"You act like we're sitting around doing nothing," Maira said. "We have helped, more than that oaf you call a first mate."

"Watch your words, syren," I warned, looking back at her. I pulled the knife away and easily removed her hand from my throat, flinging her arm by the wrist like I should have done the moment her nails met my skin. Stepping back, I looked at both syrens and Cameron, who stood between them, crossing and uncrossing his arms and shifting his weight, ready to step in if needed. "You're antagonizing me and my men and arguing with us constantly. You do nothing to search for Brigid, nothing to look after the children we saved, nothing to help keep up the house we are staying in. All you do is huddle in your room and throw barbs at anyone who passes. At least the other syrens help with some tasks."

"I'll not bow to the likes of you," Maira sneered, taking a half step toward me, her fists clenched and ready to engage once more. "You are not in charge of us."

"No one's asking you to bow," I spat back, looking down at her. She truly was an irritating creature, and I couldn't fathom how Brigid had spent ten years without killing her. "We're asking you to help us find your friend."

Kyla moved around Cameron to stand in front of Maira, turning her back to me and effectively separating us. "You need to stop this. Now."

Maira rolled her eyes dramatically as Kyla stepped away, turning back to me. Her fire and rage died down, leaving room for the diplomatic and soft-spoken woman we'd come to know. The sun peeked out from behind the clouds fully, settling on Kyla's face and lighting her skin from within. It only made her look more regal, more... in charge.

"I understand your frustration, Caelum, truly I do. But with no clues where Brigid is, we simply cannot go out and search the seas from top to bottom. It would be an impossible task," Kyla said, trying to placate me as her hands stretched out towards me, palms up. "The only place we all knew was the caves, and they're empty."

"Surely you know of other places beneath the seas where Cliodhna could possibly be holding her. You haven't even looked," I snapped. Sighing, I rolled my shoulders to ease the tension and lowered my voice. Kyla was not the one who inspired my anger, and while she needed to hear the words, she didn't deserve my tone. Not like Maira had. "You know these waters better than any of us. But you all sit here, doing nothing instead, while your queen has Brigid."

"And what are you doing about it, pirate?" Maira leaned around Kyla to speak. Kyla closed her eyes and sighed, reaching up to pinch the bridge of her nose. I felt vindicated that Maira irritated even the most mellow of the syrens.

"*I* buried Sorcha, who was one of you, in case you forgot. *I* buried my *father*, whom I *killed,* to save these children. The children *your queen* was ready to murder to strengthen her own power. *I* took the children to an orphanage where they would be safe and taken care of," I said, taking a step closer to them with each sentence. Kyla stood her ground, staring me down. Maira's eyes glowed a fiery blue, and her lip curled up to reveal her teeth. I was so close I was nearly touching Kyla, but my focus remained entirely on Maira. "So, do not stand there, in the clothes *I* provided for you, staying in the house of one of *my* men, and tell me *I* am doing nothing. If I could breathe underwater, I would be out there looking for her and wouldn't return until I found her."

"You think we don't care about her?" Kyla asked softly, thankfully speaking before Maira could again. My eyes flicked toward Kyla briefly. I saw her staring at me with sadness in her amber eyes.

"Admittedly, it doesn't much seem like it," Cameron said quietly from the side, pushing the sleeves of his sweater up his forearms to reveal the dark smattering of hair that covered the skin there. He stepped towards us, his hands out toward Kyla and Maira in a gesture of peace. "Caelum's right. If any of us could do what you could, we'd be searching the seas for Brigid, trying to get her back. And we have only known her for months compared to your decades."

Kyla sighed, closing her eyes for a moment. She glanced over her shoulder at Maira before looking back to me, meeting my gaze with purpose. "Then I suppose we all must sit down and have a conversation."

"Perhaps a productive one, for once?" Cameron asked, the humor in his voice falling flat amidst the tension between the rest of us.

I didn't want their help, but I couldn't deny we needed it. "Hopefully this time will go better than the last few."

Without another word, I turned my back on both women, walking past Cameron and back up the hill to Finn's cottage. *Damned syrens,* I thought to myself, exhaling loudly.

Eliz
@ELIZIAN

BRIGID

CHAPTER TWO

Cold water splashed on my face, waking me. It trickled down my neck and chest like blades of ice, drenching me. The cold air met the even colder water, making my muscles tighten painfully, and I shivered involuntarily. Twisting my wrists against the ropes behind my back, I shook my head, blinking the water from my eyes. Squeezing my eyes shut, I took deep breaths, trying not to use up the precious energy I didn't have.

These past weeks had not been kind to me. *Cliodhna* had not been kind to me.

"Wake up." Cliodhna's voice was harsh and angry, a far cry from the melodic and regal voice I had heard for years. This noise grated on my nerves and made me want to grit my teeth, but I needed to save my strength to endure the upcoming torture that surely awaited me.

It took more energy than I wanted, but I managed to raise my head high enough to look at her, narrowing my eyes at the sight of my former queen looking down at me. Her pale skin, white hair, and eyes like diamonds. All of her was cold and sharp.

My voice was flat and dull as I spoke. "What do you want?"

"We are not done, my child," she cooed, reaching down to hold my chin in her slender fingers. Her nails were long and pointed, even in her human form, and they dug into my skin uncomfortably.

"Just kill me already," I whispered, meeting her icy blue gaze. She had held me captive for nearly two weeks now, and the daily torture was wearing on me, just as she hoped. I had given up hope the others would find me, that Caelum would find me. My body could not take much more of this, and I doubted my mind could either.

The only things that kept me going were my dreams of Caelum, my memories of Sorcha, and my fantasies of ripping Cliodhna's beating heart from her chest.

Cliodhna's wicked grin filled my vision as she bent down, placing our faces level. Her eyes blazed with delight. "Oh, no, my daughter. You owe me for what you stole. And you will be punished."

She straightened up, releasing my face. Exhausted, my chin fell back against my chest. At least the shaking subsided. I mustered up what strength I could, filling my voice with venom. "They weren't yours to begin with."

I heard skin meeting skin, but it took a moment for my body to register the pain radiating across my face. My cheek stung, and the pain faded into a dull ache that echoed through the rest of my body.

"They were *mine*," she snarled. Her fingers tangled in the knots of my hair, yanking my head back up.

Copper flooded my tongue as I licked my lip, and I grinned at her, pulling my lips off my teeth to show my bloody smile. She would try to break me, and she might succeed, but it would take far more than a slap across the face. "You'll have to do better than that."

Her eyes narrowed, hiding her frustration behind a self-important smirk. "We're only just starting. You have no idea what I'm capable of, you little urchin."

My body was exhausted, my mind even more weary, but I wouldn't let her win. Not now. I would take any punishment she inflicted and would not give her the satisfaction of seeing me break. That was her goal, after all. That was clear to me after the second or third day here. She was careful not to use the full extent of her powers, to not injure beyond what could heal. No, this was a game to her now, as I had no information for her and no value beyond her enjoyment of inflicting pain. And I would do whatever it took to not give it to her.

As she took a slight step back and studied me, I focused on my breathing, on the feel of the chair beneath my legs and the rope rubbing against my wrists, the smell of my own stench, the hunger twinging in my stomach, on anything but the pain she would deliver at any moment. The first slice of her claws came down across my thigh, slicing deep into the skin and muscle. I flinched, but closed my eyes and turned my mind inward, not allowing myself to feel the pain. If I looked down at my leg, at the bloody mess of flayed skin and exposed muscle, I doubted I could keep from screaming. It was better to sit in denial of how bad the wound was.

Instead, I clung to the memories of my friends. Memories of nights spent up with Sorcha, telling stories, our bodies pressed together as we lay on our backs in the dark. Memories of Caelum and his rough hands on my skin, of his lips against mine, of the smell of his neck as I curled into his arms. They were my only reprieve. My haven.

And here, in the recesses of my mind that she had not broken into yet, I was safe. For the moment. It would be over eventually. One way or another, it would be over.

Elizianna
@ELIZIANNA.THE.ONE

CAELUM

CHAPTER THREE

Walking into Brinemoor, the anxious rush to do *something* knotted up my stomach and buzzed in my chest. Clenching and unclenching my hands, I picked up the pace, moving toward my destination. Despite Brigid's kidnapping, I had been regularly visiting the children we saved, checking in on them. I grappled with the decision at first, wanting to put all my energy into finding and saving Brigid, but I knew if she discovered I abandoned the children we had worked so hard to save, she would not be pleased.

Turning down a side path from the main street through Brinemoor, I could almost imagine what she would have done, standing there with her hip cocked, her arms crossed, and one of her rust-colored eyebrows arched as she stared me down, waiting for me to take back whatever words I had had the gall to say. A smile tugged at my lips, but couldn't quite form fully, stopped in its tracks by the sorrow that had made its home in my chest.

The sounds of laughter filled my ears as I neared the orphanage, and this time, the smile got past that hurdle. My chest felt lighter with every step I took. These children had saved me in the little time I had known them, just as much as I had saved them. And I knew that despite Brigid's capture and Sorcha's death, it would have pleased both women to know we made a difference in their lives.

"Caelum, Caelum!" a little boy yelled, and soon, the children overran me, clinging to my legs, grabbing at my hands, and vying for my attention. Rory, a child of about eight years old, had taken to me rather quickly, growing attached at our first meeting. He was always the first to spot me when I came to visit, and the last to bid me goodbye when I left. "You're back!"

While the orphanage in Brinemoor wasn't an ideal solution for these children, it was better than being held captive in the hands of my father, or dead at the hands of the murderous syren queen. Here, at least, they remained fed, clothed, and relatively safe. And I would make sure they stayed that way, no matter what it cost.

Laughing for the first time since I was here last, I reached down and ruffled the bright fiery head of ginger hair, hair that reminded me of the woman I had lost. "How are you, Rory?"

"We're learning to read!" he exclaimed, nearly screaming the words at me. His arms swung as he continued to talk about all his adventures that day.

I listened, nodding. The smile never left my face as the other children chimed in. I never even responded, and honestly, I don't think they wanted me to.

The orphanage was small and barely had enough space for a room with rows of cots and a kitchen. At first, I wasn't sure they could handle the fourteen young children I brought, but the matron had been more than willing to take them all in, waving away our concerns and simply rearranging the cots to make room for everyone.

"How long are you staying? Can you come to dinner?" Rory asked, pulling me from my thoughts.

I ruffled his hair again and did the same to the other children still hanging around, looking up at me. As if on cue, they all started pouting, their eyes widening and their lower lips dropping. I narrowed my eyes. *Curse whoever taught them that,* I thought.

I sighed dramatically, sticking my lip out and tilting my head dramatically, as if I were considering the question. "Fine, I suppose

I'll come for dinner. I've got to go into town for a bit, but I'll be back in time."

They cheered and grabbed my hands, pulling me toward the building. We walked past the gray-haired matron, Isla, who smiled widely at me, the movement pulling at the slight wrinkles in the corners of the sun-aged skin there. "Trouble, aren't they?"

I motioned for the young ones to go on inside and offered her a small smile. It was all I could muster. "Aye, whoever taught them that did not have you in mind."

She laughed. "Och, it doesn't work on me, boy. Don't worry your head."

"Are you okay if I come back for dinner? The little cretins may not take no for an answer, but I will," I muttered. I knew the orphanage was short on money, despite my father's unwilling posthumous donation, made when I dropped off the kids. Children were expensive to raise, clothe, and feed, and it was a wonder the orphanage stayed open sometimes. Isla had a kind spirit, and despite having little, she gave all she had to the children.

I didn't have much, but if there was one thing I was willing to spend my creatively earned money on, it was the kids. And as soon as I had Brigid back in my arms, I would do whatever it took to earn more money to give them.

Her smile dipped slightly, but remained steadfast across her face. "Aye, Caelum. Join them for dinner. One more plate will not break us."

"I'll send money soon," I promised, vowing I would do whatever it took to ensure this orphanage stayed funded. "Over half these kids are here because of me, anyway."

"I know you'd take them all if you could," she said. Her smile dropped, and she leaned in closer, attempting to avoid prying ears. "You're so good with them, and I know you want to help. That means a world of difference in their lives."

"I wish I could help more," I admitted, agreeing with her. I had considered offering my family's home to the orphanage. It would have been much larger, and better equipped to handle this many children, but it was too dilapidated, and there were far too many ghosts there for me. Fixing it up would have taken time and money, both of which we currently did not have, and these children deserved stability and a real life, not one lived by the whims of the sea.

"You help plenty," she said, putting her hand on my arm and squeezing gently, her skin pale against the sun-tanned gold of my own. "You help more than anyone else in this town."

I nodded at her, offering her another small smile. While it might be true that I helped more than anyone else in this godforsaken town, I knew I could do more. And once I found Brigid, I would do more. *We* would. Both Brigid and I had grown up feeling unloved, and I would be damned if these children ever felt that way, even for a moment.

"I'll be back before dinner, Isla," I said. "I just need to pick up some supplies from the market."

"Dinner will be ready in an hour, Caelum. Take your time." Her kind eyes locked with mine, before turning to walk inside the orphanage. As the door closed, the smile dropped from my face. The energy these children brought always stayed with them, but as soon as I was out of their presence, the oppressive reality swarmed back in, pushing down all feelings of joy and optimism. Brigid was gone, and I had no way of finding her.

Pulling the doors shut behind me with a sigh, I turned toward the town, kicking at the dirt on the path in front of me. The past few weeks had worn me down, and I knew I needed to pick up the food and other supplies we had ordered from the market, but the thought of being around more people was daunting. Instead, I turned away from the market and began walking. Maybe a nice stroll would clear my head, and I could just pick up the supplies after dinner instead.

Unfortunately, the world had other plans for me.

Alan and Duncan were walking toward me from down the road. Kyla and another syren, Nerina, were with them. Alan noticed me first, and they changed their course. "Captain, what are you doing here?"

"Went to see the kids," I replied, nodding my head back toward the orphanage. I didn't have the energy to talk to them, but they wouldn't let me get away with being alone. Alan was an undeniable ray of fucking sunshine, while I was perfectly content to keep my head stuck in my storm clouds. But Duncan would never let me get away with my brooding for long.

Duncan nodded, a strand of his sandy blond hair flipping down onto the pink strip of sunburn across his forehead, but said nothing else.

Alan also nodded, but as he was not as wise as my best friend, he continued on. "It's so great that you go visit them, especially after all that's happened."

"Aye," I agreed, my voice blunt. I wanted this conversation to be over.

"I hate to bring more bad news," Duncan interrupted, thrusting a wound-up piece of parchment at me. Kyla peered at him, as if she hadn't seen the paper in his grasp.

"What is that?" Nerina asked, leaning around Kyla to get a closer look. She tucked a strand of her golden-brown waves behind her ear, bringing her hand to mouth as she chewed on a fingernail.

I narrowed my eyes at Duncan, trying to decipher the blank expression on his face as I unrolled the scroll. Tearing my gaze from him, I looked down, only to see my own face peering back up at me. The ink was smudged, but I could read it clearly.

WANTED FOR PIRACY AND MURDER.

"You've got to be fucking joking," I groaned, balling up the paper, my hands dropping to my sides. This was just what we needed right now. "Where did you find that?"

"They're everywhere, sir," Alan muttered, avoiding eye contact and reading the mood for the first time ever. Thankfully, he understood my anger. If he hadn't, I wasn't sure what I would have said or done, but it likely would have hurt his feelings.

"We've got to get back to the others," Duncan said, "before someone realizes this is you."

"What did it say?" Nerina asked, sharing a look with Kyla. Her light bronze skin had visible goosebumps as she wrapped her arms around herself to fight off the sharp gust of wind.

Kyla stepped closer to her, wrapping an arm around the other syren. "It's a wanted sign."

I nodded in agreement with Kyla, running my other hand through my unruly hair as I considered Duncan's words. If someone recognized me and realized there was a reward involved, there would be a mob in an instant. "Aye, aye. We will, but I promised the children I'd be back for dinner. And I still need to pick up the supplies from the market."

"You cannot be serious." Duncan raised an eyebrow. "We need to get back."

"I promised them," I snapped. I had experienced too many broken promises in my own childhood, and I would never subject these children to that if it could be avoided. And I could avoid breaking this promise. "You can either come with me or go on back yourself."

"I'd like to come to dinner with you." Kyla spoke softly, once again diffusing the tension with a practiced ease. Nerina stood beside her, her topaz eyes observing every movement we made, analyzing and calculating. Kyla cast her a quick glance. "I'd like to see how they're settling in."

"Okay, then let's go," I said, looking at the woman for a moment and searching for any hidden motives in her face, but all I saw was genuine interest and concern. I turned to Duncan and Alan. "One of you can stop to get the supplies after dinner if you're concerned about me being spotted."

She nodded softly and reached down to take Nerina's hand. The quiet syren flexed her fingers around Kyla's and nodded as well. "Yes, I will go, too."

As a group, we turned and began walking back to the orphanage. Dinner wouldn't be ready yet, but I knew the children still had energy. And four new people meant four extra sets of ears to listen to their stories and four additional sets of hands to play with them.

I knocked on the door, three quick raps, and Isla answered the door almost immediately. I clearly surprised her by returning so soon, and with guests in tow, but she covered it well. "Hello, welcome."

"If it's all right with you, they'll be joining us for dinner," I murmured. Catching her gaze, I made sure she saw how serious I was. "If there's not enough, please tell us."

"Nonsense," she replied, waving her hand. She smiled widely at Kyla and Nerina. "The more the better. Come in, please. I am Isla."

Kyla stepped up first, extending her hand. "Kyla, and this Nerina. It's lovely to meet you."

And just like that, the tension that had been permeating the air disappeared, and even Duncan's shoulders relaxed as we followed Isla into the orphanage.

Isla happily watched as the children swarmed the visitors, all vying for attention. Smiles contagiously filled the room. We all sat down for dinner, eyeing the meager stew and bread that had been served. I had taken only half a serving, and the others followed my lead. The orphanage was making do, but until I could get our usual business operations back up and running, I didn't have enough money to send to them.

"What's your name?" Rory asked, sidling up between Kyla and Nerina as we took our seats along the benches in front of the long table. "I'm Rory."

Kyla smiled, her face softening. "Hi Rory, it's nice to meet you. I'm Kyla, and this is Nerina."

Rory's eyes lit up, and he leaned closer to Kyla. "You sound like my mother."

Silver lined her eyes almost immediately, and I leaned over, ready to step in and take the conversation, but she caught my eyes over Rory's head and gave a tiny shake of her head. Turning her attention back to the boy, she smiled. "Your mother was from southern Bhodheas, then?"

He shrugged, picking at his food. "I dunno. I don't remember much about her. All I remember is being with her in Prìomh. She died when I was little and they sent me to an orphanage there."

"I'm sorry," Kyla whispered, wrapping her arms around his shoulders. "If she sounds like me, she was likely from the south of Prìomh, along the coast. Have you ever been there?"

He shook his head. "No. Is it pretty?"

She widened her eyes dramatically. "Oh, it's gorgeous. Some days, the cliffs go up so high that the sea below gets lost in the clouds."

His food long forgotten, Rory leaned forward on his elbows and began pelting questions at her about what the area and the people were like. She took it in stride, answering quickly and never letting her attention stray from him.

Nerina caught my gaze from the other side of Rory and smiled, nodding toward the two new fast friends. I returned the smile. Perhaps there was hope for peace with the syrens after all.

Both of us turned to watch Kyla, who was now regaling Rory and the other children with stories of the mythical creatures said to live in the clouds, who came down on the echoes of rainbows after a storm to grant wishes to those who could catch them.

While I had heard those stories before, I hadn't heard them since I'd come face to face with another mythical creature—the syrens. I raised an eyebrow at Nerina and mouthed, "Are those real?"

She grinned and shrugged, turning her attention back to the story.

Kyla was truly a natural with the kids, and I tried to remember what Brigid had told me about Kyla and Nerina's pasts, but I could recall nothing other than they both had suffered violent histories. For a moment, watching Kyla with Rory, I never would have guessed it to be true.

Soon, the sun began to sink below the horizon, and Isla stood from the table, clapping her hands. "All right, now. Time to go clean up, all of you. You know your chores and duties before bed."

The children groaned, but reluctantly scampered off after a firm look from Isla, who smiled at us gratefully before turning and following them out of the room.

"We should go too," I said, and we all stood. Leaving the orphanage, I pulled the heavy door closed behind us and raised an eyebrow at Duncan as we began our trek back to the cottage. "So, now what?"

He just laughed and clapped a large hand on my shoulder. "We'll get through it, Cae. We always do."

"How do you think Cam will react to the poster?" I asked, a genuine grin spread across my face at the thought of Cameron's reaction. He'd either be upset that I was on a wanted poster, or, more likely, he'd be upset that he wasn't.

Duncan laughed again.

Elizianna
@ELIZIANNA.THE.ONE

CAELUM

CHAPTER FOUR

"You're *what?*" Cam asked, his eyebrows shooting up under his brown hair. It had grown in the past few weeks and now hung over his forehead and curled around his ears.

"Wanted," I replied, thrusting the wrinkled parchment at him. "I'm wanted."

Taking the paper from me, he studied it intently, as if the answers to all our problems hid in the smudged ink. He sighed heavily. "How did anyone even survive to post this?"

I shrugged. "I'm sure Kellan had plans in place in case of his death. We couldn't kill all his men. Some of them got away."

"We need to go back to town and see if we can find anything out," Cam said, setting the paper down on the table and crossing his arms. "Do they know we're staying here?"

I shrugged again. "I don't know. I'm in town most every day to visit the children, and I haven't been hiding. I don't think anyone's been following me."

Cam locked eyes with Duncan, hazel against blue. "We'll need to make sure. You'll have to stay here for a bit, Captain."

I slammed myself down in the chair, not caring about the way it stung my thighs. The last thing I wanted was to be stuck in this house with the syrens. I dragged my hand over my face, sighing heavily. "I know."

Narrowing his eyes, Cam studied me for a long moment before finally sighing and turning to Duncan. "Were there posters of the rest of us?"

"Nay," Duncan said, shaking his head. "Just Caelum."

"There's nothing we can do tonight," I pointed out. "I'm back. I'll stay here and won't visit the children. And once we find Brigid, we'll deal with this. It's not a priority right now."

"Not a *priority*?" Duncan asked, his voice rising. "You can't be a wanted man, Caelum. You're not even a pirate!"

"I know that," I said, keeping my voice flat. I barely had the energy to go see the children I had saved, and I certainly didn't have enough energy to argue with my best friend. And now, being stuck in this house would only delay our search for Brigid. My stomach was in my boots, and rage grew inside me. I wanted nothing more than to destroy everything in my path; I needed to get it out of my system.

Duncan threw his hands up in the air, scoffing before he turned and walked down the hallway, into the room he now shared with Cameron.

"He just worries, Caelum," Cameron muttered, pulling out the chair across from me and sitting down.

"We need to worry about finding Brigid, not clearing me of piracy," I pointed out. We needed to prioritize things, and dealing with what passed for the local government here was not high on my list.

"Is this about that wanted sign we saw?" A soft voice came from behind us.

Fucking syrens, I thought, turning around to see Kyla walking into the cottage, a basket of vegetables in her hands. She must have gone out to the garden when we returned from the orphanage. She'd stayed quiet when Alan and Duncan told me about the poster earlier, but now it seemed she had questions.

"Aye, I'm wanted for piracy and the murder of my father," I said, motioning toward the paper.

"You're not a pirate, though," she said, tilting her head to the side. "Are you?"

"Not technically." I didn't feel like going through the intricate nuance behind my status as a pirate or not. It was messy and complex, and would take more words than I cared to expend. "But I did 'steal' from Kellan, so his crew would likely consider me one."

"The children?"

I nodded. "They think I stole the children from them, and that the children were rightfully their property, along with the loot we took from his ship after I killed him. In their eyes and in the eyes of the law, I am a pirate. Or at least, a thief."

"How will this affect the search for Brigid?" She set the basket down and wiped her hands down the legs of her borrowed pants. Reaching up, she tucked a strand of hair behind her ear, though it did little good as the curl sprang right back to its original place as she sat down at the table next to me. Studying her for a moment, I contemplated the stark difference between this syren and the one who had burned her way into my heart.

I could understand women like Brigid and Maira being syrens. They *fit* in my mind. But women like Kyla and Sorcha... they did not. I had not been around any of the others long enough to know. Cordelia, a syren whose hair was a few shades lighter than Brigid's and skin a few shades pinker, seemed to be close with Maira, which said something for her taste. I was still unsure about Nerina and Iona, though. Those two syrens could have been sisters, apart from Iona's sharper cheekbones and cooler eyes. They seemed nice enough, but were quiet around us all. Today had been the most I'd ever heard Nerina speak.

"It shouldn't. Why do you suddenly care about searching for her?" I shrugged. It seemed to be the only movement I could bring my body to complete. The hurt across her face was instant, but I couldn't bring myself to feel sorry for my words.

"Whatever you choose to believe, know that we do care for Brigid, and we want to find her."

"Then prove it."

"How?" she asked, her brow raising as she crossed her arms. "How can we prove we care for the woman that was with us for a decade? The woman that we shared a home with, a bed with, our lives with?"

"You could have started by not turning your backs on her." My words were like deadly venom, but I couldn't keep them behind my teeth. "She cared about you enough to go back and warn you when those fishermen attacked us, and you exiled her instead."

She flinched, her voice cracking. "That was Cliodhna's order."

I opened my arms wide, gesturing to the nothingness surrounding us. "And *that* is why we are here."

Sighing, Kyla sat down. "Whatever Maira has made you believe about us—whatever Cliodhna has made you believe—we were a family. And we will help to get her back."

"We'll see about that," I snapped, my arms dropping to my sides. I had a hard time believing that was the case, since Brigid had been quick to find a home with my crew, but the emotion on Kyla's face clarified that at least *she* believed her own words.

"Iona and Maira went out searching today." Her voice was calm despite the tears pooling in her eyes. She sniffed delicately but held my gaze.

"Did they find anything?" Cameron asked, filling the silence as I sat looking at her.

"They're not back yet," she replied, finally turning her gaze to him.

I stood, abruptly pushing back from the table, unable to sit here any longer. Kyla was a nice woman, but I feared if I stayed, I would say something more venomous than even Maira could muster. "When they're back, come get me."

Cameron cocked an eyebrow at my behavior, but nodded. I returned the gesture before turning to walk to my room. The room Brigid and Sorcha had shared, and the one I now claimed as my own, and would not share.

Logically, I knew I was being rude and should have stayed to discuss things more with Duncan, Cameron, and even Kyla. But I didn't have it in me. I just wanted to lie in the bed Brigid once shared and miss her for a moment. Settling into the blankets, I closed my eyes, imagining she was next to me, imagining that Cliodhna had never taken her in the first place. I reached over and pulled the pillow she had used to my chest. I inhaled her scent as my throat burned with the tears I refused to let fall.

I would find her, and she would be back in this bed, no matter what it took. No matter what it cost me.

A knock on the door pulled me from my half-sleep. Opening my eyes, I took a deep breath and sat up, steeling myself for interaction I didn't want.

"They're back," was all Cameron said before he turned and went back out to the kitchen.

Despite not wanting to do anything other than lay here, my feet swung themselves over the bed before I was fully aware of what I was doing, nearly causing me to fall flat on my face. My palms dampened at the thought of what Maira had—or had not—discovered. Either way, I needed to know.

In the kitchen, the syrens stood with Duncan, Finn, and Alan. Finn smiled at me, an expression that seemed permanently etched on his deep bronze skin, though I didn't return the gesture. I wasn't sure where the rest of Alan's men were, and I honestly didn't care. Wiping my palms on the sides of my pants, I crossed my arms and caught Kyla's gaze. "What's the news?"

"They were just about to tell us," she said, her eyes serious with determination. Neither of us would apologize for earlier, and that was fine. Hopefully, this news would be enough. Turning to the others, she kept her voice flat and motionless as she addressed Maira and Iona. "Tell us what you found."

"Not Brigid," Maira said, her eyes darting to me. She seemed hesitant, her words slow and carefully chosen. "We ruled out many locations large enough to hold someone captive. If Cliodhna is holding Brigid in the seas, it's not anywhere close by."

"You think she might be holding her on land?" I asked, picking up the underlying message of Maira's words. I tried to push back the rage I felt, knowing it had taken only one outing to discover this, and we could have done it weeks ago.

"I don't know. All we know is we checked all the places big enough to hold someone captive in the seas nearby, and they weren't there. But that doesn't mean they're not in the seas farther away."

I sighed, reaching up to pinch the bridge of my nose. I just wanted good news, for once. Blowing out a large breath, I turned to the syrens who had searched. "Thank you for looking."

Maira snorted. "Oh, now you're being nice about it?"

"Would you rather him say the truth?" Duncan shot back.

"Sure, why not?"

"Thank you for *finally* looking. I'm so glad we wasted two weeks to discover she wasn't in the seas in a single day," he replied, contorting his face, mocking her. Had it been a different situation, I might have laughed at how closely his words echoed my thoughts, at how well he really knew me, but his words were the truth. And I was glad he had said them aloud.

"Should we begin our search on land, Captain?" Cam asked, interrupting what would have turned into an argument. Maira narrowed her eyes but said nothing more. I appreciated his intervention, though I would not have been sad to see Duncan put Maira in her place once more.

"Aye, we should." I nodded. Knowing she wasn't in the sea nearby, both raised my spirits and dashed them. If she was on land, I had no idea where to search. But if she was in the sea, the syrens would have to travel far and wide to search. "We need to find my father's men who escaped and are still in Brinemoor. If Kellan was working with Cliodhna, maybe he knows more information about her plans. That could give us a starting point."

"I'll get rotations set up," Duncan said, nodding. He pointed at me. "You must stay here, though."

"Why does he have to stay here?" Maira asked, outrage coloring her words. I knew she didn't like me, and it wasn't a secret that I didn't like her, and as the syrens often stayed at the cottage during the day, us being in the same space for an extended period of time was not appealing to either of us.

"My father's men put out a bounty on me for piracy and his murder. If I'm seen in town and recognized, they'll hang me," I said, my tone matter of fact. "And while I'm sure you'd love that, I'm not quite finished with my life."

She rolled her eyes but didn't reply. Thankfully, Kyla was tolerable, and the others stayed out of my way. But Maira seemed to thrive on making my life difficult. I didn't know how long I would make it stuck in close proximity to her.

"We'll be fine," Kyla said, looking pointedly at Maira, who huffed but said nothing else. "We'd be happy to help in any way."

"I need someone to check in at the orphanage every day." The children were my responsibility, and if I couldn't show my face in Brinemoor, someone would need to do it for me. "I don't want them in danger again, and if my father's crew finds out they're still there..."

"We'll take care of it," Cam promised.

I nodded, and without another word, turned and went back to my room. My mood had soured, and I wanted to be alone again. I stopped at the foot of the bed and stared at the rumpled blanket. Closing my eyes to keep from seeing Brigid lying across that same blanket, I turned and drove my fist into the wall, again and again, as hard as possible. I stopped only when the skin across my knuckles split open, blood oozing down my hand. I leaned my head against the brick and tried to steady my breath.

Brigid was likely dead by now, and all because I hadn't been able to find her in time. It was my fault. Another person dead because of my failures. And now, I would never know what our future may have held.

Sighing, I dropped onto the bed and curled up around the pillow Brigid had once used. I knew I was being pathetic, but I didn't have it in me to care anymore. Failure after failure, all culminating in Maddock's death, then in Sorcha's death and Brigid's capture.

That's all I was.

A failure.

Eliz
@ELIZIAN

CHAPTER FIVE

Cliodhna yet again roused me from my pain induced unconsciousness with water. This time, instead of splashing me in the face, she submerged my entire body. My muscles screamed in agony as they tightened in the icy cold, and I flailed, trying to see my surroundings through the murky water.

She had dumped me into a large glass enclosure filled with what tasted like seawater. Before I could get my bearings, she slid a heavy metal grate over the top of the enclosure, stepping back onto the platform beside it. Inside the tank, the water glowed red, tinged from my wounds, and the salt stung as I kicked my legs, drifting toward the surface.

I wrapped my fingers around the grate and pulled my face out of the water. My lips met the grate as I took a deep breath, gasping to ease the ache in my lungs.

Cliodhna climbed down from the platform and was now standing in front of it, watching me with an amused expression on her face. I eyed the gouges, still healing, on her otherwise perfect face, and satisfaction flooded through me, dulling the pain a bit.

The gash nearest her lip twitched as she sneered at me. "Have you forgotten you're a syren? Panting for air like one of *them*. What a shame."

Still sucking air into my lungs, I let my legs go still as my body weight hung from my fingertips, clinging to the metal grate. She wanted me to transform, knowing it would be painful for me. Maybe even more painful than what she had already done to my body. But I wouldn't give her what she wanted. "Why am I in here?"

"We're going to try something new, my dear," she said, and the glint in her eyes told me whatever it was, it would not end well for me.

I didn't speak. I let the burning of the wounds in my legs numb me as I prepared for whatever hell she had in mind.

"Transform, you petulant child," she snapped, taking a harsh step toward me. "I gave you magic, and here you sit, wasting it, gasping for breath."

I tightened my fingers, but did not follow her instructions. My body may eventually give out to the torture, but my mind would never be hers to break. I would no longer follow her instructions. Willingly giving her my pain would mean that she'd won. That she'd finally broken me.

In an instant, she jumped onto the metal grate as the ends of her dress slipped between the holes and dripped down into the water. She bent over and caught my hair, her long fingers reaching through the metal to haul my face against the grate. "Transform. Now."

I kept her gaze as my face pressed painfully against the cold metal, careful to not show any pain. The open wounds on my legs throbbed, my fingers hurt from holding onto the metal, and now my face and scalp ached. But I had not given in, and for whatever reason, she had been careful not to kill me—yet.

My hair still wrapped around her fingers, she stuck her other hand through the grate into the water. Power flooded through the small tank, and without my consent, my body transformed, bones cracking and muscles tearing.

The bitter taste of copper flooded my mouth as my teeth sharpened and tore through my gums. The water, slightly pink, turned a deeper red, trailing from my fingers as talons ripped open the flesh of my nail beds. I bit the inside of my cheek to keep from screaming out as the muscles of my legs tore apart and reformed into my tail. I panted, blood dribbling from my lips and down my chin. My core ached and burned, like the fire of a thousand red-hot forks pulling away from the very strands of my being.

Finally, the transformation was over. Blood swirled in the water, settling into ribbons of red, sinking toward the bottom of the tank. I closed my eyes and tried to focus on calming my racing heart, and not on the residual pain that radiated through me.

She released my hair, and I floated down into the water, now able to breathe beneath it as my tail folded awkwardly against the glass. The enclosure was too small for me to stretch out. An intentional decision, I suspected. Sinking to rest on the bottom of the tank, a plume of blood-red water pushed up around me.

Cliodhna elegantly jumped down from the top of my enclosure, dusting off her stark white dress as she stood next to the tank, once again level with me. My body was crying in relief as my healing powers could finally work again. The transformation made me sore, but the magic eased the ache of the other wounds she had inflicted.

"That wasn't so difficult now, was it?" she asked, watching me closely. "How does that feel?"

Amazing, wonderful, pain-free, was what I wanted to say, but I knew I couldn't give that information to her. It would just be something else for her to take away later. I remained silent, watching her as she studied me. For the moment, I was thankful I couldn't communicate in my syren form beneath the water.

"It feels better, yes?"

I narrowed my eyes, to keep from giving the impression I was grateful for the transformation and the relief that came with it.

"I've always wanted to know exactly how much a syren's healing power can overcome." She smiled at me, a feral expression devoid of joy.

My blood ran cold. She was not curious. I knew that much. This was just her newest plan to break me. She would tear me apart and then throw me in this tank to heal. Over and over and over. She wouldn't stop. Not until she became satisfied with my suffering, or until she grew bored.

I must have slipped and shown horror on my face, because Cliodhna broke into a wicked grin. "Oh, yes, I thought that might elicit a reaction. I told you we were just beginning, my child."

Closing my eyes, I prayed to anyone who could hear me to please end this suffering. Or to end me before she did. Not even thoughts of Sorcha and Caelum could keep the fear away this time.

Elizianna
@ELIZIANNA.THE.ONE

C AELUM

CHAPTER SIX

"You know that will not solve your problems, right?" Kyla asked, sitting down in the chair next to me.

I paused and looked at her, the mug of ale still at my lips. Swallowing the mouthful, I set the mug down in front of me. "Oh, and what will?"

She shrugged, a sweater I was nearly certain I'd seen on Cam yesterday slipping off one of her shoulders. "I'm not entirely sure, but I know that it's not drinking at dawn."

"I have nothing better to do, and I can't leave the cottage," I pointed out, taking another long sip. After waking from a nightmare, I needed a distraction, anything to get the image of Brigid's broken and bloody body out of my head. I certainly didn't need Kyla coming in and telling me it was a poor decision.

"So you're going to sit and drink yourself into a stupor instead?" Her voice was harsh.

"Not a stupor, just a blur."

She shook her head, and I sighed, setting the mug down carefully on the table and looked up to meet her gaze. It appeared I would not be drinking myself into a blur, so a battle of words with a syren would have to distract me just the same. "What would you have me do, then?"

"You were furious with us for not helping more. And now, as soon as you encounter a slight setback, you do the same thing. Would Brigid allow this?" She leaned back in the chair, tilting her head as she looked at me, her eyes unyielding.

"Brigid isn't here," I replied, my voice flat. I was proud of myself for not erupting in rage, screaming and cursing at her for abandoning Brigid—for allowing her to be taken. "And you have no right to say that."

"Don't I? I knew her for over ten years, Caelum," she said, her voice softening. "*I* was the one who rescued her after she was thrown overboard. *I* taught her and befriended her. During her first years here, *I* was the one she confided in. You are not the only one who cares for her and wants her back."

"Then why did you leave her?" I asked, my voice cracking under the weight of the burning tears lodged in my throat. I swallowed, pushing the tears down and rubbed my forehead with both hands. Kyla had explained herself plenty, and doing it again wouldn't be enough. She was right about one thing: Brigid would not have approved of me drinking my sorrows away. "Aye, you're right. I apologize."

"Don't apologize to me," she said, reaching over to take my hand, pulling it gently from my face. "I know you blame yourself, but it's not your fault."

"If I had been closer, maybe..."

"No," she cut me off, her voice stern and angrier than I had ever heard. "Cliodhna is the one to blame here, not you. Not any of us. Cliodhna is the one who took her."

"How did none of you know what she was doing?" My voice was quiet, barely audible. I didn't want to anger her, but the thoughts had churned in my mind constantly since the moment my father revealed the truth. How could they have not known? "If you all lived together, why didn't you know?"

"You must understand, Caelum. She wasn't one of us. She was our *queen*. We never questioned her, we obeyed her."

"And look where that got us." I couldn't help the words that escaped. As soon as they left my mouth, I regretted them. Seeing Kyla's face harden, I ducked my head slightly. "I'm sorry."

"No, you're right. Look where that got us. Sorcha is dead, Brigid is gone, and we are stuck living in a house instead of the ocean where we belong," she replied sharply. She took a deep breath. "Don't apologize. I understand your anger. We are all angry, though, and I need *you* to see that."

I nodded. "You're right. I... I admit my perspective of you is skewed. I was with Brigid after you all exiled her, and I'm letting that decision cloud my judgment. We all lost Sorcha, and maybe we've lost Brigid, too."

"Maybe if we had not exiled Brigid, none of this would have happened," she said, shaking her head. "But we'll never know. We're facing a new reality, and now we must either accept it or find a new path."

"You're very wise, you know that?" I remarked, the corners of my mouth lifting slightly.

She snorted, a sound no one else could have made sound so delicate. "Years of experience, I suppose."

I tilted my head and studied her. "What were you before?"

"Before?"

"Before you were a syren?"

"I was nothing. A waste of space and breath. A nameless body to bear children and to abuse." She held my gaze. "My husband threw me off a cliff. Did you know that?"

I sucked in a breath. "No, I didn't."

She nodded, but didn't look away. Her lips pursed, and for a moment, I could have sworn tears lined her lashes, darkening them subtly, but she blinked and they were gone. "Yes. I told him I wanted our daughters to have reading lessons, and he... did not agree. He said I was overstepping my bounds, dragged me from our manor, and threw me over the edge."

"And you survived?" I wasn't sure where she was from exactly, but I'd heard her tell Rory about Prìomh, and the cliffs there were jagged, rocky, and extremely high.

"Luckily, I missed the rocks on the way down. The impact with the water knocked me unconscious, and the next thing I knew, Cliodhna was explaining how she saved me. I was the first she transformed." Her eyes turned hard, and she shrugged. "Well, if I'm to believe her."

"And you all…" I swallowed hard, unable to get rid of the lump clogging my throat. "All of you came to be syrens this way?"

She tilted her head. "You didn't know?"

"I knew Brigid's story," I admitted, "but she didn't tell me any of yours."

"We all came to be syrens from the violence of men, yes. We all died in the water and were reborn there as well. None of us are here because we simply wandered into the water and chose this life. My story may be one of the more dramatic ones, but it's far from the most violent."

I wasn't sure what to say, so I kept my mouth closed. The sadness in her eyes was like a punch in the stomach. Maybe I had been too hard on the syrens. Their determination for revenge against men and our ships made sense now.

She stood from the table and wiped her hands on the sides of her dress. "I'll leave you to your breakfast, I suppose. But think about what I've said."

"I will, Kyla," I said. "Thank you for your perspective."

She smiled at me before turning to walk down the hallway and into the room she shared with the other syrens.

With a heavy sigh, I turned my attention back to the mug of ale sitting on the table in front of me. Might as well finish it now. Pulling over a map of Caladhan, I sipped my liquid breakfast and studied the parchment, hoping that something, anything, would jump out at me.

Later in the afternoon, the front door of the cottage burst open, and the frantic look on Cam's face as he entered made me jump up from the kitchen table and move toward him. They had gone to town this morning, and from the looks of it, something happened.

I met him just inside the door and grabbed his shoulders with both hands, searching his face for answers. "What did you find?"

He grimaced, looking over at Duncan, who was slowly walking in behind him. Cameron turned back to me, raising a hand to settle me down. "Look, it may be nothing, but we *might* have a place to start."

Duncan rolled his eyes and stepped around us, moving into the kitchen. "You're really going to believe that old drunk? Cameron, it's a fairytale. It's not true. It can't be true."

I raised an eyebrow at my friend. "Technically, Brigid and the others are fairy tales, too. So, what did you find out?"

Duncan sighed, motioning for us to come sit at the table. "We were out looking for your father's men when this old drunk man came up to us, blathering on about a witch. I wanted to leave, but Cam entertained the old coot."

"What did he say?" I asked, turning to Cameron. It was not surprising that Cameron had been too polite to turn away the drunk, but I was wary. Although the word of a drunk was unreliable at best, I still wanted to hear about it. If Cam was this excited, this eager to get back and tell me, there must have been something to it. My heart sped up in anticipation.

"He said there was a witch down in Bhodheas who could find anything and give you anything you wanted. He told us he overheard our conversations and said she could help us if we went to her. I thought maybe we could use the witch to find out where Brigid is."

"Did he know her name?"

"Well, no," Cam admitted, rubbing the back of his neck. "And he didn't know exactly where to find her, either."

"See?" Duncan said, crossing his arms over his chest. "It's nothing useful. Just a waste of time. 'Down in Bhodheas' could mean anywhere."

"I've heard about her before," Alan added, coming down the hallway. "Sorry, didn't mean to barge in, but I've heard about that witch before."

"Really?" I asked, pulling out a chair for him. I noticed Kyla had returned to the kitchen too and was leaning up against the counter. For a moment, I wondered how long she had been there, quietly listening to us.

"Yeah," Alan continued, "one of our old crew had a former captain who supposedly met her. She can give you anything you want, but you must pay a price for it."

"Naturally," I replied, my hope diminishing. I had nothing to give for payment, not anymore. I had pledged it all to the orphanage.

"What did your old captain want?" Kyla asked. She tilted her head to the side as she studied Alan. "And what price did he pay?"

"Well, he wanted treasure, of course," Alan said, as though that were the only logical answer. He scratched his beard. "I don't know what he gave her in return; he would never tell us."

Kyla hummed, nodding slightly as she waved a hand for us to continue. "I apologize. I was just curious."

Alan continued as if she hadn't even spoken. "And I've also heard stories about her being able to locate anyone or anything."

I desperately wanted to find Brigid. At this point, I was willing to try anything, including seeking the help of a witch. "What is the price?"

"From what I've heard, it varies. She makes it unique to each person."

"And do you know where she is?" I asked, pinching the bridge of my nose. As much as I hoped this was true, with no idea of where this witch was, it was a waste of our time.

"Not exactly, but I have heard she lives near Treòir Cove. Supposedly, she makes herself difficult to find on purpose," Alan added, once again oblivious to the tension in the room. "That way, she only helps those determined enough to find her."

I knew where Treòir Cove was, and while I wasn't fond of the witch making herself intentionally hard to find, it wasn't unreasonable for us to go there to investigate. It would take several days to get there by sea, but given that we had been searching fruitlessly for weeks, I would try anything. "But does she help anyone who finds her? Or only those she wants to?"

"I suppose she helps anyone who finds her," Alan said, scratching his beard again. "But as I said, I've only heard stories."

"Lovely," Kyla said dryly, rolling her eyes.

I rubbed my chin, seriously considering what we would need to make this trip happen. If we could find this witch, surely I could convince her to help us find Brigid. I was desperate, and whatever this witch wanted for payment, I would make sure she got it.

"Are you actually considering this, Caelum?" Duncan asked, his cheeks ruddy and his brows pinched as he stared at me.

"Do you have any better ideas?" I snapped. "Brigid has been gone for weeks, in the hands of a ruthless syren queen. If we don't find her soon, we may never find her. I know you never liked her, but you can't let her die." My voice caught in my throat and my eyes fell to the floor.

"Caelum, we will find her," he reassured, softening at my words. Maybe I shouldn't have said it here in front of everyone, but they needed to hear it. We hadn't been able to sit down and really talk since Brigid disappeared, but I knew we needed to soon. Especially now.

"Let's go south," I said, spreading my hands. Turning to Kyla, I inclined my head. "Will the syrens join us?"

"Absolutely," she said. The other syrens weren't here, having already retreated to their room, but the confidence with which she answered made me believe there would be no changing her mind, even if the others disagreed.

I looked at Duncan, a faint thread of optimism tugging at my chest. "How quickly can we get *The Voyager* ready to sail?"

"I'll send Finn and Cam to prepare it tomorrow. We can leave the next day," Duncan said, still staring at me, as if I had lost my mind. And maybe I had, but Brigid being gone had truly made me realize how much she meant to me. Everything felt... blank without her. Cold. Like she had taken the sun with her and left us all in the frigid dark.

I had to get her back. No matter what it took.

Elizianna
@ELIZIANNA.THE.ONE

C A E L U M

CHAPTER SEVEN

"Stay safe, please." The murmured goodbyes amongst the syrens huddled in the room's corner caught my attention. While most of them would come with us, one of them, Iona, would stay behind with one of Alan's men to continue the search here.

It had not been an ideal situation. None of the syrens wanted to leave one of their own behind, especially with someone they did not know well, but in the end, they all agreed it was a smart decision. Ultimately, Iona had volunteered for the duty, citing that she was comfortable staying behind with an equally quiet man named Malcolm, who had proven himself extremely helpful since he'd joined us along with Alan and his small crew. Of all of us here, those two staying behind were the safest choice, and least likely to kill one another.

"We will," Kyla whispered, hugging the syren. They separated, and she turned to me. "We're ready, Caelum."

I nodded at her before turning to Duncan and Cameron. "Let's go. We have to be careful entering Brinemoor and the harbor."

"Aye, I don't think that beard will disguise you, Captain," Cameron said, with a hint of a smile in his voice.

I stroked my beard, running my fingers through the few inches of scratchy hair. Keeping my hair and beard groomed had not been a priority lately, and over the past month, both had grown wild. Still running my hand over it self-consciously, I wondered what Brigid would think. Would she like my scruffy beard? Or would she demand I shave it off because it irritated her skin when I kissed her?

"It's better than nothing," Duncan huffed, pulling me back from my thoughts.

"Iona," I called, hesitating slightly as I looked over at the other syrens. I had barely spoken to her, but I needed a favor now that Cam and Duncan were leaving with me.

She raised a delicate eyebrow and walked over to me, apprehension written clearly across her face. She had always been pleasant, but never actively sought interaction or conversation with any of us. "Yes?"

"I... I've been going to the orphanage," I started. Pausing, I swallowed, trying to figure out how to word my request. Admitting a vulnerability was hard, especially to these syrens I barely knew. But the children were more important than my pride, and they needed to be taken care of.

Her face softened, and she reached out, placing a hand on my shoulder. It only stayed a moment before she pulled it back, but I appreciated the comforting gesture. "We will check on them. Don't worry."

My shoulders sagged as I exhaled a sigh of relief. "Thank you. Truly."

"It's no problem. I had children... before," she said, her mossy eyes turning down as they filled with tears. "I would be happy to check on them."

"The matron's name is Isla. Just tell her you're there for me and she'll update you on the children." My voice grew soft. As much as the syrens irritated me, Kyla's story had reminded me they were all like Brigid. All of them had overcome something horrid in their lives and became something new.

"I will," she promised. She pushed my shoulder gently, turning me toward the door. "Go find her and bring her home."

Nodding, I turned and followed the others out of the house, starting our trek to Brinemoor, where Finn was waiting on *The Voyager*. We'd leave as soon as we got there, heading toward the Straits of Marbh and Treòir Cove beyond that.

"Och, it's about time you lot showed up!" Finn yelled, peering over the railing above, his voice filled with joy. The wide smile on his face echoed the sentiment as he waved to the others.

"Is the ship ready?" I called back up to him. The afternoon sun was sinking lower in the sky, casting rays of gold and orange across the docks, and I knew by the time we got out of the harbor and into the open sea, it would quickly grow dark.

"Aye, Captain, all ready," he replied with a sloppy salute. Lately, I'd found Finn and Alan's carefree nature extremely irritating to be around. None of us should be joyful right now. One of our own was gone, and two of our own were dead.

I rolled my eyes and waved a hand back at him, turning my focus back to the others as we began boarding the ship and hauling up our supplies. The trip through the Straits to Treòir Cove would take a day and a half if the weather was on our side. The Straits were deadly, and ships could not sail through at regular speeds. We would have to take it slow and steady to survive the deadly passage, being careful to avoid the jagged pillars of rock lurking beneath the surface of the sea.

We had made the trip once before, traveling from Whitcairn to Brinemoor, but the weather had been fair, and we had been extremely lucky. This trip would be longer, and I doubted luck would be on our side a second time. At least we wouldn't have the threat of the syrens to contend with, but the Straits were deadly enough without them.

With the ship prepared, it didn't take long to leave the harbor and enter the open water. But it would take all of us to crew *The Voyager* through the seas.

I took up my position at the helm, studying the horizon before us and the ship below. Duncan and Alan were talking about something and pointing out at the water. Cameron was with Kyla, showing her how to tie up the lines. The smile on his face differed from any I'd seen before, almost nervous. It was less friendly, like he had been with Brigid, and more coy, like he was trying to impress Kyla. I grinned. Cam would have his work cut out for him if he wanted to impress that headstrong and grounded woman, that was for sure.

The journey from Brinemoor to the beginnings of the Straits felt quicker than I remembered. My anxiety was likely the cause, but it felt like only seconds had passed before the coastline fell away, leaving rise to sheer jagged cliffs that towered over us on either side.

I adjusted my grip on the wheel, preparing myself for the challenges that lay ahead. Looking across the horizon, I watched the sun share its last rays over the water, and I grimaced. Traveling through the Straits in the dark was less than ideal.

"What's with that face?" The soft voice startled me and I jumped. I turned to see Kyla standing behind me, an amused smile on her face. "I apologize for startling you." She crossed her arms over her chest and ticked an eyebrow up, reminding me so much of Brigid. "So, why are you making that face?"

"Sailing through the Straits in the dark is incredibly dangerous," I replied. I thought about the rocks beneath the surface. They would be the most dangerous, but the wind was picking up, and that too could prove deadly. We had to remain vigilant and take care not to swerve to miss any rocks. If we over-corrected, we risked slamming into the steep cliffs that towered over us on either side.

She tilted her head and gazed out at the ocean beyond me, the setting sun reflecting in her eyes. "Why are you worrying? We're on the boat with you."

A laugh escaped, startling us both. "Do you think you are the only things to worry about on the seas?"

Her eyebrows wrinkled. "No, of course not."

"There are rock pillars beneath the surface that are not always visible until you're right up on them, and by then it's too late. When the ship hits the rock, there's no salvaging it—and that's in broad daylight. In the dark, we won't be able to see them at all," I explained. I gently ran my hands over the ship's wheel. "This lady is old. Running into one of those pillars, or into any rocks, would spell her end."

She chewed on her lip, nodding slightly as she took in my words. "I suppose I never thought about the rocks from a sailor's perspective. They were just fun to swim around."

"Brigid brought me here in syren form once," I admitted quietly, thinking back to one of our stolen moments, hiding from the world and our responsibilities for just a moment to simply enjoy each other. "She took me out exploring, and we ended up in the mouth of the Straits. It was beautiful."

"Yes..." Her voice was wistful as she gazed at the horizon. She wrapped her arms around her waist, hugging herself. I recognized that movement too and wondered how many of Brigid's mannerisms had come from watching Kyla. I swallowed hard, past the lump in my throat.

"We'll get you back to the seas," I promised. While I hoped Brigid would at least spend part of her time with me, I knew I couldn't ask her to leave the waters for good. I couldn't ask that of them. "We'll stop Cliodhna, and you will all be free."

"But free to do what, exactly?" She smiled sadly at me. "We'll never be truly free, Caelum. It's a pleasant notion, but the sea will always call to us, no matter where we are."

I closed my mouth. There wasn't anything I could say, not without sounding like a superstitious fool. Instead, I simply nodded at her.

We stood in silence, watching the ship slice through the waves and listening to the wind catch the sails and pull us further into the Straits. The sun had set, turning the world a bluish gray that could only mean night was coming.

"I can go in the water and guide you," Kyla said, breaking the silence. She stared out at the waves crashing against the hull. She turned and met my gaze. "I can keep you from hitting the pillars."

"But how would we see you?" I asked, thinking through the logistics. It wasn't realistic. "We'll be fine. We'll survive."

"We could hang a lantern on the bow, and if I stayed close enough to the surface, the light would reflect off my tail," she said, walking over to the railing.

I watched her for a moment. If we could pull that off, we might survive. But would it put Kyla at risk? After another moment, I made my decision. "No, Kyla. We'll be fine. Please stay aboard the ship."

She looked up at me, fire and determination shining in her eyes. "You think I'm not capable?"

"Not at all. I just don't want anyone harmed on my watch," I explained, brushing off her anger.

"So, you'd rather wreck, and risk putting us all in danger?" As soon as the words were out, she frowned, her shoulders slumping. "I'm sorry. I don't mean to fight with you. I just... want to help."

Again, this conversation reminded me of one I'd had with Brigid. The stubborn determination to do *anything* to avoid feeling useless. It was something I had dealt with many times myself, and I smiled at her. "If we wrecked, I'd much rather you all help us get to safety."

She contemplated that, chewing on her lower lip for a moment. "I suppose."

I exhaled. "All right. Go with the others and get some sleep. It'll be dark soon."

Kyla started toward the stairs but paused, turning back to me, concern pinching her forehead. "Will you sail through the night? You need rest too, Caelum."

"Don't worry. I'll send Duncan to bed now, and he'll take over for me at some point."

"Okay. Be careful not to fall asleep at the wheel." She smiled and descended the stairs.

I watched her walk past Cameron, grinning at him, before approaching the other syrens. As a group, they disappeared below deck. Cameron caught my gaze and gave me a quick salute before following them.

"Duncan!" I called. He looked up at me from the deck. "Get some sleep. I'll need you to take over at some point."

He nodded and followed the rest below. Alan, Finn, and a few other men stayed up, tending the ship with me. I took a deep breath and looked out at the sea ahead of us. The wind whipped around, and the tips of the waves turned white as they crashed against the hull. I wouldn't turn back now. Not when there was a chance this witch could help us find Brigid.

But a sinking feeling grew in my stomach, as heavy as the anchor on the side of the ship. I had a bad feeling about this journey...

Elizi
@ELIZIAN

B R I G I D

CHAPTER EIGHT

"Since you stole my power source, I will use your pain," Cliodhna said, stroking a talon down the side of my face. I forced myself to hold still as she dug into my skin.

Instead of being in the tank, I was on top of the metal grate this time, hovering inches above the water. If I had the energy, I could reach out and touch the cool water, but I could barely keep my eyes open.

I was still in my syren form and being this close to the water was physically painful. My scales itched and my skin felt painfully tight. My lips were dry, and my fingers flexed, searching for a drop of liquid.

She bent down, bringing her face closer to mine and baring her teeth in a sadistic smile. She enjoyed this. How had I never seen this side of her before? She held herself apart from us, always poised, but it had never seemed cruel. As our queen, it made sense. She wasn't our friend. She hadn't spent nights with us, up in our rooms, talking and comforting one another as we dealt with the horrors inflicted upon us by men.

Now, though, her narcissism was as clear as her cruelty.

That she had not yet wounded my face surprised me, especially since I marked her cheek. Her wounds had healed, but not faded, the lines still pink and angry against the smooth and unmarred porcelain of the rest of her face. It satisfied me greatly to see the gashes running across her cheek, marring the side of her face from her temple down to the corner of her mouth. It was *almost* worth all the pain I endured.

"Maybe I'll return to the city and find my power source," she mused, continuing to trail a talon down my neck and over my collarbone. She dug in slightly and I tried to stifle a reaction as my muscles winced reflexively.

"They were *children*," I seethed, ignoring the twinge in my jaw as I gritted my teeth. Her last strike to my face had dislocated my jaw, and though I had popped it back in place, the ache slow to fade. "They were not a power source."

She scoffed. "Age doesn't matter to me. Over the years, I have taken men, women, and children. Pure souls are pure power, and power is what I need. What I *deserve*."

I ignored her, refusing to meet her gaze. If she was planning to use my pain to feed her powers, then I was in for a much longer stay than I had expected. While I clung to hope Caelum might find me, I knew it was unrealistic. He had no idea where I was, and even if he did, he had no way of stopping Cliodhna. After all, he was only a man. She was a goddess.

"Why, if little Sorcha had not chosen to be a syren, I might have taken her soul as well," she cooed, bending closer to my face. "She had one of the purest souls I'd ever seen. Not all who decline us do. Some of them deserve to be cast aside. But Sorcha... She was *special*."

The room faded away as rage filled my body. My vision tunneled, focusing solely on the face of this despicable creature in front of me. A buzzing filled my ears, blocking out her taunting words. I wanted to lunge at her, to use every last ounce of energy to make her pay for those words, but I would not allow her to use Sorcha to break me. I knew that if I showed her how much it affected me, I would only cement the constant reminder of my friend.

If I wanted to make it out of this, I had to smother my rage and hide my sorrow. I could do this—for Sorcha. I would not let Cliodhna tarnish her memory.

"Yes, her soul was pure," I said, keeping my voice flat. "And yours is so dark you don't deserve to be called a goddess. You're a monster."

"I am both. You are *weak*, Brigid. Remember that," she said, reaching out to caress the raw, bloody mess of my tail. "Now, where were we, my child?"

My body flinched as she touched the exposed muscle. I tensed my stomach and clenched my fists, not willing to give her a greater reaction. She dug her nails in deeper, and I hissed, but kept my body still. Cliodhna wanted a response from me, and I would be damned if I gave her one.

She grinned and slowly plucked out a scale. The skin beneath turned a sickly white, before blood rushed to the surface. She plucked another one, and then another, and another, until blood covered my tail and poured into the water below.

I needed to regain my composure, but I knew she wouldn't stop. She wanted my pain. She needed it, and I was powerless to stop her. My only hope was Caelum, and possibly the other syrens, if they had stayed with Caelum after. I couldn't imagine the confrontation that had happened after, but I knew it certainly wouldn't have been easy for anyone involved.

"The others will find me eventually," I panted through the pain, trying not to move. "Maira will want her vengeance for your betrayal."

"I am not worried about them." She dismissed my words with a wave of her hand. "They are still upset over your own betrayal."

"You killed Sorcha. If they decide to kill me after they're finished with you, that's my fate. But you will die first." I wondered if they had buried Sorcha. I hoped the syrens let Caelum bury her on land. She didn't belong anywhere Cliodhna had control.

She stood, stalking over to me, contemplating her next move. Before I could brace myself, her nails were back in my tail, scratching down the already bloody scales, ripping and gouging deep into the muscle.

The burning consumed my body, and I closed my eyes, clenching my jaw so hard my teeth cracked. I cried out, my mouth opened so wide I felt my jaw dislocate once again. I flexed my jaw, popping it back into place and panted for breath, trying to control the pain and calm my body.

"I will watch you die," I snarled, fueled by the pain. "I promise you that."

"Go ahead, bare your teeth at me. I will pull them out, one by one." She ran her fingernail down the side of my face. Her voice could have been soothing, if not for her sadistic words.

Recoiling from her touch, I watched her, refusing to let my expression give way to the nausea forming in my stomach.

She smiled at me and closed her eyes, bathing in my agony. "They will never find us. It will be you and me for eternity."

"I will give you nothing," I snarled, ignoring the throbbing in my temples and cheeks.

She grabbed my face, my blood smearing over my cheeks. "You will give me *everything*. Even if I must pry it from your bones."

Elizianna
@ELIZIANNA.THE.ONE

CAELUM

CHAPTER NINE

Rain pelted the portholes like nails tapping on glass, startling me out of my sleep. My heart raced as I sat up, trying to calm myself. I couldn't remember my dream, but my shortness of breath and my sweat-soaked shirt told me it hadn't been good.

Gray light filtered in through the dusty porthole. It was near dawn, and a storm was bearing down on us. Now that I was awake, the harsh swaying of the ship was noticeable. Grimacing, I pulled my boots on and stood from the bed. We would need all the help we could get to make it through this storm. I cursed Duncan for letting me sleep. I should have been awake to help.

On my way back to the deck, I stopped at the syrens' room and knocked loudly on the door. "Aye, storm's coming. We'll need your help on deck."

Hearing movement behind the closed door, I turned and took the stairs two at a time. Stepping out onto the deck, the rain immediately drenched me. I grimaced as the cold water soaked through my clothes, and the wind chilled me to the bone.

Gritting my teeth, I made my way to Duncan, who stood at the helm, his blond hair dark from the rain and whipping across his face, which was much paler than usual. "How're we doing?"

A sharp gust of wind caught the sails and yanked us to the left. Duncan cursed and wrestled the wheel back, trying to keep us straight. "How you'd expect."

"We need to get out of the Straits," I said, even though I knew there was little we could do. Looking ahead, we still had quite a long way to go. Once you were in the Straits, you stayed until the end—and we were not near the end. We traveled slowly overnight; the weather had been against us.

Thunder clapped, and we flinched, ducking low to avoid being struck. Lightning was the last thing we needed, as we were an easy target out on the water.

The syrens emerged and made their way onto the deck, rumpled from sleep, but their eyes were wide as they took in the scene of the raging storm. Kyla turned toward me and rushed up the stairs with determination written all over her face.

"What can we do?" she yelled over the howling wind. She swayed, in sync with the rocking of the ship, and I reached out to steady her. The other syrens stayed on the deck as rain drenched them and wind whipped their hair about. They remained steady, waiting for instruction.

"Be ready if something happens," I said, ducking again as another streak of lightning crossed the sky. "And watch out for the lightning."

She nodded and returned to the main deck to address the others. They listened carefully, nodded, and split off, heading toward the railings to watch the seas. Kyla met my gaze and nodded firmly. I returned the gesture, grateful they were on our side. The rest of the crew filtered out, quickly securing lines to ensure nothing broke free in the howling wind.

"Fuck," Duncan said behind me. I turned to see him wrestling the helm again.

Before I could step forward to help, the ship lurched, and the sound of splintering wood filled the dawn, echoing over the howling wind.

We had hit the rocks.

My stomach lurched. I knew I had to save us from the fate the sea had dealt. I could be angry later, but for now, I needed to get us out alive. Gritting my teeth, I raced down the stairs, yelling to alert the crew of our situation, although I was sure they had already realized what happened.

Fighting the wind every step of the way, I grabbed the railing and looked over to assess the damage. A large piece of splintered wood stuck out of the hull, and my heart dropped to my boots. Water was gushing in the gaping hole. There was no fixing that.

This ship was going to sink. I closed my eyes, my hands balled into fists, and tilted my head back, letting out a frustrated yell that was swallowed up by the roaring storm.

Another gust of wind swept the rocking ship, and another splintering sound filled the air. I pitched forward, narrowly catching myself on the railing as the ship tilted suddenly. My stomach lurched as I realized we were already sinking—fast.

Fuck.

"We're sinking," Kyla gasped, her eyes wide as she approached me at the railing. "What do we do?"

I pushed a hand through my hair, wiping the water from my face. I needed a fucking *second* to think, but time was not on my side. Instinct kicked in, and my mind ran through all the things I had studied as a child, and the lessons learned from the wreck of *The Nehalennia*. "We need to get off this ship. If we're on it when it goes under, we'll be trapped in the wreckage."

The ship lurched again and tilted forward. The bow was sinking, dipping closer toward the waterline. We needed to go now. I grabbed her arm and shook it slightly, breaking her trance.

"Brigid could make air bubbles so we could breathe underwater," I said, looking at the other syrens while counting my men. "How many can you hold in one bubble?"

"One or two," she said. Her eyes lit up as she followed my thought pattern. She turned to the syrens, gathered on the deck watching us, and shouted, "Get everyone into the water and cast an air bubble."

"We've got to go *now*," I shouted, attempting to be heard over the howling wind.

Without hesitation, the syrens slipped over the railing and into the roiling sea, followed closely by my men. I waited, ensuring each man was accounted for and in the sea with the syrens. Cam was the last one left on board. He came running up with a canvas bag in his hands, working clumsily to strap it across his chest. "Ready, Captain?"

I nodded, glancing down at Duncan, already in the water. I grabbed Cameron's arm and together we climbed over the railing and dropped into the sea.

The cold water rushed up to meet us, but before I could get my bearings, the familiar magic engulfed me. Opening my eyes, I saw Kyla had enclosed Cam and me in a bubble. Her gold tail shimmered as lightning lit up the seas.

"Can you hear me?" I asked Kyla.

She nodded, careful not to speak. I realized if she had, we could have been in a far worse situation.

I pointed toward the jagged cliffs of the coast. As much as I wanted to take a second to breathe and mourn the loss of another ship, keeping everyone alive was my most pressing concern. "We need to find a way out of the water. Preferably somewhere we can take shelter."

She nodded once more and grabbed our hands, pulling us forward with a powerful swish of her tail. The others followed behind, safely in their own bubbles. I was grateful the numbers had worked in our favor, with each syren taking two men, in line with Kyla's original estimation. In a different moment, I'd have wanted to stop and study the other syrens, to see how their tails and forms differed from Brigid and Sorcha's, but we didn't have time for that, and I didn't have the energy.

After what felt like hours, an accessible shore finally appeared. It seemed like a small spit of land, just next to the jagged cliffs, but it had a beach where we could get out of the water. Kyla pulled us toward the surface, our heads breaching. We looked around and saw trees looming overhead, which meant shelter.

This would do.

I could feel the tiredness set in as Kyla pulled us closer to land. She had slowed significantly since we first set out, and I wondered how taxing it was to have both Cameron and me in this bubble. The other syrens had taken more passengers than she had, and as I looked over my shoulder at them, I saw they were just as tired. Their faces pinched and the hollows beneath their eyes more pronounced as they slowly approached the shore.

At last, we made it into shallow waters. The bubbles disappeared as we pulled ourselves out of the water. The syrens began transforming, leaving the water behind.

Cameron handed Kyla a bag of clothes he salvaged. He grimaced. "They're soaking wet, but it's better than nothing."

She nodded and began handing out clothes to the others. As they dressed, I looked out at the water, back toward where *The Voyager* had been. Frustration built, and I ran my hands through my hair, pacing on the beach. I watched as the bulk of the ship sank beneath the waves, slowly disappearing on the horizon. I had known something bad would happen when we first set sail, but it didn't calm the rage building in my chest.

Another ship. Lost. And another delay in finding the witch and Brigid. Two weeks had been bad enough, but the more I watched the ship fade away, the more I felt like it was Brigid that was slowly slipping through my fingers, and I could do nothing to catch her.

"Fuck!" I yelled, kicking at the rocks in front of me. My hands tore at my hair, and I fell to my knees. We would never find Brigid. And now had no way to return home. I had failed. Again.

"Cae," Duncan said, squatting down beside me. "Pull it together."

I bared my teeth. I didn't need his opinion, given that he had made it clear many times that he didn't like Brigid. "Fuck off, Duncan."

"Get over yourself. This pity party will accomplish nothing," he snapped, standing back up.

"Finished with your tantrum, *boy*?" Maira sneered, as she sat on a piece of driftwood and rung out her sopping hair.

"Shut your fucking mouth," I warned, pointing at her.

She rolled her eyes and turned away from me as Duncan stared, his eyebrow raised. My fingers itched to punch the glare off his face, but I inhaled deeply and rolled my shoulders back, flexing my fingers at my sides.

"We don't have time for this right now," he hissed, looking over his shoulder at the rest of the crew standing with the syrens, watching us. Watching me.

Sighing, I nodded. He was right. I was the captain here, and despite only leading my crew into shipwrecks, I was still responsible for them. Shoving my emotions down, I took a deep breath and cocked my neck back and forth. "We need to find a way off this beach."

"We can search for the nearest accessible mainland," Kyla tentatively offered. She seemed apprehensive, and for a moment, I wondered why. Then her story came rushing back, and shame roiled through my stomach as I realized my outburst had frightened her. She continued, though, despite the obvious apprehension in her eyes as she chewed on her lower lip. "The storm won't affect us underwater."

"No," Cam replied instantly. I raised an eyebrow, but he shrugged me off. "We need to stay together."

"We would be fine," Maira said, rolling her eyes. "We have lived through storms before."

"No, Cam's right," I responded, crossing my arms. While I wanted off this spit of land as soon as possible, Cameron *was* right. The last thing we needed was the syrens to leave and never come back. "We can't risk being separated right now. If something happens to you and we're stranded here, we'd all be in danger and unable to help. It's better to wait until the storm passes. And then we'll all go together."

"You forget, we are the most dangerous things in the ocean," Maira retorted.

I sighed, pinching the bridge of my nose. "Please, don't fight me on this. I'd prefer we stay together, so we can be sure everyone is safe."

Kyla placed a hand on Maira's arm, stopping the syren from speaking. "He's right, Maira. We will wait until the storm passes and then figure out our next steps."

"So, we just sit here, waiting and staring at one another until the rain stops?" she asked, holding her palms up toward the sky. She tossed a glance over her shoulder at Cordelia, the syren with pale orange hair that stood, shivering, with her arms wrapped around herself. "I fail to see how *that* would serve any useful purpose."

"The venom you keep spewing is also far from useful," Duncan snapped. "Yet you continue to speak."

Gritting my teeth, I motioned to the trees we sat under. They blocked the rain slightly, but did little for the wind. "We need to build shelter, and a fire. You may be impervious to the cold while you're in the water, but you'll need warmth just as much as us on land."

"Can we build a fire in this?" Kyla asked, peering up at the sky as it continued to spit rain down at us. She looked around at the other syrens and crew, all of whom were visibly shivering in their drenched clothing.

"That depends on if we find any dry wood. Let's start on the shelter first. The wind is going to be the worst of it," Cameron said, taking the lead. He moved behind the brunette syren, placing his hand on her lower back and guiding her toward the tree line. "Let's get going before the coldness of night sets in."

"Cae?" Duncan asked, sidling up next to me as we trailed behind. "Share the load."

This had been something we had done for years when one of us was upset. *Share the load.* Tell the other what was wrong and let them help. We hadn't said it since before *The Nehalennia* wrecked. "We're stuck here."

"No, we're resting here momentarily. We'll formulate a plan, and once the storm passes, we'll get back on track. Even if we have to walk there," he said, squeezing my shoulder. For a moment, he was my best friend again, and not the man who was angry with me for hiding Brigid's existence from him. "Now, let's go help with the shelter and fire."

Elizianna
@ELIZIANNA.THE.ONE

CAELUM

CHAPTER TEN

Morning came, and as I stirred, I immediately remembered our less-than-ideal sleeping quarters. Sandwiched between Cameron and Duncan was not exactly my favorite way to wake up, but seeing how cold it had been during the storm and throughout the night, I welcomed the warmth.

Moving carefully so as not to wake the others, I extricated myself from between my two friends and stood, relishing the sunlight that poured into the shelter. On the other side of Cameron, I found Kyla tucked tightly in against his chest. I raised an eyebrow at the sight and vowed to question Cam once we were alone.

Stepping outside, I saw Maira standing at the edge of the water, looking out at the open sea. I couldn't muster the energy to deal with her, so I moved to tend the fire instead, bringing the smoldering embers back to life. Brigid was the only thing on my mind as I watched the bright orange flames grow as wild as her unruly hair. The sharp popping of the burning wood mirrored her quick wit. My throat burned, and I sniffed harshly, pushing back the tears that were threatening to fall.

Brigid needed me to be strong. She needed me to find her before

Cliodhna decided she was better off dead. My stomach churned at the thought. I could not lose anyone else, especially Brigid. She had pulled me from my life of complacency and filled it with fire and passion. And now, that fire was fading, and life was slowly becoming cold and empty.

I poked at the fire. We had to find that witch and convince her to help find Brigid. It was our only hope, and I would cling to it. Whatever it took, we would make it to Treòir Cove.

The others slowly awoke as the sounds of crackling wood filled the morning air.

"Good morning." Kyla came over and sat down next to the fire, the flames reflecting off her skin as she held her hands out towards the warmth.

I looked over at her, poking the fire a few more times before moving to sit next to her. "Morning. Sleep decent?"

"It was cold. The wind was brutal." She shivered, and her shirt slipped off her shoulder, exposing the deep umber of the skin there. She pulled it back up, scooting closer to the fire.

Nodding, I jerked my head to where Duncan and Cameron were still sleeping, now curled up facing each other. "You can go lay between those oafs. They're pretty warm."

The corner of her lip twitched up in a ghost of a smile. "Cam was fairly warm, yes. I was talking more about the wind, though."

"We'll be back to civilization soon," I promised, turning my gaze back to the ocean. "Do you think we would make it to the mainland in your bubbles?"

"It depends on how far it is," she said with a shrug. "At least one of us should go to check the distance. If it's too far, we may tire out, especially after yesterday."

"We have to get to land," I said. She knew as well as I did we needed to get off this beach. But after everything that happened, I was questioning my abilities as a captain. If I couldn't get us through the Straits without incident, what hope did I have to lead us to Treòir Cove? Maybe I should just go on my own and send the others back to safety.

Before she could reply, Duncan woke, loudly making noises as he sat up and stretched. We watched him with amusement as he slowly woke up, oblivious to the audience he had garnered with this dramatic routine.

Duncan's noisy wake up roused everyone in the shelter. One by one, they came to join us by the fire. With no food to offer, we desperately needed to come up with a plan.

"So, how will we get off this spit of land?" Duncan asked with a heavy sigh.

"You could swim," Maira suggested dryly as she walked back over from the water.

I sighed, rubbing my forehead. These two were exhausting. Since the minute the syrens joined us, they were suspicious of each other, throwing insults, and trading glares. Kyla sighed and stood, moving to pace around. I could tell they were irritating her as well.

"We will set off to find the closest body of land, and then return to take you all there," Kyla said, looking out at the sea with her arms crossed.

"You will all go?" Duncan asked, the suspicion clear in his voice.

Maira rolled her eyes and scoffed. "We will not leave you stranded, fool."

"I wouldn't put it past you, *syren*," he shot back.

"Both of you stop," I snapped. "We've got enough to deal with."

"Just two of us need to go," Kyla interrupted, nodding at me. "Caelum was right. Staying together is important. And it will be quicker if only the two of us go."

"I'll go," Maira said, jumping on the opportunity.

"No, Nerina and I will go," Kyla replied firmly. Maira scowled at her and opened her mouth to protest, but Kyla simply smiled at her and continued on in her even tone. "You will stay. We must cooperate to save Brigid. We are all invested in that."

"Fine," Maira huffed and crossed her arms.

Kyla turned to Nerina, motioning her toward the water. She turned back to me. "We'll be back as soon as we can. Hopefully, we find a port close by, but if not, we will find some way out of the Straits and onto the mainland."

I offered a soft smile and nodded. That would be a start. Hopefully, they could find a port. I wasn't sure where we were in the Straits, but I hoped we were near Dàrna Cothrom, a small fishing town near the end of the Straits. I turned away as the two syrens removed their clothes, only turning back once they had entered the water. Their transitions were seamless, like breathing. It was so very different from the painful transitions Brigid suffered through. My gut clenched, thinking of Brigid in pain.

It wasn't fair, and I knew that being unable to answer the call of the sea brought her both physical and mental anguish. Kyla and Nerina disappeared beneath the waves as we sat in silence for a few moments, looking out at the ripples they left behind.

Maira's heavy sigh broke the peace, the icy wind turning her usually pale nose and cheeks a bright pink. "Are we just going to sit here and stare at the water until they get back?"

"What would you rather we do? Build a new ship right here on the beach?" Duncan's snarky comment made me crack a smile.

"I'd rather do something." She turned to stare at Duncan, her stubbornness on full display. She held his gaze for a moment before looking at me. "After all, isn't that what you were so worked up about, *Captain?* Us not doing anything?"

"Stop it, Maira," a syren named Cordelia warned, pulling her back to her seat. Her cheeks were pink from the sharp wind as well.

"That was when we had the ability to do something," I said, clenching my fists to keep my anger in check. The other syren may have softened Maira's blow, but the words still landed. "I'm not sure if you noticed, but we're on a spit of land with no buildings, no other people, and no way off."

"The impossible never seemed to stop you when it was us you were angry with," she spat back. Cordelia tugged on her arm again, but Maira shrugged her off, still staring at me.

"That's enough." I took a deep breath through my nose, closing my eyes as I exhaled. "We need to keep the fire going and try to find some water. Fighting will not help."

"You're the captain," she said, rolling her eyes.

It took every ounce of willpower to turn away from Maira and focus on the rest of my crew. Thankfully, we all made it through the wreck uninjured. "We need to find some water. Duncan, you stay here with Maira and Alan and keep the fire going. The rest of you, help me find some water."

"I'm not staying here with him," Maira spat, stepping back into my field of vision.

"I don't exactly fancy your company either," Duncan retorted.

"I'll stay here," Cam volunteered, catching my eye.

"Thank you," I said. The constant bickering was exhausting, and it was pissing me off.

The rest of us split up, going in opposite directions to search for any source of drinkable water.

"Do you want to talk about it?" I asked, after Duncan and I had stepped into the trees.

"She infuriates me," came Duncan's immediate and emphatic response. "She's a fucking murderer and acts like she's better than of the rest of us."

"We need to work together," I said, sighing. "I know you don't like the syrens, but we have to get Brigid back, and we need their help."

"Why do we still need their help if we know she's not in the seas?" He stopped walking and crossed his arms. "We can find Brigid ourselves, without the help of those damn fish."

I raised an eyebrow at him. "You do remember Brigid is a syren, right?"

"She's different from the rest of them…" he whispered after a moment of silence. "And I'm sorry I picked so many fights with her. It's clear she means a lot to you."

"I appreciate that, Dun." I rubbed a hand over my face and smoothed down my beard. It was a far cry from making things right, but it was a step in the right direction. "I just want her back."

"I know you do, Cae. We'll get her back."

"What if we can't?" I asked, my voice cracking. I shuddered and took a deep breath to calm myself. Looking up at the sky, I blinked to keep the tears that had suddenly blurred my vision from falling down my cheeks. "What if she's already dead?"

"There's no water," Alan said, breaking the tension. His quiet approach startled us as we turned toward him.

"We'll keep looking," Duncan said, waving him off.

With a quick salute, Alan turned and trudged back toward the beach. Once he was out of sight, I turned back to Duncan and sighed. "Where were we?"

He tilted his head. "You think Brigid is dead?"

I reached up to rub at my beard. "What do we do if she is?"

"Well, if she's already dead, then we'll bring her home and bury her with Sorcha and Maddock. And then we kill Cliodhna." He stopped in front of me, resting both of his hands on my shoulders. "But do you really think she's dead? Do you feel it in your soul?"

I considered his words and finally shook my head. Her existence was so large and so vibrant; there would be a sign if she was gone. I would feel it. "No. I think she's alive and fighting."

He smiled. "And we'll get her back."

I offered him a smile, and thankfully, my tears dried up as I let out a small laugh. "We'd better go see if we can find some water."

"Cae, she makes you happy," Duncan murmured, stopping me in my tracks just as I had turned away.

My heart clenched at the approval my friend was *finally* giving me. Having his approval now, when we might not get Brigid back... it didn't make me feel more optimistic. It felt too late. Yes, Brigid had made me incredibly happy. She had brought a joy into my life that I didn't know I was missing.

"Aye, she does," I whispered back.

"Then let's go get your girl, Captain." He saluted, breaking the serious mood, as we both started laughing.

"I hope this means you'll be nice to her when she returns," I said dryly, raising an eyebrow. I didn't enjoy being vulnerable, and I was glad to return to our normal sarcastic humor.

He snorted and kept walking. "Of course not, but I suppose I can be a little nicer about it," he called over his shoulder.

Shaking my head, I laughed as we made our way back to the beach. Upon our return, it was apparent that Alan had informed everyone about the lack of water, because Cameron immediately came up to us.

"What now?" he asked, crossing his arms over his chest. He licked his lips, which were cracked and dry, flaking from the sun and salt water. I'm sure mine did not look much better. "How long do we think the syrens will take?" Concern rose in his voice as he looked out at the sea.

I turned to look at the syrens, who were sitting at the fire. Maira bristled. "Why are you looking at us?"

"How long do you think it will take for the others to return?" Cameron asked, thankfully getting his words out quicker than Duncan, who wouldn't have been as kind.

"It shouldn't be too much longer," Cordelia said, eyeing Maira. "Unless they went a very long distance. We typically can swim quickly if we don't have anyone with us."

Maira huffed and poked at the embers with a stick, thankfully remaining quiet.

"I suppose we just have to wait," I replied, settling down next to the fire. All we could do now was wait.

"Where will we go when we get to the mainland?" Alan asked, sitting down next to Finn, who had been uncharacteristically quiet since the wreck.

"The wreck and traveling underwater disoriented me a bit. We should be close to Dàrna Cothrom, and if we can get there, we should be able to find transportation to Treòir Cove."

"I've heard of it, but I've never been," he said, nodding.

"What's it like?" Finn asked. At my quizzical look, he clarified. "Dàrna Cothrom, I mean."

I shrugged. "I've actually never been there myself. My father often spoke of it. It's a small village, a fishing town mostly, but big enough to warrant being on a map."

"They're back," Maira interrupted, standing from the log and moving toward the beach.

We all stood and followed Maira and Cordelia down to the water as I tried to keep my optimism in check. My legs went slightly wobbly with nerves and I wiped my sweaty palms on the sides of my pants as we neared the water's edge.

I was careful to keep my eyes on Kyla's face as she exited the water. The syrens had no problem with their nakedness, which didn't surprise me, as Brigid hadn't either. But I still wanted to be respectful. Her face was neutral, and for once I cursed her level-headedness. While I could read every emotion on Brigid's face, Kyla's was always so... carefully blank. I searched her eyes for any hint of what news awaited us. "What did you find?"

"There's a small harbor not far from here. We couldn't see it during the storm, but it won't take us long to get you all there," she explained, reaching up to squeeze the water from the long ropes of heavy curls.

"Is there a spot that we can exit the water without being spotted?" I asked, cautious of exposing the syrens, as it would be very suspicious if a group of naked women entered the harbor with no boat.

She nodded. "There was. We'll be safe. I appreciate your concern."

I heard Maira snort behind me and forced myself to ignore her. "Then, let's go. I don't want to lose any more time."

"We're going back in those bubbles?" Duncan asked, moving to stand next to me. "Those things are unnerving."

"We could let you swim by yourself," Maira snapped back.

My head fell back, and I closed my eyes as I prayed for patience. I did not have the energy to deal with this bickering. "Spare us. Both of you."

"Can we just get going?" Cam asked, becoming increasingly irritated.

"Aye, yes. Let's go," I said, moving toward the water.

In front of me, Kyla motioned back to the fire. "Someone put that out, please. We don't want to burn down the few trees left on this island."

Cordelia turned, quickly extinguishing the fire with a practiced ease that must have been learned before her rebirth as a syren, and we all entered the water. The syrens transformed once they reached shoulder depth. Kyla turned to address my men. "Just try to breathe normally. I know it's unnerving, but the magic will protect you. Trust us."

With those words of wisdom, the syrens pulled us into the magic bubbles, and began our journey toward land. And hopefully, toward some good news.

Eliz
@ELIZIAN

BRIGID

CHAPTER ELEVEN

There was a certain calmness in knowing death was approaching. I could tell my health was fading. It was taking longer and longer for me to heal after each torture session, and although Cliodhna fed me sporadically, I could feel my ribs more prominently than ever. The effort to simply keep myself awake was immense, and I doubted I could keep my pain at bay much longer.

Since the last session with Cliodhna, I had stayed in my syren form. I was just barely inside the water tank, bound to the metal grate that had been lowered only mere inches into the water. With no way to track the passing days, I had no concept of time. I knew it had been weeks since Cliodhna took me, but I had no idea exactly how long I'd been here.

The wounds on my tail were not healing, and infection was setting in. My body burned as my exposed skin and muscles turned red and swollen. Cliodhna would notice that soon—if she hadn't already. My strength was waning and my spirit was, too. I needed to get out of here.

I dipped my fingers through the grate, trying to reach more water. Maybe, if I could submerge any of my extremities entirely, I could channel my healing powers. The harder I pushed, the more the metal dug into the webbing between my fingers. The pain was minimal compared to what radiated throughout the rest of my body. I kept pushing, but the water was still barely reaching my knuckles.

"What are you doing?" Cliodhna's cool voice filled the room, and I looked up to see her standing in the doorway.

I turned my head to look at her. Answering would do me no good; she had already decided what she was going to do to me before she even set foot in the room.

"Trying to heal yourself?" She walked closer to me, stepping up beside the tank.

Again, I stayed silent and still. If she wanted a reaction out of me, she would have to work for it. I would not give in willingly. All I had left was my willpower, and I would hold on to it for as long as I could.

"Only I can heal you, and I'm not quite finished with you." She smiled at me, a sickly-sweet expression that I knew was as fake as the notion that I would make it out of here alive.

My anxiety spiked thinking about what she would do next, but I couldn't let it show, or she would use it to further whatever sick and twisted game she was playing. I took a deep breath and turned inward, locking my emotions away. I let my face fall flat as I turned to look at her. "You keep saying that, and yet I'm beginning to think you have no actual plan."

She grabbed my chin. "I will do whatever I want."

"Oh, sure," I said, my words garbled as she squeezed my cheeks. A surge of defiance flooded through me. If she was going to destroy me, I would make sure she knew how despicable and alone she truly was. "That's all you have left *to* do. No more children, no more syrens... I'm all you have left. How pathetic of you to seek vengeance on us for saving children from being murdered."

She narrowed her eyes and lashed out, slapping me across the face. Her talons scratched across my skin, tearing the flesh of my cheek. The wound burned, and I bit the insides of my cheeks to keep from screaming.

That only seemed to irritate her more, and the torture began anew.

She slammed her hand down on my chest, and the transformation ripped through my body. I squeezed my eyes shut and tried to breathe through my mouth, but the pain was excruciating. It felt like liquid fire being poured over my extremities as my infected tail separated, and my legs ripped apart. When the transformation was complete, I tried to calm my body, but my legs ached as the wounds on my tail had simply transferred themselves to my legs, the torn skin tender against the slightest breeze.

"You are mine. Forever," Cliodhna hissed.

"What a sad future," I said, holding back tears. I was proud of myself for keeping my composure, but my throat burned, and my chest tightened from the agony raging through my body.

She scowled and bent down to pick up a bucket at her feet. Without hesitating, she dumped the contents all over my naked body. The salty water stung my wounds, and I couldn't hold back my cry this time. As soon as the noise escaped my lips, I regretted it as a smile formed on her face.

She reached out and yanked me by the hair, pulling me from the platform. My body crashed to the floor, and I felt my bones snap. The impact had jarred my shoulder and as I gingerly tensed the muscles, I knew immediately it had popped out of the socket.

"Get up," she snapped, kicking at my stomach.

I gritted my teeth and pushed myself up with my good arm. Looking down, I stretched my legs out in front of me, examining the injuries. They were horrific, and I was immediately nauseous. Looking away from my torn and bloody skin, I turned to Cliodhna, my face void of emotion.

She grabbed a wooden chair and pulled it to the center of the room. "Sit here," she demanded.

I knew standing would not be possible, and that was likely her intention. But I would try. I slowly tucked one leg under me and held my limp, dislocated arm across my stomach. Trying to rise, I cried out as my leg buckled and I fell back to the ground.

"Useless," Cliodhna spat. She grabbed me by my hair again and pulled me across the floor. I clenched my teeth as the pain ripped through my scalp and traveled down my body. Gingerly, I pulled my injured arm across my body and cradled it in my lap, shifting uncomfortably as the wooden chair dug into my bare skin.

She pulled a rope out and bent to tie my legs to the chair. She took special care to ensure the ropes landed directly over my open wounds, ensuring that any movement would cause my infected injuries to rub against the coarse rope. I bit down on my cheek, and a metallic taste flooded my mouth as I swallowed back the blood that covered my tongue, tensing every muscle to keep from flinching. Moving up my body, she tied another length of rope around my thighs, and smiled as she wrenched my arms back, tying my wrist together.

Tears sprang to my eyes as a searing pain tore through my shoulder. This position was infinitely worse than laying in my syren form above that tank. She specifically intended to keep me in constant pain.

"I will kill you," I whispered, my voice hoarse.

"I doubt that." She whirled around and left. I was finally alone. My body sagged, and my mouth fell open. Panting, I lifted my head, fighting through the pain consuming my body.

My mind swirled with possibilities as my eyes traveled toward the door. Cliodhna had not locked it behind her this time, something she had always been careful about. I had heard no one else during my time here. Perhaps it really was just the two of us. And that gave me hope.

Consumed by the constant torture, I hadn't been able to ponder a true escape plan yet. But she was slowing down, allowing more time between sessions, and despite my body not catching up, my mind was grateful for the extra time.

She was going to kill me soon. I was sure of it. My lack of response infuriated her, and if she wasn't careful, her frustration would end me sooner than she intended.

I had to escape. I couldn't wait for Caelum any longer. I needed to rely on myself once more.

Elizianna
@ELIZIANNA.THE.ONE

CAELUM

CHAPTER TWELVE

Finally, we surfaced, and the syrens dropped the magic bubbles that had protected us under water. When the bubbles dissolved, the cold water shocked my system, and I shivered, clenching my teeth.

Cameron looked at Kyla, who was swaying slightly. He rushed to her side and held out an arm to steady her if she needed it. "Whoa, are you okay, Kyla?"

"I'm just tired. Moving that many people takes a lot of energy," she said, forcing a smile on her face.

We all exited the water, and the syrens quickly dressed in the clothes Cam managed to save. We made our way up the grassy embankment to look for signs of life.

"Do you know where exactly we are?" Cam asked, looking over at me. He was still hovering protectively near Kyla, though all the syrens looked as tired as she did.

"I think we're in Dàrna Cothrom, but I'm not certain. We need to find someone to ask." I looked around, searching for clues as to where we were.

"You are in Dàrna Cothrom, boy." A quiet voice came from the right of us.

My hand instinctively reached for the sword at my waist, and I whirled around to see an older man looking at us curiously, leaning against a knobby walking staff.

His unruly brown hair streaked with white matched an equally wild beard that covered half of the rich brown skin of his face. My fingers slowly flexed around the hilt of my sword. Appearance meant little, and the way he leaned against the stick in his hand, carelessly resting his weight on it... he clearly didn't need it to get around. It was a weapon. "Who are you?"

"I live here," the man snapped, dismissively waving his hand at me. "Put that away. I'm not here to harm you."

"Why are you here?" I asked, relaxing my grip on the sword, but not dropping it completely. In the wreck, we had lost all the weapons we'd gotten from Galen's blacksmith shop, but thankfully, I had been wearing my sword. Other than the syrens, and Duncan and Cameron's ability to fight, we didn't have any protection. My father had connections in Bhodheas, and I was wary of everyone right now. Even though this town seemed small, I needed to be careful.

"I saw you all coming out of the sea and wanted to see what you were up to," the man said, shrugging. "Seems like you might need some help."

"We don't need help," Duncan huffed, crossing his arms over his chest.

The older man snorted. "Right. Where do you plan to go dripping sea water everywhere?"

"Why would you help us?" I asked, studying him. His face looked weathered and wrinkled, and I knew he had seen his fair share of life on the seas.

"Boy, I know a syren when I see one. And I know they wouldn't be with a bunch of sailors without a damn good reason."

We all froze, a group of collective statues.

"How do you know about syrens?" Kyla asked, her eyes narrowing.

I stepped protectively in front of the group, pulling the man's attention back to me. Cam followed as Duncan shifted into a defensive stance. Out of the corner of my eye, I watched Maira step in front of Cordelia. I wasn't sure how he knew about syrens, but it probably wasn't a positive experience. "What are you offering?"

"I thought you may need a place to stay. Clothes. Food. And we can talk about what else you may need from there. My wife would be happy to have other people to dote on," he said, as a smile lit up his brown eyes. He took a step forward and extended his hand. "I'm Faolan."

"Caelum," I replied, moving to shake his hand. The rough calluses on his hands confirmed that this man had made his living around boats.

"All right, Caelum," he said, nodding at me. "Let's get going. You lot are going to get cold if you stay in those wet clothes much longer."

"Why should we trust you?" Maira said, stepping next to Kyla. Despite the harshness of her voice, I could see hesitation in her eyes.

The older man's face softened, and he took a step back. "No one knows you're here, and no one even believes you're real. The town would laugh at me if I told them. You have nothing to fear."

"You'll forgive us for being skeptical," Kyla said diplomatically, swallowing hard as she stepped forward. She looked over at me and nodded. "We'll go with you."

"I know you could kill me if you wanted, but I suggest waiting until my wife has fed you, at least." He smirked and turned to me for confirmation.

At the mention of food, my own stomach growled loudly. I looked at Duncan and received a small nod.

"Yes, we'll go with you. We appreciate your hospitality," I said, moving to stand next to Kyla. "Please, lead the way."

Faolan led us away from the collection of buildings by the harbor and toward a spattering of houses on the outskirts of town. We continued until we reached a house that showed its age as much as the man did. Weathered wood covered in creeping moss led to a thatched roof that, while solid, clearly had not been repaired for a while. One shutter on the front windows hung crookedly, and a wooden flower box sat beneath it, the flowers inside flourishing while the wood rotted along the bottom, giving way to the upturned earth beneath.

Faolan reached the door and looked back at us, his hand resting on the handle of the smooth wood door. "You will respect my wife and do what she tells you."

The tone of his voice brokered no arguments, and we all nodded. This couple was opening their home to us, and I would ensure they received nothing but respect from us all. And if that meant Maira had to sleep outside, then so be it. I turned and caught her gaze as she huffed and rolled her eyes at me.

As we stepped inside, it was obvious the house was truly a home. An eclectic mix of well-worn furniture filled the main room. Warmth rushed to meet us as Faolan closed the door. The fireplace on the far wall was roaring and crackling as an older woman, whose kind eyes twinkled, smiled and stepped back from the pot at the stove.

Wiping her hands on her apron, she reached a hand up to smooth her graying hair, securing it back into the bun at the nape. Her smile grew wider, stretching across her tawny face, genuine and welcoming. "Well, now, who are you?"

"Found this lot coming out of the water by the docks," Faolan said. He nodded his head slightly toward Kyla and the three other syrens. "Figure these ladies here are syrens. Don't know about the men. I've never heard of a male syren, so I figure they're human."

"Oh, syrens!" the woman said, clapping her hands together. Her excitement was not the reaction I had expected. "I'm so glad you're here. Let's get you all into dry clothes."

"You know about syrens too?" I asked, before Maira could. I saw her mouth open, and I knew my line of questioning would be far less likely to get us kicked out than hers. "How?"

The woman's eyes turned sad, and she wrung her hands together. "Well, they saved me once. When I was younger."

I saw Kyla's eyes widen, the fire reflecting in her irises. "We saved you?"

The woman smiled, reaching out to Kyla and patting her knee. "Yes, dear. I remember you. There were two of you who saved me and brought me here to Bhodheas. I came here, to Dàrna Cothrom, met Faolan, and never looked back. But I never forgot your kindness."

"They should have wiped your memories," Kyla whispered in disbelief.

"Oh?" The woman's lips quirked. "Someone forgot to tell me that, then."

"All right, let's talk more once they're warm and dry, Alys," Faolan said, leaning over to kiss her temple.

The sight made my heart clench, and I longed for Brigid. Seeing them made me wonder what our own future could have been like. Would we even have one now? I missed her more than I thought possible, and all I wanted was to have her back in my arms.

"Yes, of course. Let me get you all dry clothes," Alys said, smiling softly. She motioned us through a doorway and into a room filled with cots. "You can stay in here. I know there are not enough beds, but I'll bring in more blankets."

"Put your wet clothes in this bucket," Faolan said, kicking a wooden bucket over to me. "We'll hang them to dry by the fire."

"Do you harbor people often?" I asked, nodding toward the cots. It reminded me of the safe houses I used when I smuggled people to safety. Perhaps I could gain a new contact from this.

The older man raised his eyebrow. "I bet you'd like to know..."

"Here, change into these. There should be enough for you all." Alys came back into the room with a bundle of clothes. Recognizing the tension between her husband and me, she stepped between us and pressed the clothes into my hand. "Enough, both of you."

Faolan gave me a long look before turning to follow his wife out of the room, pulling the door closed behind him.

"Change fast. I want to talk to them more," I muttered, passing out the clothes.

"Are we really staying here tonight?" Duncan asked quietly as we peeled off our wet clothes and pulled on the new dry clothes.

"Aye, we are," I sighed. "They seem to know what's going on around here, and they might have insight into where the witch is."

Duncan nodded, thankfully accepting my answer without argument.

We needed to find Brigid. And to do that, we needed to find this witch.

Once dressed, I turned to survey the group. Wet clothes filled the bucket, and everyone was in dry clothes once again. I moved next to Kyla, my brow furrowed at the haunted look in her eyes. "You okay?"

"Yeah," she croaked, clearing her throat. "I just wasn't expecting that. I remember her, too. She was one of the first girls I saved after I joined Cliodhna."

"I'm sure you'll have time to speak to her more," I said, reaching out to squeeze her hand. "I promise."

Cam moved over and wrapped an arm around Kyla's shoulders, pulling her into a side hug. She stiffened slightly, but didn't pull away. Instead, she smiled up at him, her eyes lighting up. "Thanks, Cam."

I raised an eyebrow at them. There was something about seeing the two of them together that seemed to work. A balance. Hardness and softness, serious and light-hearted.

"Let's go," Maira said, roughly pushing past Cameron to leave the room.

Faolan and Alys were waiting for us in the main room, setting the table with bowls of steaming soup and plates of crusty bread. Alys waved at the collection of mismatched chairs crowded around the table. "Sit. Eat."

Following her directions, we all sat down, bumping knees and elbows as we crammed our bodies into the small space. The soup smelled delicious, and we all dug in, eating with fervor. It felt like days since we'd last eaten, and the warmth of the soup was fantastic. I forced myself to slow down and savor the taste. I didn't want my empty stomach to immediately throw it back up.

"This is delicious, Alys," I said, swallowing every bite. "Thank you."

She smiled, patting my shoulder. "Good, I'm glad. Eat as much as you want."

We ate in silence as our hosts watched us, amused.

Finally, we slowed down, and I felt overly full for the first time in months. Now we had business to attend to. Turning toward Faolan, who was leaning against the windowsill, I raised an eyebrow. "You seem to know what goes on in this town. Have you heard anything about a witch?"

His eyes sparkled. "A witch who can grant you anything you want?"

"Aye."

"Aye, I might've heard a thing or two," he said, crossing his arms and raising his chin. "Why do you want to find her?"

I glanced over at Duncan, who shrugged. "We're trying to rescue a syren. She was kidnapped, and we must find her."

"Sure." He smirked. "And Alys is just a woman I met in town."

Could everyone tell that I had feelings for Brigid? I didn't think I was this transparent, but apparently, I was mistaken.

"Aye, boy. You should go to the pub and ask around there. I bet you'll find out something," he said with a chuckle.

"Can they stay here with you?" I asked, gesturing to the syrens and the rest of my crew. I wasn't sure what it was about Faolan and Alys, but they felt safe and trustworthy. "Duncan and I will go to the pub tonight."

"Of course. You're all safe here," Alys said, her voice firm. "No one will harm you while you're here."

"Thank you," I said as a genuine smile spread across my face. This woman reminded me of my mother, and if I had known Alys longer, I might have asked her for a hug. But I needed to keep my emotions under control, especially since a stranger could so easily read my face.

Eliz
@ELIZIAN

Caelum

CHAPTER THIRTEEN

Faolan had given us directions to the pub, and said he'd go with us, but he didn't feel right leaving Alys alone with strangers. I respected his wishes, and the protectiveness he felt for his wife, so Duncan and I set off into the afternoon sun alone.

"What do you think about them?" he finally asked as we entered the town and began our walk down the main path.

"I think it's about time something went our way for once." I turned to look at him as we approached the pub. "Kyla remembered Alys."

He grabbed my arm and pulled me to a stop just before we reached the door, furrowing his brow. "And that's enough for you to trust them?"

"Yes. Why isn't it good enough for you?" Duncan was always suspicious, and while I was thankful for it on some occasions, it didn't feel warranted here. "Faolan didn't have to help us or take us to his home, but he did because he knew the syrens had helped his wife. He's certainly suspicious of us, but cares enough to help."

"I don't trust the syrens. They are fickle and always have been."

Of all the things I'd been waiting for him to say about the syrens, that had not been one of them. I laughed at the absurdity of it. "Are you serious? You would rather they stayed with Cliodhna and worked against us and Brigid?"

He scowled. "That's not what I meant. I am glad they are helping us, for your sake and Brigid's. I just..."

"No one is asking you to be friends with them, Duncan," I whispered, seeing the apprehension and frustration on his face. "But we need to work together to get Brigid back."

There was clearly more he wanted to say, but he closed his mouth, nodding once and pushing open the door.

Despite it being late afternoon, the pub was busy inside. A band in the corner played a merry but slightly off-beat tune as people spread out, drinking, talking, and dancing to the music. Duncan motioned toward the bar and the tan woman behind it, who was busy cleaning mugs.

In a place like this, the barmaid was always the best place to start.

"What can I get you men?" she asked, putting down the rag as we stepped up to the bar and smoothing a hand over a strand of her brown hair that had escaped the low bun at her nape.

"Information?" I asked, raising an eyebrow.

She leaned forward on her elbows, a curious look on her face. "About what?"

"Rumor has it there's a witch somewhere near Treòir Cove. How would one go about finding her?" I asked. I would have been more subtle, but I didn't want to waste any more time.

Her eyes narrowed. "Why are you looking for her?"

Duncan elbowed me in the side, a warning not to tell this stranger the real reason. He cleared his throat. "Does it really matter?"

She huffed, picking up the mug and rag she had been using. "I may have heard a thing or two, but it will cost you. A girl's got to make a living somehow."

A laugh escaped from Duncan's lips, a genuine sound I hadn't heard in days. "Aye, I suppose you're right. We'll both have some ale then."

"Good choice. Coming right up." She grinned and stepped away to fill our mugs. "Now, what were you looking to know?" she asked when she returned to place the mugs in front of us.

"How can we find the witch?" I repeated, taking a sip as Duncan placed some coins on the bar.

She slipped the coins into the pocket on her apron and leaned forward. "You can't find her. She finds you."

"How unhelpful," Duncan said dryly. "And how does she know we're looking for her?"

The barmaid shrugged and her eyes twinkled as she looked at my friend. "Suppose you'll need to hang around and find out."

"We're kind of in a hurry." I felt a little guilty interrupting the flirting since Duncan rarely let himself engage in this behavior, but we were in a hurry and had no time to spare. "Is there any way to get word to her?"

She looked at us for a moment, her eyes flicking back and forth between Duncan and me. Finally, she nodded toward an empty table. "Go have a seat. I'll see what I can do."

"Thank you," I said, leaning forward to make eye contact. "I appreciate any help you can give."

My words made her pause, and she held my gaze for another moment before nodding. "Of course."

Taking our mugs, we made our way over to the table. We both sat with our backs to the wall and quietly observed our surroundings.

"How long do you think this will take?" Duncan asked under his breath.

"Hopefully not too long." I nodded back toward the bar. "She's gone, so hopefully she's talking to someone about us."

Nearly an hour passed, and I was growing restless. My leg bounced under the table as I fiddled with the splintered wood on the table, pulling back strips of it and flicking them to the floor. I had long since finished my ale, and I couldn't wait any longer. We would just have to try somewhere else to find information.

Shoving back from the table, I stood, facing Duncan, who was still sitting with his back to the wall. "Let's go. This is pointless."

"I hear you're looking for a witch."

I spun around to see a young woman standing behind me. We hadn't seen her during our hour-long observation of the bar. It was as if she appeared out of nowhere. She wore a long moss colored cloak, with the hood pulled up over her head. Waves of dark hair spilled out over the font of the cloak, framing her sepia brown skin, which was darker under the shadow of her hood and brighter where the light hit. She couldn't have been much older than Sorcha, yet as her nearly black eyes bore into mine, studying me, I could tell she had been around for a long time.

I raised an eyebrow. "Aye, who are you?"

She cocked her head to the side as her full lips quirked up. "Someone who can help you."

I fixed a look at Duncan, who wisely stayed quiet, his gaze fixed on the woman in front of us. "I'm supposed to trust you?"

"No, but I can take you to the woman who can find your syren." Her eyebrow raised. "Isn't that what you are looking for?"

All the muscles in my body tensed. How did she know exactly what I was looking for? We hadn't told the barmaid, and we certainly hadn't talked about it while we were sitting here.

"Who are you?" Duncan repeated, his voice firmer than mine had been. His suspicion was clear, and I was grateful he stepped in as I wrapped my mind around the girl in front of us.

"As I said, I am someone who can help." She stood there, completely still, never breaking eye contact. "I was told you were looking for the witch, and I can take you to her."

"And how are we supposed to trust you?" Duncan repeated my earlier question, narrowing his eyes. "How do you know what we're looking for?"

"You don't have to trust me." She shrugged. "You won't be able to get to the witch without me. It's your choice."

As she turned to walk away, I looked at Duncan, warning him to stay quiet. This was our one shot to find the witch. "Wait."

She turned back, an eyebrow raised.

"You can take us to her?" While this was a stranger, and I absolutely didn't trust her, we had come too far to stop here. And if this stranger said she could take us to the witch, I had to give it a shot. I chewed on my lip, watching her as I thought about all the poor decisions I had made lately, and the pain they had resulted in.

"I can." Her voice was confident and steady.

"I'd need to get the rest of my crew first," I replied slowly. The syrens were still with Cameron, Finn, Alan and the others at Alys and Faolan's, and we needed to stay together.

"Then go get them and meet me at the edge of town by the blacksmith's forge before sunset."

"Sunset is nearly upon us," Duncan said.

"You should move quickly, then. I will not wait." And with that, she turned and left the tavern, her cloak billowing behind her.

Duncan exhaled slowly. "Do we believe her?"

I pushed back my chair and stood up. "We don't have a choice." Throwing some coins on the table as an extra thanks to the barmaid, I turned toward the door. "We better get the others."

The sun began dipping below the horizon in the distance, and the wind picked up, cooling the night down quickly as we approached the blacksmith's forge on the edges of town, leaving behind the activity of the townspeople and approaching the quiet calmness of the forest.

Alys had tried to convince Faolan to come with us. He was hesitant to leave her alone, and even more hesitant to bring her along, especially since we did not know where this meeting would take us. In the end, Faolan won the spirited discussion, and now the syrens and my crew were the only ones standing in the shadows by the blacksmith's forge. The light from the forge's fire danced across the dirt at our feet as my eyes darted back and forth, watching for the young woman to appear.

"Where is she?" Maira grumbled, stomping up next to me. "I thought you said sunset. We don't have all night."

"I'm right here, syren," said a voice from our left. My heart took off at a run, but I was grateful I hadn't jumped at her sudden presence. She stepped out of the shadows, pausing directly in front of me. She turned and studied the group of us, her eyes lingering on the group of syrens, spending extra time fixed on Kyla, who merely returned her careful stare. "It's time to go."

"Go where?" Maira asked.

"Follow me. It will take some time." Our mysterious friend turned and began walking into the darkness of the woods.

We followed the cloaked woman into the tree line, weaving through the tall trunks. Darkness descended quickly, and the woman pulled a lantern from her cloak, lighting it. We continued to follow her, a trail no longer distinguishable.

"If she's leading us into the woods to sacrifice us…" Duncan's muttering trailed off.

"We can take her," Cam muttered back.

At least their words made me crack a smile as we walked in silence, even as all our suspicions rose.

Finally, the trees parted, revealing a bog ahead. Lanterns hung in the sparse trees that stuck up from the mud and water.

The cloaked woman stopped at the edge of the bog and turned back to us. "You're here."

"Where is here, exactly?" I asked, looking around. There were no people, no structures, nothing.

She waved her hand to the left, and two canoes appeared in the darkness. "Follow the water to the house at the end. She's waiting for you."

I leaned over to inspect the boats, and when I turned back, the woman had vanished. She was nowhere to be found as I looked around. I turned to the others. "Are we doing this?"

"We've come this far," Kyla muttered. "We have to see if she can help us find Brigid."

The others nodded. Even Maira and Duncan.

Cautiously, we all loaded into the canoes and began rowing through the swamp. My stomach twisted with nerves, more gnarled than the roots of the trees we passed. My eyes flitted around, and with every chirp of an insect or rustling of the wind between the leaves, I grew more unsettled.

Lanterns hung from the trees, spaced out to provide just enough light to see a few feet in front of us, but nothing beyond the edge of the water was visible. We rowed through the shadows, heading deeper into the bog, until it grew completely silent except for the sound of the water moving. We no longer heard the sounds of bugs or creatures, and even the wind had quieted. I kept my head on a swivel as my eyes constantly gazed into the darkness. My body was tense and ready to react to whatever lay ahead.

Finally, darkness gave way to a cottage, lit by even more lanterns. We slowed our approach and glided up onto the muddy bank. Glancing around the darkness, we left the boats and slowly approached the small cabin.

As we moved closer, a figure appeared in the doorway, backlit by the plethora of lanterns in the house.

"I've been expecting you," echoed the voice.

The figure stepped forward, and as our eyes adjusted to the light, we saw a woman standing there. Her hair was dark and hung in loose, messy waves over her thin shoulders. She wore a faint blue dress, covered by a frayed and tattered off-white shawl. Her skin was pale, almost gray against the color of her dress, and as we approached, I could see the same gray shade reflecting in her eyes. A shiver went down my spine as those gray eyes landed on me.

"You can help us?" I asked, my voice quiet and hoarse.

"That depends on what you want."

"Someone was taken from me, and I need to get her back," I said, hesitant at how much information to reveal. The young woman who led us here had known Brigid's name, and that she was a syren, but that didn't mean this witch knew. "I was told you can help me find her."

"Come inside, and let's talk." She turned and walked back into the house, expecting us to follow her.

One by one, we filed through the door and into the small house. Jars of various... things hung from the ceiling, along with the lanterns. I was careful not to look at the jars too closely. We ducked and moved through the cramped space, following the witch to the back of the house. She sat down at a large round table, covered with a stained cloth, and motioned for me to sit in front of her.

"You can help?" I asked again as I took a seat. This was unnerving, the hairs on the back of my neck standing at attention in the small cabin. My hands sweat as I wrung them together under the table.

She looked up at me. "Aye, I likely could. But why should I? Why do you want to save her?"

I shifted uncomfortably. Admitting my feelings about Brigid to Duncan had been one thing, but saying them aloud to a stranger, surrounded by the other syrens, had me feeling twisted inside. It felt like a betrayal to share them with anyone but Brigid first. She deserved to know my feelings before anyone else, and yet, it seemed she would be the last to know. I wanted to protect *something* from this stranger, to keep something for just me and Brigid. "She's a friend..."

The woman raised an eyebrow as her eyes danced with laughter. "Quite the lengths you've gone to rescue a *friend*. Who is she really?"

Swallowing hard, I cleared my throat, suddenly unable to steady my voice. "I care about her."

Loud laughter burst from the woman's lips, and I grit my teeth to keep from saying something that would surely get us kicked out, or worse. I was not Maira; I could control my words. Nevertheless, I needed this woman's help, and she was laughing at me. Her laughter ceased as she laced her fingers together and leaned forward on the table. "How can I help you find her when you cannot even admit your feelings?"

Images of her face, her hair, her skin flashed through my mind. Memories of her hands on my skin, her lips on mine. The feeling of unending loss when I saw her sink beneath the waves. The cold disregard I'd had for everything since she disappeared. All of it slammed into me at once, stealing the breath from my lungs and the warmth from my body.

"She's everything to me," I whispered, my voice thick with emotion. I hadn't admitted that to myself, let alone Brigid, and now I was telling this witch. It felt wrong. Tears stung my eyes, but I clenched my fists beneath the table, forcing them back. When I got Brigid back, I would tell her my feelings. She deserved that much.

"That's better." The witch smiled at me, her silver-gray eyes staring at me with such intensity.

"Can you help us find her?" Maira said, stepping closer to me.

"Step back, child," the woman replied, holding up her hand. She motioned to herself and then to me. "This is between us, for now."

Maira scowled but didn't resist when Kyla yanked her back to the others.

"Can you?" I asked, echoing Maira's question. We needed to find Brigid. My stomach twisted at the thought of what Cliodhna was doing to her. If she was even still alive. No, I couldn't let my mind go there. She was alive, and we would save her.

"For a price." Her voice was calm, warring with my inner emotions that were anything but. She smiled, showing her teeth. "Are you willing to pay?"

"What's the price?" While I was willing to do anything to get Brigid back, we were low on money. Although I had a lingering feeling that money was not what the witch had in mind.

"No, Caelum," she said, though I had not told her my name. "I asked if you were willing to pay."

I swallowed hard. How could I know if I would pay if I didn't know the price? My mind went back to Brigid, the curve of her smile and the brightness in her eyes. Then the memories shifted to a vision of me holding her bloody and lifeless body, her limp hand and dull face. I squeezed my eyes shut, trying to erase the image from my mind. I knew my answer. I would give anything to get her back. Alive. "Aye, I'll pay it."

"Good," she said, nodding her head only once. "Then let's begin."

Elizianna
@ELIZIANNA.THE.ONE

C A E L U M

Chapter Fourteen

The witch reached down and pulled a large iron cauldron out from beneath the table. She hefted it up, as if it weighed nothing, though the table groaned beneath its weight. "This will tell us where to find your syren."

"And the price?" I asked, raising an eyebrow. My leg bounced uncontrollably as I watched the woman work. I might give anything to get Brigid back, but the mystery of this whole situation was grating on my nerves. I needed to understand what was happening and mentally prepare for what lay ahead.

Duncan reached over to steady my shaking leg. He looked at me and shook his head slightly, mouthing the words, "Calm down."

I took a deep breath and clenched my fists, letting my nails bite into the flesh of my palms instead as I watched her move around the cauldron.

"It will tell us the price, too." She picked up the cauldron and moved to hang it on a hook above the fireplace. The fire was smoldering, and she poked at it, bringing it roaring back to life.

The small room grew uncomfortably hot as we watched the witch gather jars and other objects, adding them to the cauldron. She added various plants, powders, liquids, and what looked suspiciously like small bones. She gave it a slow stir and returned to sit at the table.

"It must heat through." Her voice was calm and casual, as if she did this every day. Maybe she did.

"What will it do?" Maira asked, her eyes narrowing at the gray-eyed witch. I sighed and pinched the bridge of my nose. Maira was going to get us all turned into toads if she didn't shut her damn mouth.

"Quiet child. What you want differs from what Caelum is looking for," the witch replied, with far more patience than I had.

Her words resonated, and my eyes narrowed. I hadn't told her my name, and she'd now said it twice. "How do you know my name? And what is yours?"

"My name has long been forgotten," she replied.

I snorted. Of course, she would say something mysterious.

She ignored me and continued. "And as for knowing your name, I know a lot of things."

"So, you know where Brigid is?" My patience was wearing thin at the witch's vague words and casual attitude. If she could find Brigid, she needed to stop dragging everything out for the sake of mystery. Beside me, I could feel the irritation rolling off Duncan and I cast him a quick glance. He offered a grim smile.

The others stood behind us, observing. Kyla caught my gaze and nodded her head once. I wasn't sure what the movement meant, but it was reassuring, and I returned the gesture.

"When the spell is complete, I *will* know where she is." She peered over the cauldron.

"And how long will that take?" I unclenched my fists and spread my fingers, running them over my thighs and breathing deeply through my nose.

"As long as it takes."

I sighed, reaching up to smooth my beard. *Of course.*

"Your impatience will only prolong the process," she said, her voice amused, and her bright gray eyes twinkled.

Begrudgingly, I settled back into the chair and watched the flames lick up the side of the cauldron. Wood crackled, filling the silence, and I was immensely grateful that no one spoke. Specifically, Maira.

It felt like an eternity had passed before the sound of bubbling liquid filled the room. The fire beneath the cauldron hissed as the contents bubbled over the sides.

"It's ready." The witch stood suddenly.

Finally. Jumping up, I followed the witch over to the fire.

She raised an eyebrow at me. "Patience, Caelum."

Patience was the last thing I was feeling, but I stepped back slightly, watching as she stirred the bubbling mixture. She sprinkled something else into the cauldron, muttering as she closed her eyes and tipped her head back.

The fire surged, flaring up around the cauldron sides and licking the fireplace walls. Heat washed over my face, and I took a step back to avoid losing my newfound facial hair to the flames. After a moment, the witch opened her eyes, and the flames died down to a normal level, simmering beneath the pot.

She cast me a quick glance before leaning over the cauldron, holding her skirt back from the flames.

"The cauldron demands your ability to father children," she said, peering down into the liquid. She looked up at me, the curiosity clear in her eyes. "What an odd price."

"What does that mean?" I asked warily. My mind immediately went to the removal of a certain body part, and I wasn't sure I was comfortable with that, despite my earlier promise to give anything to find Brigid. But if that truly was the price to pay, I would have Duncan knock me out, so I didn't feel any pain.

She laughed, noticing my discomfort, and stepped away from the cauldron and the fire. Waving a hand at me, she moved toward another wall and grabbed a jar, coming to stand in front of me. "It's magic, my boy, not medicine. I will physically remove nothing from your body. I promise you that."

I relaxed slightly and nodded. If that was the case, I was more than willing to pay this price. Despite the heavy weight of eyes on my back, I locked eyes with the witch. "Okay."

"Aren't you curious why it chose that price?" she asked,

studying me intently. Her gray eyes pierced through my skin and bore into my soul.

"Not really," I admitted. Although it may seem like an odd price to her, it made sense to me. At her silence, I continued. "Children are valuable to me. It's part of why Cliodhna took Brigid in the first place. I put children first, over her, so it makes sense that the magic would demand children as the price to get her back."

"And you're willing to pay this price?"

"Aye." I nodded, sighing. As much as I wanted my own children, Brigid was more important. The children at the orphanage needed as much love as any biological children I could have. I would turn my attention to them instead—if they wanted it. My life would not be unfulfilled if I had no children. "Do what you must. I'm willing to pay the price."

She nodded, her chin dipping to touch her breastbone. When she raised her head, her eyes shone a bright and burning silver, as if illuminated and molten. "The price shall be paid."

Warmth washed through my body, tingling as if my insides were lit ablaze. It was an odd sensation, like bugs crawling through my veins. Fighting hard to keep still, I clenched my muscles, bracing against the foreign feelings. "Is it supposed to do that?"

The corner of the witch's lip curved up. "Yes, that's normal."

"I don't like it," I admitted when the sensations finally faded. I extended my hands out in front and pushed my sleeves up to inspect my skin.

"You'll see no physical changes, boy. I told you, it's magic."

"I just needed to check," I said, pulling my sleeves back down. Magic was absolutely not my world, and I would be amiss if I just took this witch's word that she changed nothing on my body.

"If you're done examining yourself, I'll do the location spell now," she said, amused.

She circled her palms over the top of the cauldron as she closed her eyes and tipped her head back. Her eyes flew open, gazing up at the ceiling, and I could see them glowing a bright silver as smoke distorted the air around her face.

When she spoke, her voice was otherworldly and echoed through the house, shaking the furniture and rattling the windows.

"*Tro shùil an fheannag... Seall dhomh far a bheil an teine a 'falach.*"

Without another word, the witch lowered her head and tipped the cauldron, letting the liquid flow out and onto the paper map. I lurched forward to grab the map, to save it from being ruined, but the witch slapped my hand away and pointed back to the map. The liquid ran over it, but avoided one area, pooling around it.

I recognized the old language she had spoken from my childhood lessons with my mother. I heard the word for fire, the nickname I had given Brigid, but she spoke the other words too quickly for me to decipher.

"She's there." The witch pointed at the only undisturbed area of the map.

I peered down, inspecting the map. My hands rose to cradle my head and cover my eyes. The breath rushed out of my lungs and my knees buckled, nearly sending me to the floor. I reached out to grab the back of the chair, steadying myself. "She's that close?"

All this time, and she had been this close to us. We could have reached her three times over.

"It appears so," the witch said, her voice grim. Her eyes returned to normal, the pale gray now dull compared to the blazing molten silver they had been. "Now, what will you do?"

Eliz
@ELIZIA

BRIGID

CHAPTER FIFTEEN

The room was empty. Cliodhna had given me a brief reprieve, dumping me in the tank after our latest session and leaving the room. The water stung the new wounds across my chest and neck, but now that I was alone, I could show my weakness. Thankfully, the healing process had started, though it was agonizingly slow, draining my energy as it worked to heal the many injuries I'd sustained. My body slumped against the glass, and I stared out at the room.

Maybe I could escape if I had time to heal and be whole for more than half a day. But with how often Cliodhna visited me, I doubted I could formulate a plan.

As I pondered my situation, a crow landed on the windowsill outside the thick iron bars that covered the windows. I moved closer to study it, as this was the first time any creature had stopped at my window. It stood there, unmoving, as I watched it. It tilted its head at me, its eyes widened, turning molten silver, so bright I could see it even from my tank.

I slowly rose to the top of the tank, pressing my face against the grate. "Who are you?"

But the crow didn't answer. It simply tilted its head in the other direction and flew off. As quickly as its presence arrived, it left, leaving the room feeling noticeably empty.

Dejected, I sank back into the tank, letting my body lie heavily across the glass bottom. The strange crow was not, in fact, here to rescue me. I clenched my hands into fists, ignoring the pain radiating through my nail beds where Cliodhna had ripped some of my talons from my hands earlier. If no one was here to rescue me, I was just going to do it myself.

And that meant getting out of this tank.

From where I lay, I could see most of the room. The tank sat against the wall, and besides a single chair, the room was empty. There was a door to the right of the tank that Cliodhna kept bolted shut. I could tell that even without seeing it. Every time she left the room, I could hear the key sliding in the lock to secure it.

My first course of action would be to get out of the tank. And then, I'd need to get out of the room, out of the building, and finally find my way to safety.

The only windows in the room were along the top of the wall to my left. Too high for me to reach, and even if I could, they were too narrow for me to fit through. Not to mention, I had heard Cliodhna walk upstairs before entering my room, so I had no idea how high up these windows really were. My best plan would be to escape through the front door, no matter the challenge it would pose.

Trying to conserve my energy, I examined the lock on my tank. It had a keyhole, and with nothing nearby to break it off, I was stuck.

Unfortunately, it seemed my best chance of escape would be while I was actively being tortured outside the tank. Closing my eyes, I let my head fall back against the glass. *Great.*

Elizianna
@ELIZIANNA.THE.ONE

Caelum

CHAPTER SIXTEEN

"How are we going to get there?" Maira asked, leaning over and tracing her hand along the map.

The witch reached over and slapped the top of her hand. "No touching, child."

Maira snarled and pulled her hand back, the top of it reddened where the witch had struck. Her glare didn't soften as she turned her gaze to me and repeated her question. "How are you going to get us there?"

I was still at a loss for words. I heard her speaking, but my mind was only replaying the thought that we could have already saved her. She was so close. My stomach churned as I choked back the sour bile filling my mouth. We could have *saved her already.*

"Cae," Cameron muttered, touching my elbow. His touch jarred me from my thoughts and my eyes refocused on the people standing in front of me, staring at me. "We're going to get her."

"Yes, you fool," Maira said, rolling her eyes, "but I'm asking how?"

Thankfully, the witch interrupted before Maira could say anything else. "You can get there by land, but it will take you several days to walk through the forests and cross through the mountains."

"Do we have another option?" I asked wryly, raising an eyebrow. "We don't exactly have a ship anymore."

"You don't?" She studied me, amused. "What about the ship you had, named after the lost goddess, Nehalennia?"

My eyes narrowed, and my hackles immediately rose. How the *hell* did she know about that? "The syrens wrecked it."

She tilted her head, not breaking my gaze. "Did they?"

"Yes," I replied assertively, crossing my arms over my chest. How did this witch know all of this? It was disconcerting and very suspicious. After what had happened with Cliodhna and my father, I couldn't afford to allow any more mysterious people into our lives. "It was destroyed when the syrens attacked. Brigid saved me from that wreck, but we watched it sink. How do you know about that?"

"I told you, I know many things." She stood and wrapped her shawl tighter around her small body. Walking over to the far wall, she fingered several jars hanging from the ceiling, causing them to chime together. She paused and turned, looking at me over her shoulder. "But I am curious why you named it after a goddess lost to humans long ago."

"I'll answer your questions once you answer mine."

She turned fully to stare at me as if she couldn't decide whether to smile at me or strike me. "Very well."

"This is a waste of time," Maira snarled. She stepped toward the witch, but Kyla grabbed her wrist and pulled her back with a force I hadn't expected from the quiet leader of the syrens.

"Stop it." Kyla's voice was like ice as she stared at Maira. "We need her help. Calm down. *Now.*"

Maira huffed, but stopped her movements.

The witch looked amused and continued pacing around the cottage, tinkling the knick-knacks along the walls as she passed. "If you decide to sail out from Dàrna Cothrom to reach your syren, ask for Abria at the harbor."

I narrowed my eyes at her. "How can she help? Why not you?"

She raised a challenging eyebrow at me. "She'll get you a ship and a way to get to your syren. I haven't left this cove in years, boy, and I'll not be starting now."

"Why not?" Cameron asked. Whereas Maira's questions were challenging, Cam's soft inquiries were genuinely curious.

The witch turned and smiled at him, revealing a mouth of unnaturally white teeth. "I've had no need to leave. And more importantly, no one to notice if I wasn't there."

"We need your help," Maira snapped. "Enough with the riddles you're so fond of. Speak plainly."

"There's so much anger within you," the witch cooed, turning toward Maira. She stepped closer, fingering a strand of Maira's hair and continued on, stopping in front of me. "Why did you name the ship after the goddess, Caelum?"

I stared at her for a moment, wondering what she was getting at. If she truly knew all that she claimed, she would know why I chose that name. Why did she want me to say it out loud?

She raised an eyebrow at me, a challenge glinting in her eyes. And suddenly, I knew that if I didn't answer her, she would turn us away. An answer in exchange for her help was a measly cost, and another I would willingly pay.

"The only memory of my mother is her telling me stories of the old gods and goddesses. Nehalennia was the goddess of seafarers, protector of those who traveled the seas. It seemed fitting," I explained. Duncan and Cameron knew why I had chosen the name, but if the syrens were surprised, they didn't show it.

"Fitting," the witch repeated slowly. She nodded. "It gave you hope."

"Hope?"

"Hope. That you would have protection on the seas," she explained. "Hope that you could achieve your purpose."

I couldn't help but snort. "Well, it didn't exactly work. The syrens wrecked it and slaughtered us."

"But you received something valuable, did you not?" She leaned forward and raised an eyebrow, observing me.

My mouth opened, but words didn't come out. Yes, I had gained something—Brigid. But at the cost of thirty men who had done nothing to deserve their fate. It was hardly a fair trade, no matter how grateful I was to have met Brigid. "How can you say that? I lost thirty men in that wreck."

"Then it was their time," she said with a casual shrug.

White-hot fury surged through my veins, and my fists clenched at my sides. I took a deep breath to keep from doing something I would regret.

The witch noticed and smirked. "Anger doesn't suit you, Caelum. You are too peaceful a man. If your men died, it was their time. Continuing to blame others will only poison you in the end."

"They were *good* men." My voice cracked, as I could barely contain my emotions.

"They were," she said, nodding in agreement. "But that doesn't change the fact it was their time to die."

"Okay, let's move on," Cameron said, stepping up next to me and raising his hand. He gave me a pointed look, one that I was very familiar with. A look that meant I needed to calm the fuck down. Now.

Taking a deep breath, I clenched and unclenched all the muscles from head to toe and let the anger and tension drain from my body. "Okay, how do we save Brigid?"

"We need to get her away from Cliodhna, obviously. But the best way to do that..." Kyla trailed off, shifting her weight on her legs. "I am not sure."

"Cliodhna?" The witch's head snapped up, and she lunged toward Kyla, moving faster than she had all night. Kyla stepped back, surprised by the sudden intrusion into her space. The witch paid her discomfort no mind. "Did you say Cliodhna? The goddess?"

The urgency in the witch's voice piqued my curiosity, and I raised an eyebrow at her, crossing my arms over my chest. While I had been suspicious of this witch since the moment we met, the revelation that she knew of Cliodhna only increased my wariness. "How do you know her?"

"She's the one that took your syren?" She turned her gaze back to me, her silver eyes blazing with irritation. "Why didn't you tell me that?"

"How was I supposed to know I needed to?" I asked, rolling my shoulders back, trying to ease the tension that was building. "How do *you* know her?"

"She's the syren queen? She creates syrens?" The witch's voice was harsh and icy, looking between Kyla and me.

I frowned and looked to Kyla for direction on how to respond. My brows furrowed as she met my gaze and shook her head slightly.

"We're all syrens," Kyla said slowly, motioning to herself and the others. "Cliodhna was our queen."

The room's temperature dropped noticeably, and the witch's eyes blazed molten silver once more. "Tell me everything."

"Wait, stop. Stop," I said, holding my hand up. "You need to tell us what you know first."

"Cliodhna is a petulant child who will burn down this world to get what she wants," the witch snapped. "If she's involved, no good will come from it."

"How do you know?" I pressed.

"I told you—" she started.

Rolling my eyes, I interrupted. "You seem to know a lot of things."

"Now, you tell me what you know. From the beginning," she said as her eyes flicked to Kyla. "From the first time you met Cliodhna."

Elizianna
@ELIZIANNA.THE.ONE

CHAPTER SEVENTEEN

Listening to Kyla tell the witch the story of their creation was interesting. Learning what they each had faced on their path to Cliodhna, learning that their queen manipulated vulnerable women into servitude... it enraged me. These women had suffered at the hands of men, and instead of being truly rescued, this goddess took advantage of their sorrow and anger.

It enraged the witch, too. As Kyla spoke, I watched the witch's hands ball tightly into fists and her jaw clench. By the time she finished speaking, anger radiated off each of us, even the laid-back Cameron. The syrens looked uncomfortable, sharing uncertain looks with each other. Kyla held her chin high, but I could see it wobble slightly.

"She used you all," the witch spat, wringing her hands together.

"No," Maira immediately retorted, stepping forward. "She *saved* us."

Kyla held up her hand to stop and closed her eyes tightly. "Maira, stop."

"How can you all just turn against her like this?" Maira asked, ignoring Kyla's plea. "Just because she made a poor decision doesn't mean she didn't save us. It doesn't make her evil."

"'A poor decision?'" My rage nearly blinded me. "She was killing *children.*"

"Only some of them," Maira snarled, curling her lip at me.

Unbidden, I took a step forward, ready to unleash my rage. How could she say that? Did she truly not care that the queen killed *children* for her own power?

Strong arms wrapped around my chest, holding me back. Duncan's gruff voice was in my ear. "Stop it, Captain. She's not worth it."

"What the fuck is wrong with you?" I shouted from Duncan's arms, struggling to free myself. Duncan's grip remained tight as he held me back. My gaze flipped to Kyla as I searched her face for any sign she agreed with Maira's vitriolic statement. My lip snarled as I stared her down. "Is that how all of you feel? If it is, leave now. I'll save Brigid and stop your queen myself."

"You know it's not, Caelum," Kyla snapped, not backing down. She turned to Maira, anger simmering behind her amber eyes. "You need to stop this. Cliodhna wasn't who we thought she was, and you must accept that. I understand it's hard, but picking fights is not the way to do it."

Maira scowled, crossing her arms over her chest.

"She's not a saint, stubborn child," the witch said, her voice grave. "Gods and goddesses were never supposed to create new creatures once humans came to be. They were created to *guide* humanity, not compete with it. She made you because she was lonely and wanted to cling to her relevancy before man forgot her, too."

I shrugged out of Duncan's grip, my anger under control now. "You speak like you know something about that."

"I know a lot of things," she replied, smirking.

Gritting my teeth, I rolled my eyes. Apparently, that was all we were going to get from her. "Yeah, I gathered that."

Kyla sighed heavily, moving to take an empty chair at the table. "We didn't know what Cliodhna was doing. We truly thought she saved us."

"You didn't stop to question the lives you took in her name?" Duncan asked coldly.

"No, we didn't," Kyla admitted, without remorse in her voice. "Why would we? Men had sentenced us all to death at the hands of the sea. Why would we question avenging ourselves?"

"Because you were killing innocent men?"

"Were they all innocent?" Kyla said, raising an eyebrow. "Truly?"

"Let's not continue this line of discussion," the witch said, wrapping her arms around herself. "It will only fuel more anger."

As much as I wanted to continue arguing with the syrens about their life choices, I agreed with the witch. We were wasting time. We needed to make a plan to save Brigid and stop Cliodhna. I nodded toward the witch. "Is there anything more you can share with us that will help stop her?"

"There is, but I've decided I will help you myself."

My eyebrows shot up. "You're going to help us?"

Her mouth curved into a smile, and her gray eyes sparkled. "Yes, that is what I said."

"How will you help us?" Kyla asked cautiously, narrowing her eyes. "Why now? You said you never leave your cove."

"I may have some insight that could be useful..." The witch's coy smile made it clear there was more to her reasoning, and it was even clearer she had no intention of sharing it with us.

"So helpful," I said dryly, rubbing at my beard. While I was grateful for her finding Brigid, I was ready to get things moving again. I wanted answers and a way to get to Brigid as quickly as possible.

"You need a ship," the witch pointed out, raising an eyebrow.

"Aye, we do," I replied. "Know any we can borrow?"

"I might have one available. Do you have a crew?"

"Depends on the type of ship, but we should be able to make it work."

"Then let's get back to Dàrna Cothrom and prepare for our journey." She smiled sagely, clasping her hands together.

The witch coming with us was not what I had been expecting, but she had definitely said 'our' a moment ago. "You're truly coming with us?"

"Of course. Cliodhna needs to be stopped, and I can help. I will go with you."

Unless this witch was hiding something significant, I doubted she could help us stop a goddess. And given that her body looked like a strong breeze could break her in half, I wasn't even confident in her ability to help us as part of the crew.

"It's dark out," Cam pointed out. "Shouldn't we wait until morning?"

The witch paused on her way toward the back of the cottage and waved her hand around the room, grinning. "Where exactly do you think we can all fit in my home, boy? Unless you'd like to sleep in the marsh, our best option is to return to Dàrna Cothrom."

Without another word, she disappeared into a room at the back of the cottage, leaving us alone.

"What are we getting ourselves into?" Duncan whispered out of the corner of his mouth, watching after the witch.

I sighed and ran a hand over my face. "I was just wondering the same thing."

Elizi
@ELIZIAN

B RIGID

CHAPTER EIGHTEEN

T rying to escape from a room with barred windows and only one door, while also being locked inside a glass tank, was harder than I expected. But I couldn't give up now. I needed to get out of here before Cliodhna broke me entirely.

She was getting close. I could feel it in my bones—the ones she hadn't broken yet. I was dangerously close to giving up.

She left me alone between sessions of torture, which left my mind in a less than favorable position for constructing a plan.

If I could reach a claw into the lock, I might be able to get the grate off the top of the tank. But given how utterly heavy it looked, I doubted I'd be able to move it in my current state. I would try, though. Anything to get out of this hell.

Twisting my body underneath me, I reached my fingers through the grate, inching toward the lock on the end. I slid my talon into the keyhole and wiggled it around. I had never picked a lock before, but the threat of torture made me a quick learner.

I continued to twist my talon in the lock, forcing myself to ignore the sharp twinge in my nail beds and the throbbing of the joints in my fingers as I tried to feel for the sweet spot that would put me one step closer to escape.

Being underwater muffled the sounds of the room, so I pulled my head out of the water as much as possible to listen for any sign that Cliodhna was coming back. I could only imagine the pain she'd inflict if she came in and saw me trying to escape.

Twisting once more, the lock finally clicked and opened. Letting out a heavy sigh, my head fell to rest against the glass just above the water level. My fingers were screaming in protest and even that simple act exhausted me. My hope of escape waned. Cliodhna had simply done too much damage to my body.

Finally catching my breath, I reached my fingers through the grates again, pulling the lock free and dropping it to the side. It fell with a loud clanging noise, and I held my breath, waiting for the door to open. A moment passed. Then another. Only the sound of the wind whispering through the small windows along the top of the wall filled the room. My heart raced as I stared at the door handle, waiting for it to click open and my hope to be taken once more. But it didn't.

This was my chance. I had to get out of here. Now.

Tucking my tail beneath me for leverage, I pushed up, bracing my shoulder against the grate and shoving with all my force. But it didn't budge. Sucking in a breath, I pushed harder. The metal grate dug into the skin of my neck and shoulder, but I didn't stop. It still wouldn't move.

Slumping back into the water, I rested for a moment, considering my next move. If I couldn't get out of the tank, I would have to make Cliodhna pull me out herself. I wasn't sure how I would do that without subjecting myself to more torture, but it seemed to be my only option.

Noise sounded outside the room, and I glanced up, watching to see what would happen.

The door swung open and Cliodhna stepped in, a brazen smirk across her face. Despite my current physical weakness, seeing the look on her face made me burn with anger. The only thing tempering it was the reminder that I needed to get out of here, and I needed to think carefully.

"So, what shall we do today, my child?" Cliodhna cooed, stepping up to the tank and dragging her nail across the glass.

Forcing myself to keep my face neutral and weary, I stared back at her and remained silent.

"No matter," she said, waving her hand. "We're going to try something new. I've been curious to see how long we can stay in syren form outside of water."

She couldn't mean to... But she did. Suddenly, she pulled the grate off the top of the tank and reached in, wrapping my hair around her hand and yanking me up. I cried out as the sharp sensation radiated across my scalp. Surely, she had yanked out several clumps of hair as blood trickled down my forehead. I bit down on my lip to keep from making another sound, and my eyes watered as she tugged harder. I had wanted out of the tank, but not like this.

Pulled free of the water, she threw me to the floor. The cold concrete was startling against my scales. Tensing my muscles, I fought back a reaction. The more I gave, the more she would try to take.

I saw Cliodhna's bare feet as she stepped up next to me, and reaching down, she grabbed my hair again. She yanked me up and growled as I let my body go limp. Despite trying to make myself hard to maneuver, she pulled me back on top of the grate, securing my wrists and tail with leather straps.

I tugged at the bonds, grimacing when there was no give. Cliodhna had strapped me to this grate, dangling above the water. I had never been fully out of the water in my syren form for a prolonged period, and the thought of whatever was to come made my heart race. Despite the cold metal of the grate against my skin, I felt uncomfortably warm as sweat beaded on my spine and dampened my palms.

I writhed against the bindings, which only made my heart race faster, blood pounding in my ears and drowning out any sounds in the room. Squeezing my eyes shut, I tried to focus on anything but the sensation of the bindings grinding against my skin. Cliodhna had me trapped, and I was afraid of what lay ahead. I had no way of fighting back.

Inhaling deeply, I tried desperately to push my anxiety down and focus on my breathing. I steadied the rise and fall of my chest as it pressed against the bindings. Any visible panic would only make things worse, and I knew I needed to remain as calm as possible to conserve my energy. Slowly, the pounding in my ears lessened, and I opened my eyes, taking in Cliodhna standing before me, watching and studying my weakness.

She stepped up closer, running a hand through my hair and smiling widely. "This will be so much fun."

"I am going to kill you one day," I vowed, locking eyes with her.

"We'll see…" She stood and turned toward the door, grinning. "I'll be back later to check in. Don't go anywhere."

I shifted against my bindings, but they held tight. I wouldn't be able to get out of these. And she knew it.

Hours passed as my body grew tighter and tighter. It felt as though my skin was shrinking around my body with each passing minute. Being this close to the water but unable to reach it was torture, and my muscles *ached* for relief. The pain was so deep and resounding that I could barely remember what it felt like to not be in pain. Even breathing sent a fresh course of throbbing through my limbs. My scales were itchy and dry, and swallowing felt like needles in my throat.

I had no doubt this was exactly what Cliodhna wanted.

If I could transform, it would take away some of the discomfort, but I needed to conserve my energy, and going through an excruciating transformation would not be ideal.

Staring up at the ceiling, I counted my breaths, trying to focus on anything but the discomfort in my body and my tail. Cliodhna would not give up on this experiment of hers so quickly. I knew I had more suffering ahead of me.

All I could do now was try to take my mind off the pain and

retreat into myself, focusing on my memories. Memories of Caelum, of feeling his body next to mine as we lay face to face in the darkness, savoring the touch of one another. Memories of the other syrens, of learning the seas and swimming with the creatures that filled it, of lonely nights when I first joined them, pressed against Kyla as we slept, of Nerina and Iona taking turns braiding my hair and telling me their own stories. Memories of Sorcha, of nights spent awake in our shared room, talking about our childhood, about our hopes and dreams, about stories we heard and places we wanted to visit one day. Those memories of Sorcha quickly morphed into seeing her limp and bloody body resting in my arms, submerged in the water, her dark blue eyes closing for the last time.

I bit my lip as tears clogged my throat and burned my eyes. Sorcha was *dead*. And there was nothing I could do to change that. I had failed to protect her. She had died taking a blow meant for me, and I would carry that burden for the rest of my life. Thankfully, Cliodhna was more focused on physical torture instead of mental. If she threw Sorcha's death at me, I would surely break.

Just thinking about it made me crack.

I took a shaky breath, trying to ease my tears and turn my mind to happier memories. Anything to keep the sensations of my scales drying up at bay.

Hours passed before the door finally swung open again.

I didn't open my eyes, trying to hold on to the feel of Caelum's muscles under my fingertips and the brush of his lips against my forehead.

"Well, you're faring worse than I expected," Cliodhna tutted. Her sharp nails landed on my tail and my eyes shot open as she dragged her talons down, pulling off scales as she went. "This is progressing faster than I had planned."

I watched as my dried scales flaked off her fingers, falling to the floor. The skin beneath the scales was dry and cracked, and I moaned, letting my head fall back against the grate.

"Let's give it a few more hours."

Elizianna
@ELIZIANNA.THE.ONE

CAELUM

CHAPTER NINETEEN

"Is there a place we can stay in Dàrna Cothrom once we arrive?" I asked as we made our way out of the cottage and back toward the row boats. "We've been staying with a local man, and we must stop and tell him we are leaving. I'm sure he would have room for you as well."

The witch shrugged casually, lifting her skirts to climb into the boat. "I believe my assistant knows of a place. If not, we could stay on the ship that's waiting for us."

"Your assistant?" I questioned. "Is that the woman who led us here?"

"Yes, Abria is my assistant. I'm teaching her the ways of my magic," she said, settling her bag at her feet. She looked up at us all, still standing on the muddy banks. "Well, are we going to get moving?"

Duncan, Cam, and I shared a look. As much as I wanted to ask more questions, we were losing time. "All right, let's get going."

We loaded up the boats and began our journey back through the dark marshes. Finally, we reached the forest once again and left the boats behind as we trekked through the trees back to Dàrna Cothrom. Most of the town's buildings were dark and closed up, but there was still life coming from the tavern, as laughter spilled into the night.

"Where does this man live?" the witch asked, pausing on the main path and shifting her bag from hand-to-hand, scanning the surrounding buildings. "How long will this take?"

I turned to the witch, ready to rebuke her rushing us, but her impatience gave way to fear as her eyes frantically darted toward every noise that sounded. My annoyance and tension lifted at the realization. "Not long, and the route back to his house is isolated."

She stiffened, narrowing her eyes at me, but nodded after a moment, extending her hand toward the town. "By all means, after you."

The walk back to Faolan's felt quicker than the walk to get to the town center, and before long, we were standing in front of his home once again. I hesitated at the door, wondering whether I should knock or just enter. Knocking was the polite thing to do, but Alys had been so welcoming that I almost walked right in.

Before I could decide, the door swung open, and both Faolan and Alys stood on the other side. Alys let out a grateful squeal, clasping her hands together at her chest. "Oh, you're back. We were getting worried."

"Did you find her?" Faolan asked, raising a brow.

I stepped aside to reveal the witch standing between Cameron and Kyla. "Yes, we did."

His eyes lit up as he studied her intently. "You're going to help?" he asked her.

She shifted on her feet, meeting Faolan's gaze with a forced neutrality, one I recognized from the furrow between her brows and the slight shaking of the bag in her hands. "Yes, I am."

"We are leaving soon," I said, turning my attention back to the couple that sheltered us. "We're heading further southwest, along the coast."

"Come in for a moment," Faolan said, stepping to the side.

"We do not have time for this," Maira snapped. "Are we going to save Brigid or make friends with every person we meet?"

Faolan simply let his arm fall and raised his eyebrow at her before turning back to me. "I understand, Caelum. Do be careful, and if your journey brings you back this way, I'd appreciate you stopping in to let us know you got your girl back."

My heart squeezed at the care they had shown for a man they had barely just met and a woman they had only heard of. In another life, I would have loved to have them for parents. Longing rose in my chest, but I pushed it back and cleared my throat, extending my hand to Faolan. "Absolutely. Thank you for your help. We truly appreciate your kindness."

He scoffed at my hand and softly slapped it aside, pulling me into an all-consuming hug. He clapped my back and squeezed tightly. "Go find your girl."

Stepping back, I smiled at them, grateful tears clogging my throat. Alys smiled warmly at me and reached her hand out to squeeze mine. She turned to the syrens. "I'd enjoy it if you all came back. I'd love to talk to you more."

"Absolutely," Kyla responded immediately. She stepped up and hesitated for a moment before pulling Alys into a hug of her own. It was brief and stiff, but I knew it was a big step forward for Kyla.

"Can we go now?" Maira asked, the annoyance audible in her voice.

I sighed. This syren would never change. "Yes, we can."

With another wave goodbye, we began our trek toward the coast. Darkness had engulfed the town completely. It was a cool, quiet night, and thankfully, the wind was not sharp at the moment.

"Is the ship in the harbor?" I asked, glancing over at the witch as we neared the docks.

"Not exactly, but it will be soon," she replied with a knowing smile.

I shook my head and kept walking. The mystery surrounding this woman was too much for me. I needed straight answers, not these vague statements and word play.

"Do you trust her?" Duncan asked, sidling up beside me and lowering his voice to a whisper.

"Not at all, but what choice do we have?" I whispered back, tucking my hands into my pockets as we continued on. Of course, I didn't trust her, and Duncan likely knew that, but I understood why he asked. Nothing else had proven fruitful, and the image of me holding Brigid's dead body in my arms continued to haunt me.

He huffed and shook his head, but said nothing else.

When we finally reached the harbor, I turned back to the witch, who had fallen into step between Cameron and Kyla. Cam had taken her bag, carrying it over his broad shoulders. The witch looked around suspiciously, her eyes flitting toward every noise in the night. It seemed she really hadn't left her secluded cottage in quite a while. Despite my own suspicions, she *was* helping us, and I needed to make sure she was comfortable continuing along this path.

I nodded at Duncan and fell back a few steps in line with Cam. "How are we doing?"

"Fine, Captain," Cam said, sharing a questioning look with me.

Jerking my head toward Duncan, he got the message and motioned for Kyla to follow him, as they caught up with the others ahead, leaving me and the witch alone.

"Very subtle, boy," she said, keeping in step with me.

"I wasn't trying to be subtle," I replied, raising an eyebrow. This witch's dry wit both irritated me and reminded me of Brigid at the same time. I just hoped she would keep her word. "I wanted to check on you. You seem uncomfortable."

"You're observant."

She hadn't asked a question, but I answered anyway. "Aye, I am. Have to be."

"I suppose so." She hummed, turning her eyes back to the path that led to the harbor. "You need not worry about me, Caelum."

"You're helping us, and you're obviously uncomfortable being away from your cottage. The least I can do is try to make things easier."

She stopped walking and turned to fully face me, pulling me to a halt beside her with a hand on my arm. Her eyes swirled for a moment, staring at me, before they returned to their steady gray. "You are nothing like your father, boy. I hope you know that."

My throat dried, and I swallowed hard several times before I could speak again. In the fleeting moments I had known this woman, she had landed on every insecurity and tough emotion that passed through my mind. "Did you know my father?"

"No, not personally," she said, tilting her head. "But I know many things, and that is one of them. Your father was a monster, just like Cliodhna."

"Aye," I croaked, the words still clinging to the insides of my throat.

"But you," she started, staring up at me. "You have a good heart."

Getting compliments from anyone, let alone a strange woman I had just met, was unnerving, and I wasn't sure how to respond. So instead, I just nodded and held my arm out toward the others. "We'd better catch up."

"Yes, let us go rescue your fire," she said wryly.

My mouth fell open. How had she known what I call Brigid? Earlier, I thought her use of the word fire in her spell had merely been a coincidence, given that she had been casting it over an open flame. But this was not a coincidence. She knew. My mind flooded with questions, but I knew I needed to focus on saving Brigid first.

I hurried to catch up to the others, nearing the harbor. Duncan cast me a questioning glance as we descended the stairs to the docks, but I waved him off. I would speak with him later.

For now, I wanted to know what this witch had up her sleeve in terms of a ship.

"Down at the end, just as you requested," a soft voice whispered from the darkness behind us.

We whirled around, Cam and I drawing our knives at the intruder. The witch walked forward, calmly putting her hand on my arm. "Easy, it's just my assistant."

As my eyes adjusted, I recognized the young woman who had led us from the tavern into the darkness of the forest. Slowly, I returned my blade to its sheath and watched Cam do the same.

"It's ready?" the witch asked, looking at the girl, who nodded in return.

"You may leave. I will be back once this is over." The witch turned back to us and grinned wryly. "We have a ship, as promised."

I watched as the assistant stepped back and melted into the shadows of the night. I turned around, moving to follow the others down the docks toward whatever ship awaited, hoping it would be in decent enough shape for the journey.

Watching the waves lap against the wooded dock, I kept walking. Not watching where I was going, I ran into Duncan's broad back as he halted.

"What's wrong?" I asked, immediately scanning our surroundings for a threat.

"Caelum, the ship," he whispered, his eyes wide.

I stepped around him, looking at the ship in front of us. I took in the woman on the figurehead, the worn wooden rails, and the sturdy linen sails. My heart leapt to my throat. That was my ship. The one that the syrens had sunk.

The witch had brought back *The Nehalennia.*

Elizianna
@ELIZIANNA.THE.ONE

C AELUM

CHAPTER TWENTY

I was speechless, staring at the ship I had poured my heart and soul into, sitting before me once again. It was whole; with no trace of the massive gouges and splinters that had caused her to sink. How had the witch done this?

"How?" Duncan asked, breathless. He had put the same love and effort into this ship as I had, and it was as much his as it was mine.

The witch's lips curled up. "A lady never reveals her secrets. But I trust this will do?"

"This will do. Thank you," I said, my voice cracking as emotion clogged my throat.

"What's so special about this ship?" Maira grumbled, pushing around us and squinting at the hull, as if the answers would be written there.

"This is the ship you lot wrecked when Brigid saved Caelum. We thought the seas had swallowed it up," Cameron answered, flicking his eyes to me.

"How did you get it here?" Duncan asked, eyeing the witch curiously. "It sank near Fairport."

"As I said, I don't reveal my secrets," the witch replied, grinning. "But might I remind you I *can* do magic?"

I forced myself to remain in place, even though all I wanted was to approach the ship and run my hands over her sides. This ship had saved me from my father, and the sight of it back afloat in front of me would be my undoing. But I had to keep up my appearance, especially in front of the syrens and the witch. I could give in to my emotions later.

"But..." Maira started.

"Did you question Cliodhna this much?" the witch snapped, also impatient with Maira. I stifled a grin, amused that I wasn't the only one Maira annoyed.

"No, but she was a goddess, not a witch," Maira bit back.

"And how do you know what I am, little fish?" the witch asked with a feral grin. Magic crackled through the night, making the hairs on my arms stand on end.

"Okay, we better get moving," I said, eager to diffuse the tension. "The moon is bright; we should be able to make it to Brigid by midday tomorrow if we leave now, so long as the weather is on our side."

The witch pulled back her magic, and the night calmed. She shuffled over to Cam, taking back her bag. "Caelum is right. Brigid is running out of time."

"What?" I asked, my heart falling. "What do you mean?"

"Did you think Cliodhna has been dancing around all this time?" she snapped. "She's been torturing your girl, and there's only so much a body can take before they break."

My knees buckled, and I reached out to catch myself. I had suspected as much, but hearing it aloud made it even more real. Bile rose in my throat.

"Brigid would never break," Maira said defiantly, and for once, I agreed with her.

"I didn't say her spirit would break, little fish. I said her body would," the witch snarled.

I swallowed hard, trying not to think about the pain Brigid had endured. "We must go. Now."

Thankfully, even Maira nodded, and we began boarding *The Nehalennia*. It was time to go get Brigid and stop that bitch goddess once and for all.

Eventually, we got *The Nehalennia* out of the harbor. Having a crew of three syrens, a handful of men, and a mysterious witch was a far cry from the thirty experienced sailors I was used to having, and it was a rough learning curve. But with a ship this big, I needed everyone's help.

Thankfully, the syrens had elected to actually listen to us for once, as we instructed them how to prepare the ship. Even Maira had pursed her lips and continued on, following Duncan's barked instructions.

It was nothing short of a miracle.

Now, as we set sail on the open water, I ran my hands over the rough wheel, savoring the feel of the wood beneath my hands, and relishing the ship I thought I had lost.

The air stirred, though not from the wind.

"So, are you ever going to tell me how you saved my ship?" I asked, feeling the witch step up behind me. Something about her presence made the hairs on the back of my neck raise.

She moved to stand beside me, the wind pushing her hair back off her slender shoulders. "Why do you want to know so badly?"

I glanced at her out of the corner of my eye before turning my attention back to the sea. "Well, it was mine. I watched it sink beneath the waves and lost thirty men. I think I'm allowed to be curious."

"Perhaps, but you wouldn't believe me if I told you, boy," she said, the humor audible in her voice. "Trust me, it was truly magical."

"I have no doubt." I turned to face her, realizing something that had me kicking myself in foolishness. "What's your name? You've never told us."

She waved a hand flippantly. "Names do not mean nearly as much as you think they do."

"But what should I call you?" I pressed. "I don't exactly enjoy referring to you as 'that witch.' It feels disrespectful."

"Only you would worry about respecting a witch, Caelum. Most do not even deign me worth a thought." Her tone was teasing, but when I looked at her, I could see the admiration in her eyes.

"I respect those who help me—until you prove you don't deserve it."

She turned to stare at me, her silence lasting so long that I turned my eyes back to the seas, leaving her to her thoughts.

"You may call me Lena," she said, her voice so quiet the wind almost swallowed it up.

The name, and the way she phrased her sentence, set off warning bells in my head, but I wasn't exactly sure why. And even more so, I wasn't sure I trusted my intuition lately. So I nodded, accepting her name. "Lena it is."

BRIGID

CHAPTER TWENTY-ONE

Something felt different today, as the sun rose and cast its rays into my cell.

My body was beyond tired and endlessly sore after yesterday's torture session, but Cliodhna had thankfully dumped me back into the tank to heal before leaving for the night. And by some miracle, she had not bothered to lock the grate over the enclosure. Maybe she assumed I was too weak to do anything about it until she returned.

No matter, I would take advantage of it.

I had no idea how long it would be before she returned, so I needed to make a move while I still could. Since escape would be hard with a tail, I had to transform. I gritted my teeth and tensed my body as my muscles ripped and changed, leaving me with legs once more. I had been saving as much energy as possible, and this was going to be my moment.

Tucking my legs under me, I wrapped my fingers around the metal grating, pushing with all my might to move it off the tank. I ignored the burning and screaming of my muscles and the limitations of my body. I just kept pushing with my legs and shoulders as the metal made a horrible screeching noise. Thankfully, it moved just enough to create a gap I could slip through, but I needed to move faster.

Moving the grate was louder than I had expected, and surely someone had heard it. Biting the inside of my cheek, I pushed past the pain in my body and pulled my body out of the tank. My feet hit the concrete floors, and my legs wobbled as I tried to stand. I reached out, slapping my hand against the tank to regain my balance. I wanted to scream in agony, but I had things to do. This was my only chance to escape, and I needed to take it. Shoving my pain aside and locking it away, I gritted my teeth and forced my legs to hold my weight as I stumbled toward the door.

I grew steadier with each step. I could finally hold myself upright as I neared the door, the muscles supporting my weight once more.

Just as I was about to reach out and grab the door, it swung open. My breath caught in my throat, expecting to see a head of white hair. But a large burly man stood in the doorway. Panic built in my chest and my body vibrated with fear, causing the pain and soreness to fade slightly in its wake. There wasn't supposed to be anyone else here. Who was he?

"How the fuck did you get out of that tank?" he growled, advancing and reaching toward me.

There was one thing I was absolutely certain of. Letting this man live would surely mean death for me.

Taking another life was not what I had in mind, but I had done it before, and I would do it again if it meant getting back to Caelum and the others. I would kill a hundred men if it meant getting vengeance on Cliodhna.

I braced myself as he lumbered toward me, ready for his wild swing when he reached to grab me. Kicking at his knees, I brought him down. In doing so, I fell to the ground myself, my legs unable to hold my weight. Quickly, I jumped on top of him, straddling his chest and wrapping my thighs around his neck, locking my ankles together.

Even though my leg muscles were weak and had only healed mere moments ago, they were still my strongest feature. My nakedness worked to my advantage because as he clawed at my legs, there was no clothing for him to grab on to, only skin that could not be used to pry my legs apart. His face grew red and then purple as he struggled to breathe.

I felt his nails scratching into the skin of my thighs and calves, but I ignored it, squeezing harder. I also ignored the ache of my own muscles, screaming at me to stop. This man had to die.

Slowly, his attempts to fight me off weakened, and his eyes drooped. Satisfaction flooded through me as I bit down on my lip. Almost there. I increased the pressure, locking my ankles together and squeezing so tightly my bones ground against one another. I winced, but didn't stop. My pain was nothing compared to the freedom I could nearly taste.

His body fell limp, but I held on a moment longer. I had to be sure he was truly dead. I unlocked my legs, wincing at the pain shooting through my hips and ankles, and I pushed his dead body away. Brushing my knotted hair out of my face, I bent over him, checking for a pulse. There was none. Good.

I scrambled to my feet, taking a moment to lean against the tank and catch my breath. A pang of regret flashed through me as I looked down at the dead man, but I pushed it down deep. I could feel remorse later. This man obviously wasn't one of the good ones, not like Caelum. This man deserved to die.

And now, I needed to get out of here.

Before I could stop to think about my actions, I bent back down and pulled the shirt off the man. It was damp and stained from sweat, but it would be better than running naked. If I managed to get out of this building and find help, it would be best if I had some form of clothing on.

The shirt only reached my mid-thigh, but it covered all my private bits and allowed me to keep my range of motion. It would do.

Pulling open the door to my room, I stepped out into the hall-way, frantically looking both ways. I needed to stay calm and get out of here. Rushing would only cause mistakes. I glanced to my left and saw only one other door as the hall ended abruptly. To my right, the hall extended much farther down.

I turned right and rushed down the hallway, staying as light on my feet as I could with my shaky legs. I crept down the hallway, listening closely for any sign of Cliodhna. As I reached the end, the hallway opened to a staircase that overlooked a large entryway. I stopped, peering over the banister to ensure my path was clear.

There was no one around, and I heard nothing except my ragged breathing and pounding heart. Clutching the railing for balance, I made my way down the stairs, cursing how long it took my legs to cooperate. I was losing precious minutes because my knees kept buckling under my weight.

Finally, I reached the bottom and wanted to cry out in satisfaction, but I wasn't free yet. I needed to make it to the large wooden door and hopefully, out into the world again.

My bare feet scraped against the rough stone floor as I hurried forward, as fast as my legs would go. As I reached the door, I grasped the metal handle and pulled. *Locked.*

Fumbling around, I found a latch and frantically turned it. I pulled the door again, and daylight poured into the dark entryway.

I almost wept at the smell of fresh air.

As quickly as the sun poured in, it stopped. A shadow crossed over my face, blocking the blinding sun. Squinting, I looked at the figure. As my eyes adjusted to the light, I saw a mass of white hair, glowing with the light of the sun's rays. Both amusement and fury shone through a pair of icy eyes as a smile crept up to meet them. Cliodhna.

"Did you think we finished, my pet?" she cooed menacingly. Her hand reached up and grabbed my hair, yanking my face close to hers. "You're never leaving here."

I was so close to freedom that I could have tasted it. But now I knew what I had been feeling this morning. Something *was* different today. Today, I would die.

Elizianna
@ELIZIANNA.THE.ONE

Caelum

CHAPTER TWENTY-TWO

My stomach twisted as we approached the coast, looking at the looming building on top of the cliffs. It was a fortress, with its stone towers and metal gate. Seeing its size, I feared how it would take forever to search. It was undoubtedly a house fit for a queen—a syren queen.

Brigid was in there, suffering through whatever torture Cliodhna had dreamed up.

I needed to get in there. *Now.*

The structure sat on the top of a cliff, where its inhabitants could see anyone approaching. It was an extremely strategic position. If Cliodhna had anyone keeping watch, they would spot us easily, and I cursed the goddess again, this time for her ingenuity and planning.

Cameron stepped forward, his eyes fixed on the fortress ahead. "What should we do?" he sighed, crossing his arms. "There's no good way to approach."

"We need Maddock," I muttered, rubbing a hand over my face. My friend would have had a plan set, and even a backup plan ready, before the anchor dropped. I missed him desperately, but I would wait until this was over to mourn. For him and the others I had lost.

"Aye," he said grimly. "But unless you've figured out a way to talk to the dead, that's not an option."

"Maybe Lena knows a way," I suggested, only mostly joking. The witch *did* seem to know about everything, and if there was a way to get information from the dead, I'm sure she knew of it. But talking to Maddock was a fool's dream, and I couldn't get my hopes up.

"What do I know?" Lena asked, stepping up behind us.

"We were just lamenting a friend's death," Cam explained softly. "He would have had three or four plans ready for us to infiltrate that fortress."

She shrugged. "I say we just walk in the front door."

"I thought the goal was to get Brigid without Cliodhna noticing," Cam said, raising an eyebrow. "Wouldn't that be the exact opposite of what we should do?"

The witch returned the gesture and crossed her arms. "Do you really think there's a way to get Brigid without that wretched fish knowing? I say we meet her head-on. She won't be expecting it."

"Will you join us?" I asked, resting my hand on the sword at my side. "Can your magic help us?"

"I will come," she said solemnly, her eyes fixed on the stone building above. Her shoulders were back and her jaw set as determination swirled in the silver of her eyes.

"We must get ready, then." I turned to look out at the land, where the sun was dipping below the horizon. She hadn't answered my question about her magic, but I knew pushing would bring nothing but frustration. "Let's move at dusk."

"I'll tell the others," Cam said, before turning and leaving us alone.

"What are you afraid of?" Lena asked, her voice firm.

"Losing more people in this fight." This was *my* fight. One that I pulled my crew, Brigid, and her syrens into. And maybe it turned into their fight when Cliodhna got involved, but I wouldn't let anyone else die on my behalf. "No one else needs to die, except Cliodhna."

"I have a good feeling about this night," she said cryptically, looking up at the sky. "Better go get ready. And I'd keep some of your men aboard for a quick getaway."

"Was planning on it," I called after her. Sighing to myself, I ran a hand over my face. Dusk was at least an hour away, and even with the time spent preparing, I knew I would be restless until it was time to leave. Along with leaving Cameron and some others on the ship for a fast departure, I wanted to get any medical supplies prepared. I didn't know what shape Brigid might be in, but I knew she'd likely be injured, and I wanted to be ready to help.

Although we didn't have a lot, I was grateful the witch resurrected *The Nehalennia* with the supplies we had when she originally went down. I forced myself to organize the supplies and keep my mind off the injuries Brigid had no doubt endured. I could only hope she was still alive.

This was going to be a long night. And if I didn't have Brigid back in my arms by the time it was over... I honestly wasn't sure what I would do.

Elizi
@ELIZIAN

B R I G I D

CHAPTER TWENTY-THREE

Blood poured into my eyes from a gash in my forehead. It clung to my eyelashes and turned my vision red as it ran down my face, dripping off my chin and pooling in my lap.

"Is this the best you can do?" I croaked, goading Cliodhna once more.

We had been at this for hours since she had found me this morning in my escape. My body was a shredded and bloody mess, but she continued to keep me alive. My pain no longer fueled her powers. That much was clear by the venom in her eyes. The pain was for her own enjoyment now.

"You have seen nothing, urchin," she hissed, grabbing my face in her hand.

"You keep saying that," I wheezed, breathless from the pain, "but we've been at this all day. I'm getting bored."

Curling her lip, I felt her talons extend as she continued to hold my face, puncturing the skin beneath my chin. Blood trickled down my bare chest and dripped onto the floor. "I spoke to your pirate's father when I learned you two were working together. He told me what he did to his own child. Men truly are vile creatures."

I didn't reply. She already knew I agreed with her, at least in terms of Caelum's father. But correcting her that Caelum wasn't a pirate, or telling her she was just as vile as Kellan was, would do nothing but anger her or satisfy her. And I wanted to do neither.

"How do you feel about matching scars?"

If I had any blood left in my face, it would have drained out. I had seen the scar around Caelum's wrist and the ones on his back. I wasn't sure which she was referring to, but both were horrific. Remaining silent, I kept my gaze locked with hers. No matter what she did to me, I would not show fear or subjugation. Not any longer.

Her talons retracted from my jaw, and more blood flowed from the punctures. My legs were a bloody mess, and the gashes along them continued to weep. If she wasn't careful, I'd die from the blood loss. I'd already grown dizzy from it, having to sit incredibly still to keep the room from spinning. Cliodhna had taken my stolen shirt back, but my blood soaked my torso just the same.

"What did you plan to do if you escaped?" she asked, reaching down to untie my right arm from the chair I was bound to.

"Get as far away from you as possible."

Her malicious grin sent a chill down my spine. "You are my creation, Brigid. You will never be free from me."

"Once you're dead, I will be," I said, spitting blood at her feet.

A rough laugh escaped her lips. "You insolent creature. I'm a goddess. You can't kill me."

"Give me time, I'll figure out a way," I promised.

"You're out of time," she said, pursing her lips. She reached out and swiped her finger across my collarbone, smearing the blood. "Now, let's give you a scar to match the man you chose over me."

Without another word, she extended one talon and brought it to my wrist. Burning pain seared through me as she slowly dragged it around my wrist. Blood poured out, and I clenched my teeth, bracing against the pain as I tipped my head back.

"I won't remove your hand," she said, smiling widely as she continued to slice, pain searing down to the bone. Her other hand grabbed my chin and forced my gaze back to her. "But I will make sure it hurts as if I had."

"I'm waiting," I gritted out between my teeth. The pain was clear in my voice, but I couldn't resist antagonizing her.

She dug her talon deeper, and I could feel the muscles tearing. Blood welled to the surface rapidly, dripping over my hand and thigh and running down my calf, pooling around my feet.

"Does it hurt yet?" she asked, still smiling.

"Let me do it to you, then you can tell me," I spat back. Closing my eyes tightly, I clung to my memories, to anything other than the pain burning through my body. Anything to distract me.

The agony continued, and the world tipped, spinning as I lost more and more blood.

"Ah ah ah," Cliodhna said, tucking her bloody finger under my chin. I felt blood smear across my skin as she lifted my head. "We can't have you passing out now. I want you awake for this, my child."

"You... won't have... a choice," I panted, fighting to stay conscious.

She growled low under her breath and pressed her palm flat against my breastbone. Warmth surged through me, and I felt some minor wounds begin to knit themselves back together. My head cleared, and the room stopped spinning. She was *healing* me.

"We are not done yet," she said, bending down to whisper in my ear as she removed her hand from my chest.

Elizianna
@ELIZIANNA.THE.ONE

CAELUM

CHAPTER TWENTY-FOUR

Finally, the sun began sinking behind the cliffs and the sky turned a dusty purple. It was time.

Nodding to Cameron, Duncan and I slipped over the side of the boat and climbed down the side into the skiff waiting below. Lena, Kyla, Maira, and Alan joined us. The others stayed behind to help Cameron ready the ship for our return and a quick escape.

I was apprehensive about being separated, much preferring everyone in my sight so I could ensure they were safe, but given how quickly we would likely have to depart once we got Brigid—and we *would* get her—I understood the need to keep some people aboard to prepare for our departure.

We silently rowed toward the shore, pulling the boat up onto the sand once we arrived. The sand and rock crunched beneath my boots as we walked further up the shore, watching the towering building above. My palms were slick as I unsheathed my sword and switched it from hand-to-hand as we walked, wiping the sweat on the side of my pants.

Thankfully, we were able to climb up the rocky coast without notice and found ourselves standing in front of a large wooden door set inside the face of the stone building. It towered over me, double my size, and cast-iron hinges only added to its intensity. I could see why Cliodhna had chosen this place. Apart from the soft waves lapping below and the wind rustling, it was silent. It was remote, not another building in sight. We were completely alone with this goddess. Just like Brigid had been.

I only hoped we weren't too late.

We all held our breath as we approached the door, bracing for whatever waited on the other side. The syrens stood in front of Lena, their talons unsheathed and poised at their sides. Duncan, Alan, and I were in front of them with our swords drawn. Beyond the extra dagger in my belt, we had no other weapons. Nodding at Duncan and Alan, I pushed the door open, and they stepped through immediately. I entered behind them, sword raised.

I wasn't sure what I expected, but a completely empty entry way was not quite it. We paused, listening, but the only sounds we heard were the echoes of our heavy breathing. My sword dropped slowly to my side as my head swiveled, looking for guards. Lena had been right. Cliodhna was truly arrogant in her pursuit of vengeance for her imagined wrongs.

The building was massive, but remarkably as empty of furniture as it was people. But I supposed one didn't need much to torture a syren.

"What now?" Alan asked softly, searching the entry way for signs of someone or something. Two halls extended off either side of the foyer, and in front of us stood two curved staircases that met at an upper landing. Looking up, I could see two halls branching off each side of the landing.

"We search," I stated. I turned over my shoulder to look at the syrens and Lena. "Stay together." Duncan and I moved first, tiptoeing down the first hall as the syrens and Lena followed.

We cleared the lower levels, finding the rooms empty and silent, and made our way back to the curved stairwell. They *had* to be here. Brigid *had to be here.*

"She knows we're here," Lena whispered from behind as approached the entryway again.

I tightened my grip on the sword and clenched my teeth, turning toward the stairs and the only way someone could approach us now. I was ready to face the goddess once more, ready to let my rage consume me and dole out the same mercy the syren queen had shown to others. "Let her come."

As if she had heard me, Cliodhna threw open the door above us and stepped out onto the upper balcony. She looked down at us as if we were a mere annoyance, despite the anger that seemed to radiate out from her milky white skin. "You dare come into my home?"

I took a step forward, raising a challenging eyebrow at her. "Where's Brigid?"

Cliodhna threw her head back and laughed loudly, the sound echoing off the stone walls. As her head fell back, I noticed streaks of red smeared across her throat. Blood. But it wasn't just her throat that was covered in streaks of blood. Her arms were slick, nearly solid red, and blood dripped from her fingertips, leaving a speckled trail on the stone floor. Her white dress looked heavy as the hem dragged behind, leaving smears of blood in her wake. My stomach churned, and I swallowed back the bile that surged as I realized it must be Brigid's blood.

"What have you done to her?" I demanded, fighting to restrain the panic that rose.

"Nothing she didn't deserve," she replied, stepping forward, beginning her descent down the stairs.

The others moved closer behind me, readying as she neared the bottom of the staircase.

Cliodhna studied us, and as her eyes ran over our group, they paused on Lena, narrowing. Her top lip curled in a snarl as she examined the other woman. "What are *you* doing here?"

"Who's blood is that?" Maira snapped, interrupting the queen.

Cliodhna stared at Lena for a moment longer, before turning her gaze to Maira. "Surely you aren't stupid. It's Brigid's."

"Is she still alive?" Kyla asked, her voice quiet yet steady.

"For now." She turned back to Lena. "Now, I'll ask again. What are you doing here, *witch*?"

I turned to see Lena smiling widely, her eyes churning bright silver. "When I heard it was you, how could I stay away?"

"You've never cared before."

"I never needed to care before."

Cliodhna stepped off the final stair, moving closer to us. "Do not come into my home with that pretentious attitude. You are *nothing* compared to me."

I wanted to stop and ask Lena how she knew Cliodhna and what their history was, but this was not the time. Brigid's blood covered Cliodhna. Blood that should have been in her body. And we were running out of time.

"Perhaps I am nothing... or perhaps I'm everything you wish you could be," Lena said, her voice eerily calm. She raised her hand, and her voice hardened. "Let us find out."

Before Cliodhna could respond, a blast of silver energy left Lena's hand and blasted into her chest, driving her back.

"Go! Find Brigid!" Lena yelled to me, while raising her other hand and sending another blast of magic toward Cliodhna.

I looked at Duncan, my eyes pleading, and he nodded once. We broke off from the group and darted up the stairs, taking them two at a time in a desperate race to the top. We had to find Brigid, and quickly. Down below, the syrens joined Lena in the fight, circling Cliodhna.

As we reached the landing at the top of the stairs, paths of blood smears went off in both directions. Duncan pointed down one hallway. "She's lost too much blood. Go that way."

I had wanted to avoid separating, seeing how much blood covered Cliodhna's dress... I didn't care. Duncan could handle himself and anything that awaited. And so could I.

I couldn't bring myself to speak, so I just took off running down the hallway, following the trail of blood across the floors and tearing open doors as I went.

My heart sank with each empty room. Where was she?

One last door stood at the end of this hallway. It was my last hope. Perhaps Duncan found her, but I desperately—and selfishly —hoped to be the one to rescue her. I pulled open the heavy wooden door, and my breath caught as if someone had punched me in the gut. My sword fell to the ground with a metallic clanging that I barely heard.

Brigid.

She was there.

Slumped over and tied to a chair in the middle of the room, completely covered in her own blood. I froze, staring at her. A deep cut on her forehead dripped blood down her face, pooling in the large puncture wounds that lined her cheeks. Gouges and gashes on her chest and stomach oozed blood, and—*oh, god*—Cliodhna had sliced her wrist all the way around. Acidic bile flooded my mouth, and I leaned over to spit it out, swallowing hard.

Finally, forcing my body to move, I rushed over to her. My knees hit the stone floor with a sharp crack, but I ignored the stinging pain as I reached for her.

I cradled her head, my hands cupping her chin, but it immediately flopped back down. I could see she was struggling to keep her eyes open as they fluttered. Her lips moved, as if she wanted to talk, but no sound escaped. Her chest barely moved as she struggled for breath. Watching her took the breath from my own lungs, making my own chest seize along with hers.

"Brigid, I'm here," I whispered, pushing her hair out of her face. "Shh, it's okay. I've got you now, *teine*."

I gritted my teeth as I watched the blood drip from her forehead, unable to pull my hands away to find something to stem the bleeding. There was too much blood, too many wounds that needed attention, and as my eyes roved from one to the other, I felt overwhelmed, unsure of where to start. My vision tunneled, focusing only on those drips of blood. I needed to do *something*.

That bitch of a goddess was going to pay if it was the last thing I ever did. I only hoped Lena and the others had kept her busy.

If Brigid died here, I would burn this entire fucking place to the ground.

Elizi
@ELIZIAN

BRIGID

CHAPTER TWENTY-FIVE

My body was heavy, and I couldn't tell what was up and what was down. I could barely open my eyes, but even with them closed, the room was spinning. Nothing made sense. The pain was making me delirious, I was sure of it. Otherwise, how was I seeing Caelum? I tried to speak, to ask if it was really him, but the words wouldn't come out. A heavy puff of air washed over my face, and if I had any energy left, I would have winced at the pressure against my skin. My eyes drifted closed again, and I didn't fight it.

There was no way Caelum had found me, and no way he had gotten past Cliodhna. It was another dream, a hallucination driven by my pain and blood loss. Once she healed me again—if she healed me—I would realize that.

Rough hands cupped my cheeks gently, relieving the unbearable weight of my head. Fingers tapped my cheek, and I opened my eyes again. All at once, I was drowning in concerned pools of green.

"Oh, god," the eyes whispered, horror lacing every word. "What has she done to you, *teine*?"

"Caelum?" I tried to ask. I didn't know if I was successful, or if I had only made incoherent noises, but I knew those eyes. That beautiful shade of green, framed by full black lashes and sun kissed bronze skin.

"Yes, it's me." The voice pleaded, full of pain. I tried to focus on Caelum, but I couldn't. Everything remained a blur of green and tan. "It's me, Brigid. I need you to stay with me. *Please.*"

"The... the tank," I panted, letting my eyes fall shut once more. If I could get back to the tank, I could transform and heal my injuries. It would take too long to heal fully, but I could at least mend some of my wounds and hold my head up again.

His shape was still a blur, but my vision was starting to focus as he looked over at the large tank. His hands fell to my ankles, untying the rope that bound me to the chair. I winced as it scraped against my skin, and while I could hear him muttering as he worked, my mind wasn't able to focus long enough to make out the words.

He finished and pulled me into his arms. Pain tore through my body, but I tamped it down and clenched my jaw. The pain provided some clarity, and I forced my eyes open once more, watching his face alternate between utter horror and palpable rage. I flopped my injured arm onto my lap, which did little to staunch the flow of blood still trickling out, but it slowed some.

"Should I just toss you in?" Caelum asked, his voice desperate.

I slowly nodded, finding it difficult to keep my eyes open. Unable to fight it any longer, I let them slide closed.

Cold water surrounded my body, bringing it back to life. I needed to transform to heal. *Transform, Brigid,* I told myself. *No one is going to do it for you this time.*

Gritting my teeth and squeezing my eyes closed tighter, I began the transformation. Ironically, the pain of this transformation was nothing, a mere whisper of discomfort across my consciousness as my legs welded together and my teeth and nails extended.

Relief washed through my body as the transformation completed and the pain eased, shifting to a dull ache. I opened my eyes, finally able to focus on Caelum watching from outside the tank. Blood clouded the water, but I could see his hand splayed against the tank, worry etched in the deep lines of his face, and I reached up my own uninjured hand, meeting his on the other side of the glass.

"We've got to go, *teine*. Are you able to transform back and walk?" he asked, his voice muffled by the glass and the water.

While my mind had cleared a little, I was still hazy from the loss of blood, which would only replenish with time. I tested my limbs, looking down at the torn skin of my wrist. I could likely transform back, but I doubted I could walk without help. Even with my powers, I would be slow to heal. My injuries were too severe.

I shook my head, letting it drop to my chest in disappointment. He would have to leave me here if I couldn't transform back. I was too heavy for him to carry in my syren form. My heart broke at the thought of watching him walk away again, but he couldn't fall into Cliodhna's hands. I couldn't risk it.

He smiled softly, and without hesitation, climbed up to the platform and reached down into the water. I surged to the surface, reaching out for him.

"Is she dead?" I asked as I surfaced, careful to keep the hope out of my voice. Caelum had enough to worry about without the added pressure of killing a goddess. A goddess that would sooner rip out his throat.

He shook his head. "No, not yet. But let's get you out of here, then we'll talk."

"How?" I asked, letting my hand fall from his cheek and motioning down to my body. "I'm too weak. Changing back would make it worse, and I won't be able to hold my own weight."

"Let me hold your weight, then," he begged. "Please."

"You need to leave me before she comes back."

"I'm not leaving you, Brigid. We've got to go," he said, looking over his shoulder just as someone pushed open the door. Both of us tensed and he spun around, poised to fight, relaxing instantly, as Duncan stepped into the room. "Duncan. Please, come help me."

Duncan walked over to us, taking in the scene in front of him. He passed the chair, his eyes stopping at the pool of my blood surrounding it. He swallowed hard and turned his gaze to me. "You all right there?"

While I knew he was trying to make a peace offering, I didn't have any energy to pretend I was in anything other than agonizing pain, so I didn't reply.

"Transform, Brigid, please," Caelum begged.

Unable to deny him anything, even now, I did as he asked. Closing my eyes against the wash of pain, I pulled myself back to my human form. The water was cold, too cold around me and the room began spinning again. My feet slipped against the glass of the tank and I slipped beneath the surface. Caelum's hands dove in after me, grabbing me beneath my arms and pulling me back into the air.

"We need to get her out of the tank," Caelum said harshly, nodding down at me. "Come help me."

Together, they pulled me from the tank, my body dangling like a heavy weight as Caelum took me in his arms. Duncan reached out, wrapping my arms around Caelum's shoulders, and gasped when he saw my injured wrist.

"What happened?" he breathed; horror was clear in his face. I shut my eyes and curled my head down into my chest to avoid looking at the jagged flaps of skin.

"Not now," Caelum snapped. He moved from the tank, holding me effortlessly in his arms as we left that damned room behind. "We've got to get back to the ship."

Elizianna
@ELIZIANNA.THE.ONE

C A E L U M

CHAPTER TWENTY-SIX

Carrying Brigid down the stairs was worse than sailing through the Straits. With how much blood she had obviously lost, every step or jostle of her body had me holding my breath, waiting for the moment she lost consciousness again.

As we descended, I scanned the entryway but saw only the syrens and Lena. My eyes locked with Kyla's, hers widening as she rushed over to meet us.

"What happened?" Her voice was firm and commanding. Her hands fluttered over Brigid's body, ghosting over the skin, careful not to make contact. Reaching her wrist, Kyla's fingers recoiled, and she gasped. "What did she do to her?"

"Where is Cliodhna?" I demanded, searching the room as I held Brigid tightly to my chest. Surely, if they were all just standing here, there was no immediate danger, but I needed to be sure. Brigid needed me to be sure.

"Lena banished her. The magic won't last long, so we must move quickly," Maira said, her eyes glued to Brigid in my arms. For a moment, I thought I saw sorrow flash across her face. But her usual scowl quickly returned. "What happened to her?"

"I don't know, but we need to get her to the ship. She's lost too much blood," I said, stepping around the syren to continue down the stairs. "Let's get out of here," I called to Duncan, who stood behind me.

The syrens held watch, ensuring Cliodhna didn't come back and catch us by surprise as we descended the cliffs back to *The Nehalennia*. Every wince Brigid made was a dagger in my stomach and only fueled my anger. Some of her cuts and gashes had healed, slowing the actively leaking blood, but it wasn't enough. My stomach churned looking at her hand and wrist. It absolutely wasn't enough.

How much had she endured while we looked for her? It made me sick to think about how often this had been her reality.

Lena approached, her eyes sad and apologetic.

"Cliodhna is gone? For how long?" I asked. My voice echoed with a harshness I didn't recognize.

Lena shook her head. "There's no way to tell. It depends on how much power she exerted doing..." She looked at Brigid and swallowed visibly, "that."

"We need to get out of here."

"Yes, we do."

After some careful maneuvering, we were all back on the deck of *The Nehalennia*. I let out a sigh of relief, grateful we had finally brought Brigid back to us. But looking at her, I knew that if we didn't heal her soon, it would all have been for nothing. My stomach sank as her eyes fluttered shut and her body went limp, falling back into unconsciousness.

Cameron rushed over to us as I laid her on the deck, unconscious and naked. "Caelum, what happened?"

I took a deep breath and shut off my emotions, going into my captain mode. I needed to get us out of here. Then, I could freak out with everyone else. "I need fresh water, blankets, and bandages. Now."

"How can I help, Cae?" Duncan asked, squatting beside me on the deck, his eyes focused on Brigid's pale face. He shrugged off his shirt, offering it to me. I shook my head. As much as I wanted to cover her, we needed to see her wounds. All of them.

"Get us out of here and back to Dàrna Cothrom." We couldn't risk going all the way back to Brinemoor, and hopefully, Alys and Faolan could help us heal Brigid.

"Will she make it that far?" It wasn't a long journey, but it would take the rest of the night to get back to the harbor. He stood and pulled his shirt back on.

"We don't have a choice. We need to find help," I replied, moving Brigid's hair off her face as I gazed down at her. "Alys and Faolan are our best option now. Until we can get back to Brinemoor."

Duncan nodded, heading toward the wheel with quick steps.

Cameron came running back with the supplies in hand and Lena trailing close behind. "Here, let's get her cleaned up."

Lena set a bucket down roughly, sloshing water over the sides. "Move out of my way."

"Are you a healer?" I asked, trying desperately to keep the panic from my voice. Brigid did *not* look good, and I genuinely worried she might not make it.

"I'm better than a healer," she said, dropping to her knees beside Brigid. Seeing Lena's pale hands flutter over Brigid's body made me realize just how much blood Brigid had lost. Brigid's once porcelain skin, usually flushed with color, was now paler than Lena's own nearly gray skin.

Invisible hands clenched tight around my throat.

"What happened to her hand?" Maira asked, her voice uncharacteristically quiet as she stepped up beside us.

"I don't know." I took Brigid's good hand and squeezed it. Her eyes fluttered open, and I leaned over, cupping her cheek. "Brigid, stay with us. We're getting you some help."

"Cae... Caelum?" Her voice was so weak, it physically pained me. Her eyes slid shut again and her chest heaved, straining to breathe.

"Does she need to get back in the water?" I asked, looking at Maira and Kyla. When they did not immediately reply, I spoke louder. "She seemed better when she was in her syren form. Does she need to transform?"

Kyla's eyes filled with tears, but her voice remained strangely calm. "If the transformations weren't painful for her, changing forms back and forth in the water would heal her quickly. But..."

"But that would just make this worse," I finished for her.

She nodded.

"Caelum, wipe all that blood off her," Lena barked, her hands hovering above Brigid's body, her fingers splayed and palms down, as if she were scanning. Her brows pinched. "The rest of you, get us as far away from here as possible."

The others heeded her words and turned away, following Duncan's instructions to get the ship moving.

I dipped a rag into the bucket, wringing it out before I started to gently wipe the blood from Brigid's skin.

"Can you help her?" I asked quietly, afraid to look at Lena as we continued working.

She sighed. "I can make sure she doesn't die while we're on the water."

"I suppose that'll have to do," I replied, rinsing the bloody rag.

We continued until Brigid's body was mostly clean of dried blood, and only the fresh wounds remained. Lena pointed at the bandages Cameron brought over, and we silently wrapped her weeping wounds.

"I need seawater," Lena called out.

Kyla quickly brought another bucket.

"Hold her still. This will sting." And with no hesitation, she dumped the bucket over Brigid's mutilated wrist and began chanting as she waved her hands over the skin.

Kyla dropped to her knees, with barely enough time to help me hold Brigid's shoulders and hips to keep her from moving. She moaned, and her chest heaved as she panted for breath, never opening her eyes. Panic clawed at my chest, wrapping tightly around my lungs and squeezing as I watched her struggle to breathe. My fingers twitched, wanting to do something, *anything,* to help her. I knew quick wound care, how to stitch up a cut from a dagger, or how to bandage a rope burn, but I didn't know what to do with injuries this severe. I swallowed. This was beyond anything I'd seen.

Thankfully, Lena picked up the bandages and wrapped them around Brigid's wrist. The cuts along her forehead, torso, and legs were less serious, but Lena still bandaged them. I itched to help, but her fingers were much nimbler than mine, and I feared I would damage something with how badly my hands were shaking.

Cameron knelt beside me, resting a hand on my shoulder. "She'll be okay."

"She lost more blood than Maddock did," I muttered. It was all I could see, the vision of Maddock lying on that couch while the apothecary owner had tried in vain to save him. Saying it out loud made my heart thunder in my ears.

"She's healing, Cae," he said. "He didn't have that. She does."

"I threw her into the tank, but I don't know if it was enough."

Kyla looked up from her spot at Brigid's waist, sorrow and pain filling her eyes. "She'll live, Caelum. If she's made it this long, she will heal."

"I need quiet," Lena snapped, ghosting her hands over Brigid's body once more. She began muttering, her lips moving quickly, but I couldn't understand the words she was saying. Hell, I could barely hear anything over the roaring wind and the pounding of my blood in my ears.

I ached to squeeze Brigid's hand, to reassure her everything would be okay, but there wasn't one part on her body I felt safe touching. I couldn't even bring myself to push an errant strand of hair from her forehead, for fear the gash would begin bleeding again.

Panic rose as I realized just how *useless* I was in this situation. I closed my eyes, but that only brought back the flashes of Maddock's lifeless eyes staring up from that couch. I snapped them back open and focused instead on the wood beneath Brigid's body and the small circular wounds on her legs.

I began counting them, noticing how they grew larger as they neared the swell of her hips. *Thirteen, fourteen, fifteen, sixteen...* I paused. Their shape was exactly the same as the scales that covered her tail. Bile rose in my throat as I realized what the wounds were, and I exhaled harshly. I finished counting how many circles there were, vowing to remove the same number from the bitch goddess. Twenty-three.

"She'll live—for now," Lena said, sitting back. She ran the back of her hand over her forehead, smearing some of Brigid's blood across her face, and my fingers twitched to reach out and wipe it off. "We need her to transform as soon as possible."

Kyla grimaced. "We can take her to the water once she wakes and help her transform. Cliodhna made it painful for her, but we can help her through it."

"When we get back to Dàrna Cothrom," Lena said slowly, "I think I can help with that. But I'd need supplies."

"Whatever you need," I promised her, nodding my head deeply. For Brigid, I would get Lena absolutely anything. Locking eyes with Kyla, I could see the horror in her expression. "Can you stay with her? I need to help get us out of here."

"Absolutely. And the others will help with whatever you need," she said, raising her voice on the last part, so Maira, Nerina, and Cordelia, who were lingering nearby, heard her. At her words, they straightened and looked to me for direction.

"Let's go. We must put as much distance between us and this fortress as possible," I said, forcing my focus away from Brigid for the moment. The best way I could help her right now was to get us home and far away from Cliodhna. Standing, I turned away from Cam and Kyla, who were still at Brigid's side, and made my way back to the helm where Duncan was.

I needed to be a captain. I owed that to Brigid.

Eliz
@ELIZIAN

BRIGID

CHAPTER TWENTY-SEVEN

The first thing I noticed when I woke was that my body was numb. There was no pain. I didn't dare move a muscle or even open my eyes. I wasn't in my tank, or tied to that chair, and any advantage I gave to Cliodhna would be my undoing. Before letting her know I was awake, I needed to learn as much as I could about my new situation.

Kicking my other senses into overdrive, I took advantage of the pain-free moment to scan my body and surroundings. There was canvas beneath my body, pressing into my legs and my skin, but it wasn't uncomfortable. To my right, I heard heavy breathing, the noise steady and even, as if someone were sleeping. The world shifted, my stomach rolling to the side. I was on a ship.

My eyes snapped open, and the wooden planks above me confirmed I was indeed on a ship. Had Caelum really saved me? Was it not a dream? My heart raced at the possibility. Had I truly been rescued?

"You're awake." A soft voice came from my left, and I slowly turned toward the noise. A slender hand reached out, pressing me gently back into the canvas. *Kyla's* hand. My body sagged back into the canvas, and what I now realized was a hammock. "Shh, Brigid, don't move."

"Wh…" my words came out garbled and cracked. I cleared my throat, trying not to move. My eyes roamed over the room I was in, taking in a small desk in the corner, covered in maps and several lanterns, and the cot pressed against the opposite wall. Portholes stretched along the wall above the cot, allowing dingy light to filter in through the dirty glass. "What happened? How did I get away?"

"Shh, we'll talk about all of that once you're better," she said, running a hand over my forehead, her thumb soothingly stroking the skin. Her eyes shone with worry.

"You gave us quite a scare," said a male voice, as Cam stepped into view.

Relief washed over me once more. I was finally *safe*. Taking a deep breath, I studied them both. Cam's hair had grown since I'd seen him last, brushing his eyebrows now. Beneath his hazel eyes, dark circles had formed, and I wondered just how long I'd been gone, and just how much effort they had put into finding me. I wanted to reach up and put a hand on his cheek to reassure him and lessen the worry I saw on his face, but I was terrified to move for fear the pain would return.

I swallowed hard, actively trying not to look down at my body. I knew the injuries Cliodhna had inflicted upon me, and frankly, I couldn't believe I lived through them. "How bad is it?"

Kyla's thumb stilled on my forehead. "It was bad, Brigid. It was very bad."

I closed my eyes, clenching them tightly, trying to stay calm. "Was?"

"Caelum helped you to transform into your syren form and back. It kick-started your healing, and then Lena healed you as best as she could. You will live," she explained, her thumb beginning to move once more. She repeated the words in a whisper, "You will *live*."

"Lena?" I asked, keeping my eyes closed as I focused on the gentle feeling of her hand on my head. I hadn't heard that name before, but I knew if Kyla was talking about her so casually, that she had earned their trust.

"She's..." Kyla trailed off, unsure of what to say. Maybe this Lena hadn't earned their trust after all.

"She's a witch," Cam added, his voice tired but amused. "We found her in Dàrna Cothrom and she agreed to help us, for a price."

"What was the price?" I asked. I had heard of witches as a child, but had never met one. Even so, I knew that the price for their services was often harsh.

"You'll have to ask Caelum that," Cam replied, his tone firm.

As Cam said Caelum's name, my heart fluttered. Why was he not down here with me? I wanted to see him. My mind raced, thinking about what Cliodhna could have done to him. "Where is Caelum? Is he hurt?"

"Shh, shh," Kyla said, smoothing my forehead while using her other hand to gently press against my shoulder and keep me from moving. "He's fine, Brigid. He's fine. Caelum is at the helm, taking us to safety."

"I'll go tell him you're awake," Cam said, reaching down to rest his hand on the crown of my head gently before turning to leave.

I waited a few moments until I couldn't hear his heavy boot steps anymore. "How bad was it really, Kyla?"

"You nearly didn't make it," she said, her voice flat. "You lost a lot of blood."

"Was anyone else hurt?" My stomach lurched at the thought of Cliodhna putting her hands on someone else. If anyone else had gotten hurt—or had died—because of me, I would never forgive myself.

"No, just you."

"Good." I exhaled, feeling a sense of relief. I could deal with being injured, as long as no one else had been.

Kyla looked down at me, not saying anything, but her lip began trembling and tears sprung to her eyes. "We thought we were going to lose you, Brigid. And you would have died without knowing how much we all care about you."

Bracing myself for the pain, I lifted my left arm to grab a hold of her wrist, running my thumb along the inside. There was nothing I could say to comfort her. But I had a feeling my near death had changed things for her, and hopefully for the other syrens as well. I knew we would never be the same, but hopefully, this meant they would accept me and Caelum.

She sniffled and pulled her hand away, wiping at her eyes. When she met my gaze again, she was all business. "We need to get you into the water. You need to transform more to help with the healing."

The thought of moving made my stomach churn, and transforming made me want to cry. I was finally pain-free. "I don't want to," I whispered.

Her brows furrowed together. "Don't want to do what? Heal?"

"Transform," I admitted, my voice small. "It will hurt."

"We will be with you," she said, her face softening. She took my hand, squeezing my fingers gently. "You won't ever face it alone again."

"We?" She and Cam had been the only ones here, and despite assuming Duncan was nearby, I doubted he would support my transformation.

"Did you think I was the only syren who came to your rescue?"

"I..." I swallowed, the words stuck in my throat. "I honestly wasn't expecting any of you to come for me."

Kyla sighed and closed her eyes for a moment. When she opened them again, they glistened with tears, mirrors of amber shining back at me. "I know we've let you down, Brigid. But we're here to make up for that. All of us."

"What changed?" I asked, my voice barely audible. My emotions were all over the place. The notion they rescued me, and that they had worked with Caelum and his crew to do so, was hard to take in, given how easily they'd dismissed me before.

"Sorcha dying in front of us, and Cliodhna taking you changed us, but..." She took a deep breath, squeezing my fingers. "Hearing the truth about what Cliodhna had done was eye opening. We should have been there for you. You were family, and we turned our back on you. We realize how wrong we were to follow Cliodhna's orders to exile you, and we're so sorry."

Sorcha. Goddess, Sorcha. I closed my eyes, fighting the tears building at the mention of her name. "Was she..."

"We buried her," Kyla whispered, answering the question I couldn't bring myself to ask. "Next to your captain's friend."

"Maddock?" I asked, opening my eyes. "You buried her next to Maddock?"

"I think that was his name, yes," she said, nodding. "Caelum was very insistent."

I smiled even though the movement pulled at the scabs on my face. "Good, I'm glad she's with him. She'll be safe there."

"And you're safe with us now," she said, bending down to press a light kiss on my cheek. I kept my eyes on her, relishing a comforting touch for the first time in weeks.

Tears clogged my throat, but I smiled through them. "Thank you."

Elizianna
@ELIZIANNA.THE.ONE

CAELUM

CHAPTER TWENTY-EIGHT

Up on the deck, I gripped the wheel tightly in my hands, trying to keep my mind off Brigid lying down below. She was with Kyla and Cameron, and I trusted them to care for her.

Duncan stood beside me, watching silently. I was waiting for him to speak, but he didn't.

"Are you going to say it?" I finally asked, turning to lock eyes for a moment before focusing back on the seas ahead.

"Do I have to?" he sighed.

"You saw her hand," I said quietly, guilt gnawing at my stomach. There was only one reason Cliodhna had inflicted that injury. I looked down at her inspiration: the silvery and smooth line that circled my own wrist. Disgusted, I dropped my hand to my side, shoving it in my pocket. "Fuck, you saw her entire body."

"It isn't your fault, Cae," he replied, placing a hand on my shoulder. He tugged gently until I turned my gaze back to him. The sadness in his eyes was almost my undoing. "Let me say it again. This is *not* your fault, Caelum."

"We should have gotten to her sooner," I said, my eyes burning with unshed tears as images of the bloody mess of Brigid's body filled my mind. I cleared my throat, pushing back the emotions. "It shouldn't have been this bad."

"But it is, and now we move forward," he said, his voice unnervingly calm. I was grateful for his steady poise. It grounded me. "You can't blame yourself."

"If she doesn't make it..." I couldn't bring myself to finish the sentence.

"Don't. Don't think that. Lena is helping her. She'll make it."

"I just can't lose anyone else."

"You won't." He rubbed my shoulder before letting his hand drop, waving out toward the ship. "We got *The Nehalennia* back, Caelum. We can handle this. Brigid will be okay. We'll get back to Dàrna Cothrom, regroup with the others, and figure out the next steps once we return to Brinemoor."

"Fuck, the Straits," I breathed out, remembering that we would have to travel them again to get back to Brinemoor and our home base. Taking the newly resurrected ship back through the most dangerous parts of the seas for a second time filled me with dread.

"We'll worry about that when we get there," Duncan grimaced. "Why don't you go back down with Brigid? I'm sure she'll want to see your face when she wakes up. We should be back to Dàrna Cothrom soon."

I shook my head. While I wanted nothing more than to watch over her, I needed to be more for her, to do more for her. "Nay, I can't just sit there and watch her unconscious. I need to be doing something."

Footsteps sounded on the deck behind us. We turned to see Cameron walking toward us, his hands shoved deep in his pockets. "She wants to see you, Caelum. She's awake."

My breath caught in my throat.

"Is she okay? What does she need?" I realized this was a stupid question. Of course she wasn't fucking okay; she spent weeks tortured and abused.

"You, Captain," he said with a nod. "She's asking for you."

I shifted my grip around the wheel spokes. I couldn't face her yet. The guilt of knowing I had left her to suffer at the hands of

Cliodhna for so long was eating me alive. "Kyla is taking care of her."

"She needs *you*."

"Go, Cae," Duncan said, nodding toward the stairs. "You need to see with your own eyes that she's okay."

"We can handle things up here," Cameron added.

Duncan gave me a small shove. "Go."

Sighing, I ran a hand through my hair and made my way below deck. The sight of her was like a sucker punch to the stomach. Stretched out on the hammock, her pale skin looked worse against the dark canvas. I stifled a sob, thinking about how I had almost lost her.

Kyla stood as I walked in, smiling softly at me. "I'll leave you to it."

"I'll get you when I'm done," I breathed. "Thank you for sitting with her."

She smiled wider, reaching out to squeeze my hand before slipping between me and the door.

I moved to sit down in the chair Kyla had occupied next to Brigid. The sight of her bandaged wrist made my stomach churn. She would now have a scar to match mine, and I swallowed hard, nausea burning in my throat.

"Hey there," I whispered, reaching out to rest my fingers against hers. "How are you feeling?"

"Mostly numb, thankfully." She smiled at me, and the pure adoration in her eyes would have made my knees buckle if I hadn't already been sitting down. "It's good to see you, Caelum."

The dam I had built around my emotions crumbled at the softness of her voice, and I bent my head to rest against her thighs. "I'm so glad you're alive."

"Shh, I'm okay. You saved me," she said as she ran her fingers through my hair, her nails scratching against my scalp. "Your hair is longer."

I lifted my head, thankful that I was a quiet crier and not sobbing like a child. My vision was blurry, and she lifted her non-injured hand to wipe my tears away. As she pulled her hand back, I gently grabbed it, holding her palm to my cheek and turning my face into it, softly kissing her skin. "I'm sorry it took me so long, *teine.*"

"I almost got out on my own yesterday," she said after a moment, rubbing her thumb along my cheek as her eyes inspected the new beard I had grown.

My head snapped up, and I looked at her. "What do you mean?"

"Cliodhna locked me in that tank, but I got out yesterday. I killed the man guarding me, and made it as far as the doors," she explained, her voice cracking. "But then Cliodhna found me. But I almost made it."

A laugh bubbled out of my chest. Of course, she had been trying to rescue herself. *Of course.*

"We'll get her, *teine.* I can promise you that," I said, pressing another kiss to her palm. "She won't live after what she's done."

"I know we will," she said. "Thank you for saving me."

"Nothing could keep me away," I vowed. And it was true. *Nothing* would keep me away from her ever again.

Her eyes drooped, and she shifted in the hammock, adjusting her body.

I stood from the chair, slowly leaning down to kiss her forehead. The cut there had scabbed over, but I still wanted to be careful. "Get some rest. One of us will be here when you wake. The syrens want you to transform to speed up your healing."

"Will you come with me?" she whispered, her eyes already closing. "I don't think I can do it alone right now."

"Of course," I promised. I didn't know how, but I would make it work. I would give her the world.

Her eyes closed all the way, and her breathing steadied, her chest rising and falling evenly. Letting go of her hand, I watched her for another minute before turning to find Kyla and the other syrens.

We needed to talk about getting Brigid in the water.

Eliz
@ELIZIAN

BRIGID

CHAPTER TWENTY-NINE

The next time I woke up, Maira was sitting beside my hammock, her gaze fixed on the porthole. My entire body was stiff and sore, and as I tried to adjust my body, she turned her attention to me.

"Do you need help?" Her voice was blunt as she slowly stood and looked over my body.

I shook my head, shifting my upper body some. As much as I didn't want to, I knew I needed to transform. My injuries were an inconvenience, and one that I could remedy. If I wasn't so much of a coward. "I'm fine."

She hesitated, clearly wanting to say something, but held her tongue. Instead, she simply nodded, settling back into the chair.

"Why did you come?" I asked, turning my head to look at her. Maira had been a staunch supporter of my exile. Of all the syrens, she was the last one I expected to be on this rescue mission, and the last one I had expected to be working with Caelum and his men.

Her pale skin flushed, and she ducked her head. "I was wrong."

There were so many things I wanted to say. I wanted to rage, and scream, and throw things, and ask why she had abandoned me, but I didn't have it in me. Nothing I said now would change what had already happened. And nothing she could say would make up for the pain she and the others had caused me. I turned my head away from her and let my eyes fall closed.

"We were close once, when you first arrived," she said, her voice uncharacteristically soft. "Do you think we'll ever get back there?"

I opened my eyes, but kept them focused on the wooden planks above, remembering all the hateful words Maira had said in the past, and the absolute disregard she had for anyone's feelings but her own. She had been the first to condemn me for saving Caelum, and I thought nothing could ever heal that wound. "No, I don't think we will. Not after all that's happened."

I owed it to both of us, to be honest, and after the venom Maira spit out and how quickly she had turned against me, I doubted I could ever be close to her again. At least the others had been reluctant to abandon me, and were sympathetic to my plight, though they had still followed Cliodhna's orders.

"That's fair." Her shoulders slumped as she shifted in her chair.

We fell into an uncomfortable silence once more, the kind that cloyed the room and suffocated you. I cleared my throat. "Kyla and Caelum said they want me to transform."

"Yes, the witch thinks it will help you heal faster," she replied, standing from her chair.

"Who is this witch?" I asked, trying to lean forward slightly. Gathering all information on the newest addition would be helpful for when I finally got out of this hammock.

"A woman your pirate found in the swamps. She said she could help us find you. And I suppose she did, but she's been mysterious and vague this entire time. Somehow, she knows Cliodhna, but won't give us any details. I don't trust her."

My heart sped up at the mention of Cliodhna's name. Had I walked right back into her clutches by being on this ship with this witch? I felt my breath come faster, and I closed my eyes.

"What's happening?" Maira asked, her voice concerned as she stood over me. "Brigid, are you okay?"

I nodded, trying to focus on her voice and settle the erratic beating of my heart. I was safe. I didn't need to panic, but I couldn't seem to push it down. It bubbled up, and a sob escaped my lips.

"Kyla!" Maira shouted, dropping to her knees next to me. Her hand rested on my forehead and pushed against my hair, but all I could feel was Cliodhna's hand. The sharp nails, the long fingers.

I squirmed away from her, my chest heaving as my breath came out in sobbing pants. "No, no, stop."

The door swung open with a loud bang, and my entire body flinched.

"What happened?"

"I don't know," Maira said, frantically. "I was telling her about the witch and then she started crying and gasping for air."

"Brigid." Kyla's soft voice began to register in my mind. "Brigid, can you hear me?"

My heart slowed, and my vision cleared as I opened my eyes to check it was truly *Kyla* touching me and talking to me. Kyla's voice was calm and kind, soft against my ears like rain, rather than the grating and bitter voice of Cliodhna. I nodded shakily, still focused on her murmuring.

"Okay, good," she said, her voice so quiet it was barely audible. "Try to slow your breathing. Take some deep breaths."

I nodded again, trying to listen to her words and slow my breathing. But it wasn't working.

"Can I touch you, Brigid?" her voice almost cooing now, as if she were talking to a babe. It calmed me even more. "Can I put my hand on your chest?"

I nodded again and immediately felt pressure on my chest. It was grounding, and not at all like the way Cliodhna touched me. Kyla's hand was gentle and light, resting on my chest.

Focusing on her touch helped, and slowly, I regained control of my breathing. I opened my eyes, and the world was familiar again. I was on Caelum's ship, not trapped in that room. Not in that tank.

"Are you feeling better now?" she asked, peering down at me.

"I think so," I croaked, my voice hoarse. "I don't know what that was."

"I think it was a panic attack. You were just tortured, Brigid," she said, still holding her hand to my chest. "And even before that, you struggled with anxiety. It's not surprising that you're exhibiting these feelings."

"Anxiety?" Maira asked from beside us. I had forgotten she was in the room. "I never knew you had anxiety."

"I didn't want you to know," I said, still trying to slow my still racing heart. Kyla had been there when I had my first anxiety attack after joining the syrens, and she held me through it while I cried and shook. The others had never seen that side of me. "Where's Caelum?"

"I'm right here, *teine*," his voice sounded from the doorway. He moved into my line of sight, switching spots with Kyla as she stood and stepped back. He bent down and took my hand, gently pressing it to his lips. "What do you need?"

I wanted to tell him I needed him. That I needed to feel him next to me. But I didn't know how to say that, especially not with Kyla and Maira staring at me. Besides, we had bigger things to worry about right now. "They said I need to transform. Can we do it soon?"

"Yes," he said, rubbing his thumb over my hand. "Maira, can you go get Lena?"

Without a word, Maira left the room, pulling the door shut behind her.

"Are you sure you're okay?" Caelum asked, bending his head down closer to me. "What do you need, *teine*?"

"Just you," I whispered, my voice cracking slightly. While I had been in that room, I had come to terms with the fact I would die there, and never see Caelum again. And that had made me realize the depths of my feelings for this man. "I just need you."

"You have me," he said, leaning in to kiss my cheek. "For as long as you want me, I'm yours."

The door opened again before I could tell him I felt the same, and a petite woman with unnervingly pale gray eyes and similarly colored skin entered the room. As she came closer, I noticed her familiar eyes.

"The crow," I breathed out. "You have the same eyes."

She smiled at me. "Ahh, you saw him, did you?"

"The crow?" Caelum asked, standing and turning to the witch. "What are you talking about?"

"The spell," she explained, her voice patient and kind when addressing Caelum. "I sent a crow to find her, and I could see her through its eyes."

"She's ready to transform," Maira said, interrupting Lena and crossing her arms over her chest. "We must heal her."

"Patience," the woman tutted at Maira, who scowled back at her. The woman turned to me. "I need you to transform into your syren form and back again, little fire."

My eyes flicked to Caelum, alarmed that this strange woman knew what he called me. He just shrugged, as if it were a normal occurrence. I turned back to her slowly. "It's going to hurt."

"Of course it is," she said, scoffing, "but only for a few moments, and then you'll feel better."

I nodded and took a deep breath. She was right. Transforming back to my syren form would allow me to kick-start my healing once again. Though transforming in the water was always easier, I didn't want Caelum to have to carry me and my useless body up to the deck. And I certainly didn't want him to have to throw me over the side. It was too reminiscent of our first meeting, and I wouldn't do that to him. Not now.

"Can I try to transform here?" I asked. "I don't want to get in the water. She could find us."

Kyla looked at me. "*Can* you transform out of water?"

Caelum's eyes snapped to Kyla. "What? She can sense you?"

Kyla sighed, rubbing her forehead. "Yes, I forgot about that. She always said she can tell when there's a woman in the water, and can locate all of her syrens."

"Then we can't risk it. We can't let Brigid enter the water to transform again," the witch said, crossing her arms over her chest.

"How could you forget to tell us that?" he snapped, squeezing Brigid tighter to my body. "That's important, Kyla."

I squeezed my eyes shut, gritting my teeth. I didn't like the fighting, the arguing. I wanted it to *stop*. Answering Kyla's question, I pulled the attention back to myself. "She made me do it before. Out of the water. Just to see if I could."

Caelum tensed beside me, gripping my hand even tighter. "I'm right here, *teine*. You won't be alone."

I let my eyes slide shut and focused on the feel of his hands around mine as I began my transformation. The pain was instantaneous, but it still wasn't as bad as what I experienced with Cliodhna. My bones snapped and my flesh tore as my body remade itself, and I gritted my teeth to keep from crying out. The sharp gasp from Caelum told me that despite healing some, there were still missing scales and other wounds on my tail.

"Almost there," the witch murmured. "One more time."

"I'm right here, *teine*," Caelum whispered, squeezing my hand.

Finally, it was over. I wiggled my toes and unclenched my jaw as the pain in my legs lessened. Opening my eyes, I looked up at Caelum, who was watching me with undisguised concern.

"How do you feel now?" the witch asked, stepping up next to Caelum.

"Sore," I admitted as I scanned my body, "but other than my wrist, my injuries feel a little better."

"Your wrist will take a while to heal," the witch tutted, reaching down to take my injured hand, inspecting the bandages still wrapped around it. "Once we get to Dàrna Cothrom, I can do more for you."

"You're coming back with us?" Caelum sounded surprised as he turned to look at the witch. Clearly, she hadn't shared her plans.

The woman scoffed, gently placing my hand back down on my lap. "Yes, boy. Cliodhna is not dead. This is far from over."

I opened my mouth, ready to ask about her history with Cliodhna and why she wanted her dead, but she clapped her hands, causing a flinch that I felt down to my very bones.

"Let's get your fire up and about," she said, motioning to Kyla. "Grab that blanket. Caelum probably won't want the rest of the crew to see you naked."

I shrugged, looking down at my body. I hadn't even realized I was naked, but she was right. Caelum wouldn't want anyone else looking at me. In fact, it surprised me that he didn't mind that Kyla and Maira were in the room with me. But I'm sure he didn't know about our past, and how, at one point, we all sought the comfort and company of one another.

He reached down to help pull me from the hammock, and my body protested the entire way up.

Elizianna
@ELIZIANNA.THE.ONE

CAELUM

CHAPTER THIRTY

Wrapping Brigid in a blanket and helping her stand on her own feet was nerve-wracking. My heart skipped with every movement, watching her so intently for any glimmer of discomfort. Despite Brigid admitting she felt better, I was afraid to touch her. Cuts and puncture wounds still covered her entire body.

Cradling her injured hand, she smiled at me as I pulled her into my arms. I needed to hold her, even if just for a moment. With my heart safely tucked under my chin, I looked over Brigid's head at Lena and Kyla. "How close are we to Dàrna Cothrom? Should we wait until we arrive to have her transform again?"

"Transforming several more times would help heal her other injuries," she replied, her eyes roving over Brigid's body. "But she'll be able to make it back, as long as she rests."

"I don't think the water casks aboard the ship wouldn't be large enough to submerge yourself in," Kyla said, rubbing at her chin. "But we could likely improvise a tank if you don't want to transform out of the water again."

"No," Brigid and I both said at once. Brigid shuddered in my arms. "No, please no tank."

"There was a tank in the room Cliodhna held her captive," I murmured to Kyla, running my soothing hand down Brigid's back as gently as possible.

"I'll kill her," Maira snarled from the doorway, her fingers curling into fists.

"Can I go up on deck?" Brigid asked softly. "I'd like to see the others."

"Of course, *teine*," I replied. "Let's get you some clothes and food first."

Brigid dressed in loose clothing and ate small bites of bread and dried meat. She drank a cup of fresh water and we waited, ensuring it would stay down before I led her above deck, careful of her injuries and sore muscles. I knew she wanted to walk on her own, but I held my hand behind the small of her back, ready to catch her if she stumbled.

Out in the sunshine, Brigid stopped, closing her eyes and tilting her head up toward the sky. The relief of the fresh air washed over her face and made anger burn in my chest. We should have rescued her sooner. How much had she suffered? Could she ever recover?

"You're up," said Cameron, approaching us with a wide grin. He raised an eyebrow at me, silently requesting permission to hug Brigid. I nodded toward the woman in front of me. She had all the control here. His smile softened, and he reached out to her. "Can I give you a hug, Brigid?"

Her body froze for a moment before she reached out to wrap her arms around his middle. His eyes closed as he rested his chin on her head and clenched his jaw, fighting off tears as he hugged her back.

"We missed you, Brigid," he whispered, his voice lost to the wind.

She sniffed, wiping her nose with her good hand as she stepped back. She pasted a forced smile on her face, but given the circumstances, I was grateful she was trying at all. "Thank you for coming to get me."

"Like you could have kept us away," he said, dropping a kiss on her hair. "You're one of us now, whether you like it or not."

Her gaze tracked toward Duncan at the wheel, and her shoulders slumped. "I'm not, but thank you for saying that, Cam."

Cam met my eyes over her head, holding my gaze for a moment before looking at Duncan, who was watching this exchange with a blank expression on his face.

"*Teine*, you be okay with Cam for a bit?" I asked, careful to not touch her as I stepped forward.

She nodded, tucking a strand of hair behind her ear. "Aye. I want to see the other girls, anyway. Go on, Captain. Get us home, please."

Without thinking, I cupped her cheeks gently in my hand and pressed a soft kiss to her lips. When I pulled back, I saw her eyes rimmed with tears and she smiled, reaching up to press another kiss to my lips. I wanted to squeeze her so tightly, to kiss her for so long, but she needed to heal, and I needed to talk to Duncan.

I dropped my hands from her face and squeezed her good hand once before turning to head toward Duncan at the helm. Glancing back over my shoulder, I saw Cam had walked her over to where the rest of the syrens sat on deck.

"How is she?" Duncan asked, as I stepped up next to him.

"Not herself," I replied, crossing my arms over her chest. "She needs our support."

"The syrens are supporting her."

"You saw that room she was in," I snapped, losing my patience. "You saw the blood. Imagine what she went through. Why are you still doing this? I thought things had changed."

He sighed. "I'm not doing anything, Cae."

"You are," I argued. "Every time you see her, you pick a fight and point out what she was a part of. She knows that. She went against her queen and look where it got her. And that still isn't enough for you to trust her?"

"The others have done the same thing. Do you trust them?" he asked, rolling his eyes.

"I trust them enough to help see this through."

"Then I guess that's why you're the captain," he said, turning his attention back to the wheel.

My heart burned at the dismissal of my best friend, but I didn't trust myself to say anything back. We needed to talk more, but this harsh and emotion-driven conversation would not help. I thought we had addressed things back on the beach, but apparently not.

Nodding, I watched him for another moment before clearing my throat. "How are the seas?"

"They're fine. We're approaching Dàrna Cothrom."

My gaze went to Brigid, who was standing next to Cameron and Kyla. Even from this distance, I could see her discomfort. It was clear in the tenseness of her shoulders and the way her eyes continually scanned the horizon. While I wanted nothing more than to go comfort her, Duncan and I had unfinished business that needed to be addressed while Kyla kept her distracted. His opinions would only hurt her right now.

"Go on, Caelum," he sighed, jerking his head toward Brigid. "We'll talk later."

I raised an eyebrow, but nodded and headed down the stairs. I would never turn down an opportunity to go to her.

Eliz
@ELIZIAN

CHAPTER THIRTY-ONE

Standing with the other syrens, acting as if nothing had happened, as if they hadn't turned their backs on me, was grating on my nerves, making my fists clench. Only Kyla had apologized, and even though they were clearly on our side now, the betrayal still stung. Perhaps one day, things between us would be closer to what it had been in the past, but I feared it would never be the same.

"Are you okay?" Caelum's soft voice startled me, but I leaned back into him, relishing the warmth of his body against my back.

"Yeah, just adjusting," I replied, turning to look up at him.

He wrapped an arm around my shoulders, pulling me into an embrace. "I've got you, Brigid. Nothing will hurt you."

"Do you need our help, Caelum?" Cam asked from his position next to Kyla. "We should arrive back at Dàrna Cothrom soon."

"What can I do?" I asked, looking between Cam and Caelum.

"You can go back down below and rest until we're moored up," Caelum said, leaning over to kiss my forehead. "We can handle it."

"I'll be fine," I said, looking into his green eyes and trying to convey my strength in those words. "Thanks to you, I will be fine."

"You still need more rest." He cradled my face in his hands, rubbing his thumbs in soothing circles on my cheeks, and I closed my eyes. It felt right, like coming home.

"I don't want to be a burden," I whispered, afraid that if I said it any louder, the other syrens and crew would hear. It was hard enough to admit it to Caelum, as I never enjoyed sharing my weaknesses, and though I knew Caelum would not judge me, old habits were hard to break. "I want to help."

"Brigid," he said firmly, the grip on my face tightening slightly but still gentle. "No one here thinks you're a burden. You almost *died*. We all understand that you're going to need time to heal."

He was right, of course, but that didn't make it any easier. These people had risked their lives—again—to save me, and I needed to make their efforts worth it. I had to get better and help us prepare for Cliodhna's inevitable return.

"Come on," he said, taking a step back. His hands fell from my face and found mine resting by my side. Slipping his fingers between mine, he squeezed gently and said, "Let's go."

I followed him back down below to the room I'd been staying in, sighing in relief when he closed the door behind us. There were so many emotions swirling through my body, and I wasn't sure how to balance them and the physical weight I still held, too.

"Can you hold me?" I asked, my voice meek and barely audible. I didn't enjoy sounding weak, but I was woman enough to admit that I needed a comforting touch right now.

His face softened, and he immediately pulled me into a fierce hug. "Of course, *teine*. Whatever you need."

Instead of the hammock I had woken in, he pulled me over to the small cot in the corner of the room.

"Can we both fit?" I asked, smiling teasingly as he laid down on top of the blankets.

"We'll make it work," he said, returning the grin and pulling me gently down next to him.

After some gentle and creative maneuvering, we both ended up fitting. Curled tightly into his side, I closed my eyes, letting myself cherish the feeling of knowing, without a doubt, that I was *safe*.

"I was so worried about you, Brigid," Caelum said, his voice a hoarse whisper. "When I saw you in that chair... I thought we were too late."

Bringing my good hand up to his cheek, I stroked his beard, trying to figure out what to say. Tears filled my eyes at the pain in his voice. "But you weren't. You saved me."

"I..." He swallowed, closing his eyes. "I didn't realize how much you meant to me until you were gone."

My heart melted in my chest hearing him admit he cared for me, that I mattered enough to him to risk everything and rescue me. It was overwhelming, but I knew I had to share my own feelings, too. "Cae, I thought about you every single day. It was the only thing that got me through."

"No one will ever hurt you again," he said, leaning his forehead down to touch mine. "I promise you that."

"You can't promise that, Caelum," I said, turning to rest my head against his chest and bringing my injured hand up to rest on his stomach. "But I appreciate the sentiment."

"I *can* promise you that," he objected.

"This world is not made for that. I'll eventually get hurt again, and so will you. It's the way of life. But we can be there to help each other heal," I whispered, tracing the fabric lines of his shirt.

"If you weren't a day away from dying, I would kiss you right now," he said, smiling.

"Don't let that stop you," I said, tilting my head up toward him. I had missed him desperately while held captive, and maybe his touches would drive away the last ghosts of Cliodhna's hands. "Ravage away, Captain."

He laughed, pressing his lips to my hair and wrapping his arms tighter around my shoulders. "Not a chance, *teine*. You need to rest. We'll save the ravaging for when you're well."

"Maybe ravaging is what I need to get well," I said, teasing. My body likely couldn't handle Caelum's version of ravaging, but I doubted some kisses would do any harm.

"One kiss," he said, holding up his index finger. "Just one."

Not giving him time to change his mind and ignoring the

throbbing in my injured wrist, I lifted my hand to his cheek and pulled his face down, joining his lips with mine.

Warm pressure and prickly facial hair felt so *right* against my face and lips. Moving my lips in sync with Caelum's, I lost myself in the sensations, finally feeling like myself again. This was what I had needed. And I needed more of it.

Using my good arm, I tried to prop myself up to change the angle and deepen the kiss, but my lofty goals failed, and I lost my balance, falling onto Caelum's chest with a soft laugh.

"I want a do-over," I said, smiling at him. The joy I felt radiating in my heart was both a foreign and welcomed feeling.

He laughed, rolling out from his spot under me until he was hovering over me. "Not happening. You had your kiss. Now it's time to rest."

I pouted in protest, but I knew he was right. My body was already fatiguing, and my wrist throbbed. "Fine."

He stood from the cot and pulled another blanket off the hammock, nestling it over me. "I'm sure you won't be able to fall asleep, but at least lay here and rest until we're moored."

"Why are we stopping here?" I asked, looking out above the blanket that he had tucked around me. Despite the comfort quickly making my body want to rest, there were so many things that rushed through my mind. "Why not go straight back to Brinemoor? What about the children? What about—"

He put a finger to my lips. "Shh, don't work yourself up. We're stopping here to get you healed up the rest of the way. Then we'll get back to Brinemoor. The children are okay; Iona and Malcolm are watching over them while we're gone. It's okay."

"I don't want to slow us down," I said, reaching up to pull his finger away from my mouth. "I can make it back to Brinemoor."

He just smiled. "I know you can. But if Cliodhna comes back, I don't want you to be vulnerable. I want you at your best. So, we're going to stop, we're going to stay with a friend, we're going to get you better, and then we're going to go back to Brinemoor and deal with whatever comes."

"She will come back. You know that, right?" I asked, my chest tightening at the thought. There was one thing I was sure of: my escape would surely enrage her. She didn't like being made a fool of.

"Let her come, *teine*," he said, taking my hand and kissing my fingers. "We'll be ready."

Tears burned in my throat. Despite our relatively short time together, Caelum understood me, which was more than I could say for the syrens with whom I had spent over half my life with. It made me want to get up and kiss him again. But my body fervently disagreed with that plan, so instead I returned the smile and settled in beneath the blankets.

For now, I would rest.

Elizianna
@ELIZIANNA.THE.ONE

CAELUM

CHAPTER THIRTY-TWO

Pulling the door closed behind me, I slumped against it for a moment, catching my breath. Brigid had been *so close* to dying. She may think she felt better, but I needed to be careful with her, both physically and mentally, despite her protests. I knew she didn't like appearing weak, especially not around my men, but she was weak right now. And that was okay.

I would protect her until she could stand on her own again, which I doubted would take long, given her tenacity. She would heal, both physically and mentally, eventually. She just needed me to remind her of her limits for a bit.

But right now, I had things to do. Namely, getting us back into the harbor. Pushing off the door, I climbed the stairs back up to the deck, the cool night breeze pushing my hair back off my forehead. As I stepped out into the cool air, I spotted Cam and Kyla leaning against the railing, so I turned my path toward them first.

"How is she?" he asked, leaning against the railing on his elbows.

"She's resting now," I said, joining him against the rail. I looked out over the seas, seeing the harbor approaching in the distance. "As soon as Brigid is better, we need to get back to Brinemoor."

"Do you think Cliodhna will come for us again?" Cam asked.

I looked at Kyla. "Brigid thinks she will. What about you?"

She sighed. "She will. She's never liked being wrong about anything, and this will be no different. We've offended her, and she'll want to make us pay."

"Why do we have to rush back to Brinemoor, though?" Cam asked, furrowing his brows.

"She'll likely go after the children again," Kyla said quietly, her eyes locked with mine, voicing the fear I'd been avoiding. "She knows they're important to us."

Cam let out a long exhale, rubbing his hand over his face. "Then, yeah. We need to get back to Brinemoor. How long do we think it will take Brigid to heal?"

"I believe that is a question for me," Lena said, suddenly appearing behind us without so much as a noise to announce her presence.

"Okay, how long do you think it will take Brigid to heal?" Cam asked, turning to the witch and repeating his question.

"It will take as long as it takes." She returned the smile. "Healing is not linear."

"Must you be so mysterious?" Kyla sighed, turning her gaze back out to the sea. She let out a small laugh. "We are on a resurrected ship with magical sea creatures, and we just fought a goddess."

Lena dropped her head back and laughed so loudly and fully it shook her entire body. "Child, you are refreshing. You will be a good leader for the syrens after Cliodhna is gone."

"Gone?" I asked. Of course *I* had planned to kill the goddess, but Lena had not seemed to be one for violence.

She turned to me as if I were the dumbest creature she'd ever laid eyes on. "Yes, boy. Of all the people here, I did not think you would be the one advocating to keep that wretched beast alive."

Cam huffed out a soft laugh, and I turned to glare at him. My cheeks burned slightly at the admonishment from the witch. "No, of course not. I want to be the one to kill her. But I just didn't expect *you* to be the one advocating for it."

She waved her hand, dismissing my words. "Ah, you know nothing about me, Caelum. I am willing to do the difficult things and make the tough choices. She needs to be killed for what she's done. And she will be."

"You said I'd be a leader," Kyla said slowly, as if it had taken her this long to process what Lena had told her. "If we kill Cliodhna, will we lose our powers, too?"

"Of course not," Lena replied, turning her back to me and moving to stand in front of Kyla, resting a hand on her shoulder. "Cliodhna *gave* you those powers—her powers. They won't disappear with her death. They're not *hers* anymore."

"But she took back Brigid's power when she banished her."

I watched with rapt interest as Lena and Kyla leaned in closer together. Kyla would be a great leader for the syrens. Fuck, she would be a great leader for anyone. But I was just as curious about what would happen to the syrens after we took care of Cliodhna.

"Yes, because Brigid let her," Lena explained. She held up a finger to stop Kyla from interrupting. "Ah, ah. I didn't say Brigid knew she was letting her. But by believing that Cliodhna *could* take the powers back, she let her take them."

"Then why didn't she take all of Brigid's powers and turn her back to a human?" I asked, unable to keep from interjecting into the conversation.

"Because," Lena said, turning her head over her shoulder to look at me, "even Cliodhna cannot undo that kind of magic. When she turned you all into syrens, it wasn't a *gift*. It fundamentally changed your being. It's not something she can take back, even if she wanted to."

"You said when we first met that gods and goddesses weren't meant to create new creatures," I said, remembering the words she spoke. "If that's true, then why did Cliodhna?"

"Cliodhna never cared for rules," Lena said dismissively. "That will be her downfall."

"What will happen after?" Kyla asked. "If we kill her?"

"Why, you will do whatever it is you please," Lena said, as if it were the most obvious answer in the world. "You are your own person, my child."

Kyla looked uncertain, though.

Cam looked over his shoulder at me, questions in his eyes. I nodded my agreement. We would do whatever it took to help the syrens find new lives after this.

"Now, enough of that," Lena said, waving her hand. "How much longer until we reach land?"

I straightened up from the railing, looking out ahead of us. The harbor was clear now, no longer a vague shape on the horizon. "We will pull in shortly."

She hummed, nodding as she followed my gaze. "All right. We best go gather our belongings then. Kyla, dear, would you accompany me? I want to check on Brigid before we deboard."

Kyla turned a questioning gaze to me, and I nodded, telling her it was okay. Together, the two headed across the deck and down the stairs.

I blew out a harsh breath when Cam and I were finally alone. "Well, that was a fun talk."

"Yeah, I don't really know what to say to that," he said with a laugh, clapping me on the back. "You got us mixed up with some interesting ladies, Captain."

I let out my own laugh. "Yeah, I suppose I did, didn't I?"

"Might be the best thing that's happened to us, though, huh?" he said, smiling softly.

"Kyla?" I asked, raising an eyebrow at the dreamy look in his eyes.

He smiled a little wider, looking wistfully over the railing. "Maybe... Maybe in another life. We'll see. I'm not pushing anything. She's a wonderful person, though."

"Aye," I said, bumping my shoulder into his. "I'm just glad it's not someone like Maira."

He laughed loudly at that before his face dropped and he let out a heavy sigh. "We should get to work."

"Aye, get the men to their stations. I don't want any issues pulling in and tying up."

He nodded and turned around, heading over to the rest of the crew. I leaned my forearms back against the railing, looking out at the dark water for a moment longer before pushing off and heading up to Duncan at the wheel.

Eliz
@ELIZIAN

BRIGID

CHAPTER THIRTY-THREE

Asoft knocking at the door roused me from the restless sleep I had been drifting in and out of since Caelum left.

I cleared my throat, trying to get rid of the dry grogginess. "Come in."

The door squeaked open slowly, revealing Kyla. She stepped in and closed the door behind her, moving over to sit in the chair still beside my bed. "How are you feeling?"

I scanned through my body, noting the tightness of my muscles, the itch of the scabs forming, the dull throbbing of my wrist. I shrugged. "Better than I'd expected to feel."

She nodded. "Good." She hesitated for a moment, closing her mouth before taking a deep breath. "Lena wants to check on you before we leave the ship. Would that be all right with you?"

I sucked my bottom lip between my teeth. I didn't really know this witch, and even though Kyla and Caelum both seemed to trust her well enough, I was less certain. She knew Cliodhna, and still no one knew how or why. "Why? Is she a healer?"

"She healed you some when we first rescued you," Kyla explained. She looked down at my hand and reached for it slowly, waiting for my permission. I nodded, and she took it between her own hands, grasping tightly. "To be honest, I'm not entirely sure what she can do."

"What's her story?" I asked, using my good hand to push up to sitting. The witch intrigued me, and I got the distinct feeling the rest of them were curious about her, too.

"Caelum sought her out to help find you. We don't really know much about her," she admitted. "She's been very... secretive. Helpful, but secretive."

"What do you think about her?" I valued Kyla's opinion. She had been the most level-headed and objective one of us, likely because she'd had more time to adjust to the syren life. Kyla didn't have a malicious bone in her body, so if she trusted this witch, Lena, then I would, too.

"I think there is more to her than she's letting on," she said after a moment, "and I'm very curious to find out what it is."

"Do you think she'll betray us?" Panic rose in my tightening chest and sweat pooled on my lower back. I breathed deeply through my nose, closing my eyes. Kyla was here with me. I was safe. I opened my eyes again.

She watched me for a moment, making sure I was okay, before continuing. She shook her head. "No, I don't think she will. I'm not sure what the history is between her and Cliodhna, but I get the feeling it's not a pleasant one."

I nodded, taking in her words. She had answered so quickly and confidently. I believed her, or I wanted to believe her. I supposed I would need to talk to Lena myself.

"She can come in then," I mumbled. She stood, but I reached out to grab her hand again. "But I want you to stay. Please?"

Her eyes softened, and she squeezed my hand. "Of course."

She moved to the door, opening it and stepping out momentarily before returning with the witch, Lena. Her appearance alone was unsettling, and nerves fluttered in my stomach. She was clearly powerful, as she carried herself with confidence. Her shoulders were back and her chin high. She knew what she was capable of. "You are awake. That is good."

"You wanted to check on me?" I asked, shifting in a pitiful

attempt to sit up. Kyla quickly moved to my side, putting her arm behind my shoulders, and helping me sit up against the wall.

"I do," the woman said, nodding her head deeply. "How are you feeling, little syren?"

"Better. Thank you for healing me."

She waved a hand. "It was nothing. Having you die would not have been ideal."

I raised an eyebrow at the pragmatic tone. "And why not?"

"Well, your captain would be upset, of course. And Cliodhna would believe she had won." She raised an eyebrow as if I should have known that.

"Why do you care if Caelum's upset?" She spoke of him so familiarly, as if she truly knew him. But from what I had heard, they had met only days ago.

"I believe that's my concern and not yours," she replied. The silver of her eyes glinted disconcertingly in the rising sun. There was something... off about this woman, and I suddenly understood Kyla's words from before.

"Caelum is my concern," I said, my voice frosty, even to my own ears. This woman may be private with her motivations, but Caelum held a special place in my heart, which was quickly growing, and I would do whatever it took to protect him, just as he protected me.

"Then we won't have any problems, will we?" she asked, smiling. Her eyes traveled over my body where the blanket covered it. "Now, let me see to your wounds."

I watched her for a moment, trying to figure out what she was hiding, but her face was impossible to read. Her silver eyes stared back at me, unblinking. Sighing, I nodded and pulled the blanket down.

She moved over to take Kyla's place by my side and bent to tug at the bandages across my torso and legs, peeking beneath them and humming to herself. Moving to my wrist, she pulled the bandage back slightly, but the fabric stuck to the skin.

I yanked my arm to my chest with a hiss, holding my injured wrist protectively with my other hand. "That hurt."

She paused, her hands still reaching for my wrist. "I apologize, but I need to look at it still. I will be gentle."

Slowly, I offered my arm back out to her. Her fingers, cool and gentle, eased back the bandage, carefully working it away from the dried blood and torn skin. She ducked her head, looking beneath it. "It's not infected, which is good, but it is healing more slowly than I'd like."

"My healing is faster in the water, but it's slowed down since..." I couldn't bring myself to finish the sentence, swallowing down the bile that rose.

"Since you were tortured?" Lena finished my thought. She hummed. "Yes, well, I'd expect so. Once your body fully heals, the rate of your healing should go back to normal. You're just trying to heal too many things at once."

The ship shuddered and halted abruptly, knocking us all slightly off balance. We must have pulled into the docks.

Lena stood, brushing her pale hands down the front of her dress. "When we get to where we are staying, I will change your bandages, and we'll see what else we can do to get that wrist healed up."

I nodded, comfortable with that plan. I still didn't know where we were going, but no one else seemed concerned about it. While I regained my footing, I would try to go with the flow. "Thank you."

She smiled at me, a knowing smile that made her eyes twinkle like liquid silver. "You don't have to thank me, child."

Without another word, she picked up the ends of her dress and turned, leaving the room and pulling the door shut behind her. With her absence, the room seemed even more still than it had been, as if something keeping it alive had left with the witch.

I looked at Kyla with a wry smile. "I think you were right about her."

She grinned and held out her hand. "Let's get up and get you ready. It seems like we've docked, and I imagine someone will be down soon to collect us."

Gingerly, I managed to get out of bed with minimal wincing. I paused once I was fully upright to catch my breath and get my bearings. I was sore, my wrist most of all, but I could walk on my own. Kyla busied herself behind me, pulling things out of a bag by the bed. She stepped back around me, a bundle of fabric in her hands.

"Here, you'll need pants, I suspect." She handed me a pair of linen pants that appeared to be quite loose, even on the generous curve of my hips. Holding one hand on her shoulder, she bent down and helped me step into the pants, pulling them up around my hips.

The door pushed open once more, revealing Caelum. He stopped short and smiled. "Oh, good, you're up. I was just coming to help you get ready."

"She's all ready to go," Kyla said, standing and smiling at us both.

"It's just about dawn. We better be getting to Faolan's before people wake up," Caelum said, his eyes roving over my body. It wasn't a heated look of passion, but one of concern, as if he were checking me over for injuries.

"Then we should be off," I said, raising my chin in a muster of confidence, despite the throbbing of my wrist still cradled against my chest.

He hesitated for a moment, his eyes glued to that same wrist. Finally, his gaze shifted, and he cleared his throat, holding his hand out for me. "It shouldn't take long, and I'll carry you if you get tired."

I rolled my eyes, but appreciated the gesture, nonetheless. Reaching down to take his hand with my good one, Kyla and I followed him up the stairs, and we began our journey to wherever this Faolan was.

The walk was short, thankfully, but I was growing tired by the end, my breathing labored and my steps shaky.

"We're almost there," Caelum murmured from beside me. "Do you need me to carry you?"

I shook my head but didn't have enough breath to speak. Instead, I squeezed his hand and smiled up at him reassuringly. I wanted to prove to myself that I could, at the very least, walk under my own power.

"There it is," he said, pointing to a small cabin that appeared over the hill we'd crested.

Just a few more steps.

We reached the door, and Caelum stepped forward, knocking loudly. Cameron immediately filled the space beside me as we all stood waiting.

For a moment, I feared no one was home, but then the door slowly creaked open to reveal an older man, suspicion in his eyes. The minute they landed on Caelum, they flashed with relief and joy. "Oh, good, you're back. Did you get your girl, Caelum?"

Caelum glanced over his shoulder at me before turning back to the man. "Aye, we did."

The man's eyes tracked over to me and the smile that crossed his face was bigger than any I'd ever seen. He turned his head to shout into the house. "He got her, Alys!"

Beside me, Cam chuckled under his breath.

"Come in, come in," the man said, ushering us inside. Cam's hand on my lower back guided me inside, behind Caelum.

The smell of freshly baked bread filled my nose and made my stomach growl. I breathed in deeply and closed my eyes, taking it all in. It smelled heavenly.

"Smells good, doesn't it?" an older feminine voice chimed in, pulling my eyes open. She stood by the small wooden stove in the corner, a smile stretching across her face. She turned to Caelum with a quizzical look, and he smiled widely, nodding at her. Putting down the rag she had been holding, she stepped up to me, her soft brown eyes roving over my face. "I am Alys. Caelum was very worried about you, and we're so glad you're okay."

Tears sprang to my eyes, blurring my vision. This kindness from a complete stranger had caught me off guard. I blinked rapidly and cleared my throat. "Thank you. And thank you for letting us into your home."

Maira coughed behind us. "This is great and all, but some of us are still standing outside."

Alys shared a look with me and rolled her eyes, ushering us all in. "Close the door behind them, Faolan."

"Now, you must share how you rescued your girl," Faolan said, pulling Caelum toward a pair of chairs in front of the burning fire.

Lena stepped forward, quietly interrupting the conversation. "I need to change Brigid's bandages. Is there somewhere we can go?"

"Follow me," Alys said, walking toward a door off the kitchen. She pushed it open, and we stepped into a small room with only a bed against the far wall. "This was my daughter's room. No one stays here now, but you will have privacy, and a bit more space than the bunk room."

Caelum moved to follow me, but I could see the excitement in Faolan's eyes. I smiled at Caelum. "I'll be fine, you stay."

I followed Lena into the small room and grew anxious when Alys stepped in, closing the door behind us. "I was a nurse for a while and can help if needed." She paused and looked at me. "Only if you're okay with it, dear."

The warmth and kindness that radiated from this woman and the concern over someone she had just met had me nodding before I realized what I was doing.

Lena guided me to the bed, and I sat down on the mattress, gratefully exhaling. Now that we stopped moving, my body was telling me I had done too much, too quickly.

"Can I lay down?" I asked, hating how clearly the tiredness came through my voice.

"Of course," Lena and Alys replied at the same time. Alys pulled a blanket off the foot of the bed, spreading it out carefully and patting it.

I lay back and my eyes slowly closed as I nestled into the soft mattress. My body immediately felt intensely heavy as I drifted to sleep. I felt fingers touch my skin, and my eyes flew open for a moment, but the gentleness left no room for my mind to panic and they fluttered shut again. I knew it was not Cliodhna. Sleep took me.

Elizianna
@ELIZIANNA.THE.ONE

C AELUM

CHAPTER THIRTY-FOUR

"I'm glad you got her," Faolan said, his voice pulling my eyes away from the door Brigid had just disappeared behind. "Tell me about it."

I sighed, looking over at the others who were busy eating the food Faolan had welcomed them to. I turned my attention back to him. "She was in bad shape. The witch, Lena, was able to help and led us right to her, though. Thank you for helping us find her."

He waved a hand. "I just told you what I knew. You did all the hard work, my boy."

"I was afraid she wouldn't make it," I said, whispering the words while I wrung my hands in my lap.

"But she did," he said. He ducked his head and caught my gaze, patting my knee. "She *did*, and you're both here now, and you're safe."

"But for how long?" He raised his eyebrow. I sighed and ran a hand over my face. While something about Faolan and Alys made me want to confide in them, I wasn't sure I could risk them knowing about Cliodhna. The less they knew, the safer they would be. I waved my hand, dismissing my own words. "It's fine. We'll be fine."

"Don't do that," he said, pointing a finger at me like I was a misbehaving child. "What happened?"

"I don't want to put you or Alys in harm's way," I said. I waved my hand around his home. "You're safe here, and you're safer not knowing what we're involved in."

Before he could reply, Duncan walked up, perching himself on the arm of my chair. "Why are you waving all around?"

"I'm trying to convince him to tell me what happened when you rescued the girl, but he's being stubborn," Faolan said, tossing me a pointed look before turning his attention to Duncan. "Thinks it'll put us in danger."

Duncan shrugged. "It probably would, to be quite honest."

Faolan huffed. "Well, we could use some excitement around here. So, come on now, indulge an old man and tell him the story."

I hesitated, looking over at the syrens gathered in the corner of the kitchen. The story involved elements of their existence, and it felt inappropriate to tell it without their blessing. I turned back to my audience and opened my mouth to say just that when the door opened to the room Brigid had gone into, and Alys stepped out.

Everyone grew silent, watching the older woman. Alys smiled. "She's fine. Continue about your business. She's sleeping."

Kyla stepped up and murmured something to Alys, pulling her back over to the syrens.

I turned back to Faolan, not wanting to interrupt the conversation between Alys and Kyla. "How much has Alys told you about the syrens?"

"Everything," he replied instantly. "We don't keep secrets from each other."

"So, she told you about their queen, the goddess named Cliodhna?" I pressed. I would not tell him the story until he confirmed he already knew all the players involved.

He nodded. "Yes, she did."

I sighed, unsure of exactly how far back I should start. With my father? With Brigid's kidnapping?

"The queen stole Brigid and tortured her," Duncan said, his voice too casual for my liking. He looked down at me.

Faolan's eyes narrowed. "Why did she take her? And why torture her?"

"My... father," I began, tripping over my words for a moment. "My father was working with Cliodhna, supplying her with children that she used to gain more power. Brigid was helping us stop her, and once we got the children out of the queen's reach, she took Brigid instead."

"You killed the queen, though, yes?" he asked, crossing his arms over his chest. His brows furrowed, and I could see his teeth grinding as his jaw worked. "She's dead?"

"No," Duncan replied. "That's why it's dangerous for us to stay here too long. She'll surely be looking to settle the score."

"Where will you go?" Faolan asked, his hands dropping to his sides as he leaned forward in his chair. "Do you have somewhere safe to be?"

Once again, the utter concern this man showed made my heart squeeze. Why couldn't my father have been like him? "Yes, we have a place in Brinemoor, up north."

He leaned back in his chair, stroking his beard. After a moment, he straightened up and raised his voice. "Alys, dear, come here for a moment, will you?"

At his beckoning, Alys—along with all the syrens—came over, pausing behind the chairs. "Yes, dear?"

"Did those lovely ladies tell you what happened to Caelum's girl there?" he asked, reaching for his wife's hand over the back of the chair.

She stepped up, taking it between her own and patting the top of it. "They didn't have to, Lena shared the story while we were changing Brigid's bandages. I know what she went through, and it's awful."

"The witch had no right to tell you anything," Maira said, her voice snappy as usual.

Kyla shushed her, turning a sharp look toward her, amber eyes blazing in the firelight. "Stop it."

Maira glowered, but obeyed, falling silent.

"Anyway," Faolan continued, turning back to his wife. "How

would you feel about a trip to Brinemoor? These lovely kids suspect the queen will come for them again."

"No," I said instantly, jumping to my feet as my heart pounded in my chest. "Absolutely not. I will not have you both in danger. This is not your fight, and you will not be involved."

Faolan waved his hand dismissively. "Please, boy. I've been in more fights than years you've been alive. This will be fun."

I was at a loss for words. On the one hand, I was grateful for the offer and the support, but the idea of putting someone else in harm's way, someone else who didn't deserve an ounce of violence directed toward them, made my stomach churn.

"This is our decision, and we want to help," Alys said, smiling at me. She released her husband's hand and reached over the chair to grab mine instead. "Let us, please."

"We can't ask you to do that," Duncan said, glancing at me. I was grateful he had spoken, because I still could not push a noise past my lips. "We won't."

Alys raised an eyebrow. "Well, it doesn't sound like you're asking at all. We're offering my dear boy."

"It's too dangerous," I finally spat out. I looked at Kyla, begging her to intervene. It would hold more weight if the words came from her.

Thankfully, Kyla understood my silent plea, and nodding once, she stepped toward us. "There will be another fight, and it will not be safe for you to be with us when it happens."

A door closed behind us as we turned to see Lena exiting the room. She paused as we all looked at her. "Yes?"

"How is she?" I asked, searching her face for answers. "Can I see her?"

"She's tired. Let her rest for a while." She wiped her hands on her dress and walked over to us. "What is happening out here?"

"We are offering to come with you to Brinemoor, and they are doing everything in their power to convince us not to," Alys replied casually, as if her life was not in danger at the possibility of coming.

Lena simply shrugged. "I see no harm in them coming. Alys

would be of great value if anyone got injured, and Faolan can handle himself in a battle. You were a soldier, were you not?"

Faolan's brows shot up his forehead quickly. "How do you know that?"

"She does that." Maira scowled, crossing her arms over her chest. "And she won't tell you how she knows, either."

He smiled, silent laughter shaking his body. "Yes, I was a soldier. Then I was a sailor. And now I'm whatever I need to be."

I sighed, reaching up to pinch the bridge of my nose. Faolan's stubbornness was clear, and rivaled by the strong will of his wife. "You are sure you both *want* to come? You're not doing this out of some misplaced sense of duty?"

Faolan scoffed. "Dear boy, I misplaced my sense of duty a long time ago."

Alys rolled her eyes, but the fond smile stayed etched on her face. "We're sure, Caelum. Let us help."

I knew a lost cause when I saw one, and this one was definitely gone. Sighing again, I spread open my arms, sitting back in the chair. "Then welcome to the crew, I suppose."

"When do we leave?" Faolan asked, a twinkle in his eye.

I turned to Lena. "When will Brigid be ready to travel?"

"Let her sleep until midday, and then we can be off." She peered out the window, looking at the rising sun. "We must gather supplies for the journey while she rests."

"What do we need?" Alys asked, her voice suddenly all business. This was clearly where she thrived, organizing and taking care of others.

"Food and water for the journey. Enough for the day and a half journey back across the Straits," I replied, going through the list in my head. Lena may have resurrected *The Nehalennia*, but we had used most of the supplies that were onboard caring for Brigid. "We can get weapons in Brinemoor. I want to keep the ship as light as possible for the trip. Clothing, bandages, and medical supplies are a priority."

Alys nodded, turning to the syrens. "Would you all accompany me to town to get supplies?"

Kyla nodded. "Yes, we'd be happy to."

Alys turned her head toward Alan and his two men. "You can come too, to help carry everything."

And with that, they followed Alys out of the house with no objections.

Now, only Lena, Cameron, Duncan, and I remained with Faolan.

"What should we expect?" the older man asked, leaning forward to rest his elbows on his knees. "How dangerous is she?"

"She can do magic," Duncan said dryly, "and avoid her talons. She'll likely try to catch us by surprise."

"Does she work alone?" he asked.

"We're not sure about that," I admitted. "She used to have the syrens. But she also had a working alliance with my father and his crew, so there's no telling if she'll turn to them for help."

"How many are on your father's crew?"

"We don't know how many survived," Cam muttered. "We fought them at the same time we fought Cliodhna. We thought we'd killed them all, but apparently not."

Faolan hummed, tapping at his chin. "Sounds like we better do some investigating once we get to Brinemoor."

"You're not worried about putting Alys in danger?" I asked, genuinely curious. If I had been in his position, and Brigid was here, I would never put her in this position, no matter how charitable I felt like being. "You didn't come with us to the witch's house, but you'll come with us on this?"

He guffawed, waving his hand. "Alys can take care of herself. Of course, I worry about her. That's my job. But if she was concerned, I would have been able to tell. She was concerned about finding the witch, which is why I pushed. She appreciated it after. With this though... Well, it's clear she wants to go. The only thing I won't ever do is leave her alone for long. Anything else is a joint decision."

I smiled wistfully. Perhaps, if we made it through this alive and intact, Brigid and I could grow old and be like them. "All right then."

"Go see your girl, Caelum. We'll get things ready here," Faolan said, shooing me toward the bedroom Brigid was in.

I turned to Lena, automatically seeking permission. I wasn't sure why, but it seemed like the right thing to do. Nothing could impede Brigid's healing, not even me. "Can I go in? Is she still sleeping?"

She smiled, bowing her head. "Go ahead. She's drifting in and out."

I didn't need to be told twice. Standing from the chair, I crossed the small house in three strides, pushing open the door as quietly as I could. Closing it behind me, I turned and looked down at the bed. Brigid was curled up, a soft quilted blanket draped over her and her hair splayed out across the pillow. I stood, taking her in. She was asleep, her eyes shut and her face relaxed. She looked peaceful and content, and I would do whatever it took to keep that look on her face for the rest of my life.

Sitting down on the edge of her bed, my back propped up against the wall, I reached down and ran my thumb over her forehead. "Sleep, Brigid. I'm here."

She stirred but didn't wake, instead rolling over toward me and nestling herself into my side. I couldn't help the smile that spread across my face. Even in her sleep, she sought me out. My heart was bursting. This girl was everything to me, and I would spend the rest of my days making sure she knew it.

Nothing and no one would ever harm her again, as long as I lived.

Elizi
@ELIZIAN

BRIGID

CHAPTER THIRTY-FIVE

"Brigid, it's time to wake up," a soft voice said, as a warm breath puffed against my ear.

I squeezed my eyes tighter, comfortably burrowing into the warmth at my side. I didn't want to wake up.

"Come on, *teine*. There'll be time for this later, I promise."

Groaning, I opened my eyes, and immediately saw Caelum's amused grin. "How long did I sleep for?"

He bent to kiss the top of my head. "It's nearly midday."

I blew out a breath. "That long? Why didn't you wake me sooner?"

"You needed the rest," he said, shrugging. He stood from the bed and held his hand out to me. "We need to leave soon. It's time to go to Brinemoor."

Unease fluttered in my stomach, and I sucked my bottom lip between my teeth, chewing on it. "Do you think we'll be able to get there before she finds us?"

The smile dropped from his face, and the hand that extended toward me changed course, reaching up to rub at his beard. "We can only hope so."

Nodding, I put my good hand down on the mattress and

pushed myself up to sitting. It surprised me to find my body noticeably less sore than when I'd first laid down. Twisting my injured wrist, I watched in awe as it moved with just a dull ache. My eyes shot up to Caelum. "It doesn't hurt."

The smile that returned was bright enough to light the room. "Good. Lena and Alys fixed you up proper then."

Pulling myself up to standing, Caelum immediately took me into his arms, holding me against his chest. I closed my eyes and pressed my nose to his chest, inhaling his comforting scent. I was safe.

"As much as I'd love to stay here, holding you," he said, kissing my forehead, "we've got to get going."

Stepping back with a sigh, I nodded. "Let's go, Captain."

He let me step back, but slid his hand down my arm to take my hand in his. "Do you want to go to the orphanage with me when we get back? I want you to meet the children you saved."

The children. In all my unending pain and torture, I'd not stopped to consider that we *had* saved them. Tears sprung to my eyes. "Yes, of course. How are they?"

He smiled again. "They're great. They're really great."

My chest tightened, and I couldn't help but mirror the smile on his face. I was glad he found a purpose while I'd been gone, glad that the children had been there to put that smile back on his face, if only for a moment. "I'd love to meet them."

Tugging on my hand, he pulled me against him once more while his other hand reached up to cup my cheek, running his thumb over my skin. He looked at me for a moment before leaning in to press a soft kiss to my lips, squeezing my hand tightly. It was over all too soon, and he leaned back, tapping his finger on the tip of my nose. "Let's go, before I forget we need to be moving now."

I grinned as he led us out of the room.

The others looked up as we exited, their conversation stopping. The smile dropped from my face, and my stomach churned. Thankfully, Caelum cleared his throat, pulling their eyes to him instead of me. "Time to go."

As a group, we made our way to the harbor, Caelum holding

my hand the entire way, even as my palms grew sweaty with the exertion I'd still not adjusted to. We boarded the ship, one by one. Caelum turned once we were on the deck, pressing a quick kiss to my cheek.

"Find somewhere to sit down, *teine*," he said, before winking and turning to get the ship ready to set sail.

Letting out a breath, I looked around the deck and found a small barrel in the corner by the stairs. I sat, watching the bustling of the men pulling lines and lowering the sails. I lost myself in the activity. Alys and Faolan followed Duncan and Caelum up to the helm, the four of them talking as they went.

Finally, the sails caught the wind, and the ship began moving, taking us out of the harbor and into open water.

Caelum came down the stairs, leaving Duncan at the wheel, and sat down on the bottom step. "Are you ready for the journey?"

I nodded. "Yes, are you?"

Before he could respond, Lena and the syrens approached, waiting for direction from Caelum.

"We're about to head back into the Straits," he said, his face grim as he looked at me and then out to our audience. "I want everyone to be ready."

"You don't need to worry about the Straits," Lena said, smiling serenely as she tipped her head up to look at the sky. She dropped her chin to look at us with her swirling silver eyes. "We won't have any problems."

"How do you know?" Caelum asked, his forehead scrunching in skepticism. "They're called the Straits of the Marbh for a reason."

She just kept smiling. "I know many things. Trust me, we will be safe."

"I'm going to need a bit more than that to navigate through this," Duncan said, his voice dry as he stepped up behind Caelum on the stairs. I hadn't heard him approach, and for a moment, my heart raced at the voice suddenly behind me.

"No," she said, tilting her head toward him. She raised a finger and pointed. "You *need* to learn to accept that things are changing around you."

Duncan didn't reply. He just grunted before turning and stomping back up the stairs.

Lena turned back to Caelum and me. "Your ship will be safe through the Straits, Caelum."

"How long will this trip take us?" Maira asked. "Not as long as the last one, I hope."

Caelum didn't respond, and instead leveled her with a look I'd never seen before. She stared back at him, a challenge clear as her brow ticked up.

"You're not going to tell her?"

Caelum's silence only clarified that I was the 'her' being referred to. I turned to him. "Tell me what?"

"Maira, that was uncalled for," Kyla reprimanded, her voice hard. "Go below." She nodded at Cordelia and Nerina. "You two go with her."

Lena hummed and drifted toward the railing, watching the sea below.

"Tell me what?" I repeated, my voice raising a bit as panic built in my chest, constricting my lungs and throat. "What happened?"

Caelum sighed, running a hand through his hair. "We had a bit of a… setback. On the way here. I didn't tell you because I knew it would only worry you."

"What. Happened?" I asked, annunciating each word. I pressed, balling my hands into fists, my nails digging into the skin to keep from spiraling down every worst-case scenario my mind could come up with.

"You noticed this isn't *The Voyager*?" he asked, nodding toward the masts.

I nodded slowly, trying to follow where he was going with this. "Yes, I noticed this ship is bigger."

"We wrecked in the Straits on the way to get you. *The Voyager* went down." He immediately reached through the railing of the stairs and took my hand, smoothing my fingers out and running his thumb over the crescent indents my nails had made in my palm. "We're all fine, though. That is why I didn't tell you."

I turned to Kyla. "Was anyone hurt?"

She shook her head. "No. We made it to safety and then to Dàrna Cothrom. The only thing lost was the ship."

I exhaled, squeezing Caelum's hand to comfort my spiraling emotions. He was fine. He was here, next to me, and I was touching him. Everyone was fine. I turned to him. "Please don't keep things from me. Even if you think they will upset me."

He nodded, squeezing my hand in return. "I promise. I'm sorry."

"Caelum!" Duncan called from the helm. "Need you up here!"

Caelum whirled around and stood. He looked at Kyla and me. "I'll be right back."

"We'll come with you," I said, standing. I needed to be close to him, to make sure he was safe and fine while I calmed my anxiety.

He nodded, turning and taking the stairs two at a time. Kyla and I followed more slowly. A presence appeared behind me, and I froze, afraid to turn around.

"It's just me, little fire," Lena's soft voice whispered.

My body relaxed, and I nodded. I clenched my fists at my sides and resumed my ascent.

"What's going on?" Caelum asked, approaching Duncan.

"We're concerned about navigating once night falls," he replied, nodding to Faolan and Cameron, who appeared somehow without me noticing.

"There's no need for that," Lena replied, stepping forward. "We will all be safe. I promise. The Dead Waters will not harm us."

Caelum turned his head quickly, and his eyes narrowed into slits. "Dead Waters? No one has called the Straits that in years."

I watched their interaction with wide eyes. I'd only ever heard the passage between Tuathnach and Bhodheas called the Straits of Marbh.

"That's their name, is it not?" she asked, raising her eyebrow with an amused expression. She waved her hand out toward the water. "Just because man changed the name doesn't mean the water agreed to it."

"How old are you?"

"Old enough to refrain from calling things an incorrect name," she said, carefully avoiding his question. She nodded at the horizon that lay ahead. "We will be safe."

No one else replied; they simply watched Caelum and Lena face off.

After a moment, Lena hummed, breaking eye contact with Caelum and turning to me. She held her hand out. "Brigid, be a dear and come let me check your bandages."

We, thankfully, had an uneventful afternoon and night passing through the Straits. As the ship pulled back into Brinemoor Harbor, I exhaled and watched the men toss down the mooring lines. I turned to hear Duncan say something to Finn, who took over the wheel, beginning to secure it as Duncan left the upper deck and approached Caelum and me at the railing.

"Cae, you won't be able to pay the harbor master the mooring fee," he whispered, looking back and forth between us.

"What's going on?" I asked, raising an eyebrow at Duncan. Even though he may not like me, I'll be damned if I was going to be left out of any information.

"There's wanted posters for me in town," Caelum replied quietly, rubbing the back of his neck. My eyes widened. "For piracy and the murder of my father."

I took a step back and my hand rose to my chest as if the words had physically struck me. Of all the things I had been expecting him to say, that had not been it. Although I could understand the murder charge, the piracy one was one I had not expected. "Why piracy?"

He shrugged. "Doesn't matter. But I can't show my face around here quite so easily anymore."

"Do you want Cam or me to handle it?" Duncan asked, before I could ask more questions.

"You go," Caelum sighed. "The rest of us will start unloading the ship."

Without another word, Duncan turned and headed off the ship. I raised my eyebrow at Caelum. "What was that about?"

He shook his head. "We're just not seeing eye to eye on things right now."

My heart sank. While I had gathered that to be the case, given the palpable tension between them, hearing it confirmed didn't make it any easier. This was my fault, and surely the fault of the syrens Caelum brought aboard to help find me. "Is it the syrens?"

He laughed. "No, not the syrens."

"Then just me still," I muttered, nodding. It made sense. I couldn't expect Duncan to forgive me just because he helped rescue me, but it still stung. I had hoped we'd be able to move past it.

Caelum nodded, dropping a kiss onto my forehead. "Don't worry about it, Brigid. We'll deal with it later."

"We need to deal with it soon," I protested. "I can see this is tearing you up. When we get back to the house, I'll talk to Duncan."

"Let's get you completely healed first," he said, pulling me to his side, smiling. "Then you can take on my best friend."

"Deal."

Once the ship docked, we made our way into Brinemoor. Caelum wanted to stop by the orphanage to check on the children, and while I desperately wanted to go with him, I had something else to do first. Sorcha was here, and from the moment I set foot on this land, the only thing I could think of was seeing her.

"I promise I will go with you to visit the children when I'm done," I murmured to Caelum, reaching out for his hand.

"I know, *teine*," he said, leaning forward to kiss my forehead. He pulled back and bent down to meet my eyes. "Are you sure you don't want me to come with you?"

I nodded, placing my hand on his cheek and rubbing the hair out of his eyes. His eyes were so soft, so open. I wanted to drown in them. "You go see to the children. This is something I need to do alone."

Despite wanting to be alone, Kyla and Cam insisted on accompanying me to Sorcha's grave. Afterwards, we would meet up with everyone else and continue the trek to Finn's house to regroup and figure out what to do about Cliodhna.

I had seen the ruins of the house when we buried Maddock, but walking up to it this time was different. Maybe because this time I wasn't in shock and covered in blood. The ivy crawled up the sides of the house, like hands reaching up to pull a body deep into the abyss. Like tendrils dragging the house back down into the earth.

We walked around back, toward the overgrown garden of wildflowers. The two mounds of dirt made my knees buckle.

I knew Sorcha was dead. I held her as she took her last breaths. But nothing could have prepared me for seeing where her body lay interred next to another good and kind person who had died at the hand of my former queen.

My breath shuddered out of me and sent me crashing to the ground.

I wanted to rage, to scream, stomp, and beat my fists against the earth, to shout at the sky. But it wouldn't change anything. One of the people responsible was already dead. Caelum had seen to that. And now I would see to the other.

Cliodhna would die for what she had done.

My eyes fixed on the mounds of dirt and I crawled my way over, sinking back onto my heels on the ground between Sorcha and Maddock, who both lay buried beneath the earth. The reality that they were both gone finally hit me as tears burned in the back of my throat. I was grateful that Cam and Kyla stood back, letting me have my peace with my friends.

While I wanted to stay here with Sorcha, we had a goddess to find and kill, and I couldn't accomplish that sitting in the dirt crying. Sniffing, I stood and wiped the tears from my face, casting one more glance at the two piles of dirt set among the wildflowers. Then I turned and walked back to Cam and Kyla.

"You okay, B?" Cam asked softly.

"No," I answered. "But I will be once we kill Cliodhna. Let's go meet the others."

"We'll get her, don't worry," Kyla said, reaching down to intertwine her fingers with mine. "We're a team."

Tears filled my eyes, and a smile crept over my face. We were far from a team, but maybe our rag-tag group of enemies-turned-alliances could pull off the unexpected.

Elizianna
@ELIZIANNA.THE.ONE

CAELUM

CHAPTER THIRTY-SIX

I had wanted to go with Brigid to visit Sorcha's grave, but I also needed to check on the children. Even though I trusted Iona and Malcolm to watch over them while we had been gone, I needed to see with my own eyes that they were truly fine. I tried not to think about them while we were gone, focusing on one thing at a time to avoid getting distracted, but it only worked sometimes.

Duncan and I took the back roads to avoid being seen. As we approached the orphanage, I felt eyes on my back, watching us. We made the final turn down the road that led to the doors, and the eyes followed. I stepped closer to Duncan as we walked.

"Don't go toward the orphanage," I whispered, trying to keep my lips from moving. "Someone's watching us."

"Where?" He kept his head straight and his body loose.

"Alley."

We continued past the orphanage, and I prayed none of the children were out. If even one of them spotted me, they would all come running, and though I missed them desperately, I didn't want whoever was watching us to know that.

Passing the next alley, I casually glanced down it. I hadn't expected to see whoever was watching us, but I glimpsed someone slipping around the corner. So, they were watching *and* following. Two could play that game.

Changing course abruptly, we snuck down the alley, following whoever it was. Turning the last corner, I pulled my dagger.

"Aye, easy there boy," a gruff voice sounded.

Tension escaped my body at the sight of Galen in front of me. "Why the fuck are you following me?"

"Knew you'd notice," he chuckled, rubbing his hand over his beard. "Had to get your attention somehow."

Well, that certainly wasn't a good sign. Galen rarely involved himself in the happenings of town, so if he was seeking me out, something was definitely wrong. "What's happened?"

"I saw your face plastered around town, so I kept an ear out. Turns out your father's crew is trying to rebuild." He crossed his arms over his broad chest. "Saw some of your crew leaving the docks and figured you were finally back in town."

My stomach sank. This was not what I wanted to be dealing with right now. "Have you heard any details?"

He shook his head. "Not really. They came in looking for weapons, but I turned them away."

"Fuck," I said, rubbing a hand over my face. "How many weapons did they want?"

"Enough to give you some problems," he said with a grimace. "Sorry, boy."

"Well, thank you for not supplying them with the means to kill me, I suppose." I had to give him that. It was support I didn't expect. Galen was a businessman, through and through. He may care for me, but at the end of the day, he wanted to make money, and declining that big of an order couldn't have been a straightforward decision for him.

"Believe it or not, Caelum, I am fond of you." He smiled widely. "If they want to kill you, they'll have to put some effort into it."

"That's not exactly reassuring," I grumbled. Galen may be the best blacksmith in Brinemoor, but he wasn't the only one. "Do you know how many men they have?"

"At least twenty, based on what they were asking for."

"Thanks for the heads up, Galen," I sighed. There was nothing I could do about this now. We needed to get back and gather everyone to formulate a plan. Cliodhna was at the top of my list, but now dealing with my father's crew would need to be addressed as well.

"Where are you staying?"

"Somewhere safe." My hackles rose at the question. Galen may seem trustworthy based on our past, but the fewer people who knew where we were, the safer we would be. "Why?"

"If I hear anything else, how will I let you know?" He raised a bushy eyebrow.

"One of us will find you once we have a plan," I replied. Normally, I would have met him at the pub, but because of the wanted posters, being seen in town was unwise. And I certainly didn't want him to be seen dropping messages at the orphanage.

"Stay safe, boy," he said, clapping a hand on my shoulder before turning to leave the alley.

"That was... odd." Duncan said quietly once Galen was out of view.

I nodded, agreeing with his suspicion. Galen, asking where I was staying, put me on edge. "Aye, it was."

"I don't like us being separated. Not after that. We need to regroup."

"Aye, let's go." The orphanage would have to wait until I was sure it was safe to visit. I would not risk the children's safety just to satisfy my need to see them. "Everyone needs to get back to the cottage and stay together."

Once we'd all gathered back on the path out of town, my breathing eased. Seeing everyone safe with my own eyes was reassuring.

Alys and Faolan elected to stay at the inn in Brinemoor, keeping an ear out for anything that might help us. Playing the role of a visiting couple would attract far less suspicion than the rest of us could.

The aged structure of Finn's cottage appeared over the hill, and approaching it felt like a breath of fresh air. While it wasn't my home, it still felt like coming home.

Brigid had been quiet the entire way back, and the red rings around her eyes told me all I needed to know. Once we all got settled, I would go to her and make sure she was okay.

The crew members quickly scattered to their claimed rooms as we entered the house, leaving Brigid, Lena and me standing in the entryway. Iona stepped out of the kitchen, and her eyes widened as she saw Brigid. She rushed up to her, but hesitated, unsure whether Brigid would welcome the touch. Brigid nodded, welcoming the embrace. I could not hear their murmured conversation, but it was clear the reunion pleased both women. The other syrens lingered nearby, observing their interaction.

Duncan and Cameron moved to sit in the kitchen, slumping into their chairs. Brigid looked tense as she stepped away from Iona and moved toward the kitchen, her eyes flitting over at every sound and movement. Stepping up next to her, I offered whatever silent support I could. I was still wary of pulling her into my arms for fear of hurting her, but I would let her know I was there if she needed me.

She leaned back into my chest, and my heart swelled. Carefully, I raised one hand to rest on her hip, squeezing gently to let her know I was here.

"What do you need to make the spell?" Brigid asked Lena, her voice hopeful.

I raised my eyebrow looking at the two of them. "What spell?"

She tilted her head to look up at me. "Lena thinks she can make my transformations painless again."

My eyes widened. "Really?"

"Here," Lena replied, ignoring my surprise, and reaching around Brigid to hand a piece of paper to me. "Get me these things, and I should be able to complete the spell."

My eyes scanned the list, reading her neat script. I recognized some ingredients, but most were foreign to me. The apothecary that we had taken Maddock to was well stocked, and I figured I would have the best luck there. "I'll need to go back into town for most of these."

"Caelum, you shouldn't be going into town at all," Duncan grumbled from the kitchen, crossing his arms over his chest and frowning. "One of us can go."

Begrudgingly, I admitted Duncan was right. The less of an advantage we gave my father's crew, the better. "Fine. Duncan, can you or Cam take Lena to the apothecary to get what she needs?"

"Of course," Duncan replied, nodding.

"As for the rest of you," I said, turning my attention to the newly reunited syrens lingering nearby. "We are at a disadvantage fighting Cliodhna in the water, so I'm going to teach you all how to fight on land, using weapons."

Maira scoffed, stepping out from the group and propping her hands on her hips. "Cliodhna cannot overpower us all in the water if we work together."

"But *we* won't be able to help you in the water. Our best course of action is to stay together and defend one another, especially now that my father's crew is up to something." I tried to be patient as I explained my reasoning, but I could tell my irritation with Maira was clear in my voice.

"It will be valuable to learn to defend ourselves in any form," Iona said, surprising me. She and most of the other syrens had been intentionally quiet around me and my men since they joined us. "If Cliodhna attacks the orphanage or this house, we won't be able to help defend it. We must learn."

Well, it seemed the children had won over another heart. I smiled at Iona, bowing my head in thanks.

"Yes, I agree," Kyla said, looking at Maira, who just rolled her eyes and huffed. Cordelia put a hand on Maira's shoulder, rubbing soothingly as Kyla turned back to me. "When do we start?"

"I think we should take tonight to rest and regroup, and then tomorrow morning, Duncan and Lena will go into town while the rest of us start to prepare and train."

I looked around the room, listening to the quiet murmurs, and watched as everyone slowly dispersed to their bedrooms. My crew had already claimed theirs, and I figured the syrens would share rooms as they had before our journey.

Lena and Brigid lingered.

"You can take any open room," I told Lena. "There should be one left at the end of the hall."

She nodded. "Thank you, Caelum. Brigid, I will see you in the morning. Get some rest, please. Tomorrow will not be easy for you."

Brigid cast me a concerned glance as Lena left, turning down the hall. "What do you think she meant by that?"

I sighed. Lena's words were often mysterious, but none of the ingredients I recognized would cause any harm to Brigid. "I'm not sure. Did she say where she got the spell from?"

She shook her head. "Do you think I should tell her I don't want to go through with it?"

"I don't think she would do a spell that would harm you," I said, pulling her into my arms. Lena's actions had only been out of concern for Brigid's safety and healing. I couldn't imagine the witch deliberately trying to injure Brigid. I sighed again, squeezing her tightly. The warmth of her body against mine was something I thought I would never feel again, and something I would never take for granted. "We will question her in the morning, before she begins, and if you don't want to go through with it, we won't."

She nodded into my chest, her arms tightly wrapped around my body. She slowly let go, pulling my hand into hers as she stepped away. Happily, I let her lead us down the hall to the room she had shared with Sorcha.

Her steps faltered as we reached the door, and she saw Sorcha's empty bed by the window. My heart ached for her. She hadn't been able to properly mourn the younger syren.

"After this is over," I said, kissing the side of her head, "we will mourn them all."

"She deserved better," she whispered.

"You'll get your revenge, *teine*. I promise."

She nodded, stepping away from me and turning toward the

bed we would hopefully share. Sitting down on it with a heavy sigh, she looked up at me. "Will you stay with me tonight?"

"Nothing could keep me away," I whispered, smiling down at her. "Now, can I help you out of those clothes?"

The answering smile was brighter than the sun, and my heart sped up.

Elizi
@ELIZIAN

CHAPTER THIRTY-SEVEN

Waking up to Caelum's soft snores startled me at first, my body fighting to remember where I was. Feeling his arms wrapped around me and his warm body pressed against my back relaxed me. I was safe here. Caelum had rescued me.

Breathing deeply, I tried to calm myself. I wasn't with Cliodhna; I was curled up against the man who was stealing my heart piece by piece. Closing my eyes, I pressed myself back against Caelum, gently weaving my fingers with his, resting over my stomach.

"Good morning," came the sleepy reply behind me. His voice rumbled through my body, warming me even more.

Careful to avoid straining my still sore body, I rolled over, resting my head on his chest and looking up at him. His eyes were still heavy with sleep, but the smile on his lips was as bright as the new day. Gingerly, I pushed myself up to kiss him. "Good morning, Captain."

Immediately, his hand slid up into my hair, and he deepened the kiss. I could tell he was still being gentle with me, which I both hated and appreciated, but I knew if I pushed, he would stop kissing me all together, and that was definitely not what I wanted. So instead, I just enjoyed his slow and sleepy kisses.

We kissed, just relishing each other's company after our time apart, until he finally pulled back and rested his forehead against mine. "As much as I want to stay in bed with you all day, we both have matters to attend to."

I sighed. We did, and I was absolutely not looking forward to whatever Lena had planned. Despite the syrens' obvious reservations about the witch, Caelum seemed to trust her. "Can I help you with the training while Duncan and Lena go get supplies?"

"Of course." He stood and walked over to the chair, pulling his clothes on. "Hopefully, they've already left. I can't imagine Duncan would still be sleeping."

"He still doesn't like me, does he?" I asked softly, sitting up in bed and watching as he pulled his boots on.

He paused in the middle of buckling his boots and looked up at me. "*Teine...*"

"No." I immediately cut him off. Seeing the pity and guilt in his eyes was too much. "It wasn't really a question. I know he doesn't like me."

"After this is over, we're going to fix it," he said. I could hear the determination in his voice, though I wasn't sure how he expected to fix anything. I wasn't even sure he could.

"We'll see," I said, sighing as I climbed out of bed. My body was still sore, but I felt better than yesterday. At the very least, there was no throbbing pain that accompanied every beat of my heart. It was now just a dull, lingering ache I could ignore if I tried hard enough.

Caelum pulled me into his arms and looked into my eyes with such ferocity and determination that I suddenly didn't want to leave the room—or the bed—at all. "*Teine*, we're going to fix this, and then you and I are going to spend at least a week alone where no one can bother us."

I smiled. "That sounds nice."

"Now get dressed. We've got some syrens to teach," he said, reaching down to squeeze my hips before stepping back. He reached over and grabbed my clothes, handing them to me while pressing a quick kiss to my lips.

After a long morning of training, the syrens were at least passable in hand-to-hand defense. We all had some experience, but the adjustment was learning to fight with our legs and not just our arms and talons. Maira had taken to it quicker than the rest of us, after some initial clumsiness. My own movements were stiff, still hindered by the soreness lingering in my muscles. Despite it, I absorbed every instruction and every correction.

Caelum and Cameron were patient teachers, more patient than I would have been.

As we took a break to get some water and eat, the door swung open, and Duncan and Lena entered. Lena looked satisfied as a large basket hung off her arm, while Duncan just looked irritated. I wondered if it was something Lena had done, or if that was just his default expression now.

Duncan motioned for Caelum, who straightened from his spot against the wall and followed them both down the hall toward the room Lena had claimed.

"Wonder what happened," Cameron said, moving to stand behind me.

I turned to look at him. "No clue. But I guess we'll find out soon."

Only a few moments later, Caelum and Duncan emerged.

"Okay," Caelum said, walking up to the table and clapping his hands. "Brigid, Lena is ready for you. The rest of you, it's time to return to your training."

My throat clogged with anxiety. "Are you coming with me?"

He smiled at me reassuringly, reaching over to squeeze my hand. "Lena said it had to be just you and her, but I'll be just outside the door."

I nodded, squeezing his hand in return.

"Then who will train us this time?" Maira asked, her eyes narrowing as she looked over at Duncan smirking from the kitchen.

"Duncan and Cameron," Caelum replied, crossing his arms. "You'll cover dagger work next."

"Why doesn't Brigid have to train with us?" I almost smiled at Maira's petulant tone, but I understood her frustration. For years, we had been the deadliest things in the sea, but on land, we were vastly under prepared.

"Brigid has other commitments." The patience in his voice was astounding. "Now, please get started. We don't know how much time we have."

"Fine," she grumbled.

"Brigid, Lena is waiting for you in the back room," Caelum said, turning his gaze back to me. "I'll be right outside the entire time, I promise."

Nodding, I stood and pressed a quick kiss to his cheek before turning to walk toward the back of the house. He followed closely behind, pulling a chair up next to the door. He smiled at me, pushing me gently through the threshold.

Lena had her back to me, spreading supplies across the table that stood in the middle of the room. I wanted to have my transformations back and be able to enjoy the sea without pain, but I froze in the doorway, panic clawing at my throat.

She turned and looked up when I entered, smiling widely. "Ah, Brigid. Please come in. Close the door behind you."

I couldn't move, still frozen in place. She tilted her head, studying me for a moment before walking over to take my hand. She gently pulled me into the room and closed the door behind us, leaning against it. "You will get through this. It will hurt, but will not harm you."

Taking a shaky breath, I nodded, digging my fingers into my palms, the pain grounding me. "What do we do first?"

"First, you help me prepare the ingredients for the spell," she said, motioning to the table behind me. "Next we perform the spell and then you must rest for the remainder of the day."

"How badly will it hurt?" I asked, my voice shaking more than I had intended it to.

Sympathy flashed in her silver eyes, and she stepped up in front of me, placing her hands on my shoulders gently. "It will not feel pleasant. You will feel a burning sensation, but once it's over, your transformations will be painless once more."

"What about my song?" I asked before I could stop myself. It was selfish, I knew that, but the transformation problem didn't make me a full syren again. Without my song, I was still incomplete.

She grimaced and stepped back, moving around me to her table. "That, I cannot solve. Cliodhna should never have given you that power in the first place, and no spell I know of will give it back."

My heart dropped, but I nodded. I would learn to live without my song; I had already made it this long. "Okay, thank you. I appreciate your help."

She stopped piddling with the supplies and turned to fully face me, stepping up close. "Child, you *never* have to thank me for this."

Staring at her for a moment, I finally nodded, and she returned the gesture, turning back to the table. "So why are you really helping us, Lena?"

"You are suspicious," she said, continuing to organize ingredients, moving things around on the table. Her words weren't a question.

"Yes, I am. The others told me you knew Cliodhna." I stepped up to the table next to her, taking a deep breath to steady my nerves. If I survived two weeks with Cliodhna, I could survive questioning this woman. "I'd like to know more."

"I'm sure you would," she said, turning her head to smile at me. "At least you asked nicely. That's more than I can say of the others."

"Maira." I shook my head.

"Yes, that little fish certainly does not trust easily." She thrust a bowl into my hands. "Here, hold this."

I took the bowl, watching as she began placing herbs and various items into it. "No, she doesn't. And she has a long memory."

"Cliodhna and I were close once," she said after a long pause. "But when man forgot about her, she changed."

That surprised me. According to Cliodhna, man forgot the old gods and goddesses a very long time ago. "How old *are* you?"

She paused, smirking at me. "That is a bit intrusive, don't you think? If I did not answer when Caelum asked, what makes you think I will answer when you ask?"

My cheeks burned, and my eyes fell to the ground. "Yes, I apologize."

She laughed, placing her thin hand on my shoulder. "I am much older than I look, my dear. Now, let's get this spell started. Hold the bowl. And once everything is in there, you'll grind it into dust," she said, adding things from the table to the bowl. It was quite full now, but she didn't stop. "Then, we'll add sea water and mix it into a paste. I'll apply it to your body, focusing on your legs, and will say the spell, and then the magic will take over. You can stay in your human form the entire time."

I appreciated her telling me exactly what we would be doing. It helped ease the anxiety building in my chest, especially at the thought of more pain. "How long will the pain last?"

Her eyes softened. "Not long. And I'll be with you the entire time."

I nodded, taking a deep breath in through my nose. I could do this. One more bout of pain and then, hopefully, no more. I had endured far worse during my weeks with Cliodhna. This was nothing compared to that. Caelum was right outside, too, and I was sure he was ready to burst in at a moment's notice. With that thought, my shoulders released some of their tension.

She handed me a stone pestle. "Here, grind that into a fine dust. I will answer more of your questions while you work."

Taking the pestle, I began pushing it against the herbs and bones in the bowl, crunching and grinding them. Focusing on the work helped ease my worries about what was to come.

"I knew many gods and goddesses." I looked up at her, but her gaze was far away as she looked out the window, so I went back to my work and let her tell her story. "They were my friends, or so I thought..."

"What happened?" I asked, my voice barely audible.

She sighed. "As man turned away from the gods, their powers waned, and they became more human with each passing year. It frightened some and angered others. Some, like Cliodhna, clung to any power they still had while others embraced their newfound humanity and learned to live among the people who had once worshiped them."

"Were you a worshiper?" I asked, pausing.

"Keep going," she said, snapping her fingers at the bowl. "And no, I wasn't."

"Then—" I began.

"That's good enough." She interrupted me, taking the bowl from my hands. "Let's begin."

I took a deep breath, readying myself for what would come next.

CHAPTER THIRTY-EIGHT

Lena added sea water to the finely ground mixture, creating a thick paste as she instructed me to remove my clothes and lay down on the bed. I obeyed and was now laying naked on top of the blankets, completely exposed to this witch. My fingers twitched, wanting to cover my body, but I twisted them into the blankets instead, closing my eyes and breathing deeply through my nose. I knew she had seen my body before, but I had been delirious with pain. This time, I was acutely aware of her eyes studying me.

"You are safe with me, Brigid," she whispered, as she picked up the bowl of paste and moved toward my legs. She paused with her hand in the bowl. "Are you ready?"

Taking a deep breath, I nodded. I was as ready as I ever would be.

She looked at me for another moment before pulling out a scoop of the gray-green paste we had made. It was pleasantly cool as she spread it over my legs, and it tingled slightly. She started at my feet and continued up my legs, spreading the paste evenly to cover the front of my shins and thighs, stopping at my belly button.

"Do you need to do the back of my legs?" I asked, watching her meticulous work.

"No, just the front will do," she said, scraping out the last of the paste and smearing it across my stomach. She set the bowl down on the ground by the bed and wiped her hands on the tablecloth. "Are you ready for the spell?"

"Yes, do it," I said, closing my eyes. I tried to focus on the sensation of the drying paste against my skin, the itchiness of it and the slight tingling spreading through my legs.

I jumped slightly as an icy hand rested on my forehead, but Lena's soft noises soothed me. Keeping my eyes closed, I slowed my breathing as she began to chant. I didn't understand the words she was saying. They sounded like the old language, and I was far from fluent in it. The only words I recognized were *pian*, which I knew meant pain, and *casan*, which meant legs.

She stopped chanting and pressed her other hand firmly against my sternum. All at once, pain flooded my body, my legs tensing and spasming. I gritted my teeth to keep from crying out and clenched my eyes shut. Though the pain was intense, it was over in a moment, the muscles of my body relaxing and the pain fading almost as quickly as it began.

My focus turned back to Lena and the room around me as I slowly opened my eyes. The witch was looking down at me with swirling silver eyes and a concerned expression. I saw why Caelum had trusted her. She was genuine. "Are you okay, Brigid?"

I cleared my throat. "Yes, the pain is gone. It faded quickly."

She nodded, brushing my hair back off my forehead. "Good, that's good. Let's get you cleaned up and then you must rest for a bit."

"No, I'm fine. I don't need to rest," I protested, moving to sit up. But as soon as I moved, my muscles screamed in protest and I winced, laying back down against the bed. "Okay, maybe I will rest for a bit."

Lena smirked, reaching to hand me a vial of purple liquid. "Here, this will help with the pain. Drink it while I wipe the paste off you. Once you wake, I imagine you will want to test our work?"

"Yes, please." I tipped the liquid into my mouth, grimacing at the bitter taste. Lena began wiping the paste from my body using the cloth and the seawater. My eyelids drooped as the smell of the salty water and the gentle motion of the rag against my body comforted me. As I drifted off to sleep, I had the sudden realization the liquid contained more than just something to help with the pain.

But my eyes closed before I could chastise Lena.

When I woke again, I heard people whispering. My body tensed, and I kept my eyes shut, trying to assess who was here. I didn't like that people had been in while I was asleep. Caelum was one thing, but this sounded like several people. Slowly, I recognized the voices, and my body relaxed. I opened my eyes to see Lena and the syrens. Seeing me awake, they all quieted.

"Ah, you're awake," Lena said, standing from her chair and stepping up beside me. "How are you feeling?"

Trying to keep from squirming beneath their collective scrutiny, I tested my body, pleasantly surprised to find that I had no lingering pain, not even the soreness in my wrist. "Good, actually."

She nodded, smiling. "Good, the sleeping draught helped. It should ease any soreness while your body heals."

"I want to go to the sea," I said, looking over at Lena. She told me we could test my transformation once I woke, and if I could transform without pain, I wanted to do it as often as possible.

"Patience," Lena chastised, handing me my clothes. "I know we said when you woke up, but give it a moment first. You may not feel any pain or soreness, but it doesn't mean it's not there."

Impatience hummed in my blood, but I pulled on my clothes and settled back into bed. "Why are you all in here?"

"We got a reprieve from training, so we wanted to check on you," Kyla said, smiling. "And Lena was telling us more stories about Cliodhna and the other gods."

"Are you ever going to tell us how you know Cliodhna?" Maira asked. It was clear she still didn't trust the witch, but at least she wasn't as combative as she was with Duncan.

"Does it truly matter how I know her? Or are you asking me if I knew she was evil all along?" Lena raised an eyebrow. "Because if it's the latter, yes and no."

"What do you mean?" I struggled to make sense of her answer.

"Cliodhna has always been... ambitious. But I never thought she would stoop to breaking the most sacred laws of the gods."

"Gods have laws?" Maira asked.

Lena scoffed. "If there are no rules, the world would be chaos, even for the gods. Yes, little fish, the gods had laws. And the most important law was that gods were meant to guide humanity, not create it."

"Then why did Cliodhna make us?" I asked, very interested in Lena's insight.

"She likely felt she was being forgotten."

"What do you mean?"

"Man forgets, over time, but the sea always remembers," she said solemnly. "And Cliodhna only ever cared about humanity's opinion of her."

"But man didn't know we truly existed," I protested, confusion still reigning. "If Cliodhna cared about man's opinion, wouldn't she have wanted us to be widely known and feared?"

Lena shrugged. "I won't pretend to understand her motivations, but I suspect your existence was enough to satisfy her. That, and the legends of the syrens, likely sustained her—for a while."

"People really worshiped her?" Kyla asked, leaning forward.

"Oh, yes. People worshiped all the gods. There were temples and some had priests and priestesses to manage them," she said, rubbing at her chin. "But over time, it just... faded."

"How do you remember them all?"

She smiled. "I am much older than I appear, but there will always be people who remember the old ways." She nodded her head toward Caelum. "Like Caelum's mother, for example."

"You knew Caelum's mother?" I asked, reeling back. Caelum

hadn't mentioned that. Actually, he hadn't mentioned his mother at all.

"Yes, I did," she said, gazing wistfully toward the sky. "She was a wonderful woman."

I had so many questions, but I knew Caelum wouldn't want me to find out the information from Lena. Later, when I was alone with him again, I would ask him directly.

"Now, that's enough of that. We have a rough time ahead of us, my dears. It's time to prepare for the days to come," Lena said, clasping her hands together.

Elizianna
@ELIZIANNA.THE.ONE

C AELUM

CHAPTER THIRTY-NINE

The syrens had been in the back room with Brigid all morning. Despite my overwhelming desire to check on how things were going, Lena had assured me Brigid was resting and fine. I ground my teeth when she'd invited the other syrens back into the room, but her knowing smile and a raised eyebrow stopped my protests.

Though I agreed to give the syrens their collective space with Brigid, it did little to ease my impatience. Brigid had been on the brink of death, and Lena's cure for her transformation pain had also involved pain, something I was not keen on.

Just as I was about to head to the back room, the front door burst open, and a breathless Cameron filled the space. "We have a problem."

My stomach dropped as I jumped to my feet. Whatever he had to say would not be good. He went into town to check on the ship and keep an ear out for any news. "What's happened?"

"Galen caught me as I was leaving. Said he'd heard your father's men were planning an attack on the orphanage," he said, panting and wiping the sweat from his forehead as he stepped further into the house.

Fuck. This was exactly what I was afraid of. "When?"

"He thinks today. Said he'd been looking for one of us all morning. I ran back as soon as I heard."

"We need to go. Now," I said as dread filled my stomach. Kicking myself for not staying closer to Brinemoor, I grabbed my sword from the table, strapping it on as I moved down the hallway. I flung open the door to the syrens' room. "There's going to be an attack on the orphanage. We need to go."

I locked eyes with Brigid, who stood by the bed. While I was happy to see her up and about, I didn't have time to savor the moment. I was already moving, turning down the hall to collect everyone else. We would have our reunion later.

Within minutes, we had left the cottage. Brigid rushed to my side, tightening the dagger belt around her waist. "What's happening, Caelum?"

"Galen told Cam that my father's men were planning to attack the orphanage," I said, looking back over at my shoulder at the others trailing behind. "I can't let that happen."

"We," she said firmly, reaching down to grab my hand. "*We* won't let that happen, Caelum."

I squeezed her fingers quickly. "Thank you, *teine*."

It was a tense journey from the cottage into Brinemoor, and I again cursed myself for not electing to stay on the ship or somewhere in Brinemoor. I should not have let the sentimentality of Finn's cottage overshadow the need to protect these children. We should have been closer.

Brigid, walking beside me, looked over for a moment, never breaking her stride. In one wordless gesture that made all the anger bleed from my body, she reached her hand down and worked her fingers inside my fist until I was squeezing her hand instead of my own. She smiled at me, squeezing my fingers.

The town was quiet as we approached. Cautiously, I held up a hand to slow everyone down. If my father's men were watching, they would notice such a large group, and we would be an easy target.

"We need to split up. Surround the orphanage and approach it slowly," I said, turning to look at Duncan and Cameron. "We must protect it."

"No one will get past us," Cameron said, nodding. "What if they're already inside?"

"Brigid and I will go in the front door," I said. On the trek here, I had considered what Cam had said. If Kellan's men were smart, they would already be inside the orphanage. These children would not be pawns in whatever game Cliodhna was playing. Children should not be involved in the battles of men. "We will protect them from the inside."

"Then let's get going," Duncan said, tightening his grip on his sword. He turned to the syrens. "Split up between Cam and me, and keep an eye out."

With that, we all went separate ways, Brigid and I taking the main road into Brinemoor, walking straight toward the orphanage.

"How are the children?" she asked quietly as we picked up our pace. She had unsheathed her dagger and her eyes roved our surroundings, searching for any sign of a threat.

For a moment, I regretted bringing her. The idea of putting her right back in danger, in such an emotional situation, was not ideal. I could tell by the tension in her shoulders and the way her eyes darted around that she was still dealing with the aftermath of Cliodhna's torture. I reached down to squeeze her free hand. "They are good; they bounced back quickly. Some of them are learning to read now."

She smiled, and even though it didn't quite reach her eyes, it was still radiant. "Good, I'm glad."

"We'll get her, *teine*," I promised, squeezing her fingers again. "We'll stop her."

"I know, Captain," she replied. "But for now, let's protect the children."

Reaching the orphanage, I released her hand and pushed against the heavy wooden door. It swung open, and silence greeted us. The halls were quieter than I had ever heard them. I slowly unsheathed my sword. Silence was not a good sign. Not in a place where children's laughter was louder than any other noise in this town.

"Do you think they're okay?" Brigid whispered as we walked down the hall toward the dayroom.

"I don't know." I wasn't sure what I would do if they weren't.

As we continued down the hall, I could barely breathe. My heart pounded in my chest and my palms were so sweaty I struggled to hold on to my sword. If someone had hurt these children because of me, I vowed to make those responsible pay. And from the look on Brigid's face, I knew my fire would help me burn them down.

Pushing open the door to the dayroom, I held my breath, readying myself for what might be on the other side.

"Caelum! You're here," a small voice shouted. My breath rushed out of my body as Rory ran up to me, wrapping himself around my knees.

I twisted my sword behind my back to keep it out of his reach as I squatted down to his level. Looking over his head, I took in the other children, huddled in the corner with Isla. "Rory, what happened?"

"Bad men came in," he said, sniffling.

My head snapped up to Brigid, who nodded and turned her back to me to guard the door, raising her dagger. I turned back to Rory, dropping to a knee. "Are they still here? Are any of you hurt?"

He shook his head, wiping at his nose with the back of his arm. "No, they just shoved us all in here and told us to stay quiet."

"Where did they go?" I asked, looking over Rory's small body. He didn't appear injured, just frightened.

He shrugged, oblivious to the dangers that lay ahead. "I don't know."

"Okay," I said, leaning in to kiss the top of his head and ruffle his bright orange hair. "Go back to the others. We'll keep you safe."

Isla stood as Rory went back over to the group, ushering him behind her with the other children. I stood, keeping my sword out as I walked to meet her. "Caelum, we're so glad you're here."

"How long ago were they here?" I asked, studying her face. Her cheekbone looked swollen, and I reached out my free hand to brush it. She winced, pulling away before I could touch the skin. "Did they hit you?"

"A little under an hour ago," she replied, avoiding my second question.

"Isla, they hit you." It wasn't a question this time, and the anger burned in my chest at the thought of someone hurting this woman.

"They did," she sighed, "and I would gladly take it again if it meant protecting these children."

"I know, I know. I would do the same. How many men were there?"

"Four approached us," she said, tucking a loose strand of hair back behind her ear. She nodded over at Brigid, who was still standing at the door, her dagger out. "I see you got your girl back."

I couldn't help it as a smile stretched across my face. "Aye, I did."

As if she knew we were talking about her, Brigid turned around and looked at me, smiling slightly. She was nervous, that much was clear in the white-knuckled grip she had on her dagger. Her talons weren't out, which was unusual given how I'd seen her fight in the past. I watched her for a moment as she kept adjusting her grip on the hilt. Something about her fingers seemed off. I tracked the movement, tucking it away to ask about later.

"She seems good for you," Isla said. "You're both very protective."

"We'll talk about that later," I said, raising my chin toward the children huddled in the corner. "We need to get you all out of here."

"And go where, Caelum?" She crossed her arms over her chest. "This is our home, for better or for worse. I won't let those overbearing fools run us out of it."

"Your lives matter more than this building, Isla. Now, come on." I stepped around her, moving toward the children. "Once this is over, you can all return."

She hesitated for a moment, but gave in, following me over to the children. "Okay, everyone up. It's time to leave."

"Where are we going?" Rory asked, his arm cradling a younger child next to him.

"You're all coming with me," I said, even though I had absolutely no idea where to take them. The ship was the closest refuge that would have enough room for everyone, so that would have to do for now.

"Are we getting away from the bad men?" one of the other children asked, his eyes big and round.

"Aye," I said, squatting down to his level. They were all terrified, but I would do whatever it took to protect them and get them away from here safely. "I need you all to listen closely to me and Miss Isla. Can you do that for me?"

"Caelum, hallway," Brigid's voice was sharp but quiet as she spoke. Her knees bent softly as she braced herself, her shoulders tense. The hand that held no dagger sat at her belt, ready to unsheathe the second blade waiting there if needed.

I immediately ushered the children back into the corner and moved toward Brigid, tightening my grip on my sword. "What is it?"

"A noise. In the hallway," she hissed, glancing back at the children. She took a deep breath, rolling her neck and flexing her jaw. "It sounded like several sets of footsteps."

I nodded, rolling my own shoulders back and forth, loosening them to get rid of the tension. "We can't wait any longer. On three?"

"Draw them as far away from this room as possible." She tucked a loose strand of her hair behind her ear. Cam hadn't had time to braid her hair this time, so her curls tumbled wildly around her shoulders. With the knife in her hand and the fire in her eyes, she looked like a vengeful goddess.

"Aye. Should be about four of them, according to Isla," I murmured, finally pulling my eyes from her. The last thing I wanted was Brigid to be involved in a fight, but we needed to protect these children. And she seemed unlikely to follow any instructions that told her to hide with them.

"I'll be fine, Captain," she said, reading my mind. "I can hear you worrying from over there."

"I'll always worry about you, *teine*." I returned the smile, stretching my hand out to grip the door handle. "Ready?"

She took a deep breath and nodded.

I pulled the door open, and a face I had not been prepared to see stared back at me. Surprise rushed through me, almost causing me to drop my sword, but thankfully, I held on tight. "What the fuck are you doing here?"

"I'm the captain now," the brute man said with a wide grin.

Arran. A man so violent my own father had kicked him off the crew right before I departed. The fact he was now leading the remaining members of my father's crew was disconcerting. Arran had a soul as black as his oily hair, and the scars that littered his pale body told of his victories, not defeats. As long as I'd known him, he had never lost a fight he was in, and I seriously doubted he was prepared to start today.

My stomach twisted at the thought of fighting him, and my heart raced. This would surely be a fight, and despite my confidence that my skills had improved since I'd last seen him, I was not positive I would make it out alive.

"Get them out of here," I muttered under my breath to Brigid. Even though Arran had only two other men with him, I needed Brigid to get the children to safety immediately.

"Now, now," Arran said, stepping closer to me. He turned his head to look at Brigid, and I wanted to tear his eyes from his skull. "Don't be leaving yet girl. I know someone who's looking for you."

Fucking hell. Could this day get any worse? Arran and Cliodhna working together was a recipe for a bloodbath.

"Oh, good," Brigid said, a devious smile spreading across her face, "because I'm looking for her, too."

And then, without hesitation, Brigid launched toward Arran, falling to her knees at the last second as her dagger sliced across his inner thigh. He bellowed, and I sprang into action, heading toward Arran to finish what Brigid had started.

Maybe we would make it out alive after all.

One day, I would learn to stop underestimating the woman across the hall with blood on her face.

Eliz
@ELIZIAN

BRIGID

CHAPTER FORTY

I wasn't sure what empowered me to attack the giant man that met us on the other side of the door. But I had seen the look of pure fear on Caelum's face, and that wasn't something I could forget. Caelum had told me to protect the children, but who would protect him?

I turned my attention from the larger man to the two others standing behind him. Continuing my attack, I engaged my dagger and kicked out with my legs. I employed every technique I had learned from Caelum, and the knowledge of the most painful spots on the body, courtesy of Cliodhna. I slashed and kicked until both men were lying on the ground.

I stood, wiping away the moisture gathering on my forehead. Pulling my hand away, I realized it wasn't sweat on my brow, but blood. It didn't even repulse me. The time I'd spent with Cliodhna brought back the bloodthirsty syren I had been years ago, before I became numb to suffering. These men wanted to hurt me, so I had hurt them first.

Caelum continued to engage with the larger man, who was still on his feet, swinging his sword, despite the blood pouring from the wound in his thigh. Caelum nodded at me, and I returned the gesture, running to the back of the room to gather the children.

"Time to go, little ones," I said, trying to sound calm. If I'd had a moment to spare, I would have wiped the blood from my face, but we needed to get them to safety.

"You won't get away, boy," I heard the larger man say to Caelum.

Ice filled my veins. I turned back to Isla and pressed my bloody dagger into her hands. "I have to help Caelum."

She nodded fiercely, gripping the dagger as though she knew exactly how to use it. "Go. We'll be fine."

Running back to Caelum, I pulled the spare dagger from his belt in one smooth movement, just as he swung his down at the man. The metal clashed.

"I can't wait to watch you hang," the man spat, pushing Caelum back. He turned his sword to me, and a bloody grin spread across his face. "And then I can't wait to show your woman what a real man is like."

Anger threatened to erupt from my body, and my talons extended. I didn't even have a chance to revel in the realization that they'd grown back before my feet were moving toward him.

Arms wrapped around my middle, and Caelum pulled me back. "He's alerted the authorities."

"Caelum, you have to go," Isla called from the corner. "You're wanted. They'll hang you."

"The children," I exhaled. "We can't leave them behind."

"They were never going to hurt the children. They were just trying to lure me here." I could see the frustration on Caelum's face.

"If we leave, they'll just use them again," I said. Caelum was right, but now that they knew how much the orphanage, and the children, meant to us, they would absolutely use it to their advantage.

"Caelum, unless you want to see us from behind bars, you must go now," Isla said. "Please, we'll be safe."

The large man took a step toward us, blood dripping with every step. "Oh, you're not leaving yet Caelum."

"Yes, we are," I snarled, pushing Caelum behind me as we moved toward the door. The man followed, matching us step by step. Adjusting my grip on the dagger I'd taken from Caelum's belt, I lifted it past my ear and hurled it toward the man. It was risky. I'd never thrown a dagger before, but for once, luck was on my side as it embedded in his shoulder.

He staggered back with a grunt, stopping his advancement to look down at the wound.

Taking advantage of the distraction, I pulled a reluctant Caelum into the hall and away from the man, his laughter following us as we turned and ran down the hall. While leaving Isla and the children behind with only my dagger to protect them was the last thing I wanted to do, I knew seeing Caelum get arrested would be worse. We would have to come up with another plan to guard the orphanage.

We opened the back door, and Caelum immediately pulled us back against the door as a bustle of people ran past the alley. "Fuck. Stay quiet."

We pressed ourselves against the wooden door until the band of soldiers passed. We let out a collective breath, and Caelum hung his head. I turned, taking a moment to rest my palm against his cheek. "We must find the others. They can guard the children while we get you to safety."

It looked as though he would protest.

"You're no good to us locked up, Cae," I reminded him, softly patting his cheek. I took his hand and stepped into the alley. Caelum was questioning himself, and while I wanted nothing more than to stop and reassure him, we didn't have time.

"And those children are no good to us dead," he snapped. His anger surprised me, bringing me to a halt.

He had never raised his voice in anger at me before, and while I knew he wasn't directing his anger at me, he still aimed it in my direction. "Don't speak to me like that, Caelum. I know."

"My life is not more valuable than theirs," he said, running a hand through his hair. "I'm no more important."

"No," I agreed, careful to keep my voice steady and not let my quick temper seep through. "But we cannot help these children if you are dead or imprisoned."

He sighed, darting glances toward the mouth of the alley. "You're right. Let's go. We need to find Cam and Duncan and have them keep watch at the orphanage."

I nodded, grateful that our anger didn't feed off one another and escalate. "Yes, let's go find them."

Caelum hung back as I turned toward the mouth of the alley again. After a moment, his shoulders slumped in defeat, and he followed me. Scanning the side paths, we eased out of the alley and down toward the perimeter of the orphanage, where hopefully the others were waiting.

We found Duncan first, leaning blatantly against a wall, watching the town. He straightened when he saw us approaching. "What's happened? There are soldiers swarming everywhere."

"Arran is the new captain of my father's crew," Caelum said through gritted teeth.

"That bastard?"

"Arran?" I asked. My curiosity piqued as I made the connections. "That's the big man you fought?"

Caelum nodded. "Aye, Arran is possibly even worse than my father. He has no sense of loyalty, even to himself. He was so bad my own father kicked him off the crew."

"How is he back?" Duncan asked, crossing his arms.

"This conversation is riveting, and I would also like to know the answer, but we need to get out of here," I said impatiently. "Someone called the authorities on Caelum."

Duncan cursed, standing up straighter. "Fucking hell, Caelum. You should have led with that. You've got to go."

"The orphanage is still in danger," Caelum spit out as the anger rolled off him in waves. "Someone needs to stay and protect them."

"And someone will," Duncan said. "But it won't be you."

"Then who the fuck will it be?" Caelum yelled, pacing as he ran a hand through his hair. Interlacing his hands on top of his head, he blew out a breath and came to a stop in front of us.

Duncan raised an eyebrow at me before looking back at his best friend. It seemed Caelum's temper was surprising to him as well. I understood the reasoning behind it, but it still made me shy away, wrapping my arms around myself. I *knew* Caelum would never hurt me, but it was still unnerving.

"What's really going on, Cae?" Duncan asked, his voice softer than I'd ever heard it before.

Caelum sighed. "Let's just go. Can you arrange for some of the crew to watch over the orphanage? I know they will try to get my attention again."

"Should we just move the kids?" I asked. While I was wary of Caelum's anger, I could take care of myself. These children mattered more to him than anything right now. That much was abundantly clear.

"Move them where?" he asked, his voice quiet but gruff. He took a deep breath, rolling his neck. "We are living in a cottage. We have no home, no room. Especially not for children."

"We could put them on the ship. Or hide them at your family's house," Duncan suggested. "Anywhere Arran can't find them."

"Right. Sudden activity in a decrepit mansion isn't suspicious at all." Caelum rolled his eyes and waved a hand at Duncan. "Please, just have some of our men guard the orphanage. I'm going to stay on the ship so I can be close by, but we can't leave them unprotected."

"The ship is the first place they'll look for you," I pointed out. I reached out to him, but he stepped back, shrugging my hand away. It stung, and I retracted my hand, turning my back to him. He was emotionally compromised right now, and I had to make sure Caelum wouldn't put himself in danger. "You can't get arrested."

"Why the fuck not?" he yelled. He looked around again before lowering his voice and stepping closer to Duncan and me. "Why the fuck not? It's not like I'm doing any good right now, anyway."

Before I could even think about what I was doing, I turned and grasped his shoulders, shaking slightly more roughly than I'd intended to. "Wake up, Caelum."

His eyes shot open, and he glared at me, the expression only lasting a fraction of a second before it turned into shame and his eyes cast down towards his boots.

"We don't have time for self-pity," I said, moving one hand to rest on his cheek. "If you want to protect the children and stop Cliodhna, we need to do something about it. And if you get arrested, we'll spend all our time trying to keep you alive and make no progress toward either of those other things. So, it's time to get your head out of your arse and be the captain."

It was silent for a moment as both men just stared at me, stunned.

Duncan's face broke into a respectful smile. "Aye, I actually agree with her. It's about time someone talked some sense into you."

Caelum looked at us for another moment before he laughed, and a smile begrudgingly crossed his face. "Who knew this was all it took to get you two to agree on something?"

"Listen to your woman, Captain," Duncan groused. "I'll grab some of Alan's men and we'll watch the orphanage."

"Where should I go?" Caelum asked, his shoulders slumping.

"Back to the cottage with the others. Where you will sleep, eat, and come up with a plan to stop Arran, the rest of your father's crew, and that damn goddess."

"What if we can't stop them?" he asked, his voice barely audible.

I wanted nothing more than to wrap my arms around this man. This man who had literally walked through bloodstained halls to rescue me. "We can, and we will. You don't have to do this alone."

He looked at me for a moment, before nodding, as if he were trying to convince himself. "Aye, okay. Let's move then."

"The other syrens are near Galen's if you want to head back with them. I'll work out who will stay behind with Cam and Alan," Duncan said. He looked at me for a moment. "Brigid, keep him in line."

Despite Duncan's attitude toward me, it would appear my speech to Caelum had gained his respect. "Protect those children."

"Aye, we will," he said. He clapped Caelum on the shoulder. "Get out of here now and watch out for the authorities."

"We will," I promised. Even if it took everything in me, I would keep Caelum from the gallows. He had too much goodness to offer the world.

Eliz
@ELIZIAN

B RIGID

CHAPTER FORTY-ONE

"Are you sure we can't stay on *The Nehalennia*?" Caelum asked for what felt like the tenth time as we snuck through the alleys out of Brinemoor.

"Yes," I whispered, trying to keep my patience. I understood why he wanted to be close, but staying where his father's crew could easily find him was not the smart decision. And if he was thinking rationally, he would agree. "We're finding the syrens, and then we're going back to the cottage."

He grumbled something unintelligible, but continued walking with me.

"Brigid," a voice hissed off to the side.

We turned to see the other syrens huddled together in a small alleyway behind a building. Looking around for any evidence of the constable or his hired enforcers, we moved to join them. "Are you all safe?"

"Yes," Kyla replied. "Are you?"

"Not exactly," I replied, glancing briefly at Caelum. "The others are staying behind to guard the children, but we need to leave now and get back to the cottage."

"Why do the children need guarding?" Maira asked, her eyes narrowing.

"The remaining members of my father's crew are using them to get to me," Caelum explained, his face stony.

"And you're running away, because?" her voice was sardonic and the smirk on her face showed her true thoughts.

In an instant, red flooded my vision, and I had Maira pressed up against the building, my forearm across her throat. Her eyes were wide and, for the first time since I'd met her, she looked scared. "Do not speak like that to him," I hissed, not recognizing my own voice.

"That's enough, Brigid," Caelum said, resting his hand on my shoulder. When I didn't let go, he pulled slightly. "Come on. We need to go."

Glaring at Maira for a moment longer, I pulled my arm back, and her hand immediately went to cup her throat. "He is leaving to protect those children. Which is more than you've done." I stepped back with Caelum and let him guide me away from the syrens. I didn't look back to see if they followed us as we walked away from Brinemoor and down the path leading out of town.

"*Teine* now is probably not the time to tell you how much I appreciate it, but thank you for defending me. It means a lot."

I looked at him as we walked, trying to cool my anger. "Why isn't this the time?"

He grinned wickedly, the dejected frown now erased from his face. "Because it would involve showing you just how much I appreciate it—without clothes involved."

And just like that, the remnants of anger rushed out of me, and a laugh bubbled up. "You're right. Now is not the time."

He reached down to squeeze my hand. "Thank you, *teine*. For all of it."

"Even for yelling at you?" I asked, raising my eyebrow as we walked.

"Aye, even for yelling at me," he sighed, more serious than I had been expecting. "I needed it."

"You did," I agreed, "but for now, let's just get back. We can talk about it more later."

He nodded, pulling me in to press a quick kiss to my forehead before lacing our fingers together as we walked. I felt the syrens behind us, trailing at a distance. I briefly felt regret for what I had done to Maira, but it faded as quickly as it came. She needed to understand that her words had consequences, and since no one had ever dared show her that before, the responsibility fell to me.

No one would harm Caelum. Not Maira, not Arran, not Cliodhna. And especially not Caelum himself.

I could feel Caelum's hesitancy as we moved further from Brinemoor. He didn't want to leave the children, which I respected, but we needed to keep him out of jail. Being arrested would be worse for us all, including the children.

Arriving back at the cottage, I squeezed Caelum's fingers. "We're safe, Caelum."

He shook his head and laughed. "For now."

"We will stop them," I said, pulling him to face me. The other syrens looked at us, but continued around into the cottage. I met Caelum's gaze. "Anyone who needs to use children in a war between men deserves to suffer."

He looked at me for a moment, then smiled widely. "And who is going to make them suffer, *teine*?"

I returned the grin, the smile coming easier than I had expected given the past weeks. "Us, of course."

"Now, you know I'm not that kind of pirate," he teased, tapping my nose with his finger.

"But I am that kind of syren. And you're able to be that kind of pirate if it's called for."

Laughing again, he pulled me into his chest, wrapping his arms tightly around me. "I am so glad to have met you, Brigid."

I snuggled into his chest, inhaling his unique smell of sunshine and sea salt, relishing feeling safe and cared for. "Same to you, Caelum."

"Let's get inside," he said, cupping my face in his hands. "I've been going crazy without you."

"You saved me, Captain," I whispered, reaching up to rub my thumb over his beard. "Thank you."

His green eyes darkened, and he leaned down, pressing his lips against mine. I groaned at the contact, opening my mouth to deepen the kiss. Caelum's chest rumbled as he slid his hand up from my cheek to tangle in my hair, tipping my head back. His tongue slid against my lower lip, and I eagerly opened my mouth, gripping his shirt at his waist as our tongues met. I had desperately missed this. I had desperately missed *Caelum*.

His other hand slowly ran down the side of my body, squeezing at my waist and my hip. The kiss deepened, and Caelum pulled me impossibly closer to him. I wrapped my arms around his neck, moving my lips with his. I couldn't get enough of him, the feel of his body pressed against mine, the smell of him, the roughness of his palms even through my clothes. It was intoxicating, and I wanted more.

We pulled back slightly, our foreheads touching as we both panted for air. His breath puffed against my face as he whispered. "I missed you."

I smiled, my lips brushing against his chin, beneath his lower lip. I leaned up on my tiptoes and pulled that swollen lip between my teeth. He groaned, the sound vibrating through my body and sending tingles down my spine. I pulled myself closer to him, and we resumed kissing, his hands moving over my body and coming to rest on my lower back.

"Hey!" a voice shouted from the house. We pulled apart, but remained in each other's arms as I looked over my shoulder to see Maira glaring from the doorway. "Are you two going to come in and use the perfectly good bedroom? Or are you going to lie down and fuck right there in the grass?"

"One day, I'm going to snap and kill her," Caelum muttered under his breath. He took a deep breath and pressed another quick kiss to my lips before stepping back. Looking down at the impressively large bulge in the front of his pants, he cursed slightly.

I grinned mischievously, reaching down to adjust him so the bulge was at least a little less noticeable. "Suppose we should probably go inside."

"That's not helping, *teine*," he grumbled, swatting my hands away. He leaned down to press his lips to my ear, making me shiver as he spoke. "And I will get you back for that, just so you know."

My grin grew wider. This was going to be fun. I hadn't felt this free in a long time, and after what I had gone through with Cliodhna, I had honestly not been expecting to get back to this state of mind so soon. But Caelum brought out the good in me, whether I wanted him to or not. I leaned back and winked. "Promise?"

"You're trouble," he said, a warning look on his face. Without another word, he pulled me into his arms, lifted me off the ground, and spun me around. "Let's go inside."

I raised an eyebrow and smirked. "To do what?"

"Well, that depends on if we're interrupted again," he said, smiling as he carried me into the house.

Elizi
@ELIZIAN

CHAPTER FORTY-TWO

Caelum carried me into the cottage, glaring at Maira as we passed her in the kitchen. She smirked as he carried me down the hall and into our room, kicking the door shut behind us so forcefully it shook the walls.

"A little eager there?" I teased, tracing my finger over his temple and down his cheek.

"You have no idea, *teine*," he said, setting me gently on my feet. He pressed a kiss to my forehead that was so tender it made me nearly cry. This man was truly the definition of *good*. And I would never let him forget it.

"Show me," I whispered, ignoring the protests of my sore muscles as I rose on my tiptoes to brush my lips against his.

His hands found my waist, and he squeezed gently, holding himself back. His eyes burned green as he bit his lip and shook his head. "You're still healing, though."

"So, you think you can do more damage than she did?" I asked quietly. I knew within the very deepest recesses of my soul that Caelum would never hurt me. *Could* never hurt me. Not physically, at least.

He pulled back, his eyes now horrified instead of aroused. "I would never."

"Then we won't have any issues," I said, pressing into his chest. I wanted Caelum in every way I could have him. The weeks spent without him had only solidified the fact that we belonged together, for better or worse.

Caelum still looked hesitant, his hands wavering on my hips as he chewed on his lip. It made me want to nip his lip with my teeth, but I had a better idea.

Deciding for him, I stepped back and turned around, climbing onto the bed in the center of the room. I looked at him over my shoulder. "Caelum, I want this. I want you. But only if you want me, too."

He swayed, as if he wanted to move toward me, but his feet froze in place. I stared into his wide eyes, and the arousal and pure desire were clear.

Emboldened by his gaze, and honored by his restraint, I reached down to the hem of my shirt and pulled it over my head. Before I could stop to feel self-conscious about the scars that now littered my body, I tugged down my pants, wiggling to pull them over the curve of my hips and thighs. Now fully naked in front of this man I desperately wanted, I straightened up, pulling my shoulders back and holding my chin high. This was *Caelum*. There was nothing for me to be afraid of.

Apparently, taking my clothes off was all the push Caelum needed. The breath rushed out of him, his chest visibly collapsing, and then I was in his arms, his face buried in my neck.

"You're beautiful," he breathed, pulling back to let his eyes feast on me. They passed over my body from head to toe once, twice, before his lips crashed into mine.

The kiss was gentle and passionate. All-consuming. Nothing existed apart from Caelum's lips on mine. He cradled the back of my head like it was the finest treasure he'd ever laid hands on, and kissed me like I was the last drop of fresh water on a deserted island.

He pulled back slightly, just enough for us to take a breath. His eyes searched mine for any signs of discomfort, which I knew he wouldn't find. "Are you sure, *teine*? We have all the time in the world."

I smoothed a hand over his face. "I am sure, and no, we don't. Cliodhna is coming. But that doesn't change how badly I want this time with you. Even if it's just holding you against me for the night."

"I think we can do a bit better than that." He smiled widely and pushed me back gently until my head rested against the mattress.

Taking his lead, I slid over to lie in the center of the bed atop the blankets. Thankfully, I didn't have to wait long for him to join me.

I could tell he was still being careful not to put too much of his weight on me, but I was physically fine, and I wanted to feel him. Tugging him over to me, he pulled back once more.

"Caelum, please?" I said, unashamedly pouting my lip out. "I am fine, and I want this."

"I know you do," he said, peppering my chest and neck with light kisses. "And I want this too, more than you know. I just don't want to hurt you. I'm afraid."

"My body is okay," I breathed, arching up into him as he nibbled at the spot where my neck met my shoulder. "And if you keep denying me, I'm going to get very upset."

"I wouldn't dream of upsetting you, *teine*," he said, smiling against my skin. He continued pressing kisses to my body, moving from my neck to my chest and down to my breasts.

I lost myself in everything he did. The warmth of his body against mine, the scratching of his pants against my legs, the smell of him, the feel of his calloused hands as they roved over my body. I thought I might struggle with his hands roaming over me, might mistake his touches for Cliodhna's as they mapped out the planes of my body, but all I felt was my own arousal. All I felt was him.

There was no mistaking the way the torn skin on his palms caught on my sides, scraping gently against the skin at my ribs and sending shivers down my spine. There was no mistaking the prickle of his beard against my stomach as he pressed open mouth kisses there, covering every scar and mark left behind.

There was no mistaking Caelum for anyone else.

He was one of a kind. And he was *mine*.

It was more intoxicating than the ale I had drank with him that night in the pub.

And I wanted more.

Raking my hands through his hair, I tightened my grip and tugged on the strands, pushing his head down my body. He resisted my suggestion for a moment, smiling wickedly up at me before lowering his mouth to the soft flesh of my belly. Pressing kisses there, sparks surged through my body, traveling from his lips down to my core where wetness built. His teeth nipped at the skin, his tongue following closely behind to soothe the bite.

I was quickly losing my mind—and my patience. I pushed at his head again, trying to get him where I wanted him, between my legs.

"Patience, *teine*," he whispered, laughing softly. I closed my eyes as the puff of cool breath met my skin, shivering as goosebumps enveloped my body.

Before I could curse at him for denying me once more, his lips began moving toward their destination. He kissed over the tops of my thighs, shifting in the small bed so his broad shoulders spread my legs wider, settling more comfortably between them.

"Open your eyes," he whispered, tapping the outside of my thigh as his hands curled beneath them to open my legs wider for him.

I didn't want to. I knew the sight that awaited would undo me, but I wanted him to keep going. Struggling against the waves of pleasure, I opened my eyes. Immediately, I regretted and relished the decision. The look on his face, the pure and undeniable attraction, was more than I had been expecting. His pupils blown so wide the green was nearly invisible, and his cheeks flushed beneath the hair of his beard. But the determination on his face, the set of his jaw, was what really did it.

Then he winked at me, ducked his head, and tore me apart.

His lips moved rhythmically against the flesh of my core, and I writhed beneath his attention. The weight of his body pinning down my legs, the smell of him mixing with my arousal, and the feeling of his lips and tongue overwhelmed me. My eyes slid shut as

I writhed, trying to move away from him yet closer at the same time.

Immediately, his ministrations stopped, and he pulled back, blowing a soft breath against me. "Ah, ah. Eyes open, *teine*. Watch me bring you pleasure."

I groaned, but took advantage of the reprieve, opening my eyes to gaze at him. It was weak, I knew, and he laughed loudly, shaking against my inner thighs.

The vibrations of his laughter moved right through me, and I instinctively clenched my thighs together, catching his attention. The smile slipped from his face and his eyes burned with renewed intensity as he ducked his head back between my legs. "Keep them open, Brigid. You close them, I stop."

I ignored him, grinding against him to find friction.

His hands clamped around my thighs like vices, almost hard enough to bruise, but gentle enough I knew they wouldn't. He squeezed my legs when I didn't immediately answer, his voice a growl. "Say it, Brigid. Say you'll keep them open."

I glared at him again, gasping at the sensations taking over my body. I wanted to defy him, but I didn't want to prolong this anymore. "They'll stay open, they'll stay open. Don't you dare stop," I panted.

And by some miracle, I kept my word as he brought me to orgasm with his tongue, and lips, and teeth. But it wasn't enough. I wanted to be filled by him, and after my thighs stopped shaking, I squirmed, trying to convey that message with my body. I had never wanted this before, had never wanted to find pleasure in the arms of a man. But this was *my* man. My Caelum. He was different in every way.

He grinned, still holding my legs with his body weight as he traced a finger down my sternum. "Needy little thing. What do you want?"

Tracing his fingers down over my thighs now, he knew exactly what I wanted. My clit caught a bit of friction as I moved my hips against him. I moaned louder than I had expected, but it felt delicious. I should have cared that the others would hear us through the thin walls, but I finally had this man between my legs and, with no interruptions in sight, I planned to take full advantage of it.

"Words, *teine*," he breathed, moving his finger from my thigh and tracing it over my center, sending sparks through my body and causing my body to jerk slightly. "Tell me what you want, and I'll give it to you. I'll always give you what you want."

It was a great effort, but I pushed myself up to sitting, resting on my elbows to meet his gaze. "Inside me, Captain. Now."

The small sliver of green around his irises vanished, and his eyes went dark at my words. His finger stopped, and he pushed up, lingering between my thighs as he moved back up to eye level with me. "Are you sure? We can wait for this part. As long as you need."

"If you ask me that again, I'm going to hurt you," I said, patting his cheek gently. While I appreciated his caring, I was beyond waiting now. "I want you to fill me up."

He didn't answer with words, but the kiss he initiated was answer enough. The taste of myself on his lips was intoxicating and the kiss immediately turned to more. I hitched a leg around his hip, digging my heel into his back and pulling him against me.

"Impatient," Caelum whispered breathlessly as he pulled back, grinning at me. He reached down to run his hand along the outside of my leg that wrapped around him. "I have a question."

"Now?"

He shook his head, smiling, but his gaze turned serious. "*Teine*, I need to know. Have you ever been with a man?"

I had been expecting his question, but it still made me pause. I didn't like admitting my inexperience in anything, but I knew he wouldn't go any further until I answered him. "No. Only with other women."

His eyes shone for a moment, and I could tell he felt honored. He was easy to read as his eyes betrayed his every emotion. He nodded and bent down to kiss me again. "If it hurts you at all, you promise to tell me? We go at your pace, Brigid. Your pace, or not at all."

"Nothing you do right now will hurt me, Caelum. Nothing you

can *ever* do will hurt me more than they already have. Please don't treat me like I will break."

"I'll go slow." His voice was firm and brokered no argument.

"Only at first," I argued back.

"We'll see." He sighed as if exasperated, but I could tell he was trying to hide his enjoyment.

"Sounds like you need to take your clothes off," I said, rubbing my nose against his neck and pressing kisses along the skin there, breathing him in.

"Want to help me with that?" he asked, his voice hitching slightly.

"No," I replied, continuing to kiss at his neck, pleased with the growing arousal I could feel pressed against my thigh. "You're able to undress yourself."

I could feel him roll his eyes at me, but he pulled back far enough to pull his shirt over his head and then shifted his weight, removing his pants. Finally, he was naked. He paused just long enough to let me drink in the sight of him, of his toned muscles and the smattering of dark hair that led down his chest and stomach, thickening and darkening around his arousal.

He opened his mouth to speak, and my eyes snapped back up to his face.

"If you ask me if I'm sure I want to do this one more time..." I warned, raising an eyebrow.

"I'm always going to ask you if you're sure, *teine*," he whispered. I reached out to hit his arm, his eyes sparkling with laughter. The laughter didn't last long, though, as his eyes changed when he looked over my body. "You're beautiful. You're mine."

"Then come here and show me," I taunted, nudging at the back of his thigh with my foot.

Smiling at me, he wrapped his hands around the outside of my thighs, spreading my legs and hitching them up around his hips before leaning down over me. He squeezed at my legs in a warning. "Slowly, *teine*. Don't rush me. Don't rush *this*."

I opened my mouth to protest, but he reached a hand between us and slid inside of me. At first, he only slid in an inch before stopping, but it just spurred me on, and I pushed against him more. It felt *good*, and I wanted *more.*

He withdrew completely, raising an eyebrow at me. "What did I *just* say?"

"That you want me to encourage you to go faster and make me scream?" I offered with an innocent smile.

"If you need me to slow down, just say it." He shook his head and entered me once more, thrusting shallowly as he bent down to kiss me slowly and deeply.

My body wrapped itself in the sensations, and my heart burst with emotions. Tears sprang to my eyes. Not from pain, but from the overwhelming emotions buzzing through my body. I *loved* this man.

I sniffled, reaching up to wipe away the tear that had escaped.

Caelum immediately stopped, pulling back with a look of concern as his eyes scanned over every inch of my body frantically. "Did I hurt you? What's wrong?"

I shook my head just as frantically, never wanting him to think he had caused my tears. "No, absolutely not. You didn't hurt me at all."

His face softened, and he bent down to place a gentle kiss by my eye, wicking away the tear and licking it from his lips. "Then why are you crying?"

I hesitated. If I told him I loved him and scared him away, I wasn't sure I could handle the rejection. I kept my revelations to myself, for now at least. But I would tell him *a* truth, if not *the* truth. He deserved that, at the very least. "I'm happy, Caelum. You make me happy."

He smiled softly, wiping his thumb across my lips before ducking down to kiss me so tenderly I wanted to cry again. "Let me keep making you happy, then."

"By all means," I said, smiling as he entered me again. The feeling of our bodies colliding overwhelmed everything else in the room. There was nothing but him. Nothing but *us.*

"You make me happy, too," he said, tangling a hand in my hair and thrusting into me slowly, his eyes closing as he groaned. "Happier than I think I've ever been."

"We can be happy together," I said quietly, relishing the feel of his body against mine.

A deep thrust had my eyes fluttering shut and my nails digging into his arm as a loud moan escaped my lips. He stopped. His words were soft as he tucked a finger under my chin. "Eyes, Brigid. Look at me while I make you happy."

I obeyed, and then he did make me happy. All night long.

Elizianna
@ELIZIANNA.THE.ONE

Chapter Forty-Three

Holding Brigid in my arms was the most peaceful I'd felt in my entire life. And I never wanted to let her go.

It was dark now, had been for hours, but I couldn't sleep. It had been tough, leaving the children behind, and only Brigid's words and touches made things more bearable.

Despite having only had Brigid in my life for a short time, I felt incomplete without her beside me. Maybe it was my tendency to jump in feet first with everything I did, but we felt right. It was like I had been waiting for her my whole life.

I had been with other women, sure, but none had made me feel the way Brigid did. None had burrowed their way so quickly into my soul. Her fire drew me in, and I *wanted* to be burned. I craved it.

Tightening my arms around her sleeping form, I pressed my lips to her hair. She mumbled in her sleep and nuzzled her face further into my neck. Her breath tickled as it evened back out. I should sleep too, but it was the first night since we had gotten her back that Brigid was truly mine again, and I didn't want to miss a moment of it. Morning was still hours away, but I knew it would arrive before I was ready.

Our time together earlier had been exactly what I needed, and though I still worried her body was healing, I knew she needed it, too. Sighing, I adjusted myself further into the pillows and closed my eyes, content to lie here, basking in her body until morning finally came.

A loud bang rang through the house, and unfamiliar voices filled the air. I shot up in bed, my body tense as there could be no good reason that strangers would enter the house at this hour.

"Brigid," I whispered, shaking her awake. She blinked up at me sleepily. "Someone's in the house."

She sat up, sleep clearing from her face immediately as she looked around, searching the darkness for an invisible enemy. "Who?"

Before I could answer, someone was pounding on the door to our bedroom. "Caelum Loinseach, open this door."

Brigid flinched at the noise and looked at me, her eyes wide. "Who the fuck is that?"

My blood ran cold at the sound of my full name, and I froze, my eyes on the door. The formality of the voice, along with the fact they knew my last name, could only mean one thing. Soldiers. Brigid pushed at my arm, spurring me back to the moment. "Clothes, we need clothes."

Quickly, we both left the bed and pulled on the clothes we had shed. Brigid had barely pulled her shirt back over her head when the door frame splintered and the door swung open. Two soldiers stood there, shackles clanking in their hands.

"Caelum Loinseach?" one of them asked. He was tall, but scrawny, his sickly pale skin sunburned across his face and his scraggly black hair pulled into a low, greasy ponytail.

Brigid reached down to lace her fingers through mine, rolling her shoulders back and lifting her chin defiantly, despite the fact she was only in a shirt. "Why do you want him?"

"We will charge him for piracy and murder, young lady. You should thank us for taking him in," the other one said, sneering at her with crooked teeth. It made my hackles rise, and I knew it would irritate her as well.

I felt Brigid tense up beside me, and if she wasn't careful, she would find herself coming with me. I tugged at her hand and shot her a warning glance, shaking my head slightly. She had said earlier I was no use to them in jail, but it would definitely not be helpful if both of us ended up there. She argued with her eyes, but finally deflated and let go of my hand. I turned to the soldiers. "Are you really going to do this?"

"You murdered your father," the one with the ponytail said, as if that explained everything. And it did.

"You were friends with Kellan."

"I don't answer to you."

I couldn't help it but snort. I hadn't expected him to admit it, but I knew that my father's influence ran to the highest levels of this town. Despite the horrible things he'd done, money was very good at making people look the other way. "My father was a thief and a bastard. He was stealing fucking children. He was far from a good man."

The pony-tailed one shrugged. "Don't matter none. You still killed him. And now you'll have to face your punishment."

"Are you taking anyone else?" I asked, thankful that Duncan and Cameron had stayed in Brinemoor to watch over the orphanage. But if they knew anything about the true circumstances of my father's death, everyone in the house was in danger.

"You're the only one wanted," the one with the crooked teeth replied. He shook the shackles. "Now let's go. No more talking."

"You can't just take him in the middle of the night," Brigid protested, stepping in front of me. As much as I admired and loved her tenacity, it would not serve either of us well right now.

"Lady, we can do whatever we want. If he hadn't run and hid, we wouldn't be doing this now." The man tried to step around her, but Brigid stepped with him, crossing her arms over her chest. He sighed and crossed his own arms, jangling the shackles in his hand.

"You followed us from town," I said. There was no other way they could have found out where we were staying. "We returned hours ago. So, you absolutely waited until the middle of the night to come in."

The pony-tailed one rolled his eyes. "You're a murderer. You don't get to question us, boy. Come on."

He shouldered Brigid out of the way and clamped the shackles around my wrists. He bent, shoving my feet into my boots before pulling me toward the door. Brigid stumbled but caught herself, her eyes blazing. If these men weren't careful, there would be two more murders.

"Get the others, and tell them what's happened," I said, catching her gaze. "You're in charge now."

She shook her head as panic entered her gaze. "No. I can't be in charge. You're the captain."

The men shoved me again, pushing me into the hallway. I turned to look over my shoulder, meeting her eyes once more. "You're in charge, Brigid. You can do this."

She nodded, wrapping her arms around herself as they yanked me away, shoving me out of the house and into the cool night.

"So, where are we going?" I asked as they led me down the path toward a waiting horse and buggy.

"You're going to the noose, pirate scum," the one with the crooked teeth sneered.

I froze as my stomach dropped to my feet. They wouldn't hang me outright. Would they?

"There's no trial for pirates and murderers. You'll hang by sundown tomorrow." They threw me into the back of the buggy and secured my shackles to a chain fastened to the wooden floor.

I was going to hang, and Brigid had no idea. I had no way of telling her the fate that awaited me. Now I needed her to save me.

Elizi
@ELIZIAN

CHAPTER FORTY-FOUR

My heart shattered as I watched the horse and cart travel further into the distance. I had just made it back to Caelum, and now we separated again. Despite his assurances, I knew this was not fine. That *he* was not fine. We needed to free him.

The cart finally dipped over the last hill and was no longer visible. Caelum had left me in charge, and now I needed to step up. Taking a deep breath to steady my body and mind, I turned and went back into the house. I headed down the hallway, pounding on the bedroom doors. "Join me in the kitchen. Now," I shouted through each of the doors.

The kitchen filled up quickly, as the commotion had woken up the house. Once everyone joined me, I cleared my throat, trying to channel the energy Caelum needed me to have.

"The authorities just came. They arrested Caelum for his father's murder," I said bluntly. My anger knew no limits, but right now, my anxiety overshadowed it. Swallowing, I let myself lean into the fire growing in my belly. My anger bubbled up from where I carefully tried to smother it. "We are going to rescue him."

"That's what all that noise was?" Maira asked. "How did they find this place?"

"Caelum thinks they followed us from town."

From the corner of my eye, I saw Alan and some of his men straighten, looking at each other. "Are we in danger, too?"

Irritation surged at their selfish concerns, but I took a deep breath, in through my nose and out through my mouth. Caelum would not snap at them. Caelum would be patient and explain what was going on. "No, they said it was only Caelum they wanted."

They all visibly relaxed. "We need to find Cam and Duncan and the others to warn them."

"We're all going back into town," I said. "We'll stay on *The Nehalennia*. Between Caelum and the orphanage, we can no longer afford to stay here. We only came here because no one knew we were here."

"And now they do," Lena finished.

"Aye, now they do. So, it's time to go back to town. We need to protect the children and figure out how to get Caelum out of jail," I said. A breeze passing through the cottage reminded me I was still in only a shirt. "We're going now, so everyone get dressed and pack what you need."

"If Caelum's father's crew is behind this, won't they be suspicious if we come back into town?" Kyla asked.

I hesitated. She had a good point. If we all showed up after they arrested Caelum, they would have an even bigger reason to watch us closely, and perhaps would have enough influence to have more of us arrested. "Alan, you and your men go ahead first with Lena, and get the others back to the ship. We will meet you there."

"You'll be okay walking alone?" Alan asked, worry furrowing his brow.

"We won't be walking," I replied. "Now, get moving."

Alan and his men listened without question, quickly returning to their rooms. The syrens and Lena lingered, all moving closer to me.

"What's your plan, Brigid?" Kyla asked softly. "I know you have one."

"To get Caelum out of jail," I said, turning to leave the room. I stopped in the hallway, looking back over my shoulder. "And then to kill Cliodhna."

I left them behind, heading back to my room. Running a hand through my hair, my mind swirled. Alan and his men would leave first, making their way to the ship by land while we would approach the ship in our syren forms. Keeping the syrens out of view in Brinemoor would make it easier for us to save Caelum. Kyla was right. I had a plan. But first, we needed to make it back to town.

While packing mine and Caelum's belongings, a soft knock sounded at the door. Lena pushed it open and entered the space, closing the door behind her and leaning against it. She glanced at the items on the bed. "I suppose you're taking your weapons with you."

I nodded, shoving the daggers into my bag. I didn't have time for small talk, but I knew better than to ignore her outright. "Caelum will need them once he's free."

She was silent for a moment, and I could feel her gaze, heavy on my back.

"Can I help you, Lena?" I asked, pausing my packing and turning to her with a sigh. While there was tentative trust in the witch, I was still wary of her presence. From what Caelum had told me, she had no real reason to stay with us, other than her mysterious history with Cliodhna.

"Perhaps." I stopped packing and turned my full attention to her. She hesitated for a moment, before sighing and stepping away from the door and closer to me. "You plan to kill Cliodhna."

"Was that a question?" I asked, raising an eyebrow.

"No," she said, smiling. "My question is: how do you plan to kill her?"

I sighed and sat down on the edge of the bed. "To be honest, I haven't considered the specifics yet. But I figure removing her head from her body would be a good place to start."

Her eyes widened, and she broke out in laughter; the rich sound visibly moved through her entire body. "Yes, I suppose that would be a good start."

"Do you have any other ideas?" Lena seemed to know much more about the truth behind Cliodhna than the rest of us. If any of us knew how to kill a goddess, it would be her.

Her gray eyes twinkled as she smiled. "I might have a few tricks up my sleeve."

I smiled back at her, knowing she would not elaborate further. Turning back to my packing, I chuckled. "I imagine you do."

Hours later, pacing anxiously by the door, I waited for the sun to begin peeking over the horizon. Alan and his men had left nearly an hour ago, and I had decided it best to wait until they got to Brinemoor and boarded the ship before leaving the cottage.

Lena had left with them, carrying the bags of clothes and weapons. Now, it was simply a matter of waiting until the sun began to cast rays of gold over the water, and then we would slip into the sea and make our way to the harbor.

"Do we think she'll know we're in the water?" Kyla asked, stepping up beside me.

"I'm sure she will," Maira responded from across the room where she sat with Nerina and Caledonia. "The real question is if she'll do something about it."

"It doesn't matter right now," I replied, turning to face the rest of them spread throughout the cottage. "We just need to work together and get to Brinemoor as quickly as possible."

"Remind me, why are we risking the seas to save your pirate again?" Maira asked, rolling her eyes and picking at her nails. "Could we not just walk with the others?"

"If we approached in a large group, they would see us, making it more difficult to save Caelum," I explained, trying to keep my patience. "And if they move to arrest the other crew members, we'll need to watch over the orphanage."

Maira paused, looking at me with narrowed eyes. "Brigid, why do you care so much?"

"Why *don't* you care?" I shot back. "These children have done nothing wrong. Are they so different from us?"

"Not the children," she said, rolling her eyes. "I understand that, though I may not agree. I'm asking why you care so much about Caelum and his crew. You just left us to be with them, and now it seems you hold them above us. Are we not your family?"

"You left me too," I replied, taking a step toward her. All the anger I'd been holding, all the feelings of abandonment, surged up in my words. "Was I not *your* family? I saved a man who had tried to save me as a child, Maira. A child. And you shunned me for it. Is it any wonder I stayed with them?"

"Now is not the time for this." Kyla's voice was calm as she stepped between us. "None of us handled things like we should have, but the fact remains, we *are* a family. And we will rescue Caelum because he is a man who deserves our help."

Maira didn't reply, but held my gaze for another moment before she huffed and looked away. Turning to the window, I saw the sun had finally set. "It's time to go."

Kyla looked between Maira and me. "They should be there by now. Let's go."

Together, we undressed and left the cottage, heading down to the water. Entering the sea, I lingered closer to the shore as the others transformed. Even though Lena said her magic would make my transformation painless, I was apprehensive. Taking a deep breath and bracing my core, I slipped beneath the water and transformed.

In an instant, my body changed, and I felt nothing beyond a slight tingling sensation. Relief washed through me and if I wasn't underwater, I would have cried. Being a syren was my calling. The pain Cliodhna had cursed me with had been a punishment for choosing a man over my queen, but now I was free to make my own choices again.

The others looked back at me, watching expectantly. Even

though Kyla was our new leader, I was in charge for the moment. For an instant, I wanted to open my mouth and see if my song had returned, but I couldn't bear it if it had not, so instead I nodded and shot off toward the harbor.

We had work to do.

Elizi
@ELIZIAN

BRIGID

CHAPTER FORTY-FIVE

Approaching Brinemoor, we swam toward the end of the harbor where *The Nehalennia* sat. Our heads popped up above the water as we silently moved toward the docks. There were lanterns on the deck, and I could hear voices. Hopefully, it was our own crew and not more soldiers coming to raid the ship at dawn.

"Brigid!" a voice whispered. Looking up at the railing, I saw Cameron leaning over the side, relief clear on his face even in the fading darkness. "We've been waiting for you. Come aboard."

After transforming back in the water, we all climbed the ladder and boarded the ship, where Cameron was waiting with blankets. He handed them out one by one, but when he got to me, he paused, throwing the blanket around my shoulders while simultaneously pulling me into his arms. "I'm glad you're safe."

I tensed for a moment, shocked by the feeling of someone else's arms around me, someone other than Caelum. But this was Cam, and he had been nothing but welcoming to me. Relaxing into his arms, I let myself find comfort. "We need to save him, Cam."

"We will," he said, rubbing my back. "But for now, let's get you all some dry clothes and talk about what we know."

I nodded, taking the blanket from him and wrapping it tightly around myself. I turned to the other syrens, wrapped in blankets, waiting for me to speak. "Get dressed. We have work to do."

Cam stepped up beside me. "Head below. Finn will take you to Lena. She has clothes for you all." They nodded and stood, following Finn below deck. As they left, Cam held out a smaller bag for me. "These are yours."

Dropping the blanket to the deck, I laughed as Cam immediately jerked his eyes up toward the night sky as I dressed. "I'm decent now, Cam. And you know I don't care about that."

"I know." He grinned, bringing his eyes back to my face. "Doesn't mean I want to give Cae a reason to beat me up later."

"You've arrived," Duncan said, startling me as he walked up behind us. "Is everyone safe?"

"Except Caelum." I rolled my eyes. Duncan's newfound concern for me and the others was surprising, but I doubted it would last much longer. Remembering Caelum's words, I took a deep breath, putting aside my differences with the blond man in order to take care of everyone. "How is the orphanage?"

"Safe." He crossed his arms over his chest, never breaking eye contact. "What happened at the cottage?"

"What did Alan tell you?" There was the Duncan I had been expecting.

"They arrested Caelum and took him away in the middle of the night. And that you sent them ahead."

"That's all?"

"He's not exactly observant, Brigid." He shifted his weight from one foot to the other.

I snorted. "They must have followed us from town and waited until we were all asleep. They busted right through the front door and all but pulled him out of bed."

"What were the charges?" Cam asked, though the frown he sported told me he already knew what they'd be.

"Piracy and murder," I replied. "The men who arrested him seemed to be friends with Kellan."

Duncan cursed. "Of course they are. Kellan had nearly everyone in town in his pocket."

"We need to find out when the trial will be," Cam said, wringing his hands together.

"About that..." Duncan hesitated, gathering his thoughts. "On the way here, I heard people talking about a hanging at sunset tonight. I don't think there will be a trial."

Now it was my turn to curse. "Why the fuck didn't you lead with that information? We've got to go get him. Right now."

"You're not in charge here, syren," Duncan said, his face hardening. "I'm the first mate. And we can't go in without a plan."

"I am in charge, actually." My voice was colder than the wind cutting across the deck. "Caelum trusted me to free him and protect those children. So, if you have a problem taking orders from a syren or a woman, you better get over them quickly."

"Fighting amongst ourselves will do no good," a female voice said. Lena stepped out from behind Duncan, silent as always.

"You know nothing about being in charge of a crew," Duncan hissed.

"And you know nothing about being part of something bigger than yourself," I shot back. Duncan may have been Caelum's best friend, but it was clear he was territorial from the first moment I met him. He was unwilling to share his friend, and unwilling to let anyone be close to them, except for a select few. "We have to work together."

He stared at me for a moment and then scoffed and walked away, heading below deck.

"Caelum put you in charge?" Cam's voice was quiet.

I nodded. "Aye, he did. As they were taking him away. I will make him proud, Cam. I'll do what he's asked of me."

"I know you will, Brigid." He reached out to squeeze my shoulder. "Don't mind Duncan. He's angry he wasn't there to help stop them."

"There was no stopping them," I sighed. "They came for him, and if any of us had interfered, they would have taken us, too."

"So, the real question is: what are we going to do about it?" Lena interrupted.

I paused. What were we going to do? Caelum was in jail, awaiting the noose. Cliodhna was still out there, biding her time to strike back at us. And there was still the threat of Arran and his remaining crew to the orphanage. There were too many directions to consider and not enough people to use. We would need to handle one at a time. But which would be first?

Logically, I knew Caelum would want me to protect the orphanage above all else, but I couldn't do that. We had already lost Sorcha and Maddock. I could not watch anyone else I loved die. And I loved Caelum. I may not have told him yet, but I did. Last night made me realize it, and this had only solidified it.

He had saved me, in more ways than one. And now it was time to save him.

"Gather the crew and the syrens."

Lena raised an eyebrow, watching me for a heartbeat before nodding approvingly and turning to leave.

"What's your plan, Captain?" Cam asked with a smile.

"We're going to get Alys and Faolan," I said, ideas swirling in my head. The couple would want to know about Caelum, and I had a sneaking suspicion they would be more than willing to take an active role in his rescue. "And then we will stage a distraction while we break Caelum out of that jail."

His grin grew wider, and he reached out, tugging at a strand of my hair. "Aye. Let's get to it then."

Duncan and I ventured into Brinemoor alone, heading toward the inn Alys and Faolan were staying at. While Duncan would have been my last choice of someone to spend more alone time with, I couldn't discount that he was still the first mate, and that Caelum trusted his judgment.

"What are you going to tell them?" His voice was low as we walked through the streets. The town was just waking up, and people trickled down the paths as businesses opened. His eyes roved, searching for any threats.

"We'll tell them the truth, and ask for their help," I replied, looking up at him. I suspected that despite what Caelum would have wanted, Alys and Faolan would not be willing to merely sit back and hope. I'd only met them briefly, but that much was clear to me. "And then we'll accept their decision—whatever it may be."

He huffed, but kept quiet as we approached the inn. A picture of politeness, Duncan pulled the door open for me, nodding for me to enter. Stepping in, my eyes scanned the small sitting area.

Alys and Faolan sat in the corner by the fire, mugs in hand and leaning close to each other as they spoke. Alys noticed me first, and her eyes lit up as she waved me over.

"Brigid, dear," she said, standing as we approached. Her eyes drifted over me, concern shining through them. "What are you doing here?"

I looked around and dropped my head. Even though no one else was paying attention to us, I didn't want to risk someone overhearing. "Can we go somewhere a bit more... private?"

Faolan frowned, now standing to join us. "Yes, of course."

Wordlessly, we followed them up the stairs and into their room. Duncan leaned protectively against the inside of the door as we entered, his arms crossed over his chest.

Faolan mimicked the gesture, looking between us. "Okay, what's happened?"

I sighed, trying to figure out the best way to word the news. I needed to be detailed enough without making them feel obligated to help. If they helped us free Caelum, it had to be their own choice, and I didn't want to influence that.

"They arrested Caelum for piracy. He'll hang by sundown," Duncan spat out.

Alys gasped as her hands flew to her mouth. I whirled around, glaring at him. He just shrugged and pushed off the door, stepping toward us.

"What? When?" Faolan eyes were wide with horror.

I let my glare linger on Duncan for another moment, and then tore my eyes away and back to Faolan and Alys. "They came last night and arrested him."

"What do you need from us?" Alys wrapped her arms around her middle and looked up at Faolan, concern written all over her face. "We have to stop them from hanging him."

"That's why we're here," I said, tossing another glare at Duncan before I continued. "We'd like your help in the rescue, if you're willing."

"Absolutely," Faolan answered instantly. "Whatever you need. What is your plan?"

"We need a distraction," I said, crossing my arms over my chest. "Something to catch the attention of the guards and soldiers, drawing them away long enough for us to get in and get Caelum."

"Outside the jail, I imagine?" He reached up, stroking his beard. "I think I can manage something."

"I'll be there to help," Duncan replied. "And we can get a few other men if needed. But I want to be clear that you don't need to help us. It's going to be risky. We knew you would want to know about Caelum, though."

Faolan scoffed. "I may look old, young man, but I'll certainly be able to pull off being enough of a nuisance to attract the guards by myself."

"No," I said quickly, shaking my head. A knot formed in my stomach at the thought of Faolan or Alys being harmed during this ploy. "No one is doing anything alone. Especially not when there's the possibility of being arrested."

The older man raised a brow at me. "What are the rest of your crew or the syrens doing? Why aren't they providing the distraction?"

"They're preparing for what happens when Cliodhna returns. The fewer people involved in freeing Caelum, the better, so as not to raise suspicion," Duncan replied before I could open my mouth. I glared at him again, and he winked at me in return. "We can make it work without you, though, if it's too dangerous. Brigid and I can handle the distraction and the jailbreak."

Faolan simply laughed, and even Alys had an amused smile on her face as her husband spoke. "The danger is half the fun! I've been sitting idle for far too long. When do we start?"

"Right now," Duncan said, a smile spreading across his own face.

Elizianna
@ELIZIANNA.THE.ONE

CAELUM

CHAPTER FORTY-SIX

The ride to Brinemoor was jarring, and my bruised body ached from the shackles and the rough jostling of the cart. Finally, the cart came to a stop, just as the faint gray of the coming dawn lightened the sky. My two jailers dismounted and came around to unchain me from the floor.

The one with the slimy ponytail grabbed me roughly, yanking me down from the cart. Bound by the shackles, I could do nothing to brace my fall and winced as my body hit the dirt. My shoulder screamed in protest, but I gritted my teeth and pulled myself back up.

I could show them no weakness. It would be like asking for them to exploit it.

"Get up, scum," the other one said, kicking at my foot.

Biting down on the inside of my cheek to avoid lashing out, I managed to stand despite my hands being shackled together. Pushing back at my captors would only get me beaten, or worse. For now, I needed to keep my head down and figure out a way to escape my fate. Or at least, keep myself alive until Brigid could save my sorry ass.

They dragged me down the alley into the jail, shoving me even as I stumbled from the chains catching around my feet. As we entered the cell area, I gagged. The stench was overwhelming. Human waste, sweat, and stale air clogged my throat and my eyes watered. This was going to be miserable.

My jailers pulled me down to the end of the row of cells and unlocked the very last one, throwing me inside. The cell door clanged shut and their keys jangled as they locked the door and walked away.

"I suppose you won't be removing these?" I called out, raising my shackled hands.

They glanced at each other and laughed before turning to leave.

I sighed and let my hands drop. I guess that was a no. Wonderful. My last moments in life and I would spend it trussed up with limited movement. This would undoubtedly hinder my escape plans.

"They likely would have until you opened your mouth." A gruff voice came from the cell next to mine. "Fool."

"Who are you?" I asked, turning to my neighbor. Cloaked in the shadows cast by the meager lamps down the hall, his mysterious presence was unnerving.

"Ah, doesn't matter," he said, not bothering to move into the light. "What got you put in here?"

"Why do you want to know?" I asked, stepping closer to the grated wall between us. I wasn't about to admit to anything, not when I didn't know who could be listening nearby.

The man laughed, the sound echoing off the stone walls. "Fine. Don't tell me, boy. No skin off my nose. Just trying to pass the time, is all."

I sighed. Could it really hurt to talk to my fellow prisoner? "I'm Caelum."

"I'd say it's nice to meet you, Caelum," the man drawled, "but considering where we are, I think I'll just skip that part."

Snorting, I slid down against the wall. "Aye, I think that's for the best."

"So, what did they nab you for?" The sound of chains jingled as he scooted closer to the wall separating us. Moving into the light, I could see the wrinkles marring his deep brown skin, a crooked nose and strong brow. His hair would have been the same color as mine, but was now streaked with white. Well-muscled, even for his obviously older age, this man was not someone I would underestimate. He could clearly handle himself.

"I killed my father." I shrugged, keeping my voice even and void of emotion. There was no point in denying what I had done. "Oh, and I supposedly stole some stuff, too."

He whistled. "Well, yeah, I suppose that would do it."

"You?"

"Well, my boy, we have the thief part in common," he said, grinning widely to show off his missing teeth. "I'm awaiting my trial. So, why'd you off your pa?"

"He was trying to kill me first."

"Sounds like a hell of a father. And I thought my pa was a right bastard."

There was nothing else I could really say to the man. I had killed my father in front of witnesses. And given how highly regarded my jailers held Kellan, I doubted I could convince them he deserved it. I would hang if I didn't find a way out of here.

"When's your trial?" he asked, his feet scuffing against the dirt floor.

"Don't get one." It felt surreal saying it out loud, but it was my reality. "I'm set to hang tomorrow night."

"Well, that hardly seems fair." He was quiet for a moment.

I snorted. "This life is far from fair, my friend."

"Aye, it is," he sighed. "Well, it was nice meeting you, Caelum."

"Suppose we should try to sleep through what's left of the morning." I shifted against the stone wall in an unsuccessful attempt to find a comfortable position. Sighing, I stretched my legs out in front of me and tipped my head back against the wall, closing my eyes. Only hours before, I had been pressed naked against the woman of my dreams. How quickly life could change.

The banging of wood against metal woke me. "Wake up, murdering scum."

Groaning, I sat up, opening my eyes to see three guards standing outside my cell. The full burn of the morning sunlight filtered in through the bars above the open windows. "You lot really need some better insults."

One of them spat at me, a glob of saliva landing on my boot. "You'll hang today, trash."

"I suppose you were also fans of Kellan?" I tried to keep my temper down, and the bored look on my face. The more unaffected I seemed, the more it would irritate them.

"He should have killed you years ago."

I shrugged. "Aye. But he didn't. And now he's dead, and I'm not."

"Not for long."

"Why are you here?" I asked, sitting up straighter and crossing my arms, the shackles jangling. "Surely you have better things to do than stand about heckling prisoners."

"Your little friend is gone," one of them said. He nodded toward the cell the older man had been in. The thief. It was empty now. A strip of fabric that had been tied around his wrist was the only remnant of his presence. My stomach dropped. Had they harmed him simply for talking to me?

"What did you do to him?" I tried to keep my voice careless and light, as if I didn't care what had happened. But my heart was racing, my stomach sick at the idea of someone being killed or taken because of me.

"We moved him somewhere else to await his trial." The one who spat at me grinned.

One of them started to say something else, but a bustle of noise and shouting from outside the cellblock caught their attention. Clanging of metal, raised and panic voices... something was happening. I leaned forward, trying to hear, but I couldn't make out any of the words being shouted.

The shouting grew louder, approaching the door at the end of the hall. Suddenly it burst open, and two more guards pushed through, hauling someone behind them. "Get that cell open!"

The three guards who'd been taunting me sprang into action, unlocking the cell my neighbor had occupied, pulling the door open as the additional guards tossed the man inside. The cell door echoed loudly as they slammed it shut.

Leaning back against my cell wall, I looked at the man now occupying the cell next to me. He was bent over, his face hidden by his knees as he loudly panted for breath.

"This bastard was causing a ruckus near the doors, shouting about that one there," one guard explained, nodding toward me. He rubbed a bruise forming beneath his eye. "Decided he'd rather join him instead."

"They can die together then," the guard said. "There's room at the noose for another pirate scum."

"Och, you piss-eating infant," the man snapped. My vision blurred as I recognized the voice. Faolan. "I'm no pirate."

"A pirate sympathizer is just as dead," the guard sneered over his shoulder. He nodded his head toward the other guards and thankfully, they left the cell block, locking the door behind them.

"Faolan?" I hissed, moving closer to the cell wall separating us. "What the hell are you doing here?"

He straightened up, sitting back on his heels as he held his side, finally catching his breath. He smiled at me. "Oh, Caelum. Funny running into you here."

"What are you doing?" I whispered again, flexing my fingers around the bars. I was going to be sick. Faolan tried to save me, and now... now he was going to hang with me. "They're going to kill you now."

He waved his hand, shifting to sit on the floor, his back against the wall. "Naw, your girl won't let it get that far."

"Brigid?" My stomach flipped at the mention of her. "You've talked to Brigid?"

"Oh, aye," he said, wincing as he adjusted his position. "Her and that big blond one came and got Alys and me, asked for our help to get you out of here."

I closed my eyes, letting my forehead fall forward, resting on the bars as I took deep breaths to calm myself. "They shouldn't have done that."

"And why not? What should they have done instead?" His voice was defensive. "Risked your crew or the syrens, and then be vulnerable when your father's men or Cliodhna came back? That wouldn't be very smart."

I opened my eyes to see him glaring at me. "So, getting caught and thrown in the cell next to me was your plan?"

He scoffed. "Of course not. I admit, things did not go as planned."

"What *was* the plan?" I asked, not entirely sure I even wanted to hear it. While I'd known Brigid would work to get me out of jail, I hadn't expected her to ask Faolan for help.

"Me and the big one—"

"Duncan?"

He nodded. "Yes, him. Duncan and I were supposed to cause a big commotion and get the guards to come out. Then your girl would sneak in here and get you out. Easy as that."

"And yet you didn't even consider that you might get arrested?" Surely, they had thought things through better than this.

"Of course we did," he said, glaring at me. "We ran through multiple scenarios, all dependent on how the guards reacted. This was our second plan since the others didn't come out as expected. Our best bet was to get one of us in here with you. I just so happened to throw a punch before Duncan could."

I rubbed my temples. "This is... I don't even know what this is."

"This is genius, Caelum," he said, scooting over toward me, lowering his voice. "Brigid's thought through everything."

I furrowed my brow. "What?"

"Well, she wasn't too keen on Duncan or me being arrested as the backup plan, so she's formulating her own. First, we need to escape from the inside. I'm a little skeptical on that one, but we'll see if we can pull it off. If that doesn't work, presuming Duncan got free, he will replace the hangman at the gallows." His eyes lit up. "And I'm sure she's got a few other tricks up her sleeve, although her and Duncan weren't exactly seeing eye to eye on a lot."

"Of course they weren't," I grumbled. I took a deep breath, my shackles clanging as I rubbed at my beard. "How can we escape from the inside? We're locked in cells, I'm in shackles, and there are many locked doors and guards between us and the exit."

"Duncan said you knew how to pick a lock. That true?"

I nodded. "Yes, if I have the right tools."

He grinned and relaxed, leaning back against the wall once more. "Then there you go. That's how we'll get out. You're over-thinking this, Caelum. Relax a bit."

I couldn't believe my ears. Faolan, who didn't help rescue Brigid because of the danger to Alys. Faolan, who'd been so serious and concerned until now. "Are you insane?"

He waved a hand at me dismissively. "Naw, boy. This is the most fun I've had in ages. I'd forgotten what being entangled in adventure was like."

"This is dangerous," I said, shaking my head. My stomach twisted in knots, and my body vibrated with the need to get free and ensure my friends were safe.

"Yes," he agreed, smiling. "Isn't it grand? I haven't had this much fun since I sailed out west."

The wistfulness in his eyes made me shake my head. I could appreciate his thoughts though, being a former sailor and soldier, now living a quiet life in a quiet town. It was easy to see how this might have felt like a return to his former glory. "You are crazy, old man."

"Aye, right I am," he replied, grinning. I watched as he took off his boot and began fiddling with the heel. After a moment, he pulled out a small sliver of metal that glinted in the sun. "Aha. Got this for you."

"What is that?" I leaned closer, my heart speeding up. I didn't want to get my hopes up before I had all my facts straight.

He slid forward and discreetly passed the object through the bars separating us. "Here, see if you can get those shackles off."

I almost wept with joy as my fingers wrapped around the thin metal. I turned it over in my hand, rolling it between my fingers, examining every inch. It was a bit thin, but it should work on the shackles. Without a second thought, I twisted my hands back toward me, turning the keyhole up to face me. I inserted the small pick into the space, twisting and wiggling.

Holding my breath, I worked the pick, trying to catch just the right spot to release the lock. Pushing it in further, I twisted it once more, but instead of catching like I'd hoped, the metal snapped in half right at the edge of the keyhole.

"Did it just break?" Faolan asked, pressing his face to the bars to see.

I slumped forward as all the hope bled out of me. "Yeah."

"Is there enough left to try again?" His voice was quieter than it had been before.

I held up the remaining metal, bringing it over to him. It was barely the length of the tip of my finger, and definitely not long enough to try again. "No."

He sighed. "Don't worry, boy. We'll figure something out."

As if on cue, the heavy wooden doors at the end of the hall swung open. My heart skipped a beat, wondering if they'd known what I'd been doing. Carefully, trying not to cause the shackles to jangle, I tucked the piece of metal into my boot and leaned against the wall, away from the bars separating Faolan and me.

A fresh set of guards entered the hall, walking toward us with trays of food. Wordlessly, they stopped in front of each of our cells and thrust the trays through the slot, dropping them to the ground. The bread on my tray bounced off, rolling onto the dirt floor.

Watching until they turned to leave, I lunged forward, picking the bread off the dirt and wiping it against my shirt. The floor may have been cleaner than the shirt, but I didn't want to eat food covered in... whatever was on this cell floor.

"You should eat too," I said, shoving the bread in my mouth. I'd not eaten since the night before, and my stomach had started to voice its displeasure. I scarfed down the stale bread and dried meat on the tray. However we tried to get out of this mess, I knew I would need my energy. I had until sundown to get out of these shackles, out of this cell, and back to my crew. There wasn't time to dawdle.

Both of us ate quickly and silently. Once finished, Faolan leaned back against the wall, sighing. "Got any other ideas for getting out of here?"

"Oh, now you're getting worried, are you?"

He scowled at me. "Course not. Just giving you a chance to be the hero this time."

I glanced at him out of the side of my eyes. "Yeah, sure. Thanks for that. Obviously, we need something to pick the lock on my shackles, and then we'll need it to work again to get out of our cells."

"Okay..." He looked around the cell, picking up the fabric that the previous occupant had left and throwing it back to the ground. "All we've got are these trays now."

I picked up my tray to examine it. The wood was smooth with age, but the sides had splintered a bit. An idea popped into my head.

"Slide your tray over here. Then listen for the guards while I break off pieces of the wood. Hopefully, it'll be sturdy enough."

"I hope this works," he grumbled, sliding the tray over to the edge of the bars. "I'm too old to sit on this floor much longer."

Eliz
@ELIZIA

Brigid

Chapter Forty-Seven

The *Nehalennia* was busy with activity as the sun moved higher overhead. I'd been a nervous wreck, pacing around the deck, double checking our meager stock of weapons. Faolan being taken had not been my ideal solution to getting Caelum out of jail, but we'd known it was a possibility.

Even so, I'd been reluctant to leave the heart of Brinemoor after the guards had taken him away, only agreeing when Duncan pulled me toward the docks, saying they would arrest us both if we stayed.

Duncan was moping, standing with his arms crossed, studying me. I felt his heavy gaze on my back as I paced around the deck. Caelum was right. Once this was finally over, Duncan and I would need to address our issues. I wasn't sure if this issue was because Caelum had left me in charge, or because I was a syren.

Finally, after another scoff, I stopped, whirling around, my fists clenched. "Is there something you'd like to say, Duncan?"

"Your plan is stupid." He straightened from the railing he was leaning against.

Everything and everyone aboard the ship stopped. My eyes narrowed and my fingers flexed at my sides, my talons itching to come out. My voice was ice as I spoke. "Excuse me?"

He took a step toward me. "It was stupid to—"

"No, I heard you," I said, holding up my hand to stop him. "I was giving you a chance to take it back." My body tensed as I felt someone approach from behind. I turned, relieved to see Cam, and I refocused my attention on Duncan. "What is stupid? You sure seemed on board when we devised this plan."

"Waiting until they're at the noose to act is too late," he said, crossing his arms over his chest. "We need to act sooner."

Chewing on the inside of my cheek, I rolled the words around on my tongue before letting them escape. "Faolan, Alys, and *you* agreed that if we couldn't break him out of the jail, the best chance we had would be at the noose. If you've come to some startling revelation since then, by all means, please share it."

As I spoke, Cam moved up next to me, between Duncan and I. Alys, Kyla, and Nerina stopped what they were doing to watch us as well. The audience made my stomach sour, but I took another deep breath and kept my gaze focused on Duncan. If he genuinely had a new idea that was better, I would be open to hearing it. I owed Caelum that much.

"We get him while they're moving him," he replied, as if it were the most obvious solution.

I rolled my eyes. "This again? This is why you think my plan is stupid?"

He merely shrugged.

Rage coursed through my veins, pushing the anxiety away as I stepped up to him. We stood chest to chest, not breaking eye contact. "You are acting like Maira. You don't get your way, so you pout and spit venom at anyone who will listen. Now is not the time for this, and you know it. I know you have problems with me, with all the syrens, and that's fine, but I am trying to *save Caelum* and I thought you were, too."

His nostrils flared as he looked down at me, the muscles in his jaw feathering.

"Duncan," Cam said, exasperated and tired of our arguing. He stepped up next to me, physically wedging himself between us and turning his back to me. "We're all trying to accomplish the same thing here. Can you please cooperate to help us?"

He shrugged again. "The syren said she was in charge. I'm just pointing out an alternative option she's refusing to consider."

"You're going to let Caelum hang because of your delicate ego?" I snarled, stepping toward him, but Cam held out his arm to keep us apart. "Surely you're not that *stupid*."

"And surely you're not so ignorant to think you *actually* know what you're doing here."

"This isn't helping anyone," Cameron hissed, glaring at both of us.

"You're right. I don't know what I'm doing. But I'm trying my hardest to do what Caelum would want." I leaned around Cam, holding eye contact with Duncan.

He broke our stare, rolling his eyes. "You tried to kill Caelum less than two months ago. You don't know a fucking thing about what he would want, syren."

This time, my talons *did* leave my nail beds, and I clenched my hands into fists, letting the talons puncture my own skin instead of Duncan's throat like I would have preferred. I needed to leave this situation, or one of us would end up hurt. Biting my tongue to keep from speaking, I turned and walked away, moving toward the syrens.

As I walked away, I could hear Cameron and Duncan arguing, but I couldn't make out the words over the blood pounding in my ears.

"Are you okay?" Kyla asked, putting a hand on my shoulder as I approached.

It took a moment for her words to register, but when they did, I shook my head. Lowering my voice to a whisper only she could hear, I admitted, "I have no clue what to do."

"Yes, you do. You can do this." She put both hands firmly on my shoulders and gave me a small shake. "You know what Caelum wants. You know what we must do."

"Don't doubt yourself just because of a man," Maira sneered. "Especially *that* man."

I laughed. The syrens, the women who had abandoned me before, were now reassuring me. All I had ever wanted was this kind of acceptance and friendship, and now, with the man I loved facing death, I had it. But I couldn't enjoy it.

Wiping away the angry tears that formed at the corners of my eye, I nodded. "You're right. But Duncan will not let go of his plan without facts. I've told him they'll be expecting that, since transit is the weakest point, but he isn't listening to me."

"I agree. They'll be expecting that," Kyla said, nodding. "How can we prove that to him?"

"We need to figure out the route they will take from the jail to the noose and see how public it is and how many guards they'll have."

Kyla looked at Maira, who shared a look with Cordelia. Stepping forward, Maira nodded. "We'll go into town and see what we can find out."

"Be careful, and come back as soon as you know something," I said, extending my hand toward Maira. I wasn't sure why I did it, but despite our past, I wanted us to come to some sort of alliance. I would never forgive her, but that didn't mean we couldn't work together. And no matter what, I was still concerned for her safety.

She eyed it for a moment, and I nearly let it drop, but at the last moment, she reached out to squeeze my hand. "Aye, Brigid. We'll be safe."

I smiled, fighting back the grateful tears that had taken the place of the angry ones. "Best get on with it, then."

Maira smirked as she and Cordelia disembarked from the ship.

Watching as they walked up the docks and disappeared into the city, I let out a heavy sigh.

The sun was dropping into the afternoon haze when Maira and

Cordelia finally returned. Finn's piercing whistle from the crow's nest alerted us to their arrival.

"They're back," Cam said, setting down the map of Brinemoor we were studying.

All of us, even Duncan, stopped what we were doing to watch them climb aboard.

My heart was in my throat, waiting for them to speak. I couldn't read Maira's face, and Cordelia's was carefully blank. "What did you find?"

"They're taking him right through the center of town," Maira said, her voice sharp as she looked at Duncan. "So, your plan of getting him during transit is, in fact, the stupid one."

"Everyone in town was talking about it," Nerina added, grimacing. "They're making quite a spectacle."

Duncan rolled his eyes, thankfully remaining silent.

Alys stepped up next to me, reaching down to squeeze my hand. "If they're making a spectacle of the hanging, our plan will work, Brigid. The crowd will work to our advantage."

I nodded, squeezing her hand in return, thankful for the voice of reason she provided. Duncan would not argue with her. Her hope, determination, and sheer confidence that we could save her husband and Caelum were contagious. Anticipation bubbled in my throat. "Then let's get moving."

Lena laughed, turning from where she stood at the railing, looking out at the sea. Her eyes were a bright molten silver. "Oh, yes, I think whatever we do will turn into a spectacle now."

"What do you mean?" Duncan asked, his eyes narrowing. Lena's words had a certain air of mystery about them, as if she was talking about something entirely different from the rest of us.

She tilted her head as she looked out toward the town. "Cliodhna is here."

Elizianna
@ELIZIANNA.THE.ONE

C AELUM

CHAPTER FORTY-EIGHT

As the afternoon drew to a close, Faolan and I finally gave up on our attempt to pick the locks. The pieces of wood we'd broken off weren't ideal picks and kept splintering off until there was nothing left.

"Well, I guess that's it then," Faolan said as I threw down the last tiny splinter.

"Now what?" I sighed, leaning back against the wall. I knew Faolan said Brigid had another plan, but waiting around had never been my strong suit.

"I don't know about you, but I have no plans of dying just yet. Trust your girl, Caelum, and trust me," Faolan grinned. "They still have to move us to get to the noose. I imagine we can at least attempt to get away then."

He made a good point, but it would depend how many guards they put on us. They'd likely be expecting that, but we could at least keep that plan in the back of our minds.

"But what if our next plan doesn't work, either?" I didn't want to bring down the optimistic mood, but I needed to prepare for all scenarios, and that included one where we wouldn't escape our fates.

"Then we trust Brigid can follow through with her plan and save both our sorry arses." The calm smile still plastered on his face kept the glimmer of hope alive in me, but I couldn't bring myself to return the smile. "What is it, Caelum? You don't trust our women to save us?"

"No, I do," I said emphatically, letting out a harsh breath. "I trust that beyond a doubt. I just..."

"Facing one's death is never easy, my boy," he said, his voice soft and reassuring. "But this is not our end, I promise you that. You've got to think positively."

"I'm trying," I said, shifting against the uncomfortable floor.

"Good. Now, we conserve our energy and see what we can pull off when the guards come." He settled back against the wall, noisily trying to find a comfortable position.

I let my head tip back as my mind spun in every direction. I knew Brigid would burn the world down to get me back, and while I loved her for it, I would never forgive myself if she got hurt trying.

My eyes widened as the realization hit me. I loved Brigid. I had loved before, fleeting as it may have been, experiencing the love of friends and remembering the love of my mother as a child. That same warmth and protectiveness was what I felt toward Brigid, only much stronger.

Did she feel the same way? Something had intertwined our fates many years ago when I first saw her on that ship, but we had only just reconnected. Was it too soon? Now that I knew how I felt, I wanted to scream it from the tallest mountain. But would it scare her away and back into the sea?

Acid burned in the back of my throat, and I swallowed. There was no time for these feelings. I would deal with them after I was free. And if I didn't get free... Well, then I wouldn't have to worry either way.

Hours later, the doors at the end of the hallway opened again, and four guards entered, holding leg shackles and chains. Two of them stopped in front of Faolan's cell and the other two stopped in front of mine.

"Time to go, prisoners."

The guards hauled us to our feet, the shackles attached to our ankles and secured to the shackles already clamped around our wrists. This would make our escape a bit more difficult. I clenched my teeth as the metal rubbed painfully against my skin.

"Let's go," the guard grunted, pulling on my shoulder and roughly leading me out of the cell.

Shuffling as best I could in my shackles, I followed their lead down the hall and through a maze of passages before exiting the jail. The late afternoon sun peeked over the top of the nearby buildings, and I swallowed hard. My stomach felt like it weighed more than *The Nehalennia's* anchor.

The guards pulled us toward an alley behind the jail while even more guards filtered out behind us.

"So, we're walking to this shindig?" Faolan asked, jangling his shackles. "I'm old, you see, can't walk that far."

I bit down on my lip to keep from smiling at his overzealous ploy to get information from our guards.

"You'll walk or I'll drag you," one guard sneered. As if on cue, two horses came around the corner from the nearby stables.

Two guards mounted the horses after securing our chains to the saddles, and six other guards surrounded us as we set off on the march to our deaths. My stomach sank with each step.

We had no chance to get away, and our only hope of making it out of this was Brigid and the others. I held my head high as they led us through the streets, weaving our way to the main road in Brinemoor. Fucking hell, they were really going to make this a spectacle.

I'd not been here in a while, but I knew most hangings did not bring this much attention. Were this many people really excited about my death? My father must have paid off way more people than I thought. The horse whinnied, bucking at the noise of the crowd, and I gritted my teeth as it tugged at the chains on my wrists.

A crowd had already formed on each side of the street, heckling us as we passed. I kept my eyes up, scanning the crowd. My eyes widened as I glimpsed blonde hair and a smirking Maira in the crowd. They were here to save us. She winked at me and disappeared into the crowd, Cordelia close behind her.

As we continued moving, my eyes flicked between the ground—making sure not to trip over the chains—and the faces of the people lining the streets. I saw Kyla, Finn, Nerina, Iona, and Alan, each of them acknowledging me with a quick nod, before slipping back into the crowd.

We were running out of time as we approached the middle of town. My stomach twisted with anxiety. What were they planning?

I'm sure the publicity of my upcoming death threw a wrench in their plans, but I knew that Brigid, Cam, and Duncan adapted quickly. Faolan had mentioned they planned to replace the hangman, but with the crowd of people watching, I doubted it would be as easy as they expected.

The horses turned the last corner, entering the town square, and my stomach flipped at the sight of the noose that stood waiting. Faolan faltered ahead of me, nearly tripping at the sight of a second noose. I guessed they were planning to hang him, too.

We drew to a stop, and the three guards came to unhook our chains. They dragged me toward the platform, not even allowing me to get my footing. Shoving me toward the stairs, one of them jerked his head at me. "Go on, pirate scum."

"You lot desperately need better insults," I muttered, picking up the loose chain as I ascended the stairs. The hooded hangman stood by the lever with his arms crossed in front of him. I searched his face, trying to see if they'd been successful at replacing him with Duncan, but the hangman gave no sign I was even in front of him.

The guard shoved me forward, closer to the noose, forcing me to turn or lose my balance in the leg irons.

Facing the gathering crowd, I frantically scanned the faces staring up at me, looking for Brigid or Cameron or *anyone* I knew.

For a moment, I saw a flash of red and thought it might have been Brigid, but it was just a shawl wrapped around an older woman. Finally, my eyes landed on Lena. She stood in the middle of the crowd, smiling serenely at me, as if she had passed a friend in the street and not someone who was about to die.

Subtly, she tilted her head to the side, her eyes darting to the left and then back to me several times. I followed her gaze to where a woman with a hood stood, set apart from the crowd. Squinting through the light of the setting sun, I recognized her.

Shit, I cursed to myself. My eyes landed back on Lena's, who raised an eyebrow, a grave smile on her face. Cliodhna was in the crowd. Likely to ensure I actually died. My stomach churned, and I could only hope that if Lena knew Cliodhna was here, they had prepared for it.

The executioner, a pale, thin man dressed far too formal for the occasion, stepped up between Faolan and me, a scroll tucked tightly under his arm. He cleared his throat and turned toward the crowd. "Found guilty of piracy and murder, we have sentenced Caelum Loinseach to hang until dead."

Faolan grinned, dramatically turning to the man. "What about me? Don't leave me out, now."

The executioner grimaced, avoiding eye contact and never mentioned Faolan's name or his crimes.

The crowd heckled me, one person even throwing fruit, which I thankfully dodged just before it hit me in the face.

The executioner nodded to the hangman, who stepped up and looped the noose around Faolan's neck before doing the same to me. My breath caught in my throat. I was getting nervous. If Brigid had a plan in place, I hoped she revealed it soon.

The hangman lingered for a moment, patting my shoulder once, twice, three times before pinching the spot above my collarbone.

My eyes widened, and it took every ounce of self-control to not whirl around to look at the hooded man. It had to be Duncan. That specific pinch had been something we did as teenagers, seeing who could pinch the hardest and leave a mark on the other. He always won.

If Duncan could take the place of the hangman, I wondered what else would happen in the next few moments. Faolan hadn't given details about the rest of the plan, and I was growing impatient.

Thankfully, I didn't have to wonder much longer.

The hangman—Duncan—brought his ax down on the rope holding the trap doors shut and they swung open. We both dropped, but the rope didn't catch like I expected. Instead, both Faolan and I hit the ground below with a thud. Shaking my head, I looked up to see Brigid and Cameron smiling down at us from beneath the platform.

"Got yourself into some trouble, Captain?" Brigid asked, mischief twinkling in her eyes. My breath rushed from my body in a sigh. She did it. She was here.

"Brigid," I whispered, my voice hoarse. She dropped to her knees, her long braid flipping over her shoulder as she bent to hug me tightly.

"Told you," Faolan said, grinning as he rolled up to sitting.

"Aye, you did," I said, the smile on my face almost painful as I looked between Brigid and Cam. As much as I wanted to pull her into my arms, kiss her, and *thank* her for saving me, we had bigger concerns. "Got any plans to get these shackles off before they figure out we're not dead?"

Brigid nodded at Cameron, who pulled a key ring from his pocket, freeing me and Faolan. I shook the chains off and removed the rope from my neck.

"What now?"

"Now, we have to get out of this crowd without dying," Cameron said dryly.

The crowd grew louder, shouting from the other side of the wooden barrier that blocked us from view. A guard leaned over the hole, and we froze, looking up at him. His eyes widened, and he turned back to the crowd. "They're not dead! They're escaping!"

"Well," Brigid said, tossing me a sword she pulled from the strap across her chest. "Time to go."

Elizi
@ELIZIAN

BRIGID

CHAPTER FORTY-NINE

With Caelum and Faolan now free and armed, we opened the wooden door at the back of the platform and ran, immediately caught in a flurry of the crowd. Guards were shouting, trying to push through the crowd toward us.

"So, what now?" Caelum asked breathlessly as we wove through the crowd, moving further away from the guards.

"Syrens," was all I could respond as the shouting of the guards grew more panicked. The syrens flanked the perimeter of the crowd, working their way in. We had agreed on no killing unless absolutely necessary, but I was sure some of them, namely Maira, would find any reason to spill blood today.

The guards, redirected as they tried to make their way to us, were now moving out toward the threat the syrens posed. I smiled as we moved through the crowd, reaching back for Caelum's hand. He grabbed it, our fingers twining together as he followed me.

"STOP!" a booming voice echoed through the crowd, audible even over the panicked shouting.

Everything and everyone in the square obeyed the voice, and then, all at once, the crowd and guards broke into a run, leaving the square in a panic. Shoving to get away from the voice that seemed to be at the center of the square, people dispersed, leaving us and the syrens exposed.

At the center stood a woman in a black cloak, and a few steps away stood Lena, facing the figure with her head held high.

"Ah, we meet again," Lena cooed, stepping closer to the figure.

I squeezed Caelum's hand. The figure had to be Cliodhna. Lena had known she would be here, but facing her was not high on my list of things to do.

"It's okay," Caelum murmured, stepping up beside me as we walked toward the crew and other syrens who were gathering together.

"Give me, Brigid," Cliodhna said, her voice still loud, carrying through the square. She held her hand out toward me. "And perhaps I will let the rest of you traitors live."

I sucked the air through my teeth, biting down hard on the inside of my cheek to help stave off the panic building in my chest. She really was intent on killing me. But I knew she would never let the others go free. No, she would kill us all.

"Liar!" I shouted, emboldened by Caelum, standing beside me.

Cliodhna tipped her head back and laughed. "No, child. I said *I* would let the traitors live. I didn't say they would make it out of here alive."

On cue, footsteps and the clanging of metal sounded behind us. Looking over my shoulder, I saw the big man from the orphanage—Arran—and what remained of Kellan's crew surrounding us. They boxed us in, forcing the remaining syrens and crew toward the middle.

"Why are you doing this?" Lena asked Cliodhna, stepping closer to her.

Cliodhna sneered. "Do not pretend to be superior. I am more than you will ever be."

"We shall see about that," Lena said. She nodded toward Caelum and me. "That syren is more than you could dream of being."

Cliodhna shrugged. "Not if she's dead."

My stomach dropped. The memories of my torture at the hands

of Cliodhna crawled up from the recesses of my mind. I tried to push them back, to focus on what was right in front of me, but I couldn't. My heart sped up and my palms were sweating. The blood pounding in my ears muffled the sounds and voices, but I could see Lena and Cliodhna still talking.

Caelum pressed himself close to my back. "*Teine*, are you okay?"

I opened my mouth to speak, but could only pant out quick breaths. My vision grew black around the edges and the ground spun. I shook my head, closing my eyes tightly.

He cursed, pulling me to his side. "Okay, hold on. I've got you. Cam?"

"I'm looking for an exit, Captain," I heard Cam reply. "You need to calm her down, though."

"Have her breathe through her nose," Faolan said quietly. "It'll help."

I felt hands on my shoulders, and my vision focused, filling with Caelum's worried face. "Brigid. Brigid, listen to me. Can you hear me? Nod if you can hear me."

I managed a nod. I could hear him, and focusing on his voice instead of Cliodhna's was helping. But I couldn't face her. I couldn't go back there. She had almost killed me, and despite me wanting to fight her and end her for what she had done, I couldn't.

"Okay, good," he said. There was a thud of something hitting the ground, and then both of Caelum's hands were holding my face. "Listen to me. She will not touch you. You are safe here with me. Say it."

"I'm safe," I said, my voice a hoarse whisper. Clearing my throat, I raised my eyes to his. "I'm safe. She won't hurt me."

"Good." He smiled and squeezed my cheeks. "We have work to do, my bloodthirsty little syren."

My body was shaky, but I adjusted my grip on the dagger in my hand as Caelum bent to pick up his sword from the dirt. "She'll focus on me while Arran will focus on you."

He grimaced. "I know. Want to trade?"

I couldn't help the smile that crossed my face. He had distracted me from my panic, and knew exactly how to do it. A flood of gratitude filled my belly, warming me from the inside out. "Deal. Cam, want to help me take on the giant?"

"It would be my pleasure," Cam said, smiling at me.

"We can try to get you out of here, Faolan," I whispered, not looking at the older man standing next to me. "I won't ask you to be part of this fight."

"Absolutely not," he replied. "I won't risk Cliodhna getting away and going after my Alys. No, I'll stay and do what I can. This old man still knows a few tricks."

"Oh, Brigid," Cliodhna cooed, turning her attention away from Lena and back to me. "Come quietly, and *maybe* your man will survive."

I glanced at Caelum, and he nodded. "Let's go."

Without another word, he turned and charged toward Cliodhna, his sword raised.

And then all hell broke loose.

Elizianna
@ELIZIANNA.THE.ONE

CAELUM

CHAPTER FIFTY

As I charged at the syren queen, I realized it was likely a stupid mistake. She would allow no one to attack her head-on. But my anger over her words toward Brigid coupled with my fear watching Brigid panic... It had pushed reason from my mind. Only pure white-hot rage remained.

I swung my sword, but Cliodhna dodged it easily, just as I knew she would.

She paused, staring at me. "You think you can beat me?"

"Not on my own." Pulling my dagger from my belt, Lena stepped up next to me, the silver swirling around her hands and eyes.

Cliodhna's eyes narrowed at the woman beside me. "This is not your battle, witch."

"You've made it my battle," Lena replied, raising her hand and blasting a fire of silver toward Cliodhna. "You knew the rules, and still you ignored them."

As soon as the wave of magic dissipated, I was moving again, circling behind her as Lena continued to distract her with waves of silver energy. Despite wanting to keep my distance, I knew the sword would be useless. I dropped it, pulling another dagger from my belt, and moved in closer.

Cliodhna realized I was close to her and turned, blasting me with a wave of her own magic and knocking me to the ground. Growling, I rolled to my feet, surveying the situation for an opening.

Several of the syrens were battling with Arran's men, but Maira and Kyla came up beside me, their talons out. Maira's were already bloody. "What do you need us to do?"

"Help Lena distract her. Keep her engaged and her focus off us," I whispered, moving toward her again to distract her from Lena. I swiped at her leg with my daggers, cutting along her calf.

She roared in pain, or perhaps annoyance, and turned, swiping at me with her talons. She nearly connected with my chest, but a pale arm shot out and grabbed her wrist. Maira grinned as she shoved Cliodhna's arm away, moving to engage her queen in a flurry of strikes.

Between the four of us, we kept Cliodhna from gaining the upper hand, each of us striking out between blasts of Lena's silver magic.

Cliodhna was growing frustrated, sending out lazy blasts of her own magic at us, missing more times than not. I had caused more injury to her, with cuts now bleeding on her arms and legs. Kyla had also made contact, swiping her chest with her talons, while Maira had reopened the wounds on her face. We were winning.

"I will bathe in your blood, deceitful creatures," she snarled, panting for breath as she pointed at Maira and Kyla.

"You'll do no such thing," Kyla snarled, looking over Cliodhna's shoulder at Lena, whose magic was building into a ball at her chest.

As Cliodhna lunged at us, Maira stepped forward, grabbing her former queen by the shoulders and spinning her around to face Lena. The ball of silver magic hit Cliodhna in the chest, pushing her and Maira back several yards, falling from the brunt of the impact. I rushed over to Maira's side.

"You okay?" I asked, lifting her head up slightly. From this position, I could see Cameron, Faolan, and Brigid still engaging with

Arran. Thankfully, they seemed uninjured, but Arran was in rough shape as blood poured from his legs and a gash high on his collarbone dripped down his chest, soaking his shirt.

Maira's eyes twitched as she tried to sit up. "'M fine."

"You're not. You hit your head," I said, helping her up.

She waved a hand. "Go, help them. I'm fine."

I hesitated as she shoved me, snarling. "Go, stubborn fool."

Casting one more glance her way, I stood and ran back over to Kyla, who was battling Cliodhna once more, kicking at her legs to knock her off balance. Out of the corner of my eye, I saw Brigid running toward us, Arran's body lying on the ground behind her. She held a bloody dagger in her hand, aimed right at Cliodhna. The syren queen raised a shaky hand, sending a last-ditch magical blast toward Brigid. It hit her square in the stomach, stopping her in her tracks and knocking her onto her back.

NO!

My first instinct was to run to Brigid, but Lena cast another wave of magic, and Cliodhna stumbled. Picking up my sword from the dirt, I saw my opening. Cliodhna was weak, and this would be our best chance. I could see Brigid moving in the distance, and I was relieved to see she was okay. My gaze blurred slightly as I forced everything away—except Cliodhna.

"You'll never be what you once were, Nehalennia," Cliodhna hissed, swaying as she dropped to her knees.

Lena shuddered as she blasted Cliodhna with more silver magic just as I swung my sword. In one clean slice, her head rolled from her shoulders and landed with a thud at my feet.

Staring down at the severed head of the syren queen, I held my breath, waiting to be sure she was truly dead. I watched for one breath, two, three. She remained dead, her icy blue eyes staring vacantly out at the carnage she'd created.

My sword fell from my hand, clattering to the ground next to the goddess's head, my fingers unable to keep hold of the hilt as it finally sank in.

She was dead.

It was over.

I let out a shuddering breath, finally returning to my senses and rushing over to where Brigid lay in the dirt. "Are you okay, *teine*?"

She panted, holding a hand to her chest where Cliodhna had struck her. "I'm fine. Did you kill her?"

"Aye," I said, brushing the hair out of her face and gently pulling at the neckline of her shirt to inspect the bruise that was already forming on her ribs. The blow had been harder than it looked. "Did you kill Arran?"

"Yes," she whispered. "Cam and Faolan helped. He's dead, too."

"It's over, *teine*." I looked over to Lena, who kneeled by Cliodhna's body, her mouth moving, speaking words I could not hear. "We did it."

"Good." She winced, closing her eyes and leaning her weight into my body.

All at once, Cliodhna's last words hit me. I studied Lena, kneeling beside the blood pooling around Cliodhna's neck.

"Lena," I breathed, my eyes wide. "Cliodhna called her Nehalennia."

Elizianna
@ELIZIANNA.THE.ONE

C A E L U M

CHAPTER FIFTY-ONE

Now that Brigid was at least okay to be on her own, I pulled her to her feet and led her back to where Lena still knelt by Cliodhna's body.

The surrounding fights were dying down, now that both Arran and Cliodhna were gone. My father's crew seemed to have given up, but Cameron and Duncan handled the last few stragglers.

"Lena," I said sharply, interrupting her chant. My vision tunneled in on the witch, the blood pounding in my ears as I stepped up to her. I had been the only one who trusted her, and she had been lying about who she was this entire time. "Or should I say, Nehalennia?"

She froze and slowly looked up at me, her eyes churning silver. Her words were careful and slow. "Mind your tone, Caelum."

"You lied to me," I hissed, stepping closer. I had just killed one goddess. Another did not scare me.

She shook her head, her sad eyes extinguishing some of my anger. "I have not been that goddess in a long time."

"Why didn't you tell us?" My emotions threatened to break through. I had named my ship after this woman—this goddess. I had *worshiped* her as a child and prayed to her for safe passage as an adult. And she had known this the second she met me.

"Because I do not answer to you." She stood, casting a final glance at Cliodhna's body before removing her cloak and draping it over the fallen goddess. Her gaze met mine again. "I was lost to man, Caelum. Forgotten to all but a scarce few. I owe you no fealty."

"No, but you owe him an explanation," Brigid said, still holding her torso gingerly. "He trusted you. More than the rest of us."

Lena sighed, her eyes scanning the carnage. I noticed her gaze pause on Faolan before she continued speaking. "Let us be done with this mess, and then we shall talk."

"Where have the guards gone?" Brigid asked, looking around the square, now empty apart from my crew and the multitude of dead bodies.

"They decided that there were safer places to be," Lena said, rolling her eyes. "Pathetic."

"Well, they'll likely return soon, so we need to get rid of these bodies," I said, wiping the back of my hand across my sweaty forehead.

I caught Duncan and Cam's eyes from across the square, nodding at them to join us. The rest of the crew and the syrens followed suit.

Once they gathered around, I spoke again. "Collect all the weapons and get rid of anything identifying on the bodies."

"What do we do with the bodies themselves?" Cameron asked, looking out at the half dozen bodies, including Arran and Cliodhna.

"The guards can deal with them when they collect their spines." I waved a hand. "Just be sure to leave nothing that could lead back to us."

"We want Cliodhna's body," Maira spoke up from the syren side of the group.

"Why?" I asked, raising an eyebrow. We had just killed the vile goddess, and I didn't want Maira to resurrect her out of spite.

"To take her to the sea and bury her the way she deserves," she snapped back.

"She deserves to rot." My voice was icy as I let my gaze slide over to Brigid before turning back to Maira. "Or did you so quickly forget what she did to two of your own, in the name of her own pride?"

"I will take her body," Lena said sharply, stepping up beside me. "I will lay her to rest in a manner fitting for a goddess."

Maira wanted to argue. That much was clear, but Kyla placed a hand on her arm to stop her from speaking again. Kyla turned to Lena. "That's acceptable to us. Thank you."

Lena nodded once in return.

"Then get to it," I said, raising my voice slightly. "I want to get back to the ship before the guards return."

The crew and the syrens set out on their tasks as Brigid lingered behind. Turning to her, we both stepped forward at the same moment. I wrapped her in my arms, burying my nose in her neck and breathing her in. "We did it."

She nodded into my neck, tightening her arms around my shoulders. "We're alive."

Pulling back slightly, I moved my hands to her face, smearing some of the blood spatter there. Taking a deep breath, I took in every detail: her full lips, the freckles that spattered across her nose and cheeks, her fanning lashes, her bright green eyes, all of it. Gratitude and relief washed through me, nearly knocking me to my knees as I let out a shuddering breath.

Astute as ever, she rocked up on her toes and pressed her lips to mine for a kiss that was over far too soon. Wrapping me in her arms once more, she ran her hand through the back of my hair. "We did it, Caelum. We're safe."

"Are you two planning to help soon?" a sharp voice came from behind me. Turning, I glared at Maira, who simply smiled in return, showing all her teeth.

With a sigh, I stepped back. "We should help. We need to get out of here before the guards and soldiers come back."

She nodded, slipping her hand into mine as we turned toward the mess of bodies in the square. "Let's go."

Clearing the square of weapons and identifying information

went quicker than I expected, and now we were safely out of the town and back on *The Nehalennia*. Most of the crew was up on deck, but I had asked Duncan, Lena, and Brigid to follow me to my quarters. We needed to talk.

I invited Brigid because she needed to be involved in the discussion with Lena and Duncan because he would have hit me if I left him out.

Lena took a seat at the small table in the corner as I closed the door behind us. I had so many things to ask her, but I wanted to give her a chance to come clean about everything first. She had hidden so much from us, from *me*. Beyond her name and her history with Cliodhna, I wanted to ask how she knew Faolan. Had he not told me the whole truth about himself, either?

"Explain, now," I sat down at the table across from Lena. She raised her eyebrow at my demand. "Please," I sighed.

Brigid and Duncan stood in the corner of the room, watching our interaction, thankfully allowing me to lead the conversation.

Lena sighed, a heavy sound that blanketed the room. "I knew your mother, Caelum."

Of all the things I had expected her to say, that had not been one of them. The breath left my lungs instantly, the room spinning slightly on the edges of my vision.

My mother?

I only had vague memories of the woman, who, according to my father, had died from sickness when I was a child. I always suspected he'd had a hand in her death, especially as I grew older, but I could never confirm it.

Lena continued as I sat in stunned silence. "She was the daughter of a priestess who'd been with me when I still clung to any last hopes of worshippers. Raised in the old ways of the gods, her mother found me as a young woman, and raised her daughter—your mother—in my sad excuse for a temple."

"What..." I started, my voice clogged with emotion. I cleared my throat. "What was she like?"

She smiled at me, genuinely this time, void of her usual mystery.

"Rhiannon was a wonderful woman. Kind, loyal, and stubborn to a fault. You remind me a lot of her."

"Why did she leave you?" I asked, unsure if I really wanted to know the answer, but needing it, nonetheless. Sure, I likely wouldn't have been born if she had stayed, but maybe she would still be alive.

Lena's smile fell and her face darkened. "Only having one person worship you is not enough for a goddess, Caelum. As man forgot the old ways, turning away from the gods and toward things of their own devising, we all lost our powers. A god is only as powerful as those who remember them. Some faded more quickly than others. I was always a minor goddess in the eyes of humanity. Only important to those who traveled the seas. But your mother... your mother was determined. After her own mother passed, she stayed with me until I realized it was futile. I had become human. It was time for her to move on with her life."

"She moved on, into the hands of my father." The venom in my voice surprised me. I looked down, ashamed of my tone. "Apologies. I know that was not your doing."

She sighed. "It was, in a way. I encouraged her to continue helping those who traveled the seas. She worked as a healer, hired for any ship who needed one for their journey or for after. That's how she met your father. Or rather, that is how your father found her."

I swallowed, wanting to ask more.

Thankfully, she saw the question in my eyes without me having to voice it aloud. "Rhiannon was a beautiful woman. And your father was not always the violent and evil man you knew. Even after our separation, Rhiannon stayed in contact with me. She loved your father, Caelum. And he loved her. He simply grew to love his fortune more."

"Do you know how she died?" My voice was barely audible, and I felt Brigid shift behind me, knowing she wanted to comfort me. Hell, I needed it. Turning my head to look at her, she immediately stepped up behind me, resting her hand on my shoulder. I reached my hand up to hold hers.

Lena's gaze lingered on our hands for a moment. "No, I do not.

We lost touch after you were born. I suspect your father helped little with you as a baby and kept her busy."

I cleared my throat. "She spoke of you. Not as a friend, but as a goddess. She told stories of all the gods and goddesses."

She smiled sadly. "I suspected as much when I saw your ship."

Brigid shifted behind me again. "Can I ask something?"

"Of course, fire," Lena said, smiling a little brighter.

"If you no longer have the powers of a goddess, how do you know everything you do?" Brigid asked, squeezing my hand again as she spoke. "You knew Caelum's name, and the name of his ship, before even meeting."

"They call me a witch now for good reason," she said, smirking. But her face grew serious once more. "I kept some of my powers, one being the ability to see all the vessels on the seas of Caladhan. The others... Well, I learned to adapt to my new reality. Magic is still available for those willing to learn it."

"So, now that we stopped Cliodhna," I asked, turning the conversation back to our uncertain reality, "what do we do?"

"I suppose we can do whatever we'd like."

"What if we don't know what that is?" My voice trailed off, full of uncertainty. I spent my whole life focused on stopping my father. And while I now had the orphanage to help, I felt lost and without purpose.

"Then I suppose your new adventure will be finding that out."

Elizianna
@ELIZIANNA.THE.ONE

CHAPTER FIFTY-TWO

We left the room, making our way back up to the main deck, where the crew and the syrens were waiting, looking at me expectantly. Our mission may be complete, but there was still work to be done and promises that still needed to be kept.

"We need to make sure the orphanage is okay," I sighed, running my hand through my hair. "I'm sure they're still scared from the encounter with Arran, and we need to inform them he's no longer a threat."

"Lena, what will you do? Are you staying with us, or returning to your home?" Brigid asked.

"I suppose I need to get back to my home and Abria," she said, staring wistfully out at the waves. She turned to us. "Someone will need to take me."

"You can raise a ship from the depths of the sea, but you cannot take yourself back home?" Duncan asked, raising an eyebrow.

"There *are* limitations to magic," she replied, shaking her head.

"Will you stay here while we go to see the children?" I asked, interrupting whatever response Duncan had planned. "Or will you come with us?"

She shook her head. "No, I will stay here. You all go on."

Nodding at her, I motioned toward Brigid and Cam before turning to Duncan, who I assumed would also stay behind. "Have Alan's men watch over the ship, and find out if they plan to stay with us or go their own way."

I could see he was grateful for not asking him to accompany us to the orphanage. "Aye, aye."

Turning to the syrens, still gathered and watching us, I locked eyes with Kyla. "Would you like to join us?"

She smiled, and her eyes lit up. "Yes, I'd love to."

After a brief goodbye, Kyla, Brigid, Cameron, and I climbed down the rungs to the dock below and began our trek back into town.

Although I was technically a fugitive, the town's guards had dispersed when the fighting began, and I doubted they would be looking for me now. There was too much else they had to worry about. Even so, I hesitated slightly as we approached the main road.

Brigid squeezed my hand, smiling at me. "It'll be okay. I won't let anyone take you away again."

We were cautious as we made our way through the streets of Brinemoor toward the orphanage, keeping to the back alleys and vacant side paths, just in case.

"Are we staying in Brinemoor?" Cam muttered as we walked.

I was wondering the same thing. While I wanted somewhere permanent, somewhere other than my small cottage, to live, my life was on *The Nehalennia* and on the sea. "Do you want to stay?"

"Caelum, I have followed you for the better part of a decade." The corner of his lip twitched slightly. "You're my captain."

"This is a crew, Cam," I replied. "If Alan and his men are staying with us, we will vote."

Brigid looked at me, raising her eyebrow. I could tell she wanted to ask me something, and I had a sneaking suspicion she had an opinion on whether we should stay here. My stomach knotted, anxiety rising at just what her opinion might be. But before I could worry more, the conversation ended, and we stepped up to the orphanage doors. These children might have been resilient, but the last few days with their home being attacked were likely tough on them.

I knocked on the heavy doors, and after a moment I heard movement behind them. The door opened and Isla peeked out, her face relaxing when she saw it was me. "Caelum. You're safe."

"I am." I smiled reassuringly. "We're all safe now."

"What about that man that came earlier?" she asked, looking over her shoulder. She stepped outside, pulling the door closed behind her. "Should we be worried?"

"He's dead." Brigid spoke confidently. "No one will bother you again."

She and Isla shared a look for a moment before Isla nodded, taking a deep breath. "Good. Thank you all."

"There's nothing to thank us for." I reached out to squeeze her shoulder.

"Do you want to come in and see the children? I know they want to see you," she said, smiling widely. She looked at the rest of the group. "Please come in, all of you. We should have enough food for dinner."

"We'd love to come in to see them, but there's no need to feed us," I responded quickly. "That food is for you and the children. Do not worry about us, Isla," I said, offering a soft smile.

"Well, come on then," she said, turning to pull the door open.

We stepped over the threshold and moved down the hall toward the dayroom, following the sounds of children playing as it filtered out the open doors. The laughter was infectious. These children paid no heed to the violence that had taken place down the street from them. I smiled as the children noticed us entering the room.

As usual, Rory was the first to notice. He jumped up and ran over so quickly; it was a shock he didn't trip over his own feet. For such a small boy, he packed a large punch when he rammed himself into my legs, wrapping his arms around my knees.

"You're back!" he yelled, looking up at me.

I bent down and lifted him into my arms, settling him on my hip and ruffling his hair with my free hand. "Aye, had to make sure you lot weren't causing trouble."

Noises of protest filled the room, and I could see my friends all smiling at the children.

I set Rory down and patted his head as he clung to my leg. "I want you all to meet some new friends."

I introduced Cam and Brigid, and the children swarmed them, Cameron quickly becoming a favorite.

I stood back with Isla, watching them all. She nudged her shoulder into mine. "They'll be fine, Caelum. Children are resilient."

"I know, but they shouldn't have to be." I sighed, watching how happy they were, showing off their toys and talking animatedly to my friends. Rory had once again claimed Kyla as his own, and two young girls captivated Brigid, speaking to her with such excitement. It was good to see.

Isla turned to me, raising an eyebrow. "That's life, Caelum. You know that better than most. We can't control what happens."

"I know, but I still want better for them."

Isla nodded toward Brigid. "You need to focus on better for yourself first."

"What do you mean?" I was fine now. Brigid was back, Cliodhna was dead, and the children were safe.

"Work on building your relationship with her first," she said, smiling and nodding toward Brigid. "*Without* violence involved for once."

I fell silent, pondering her words. She was right, as usual. Brigid and I had met as children under violent terms. Violence enveloped our reunion, and nearly every moment since then. We never had a chance to learn about each other in times of peace.

That seemed like a good place to start. Our next chapter.

"I'll keep sending money," I said, changing the subject. These children and this orphanage still needed help, no matter my relationship status.

She waved her hand. "We make do. Send what you can when you can. And please come to visit."

Before I could answer, Rory popped up in front of us, hands on his hip and his head cocked to the side, pouting. "Caelum, you said you were going to play with us."

Isla grinned at me, waving her hand. "Go on. We can talk more later."

Elizi
@ELIZIAN

BRIGID

CHAPTER FIFTY-THREE

The orphanage had been emotional both in a good way and a heartbreaking way, and it was clear Caelum still felt responsible for these children. The little girls who had been so intent on telling me everything they'd done that day. The little boy who'd attached himself to Kyla and was distraught, trying to decide if he'd wanted to play with her or Caelum. All of it brought a warmth that spread through my body.

These children were amazing, and it was clear they meant a lot to Caelum. I wanted him to stay here if that was what he wanted, and I would join him, but I had one thing to do first.

Sorcha had given her life to save mine, and I would honor her last request now that I had a moment to breathe. I was going back to Bhodheas to find Owen and tell him about Sorcha. He deserved to know what happened, and she deserved to be remembered by someone other than us.

The time in captivity with Cliodhna and then Caelum's imprisonment had pushed her request to the back of my mind, but now that was over, and I knew what I needed to do.

I wanted Caelum to come with me, but his heart was in the hands of these children, and I couldn't expect him to leave with me.

I would ask him, and whatever answer he gave would be enough for me. If I went to Bhodheas alone, I would return to him when I finished my task.

Climbing back aboard the ship as the sun sank into the horizon, it did not surprise me to see Alan and his men still aboard. I had a feeling they would stay.

"Caelum, can we talk?" I pulled him aside as we approached the others gathered on the deck.

His brows furrowed. "What is it, *teine*?"

"Nothing bad, Captain, I promise."

He slipped his hand into mine as we stepped away from the others. Leaning against the railing, he spun me around to face him. "Talk to me, *teine*?"

I hesitated, taking a deep breath, as I was unsure of what I would do if he didn't want to come with me. "I must go back to Bhodheas to find Sorcha's Owen and tell him what happened."

The look of confusion on Caelum's face quickly faded to understanding. "Of course, *teine*. Once the crew votes, we can set off."

"You'd come with me?" I breathed, surprised at his immediate agreement.

He smiled, nodding as he let go of my hand to grab my face. "Of course I will come with you. I'll not be letting you out of my sight for the foreseeable future, Brigid."

Emotion swelled in my chest. The immediacy of Caelum's agreement, the tenderness I saw in his face, the openness... It solidified my feelings for him, and I needed to tell him. "Caelum, I..."

He raised a brow as I trailed off once more. "What?"

For some reason, I couldn't bring myself to spit out the words. *I love you.* The three simple words caught in my throat and refused to come out. Instead of speaking, I reached my arms up and grabbed his face, pulling his lips down to mine and pouring all the words I couldn't say into the movement. The ferocity of the kiss seemed to surprise him for a moment, but he recovered quickly, grabbing my waist and kissing me back with equal energy.

Finally, Caelum pulled away, gazing deep into my eyes. "I love you too, *teine*," he whispered.

My mouth dropped open. "How?"

He smiled. "You don't need to say a word for me to know what you're thinking."

The smile that broke across my face was so wide it hurt my cheeks. At a loss for words once more, I pulled him down for another quick but fierce kiss. "I'll go with you anywhere, Captain."

"And I with you, syren."

"Aye, you two!" Duncan shouted. "We've got some decisions to make if you'd stop snogging soon."

Sighing, I pulled away. "I doubt that relationship will improve."

"You two need to work it out."

"I will try," I replied, dreading that conversation already. Caelum stepped back, linking hands as we walked back to the rest of the crew and the syrens.

Lena had joined them, as well.

"We need to decide what to do, Captain," Duncan said, crossing his arms. "I doubt the guards will forget about your escape for much longer."

"Aye," Caelum agreed, rubbing a hand over his face and looking around at the rest of the crew. "I may be the captain, but this will be a group decision. Do we want to stay here in Brinemoor or continue sailing?"

"Where would we sail?" Alan asked.

"South. To Bhodheas," I answered, holding my chin up high. I was ready for Duncan to protest, but he never did. Still, I knew it was important to Caelum that everyone on his crew have a voice. "I promised a friend I would deliver a message for her before she died. I intend to keep that promise."

Alan looked at his men before replying with an easy shrug. "We'd be happy to sail with you."

"Will we return here?" Cameron asked, his brows furrowing as he looked over at Kyla, who watched our interactions carefully. "With the orphanage here in Brinemoor, it might be smart to establish a base here."

"But Caelum is still a fugitive," I pointed out. "Until we resolve that, that might not be wise."

"If anyone on the crew wants to stay here, my old home is open," Caelum said slowly. "It needs some repairs, but having a home in Brinemoor is a smart choice."

Cameron and Caelum shared a look for a long moment. Finally, their gazes broke and Cam spoke. "I'll stay here. To watch the orphanage and repair the house. I'll work on getting Caelum cleared of his charges, too."

"What will we do after we deliver your message?" Duncan asked, raising an eyebrow at me.

I shared a look with Lena before turning my attention to Kyla. "Women will still face the possibility of a watery grave, and without Cliodhna to notice when they have entered the sea, it might be more difficult to save them. Although we may not be able to make new syrens, perhaps we can work together to help them start a new life somewhere safe."

Alys and Faolan stepped up from behind the crew. I did a double take, not having noticed them earlier. Alys smiled widely. "We have plenty of room in our home for anyone who needs help, so long as you get them to us."

"I think we can handle that," Caelum said with a smile at me. He raised an eyebrow at Duncan. "If that is acceptable to you?"

Duncan smiled wryly. "It would be my honor."

"Well," Lena said, clapping her hands. "It appears it is time to begin our newest adventure."

I turned to Kyla and the other syrens, still standing and watching us silently. There was still one other group we needed to hear from.

Elizi
@ELIZIAN

CHAPTER FIFTY-FOUR

"I want you to know you're always welcome on my ship or in my home, Kyla," Caelum said, looking over at the syrens. "What will you all do now?"

"Carve out a new life and a new purpose. Protecting those who travel the seas and punishing those who use it for evil." She smiled. "Save the women sent to the sea to die."

I stepped up, locking eyes with her for a moment before pulling her into a hug. "Please, be safe."

"You as well, Brigid," she said, stepping back to stroke my cheek. "You're always welcome with us, no matter what."

Maira stepped around Kyla and cleared her throat. "This is all great, but I think we're forgetting something. Our queen is dead. Will we lose our powers? Where will we go?"

I felt shocked by the anxiety in her voice. Maira had never been uncertain of anything for as long as I had known her. But I didn't know the answers to her questions, either. I looked at Lena, hoping she'd take the lead.

"Those powers are yours now, little fish." Lena's voice was calm. "No one will take them."

"But you cannot keep killing innocent people." Duncan said, glaring at them. "That's over now."

"And how will you stop us?" Maira snapped, stepping in front of Cordelia, who shied back at Duncan's harsh tone. "We don't answer to you, brute."

"Now, now," Lena said, holding her hands, and separating Maira and Duncan. "Let's stay calm."

"They can't just go back to killing sailors!"

"We won't," Kyla said sternly, looking back at Cordelia and Maira as she spoke. She turned to Duncan. "Innocents will not die at our hands. Not anymore."

"That's not exactly encouraging," Duncan spat. "You get to decide who's innocent or not?"

"Stop this," I said, stepping in front of Duncan, pushing his chest and forcing him to step back. "We *all* went against our natures to help you and kill our queen. This is all we have known for decades. Give them a moment to accept a new reality."

Duncan's nostrils flared. "Well, accept it quickly. We'll not let you go about killing people on the seas."

"You aren't in charge of us, Duncan." I met his glare, raising an eyebrow.

"Us?" he asked, scoffing. "And here I thought you were on *our* side."

"That's enough," Caelum called, leaning against the mast with his arms crossed, observing the scene before him. "Brigid's right. We have no control over the syrens. They've said they will protect those on the seas and not hurt them. We must take their word for it. I believe they've earned our trust."

"Kyla is our new leader," Maira said, her voice quiet but firm. "We will follow her orders."

I turned to Kyla, smiling widely. That was an excellent decision, and one I would have made myself. Kyla was not only the oldest of us, but the wisest and most level-headed. However, Duncan's words echoed in my mind. Where would *I* go? Would I return to the syrens? Or would I stay with Caelum? Did Caelum want me to stay with him? I hoped so. I wasn't sure what I would do if he didn't. "Congratulations, queen."

She shook her head. "No, not a queen. I won't be like Cliodhna."

"This is all very touching," Duncan snarled. "But the original issue remains."

I watched as Kyla rolled her shoulders back and turned her attention to the big blonde. "As the others have said, we don't answer to you, but you needn't worry about us. We will not be the violent beasts you seem to think we are."

"Where will you stay?" Cam asked, his brows pinched. "Will you go back to the seas, or stay on land?"

"We will go back to the caves," Kyla said. "They're the only home we know."

"My home is always open to you," Lena said. "If you would like to learn from me."

"And what would we learn from you, witch?" Maira asked, her voice sardonic. "How to murder goddesses?"

"Among other things," Lena hissed with a raised eyebrow. "But I can teach you magic to help supplement anything you may have lost with Cliodhna's death."

"That's enough," I sighed. Maira would never change. "What you do is up to you, of course."

"Will you be returning with us?" Kyla asked, turning her attention back to me.

I hated that I hesitated, but I did. I looked over at Caelum, silently pleading for him to speak up, but he just smiled and inclined his head, waiting for me to speak. It was my decision. Did I want to go back to the syrens? Did I want to stay here? The warring decision tugged at my chest, my heart quite literally splitting in two, torn between my old life and my new future.

I took a deep breath, closing my eyes for a moment. Filled with peace, I looked back at Caelum once more before turning to face the syrens. "No, I'll be staying with Caelum."

"So, you're abandoning us for a man? Again?" Maira sneered, crossing her arms.

"No," Kyla said, stopping Maira's. "We've lost Brigid once before, and we're not pushing her away again. She can do whatever she wants, just like you. We all have free will, Maira."

"She's leaving us for him!"

"She's leaving us for love." I jerked at Kyla's words, my cheeks heating at the public declaration of my own emotions. I'd told Caelum, but hearing it aloud from someone else was... jarring. For so long, I'd not considered myself worthy of anyone's love, but Caelum had proven that otherwise. The crew, the syrens, the children at the orphanage.

Maira huffed, but fell silent.

"Little fish," Lena said, standing up straighter and looking at Maira with her eyes beginning to swirl, "if you continue holding on to that anger, it will poison you, just as it did your former queen. I hope we will not have to dispatch you once it does."

"Are you threatening me?" Maira asked, stepping toe to toe with Lena.

To her credit, Lena didn't back down, though Kyla and I were both poised to grab Maira if she did anything rash. The last thing we needed after the fight with Cliodhna was another fight. Lena likely had little magic, and even less patience left.

"Of course not. I do not need to resort to petty threats and words of spite." Lena's chin lifted, daring the syren to make a move.

Kyla stepped between them, sensing Maira's anger rising once more. "We will consider that, Lena, thank you. We will decide what to do as a group. No more following the orders of one person."

"You will be a good leader, Kyla Còmhan," Lena said, her eyes falling still again and turning a flat gray.

"When will you leave?" Duncan asked, crossing his arms.

"Whenever they please," Caelum interrupted, raising his eyebrow. "Lena, you are certain she is dead and no longer a threat?"

"She is gone," Lena confirmed. "Killing a goddess is difficult, and had she been at the height of her powers from centuries ago, that likely would not have been enough to kill her. But she is gone."

"I believe it's time for us to go now," Kyla said wistfully, looking out at the seas.

The other syrens moved to the edge of the ship, shifting impatiently as their new leader stood with us. I felt Cam hovering behind me, likely waiting for his chance to speak to the woman who enthralled him. They would have been a good pairing, but both were too selfless and loyal.

I leaned in and kissed Kyla on the cheek. "Be safe. Someone else wants to speak with you before you leave."

She looked confused for a moment before noticing Cam standing behind me. Her forehead softened as she gazed at him. Squeezing her hand once more, I stepped back and smiled at Cam as I moved back to join Caelum.

"They would be good together," I whispered, watching Cam fumble with his hands at his side, hesitating to reach out and touch Kyla.

"I wish they would acknowledge it," he replied.

We watched in silence as they spoke, Kyla ducking her head shyly at something Cam had said.

"Another syren lover?" Duncan sighed, rolling his eyes as he stepped up next to us. "Great."

"Maybe you should get one too," I laughed, raising my brow. "Might put you in a better mood."

Caelum laughed, joining in on my teasing.

Duncan opened his mouth to respond, but just then Cameron pulled Kyla into his arms and kissed her deeply. At first, she was shocked, and then pulled back and slapped him across the face. The impact echoed across the deck, and both Caelum and I straightened, ready to intervene.

Everything paused for a moment as both the crew and the syrens stood there watching the two. Cameron held his cheek and Kyla looked ruffled and unsure. She stared at him for a moment, and then flung her arms around his neck and kissed him again, fiercely.

Caelum and I smiled as they continued kissing. "Well, glad that worked out."

Caelum laughed. "Aye, I don't think I could handle Cam moping around for the next month."

Finally, Cam and Kyla separated, sharing one last embrace before Kyla stepped away and joined the other syrens. Kyla smiled and waved at us before they all slipped over the railing and disappeared into the sea.

Cameron walked back to join us, a dreamy look on his face.

"So, was it worth getting slapped?" Caelum asked, smiling.

He grinned, reality coming back into his eyes. "Absolutely."

Caelum shook his head, and I smiled, pulling Cam into a quick hug. "Good. She'll be back, I'm sure of it."

"She said she will visit," Cam said, shrugging, pretending it wasn't important to him. But we all knew better. "Now, where in Bhodheas are you going?"

"Teich," I said, nodding my head. "Sorcha said they were supposed to meet in Teich. We will start there."

Caelum grinned at me, pressing a kiss to my forehead. "Then let's be off."

THE END. FOR NOW.

CAMERON

A FAREWELL KISS

This is a bonus scene from The Captain's Revenge

Watching Brigid and Kyla exchange soft goodbyes was ripping my heart to shreds. Both of them were teary, their eyes reflecting like mirrors as they held each other.

I shifted impatiently. I *needed* to talk to Kyla before she left, and I only hoped Brigid would let me have the chance. Seeing Cae and Brigid together... it had only solidified my need to tell Kyla that I cared for her. That I wanted to pursue something more with her, if and when she was ever ready for that. And if she said no, I would respect her wishes and leave her alone.

But I knew I couldn't let her go without at least telling her.

Brigid looked over her shoulder at me for a moment before turning back and pressing her lips to Kyla's cheek. She muttered something into her ear and Kyla's brows furrowed as her eyes searched out across the deck. Landing on me, they softened and she nodded, acknowledging whatever Brigid had whispered.

Brigid stepped away, dropping her hold on Kyla's hand.

I hesitated, rocking back and forth on my feet as Brigid passed me with what could only be described as a shit eating grin plastered on her face.

Reaching up to rub the back of my neck, I took a deep breath and willed my feet forward. In three strides, I was in front of Kyla... and I had no idea what to say.

Her amber eyes landed on my face, searching for an answer, and all the words I'd ever learned left my brain.

"Cameron?" she asked. She tilted her head, waiting for me to speak. "Did you want to talk to me?"

I opened my mouth, but no sounds came out and I promptly clamped it shut. The clouds parted and the sun shone brightly, only on her. Her eyes caught the light, reflecting facets of brown and gold. The sun kissed her skin, illuminating the rich color that spread across her body. The wind picked up and moved a stray curl across her face.

Without thinking, I reached up and tucked it back behind her ear. "You're stunning," I murmured, my eyes still roaming over her face, drinking in her beauty while I still could. I was no worse than a drunkard, and I was happily drunk on *her*.

"Thank you, Cam." She ducked her head. "What did you need to tell me, though? We should be leaving soon."

My heart raced, and the planned words I'd carefully constructed left on the wind. "Will you come back?" I cleared my throat, trying to not seem overeager. "I mean, do you think you all will come visit again?"

She studied me for a moment, and I feared my every thought was plastered across my face. But maybe that was a good thing. Maybe she would see what I was trying—and failing—to tell her. "Yes," she drawled. "Of course we'll be back to visit."

My heart stuttered in my chest, pounding against my ribs. She would be back. She was *coming back*. Weeks in her presence had wrecked me, had ruined me beyond repair until all I could see was her and all I could think about was her. And maybe it was a fantasy, something I'd dreamed up to tell myself I had a shot with her. But on that island, and again as we walked back from the orphanage... I thought I'd seen the same desire reflected in her face.

Before I could doubt myself anymore, I swept her into my arms and bent to press my lips to hers, trying to convey all of my feelings into that one kiss. It was like the sun was coming from within her, warming me. She froze in my arms, and her inaction had me pulling back and searching her face. The apprehension there sent me back a half step, dropping my arms from her body.

Fuck, I thought, wanting nothing more than to disappear into the deck. Maybe she would take pity on me and the syrens would drown me quickly.

Her hand reached out and struck my face, a burning sting stretching across my palm as I reached up to cover it. The world seemed to still, and I could feel the eyes of every single person on the ship upon us. Waiting to see if they should kill me for my indiscretion.

Kyla's eyes were burning brightly, but her face didn't convey offense, fear, or anything of the sort. Before I could make out what her face *was* saying, her hands reached up, knocking mine out of the way as she pulled my face down to hers. Her arms snaked around my neck and I finally shook off my surprise, surging forward to meet her and wrapping my arms around her waist to pull her as close to my body as possible.

Her plush lips against mine, the feeling of her chest and stomach and thighs pressed against mine… it was a feeling I would never forget as long as I lived.

Our kiss broke and I rested my forehead against hers. Both of us were breathless, our pants mingling in the small space between our mouths.

"I'll be back, Cameron," she whispered. "I'll be back for you."

"Stay safe out there," I whispered back. "I'll always have a room for you."

She smiled, leaning up to press a soft kiss to my lips once more before she stepped away.

My lips tingled, and for a moment, it balanced out the twisting in my stomach as she moved over to the syrens. She turned back, smiling at me, sadness in her eyes. And then she was gone, waving at us before slipping over the side and into the sea.

I waited for a moment, until I was sure they'd all be gone. Sighing, I forced myself to remember her words, her touch.

She would be back. And I trusted her word, and would be waiting for her when she came.

Turning back to the crew, I made my way to Brigid and Caelum, who were both grinning at me like fools. Hell, I was likely grinning like a fool myself.

"So, was it worth getting slapped?" Caelum asked, his grin growing ever wider.

I huffed a laugh, unable to come up with the words to describe exactly how worth it it was. Instead, I settled on a breathy, "Absolutely."

Caelum shook his head, and Brigid stepped up, pulling me into a quick hug. "Good. She'll be back, I'm sure of it."

"She said she will visit," I said, shrugging slightly and trying not to make it a big deal. If I did, they would only butt in further, and I wanted this to be ours. Mine and Kyla's. No one else's. It would happen when it happened, and I didn't want to rush anything. Rolling my shoulders back, I turned to the redheaded syren and my captain, both of whom were about to leave as well. "Now, where in Bhodheas are you going?"

Acknowledgments

To my readers: Thank you. This would never have happened without you and I am beyond grateful.

To my family: Words can't describe how thankful I am for your continued support in this journey.

To my husband especially, thank you for providing a shoulder to cry on, an ear to talk through all my insane ideas, and the manual labor it takes to haul all these books up and down the stairs for my shop.

To all of the friends I've made along the way, and to all the friends I've lost, and will gain. It's hard doing this, but you all make it so much easier to endure. You inspire me every day to keep going.

To everyone who helped bring this book, and every book, to life. I'm in awe of your creativity, and gracious for your patience when I try to describe what I'm looking for and it makes zero sense.

From the bottom of my heart, from Caelum and Brigid and all the others too, thank you for being here. We hope you enjoyed.

About the Author

Jessica S. Taylor (she/her) is the author of dark fantasy romance novels. Her first book, THE SYREN'S MUTINY was an ode to her childhood love of pirates and mermaids. She's since moved onto spookier things, as one does.

As a kid, Jessica devoured whatever books she could get her hands on and when that wasn't enough, she began writing her own.

Jessica was born and raised in Kentucky, but is currently residing in New England with her husband and cat, Nebula. When she's not reading or writing, Jessica enjoys concerts, traveling, and spending time with her family.

Visit her website to learn more and join her newsletter to be the first to get exclusive content and updates! www.authorjessicastaylor.com

Glossary

As you probably guessed, a lot of my inspiration came from Celtic (specifically Irish, Scottish, Welsh, Germanic) mythology. As such, I used Gaelic words and names, as well as various Celtic gods and goddesses and their mythology, to inspire my world.

Here is a list of all the words and names and their meanings in English.

Characters:

Brigid - Celtic goddess of fire, healers, blacksmiths, childbirth, and inspiration

Teine - fire; Caelum's nickname for Brigid

Caelum - heavens (as in stars)

Sorcha - radiant

Duncan - powerful warrior

Cliodnha - Irish goddess of love, beauty and the sea, queen of the banshees and/or fairies (depending on which myth you read)

Kellan - slender

Nehalennia - Celtic (modern day Holland) goddess of well-being, prosperity, and seafarers. A goddess of healing and/or death.

Kyla - victorious

Maira - of the sea
Cordelia - daughter of the sea
Nerina - flowing waters
Iona - from the island
Rhiannon - great queen
Alys - noble
Faolan - little wolf
Abria - strength

Places:

Gaisin - warrior
Straits of Marbh - straits of the dead
Seòltan Seas - cunning
Bhodheas - of the south
Tuathnach - in the north
Caladhan - haven
Neamh Na Mara - heaven of the seas
Faileas Seas - shadow
Treòir Cove - guide
Dàrna Cothrom - second chance
Teich - escape
Prìomh - main

Terms:

"Tro shùil an fheannag...
Seall dhomh far a bheil an teine a 'falach."
"Through the crow's eye...
Show me where the fire is hiding."